My Sins
Upon You
All

My Sins Upon You All

Betty Balsam

WINDSOR HOUSE
PUBLISHING GROUP INC.

Windsor House Publishing Group
Austin, Texas

My Sins Upon You All

Written by Betty Balsam

Printing History
First Edition March, 1999

ISBN: 1-881636-62-3
Library of Congress Card Number: 98-061469

For information address:
Windsor House Publishing Group, Inc.
11901 Hobby Horse Court, Suite 1516
Austin, TX 78758

The name "Windsor House" and the logo are trademarks belonging to
_ Windsor House Publishing Group, Inc.

PRINTED IN THE UNITED STATES OF AMERICA
10 9 8 7 6 5 4 3 2 1

Dedication

To my husband and children.

Chapter 1

BY THE TIME SARAH REACHED her bedside lamp to switch the light on, the phone stopped ringing. She waited a while, then slipped back in bed and promptly fell asleep. About an hour later, it rang again. She let it ring several times before she picked it up. She heard a lot of static, followed by a sharp, piercing sound, but no connection. It was three minutes after four. She could not fathom who'd be calling her that late at night.

She tried to go back to sleep but it was futile. She rose, put her robe on and went to the kitchen to fix herself a pot of coffee. She pulled the drapes open and was greeted with a flood of sunshine uncharacteristically bright for Seattle. Seattle was not the city of her choice. All the talk about gray skies and rain had forced her to pause and consider the effect it would have on her mother dying from ovarian cancer. However, the doctors treating her mother in Bern, Switzerland, urged Sarah to move her to Seattle where The Fred Hutchinson Center and the University of Washington had extensive research projects in progress. It was too late. The metastasis was out of control. At the end of May, after seven months of suffering, Jane Allbright Sultan died, survived by an only daughter and a husband who could not be consoled.

Sarah poured herself a cup of coffee, then settled on a lounge chair on the deck to soak in the soft rays of morning sunshine. Seattle had definitely not lived up to its reputation as the rain capital of the country. Not in the summer of 1994. The sun shone every day and the temperature was just right, in the seventies and low eighties. Washington State reminded her of Switzerland where she had spent most of her school years. She loved the place, especially the University of Washington, and particularly the Jackson School of International Studies. Her goal was to learn more about the world in general, and the Middle East in particular. Of all the universities she had investigated, she felt the Jackson School of International Studies offered a program best suited to meet her expectations. She decided to give it a try.

Sarah's mother had been pleased with her daughter's interest in international studies, but did question the motive behind the institution she chose. Why a public school, she had asked. Why Seattle? Was it because Sarah felt she had to remain close to her mother while her mother underwent treatment in Seattle? Jane Albright was a firm believer in education, the best money could buy. Nothing, not even a mother's health problems were allowed to interfere in what she considered to be of ultimate importance. Education makes a person, she often said, and lack of it is like a cement tire around a person's neck – blocking his view of the world – completely. The only place it will take that person is down.

It took a lot of convincing before Jane Albright, still skeptical, agreed to her daughter's choice.

Thoughts of her mother welled tears in Sarah's eyes.

The phone rang.

Sarah rushed to the kitchen and grabbed the receiver.

"Can you hear me?" the caller asked.

"Sure can. Ramzi is that you?"

"It's me calling from Amman – from a friend's house. I called twice, earlier, from the hospital. Couldn't get through."

Sarah stiffened. "What hospital? Who's sick? What's wrong?"

"I'm not sure I'm doing the right thing by calling you. Mom said not to. She was adamant about it. But she doesn't know you like I do. I think your father would like you to be here."

"Ramzi, I'm twenty eight years old, able bodied, and quite capable of dealing with my problems myself. My aunt has to learn to mind her own business. Now, will you please come to the point. You're making me very nervous."

"It...it is Uncle Maher. I mean... I mean ... he has not been feeling well for over a month – since he returned from the States. We weren't too concerned initially. Figured it was your Mom's death and all. But he...he... he..."

"What's wrong with my Dad, Ramzi. Tell me or I'll take the next plane to Jordan. And when I get there you won't like me at all."

Ramzi always had trouble dealing with unpleasant situations, he rarely had to though since he frequently delegated a relative or a friend to take care of it for him. Sarah suspected the reason he called was because he felt he had to. He knew no one else would for fear of upsetting her. Custom demanded unpleasant news be concealed from victims and close relatives at all cost. He also knew if he didn't, it would be the end of their relationship. Sarah would never forgive him – not when it was a matter involving her parents, and, hopefully, it would win a few points in his favor.

For a few seconds Sarah heard nothing and panicked. "Hello, hello, Ramzi are you there?"

"I'm here," was the weary reply. "I don't know how to break it to you. I know how close you are to your father, and I think he'd like you to be here with him. Don't...Don't misunderstand me. Mom is with him most of the time and he has private nurses taking care of him around the clock. But I feel... I feel, I mean, I feel you should be here. You should come."

Was this a ploy, perhaps an over dramatization to lure her to Amman where he could be with her. Ramzi fancied himself in love with her ever since they were teenagers. She liked him – to a point. He was her cousin, pampered and spoiled like most males in the Arab world, a custom expected and accepted by almost all, not a matter for altercation.

"You still haven't told me what's wrong with him."

"I told you. He's not feeling well."

Sarah lost patience. She pushed away a strand of hair from her face and stuck her mouth to the receiver. "Ramzi, tell me exactly what's wrong with my Dad, whatever you know, or you'll live to regret it."

She could hear heavy breathing, a sigh, a moment's hesitation. "O.K., O.K. Uncle Maher had a stroke. I think it was a stroke. I'm not sure."

"A stroke? Did you say a stroke? How bad is it?"

"It's pretty bad. He... He can't talk. He can't move his right arm or leg. I don't really understand all the medical terminology his doctors use. But I think they suspect hemorrhage in the brain or something like that. It has something to do with blood. He doesn't look good and doesn't seem to be getting better. Actually, I think he's getting worse. That's why I decided to call you."

Sarah did not hear much after 'hemorrhage in the brain'. Hemorrhage in the brain, she repeated over and over. Ominous words, words she was not prepared to hear, words which left her stunned. Her father was her favorite person in the world, her best friend, her hero. While her friends and classmates delighted in telling malignant stories about their parents, Sarah had nothing to contribute. She felt giddy, grabbed a chair and collapsed in it. The receiver fell from her hand. A few seconds later she heard Ramzi's voice, "Sarah, Sarah, are you there?"

She pulled herself together. "I'm here. Sorry. I dropped the phone."

"Are you all right?"

"I'm fine. Is . . . Is Dad comatose?"

"I don't know what you mean – 'comatose.'"

"Does he recognize you?"

Ramzi hesitated. "I'm not sure."

"When you or your Mom talk to him does it seem like he understands you? Does he seem to know who you are?"

"I don't think so. Maybe. It's hard to tell. His eyes are closed all the time."

"Which hospital?"

"Jordan University Hospital."

"Who is his doctor?"

"There are a whole bunch of them. I don't know their names. Anyway, if you are thinking of calling, you would be wasting your time. It's almost impossible to get through to the hospital, and even if you do there's no guarantee they'll put you in touch with a doctor. The doctors do their rounds in the morning, and leave soon after to attend to their private practices. That's where they make their money."

"I'll leave for Jordan on the first flight out of here. I'll call you as soon as I get hold of a ticket."

"I hope you can. I checked. Every flight on every airline is booked solid."

"I'm not surprised. It's July. Students returning home and all. But I'll get there somehow. Trust me. I will."

"I know you will. You always do what you say you will and get what you want."

Sarah smiled despite herself. "Thanks for your vote of confidence. I truly appreciate your taking the trouble to call me. Thank your Mom for me too, please. I'll relieve her when I get there. Then she'll be happy you called."

"My mother happy? I don't believe she has ever been associated with such a state of mind or feeling. Not to worry though. Remember how you always teased me – said my mother was firmly convinced her son could do no wrong. That's what I'm counting on."

"I guarantee you won't be disappointed. Never fear. Your mother will rationalize it somehow." Sarah could see the scenario unfurl in front of her eyes, a repeat of reactions expected, predictable, undiminished for centuries.

"See you soon, I hope."

"I'll call you in a couple of hours. Can you arrange for Dad's driver to pick me up from the airport?"

"No need to. I'll be there."

"Bye."

Two days later Sarah was still trying. She had called every airline in the phone book – even Royal Jordanian Airlines, in Jordan. Nothing. The earliest available opening was September fourth. They could get her as far as New York but all seats to destinations overseas were booked solid months ahead including business and first class. In addition, every carrier had a long waiting list with priority given on a first come first served basis. Her travel agent, Doug Fox, did not fare any better. Sarah refused to give up. She packed a few essentials in her backpack, took a taxi to the airport. Destination, New York.

Despite her persistence and her willingness to stand by, all her efforts to find a seat were futile. As she sat cross legged on the floor at Kennedy airport, she tried to sort out her options. After a while it hit her. She'd heard airlines sometimes saved seats for emergencies. This was an emergency. What could be more urgent than a man who had a stroke, a man who could not talk or recognize his relatives. She decided to try Air France mostly because Air France had regular flights from Paris to Amman. She asked to speak to the manager. The manager listened. When she was done, he reached for the phone. After a brief conversation, he turned to Sarah, "We have one seat in first class. That's it."

"I'll take it." Sarah was ecstatic.

"It's expensive."

"Mr. Robuchon," The manager's name was boldly displayed on his desk. "I carry one credit card, the American Express. There's no limit on it." She handed it to him. He phoned, got the information he needed, gave her card back and asked for her passport. He studied it briefly. Suddenly his eyebrows shot up. "Is Maher Sultan your father?"

"Do you know him?"

"The philanthropist? Who doesn't?"

Sarah glanced at her watch. "You're very kind. The monitor indicated the flight should be about ready to leave. I...I need a ticket."

Mr. Robuchon reached for the phone. He arranged for the flight to be delayed a few minutes while the clerk prepared Sarah's ticket. He rose and opened the door. They walked to the counter. The clerk finished preparing the ticket and handed it to the manager. The manager gave the ticket to Sarah. Sarah paid for it with her American express card, thanked the manager and the clerk, her voice barely audible, overwhelmed by their kindness, unable to express her gratitude in words.

"You're cleared through – to Jordan." The manager reached for Sarah's hand and gave it a gentle squeeze. "Bon voyage. Hope your father gets well soon."

She had done it. The thought of seeing her father in less than a day, made her feel good. "Thanks again. I will mention you to my father." Sarah slipped her backpack on her back and ran to the gate.

Chapter 2

SARAH GREETED THE LANDING AT Orly International Airport in Paris with great relief. Half the journey was over and she could breathe freely again. Forty minutes into the flight, while first class passengers were being served cocktails and appetizers, a flight attendant had dashed in from the economy class, across the aisle to the cockpit, a worried expression on her face. She returned almost immediately, went to the back, was gone for a few minutes, came back, her lips tight, her brows knitted, and headed straight for the cockpit again. The attendant who was serving first class passengers, handed the woman passenger seated next to Sarah a gin and tonic, a coffee for Sarah, excused herself and hurried to the cockpit as well. For about ten minutes, attendants rushed back and forth as terrified passengers searched their faces for clues. "A hijacking," the passenger next to Sarah whispered as her teeth chattered. "I bet we don't make it to Paris."

Sarah stiffened. She had suspected as much but did not want to believe it. "Let's give it a few more minutes. If it is a hijacking, I am sure the captain will announce it."

The minutes passed, the commotion continued, but no announcement was made. Soon, however, the flight attendant for the first class cabin stepped out of the cockpit and proceeded to serve the rest of the passengers.

"What's going on?" It seemed the woman next to Sarah could not contain herself any longer.

"No cause for concern." The attendant's voice was reassuring, but the passenger, an elegantly dressed and coifed woman in her forties, was not pacified. "It's a hijacking, isn't it?"

"Oh, no. Nothing of the kind. We have a passenger in coach, not quite seven months pregnant, gone into premature labor. Every seat is occupied, first class and coach. There's no room to move back there. That's the problem."

"Do you think she's about to deliver?" What an awkward situation to be in, Sarah thought.

"We don't know. She's having contractions about a minute or two apart. We need a doctor. The captain... Here he is now."

The captain's voice came on the intercom. "If there is a doctor on board could that person please identify himself or herself to a flight attendant. I repeat. We need a doctor. Urgent. Emergency."

"I'm a doctor," the woman next to Sarah said her voice still shaky. "A pathologist. The last time I delivered a baby was in med. school."

"Terrific. I'll tell the captain." Delighted, the attendant hurried to the cockpit.

When she returned, Sarah had had time to mull over the pregnant woman's predicament. "Why don't you bring the woman here," Sarah offered. "She can have my seat. It will be easier for everybody."

"You mean it?" The attendant's face lit up in obvious relief. "Why that's terrific. Thank you. Thank you very much. I'll bring your food and drinks back there for you."

"Please don't. I'll be fine. Which seat is she in?"

Sarah and the flight attendant whose name tag read Nicole, were led by the attendant for the economy class to the back of the aircraft. They found the patient doubled over, her face on her folded arms pressed against her knees, tearing her shirt sleeve with her teeth, her hair wet with perspiration. She had the worst seat imaginable – in the middle of five seats, in the center of the aircraft, surrounded by passengers not one of whom spoke English or French. She was traveling alone, to join her husband in Paris, a trip authorized by her physician. "This is not exactly a prize seat." Nicole seemed uncomfortable with the arrangement. "Are you sure you want to go through with it?"

"Can you see yourselves delivering a baby in that seat?" Sarah always traveled first class with her parents and only occasionally booked coach fare, on short flights, within Europe, when she traveled with friends. Being packed like cattle in a confined space, with someone's elbow in her side, or butt in her face, was hardly a choice she would have made. But she reminded herself that she would not have hesitated to grab a seat, any seat, to get to Jordan. Meanwhile, both attendants struggled to move the man and the woman occupying the seats to the left of the pregnant woman, so she can get out. The couple seemed confused at first, but soon relented. The attendants helped lift up the pregnant woman whose pain wracked face sent shivers through Sarah. The attendants accompanied the woman to the front of the aircraft while Sarah tussled to pull herself to the woman's seat. She was five foot ten, long limbed, slim. Either the seats had shrunk or she'd grown bigger. Probably both, Sarah figured. It took her a few seconds to find a comfortable spot for her arms and legs. The discomfort heavy passengers have to put up with must be horrible, she thought, as she observed the passenger to her left re-seat herself. The woman was in her fifties, medium height, close to two hundred pounds. Yet she had less trouble squeezing herself in her seat than Sarah did. The passenger next to the woman did not do so well although he had the aisle seat and more room to maneuver in. A huge man, he almost lost his balance before gravitating to his seat like a cyclone. To Sarah's right, another couple struggled valiantly to be heard by the couple to her left. Sounded like Russian, or Polish, maybe Ukrainian. She couldn't tell. Eventually, the roar of the engines won. The couple to her right covered themselves with blankets and slept. But not the woman to her left. She talked incessantly, even while she ate. From the few words Sarah grasped, she gathered they were diplomats assigned to an embassy in Damascus, Syria.

The woman's companion did not talk or eat. He drank Vodka, continuously, with his back half turned to the woman. Sarah did not mind the woman's talking as much as she did her body odor. Every time the woman moved, especially her arms, Sarah was hit with a wave of nausea, perpetuated by body odor mixed with the smell of tobacco, permeated deep in the fabric of her clothing. By the time they reached Paris, Sarah was willing to swear in a court of law, that the woman had never heard of deodorants, and the last time she took a shower or changed her clothes, had to have been when Noah built his ark.

The coup de grace came when the woman took out a bottle of perfume from her purse and poured it liberally over her neck and chest. Sarah was hit with an instant headache so intense the slightest movement of her head felt like a ton of bricks tipping left and right. She sat still, head held high, and hoped it would go away. Meanwhile, the woman continued her monologue oblivious of her neighbor's discomfort. Half an hour later, Sarah felt like her eyeballs would pop out. She was prone to migraine headaches, something she'd rather not have to deal with on a long trip. She took a couple of Tylenols from her purse, rose, asked to be excused. The woman to her left stopped her monologue, smiled, pleased she understood and pleased to oblige. She nudged the man next to her. They rose and let Sarah pass. Sarah got water from the water fountain, swallowed her pills, walked up and down the aisle for a while, returned, her headache less in control. The man who had been drinking blocked the way to her seat while he fought to extract a large canvas bag from the bin overhead. He yanked the bag repeatedly but could not pull it out. Sarah moved a couple of steps back. Frustrated, the man threw himself at the bin, grabbed the bag with both hands, clung to it, pulled savagely, lost his balance. The bag flew out of his hands and landed like a missile on Sarah's right foot. Simultaneously, the man went down, buttocks first, in a heap, on the floor.

Sarah gasped with pain. An attendant rushed over, apologized profusely, insisted Sarah remove her shoe to check her foot. "Not a problem," Sarah protested. "I'm all right."

'The Perfumed Lady' contorted her body with difficulty out of her chair and stepped in the aisle to check on her companion. Sarah took the opportunity to retrieve her seat. Meanwhile, a male attendant helped the man off the floor, back to his seat, and gave him his bag. He inquired if anyone spoke Russian. There was no response.

"Do you know if the pregnant lady delivered or not?" Sarah asked the attendant.

"She's working on it. We'll keep you posted."

"Thanks."

The Russian unzipped the bag, pulled out a bottle of Vodka, unscrewed the cap, took a big swig, swallowed it, took another, wiped his mouth with his sleeve, dumped the bag in the aisle, put the bottle between his thighs, put his head back and closed his eyes. Within minutes, he started to snore.

Half an hour later, Nicole rushed over to Sarah beaming, "It's a boy, tiny, but looks healthy. The mother wants to know if you'd like your seat back."

"Of course not. Please congratulate her for me."

"Thanks again," Nicole said with genuine sincerity as though the favor had been done for her personally. "I don't know what we would have done had you not volunteered."

Four hours later, when the plane landed in Paris, Sarah's big toe had swollen to the point where she had to remove her shoe and limp barefoot to the airport bus to get to the transit lounge. The man who had dropped the bag on her foot hobbled past her, without a glance in her direction.

A five-hour lay over was scheduled for the flight to Amman with an hour stop in Damascus. Sarah dragged herself to a pay phone, dialed Ramzi's number and waited. After the tenth ring, she gave up. She found a bench in a quiet corner, pushed her backpack under her right foot, put her head back, and tried to rest. The many boutiques lined on the west side of the lounge were not new to her. Neither was the airport. She'd seen them before, often, with her mother, on her yearly pilgrimage to school in Switzerland. Memories of her mother, fresh, vivid, exhilarating, lurked in the shadows of her mind – always.

For Sarah, her mother was an unusual person. A woman in step with the times, in tune with the demands of the lifestyle of her daughter's generation. Sarah's mother, Jane Allbright was born in Newport Beach, California, of well to do parents. Her father had bridal boutiques in most major cities in the U.S and was actively seeking markets overseas. When Jane graduated from Stanford University with an MBA, her father offered her partnership in the business, and a chance to explore possibilities of markets overseas. Jane was delighted. After months of research, in 1965, she headed for the Gulf States, convinced ventures in countries with oil money to burn, were bound to yield great profits. By 1967, she had opened stores in Bahrain, Kuwait, Qatar, Oman and Abu Dabi, in partnership with local businessmen, the deals sealed with a handshake, the proceeds incredibly lucrative.

Jane Allbright's success in business, as a woman, in the Arab world, was not the result of her charm or business savvy. It was the outcome of a chance encounter. After months of trying, she could not arrange a single business deal. She was a woman. No one took her seriously. No one would talk to her. After yet another frustrating trip to Kuwait, she booked a flight home, via London, determined to avoid similar costly mistakes in the future. Who was she to assume that centuries old traditions would yield to her modern day ideas. She would focus on countries where gender played a lesser role. They had to be out there somewhere. She was determined to find them.

Jane checked the monitor. It indicated no change in the scheduled departure time. She moved to a bench across the Kuwaiti Airways counter to wait for the boarding call. Instead, a forty-minute delay was announced in Arabic and

English. There was not much to do but watch other passengers, wait, and hope there would be no further delays. The airport was crowded, the clerks looked lazily at the long line of passengers waiting to be checked in. She noticed a man in his late twenties – early thirties, briefcase in hand, rush towards the counter, glance at the screen, at the crowd, step back. In a moment, he seemed to have spotted Jane. He walked over, sure steps, tall, erect. "Excuse me," he said. "I missed the announcement. Was it for the flight to London? I can't tell. The screen is blank."

Jane's eyes met his. She wasn't sure she could trust her voice. "There is a delay. I believe they said forty minutes." She shifted her gaze. She'd never seen such stunning looks. It was as though he was carved out of marble, leisurely, by a master sculptor. Special commission. Every feature, every line, every curve had a dignity she'd never seen in any man before. Yet the young man seemed totally unaware of it.

"Mind if I sit here?" The young man pointed to the space next to Jane.

"Not at all. Please do." She almost stuttered. Jane admonished herself for acting like a teenager. She was twenty six and if she were to believe her father and what she saw in the mirror, she was pretty good looking herself.

"Maher Sultan. Businessman. Construction."

"Jane Allbright. Pleased to meet you."

"Visiting?"

"Not really. Thought I could do business. Learned otherwise. Great learning experience though."

"Business?"

Jane chuckled. "I was too naive to know better."

"What business are you in?"

Jane Allbright told him and Maher Sultan listened. When they reached London, he convinced her to cancel her trip to the U.S. and return to Kuwait with him two days later when he'd be done with his business in London. This was the beginning of a great business partnership, and eventually love and marriage, until Jane Allbright Sultan's death in May 1994.

As her Gulf business grew so did the need for her presence. It became increasingly time consuming for her to fly to and from the U.S. Jane decided to rent an apartment in Beirut, Lebanon, and make it her base. She also signed up to study Arabic at the American University of Beirut. These were exciting and challenging times. Jane loved it. Maher opened the doors for her and after that she took over. Her first business agreement was in Kuwait. A nod from Maher was enough for Jane to agree to invest over a hundred thousand dollars to open a bridal boutique in Kuwait, in the name of a total stranger. The stranger was a Kuwaiti. Had to be. It was the law and the only way any one could do business in Kuwait. Anytime the stranger wanted to, he could claim full ownership of the business and the person who made the investment could do nothing about it. It did not happen. The stranger signed the agreement at the Business Bureau and was never seen again. Jane had gambled big by trusting Maher Sultan, a man she'd known only for a few days, and won. After that, it snowballed. She opened boutiques in the capital cities of most Gulf States, in partnership with locals where allowed by law, presumably owned by a native when the law denied foreigners access to local markets.

After a few months, her relationship with Maher ceased to be strictly business. He was deeply in love with her and made no secret of it. She, however, held off – initially. Even though she was well aware of the perpetual negative portrayal of Arabs by the American media, she refused to allow it to cloud her thinking. She could claim without reservation to accept a person for who he or she was. She held off because he came from a prominent Jordanian family and she'd been among Arabs long enough to know that they would disapprove of their son having a relationship with a foreigner. Actually, relationships were tolerated as long as they did not lead to marriage.

What loomed large in the eyes of many had no signifi-

cance for Maher. Race, color, creed, wealth or position were
matters he never brooded over. When Jane mentioned it occasionally, he brushed them off as insignificant, minor issues
blown out of proportion by people with nothing important to
occupy their minds. And when he proposed marriage, a year to
the day they had met, she was too overwhelmed to answer. She
took a week off, returned home to talk it over with her parents.

"Does he know you're Jewish?" Jane's mother asked.

"I mentioned it several times. He ignored it. When I persisted, he pointed out that you were married to a Christian and
he could not see the difference."

They were married the next week by a justice of the peace
in Newport Beach, California in the presence of her immediate family. Ten months later, Sarah was born in Beirut,
Lebanon. The family moved to Saudi Arabia when Sarah was
three years old. Mr. Sultan was invited by the King to build a
palace for the prince sixth in line to the Saudi throne. It was
an offer Maher Sultan wanted to but could not refuse. The
thought of living in a closed society like Saudi Arabia, especially with an American wife and a daughter who would soon
need schooling, compelled him to evaluate the offer with far
more scrutiny than would have been required otherwise. In
the end, Jane prevailed. It was an opportunity of a lifetime,
she insisted, and by all accounts a coveted honor. Millions of
dollars in profit, as well as the good will of the Saudi Royal
family was at stake. Since Maher's business, as well as Jane's,
was mostly in the Gulf States, he accepted the offer – reluctantly. Maher Sultan was the best known architect in the Arab
world. His specialty was Islamic architecture, its preservation
and introduction into modern society as an exquisite, yet
pragmatic form of art.

He was given carte blanche. The only stipulation was for the
palace to be completed in ten years when the prince was
expected to marry. The prince was then six years old.

Chapter 3

IT HAD BEEN FOUR DAYS since she'd last spoken to Ramzi, two days of it on the road. Sarah's concern for her father mounted with each passing day. She tried to reach Ramzi repeatedly but failed to make contact. Getting to Jordan had taken longer than she had anticipated. She tried one last time, from Paris, before boarding. The phone rang and rang. Assuming her aunt was at the hospital with her father and Ramzi was who knows where, where were the servants? Sarah asked the operator for help. "Their phone must be out of order," the operator replied. "Happens frequently."

When the plane landed in Damascus, Syria, Sarah's toe had turned blue, throbbed, and the swelling had spread to her ankle. An ugly sight. An hour in Damascus, less than an hour to Amman, she'd check on her father, then have a doctor in the emergency room take a look at her foot.

Only a few transit passengers remained on board the aircraft in Damascus. Briefly. Within the hour, every seat was filled, including first class. The newcomers were mostly Arabs. A young woman, in her middle twenties, her head, neck and shoulders covered with a white scarf, accompanied by an older woman covered from head to ankle in a black tent-like outfit called abaaya, a man in his fifties, and a teenage girl also with a head scarf, were the first to rush in. The young woman and the teenager sat next to Sarah, the older woman and the man took the seats behind them. The young woman wearing the white scarf asked Sarah in impeccable English, if she was American but did not wait for an answer.

"I'm Mona," she said. "This is my sister Huda. Behind us

are my mother and father. We've been waiting at this airport for three days for a flight to Amman. I don't wish that experience for my enemy. Damascus airport is not the Ritz you know, but we had no choice. My father refuses to go by car. He doesn't like the roads, or the drivers, especially truck drivers. We used to vacation in Egypt – every summer. Three years ago my brother was killed by a terrorist bomb in a nightclub in Cairo, by religious fanatics, Islamists, trying to topple Hosni Mubarak's regime. He was twenty six."

Tears welled in Mona's eyes as she spoke.

The profusion of words, and the manner in which they were spoken, caught Sarah off guard. "I'm sorry about your brother. It must be very hard on your parents. From what I have read in the newspapers, turmoil in Egypt seems to have gotten worse. You'll probably be better off in Jordan. I haven't heard of any problems there. Have you?"

"Jordan is okay. But we love Egypt, especially my parents; Arab country, same language, similar customs, like Jordan. But there's not much to do in Jordan. Egypt used to be a place to have fun. Lots of fun. Inexpensive, eager to please tourists, sites to see, good food, great nightlife. No more. One never knows where or when a bomb will go off. They're meant to scare tourists away. The terrorists are doing an excellent job, I must admit. Why are you going to Jordan?"

"My father is in the hospital."

"I wish him good health. Will someone meet you at the airport?"

"My cousin would have, but I couldn't reach him. His phone must be out of order, or something. I'll grab a cab."

From the back seat, Mona's mother spoke to her daughter. "My mother understands English but can't speak it. She says it is not proper for a young woman to take a taxi, at night, alone. We'll take you wherever you want to go."

Sarah wanted to tell Mona she was fluent in Arabic, yet restrained herself. She knew it would immediately invite a stream of questions, personal questions, a ritual with Arabs, to which, for the moment, she was not disposed to contribute. "I don't think it will be necessary. Thanks anyway."

After conferring briefly with her husband, Mona's mother tapped her daughter on the shoulder. "Mother says for you to honor us – to come stay with us – at least until you contact your cousin."

Sarah shook her head in disbelief. She had spent ten years of her childhood in Saudi Arabia, yet she never ceased to be amazed at the generosity and genuine hospitality which most Arabs offered to total strangers without hesitation or reservation. "Please thank your mother for me. I truly appreciate her concern but I'll be just fine. I'll take your phone number though. Give you a call. Perhaps stop by if I have time."

"We'll be honored." Mona gave Sarah their phone number.

When the aircraft landed and the passengers were bussed to passport control, Sarah had to queue in a separate line because she carried an American passport. She was the last person to reach customs, barefoot, limping. The customs official watched Sarah drag her right foot wincing with pain as she approached the counter. He took one look at her swollen foot and waved her through. When Sarah exited from the customs building she saw Mona and the rest of her family waiting for her – in case.

"Sarah!" Ramzi's voice rang across the hall. He worked his way through the crowd, threw his arms around her and gave her a big hug. "Am I glad to see you! I was becoming a permanent fixture of this airport. I've been here every day, met every international flight, chased a dozen women thinking they were you." He reached in his coat pocket for his car keys. As he did so, he saw the bare foot. "Wow! What's wrong with your foot?"

"It's my big toe. I think it's broken."

"Where's your luggage?"

Sarah pointed to the backpack on her back. "You're looking at it."

Ramzi shook his head. "Why am I not surprised? I'll go

get my car. Wait for me in front of the south side of this building. Parking to pick up passengers is permitted there. If you're
in pain, wait for me here. I'll help you to the car."

Sarah looked up. The sign said no parking any time.
"South side will be fine." She limped toward Mona and her
family, thanked them and promised to call.

*   *   *

"I have reservations at the Marriott." Sarah was not sure
where they were headed to. Although her father was
Jordanian, this was Sarah's first trip to Jordan. "Could we stop
at the hospital first – say hi to Dad – maybe have a doctor
check my toe?"

Ramzi kept his eyes focused on the road.

"Well, could we?"

No answer.

"Is something the matter?"

Ramzi fidgeted in his seat, reached for her hand and
squeezed it gently. Darkness failed to mask his discomfort
from Sarah's probing eyes.

"When?" He did not have to spell it out for her. Suddenly,
it was as if the wall she had leaned against all her life had
crumbled right before her eyes. The one constant, the man she
loved and admired, the man who was there for her no matter
when, no matter what business engagement he had to postpone, or cancel – was no more. On few occasions, when she
had contemplated about life without her father, she had to
make a conscious effort to shift her thoughts to other, less
debilitating subjects. Somehow, she could not fathom life
without him, especially so soon after her mother's death. Yet
now that it had actually happened, she felt calm – totally
numb.

Ramzi pulled the car to the shoulder of the road. "Day
before yesterday." Tears rolled down his cheeks. "We could-
n't reach you. We ... We ...weren't sure when you'd arrive – if

you'd arrive. He was buried today – in Kerak, in the family plot."

"What? What do you mean buried? You mean he is already in his grave? What was the hurry? Why couldn't you wait?"

"Perhaps you have forgotten. Your father was a Muslim – at least by birth. He had to be buried as soon as possible, which almost always means within twenty four hours."

Sarah cringed. She wanted to grab and shake him, to scream, to explain to him and to the rest of the world who her father really was: a man who prided himself on being blind to all prejudice most people allowed their lives to be dictated by, a man who was compassionate, loving, generous, a man untainted by dictates of politics, society or religion. A citizen of the world. That's who her father was. Shout, an inner voice commanded. Let everyone know. She said nothing.

"Let me take you home." Ramzi pulled off the shoulder and merged with the traffic. "You can't go to a hotel, a woman, alone – even in Jordan. You'll probably be told there are no rooms, or we have no reservations by that name, or some other fib. But most likely they won't give you a room. It's bad for the hotel's reputation."

Sarah took several deep breaths before she could respond. She had to. She was about to lose the last shred of self-control she had left. "You said the family was in Kerak. You think they will approve of you and I staying in the same house alone?"

"I don't care if you don't. There's at least one servant at home at all times."

Of course, Sarah reminded herself. Someone will be there to attend to Ramzi's needs. She dropped her head in her palms to stop the pounding. Every word she uttered resonated in her head. Ramzi drove, silent. Thirty five minutes later, he stopped in the most exclusive neighborhood in Amman in front of a picturesque villa which could easily qualify for the cover of an architectural magazine. Actually, it had been copied from one. Sarah collapsed on a sofa in the living room, lifted her foot to check it. A sharp pain shot up her leg to her groin. She bit on her lower lip to muffle a scream. Her foot was swollen to more than twice its normal size, was purple and blue, and throbbed. She lifted her foot with both hands and placed it on the coffee table, turned to Ramzi. "Could I use your phone? I'd like to call a cab. I feel my foot should be looked at."

"The phone has not worked for days. If you don't think you can wait till morning, I'll drive you to the Jordan University Hospital. They have American trained doctors there. I doubt you can get a specialist at night, though. Only residents. From the looks of it, you need a specialist – badly."

"I'll wait." Sarah thanked Ramzi, showered and went to bed, thoroughly drained of energy. It was past midnight. She figured she'd pass out from sheer exhaustion and lack of sleep. It was not to be. Images of her father paraded in her mind's eye in connection with two incidents that never left her thoughts. A day after her eleventh birthday, her parents had to leave her in the care of her British nanny, and an aunt who lived with them to attend an urgent business meeting in London. Sarah's aunt was thirty years older than her half brother, Maher. Sarah's grandfather had married eight times, until finally, after ten daughters, he had a son, Sarah's father. What puzzled their friends and relatives though, was Sarah's father, Maher, who after twelve years of marriage had only one child, a daughter, and seemed perfectly content with the way things were. This was and still is most unusual in the Arab world where men advertise their masculinity by the number of sons they produce, and cease to be referred to by their own names with the birth of the first son. Henceforth, they carry the child's name, with the word Abu, meaning father, preceding the child's name. Consequently, they remarry as often as it takes, with or without divorcing their previous wives, until they have sons – at least one, preferably two, in case something happens to one of them.

Sarah's aunt was in her late sixties, divorced long ago because she could not have children. A uterine infection after clitoridectomy at age ten, had almost cost her her life, and left her barren. Clitoridectomy is not practiced in Jordan or Saudi Arabia. But her husband to be, an Egyptian had refused to marry her unless she was circumcised. Since the infection had destroyed her chances of conceiving, her husband moved on to other wives.

As a woman, Khadijeh could not live alone. After years of roaming from one relative's house to another, Khadijeh was invited by her brother, Maher to come live with them in Saudi Arabia. The arrangement worked well for everyone for about two years. Sarah's parents felt comfortable leaving their daughter home with her aunt while they jetted to different cities to attend to their ever-expanding businesses. And the aunt, whom no man would marry when it became known that she could not conceive, and who was forced to live with different relatives, could live comfortably with her half brother and his family.

Sarah loved her aunt. Khadijeh told her stories, mostly from the Koran, about the Prophet Muhammed and his teachings, and occasionally about her own life. Although illiterate, Khadijeh could recite long passages from the Koran without mistakes. It was because of her aunt that Sarah was well versed in the life and teachings of the Prophet. On one occasion, however, the day after Sarah's parents left on a business trip, Khadijeh had little time for Sarah. She was busy preparing for a party, a special party, a surprise.

Strange, her aunt never gave parties.

Groups of women in abaayas arrived about eight that evening. Sarah watched from her bedroom window, a dozen or more women, like black shadows being ushered in by the house boy. She could not tell who they were. Except for two slits for their eyes there was no break in the fabric enveloping them. Curious, she tiptoed downstairs. There was no one in the large room where Sarah's parents entertained guests. The dining room was also vacant, but the side tables were laden with fruits, nuts and pastries. As yet, no food had been served. Down the hall she heard music, singing, followed by ululating in the kitchen. All women, perhaps two dozen, dressed to kill underneath their abaayas, covered with gold wherever possible, surrounded the kitchen table. Sarah was puzzled. Arabs never entertained in the kitchen. The kitchen was for servants, not guests. An older woman dressed in a simple outfit of coarse black material, stood at the foot of the table, a business-like look on her face, rolling a long white cloth. She looked out of place among the glitter and the glamour surrounding her. Sarah strained to see if she could recognize anyone. She couldn't. The women were talking among themselves. Sarah heard one women say, "Khadijeh will be in big trouble when the mother finds out."

"I'd worry more about the father," said another. "He is very different. And believe me that's an understatement."

"I've never seen one done," said the first woman. "Have you?"

"I sure have. It's done routinely in Egypt before puberty."

"Once it's done, it's done," was the opinion of another. "There's nothing anyone can do about it."

"She's right," chimed in one woman wearing more jewelry than Sarah had seen on anyone. "By the time her parents get back, it will be too late."

Sarah stiffened. What were they talking about?

"Maybe the parents want it this way."

"I doubt it," said the first woman. "The mother is not one of us. She wouldn't understand."

"It doesn't matter." An old woman listening to the conversation motioned with her hands to end the discussion. "It has to be done."

"In my opinion," Khadijeh said as she joined the discussion, "it should be done on every girl. She will remain faithful to her husband and that will keep the family together."

"But I am told," interrupted the first woman, "that you

almost died from it and that's why you don't have children or a husband."

"You don't understand," Khadijeh snapped back annoyed. "It's a procedure practiced for hundreds of years. Occasionally, something goes wrong. It's God's will."

What's she talking about it? Sarah wondered. What procedure?

"What's there to understand." Sarah heard a woman's voice say in Egyptian dialect. "We've all had it done. How else does she expect to find a husband?"

"Well," another woman said with a shrug of her shoulders, "women have enough to deal with in this country. We certainly don't need yet another demand added to our woes."

Has my aunt arranged for me to meet my future husband? The child's mind failed to grasp the subtleties of the remarks being tossed around. The guests are right though, Mom and Dad will not like it if that's what Aunt Khadijeh has in mind. Of course most girls Sarah's age were already married. But she could not bring herself to believe that at age eleven her aunt was already shopping for a husband for her. While Sarah tried to make sense of the bits of conversation she could hear, she heard another guest explain in a high pitched voice, in Saudi dialect, how fortunate women were in other Arab countries, at least in that respect. Unlike Egypt and the Sudan no such restriction was forced on women living outside Africa. "The horrid stories I have heard about it are enough to make my blood curdle." She finished her remarks her hands rubbing her arms as she shuddered.

This discussion makes no sense, Sarah muttered to herself. Restriction? Africa? Her gut feeling was that she had it all wrong. I wish Mom was here. She'd know. She'd explain it to me.

Khadijeh glared at the woman in disapproval, started to say something but didn't.

The woman at the foot of the table finished rolling the white cloth.

"Ready Um Omar?" Khadijeh asked.

The woman nodded.

"I'll get Sarah."

It hit her like a bulldozer. Run, run as fast as you can, Sarah told herself, but could not move. Suddenly she saw clearly what it was all about. Horror stories, recounted by classmates from Egypt about female circumcision fit the picture perfectly. No. It was impossible. The women did not know what they were talking about. Her parents would never allow such a thing to happen to her. But her parents were thousands of miles away. Could they have succumbed to brain washing by her aunt and delegated her to have the procedure done in their absence? No. Never. The child's mind refuted the possibility instantly. Not her parents. Absolutely not. She pulled herself together with all her might and tried to retreat quietly.

Khadijeh spotted her. "Ah, there you are, Sarah. Come join us. This is the surprise. This party is for you." She reached for Sarah's hand. Sarah struggled to free herself and almost succeeded. At that moment, two big women who reminded Sarah of Sumo wrestlers she'd seen on TV, stepped out of the kitchen and helped Khadijeh drag Sarah in, kicking and screaming. She was lifted and placed on the kitchen table in a half reclining position and was held down by the women who had dragged her in. Someone pulled her jeans off, another lowered her panties to her ankles. The two women who had dragged Sarah into the kitchen positioned themselves on each side of her at the foot of the table. Each woman grabbed one foot and forced her legs open. Sarah could not kick any more but she continued to scream. Her voice echoed throughout the house. It was futile. Her aunt had given the governess the day off. The rest of the help would be too scared to interfere.

Um Omar approached Sarah, rolled white cloth in hand. She bandaged Sarah's arms to her sides and her legs to the kitchen table despite Sarah's furious attempts to release herself. She checked to make sure Sarah could not move, reached for the razor blade which was at arm's length, on an old rag, on a side table, turned back, separated the labia, pushed the clitoris up ready to cut it off.

She did not make it. Gwynne, Sarah's governess, a big, powerful woman, grabbed her and shoved her to the ground. She threw herself on the table, tore the bandages off, grabbed Sarah, pressed her against her ample bosom and marched off.

Sarah was twenty eight now, but she could still hear herself screaming hysterically as her nanny comforted her. Her salvation had come due to a chance conversation. Her nanny was given the day off by Khadijeh to prevent the nanny from interfering with her plans. However, late that evening the nanny had stopped by her best friend's house on her way back from shopping. Her friend, also British, acted surprised to see her. When asked why, since they often dropped in on each other, it was the nanny's turn to be surprised. There is a big party going on at your place, the friend explained. My mistress spent hours getting ready. It is a big day for Sarah. She is going to be circumcised.

Sarah did not see Khadijeh again. The family physician, an Englishman and a close family friend, wanted Sarah kept under strict medical observation and insisted Gwynne and Sarah stay at his house until Sarah's parents return. The offer was much appreciated by Gwynne. As a woman, moving to a hotel was out the question – staying in the same house with Khadijeh, a very unpalatable alternative.

Maher Sultan put his sister on the first flight out of the country.

It felt awfully warm. Beads of perspiration trickled down from her head to her neck. Her body felt wet. Sarah rose, tried to stand and almost fell on her face. Her right foot pulled her down, felt like it weighed a ton. She returned to bed assuming the air conditioning did not work. The power was on, though. The digital clock on the night stand pointed to three minutes after two. Her mind groped for something, anything, to stop the pain, physical and mental. How could her father do this to her? Why couldn't he hang on a little longer? At least until they saw each other one last time.

Her mind was a blur except for occasional, brief periods when she was fully lucid. It was then that she realized there was more to her father's death than her single minded focusing had permitted her to see. Her father, being the type of man he was, independent, self sufficient, always a giver, must have lost his will to live. His concern about being a burden to his family if he did not recover fully, must have outweighed his love of life. He probably welcomed death, Sarah thought, so I could go on with mine. "I can't. I can't go on living without seeing my Dad." Sarah caught herself yelling, lowered her voice. "I will see him. I will find a way. Definitely. In the morning."

Morning would arrive sooner if she could sleep. Sleep. Yes. That was the answer.

Soon after she closed her eyes, the second incident followed the first which in times of turmoil were her constant companions. Vivid scenes flashed through her mind in fragments and often in disorderly manner. A prominent Swiss psychiatrist, Dr. Bernard Chegal worked with her for over two years to help her cope. Yet the trauma was so deep, and the impact on her psyche so indelible, that even after fourteen years, it was as poignant and devastating as the day it happened. The face of a child – the terrified, uncomprehending shift of her gaze, eleven, perhaps twelve years old, hands bound to her back, feet reluctant to move. A truckload of rocks, some fist size, many larger. Mutawas – the self appointed religious police savoring the victory of their toil, in a semi circle, in the public square. The child's crime – adultery; concocted, imagined, read aloud by a mullah for all to hear – imposed. A hood placed on her head. The flogging, the stoning, on and on from all directions. Hours later, the child pronounced dead by a doctor. The show over, the crowd dispersed bragging about who threw most rocks, the biggest. Another day, another death, 'justice' dispensed in the name of

God. Special justice reserved for women.

Sarah had not chosen to be there. Their driver, on the way
to school had detoured to witness the spectacle. Sarah was left
alone in the car while the driver did his share catapulting
rocks with canny accuracy. It was a thrill he'd experienced
many times before, he explained, and would not miss it
regardless of the consequences.

The consequence came swiftly. He was fired. Another driver was out of the question. Sarah's parents would never trust
another stranger to drive their daughter. And since women are
not allowed to drive in Saudi Arabia, Jane Sultan could not
drive her daughter to school. Neither could her father because
of business commitments. After much soul searching, despite
their reluctance to break up the family, it was decided that
Jane and Sarah must leave Saudi Arabia, immediately, for
good. The mental health of both women, especially Sarah's,
was on the verge of collapse. Maher Sultan decided to import
as many skilled workers as it took regardless of cost, to complete the palace and leave the country. Although he did not let
on, the floggings, the public executions, the censors, the treatment of women, the human rights violations and mostly his
inability to do anything about them, made the millions in
profit feel like a dagger aimed at his heart. Sadly, he felt honor
bound to respect the terms of the agreement. As the construction of the palace progressed, albeit slowly, the beauty of
Islamic architecture in its most exquisite form demanded
attention even from the most sophisticated observer. Yet it
pained Maher Sultan to look at it. To him, it meant contribution to the perpetuation of an archaic social system, a system
designed for the glory of a single family, a family whose autocratic rule like most other aspects of life in the kingdom was
cloaked in religious garb. The longer they lived in Saudi
Arabia, the heavier the burden of injustice weighed on him.
He felt trapped. The palace was years behind completion
because of numerous changes introduced by the prince whenever boredom prompted him to do something with his time,

and because even for exorbitant fees few foreigners were willing to accept job offers in a country where the whim of the religious police could cost them their lives guilty or not.

Years of separation followed. Sarah and her mother lived in Switzerland when Sarah was in school, and in California in the summer with Sarah's grandparents. Maher joined them whenever he could. It was an arrangement no one liked and which eventually frustrated all three. But because their bond was strong, her parents remained in love and the family remained intact.

"I absolutely must see Dad tomorrow even if I have to dig the grave myself." In the semi-darkness Sarah heard herself talk again. Had she been awake or just woken up. She wasn't sure except that she was hot, her back was stuck to the bed sheets, her pillow, her hair, her whole body felt like it was on fire. "I need you Dad," she cried. "Please don't leave me. Not so soon. Please."

Within minutes, darkness closed in on her.

Chapter 4

SARAH'S LEFT ARM FELT NUMB. She tried to move it but could not. It remained stuck to the bed. She forced her eyes open to find herself in a different room, a different bed, with only a night light on. Her arm was taped to the bed and a needle in the back of her hand was attached to an intravenous tube. She rang the bell. A nurse opened the door and switched the light on. Startled, Ramzi shot up from the armchair he had dozed in. "What? What happened?" He rushed to Sarah's bedside. "Sarah, oh my God, Sarah, you're awake. How do you feel?"

Sarah searched his face. "I feel fine. What's this all about?"

"Thank God. Thank God." Ramzi turned to the nurse. "Please notify her doctor. He said to notify him immediately if there was any change in her condition."

After the nurse left, Ramzi sighed, relieved. He pulled his chair close to Sarah's bed, reached for her right hand and held it in his. "You had septicemia. The doctor said a few more hours and you wouldn't have made it. The infection from your toe had spread through your blood throughout your body. Your temperature was so high that despite the massive doses of antibiotics the doctors pumped in you through the intravenous and the cold compresses the nurses applied for hours, they couldn't bring your fever under control, until about" Ramzi glanced at his watch. "an hour ago."

"What day is it? What time?"

"Let's see." Ramzi checked the time again. "It's a few minutes after midnight, Saturday. We brought you here at about ten yesterday morning."

"Who's we?"

"Jim Bateson and I."

Sarah's groggy mind had trouble computing the information. Jim Bateson was her father's right hand man – in London. "Jim Bateson?"

Ramzi nodded. Jim Bateson had flown in from London to attend the funeral. He had returned to Amman the same evening and phoned repeatedly to check with Ramzi if he'd heard from Sarah. The operator told him the phone was out of order. In the morning, he took a taxi and went to Ramzi's house. Although Sarah's father's death was unexpected and sudden, he had made important changes in his will after his wife's death, and left instructions with his business manager to make sure Sarah received a copy of the revised version being prepared by his lawyers in London. "Jim Bateson waited for over an hour," Ramzi said. "He had a plane to catch, so I suggested we wake you up. I sent the housekeeper to let you know you had a visitor. About two minutes later, she came running down the stairs like a demented creature calling on the Prophet to have pity on your youth. She could not wake you up. She thought you were dead."

"Gees... I'm sorry. Has Jim left?" Sarah felt unusually lightheaded.

"Of course not. He canceled his flight. He was here all day, worried sick, convinced the doctors here don't know what they're doing. He went to the hotel to make arrangements to fly you to London."

"I feel tired, very tired." Sarah's head dropped to the right and she drifted off. Later, she heard a man's voice, in the distance, agitated, urging someone about something or other – to hurry – no he did not want the resident – no – it had to be the surgeon in charge – to hurry, please hurry. The phone rang. Yes, Mr. Bateson – surgeon – from London – can't make it to Jordan in time – should be lanced – yes – as soon as possible. Dr. Tuqan is the best. Right. Talk to him. He is still in the hospital. Should be on his way over. Here he is now. Thanks. I'll call you back.

Wheels. Sarah is pulled, put on a narrow bed, pushed, in motion, both hands placed on her chest, strapped to the bed, excited voices. Doors open, doors close. A huge ball of light penetrates the eyeballs momentarily and disappears. Darkness, deep inviting. She moves slowly through a vast expanse to a train station. It is dark, a little chilly. She does not have her coat on. She shivers. Slowly, the first rays of sunshine pierce through the thick fog and shed the barest of light directly on the spot where she stands. The train station is totally deserted. The wind, silent, caresses the leaves around her feet, moves on to penetrate her flesh and bones. She is dressed in a flimsy gown tied in the back and nothing else. Should she go back? Her attention shifts momentarily towards a faint noise in the distance. A train, a single wagon, glides smoothly towards her and comes to a halt. There is no conductor, no passengers, no baggage, nothing, except for a lone woman in the second row window seat. She is staring straight ahead. Jane Allbright turns her head, looks at her daughter. There is no expression on her face. "Come, Sarah. Come join me. Let's go," she says.

The chill wind makes Sarah's voice quiver. "I can't, mother. I haven't seen Dad yet."

Jane Allbright turns her head back to its previous position. The train starts to move and glides down the rail. "Wait, mother, wait, please."

She's nauseous. Has to throw up. Can't move. She's strapped to the bed.

*　　*　　*

Three days after the abscess was lanced, Sarah felt almost like her old self again. Her near death experience had pumped new life into her. She interpreted it to mean that she had an obligation to her father, unfinished business to take care of. Fate she was spared. Dr. Tuqan wanted her to stay in the hospital for a couple more days. After that, he was willing to follow up on her progress as an outpatient. Sarah's aunts were still in Kerak to commemorate the seventh day of her father's death and she did not want to impose further on Ramzi's hospitality. She'd try the hotels – despite Ramzi's predictions. Most likely it mattered more to Ramzi than to the hotel management if she were to have a room.

"No need to do that." Jim Bateson spent every spare moment at her bedside. "Your father owns a fifty two unit compound on Mecca street. He came to Jordan to complete a deal for its sale. It didn't happen. He collapsed while negotiating the deal and was rushed to the hospital by the two buyers. He kept a small unit for himself to use whenever he had business in Jordan. I don't know where the keys are, but I believe we have a spare in London. I'll have someone Fed Ex them to me immediately."

"Thanks Jim, but I'm not staying that long." Sarah stepped out of bed, wrapped her hospital robe around herself and took a few, cautious steps. "The doctor said to walk. A couple more days of treatment, then I'll go to Kerak, say bye to Dad and leave. What's to keep me in Jordan?"

"Plenty." Jim Bateson reached in his briefcase and handed Sarah two envelopes. "Your father wanted me to give you this – your parents' will."

"I have a copy. I've had it for years."

"He changed it substantially after your mother's death. He liquidated all his business. Everything. Wanted to stop work, live a little. He left me in London in charge of tying the loose ends and flew to Jordan. It was to be his last stop. It was. Not the way he meant it, but it was." Jim saw the expression on Sarah's face and stopped. Sarah was about to lose control. She grabbed hold of the back of the armchair and turned her face.

"I'm sorry. Perhaps I better leave. Perhaps tomorrow."

"No. No, please don't. I'm O.K." A forced smile slowly relaxed her tight lips.

Jim moved closer. "Here. Use my arm for support. You need crutches. I'll get you a pair this afternoon."

Sarah had regained her composure. She thanked him and with his arm for support took a few more steps.

"I suggest you study your father's will carefully. You have two options. I'll work with you as long as you want me to. Your father..." It was Jim's turn to lose control. His chin quivered. He had trouble with his voice. "I'm sorry. Your father was like a brother to me. Worked for him twenty one years next month. It's such a shock." He wiped the tears coursing down his cheeks with the back of his hand. He shifted his gaze from Sarah to his shoes looking uncomfortably embarrassed.

Sarah's brave facade dissolved. She wrapped her arms around him, dropped her head on his shoulder and let herself be. They hugged and sobbed, until the pain in her right foot forced her to lower herself onto the bed. "I needed this." Sarah reached for the box of tissue paper on her bedside table. Jim Bateson shook his head. "I'm forty one years old. Don't recall shedding a tear since I was a boy."

"My father did strange things to people."

"Yes indeed." Jim Bateson reached for his briefcase. "Must go now. Have to call the office in London before they close. Keys to the condo should arrive within forty eight hours."

In the afternoon, Dr. Tuqan checked her toe, replaced the soiled dressing with fresh gauze and tape. "In a couple of days, you'll be as good as new."

"I'm very fortunate to have had such terrific care. How can I ever thank you?"

"How about dinner tomorrow night?"

She thought he was kidding. He wasn't. "Sounds like fun. But I couldn't. I came with a backpack, a couple of jeans, a few T shirts. That's it."

He was paged. Emergency. "I'll stop by later this afternoon."

He did – shopping bag in hand. He handed it to her. He had thought of everything – dresses, shoes, pantyhose, even crutches. She was not surprised. Lavish Arab generosity was the norm, not the exception.

"That's very kind of you, but I can't accept it." Until then, it was strictly a doctor-patient relationship. She couldn't figure out what prompted the sudden change.

"You don't like it?"

"Oh, no. That's not it at all. I hardly know you."

"That's why you should. We'll get to know each other."

"I won't be here that long. I have to return home, to Seattle, as soon as I visit my father's grave. Summer school starts within a week."

"O.K. Fine. Forget the clothes. Wear your jeans. We'll go to a café or a bar, some place simple."

"Sounds good."

Dr. Tuqan threw his hands up in mock joy. "Success at last. I can't believe it, especially with a woman the nurses insist is Julia Roberts with an assumed name."

"Next time I see myself in the mirror, I'll be sure to ask."

Dr. Tuqan laughed. "I like it. Brains and beauty. A rare combination. You might be able to shed some light on a matter which has disturbed me from the day I returned to Jordan, last July, after five years of training in the U.S., many grandiose ideas bubbling in my head. But the Arab world had taken a hundred and eighty degree turn during my absence – for the worse, I might add. Even in Jordan. It' subtle, but it's there."

"I can't tell. I haven't been here long enough." Sarah was not quite sure what he was referring to. Most men enjoyed their special positions of superiority in the Arab world, took it for granted. With religious fanaticism on the rise delegating women to slave status, what was there for men to complain about?

As though reading her thought, Dr. Tuqan continued. "It's all over the Moslem world. Religious extremists are hard at work and succeeding. Take women, for instance. Many, some very young, are covered from head to toe. Might as well live in a monastery."

Sarah had to readjust her thought pattern. Perhaps there were other men who thought differently – like her father. She herself had witnessed changes, and not so subtle at that. And it did not happen only in Muslim countries. Religious conflict did not draw lines. It had had it's disastrous affects on Lebanon, a Christian Arab country. Although Sarah had left Saudi Arabia when she was thirteen, she returned to Beirut for part of the summer to vacation with her mother and father. Beirut was known as the fun and sin capital of the Middle East until civil war broke out in 1975 among Christians and Muslims. In the early eighties, Beirut metamorphosed from 'the Switzerland of the Middle East,' to a battlefield for different religious factions to slug it out. Muslim women traded their mini skirts and bikinis for abaayas – the young, at the least, had scarves to cover their heads. Although Jordan was more westernized, more liberal than other Arab countries, definitely more so than Saudi Arabia, if the doctor wanted to go out with a woman, his intentions better be serious. Few 'good families' would permit their daughters to date a man for any other reason. Even then, a chaperone usually accompanied the couple to make sure the couple did not indulge in any form of contact before marriage. Otherwise, the family honor would be compromised.

Dr. Tuqan glanced at his watch. "I have to go to my clinic. I'm already ten minutes late. See you tonight. I'll pick you up at eight."

They went to 'Salute,' a restaurant-bar owned by an Italian family, surrounded by a large terrace with a panoramic view of downtown Amman. The waiter who met them at the entrance, seemed overjoyed to see the doctor. He ushered them to a table he claimed had the best view of the city. The clear sky, the stars and a city lit to challenge the night, were more than Sarah had hoped for. She relaxed and almost forgot the reason for her being in Jordan and her sore foot. Dr. Tuqan however, seemed obsessed with the religious and social upheaval sweeping his country. With the fourth drink, he lounged into a diatribe against what he considered a distortion of values by politicians and clerics to serve their own ends. He was a disappointed man, an idealist who had made the decision to return home, based on factors which had changed considerably over the decade he was in England and the U.S. completing his studies. What he disliked most was what he referred to as the desecration of Islam evidenced by regression to medieval practices, practices he insisted had nothing to do with the teachings of the Prophet. "Who, in this day and age," he demanded to know, "covered themselves from head to toe, in black, in the heat of summer. Why? What are these women out to prove?"

"Women? Are you sure it's not the patriarchal society in the Arab world which forces them to subjugation – to do as they are told?"

"Sarah, I understand that logic if you were referring to Saudi Arabia, or Qatar, or Oman. But Jordan?"

"I don't know. Maybe it's a manifestation of resentment against Western culture – maybe it makes them feel special, or different. Maybe it's insecurity. Why don't you ask them?"

"How? It's so difficult to make contact with women, and men are thrilled with the way things are."

"There's the problem. Women have no recourse. They're at the mercy of men. If my memory serves me right, in Saudi Arabia, if you stepped out the front door without being fully covered, the Mutawas, the self-appointed religious police would waste no time to bring you to justice – their kind of justice. I don't know how or where they get their power from, but I do know that even the King and the Royal Family were terrified of them."

"I know. I was invited to work there. The offer was so attractive, I decided to check it out. Three months later, at the verge of losing my sanity, I quit. I've still not recovered from that experience."

This is good, Sarah thought. If more men find the oppression of women disturbing, women will have a fighting chance. But sitting on that terrace, sipping wine, she realized the confusion which engulfed the lives of most Muslims. How to reconcile the demands of modern life and still remain faithful to the religion and social structure which shaped their lives. On what grounds could the subjugation and oppression of women be justified by a society which was bombarded relentlessly by modern technology and Western ideology. Sarah remembered a statement made by a friend who had returned from Iran the previous summer and chuckled inwardly. "Neither the west with its military power, nor the Mujaheddin with their revolutionary zeal will be able to bring down the government of Iran," he said. "It will fall thanks to Madonna and Michael Jackson." Apparently, a satellite dish is the most coveted possession in Iran. Often, whole neighborhoods pitched in to buy a dish to brighten their dreary lives while they watched how the rest of the world lived. This in a country where listening to Western music, dancing, contact with the opposite sex except for one's spouse, or possession of alcohol guarantees a first class ticket to jail, sometimes never to be heard from again.

Sarah recalled a story told by another businessman, a friend of her father's about the man who had never drank alcohol in his life, never listened to any western music until after the revolution when tired of watching mullahs preach at him all day on television and radio, he decided to sink his life savings to buy a satellite dish, a cabinet which he filled with every brand of liquor available on the black market, and a CD player which he used to play the same tune from Nat King Cole – every morning upon waking, and every night before going to sleep.

Sarah looked around. The crowd on the terrace could be anywhere in Europe or the U.S. Here women seemed free to dress as they wished, drink, smoke, date. Were they Muslims? Some spoke English, others Arabic. But that did not mean they were Muslims. They could be Christian Arabs. "There's too much here that's impossible to untangle," Sarah said. "I'll be happy to return home to my simple life in the States."

"That's what I'm planning on doing too." Dr. Tuqan motioned for the waiter to bring the check. "My agreement is for another year. After that it's curtains for me. I've come to the conclusion that I cannot save the world, not this world, anyway."

What a pity, Sarah thought. Such talented, conscientious physicians are so desperately needed in these countries. Yet when circumstances become unbearable who can blame them for wanting to leave?

They waited for about ten minutes but the waiter who'd served them did not bring the check. Dr. Tuqan covered his mouth to suppress a yawn. "Sorry. I was up all night last night. Emergency. Car accident. If you're ready to leave, I'll go pay the cashier."

"Do you want me to wait here or out front?"

"Wait here, please."

The doctor had barely left when the waiter hurried to their table. His hand shook and when he spoke, his voice shook. "Sorry I'm late. I hope the doctor is not mad at me. My wife called. Our two year old son fell from his bed."

"Is he hurt?"

"That's why my wife called. He cut his forehead. He has a brain tumor which has affected his vision. He falls frequently."

"A brain tumor?"

"That's what Dr. Tuqan said he suspected. He saw our son about three months ago – ordered tests. We haven't taken him back."

Sarah did not have to ask. She knew. A waiter with limited financial resources, could not possibly afford the cost of the tests, much less surgery. "What's your name?"

"Abu Younis."

"Do you work here every day?"

"No, Ma'am. Every night. During the day I work as a taxi driver."

Dr. Tuqan returned. "Shall we go?" He placed a bunch of bills on the table.

Sarah turned to the waiter. "I'll be in touch." Although she felt the man's pain, she could not help but wonder what his reaction would have been if the child were a girl. Would the wife have bothered to call? Would it matter at all?

Perplexed, the waiter stopped and stared at her as though expecting an explanation. Sarah made no further comment. She reached for her purse, slung the strap on her shoulder, stuck the crutches under her arms and walked out with Dr. Tuqan.

"What was that all about?"

"You've diagnosed his son with brain tumor."

Dr. Tuqan thought for a moment. "Yes, yes of course. That's why his face was familiar. It was a few months ago. They didn't come back." He shook his head, a pained look on his face. "They rarely come back."

Ramzi and Jim were waiting for her in her room when she returned to the hospital. Ramzi stopped pacing when she walked in. "I've been waiting for you for two hours. I assume you have a good explanation."

Sarah cocked her head to one side and looked at him partly amused by his audacity, partly perplexed, mostly angry. "An explanation?" She sat on her bed, pulled a chair and put her foot up.

"Sarah, you're not in the States. It's eleven o'clock. You're too trusting. All these guys want is a woman to go to bed with?"

Jim Bateson gulped.

Sarah's eyes remained glued on Ramzi's face. The man seemed genuinely upset. We're back in the Middle Ages, Sarah thought. His obsession with control borders on paranoia. It must be stopped. "Let me set you straight." It took all her energy to keep her temper under control. "I'm a big girl. I take care of myself and I don't give explanations to anyone. I thank you for your concern and all the trouble you've been through on my behalf. I'm very grateful to you. But that does not give you a license to tell me what I can or cannot do. I repeat. I don't answer to anyone."

Ramzi's face turned red like a tomato. The muscles around his lips tightened. He marched towards the door and reached for the door knob. "Do you know who are the worst kind of people to deal with? It's people like you. People who are half and half. Neither Arab, nor American. Neither Muslim, nor Christian. People who have no allegiance to family, friends or society. Only to themselves – self centered know-it-alls whose sole claim to superiority is their Western background, in your case, half." He slammed the door shut and was gone.

Jim reached for his briefcase. "Good riddance, I say."

"It's been a long day." Sarah felt exhausted. "Thanks for stopping by. Will I see you in the morning? Dr. Tuqan said he'll check me in the morning and if all is well, I can leave."

"Not until noon, I'm afraid. Federal Express stops at the hotel about noon. I'm expecting the key to the condo."

"I'll probably be better off in a hotel," Sarah replied. "It's only for a few days anyway. I'll call around in the morning."

"If I were you, I wouldn't waste my time. You should check your father's will first. Goodnight."

Chapter 5

THE SMELL OF PIPE TOBACCO hit her first, a smell that lingered about wherever her father was present. She saw him everywhere she looked. His pipe half full of tobacco, in an ashtray, on the coffee table, next to three half empty glasses and *Business Weekly* magazines piled high, in a living room ten by fifteen. The bedroom, of identical size, with a simple bed, a bedside table, a lamp, a few magazines and books, her father's robe casually thrown at the foot of the bed. She expected him to walk in any moment and announce as he always did, "Hi, my loves, I'm home."

How does a person cope with a loss of this magnitude, Sarah wondered. It must be like losing a limb, or an eye, or a lung. You know it's not there, but you'll always look for it and convince yourself nothing has changed. You might succeed – for a while. You inculcate, tell yourself it's gone, it's over – try to focus on the present. But suddenly you feel that itch again, the itch from the limb long gone. You reach for it and freeze. You hear the messenger laughing uproariously at your vulnerability. It's not a learning process. You'll do it again and again, regardless of what time of day or night it demands your attention.

She drifted to the kitchen, her thoughts floating to the many wonderful times they spent together. Surely there was a mistake. He'd be back soon to explain it all.

The kitchen, small, clean, the teapot on the stove. In a corner, on the counter, a surprising find: bottles of medicine – more than a dozen, with unfamiliar names. The father she knew refused to take any medication – not so much as an aspirin for headache. What did it all mean?

A timid knock on the door intrudes. Jim wants her to meet

someone – Attiyeh, an Egyptian in his late thirties, worked as the caretaker of the compound. Attiyeh knew Jim well from his many visits to Jordan with Mr. Sultan, but had not met Sarah. His master's death, he lamented, was a blow impossible to bear. "What are we to do now?" he lamented while he rubbed his hands together fighting to control the flow of tears pouring down his face. "Allah, have mercy on us. What are we to do now?"

Jim pulled the man to a corner of the room, put his hand on the man's shoulder and whispered something in his ear. Attiyeh nodded, sniffled, then proceeded to open the windows. On his way out, he said to Sarah, "You call me if you need anything. Anytime, day or night. I'm your servant."

Sarah lowered herself slowly onto the couch. "My father did not have a stroke, did he?"

"Who said anything about a stroke?"

"Ramzi."

"I don't know where Ramzi got that information. If you feel up to it, there's a letter in one of the packages I gave you. I believe it explains everything."

Sarah tore open the first package and glanced through the pages. "This is like the will I have. Why the duplication?"

"It's not a copy. If you read it carefully you will note the changes your father made. You're his sole heir, all his wealth goes to you and you can do with it as you please. In the copy you have, the inheritance is equally divided between you and your mother."

Sarah reached for the second package. "Do you know what's in this one?"

"Your father's will. The new version. I worked with your father to prepare it. My instructions were to give it to you personally, after his death."

Sarah tore the package open. Inside, there was an envelope addressed to her. The familiar handwriting caused her fingers to twitch and her throat to tighten. Her face a portrait of grief in its assimilation of the enormity of the loss she faced, and the helplessness she felt at changing the blow fate had dealt her forced her to pause, to remind herself of the beauty of his life. She managed to hold the pages together and steady herself enough to read, – except when tears blurred her vision.

June 17th, 1994

My dearest daughter,

About a month after your mother was diagnosed with breast cancer, I had a call from my doctor in London who does my annual physicals. He had received my test results, was concerned by the report and wanted the tests repeated. They were repeated three more times and in each case the results were the same. I had leukemia – six months to a year max to live. The doctor was more upset than I was. I really don't think it matters how long we are on this earth. It matters what we do with it when we are here. I have been blessed with a wife whose unconditional love and brilliant mind made every moment seem like a lifetime, and a daughter who is the joy of my life. My only regret is that your mother and I will probably be leaving you about the same time. Yet I know I need not worry. You can deal with any situation you are faced with. That is how you always were, and I believe it will be that way all your life.

You might wonder why there are two copies of my will. The first will is a rewrite of the will you have plus your mother's share of the inheritance from me. The second will is from both of us. Your mother and I, after months of discussion and consultation with experts, decided to put the total sum, in several banks, (listed in the will) in your name. I know this will surprise you because money was never an obsession with you, and there is far too much for any sensible person to need or want. We had many discussions about this, and we concluded greed rendered life meaningless. Do you recall the coffee mug on my desk you used to tease me about? The writing on it expressed the irony of life in one sentence. "The one who dies with most toys, wins." Your mother and I had no toys. Our happiness lay in each other. Perhaps that's why we had such a fabulous life.

We considered another option – charitable donations. But after much deliberation and consultations with experts, we decided against it because we felt it would benefit bureaucrats more than the needy. Consequently, your mother and I came up with an idea. It seemed to us that many problems daunting mankind were caused by ignorance; like population explosion, devastation of the earth, subjugation of women, racism, religious intolerance. The list is endless. You're familiar with our views. We discussed these subjects with you often enough. We all know there is no quick fix. Yet we try, fail, and try again. Therefore, we concluded that we needed a radical, long-term solution. The only answer is education. We are convinced little can be accomplished without education. It's a monumental task. But it can be done. And you are the only person we can trust to do it right.

Dearest, I know how surprised you must be that your mother and I have chosen you instead of an institution to carry out our wishes. However, gradually, you will understand how crucial this matter is. Without it the world is doomed. And since we were fortunate to have so much, we want to give all we can back – with your help. We would like to educate as many people as possible, as early as possible, wherever possible. Your mother and I have been deeply concerned about the rise of Islamic fundamentalism and fanaticism in recent years, and the effect it has been having on women in the Muslim world. We think women as wives and mothers are what hold a society together. Their welfare should be of utmost concern to all. Unfortunately, fanaticism is not the monopoly of Muslims. There are radicals in all religions, in all disciplines. Islamic fundamentalism is contradictory to everything Islam stands for and we should strive to correct this misconception. We should start with the children. Children should be taught to think. A good place to start

*might be the Palestinian refugee camps in Jordan. Hire qual-
ified, intelligent tutors to teach the truth and the rest will follow. Jim Bateson can help. He is loyal, honest, brilliant, and
has promised to be by your side as long as you want him.*

*My darling, your mother and I realize this is a huge
request but we have no doubt you can meet the challenge. It
will give meaning to your life and meaning to the life and
death of your parents. This is not to say that you must fulfill
our wish. You don't have to. You can do whatever you please
with the money. That is why our wishes are expressed in this
letter rather than stipulated in the will. The choice is yours. If
you decide to give it a try, please make sure all contributions
remain anonymous. We love you and will always be with you.*

*PS Jim's instructions are to make sure you receive this let-
ter after my death. You might wonder why your mother did not
discuss this matter with you before her death, or I before leaving the States. The reason is simple. Your mother and I felt we
should not be around to influence your decision. It's an
extremely crucial decision that will demand total commitment
and great sacrifice. It has to be entirely your own. But remember. Regardless of what you decide, we love you and will
always be there with you.*

*Your parents,
Maher Sultan and Jane Allbright Sultan*

She read it twice more to grasp it fully. In life and in death,
the man she had the good fortune to have as a father never forgot those less fortunate than himself. Neither did her mother.
Sarah wiped her eyes, put her head back and tried to think. She
felt overwhelmed simply by thinking about it. Twenty-eight,
pampered, showered with the best without asking, inexperienced and like Ramzi put it, half-and-half. She did not belong
to either culture, Western or Middle Eastern. Not fully, anyway. How could she possibly tackle an undertaking of that
magnitude? What made her parents think she could?

"Are you all right?"

"Scared to death is more like it."

"I tried to talk them out of it, but failed. This was one of the few instances where your Dad and I disagreed. He seemed to think you could do anything you set your mind to. So did your mother. I'll stay and help if you want me to. I know Jordan well. I know the Arab world well – better than my hometown of New Orleans. Haven't been there for over twenty years."

"Out of necessity or choice?" Sarah studied Jim carefully assessing the man. He had to be someone special to win her father's trust. She had heard her father say on more than one occasion that Jim was his right hand man, that he'd be lost without Jim, that he trusted Jim implicitly.

"Let's say there's not much to lure me back home."

Sarah reached for her crutches and hobbled to the kitchen. She knew so little about this man who had worked for her father for over two decades. Was he a victim of discrimination? Many blacks that lived abroad claimed racism was less pronounced overseas, especially the Middle East. Many Arabs were black themselves. She, herself, could not wait to return home. Like him, she'd lived overseas, and only lived in the States for brief periods, mostly visiting her grandparents. Yet, there was no where else she'd rather live than the States. Absolutely. No doubt about it. She opened the refrigerator. It was packed with food, fruit, vegetables, and soft drinks. "Gee. Who's my guardian angel?"

"Attiyeh. I can, without reservation, declare him the best caretaker anywhere. And the best paid, I might add. That's why he was so distraught. He thought now that his master is gone, he and his entourage, which is considerable, as you might have guessed, will starve to death."

"Meaning?"

"He needs the job. If the compound changes ownership, in all probability he will lose his job. Even if the new owner keeps him, he won't get the same pay."

"He won't have much left if he makes a habit of filling my refrigerator."

"Not to worry. I compensated him amply – as instructed by your father – as always."

Sarah pulled a chair and sat down. "I have so much to learn. The enormity of it all makes me want to grab my backpack and run. But then, I realize I'll be taking myself with me wherever I go and me is very hard to lie to."

Everything about Jim was big. He was almost seven feet tall, had broad shoulders, a huge head and huge hands. He put his right hand on Sarah's shoulder. "Can't say I blame you. It's a tall order. But it's do-able. And done right the experience is bound to enrich you and the beneficiaries. But it's got to be your choice. Your parents would not want you to do it simply to please them. It won't work."

Sarah sipped her Coke. "I need time to think, to sort things out. Also I need to go to Kerak to visit Dad before I do anything else. Is it possible to rent a car?"

"No problem."

Attiyeh knocked on the door. He handed Jim a large basket of fresh flowers.

"Looks like you have an admirer." Jim brought the basket to Sarah.

"Ramzi – most probably. He wants to appease me with flowers to pave the way for his next temper tantrum. I don't feel like dealing with it now. Please put it in the living room."

Jim placed the basket in the far corner of the living room and prepared to leave. "When do you want to go to Kerak?"

"Today is Friday, right? I prefer to be alone with Dad. Ramzi said my aunts plan to return to Amman after commemorating the seventh day. That's today. I'd like to go tomorrow if you could arrange for a car. If not, Sunday would be fine."

They left early the next morning. The drive south was mostly through arid, parched fields, but the main road was well maintained, and the weather sunny and comfortable. A

couple of hours later, a town with centuries of history presented itself with ancient streets and homes mixed with modern highways. On a plateau, 4300 feet above sea level, a massive crusader castle, Crac de Moabs, built on a dizzying
height, graced the walled city of Kerak. The smell of fresh
baked bread followed the visitor through narrow streets congested with cars, a testament to a civilization past but not lost.
Arabs in traditional costumes, sitting on their doorsteps, welcomed Sarah and Jim with smiles and offers of fruit and vegetables plucked from the orchards behind them.

"Why is it," Jim asked, "no matter what country you go
to, people to people contact is an experience cherished by
most. Then the politicians take over and disaster strikes."

"Adds spice to life, Jim, and gives us ordinary people
something to gripe about."

After a brief search, they located the cemetery. It was a
small lot of land, on the east side, almost totally overrun by
the expanding city. Still on crutches, though much improved,
Sarah spotted her father's picture on a mound of earth which
looked to be freshly dug. The picture, in a narrow, plastic
frame was at the foot of a plain headstone.

"This is the way your Dad wanted it," Jim said. "He
insisted on a simple casket, a few feet of earth and his picture
on the grave so you will know where he was buried."

"I'd like to see Dad one last time. Do you think it's
possible."

"Anything is possible, for a price. But why?"

"I don't know. I guess it is to convince myself that he is
really gone."

She knew it was an unreasonable request. To ask Muslims
to disturb the peace of the dead would be blasphemous. She
lingered for a while, slow steps, up and down the site of the
grave as though the proximity of her father's body would
somehow infuse her with energy, or courage, or whatever it
took to enable her to cope. Instead the pain intensified. The
vibes radiating from the grave had a clear message. She had

to be master of her own self. No self-pity, no reliance on anyone but herself, and absolutely no doubt that she could do it.

Sarah placed a single white rose she had brought with her
next to her father's picture, watched silently as the wind
danced through its petals, then hobbled back to the car, slowly, head bent, lost in thought. Jim helped her get in without
comment.

"Dad always brought a fresh, white rose, for Mom. In
Saudi Arabia finding a rose when you wanted one, white, and
year round was a big deal. But Dad managed – always."

"Your parents lived wonderful lives. Now it's your turn.
They'd want you to concentrate on that."

"Right. I just need a little time."

"I'm starved." Jim slowed down and scanned both sides
of the street. "Let's get something to eat."

It was not quite ten in the morning. The bakeries were
open and a few stores had pulled their shutters up but the city
had not yet come to life. They bought fresh bread, cheese, and
fruits. Ate it in the car. Later they toured the crusader castle,
visited the vaulted galleries, secret passages, stables, halls.
The view from the top of the four story crusader castle was
breathtaking. As they stood on huge blocks of stone, on top of
a precipice, Sarah was awed by the grandeur of nature and its
all consuming energy. Humans seemed like minor details who
blew across the horizon, some lingered, some not, and then
they were gone. Occasionally, a human came along convinced
of his invincibility and determined to change history. One
such person was Salah Al Din. The impregnable fortress upon
which they stood, managed to resist all invaders for fifty years
until 1189, when Salah Al Din came along, conquered the
unconquerable, and changed the course of history, at least in
that part of the world.

On the way back they stopped at a small grocery store to
buy bottled water. "Do you know where Ahmed Sultan's
home is?" The thought occurred to Sarah on the spur of the
moment. The grocer stopped, searched her face, shook his

head. "You speak Arabic very well. Why do you want to know?"

"Ahmed Sultan was my grandfather. I am Maher Sultan's daughter."

The man's eyes almost popped out of their sockets. "You...You are Maher Sultan's daughter? Most folks in this town owe their existence to your father." He threw himself at her feet. "Let me kiss your hand."

"No. Please don't."

"You honor us with your presence. Permit me to take you to your grandfather's house." He did not wait for an answer. He walked out of the store, into the traffic, zig zagged through to the other side of the road before he realized he was alone.

"What about your store?" Sarah yelled from the other side of the street.

"Nothing will happen to it. We are God fearing people here. Come."

It was a two story, unpretentious, stone house, old, but well kept. "Your aunts were here for a week. They left this morning. God have mercy on us." Sarah knew he would not mention her father's death to her out of respect. "God have mercy on us."

Sarah turned to Jim. "An ideal spot for a school. Don't you agree?"

"Do I detect a whiff of excitement in your voice?"

Sarah walked around the building, checked the grounds. It was one street removed from the congested center of town, with acres of land filled with fruit trees. "No caretakers?" she asked the grocer.

"There are five. They tend to the orchards. Except for occasional visits by your aunts, the house remains locked up."

They thanked the grocer then walked back to the car to drive to Amman.

Lost in thought, Sarah slumped in her seat while Jim drove.

"What are you thinking about?"

Sarah perked up. "The shattering of my preconceived

ideas. Because Dad was Jordanian, I read everything I could find about Jordan. But it's not like seeing it. I should probably reserve judgment, but so far, I like what I see. I like it a lot."

Jim drove on without comment.

"What's wrong Jim?"

"Oh, I don't know. Fear. Apprehension perhaps."

"You don't think I should, do you?"

"That's for you to decide. Jordanians have chosen a progressive path thanks to their King and the Queen. They are not representative of traditional Arabs. You should visit a few Palestinian refugee camps before you decide. They're not pretty."

"I've seen the camps in Beirut. Shatila and Sabra are the worst. I was sick for a week after our first visit to Shatila. I remember it well. I was twelve."

Jim drove on.

"You're not much help."

"No."

"You think I should go back to the comfort of my Seattle condo."

"No."

"You've lost me. What do you think I should do?"

"Take your time. Think long and hard. Put your parents out of the picture. Think with your head. It is a decision with immense consequences."

"I hear you, and I also sense hints of disapproval. Regardless of what I decide, I want you to feel free to go on with your life any way you please. I know you promised Dad, and I don't deny that your help and advice would be invaluable to me. But you shouldn't stay, if that's not what you want to do."

Jim took a while before he answered. "My comments are not based on considerations for myself. It is you I worry about. I have no doubt you'll stay and you will carry on your parents' wishes. But your parents, especially your father, had a character flaw, a major character flaw. Don't misunderstand me. I loved the man. I owe him my life. But he could not see the evil side of people. Not even when it stared him right in the face, or poked him in the eye. Unknowingly, he's thrown you in an ocean full of killer sharks convinced none will harm you because you are you."

Sarah chuckled. "Where do you see sharks? Educating children does not seem at all like an ocean full of killer sharks to me."

They had reached Amman and a traffic light. Jim turned around. "I have this sinking feeling in the pit of my stomach, that like your father, you are blind to the myriad problems that can arise from something as simple as 'educating children', as you put it. Do you really believe that teaching the 'truth' will be welcomed with open arms? Can't you see how different your truth is from what they've been teaching for centuries? What disturbed your parents most was religious fanaticism gaining hold in all levels of society. Are you prepared to fight fanaticism, religious fanaticism at that?"

"Since you put it that way, yes, I am. I'll probably lose. But not without a fight."

"Does that mean you've made up your mind?"

"Not at all. I've got a lot of ground to cover, to research, to study. I'll need advice from experts in education and people experts like you. Are you willing to stay and help me?"

Jim did not comment.

They drove in silence through the congested, unruly, city traffic which seemed to transform the usually polite, hospitable people into instant killer machines. When they arrived at the apartment, Jim parked the car in the underground garage of the building. He got out, opened the door for Sarah, and tried to help her with her crutches. "Thanks. I can manage," she said. There was an edge to her voice, not intended but there nonetheless.

He followed her through the courtyard to the apartment. "May I come in?"

Sarah hesitated. "I..."

"Please."

They walked in. She went to the kitchen, got herself a glass of water, then settled in a chair. Jim stood close by, one arm resting on the banister which separated the kitchen from the living room. "You asked me if I wanted to stay. I'd like you to know who I am before you decide if you still want me to or not. Like I told you, your father had a major character flaw. I am a convicted killer who has served time. Had it not been for your father, I'd probably have killed again or been killed long before now."

Sarah did not believe him. It was most probably a ruse to break a commitment made to a dying man, an escape without the guilt. It did not make sense to hold a man accountable for a promise he might have felt compelled to make. "How did you and Dad meet? I know you met in the States. But Dad never said how."

Jim shifted his weight from one foot to the other. "I guess you have a right to know. I came home from school one day at lunch time. I should have been in school till three that afternoon but skipped. We lived about four blocks down the street. When the food was bad at school, I'd sneak out, grab a bite to eat at home and return back to school in time for my next class. That summer my mother had remarried. Never knew my real father. Anyway, when I walked in – I used the kitchen entrance, my mother was crouched in a corner, her face cut, her left eye swollen, bleeding from her mouth, nose, and right ear, her hair caked with blood, stuck up in shoots like rabbit ears. It wasn't the first time I had seen my mother beat up. It seemed to be her new husband's favorite pastime. Before I could reach her, I heard screams from my little brother's bedroom. I knew instantly what was going on. The bastard had tried to sodomize me on two occasions, the first time a week after they were married. I was twelve, but already five nine, a much bigger a person than he was. I told him if he ever tried it again, I'd kill him. He didn't. My brother was home sick with a fever. He was six years old."

Sarah was in a state of shock. She opened her mouth to say something – couldn't. The soft, quiet manner in which Jim explained what had to have been the most agonizing event in his life sent shock waves through Sarah's being. What an awful demand she had made of the man who her father often had referred to as the most loyal, honest, thoughtful man he's ever had the good fortune of having as a friend. She let her eyes drop. She felt too embarrassed to face him.

"I killed him," Jim said. "I grabbed the kitchen knife and stabbed him."

Sarah struggled to find the right words. "I'm really sorry. I apologize. I didn't know."

"I met your father in New York, in a parking lot. After I got out of jail, it was either starve or rob. He gave me all the money he had on him, gave me his card, told me to come to the hotel to see him the next morning and that he would give me a job. I didn't. The cops would be there waiting for me, right? Well he came looking for me, that evening, in the same parking lot – offered me a job overseas, money to get myself ready, told me to join him in London. At the time I thought any man like that had no business walking the streets. He should be institutionalized. I repeated those words to myself for three days then I went and applied for a passport. We have been together ever since – I mean until...." Jim's voice cracked. He could not refer to Maher Sultan and not lose control. It was ineluctable.

Sarah reached for her crutches and hobbled towards the man she had put through so much pain. "Thanks for telling me. You are wrong about Dad though. His major character flaw, as you refer to it, is not a flaw at all. My father knew a good man when he saw one."

"And you're not much different from him."

Sarah's response was a smile.

Jim pulled the car keys out of his coat pocket. "See you in the morning."

Chapter 6

SARAH'S APPOINTMENT WITH DR. TUQAN was at four fifteen. At five thirty she was the only patient left in the waiting room. She assumed he was running late. Another half-hour passed before the door to the doctor's office opened and his nurse walked out. She called Sarah's name. Sarah walked to the desk where the nurse stood. "Dr. Tuqan will not be able to see you," she said without looking at Sarah.

"Does he have an emergency?"

"He's busy."

"Excuse me?"

"I said he's busy." She pretended to be engrossed in a patient's file she was holding.

It did not click. "Let me get this straight," Sarah persisted. "He saw two patients with appointments later than mine. I know because I spoke to them. And now you tell me he has no time for me."

The nurse did not answer.

Sarah was outraged. What sort of stunt was the doctor pulling and why. "Please tell Dr. Tuqan since he is too busy to see me, I shall make arrangements with a doctor who has more time. Thank you and good bye." With that, she walked out, fuming.

She took a taxi to the apartment. The driver happened to be more reckless than any she had previously encountered forcing her to hold on to her seat and concentrate on the road. Still, her rage did not subside. What could have possibly prompted such rude behavior – particularly after the pleasant evening they had spent together at the 'Salute' a few days earlier.

There was a message on her answering machine from

Jim. He wanted to know how her check up went and if she wanted to go out to dinner. She called him back and told him what had happened and also that she did not feel like going out. She wanted to stay home, to relax. Jim admitted he could not explain or understand the rebuke either.

"I have more pressing matters to concern myself with," Sarah said. "Like am I really the right person to take on the immense responsibility my parents have no doubt I am capable of. Is it worth it, or wanted. I hope to find a few answers in all the material you have gathered for me which right now is staring at me from the top of the kitchen table. That's what I intend to concentrate on tonight."

She fixed herself a sandwich, poured a glass of milk, leafed through the package, picked a few pages that attracted her attention, and settled down on the sofa in the living room. The material was about the Palestinian camps in Jordan, educational needs of the children, the status of females in Jordanian society and in its schools – a subject of extreme interest and concern ingrained in her by parents who had quietly devoted their lives to it.

The doorbell rang. "It's open," she said assuming it was Attiyeh. Attiyeh made it his business to bring fresh bread, right out of the oven, every morning, and most evenings, if he knew Sarah was home. Another reason for Attiyeh's nightly visits, not verbalized but understood, was for him to make sure everything was all right with his mistress. He had assigned himself that duty automatically soon after she moved in. She was a female, living alone. Not a good idea – in his opinion. However, he was not of her social level. He could not give her advice. Nevertheless, he could make sure nothing unpleasant happened to her. After all, he was a man.

The door opened partially. Dr. Tuqan stuck his head in. "May I come in?"

Caught off guard, she searched her thoughts for a quick, smart answer. She drew a blank. "If you must." She said and quickly regretted it.

He glanced around as though searching for something. A moment later, seemingly satisfied, he joined her in the living room. "I shouldn't be here," he said as though admonishing himself. "I told myself I will never have anything to do with you again. But...but... here I am, despite myself."

"And to what do I owe this honor?"

He put his fist under his chin and watched her watch him. Finally he said. "You don't know why I am upset, do you?"

"Sorry. I can't say that I do."

"Difficult to fathom. You obviously received the basket of flowers I sent you. It's in the corner here in the living room. Wilted, I might add. If you received the basket, you must have received the card and the invitation I sent with it."

Card? Invitation? Sarah was about to fall on her face. She wobbled to the coffee table, tore open the card, and sure enough, there it was, gold writing and all. It was an invitation from the office of the Minister of Health to a formal dinner and dance the previous Saturday. "I'm...I'm so sorry. I thought the basket was from my cousin Ramzi. I did not read the card."

"You cannot imagine how embarrassed I was. I spoke to the minister on Friday, assured him I'd be there with a special friend I wanted him to meet."

"I am truly sorry. I apologize and will gladly do so to the minister. Better still, I'll invite you and him for dinner. We can dine out or I'll cook for you. I make a mean lasagna." She smiled. Her words seemed to have a soothing effect on him. "Hey, don't get any ideas. Lasagna is the beginning and end of my culinary expertise."

Dr. Tuqan rearranged his body in the armchair, dropped his arms by its sides. The unexpected explanation seemed to have comforted him. Sarah studied him shamelessly. Friend or foe? Perhaps it was the constant frown, the pained look seemingly plastered on his face, plus the long hours he put in every day which made him appear vulnerable, crumpled, like a silk shirt labeled 'dry clean only' emerging from the heavy

duty cycle of a washer, in desperate need of attention. She had
been warned by her mother, her father, and lately by Jim to be
careful of men who acted vulnerable. Western women were
not taken seriously by Arabs. Their focus of interest was sex.
Period. She must never let her guard down.

Sarah hated stereotyping. She was convinced, somewhere
under the premature wrinkles and the perpetually pained look
there was a young man, unhappy, demoralized, tortured by
events he felt were beyond his control – but a good, caring
man. "I'm impressed by your honesty," Dr. Tuqan said, interrupting her thoughts. "I'll talk to the minister tomorrow and
get back to you. Now let me have a look at that foot." He rose,
walked over to the sofa, checked Sarah's foot and pronounced
her almost cured. "I better get going and let you continue with
what you were doing."

She invited him to stay. Offered him a sandwich. When
they were done eating, she gave him a brief explanation of
what she wanted to do if she decided to stay. "You can't be
serious," he said, aghast. "The Arab world is not a place for
women. Definitely not a single woman. Not even Jordan with
its veneer of Westernization. What you see is not what you
get. There are currents, undercurrents, social, political, economic, religious. They'll fight you every step of the way.
They don't want change. No. I take that back. They want
change – backwards. They'll question your motive, especially since you are half American. I wouldn't be surprised if they
accuse you of all sorts of things."

"Like what?"

"Corrupting the youth, tempering with their values, their
morals, spying."

Sarah listened with total concentration. "How? Wouldn't
they need some kind of proof or something to substantiate
such serious allegations?"

Dr. Tuqan smiled sadly. "That's a logical question to ask.
But logic was eliminated from their vocabulary when fanaticism took over. These people kill and maim in the name of

religion with no qualms at all, no questions asked. Suicide missions are carried out by so called martyrs assured of a place in paradise for their sacrifice. Do you think they stop and think about the consequences of their actions? Do you think it matters to them that innocent people, women and children are often their victims?"

"Perhaps that's all the more reason for those who can do something about it, to do it," Sarah replied quite disturbed, yet not fully convinced. Of course the newspapers were full of stories about the atrocities committed in the name of religion. Thousands of teenagers, some claim over a million, many as young as eight or nine years old, were killed in the recent war between Iran and Iraq. The government of Iran promised its young conscripts a one way trip to paradise, sent them ahead of their troops to clear the Iraqi land mines – with their bodies – unarmed, unprotected. Despite it all, Sarah believed, given the right tools, the human mind would opt for good over bad, for reason over insanity.

"You can't be serious," Dr. Tuqan said the lines on his forehead knitted closer. "Don't let the relative calm in Jordan deceive you. Look at Egypt, Lebanon, Algeria, next door in the West Bank in Gaza, and all the way to Argentina. They strike anywhere, anytime, in the name of something or other, mostly religion, often bankrolled by Iran. It doesn't matter when or where. Not if it means a one way ticket to paradise."

None of it was news to Sarah. Discussing history, politics, religion and the daily news, (whatever the Saudi Arabian censors would permit) with her parents, was the norm when she was growing up. This had created a hunger for knowledge in Sarah and turned her into an avid follower of world events. She listened eagerly to different interpretations, especially in the Middle East, because nothing ever was what it seemed to be. "I'm aware of it," Sarah said simply. "I fear if measures are not taken to educate the public, matters will only get worse."

It took a while before Dr. Tuqan seemed ready to reply. "It

is my humble opinion," he said eventually, "that only a dictator, or a government backed by the military, like in Algeria,
can slow, not prevent the tide of fanaticism that is sweeping
these countries. It is also my humble opinion that the rising
tide is too strong to be stopped – especially by the method you
suggest. It takes time for education to take effect. Meanwhile,
the situation is bound to deteriorate further. I for one, can't
wait to get out."

"When you say 'they', who do you really mean?"

"If you decide to stay, you'll soon find out. It will be the
clerics, the teachers, the parents, the politicians, the children
you're so concerned about, and anyone who might be affected by the changes your proposal will bring about. It is a no
win situation."

His answer was not hard to guess, but Sarah wanted to
learn his take on it in his own words. He was right of course.
It could easily be a case of too little, too late. Or lots of money
and energy poured into a project no one wanted or appreciated. These were serious concerns – for her. But those were her
problems, not his. Why then was he so troubled? "More
coffee?"

"Please." Dr. Tuqan picked up where he had left off. "I
admit, I enjoy your company. You're the only female in this
city I can have an intelligent conversation with – freely. And
I'd love for you to stay. Unfortunately I can't permit myself
such luxury. I advise you not to subject yourself to this convoluted society. Your reward will be plenty of heartache – if
you're lucky. If not, you might end up by paying for your
altruism with your life."

She couldn't fathom why, but somehow, his ominous
words strengthened her resolve. It was too great a challenge,
too rare an opportunity to miss. "I don't want to mislead you,"
she said calmly. "There is very little doubt in my mind that
this is what I want to do."

He reached for her hand and held it tightly in his, his eyes
boring into hers. "Please, listen to me. I wouldn't be here and

I wouldn't be pouring my soul out to you if I didn't care about you. I felt as you do when I first got here. Armed to change the world. But the knocks have been relentless. My own mother who made two yearly visits to France to buy her clothes, won't leave the house without covering herself from head to toe with that hideous black cloth, and lately my sisters have followed suit. Educated in England, if you please. My questions are either ignored or I am rebuked. I am told to take time out and study the teachings of the Prophet. Then, instead of criticizing them, I would commend the female members of my family for their modesty and morality. Often, I have to remind myself that it is not some Hollywood production I'm watching. This is my country, my people, and my family we're talking about. Tell me, how do you reason with those whose logic has taken flight?"

Sarah was touched by his sincerity. Unlike most men who limited their involvement to lip service in regard to the plight of women in the Arab world, or internationally, Dr. Tuqan seemed genuinely concerned. Frustrated, on the verge of being bitter, yet concerned. He would make a good ally. She needed all the help she could get. So she spent the next hour explaining to him the importance of not giving up precisely because the situation was spinning out of control. She said, "If those of us who can help, who can contribute, regardless of how immutable the situation might seem at the time, pack up and leave, then we are no better than those power crazies who started this mess in the first place. If we teach children how to think, especially when they are young, we will set them free – free to choose. Granted, it will take time. But it will be worth it."

"To choose what, Sarah? Men can choose already – whatever they want, whomever they want, whenever they please. Women have lost the little they had. To think that you can reverse centuries-old traditions, customs, taboos, more oppressive now than they were a couple of decades ago, borders on ignorance or megalomania. In your case, I'd say lack of information has clouded your thinking."

Dr. Tuqan was visibly upset and made no effort to hide it. Sarah was touched. "I appreciate your concern. I really do. Don't worry. I will study the matter carefully and do all the necessary research. Only then, and only if I am convinced that my efforts will have at least a fair chance of success will I decide to stay."

"You're quite innocent, aren't you?"

"Not at all. I lost my innocence first when I was eleven, at my own circumcision party, and then again at thirteen when I watched a young girl who was probably my age stoned to death in the public square in Riyadh, Saudi Arabia. Those were the highlights of my childhood besides the daily doses of shocks inevitable in a society that values its women less than it values its camels."

Dr. Tuqan's eyes bulged, his fist automatically rose to his face to seal his lips. He had been in Saudi Arabia and witnessed several deaths by stoning, operated on numerous genital mutilations, mostly girls from Egypt, battled obnoxious infections. He recalled his first case, a girl of twelve with vaginal infection so severe, the foul smell catapulted the contents of his stomach to his mouth. He didn't make it to the bathroom. One of the many reasons he quit. Nevertheless, he would never know how it really felt to be a victim. He belonged to the privileged group. He was a male.

She was too wired to stop. "So you see Dr. Tuqan, I am not as innocent as I look."

"Please call me Suheil."

"Thanks. Neither am I naive. Young, inexperienced, yes. Naive, innocent, no. Regardless, I have to try. I've got to. I'm convinced, absolutely certain that the sea of change we are witnessing has nothing to do with religion, or politics or nationality. It's a power trip by misguided individuals who use religion as a shield, as a weapon to gain control. The key word here is control. They must be stopped."

"You think you will succeed where dictators with mighty

armies failed, right? The Shah of Iran comes to mind. The Pahlavi dynasty is dust, the people of Iran forced to live in the Middle ages. In Algeria, eighty thousand people are reported slaughtered in six years, while the secular government struggles to contain Islamist fanatics. Do you call that success?"

"Of course not. My approach has nothing to do with politics, or religion, or control. I fail to understand why anybody would choose ignorance over knowledge. I bet given the opportunity there will be plenty of takers."

"Yes, indeed." Dr. Tuqan tipped his head back. "Sure there will be takers. There will also be plenty of opponents. And you plan to wage a one woman crusade against human weaknesses which have plagued mankind since the beginning of time."

"Not exactly. Not a crusade, and not alone."

"Oh? What do you have in mind."

"A zillion ideas taxing my gray cells but nothing concrete," Sarah replied exuding a boyish diffidence. "I realize the stakes are high. I'll only embark on such a venture after I've done exhaustive research." She pointed to the pile of papers on the kitchen table. "And consulted as many experts as I can. I hope to find people who care enough to help, people who are not easily intimidated, or discouraged. I bet I will find quite a few, in due time, right here in Jordan, eager to help, given the chance."

Dr. Tuqan reached for the package of information. He scanned the pages briefly and acknowledged the contents presented pertinent information, mostly statistical in nature. Statistics, he cautioned, presented part of the picture. To learn the truth, how the minds and souls of the people were manipulated, he advised her to visit the camps, talk to the people, listen to their problems, the solutions they suggest, the interest they show in improving themselves and their lots. "I assure you, no amount of reading can prepare you for what you will see and hear."

"I plan on doing just that. My problem is my gender, my

Western looks and my knowledge of Arabic. Initially, it throws them off. They don't pay attention to what I have to say and they don't take me seriously. It would be easier if I knew someone who lived in the camp."

"You do."

Sarah gulped. "I do? Who?"

"The waiter from 'Salute.' He said there is nothing he would not do for you."

"Did he? Did he bring his son?" Sarah felt embarrassed, but not surprised. It was supposed to remain anonymous. She had been warned by Jim not to expect anonymous donations to remain anonymous. At least not in Jordan. Generous donations were the exception, spread of the donor's name inevitable.

"I operated on him Saturday. It was a benign tumor. The child is doing better than expected. Abu Younis said Jim took care of everything."

Chapter 7

A WEEK OF INTENSE SEARCH finally yielded results, a 1983 VW bug, better suited to grace a junkyard than a garage. However, cars were heavily taxed and as long as it ran, it suited Sarah just fine. Actually, she was thrilled. No more waiting in the streets, no more maniacal cab drivers, and a lesson learned in self-control. Each attempt she made to negotiate a deal with a car dealer or a seller was met with indifference or rudeness. She found herself often restraining an ugly impulse to respond to them in kind. Instead, she walked away, relented to Jim's offer of help and in no time found a car that drove better than it looked. And the price was right – three thousand dollars. Cash. Again, thanks to Jim.

Although the crime rate is low in Jordan, auto theft not too common, and most people do not own cars, Maher Sultan had built a parking garage for twenty cars adjacent to the compound. The garage added to the value of the complex and would be greatly appreciated by tenants who owned cars since there were few public or private parking spaces available in Jordan, especially Amman. A narrow passageway from the parking lot led to a small unit for the caretaker. Attiyeh was in charge of the compound, the garage, the swimming pool and all else, by choice. Seeing him work long hours all day, every day, Sarah offered to hire at least one other person to help him. Attiyeh, who never said no to anyone, let it be known through Jim that he much preferred to work alone. He received tips from tenants for running errands and was loath to share it. He had a large, extended family he supported in Egypt.

Upon Sarah's insistence Jim spoke to Attiyeh again. There

was no convincing the man. He was adamant he could do the job by himself, had done it for years. "Let him be," Jim advised. "Your Dad tried every time he came to Jordan. He becomes unglued whenever the subject is brought up."

"Why? Let's add to his pay whatever he makes from tips. It's inhuman to work such long hours fifty one weeks a year."

"It won't get us anywhere, but I'll talk to him again."

Sarah parked the car in the street and went with Jim to Attiyeh's quarters to arrange for a parking spot for her car. They found Attiyeh in the passageway. A metal bed frame covered with a blanket, a small burner in the corner, an ancient, vinyl suitcase partially open pushed against the wall, and Attiyeh filled the passage to capacity.

Attiyeh knelt in prayer.

Jim stepped back looking surprised.

It looked like Attiyeh lived in the passageway. An Egyptian, he was employed by Sarah's father a week after he got married at age seventeen. His family remained in Egypt. Although it meant being away from his wife and children, Attiyeh was thrilled he had a job, difficult to find in overpopulated Egypt. He took one week off a year to visit his family and his wife gave birth to a child a year. Unfortunately, only four daughters survived. All the males died in infancy. Attiyeh prayed five times a day for God to have mercy on him – to give him a son, a son that lived. The only breaks he took were for prayers, no compromise.

His prayer over, Attiyeh rose, apologized for keeping them waiting, folded the small prayer rug neatly and placed it on his bed.

"Is this where you live?" Sarah asked, her annoyance clearly evident in her voice.

Attiyeh seemed to have developed a sudden interest in his worn out sneakers.

Sarah turned to Jim. "You told me the unit next to this passageway was reserved for the caretaker. What happened to the unit? What's going on?"

"Of course it is. Attiyeh has lived there ever since your father bought this place. I have no idea why he is in this passageway. Let me talk to him."

Attiyeh fidgeted.

"He's uncomfortable," Jim said. "He won't talk with you in the room." A simple man, ill at ease in the presence of his master, a master who happened to be a woman.

Sarah understood. She stepped out.

Jim joined her a few minutes later. Apparently, the day after Maher Sultan's death, his two sisters, widows, told Attiyeh to move to the passageway. They rented his flat to a couple recently back from Kuwait willing to pay rent above market value since decent housing was in short supply in Jordan, more so in Amman. Both sisters owned a unit each in the compound, courtesy of their brother Maher Sultan. Although they were well provided for by their brother during his lifetime and had inherited a sizable fortune upon his death, they had no qualms about grabbing more. Legality was not an issue for them. What belonged to their brother belonged to them, but not vice versa.

Greed and Sarah never failed to clash. She lost control. "I have been here for over two weeks. I have six aunts living in this city. I have not heard a word, not one word, not from anyone one of them. It is as though I don't exist. My cousin Ramzi – the same, since his temper tantrum in the hospital, he has disappeared. I assumed they were busy mourning Dad's death. They didn't have time. How could they do this to a man who works as hard as Attiyeh does? How is he supposed to live in a narrow passage, a passage used by the public to commute, a place with no toilet or even a sink to wash in? And if my memory serves me right he has to wash five times a day before he prays. Do my aunts bother with such detail when it is not they who are affected?"

Jim reached for her arm and nudged her slowly across the football field size yard, talking, calming her. "Your father's family doesn't want you here," he said bluntly. "They will do everything they can to force you to leave. Your father wanted to dispose of this last piece of property before he died but did not have time. Attiyeh overheard your aunts and Ramzi's parents argue with Ramzi for notifying you about your father's illness. It's a huge piece of property, worth millions. And here, in Jordan. They could have sold it and pocketed the money without you being aware of the fact that it existed. Ramzi was packed off to England and told not to return until he heard from his father."

It did not compute. "It's a little late for that, isn't it?" Sarah remarked. "I'm here now."

"Unfortunately for them, yes."

"And I know this property belongs to my parents."

"That's not how your aunts see it."

"You mean they could sell the land and the vacant units without owning the titles? How?"

"It can be done, Sarah. Everyone here knows Maher Sultan was their brother. They could easily claim that he died suddenly without leaving a will."

Sarah let out a nervous chuckle. "And all the while I thought my aunts did not want Ramzi to notify me because they were worried about my feelings. What were they thinking? That I would not find out, or would not care, or what?"

"After the fact it would be a difficult legal matter to untangle. It will take years. They've figured that out. But it is not over yet. My bet is that they have plans and are worried that Ramzi might inadvertently give their secrets away. They know how he feels about you."

"Not any more, remember? I insulted his manhood by refusing to let him dictate to me how to run my life. His insight into such matters, shaped by his upbringing and the culture he lives in, limits him to a rigid, confined point of view. Limits, but does not deny. He lived in Europe, studied in England and had lots of opportunities to experience other cultures. It has not phased him. He likes things the way they are in the Arab world. In his mind men are superior to women.

End of discussion."

"He may be right," Jim teased.

Sarah smiled. "I'll settle that score with you some other time. First we have to take care of Attiyeh's problem. I can't believe Dad did not make provisions for a complex this large even if the property was for sale. Who needs such a monstrous headache?"

Jim could not give an informed answer. When Sarah's father was in the States for his wife's funeral, Jim had been dispatched to put the final touches on liquidating Maher Sultan's and his wife's assets in the Gulf States and thus was not fully informed of last minute revisions to their will. But a law firm in London that handled Maher Sultan affairs did. Jim and Sarah went to Sarah's apartment, called London to talk to Mr. Brighten, her father's lawyer.

Mr. Brighten told Jim he had left an urgent message at Jim's hotel advising him to contact London as soon as possible. He said a young man called Ramzi Itani had phoned twice yesterday and this morning had paid the law firm a visit demanding to see his uncle Maher Sultan's will. Denied, he had become belligerent, claimed he was the only male in the family, therefore the rightful heir to his uncle's wealth. He had to be removed from the premises by the police. Mr. Brighten said his records show Mr. Sultan left generous amounts in his will for his relatives, including Ramzi Itani and had signed statements from each recipient agreeing to have no further claims. The sole inheritor of the remainder of his wealth was his daughter, Sarah Sultan. He promised to fax Jim a copy of the document.

Sarah grabbed her keys. "I don't need to be told why my aunts did what they did. I already know. But I want to find out who the caretaker's unit was rented to, when did it happen, and which of my aunts did it, Khadijeh or Hamideh."

Jim rose reluctantly. "Both your aunts were involved. They threatened to deport Attiyeh if he did not comply. They advised him not to tell you about it, and if you happen to find out, he should insist that he did not want the caretaker's unit because it was too big for him."

"It's a tiny unit for heaven's sake. How could it be too big for him?"

"You forget. Given the housing shortage it can bring good rent," Jim said with a soft chuckle. "How can you expect your aunts to overlook such an opportunity."

"I want to have a talk with them. We have to draw the line somewhere."

Sarah stepped out. Jim followed reluctantly and pulled the front door shut.

"You look quite uncomfortable, Jim," Sarah said as the corners of Jim's lips drooped. "You don't have to come with me. Actually, I prefer for you not to. I can deal with it myself."

"When was the last time you spoke to your aunts, Sarah?"

"To Khadijeh when I was eleven. I probably won't recognize Hamideh if I see her."

"Your father felt his biggest mistake was to give the two units in this compound to his sisters. He hated coming here because of them. He wanted to sell the place because of them. They drove your father and the tenants crazy. They still drive the tenants crazy. Despite a serious housing shortage, there are many vacant units in this compound thanks to your aunts."

That was even more confusing. Sarah could not fathom why her aunts rented a unit meant for the caretaker instead of the many that remained vacant.

"Those units carry titles," Jim explained. "Attiyeh's place is the only unit which does not. Legally, it is not a unit for sale or rent."

Sarah put her keys in her pocket as they descended the stairs. She walked across the yard and rang the doorbell of unit three. It belonged to Sarah's seventy four-year-old aunt, Hamideh, an aunt Sarah had met once in Saudi Arabia when she was seven. After two rings and quite a wait, the door cracked open slightly and an old woman covered from head to toe in her black abaaya wanted to know what the caller wanted.

"Are you Hamideh?" Sarah moved in front of the woman so she could take a good look at her.

"Who might you be?"

Sarah recognized her aunt from her eyes. "Sarah, aunty, I am Sarah, your brother Maher Sultan's daughter," she said with forced cheerfulness. "You came to see us in Saudi Arabia long time ago, remember?" The hardest part of the encounter was to act in a civilized manner, to keep her anger contained when she knew how callous her aunts' act had been.

"What do you want?"

"I'd like to talk to you, for a minute, if I may."

The old woman did not bother to answer. She gathered her abaaya in her right fist, left the door partially open, then walked down a few steps to a heavily furnished semi dark living room. Sarah followed. She motioned for Sarah to sit on the sofa, and she sat in an armchair across from Sarah. "Why are you here?" she demanded to know, her voice bigger than the square body it came from.

A reception chilly enough to cause pneumonia, Sarah thought. To her aunt, she said, still hoping for a semblance of polite conversation, "My father was sick. Remember?"

"He is dead and buried. Why are you still here?"

Sarah felt the blood rush to her face. "Why should it matter to you? I am where I want to be."

With great effort Hamideh pulled her voluminous body out of the armchair. "Enough," she yelled with a sweep of her hand. "Enough already, I say. Go back. It doesn't matter where you go as long as you get the hell out of Jordan. We don't need the likes of you here. We have suffered enough, I tell you. Because of your Jewish mother and you we have lost all our brother's wealth. It belongs to us, to the man in the family, Ramzi. Not to you. And we will get it back. You wait and see."

Sarah was already on her feet. "Really? How do you figure to do that?"

"That ... that infidel twisted Maher's mind. That infidel mother of yours. She cast an evil spell on him. My brother was never the same after he met her. He was born a Muslim, was a Muslim until he married that woman. He was a good, decent man, a kind, generous brother."

Sarah lost it. The disdain with which her aunt referred to her mother left her shaken, as anyone would be. "And what was so indecent about my father after he got married?" she demanded to know. "I happen to know he provided quite generously for all of you. If he was an indecent man, why did you accept his support all these years. Why didn't you refuse this condo and all the money he left for you?"

"Bah! A condo, money, a pittance. That's what he gave us, a pittance. Our laws are specific about inheritance. Most of the wealth must go to Ramzi. Not to you. You are a woman. Ramzi is the male next in line. Your father managed to stash his money abroad to hide it from his family. No doubt instigated by your mother. But Allah has his ways and His will will be done."

"I am your brother's child. Not Ramzi." The accusations had reached punitive levels. Sarah headed for the door.

Hamideh pulled a kerchief from her pocket and blew her nose. "Go back where you came from. Ramzi is better off without you. Your mother was an unbearable curse for the Sultans. We don't need more Jewish blood polluting our family."

"My dear aunt," Sarah said. The word 'aunt' almost stuck in her throat. "Do not fear. I have absolutely no intention of marrying Ramzi. I would not dream of polluting the Itani blood."

"Sure, sure. You expect us to believe you?"

Sarah smiled despite herself. "I will gladly put it in writing if it will make you and the rest of my relatives feel better."

"Nothing you do will make us feel better until you get the hell out of here." Hamideh reached into her dress pocket underneath the abaaya, pulled out a kerchief and blew her nose.

Sarah's anger subsided slowly as she watched her aunt work herself into a frenzy. Her aunt, like numerous others was a by-product of the society she lived in. Uneducated, oppressed, fully indoctrinated by distorted reality, guided by blind prejudice. Troubled by the thought, her parents' request began to weigh heavily on her mind giving credence to her hunch that they must have done an extraordinary amount of research before asking her to embark on such a monumental project. The need was great. One had to be blind not to see it. "I will leave Jordan if and when I chose to do so, and not because you or anyone else wants me to," she replied calmly.

"Then what the hell are you doing in my house? Go. Get lost." Hamideh shooed Sarah towards the front door cussing incessantly.

Part of her felt sorry for the old woman, and part of her wanted to grab the woman and shake her until she came to her senses. An exercise in futility, she reminded herself. If they could think straight, they would realize that the only chance for her aunts or the Itanis to lay their hands on their brother's wealth would be if Sarah were to marry Ramzi. The money was not in Jordan. It was in London and other countries in Europe where Muslim law as interpreted by her father's relatives did not apply. Consequently they could not touch it. Sarah opened the door and stepped out.

But her aunt was not through with her. Not yet.

She heard Hamideh shout before she shut the front door. "The black man must have put you up to this." Hamideh spat. "First the mother, now the daughter. Allah have mercy on us."

Sarah was outraged but refused to dignify her aunt's words with an answer. She did not turn around, nor did she change her pace. Initially, she had intended to talk to Khadijeh after she was done with Hamideh but saw no sense in doing so. After her unpleasant encounter with Hamideh, she had no reason to believe Khadijeh would treat her any differently.

In the summer heat, without a tree in sight, perspiration ran down Jim's face. He sat on the steps, in the yard, waiting for her. She was still trembling when she joined him. "That bad, eh?" he asked.

"Money does strange things to people. The first victim seems to be loss of logic."

"I'm cooking. Let's get out of here."

She gave him the keys to her apartment. "I'll join you later. I want to speak with the tenants who rented Attiyeh's place. I will need a list of the vacant units. Can you prepare it for me please?"

Unlike her aunt, the couple from Kuwait invited Sarah in, offered her the most comfortable chair they had in their sparsely furnished living room, and immediately served coffee, pastry and fruits. Treating guests with great respect and hospitality is the custom throughout the Arab world, a custom Sarah loved. An error has been made, Sarah explained. The tiny narrow hallway is not a suitable place for the concierge to live. She offered to rent to the couple the vacant unit of their choice for the same price as the unit they were in, promised to help them move and pay for any expenses they might incur. "Please, take your time, think about it and let me know what you decide."

The couple exchanged glances. The husband told Sarah they were unaware of the fact that the concierge had to be displaced so they could have the unit. It was indeed unacceptable for anyone to live in a hallway. They would be delighted to move – immediately. It did matter to them which unit.

Sarah found them refreshing, especially immediately after her encounter with her aunt. The couple had worked for six years in Kuwait, she as a school nurse in a girls' school, he as a teacher and assistant to the principle in a boys' school in Kuwait. She was dressed in a blue, knee-length skirt and short sleeved shirt. He wore jeans and a T-shirt. There was no pretense of abiding by Islamic law here. They could be any couple in Europe or the U.S.

The wife, Nabila, took an immediate liking to Sarah. They were Palestinians. After the Gulf war, Kuwait accused

Palestinians of collaborating with the enemy, the Iraqis. Gradually, Palestinians who were issued work permits prior to the war, found the atmosphere too oppressive to remain in the country. Although unemployment was high in Jordan, and schoolteachers poorly paid, they had returned to Jordan because there was nowhere else they could go. Inevitably, a discussion of the political problems in the Middle East followed. In the Middle East, politics is topic number one – has been ever since the creation of Israel. Sarah was used to it. It had been the same way at home, in Saudi Arabia, whenever her father brought guests home. Politics aside, it was the couple's professions which interested Sarah. Her gray cells shifted into high gear. She had made tentative plans in her mind to start a school for underprivileged refugee children born and raised in camps. The camps were an ideal breeding ground for terrorists, Islamic Fundamentalists, and where Hamas, the extremist terrorist group recruited many of its radical members from to be sent on suicide missions to Israel. Education could be a powerful weapon, a means to better their lot, and hopefully temper the hatred and bitterness brewing in the camps among the old, the young, even the children. But she had no idea how to go about it, nor did she have any contacts. Nabila and her husband Samir impressed her as a couple who had the right attitude. Although young, their thinking came across clear, logical, not controlled by emotion or shuttered against all dialogue which did not extol the virtues of violence against Jews and the West.

Should she tell them about her plans? Should she ask if they would like to join her?

She decided not to. Not for the time being. She had a general idea as to what she wanted to do but had not worked out the details. She needed a lot more information before she made up her mind conclusively.

The living room window opened onto the courtyard. Sarah saw Jim approach. She excused herself and went to the door. Jim gave her the list of the vacant units.

Sarah returned, wrote her phone number on a piece of paper and handed it to Nabila with the list. "When you are ready to look at the vacant units, call me. Either Jim or I will show it to you."

"Jim?" Nabila reached for the doorknob.

"My assistant."

It was Samir's turn. "Your assistant? What business are you in?"

Sarah chuckled. "I'll have you over for dinner some time soon and tell you all about it."

Chapter 8

JIM'S DISCREET INVESTIGATIONS REVEALED CONTACT with prominent politicians was imperative if Sarah was to realize her goal of starting a school. Although her intentions were altruistic, its interpretation could vary depending on who was affected by it and who analyzed it. Sarah was aware of the pitfalls she was bound to encounter and her lack of experience in dealing with bureaucrats, even ordinary people should have weighed heavily upon her. It did not. She was determined to use her youth, her intelligence, her charm and whatever else she could muster to help reverse the tide of religious fanaticism which was insidiously creeping through the masses. The sight of teenage girls covered from head to toe in black, in the summer desert heat, sent shivers down her spine. A few even wore gloves. This was a man's world, less obvious than in Saudi Arabia, but a man's world nonetheless. Obvious to the most casual observer.

No one seemed to be bothered by it, though. There was a defiant look in the faces of mostly the young. Had they all been brainwashed? Many words, indeed many passages in the Koran were ambiguous, making it impossible to attribute precise meanings to them. To date, the interpreters – almost all men, except for Fatima Mernissi, a Moroccan sociologist, had done their job well – totally in favor of men. In the Arab world, men had no problem imposing their wishes on women disguised as dictates of Islam. A woman's job was to make the males in her family – husband, father, brothers, sons – happy. Period. The noose seemed to get tighter daily giving plenty of ammunition to the international press to brand Islam as a religion better suited to the past than the present.

A month after her arrival, the many discussions Sarah had had with her parents, her observations, personal experiences, and the voracious amount of reading she did about the subject, took on new life. They were no longer incidents of the past that would soon be wiped out by modern thought and technology. On the contrary, fear of Western influence corrupting the believer, prompted the religious leaders to further increase their vigilance, tighten their controls – all in the name of religion.

Some days, Sarah could hardly control her anger.

"You're on another wavelength again."

"Think Jim. Who do you know who has access to the Minister of Education. You've been here with Dad many times – a business associate, someone, anyone who can put us in touch with the minister. We've got to get that permit."

"I've already looked into it. It's summer. The two influential businessmen your father worked with here are in Europe. It's customary for the wealthy to vacation in Europe. I doubt they'll be back before fall. By then it will be too late."

Sarah drifted onto the sofa submerged in thought. Few minutes later, she perked up. "I promised Dr. Tuqan and the Minister of Health dinner. I bet either or both know the Minister of Education."

"It's worth a try."

Dr. Tuqan returned her call late that evening. "The Minister of Health is free Thursday night. I probably can take a couple of hours off too. Is Thursday night a good time for you?"

Sarah was overjoyed. "Terrific. Eight p.m. O.K.?"

"We'll be there."

"Is the Minister married?"

"He is. You're out of luck."

Sarah ignored Dr. Tuqan's teasing. "I'd like to invite his wife too. Do you have their home phone number?"

"No, I don't. I am sure his secretary has it but she is most probably not allowed to give it out. I have not known the

Minister to bring his wife to social functions. Actually, I have never met the woman."

"Maybe it's time she did accompany him. What do you think?"

"What I think is irrelevant," Dr. Tuqan replied. "Call the Minister's office. Tell his secretary you're a friend of mine. She'll put you through. You can ask the Minister yourself."

"I prefer to talk to his wife personally. To be sure she gets the message. Sometimes men forget such trivia." It was Sarah's turn to tease Dr. Tuqan.

"Use your charm. Maybe if you explain to his secretary why you want the Minister's home phone number, she might give it to you. If not try the Minister."

She did. Her request for the Minister's home phone number was brushed aside. The Minister of Health let it be known through his secretary that he would inform his wife about the invitation. However, he arrived on Thursday forty minutes late – alone. After a couple of cocktails, Sarah removed the fourth place setting while Dr. Abdullah, the Minister of Health watched. She waited for an explanation. There was none. "I'm sorry your wife couldn't come." Sarah could not help herself.

Dr. Abdullah was of medium height, round in the middle like a Chinese lantern, in his early forties, with a husk of hair atop each ear – out of control. The rest of his head was completely bald. He tilted his head back and a twisted smile pulled the corner of his lips and bushy moustache down. "Dr. Tuqan raved about your beauty. He wasn't exaggerating. You look exactly like ...like. What's her name? The one who acted in 'Pretty Woman'."

"Julia Roberts," Dr. Tuqan said.

Sarah felt the blood rush to her cheeks. It happened each time someone likened her to Julia Roberts. And it happened often. Although the remark was meant to please her, it made her uncomfortable. She did not know how to react to it, and she much preferred for people not to discuss her looks.

"Yes. That's it." Dr. Abdullah rubbed his hands together in glee, in rhythm with the excitement in his voice. "Julia Robert is pretty. But you are beautiful."

"Thanks." His effusive compliments left her mildly annoyed. She wanted to change the subject and get him to give her a good reason why his wife had not accompanied him. "I would have liked very much to meet your wife. Pity she's not here."

Alas, he played deliberately deaf.

A little bolder now, he moved closer practically breathing down her neck as she bent over the table to rearrange the place settings. "I have heard it said," Dr. Abdullah was on a roll. "A man should not take his wife to Paris. Some pleasures are better enjoyed without intrusion. Don't you agree?"

"Would you have felt the same way if the situation was reversed?" Sarah regretted it the moment the words left her mouth. She watched Dr. Abdullah cringe. It was apparent he was not used to back talk – especially from women. He studied her briefly, an air of arrogance about him, then said with finality, "We believe a woman's place is at home. You women in the West want equality with men." He threw his head back and laughed. "What a ridiculous notion, what a preposterous notion whose time I hope never comes. It would spoil everything for everyone."

No surprises there. It was usually what Sarah heard whenever the subject of women came up. The social, cultural, and religious consequences would be calamitous, intolerable, viewed as barbaric by some clerics. "The truth might be a bitter medicine for so called 'liberated' women in the west to swallow," Dr. Abdullah added, "but our women like things just the way they are."

Actually, Dr. Abdullah was a guest in her house and as custom dictated, more polite than he would have been otherwise. Muslim men, including many educated in the West, insisted a woman's place was in the home. End of discussion.

Dr. Tuqan reached for his tie, rearranged it around his

neck, raised his head, glanced at Sarah then back at the food in his plate. The two men seemed to have nothing in common except that they were both physicians. Dr. Tuqan walked straight, talked straight. His eyes spoke. Dr. Abdullah reminded Sarah of Miss piggy. His nose – unique, nostrils pointed at eyes that seemed governed by remote control.

"Who's we?" Dr. Tuqan stared right at Dr. Abdullah.

Dr. Abdullah stared back but did not answer.

"It's all of us men," Dr. Tuqan answered his own question. "Especially in this part of the world. We dismiss women as a sub-group of society – self interest masquerading as religious dictate."

"Religion holds a society together," Dr. Abdullah countered. "What's wrong with that?"

Her job was going to be tougher than she had anticipated. The so called educated elite was no less in favor of subjugating women than was the illiterate peasant. Fortunately for her she had met a man who wasn't.

"How long do you plan to stay in Jordan?" Dr. Abdullah seemed eager to change the subject.

"It depends."

"We want to keep her here forever," Dr. Tuqan joked. He impressed Sarah as a man who did not remain angry for long. "Anyone who can cook lasagna like this should be forbidden to leave the country. Could I have seconds, please?"

Sarah placed another serving in Dr. Tuqan's plate. She was pleased with the way the lasagna had turned out considering that she had to make a number of substitutions for ingredients which were not available on the local market. "Don't get the wrong idea," she warned Dr. Tuqan. "That's the sum total of my culinary expertise. Dr. Abdullah, would you like some more?"

"Call me Ahmed. Thank you. Yes, please," he replied absent-mindedly. "If you're still in Jordan next month, we can go to Jerash – for the festival. It is organized by the Queen. I have tickets."

Sarah wondered if 'we' included his wife. Not likely.

"Wow." Dr. Tuqan sounded surprised. "How did you get them? They have been sold out for months."

"Compliments of the Queen, thank you."

Dr. Tuqan looked at his colleague intrigued, started to speak, chose to attack the lasagna instead. But for Sarah it meant a possibility – the contact she needed. She could hardly control her excitement. "Like I said, it depends."

"On what?" Ahmed wanted to know. "I can have your visa extended."

"Don't need to. I have dual citizenship. I want to stay."

"Then what's your problem?" Ahmed looked puzzled.

"There should be a reason for me to stay. I signed up for summer classes at the University of Washington. But I can cancel. I want to do something worthwhile with my life. I feel I can, here, in this country, where my father was born and for the people he loved."

Dr. Abdullah narrowed his eyes looking baffled. "Like what?"

"I'd like to teach."

"Teach? Why?"

"I want to."

"Not to worry," Ahmed said generously. "I can get you a work permit tomorrow. What do you want to teach. English?"

"Not exactly. Do you know the Minister of Education?"

"I should. He is my brother."

Sarah took a deep breath to hide her excitement. "I'd like to start a school for underprivileged children. I've got the place and a few possible helpers. I need a permit – from the Ministry of Education?"

Ahmed pushed his chair back, lifted his chin, stuck his fist under it and stared at her. A minute later, he was still staring at her. He seemed to be assessing her, what was and was not said.

"Did I say something wrong?" Sarah could not figure out what she had said to give Dr. Abdullah reason to pause and ponder.

"I knew your father well." Ahmed leaned back further, drew a deep breath as he stuck his chest out. "I also know how strongly he opposed what he felt was the rise of Islamic Fundamentalism. Correct me if I am wrong. Although I have known you briefly, I think your views are similar to your father's."

While in her teens, Sarah had witnessed many crimes committed in the name of religion. But she believed eventually change would come, it would have to, she was convinced, no doubt about it, despite all the resistance. The world was getting smaller, communication instant, travel extensive, contact with other cultures inevitable. Change had to come. It was only a matter of time.

It did. Only backwards.

This was a sample of what she would face in the future. As calmly as she could, she said, "My father was a citizen of the world – a very open minded man. He did not approve of fanaticism of any kind. No exceptions. For him, and I might add for myself as well, fanaticism is synonymous to ignorance."

"Would that it were so simple."

"Maybe not. Why bring it up, though? What has it got to do with teaching a bunch of children?"

"Like I said," Ahmed answered his chin still wrapped in his fist, "it sounds simple enough. A generous woman. Doesn't have to work for a living. It will give her something to do. But it isn't. Whether you mean it or not, you'll be teaching the children Western values, values contrary to the teachings of Islam. Children lack judgment. It will be impossible for them to see the detrimental effects of Western ideology. Stop and think. We Arabs have little in common with Western thought. Don't you agree?"

"Come now." Dr. Tuqan cast a disapproving glance at his colleague. "Let's admit it. We're phonies. We take what we like from the West then complain about its negative affects on our society, on our culture, on our religion. But that's not what's bothering us. What we as men fear most is loss of control. We love Western technology as long as it leaves us, men, in charge. We love democracy if only it were limited to men. We flock to their movies, we buy their books, we go to their universities then return home and pretend we are devout Muslims. Fortunately for us, there are enough ambiguities in the Koran giving us lots of ammunition to twist things our way. We're doing great, I might add. In less than a decade, we have taken a giant leap backwards – back to the Middle Ages – all in the name of religion."

Sarah felt a great urge to plant a big fat kiss on Dr. Tuqan's lips. She bit her lower lip instead.

"I see nothing wrong with the way things are." Ahmed shrugged his shoulders. Although seemingly pleased with his own ideas, he fidgeted, restless, indicating he was bored when others expressed their opinions.

"Of course not." Dr. Tuqan placed his napkin on the table. "You're not a woman. No one tells you how to dress, where to go, when to go, what to do. You don't have to take your wife's permission to travel. You don't have to take her permission if you want to divorce her, or take on another wife. In fact you don't have to take her permission for anything. Like I said, you and I have it made, my friend, and every other man with the good fortune to be born in this society."

Ahmed cracked his knuckles, glared at his colleague, said nothing. However, Sarah knew the subject was like an open sore for Dr. Tuqan, a sore necrosing his flesh. Sarah decided to intervene before the situation spun out of control. "Gentlemen, please. Let's put aside our differences of opinion for the time being. I want to teach children to read and write. Thinking the only outcome would be Westernizing the children sounds a bit far fetched to me. Dr. Abdullah, what makes you think knowledge is detrimental to religion?"

"Of course it is." Dr. Abdullah sounded annoyed.

"And yet you're an educated man and you believe. Don't

you?"

"Of course I do. But that doesn't mean others have the same powers of judgment."

"Religion will be taught in any school I start."

"We have schools." Ahmed stuck his chest out – again.

Sarah was desperate. She wanted to explain, sensed the futility of it, stopped in mid sentence. However, Dr. Tuqan seemed bent on venting his frustration. "You don't get it, Sarah," he said with a weird look on his face. "Ahmed is right. We have schools. Not enough, not quality schools, but schools nonetheless. Ahmed's objection has nothing to do with teaching. It is you he objects to. You'll corrupt our children with your Western ideas. Like he said, you'll spoil the status quo for everyone."

"You're exactly right." Ahmed had totally missed Dr. Tuqan's cynicism. "The Prophet has given us explicit codes of conduct – how to live our lives, how to run our governments. The family, the tribe, the nation matter. Not the individual."

Sarah bit her lower lip, hard. She wanted to say the individual did not matter if she was a woman. She chose not to. For the moment, Ahmed Abdullah was her only hope.

The phone rang. It was from the hospital for Dr. Tuqan. Emergency. He had to leave immediately.

Dr. Tuqan seemed to hesitate, glanced at his watch, at Dr. Abdullah comfortably relaxed in his chair. It seemed as though he expected Dr. Abdullah to leave with him. The social demands which Dr. Abdullah so gallantly defended required of men not to remain in the company of women when a woman was alone at home.

Another moment's hesitation and Dr. Tuqan felt compelled to depart alone. Asking a guest to leave, especially when that person was in someone else's house was simply not done.

Sarah walked him to the door. There was a sadness, a melancholy look which clouded his eyes at all times. "Thanks for a delicious meal. I'll call you tomorrow." He squeezed her hand, hard, looked one last time past her shoulder, and left.

She returned to the dining room overwhelmed by an uneasy feeling she sensed but could not explain. It bothered her to see Dr. Tuqan go. It was his eyes. They left part of him behind. Without giving it thought, she piled the dinner plates on a tray and carried it to the kitchen forgetting momentarily about her other guest. As she scraped the plates she heard heavy breathing inches away from her face. She swung around.

"Can I help?" Ahmed reached for her hand.

She pulled it away slowly, not quite sure how to respond.

"How badly do you want that permit?" Ahmed asked an impish grin on his face. He reached for her hand again as he leaned his body against the kitchen sink.

She wanted to say not badly enough to satisfy your lust, but didn't. Couldn't. The mere thought of him touching her, sent shudders through her body. She managed to retain her composure as once again, she pulled her hand back. "Not a problem," she said. "I'll manage, somehow."

The corner of his lips pulled his mustache down on its sides. "I doubt it." His grin broadened. "We can be friends. I can open doors for you. Any door you want."

She turned around, pulled herself away from the kitchen sink. He was too close for comfort. Engaging him in conversation might buy her time. "Do you have many friends?"

He cocked his head to the right, smiled as if to say you stupid woman, of course I do. He said, "Lots."

The kitchen grew small, claustrophobic. She walked past him to the living room, bypassed her favorite spot on the sofa, settled in the armchair. He followed her, still smiling like a conqueror, moved to the back of the chair, placed his hands on her shoulders and proceeded to caress them. "You're playing hard to get. Why? You want something, I want something. We'll both win. What do you say?"

She reached for his hands and slowly lifted them off her

shoulders. "No. I don't need anything that bad."

He swung around, grabbed her head between his hands and pressed his lips against her while she struggled to free herself. The armchair tipped under their combined weights and she landed on her back, on the carpet, with him on top of her.

It took him seconds to lower his pants with one hand while he kept her pinned to the floor with the other. She fought and screamed while he assured her she'll love it. Her screams were futile. Because of the summer heat, her neighbors as well as she had their windows shut tight, their air conditioners running.

Chapter 9

AFTER A HOT BATH THAT lasted over an hour, Sarah still felt filthy. No amount of scrubbing seemed to get rid of the semen stuck to her flesh. She dried herself, put on a robe, turned the lights off and lay on the sofa to contemplate her next move. By morning, she had worked out a plan.

She called Dr. Abdullah's office and was told the doctor would be in his office at noon. No, he could not see her. He had appointments all afternoon. Sarah decided to go ahead with her plan, regardless. By noon the shaking had stopped, her anger was under control, and her plan reviewed many times and memorized.

Sarah was waiting for him when he arrived. Surprised, a broad smile swept across the doctor's face. He brushed aside his secretary's objections and invited Sarah to accompany him to his office. He offered her a chair. She remained standing. He lit a cigarette, leaned back in his chair and stuck his chest out as he had done the night before. "What a pleasant surprise," he said as he reached for a crystal ashtray on his desk. "I did not expect to see you so soon."

She remained stiff, head held high in a defiant manner and said without elaboration, "This won't take long. I will probably need several permits, beginning with a permit to use the vacant units in the compound as classrooms. I expect you to get them for me as you claimed you could, within twenty four hours."

Dr. Abdullah threw his head back and let out a paroxysm of laughter that almost choked him. Having humored himself into an expensive mood verging on hysteria, he stopped long enough and said, "And if I don't, what the hell will you do about it."

"It is simple really. I will have every newspaper, local and international, write about what you did to me last night. Let the world know who the real Dr. Abdullah is."

Dr. Abdullah's joyful countenance was instantly replaced by a look of disbelief. He stared at her long and hard. "You probably can and will," he said eventually. "You have the money and obviously the determination to do it. But that will involve you as well. I doubt you will risk it."

"Don't let my involvement give you false hope. Fortunately, I don't hold a ministerial position nor do I have to answer to anyone. I can pack up and leave this place anytime I choose and leave all the repercussions behind. You can't."

His eyes glazed over. He stared at her unblinkingly. "Let's assume you will be foolish enough to do it. But then, who will believe you?"

"That's immaterial. In your position you can't afford a scandal and you know it."

"I refuse to believe that you are willing to drag your name through the mud just to punish me?"

"Of course I will. Only it won't be just to punish you."

Dr. Abdullah cocked his head to the right and studied the woman facing him, the woman who had the audacity to threaten him. "What more do you expect to accomplish, pray tell me."

"This might be difficult for you to comprehend, but by exposing you I hope to warn other women who might otherwise become your victims."

His eerie smile was back. "I find that hard to believe."

"You can believe or not believe at your own peril. I plan to take action as soon as I leave this office. The choice is yours." Her voice was steady calm, almost too calm.

"I would hardly call it a choice. You are dictating your terms and expecting me to comply. It's a stupid threat. No one in his right mind would go through with it – definitely not a woman."

"You have made your opinion of women amply clear.

That alone gives me enough incentive to go ahead and prove you wrong."

Dr. Abdullah stuck his chest out and laughed. "You want to prove me wrong not because of what I think about women in general but because you are convinced you are different." He stopped, thought for a moment, then added almost as an afterthought, "You are probably right."

"I cannot claim credit for a universal fact. Everyone is different."

"You've made your point. Now if you will excuse me, I have work to do."

"You should have thought about your work when you decided to attack me last night. I am not here to discuss you or me. I am here with a request. I'd like an answer." Sarah drew mild pleasure from watching the doctor squirm.

Ahmed Abdullah gave her a malevolent look, crushed his cigarette in the ashtray, reached for another from a pack in his shirt pocket, tapped it on his desk a few times, but did not light it. "I'll think about it."

"I expect the permits at my apartment by tomorrow afternoon, five o'clock, the latest."

"I said I'll think about it. What will you do? Threaten me each time you need a permit?"

"I intend to do better than that. I plan to recruit you to help me fight the injustice towards women in this country, the injustice so dear to your heart."

Ahmed stuck his chest out and laughed uproariously – again. "You're crazy. I can have you thrown out of this country within the hour."

"By five o'clock. Tomorrow. Don't bother to bring it yourself. That is another thing for you to remember. If you ever touch me again, I will make sure you pay for it the rest of your life."

"That sounds like a threat."

"It is."

Sarah opened the door and marched across the reception

hall to the street like a soldier on a mission. Her mission: keeping her body from disintegrating under the pressure of what she had just done. She drove to her apartment she had no idea how, and collapsed on the sofa.

Within minutes, Attiyeh was at the door with a loaf of fresh bread and a bowl of mulberries picked from a lone tree on the compound. Attiyeh's devotion and loyalty exceeded by far the monetary compensation he received from Maher Sultan or his daughter. Ordinarily, Attiyeh delivered what he thought his mistress needed, asked if there was anything else he could do, never making eye contact, and when told no, he would leave immediately. That afternoon though, he lingered, his eyes refusing to focus, his body in restless motion like a man weighted under a heavy load. Eventually, he seemed to gather his courage, still standing at a respectful distance from the sofa where his mistress had pulled herself up to see what the problem was.

"Miss Sarah," he said, his voice shaking, "are you all right?"

The anxiety in his voice, and the fearful look on his face, prompted Sarah to get up and approach him. She took the bread and the bowl of mulberries and placed them on the kitchen counter. She did not feel like talking to anybody but Attiyeh looked like he was in agony. "I'm all right. You look like you're not. Is something bothering you?"

Before Attiyeh could answer, the doorbell rang. It was Jim. Attiyeh fidgeted, glanced at Sarah, at Jim, back at Sarah. "I better go," he said, as he reached for the front door looking resigned and defeated.

His discomfort did not escape Jim. "Hold it. What's going on?"

Attiyeh kept his eyes focused on his tattered slippers.

Jim turned to Sarah. "My timing is bad. I think he wants to talk to you in private. Right, Attiyeh?"

"It depends on Miss Sarah."

"On me?" Sarah asked surprised. "What's so serious you

can't discuss in Jim's presence?" And that's when it hit her –
her words prompting a window to open on that specific spot
in her brain. Attiyeh knew.

"Master Jim will know," Attiyeh said, his voice quivering.
"If not from me, from the others."

Sarah walked slowly back to the sofa, dropped her body
on it, and waited for the inevitable to happen. Attiyeh's words
gyrated in her head like bullets. "Master Jim will know. If not
from me, from the others."

"Go on," urged Jim. "This is getting more interesting by
the minute." He turned to Sarah. "Will you please tell me
what could have happened overnight to send Attiyeh into such
a state of agitation? He looks apoplectic. I have never seen
him like this."

Sarah pressed her aching head against the back of the
sofa. The pounding had obliterated any energy she might have
had left from her earlier duel with Dr. Abdullah. She didn't
want Jim to know. No telling how he would react. But it was
too late. Like Attiyeh said. He would hear about it – regardless of what she did. She wondered how far the news had
spread in less than a day.

Meanwhile Attiyeh continued to examine his slippers.

"Go ahead." Sarah did not recognize her own voice.

"Please, Miss Sarah. Forgive me. If you insist ... I have no
choice." Attiyeh took a step towards the front door. "Maybe I
come back later."

"It's all right." Sarah felt her head was about to explode.
"Go ahead. Let's get it over with. Tell him everything you
know."

"Do you know what this is about?" Jim asked surprised.
Sarah nodded.

Attiyeh's voice shook as he finally gathered his courage
and began to speak. "Last night I saw Dr. Tuqan leave about
ten o'clock but not Dr. Abdullah. People say bad things about
Dr. Abdullah. Very bad things. I waited in my apartment,
lights turned off. His car was parked a few yards down the

street. The driver was asleep." Attiyeh shifted his weight from foot to foot his discomfort increasing with each additional word he spoke. "Miss Sarah, do you want me to stop?"

"No. go on."

"About eleven fifteen, Dr. Abdullah crossed the yard in a hurry, got in his car, dropped himself in the back seat whistling all the while. Before the driver could start the car and shut the windows, Dr. Abdullah said 'that was the best' excuse me. I better not."

"Go on," Jim urged intrigued.

Attiyeh's eyes never left the ground. "Are you sure you want me to, Miss Sarah?"

She was sure she did not want him to but there was no stopping Jim now. The compound was like a fish bowl; all units connected like townhouses, forming a three-sided rectangle around a football field sized stone courtyard, all units within sight of each other. It didn't take much effort to see who came and who went.

"He said that that was the best fuck he ever had. Excuse me Miss Sarah, but those were his exact words. I thought you should know."

Jim did not move or say a word. His demeanor scared Sarah. Actually, it was mostly his eyes. They froze the instant Attiyeh said the word fuck. She had seen Jim angry a couple of times and each time her heart had skipped a beat. Pacifying Jim would be more difficult than warding off a rapist. Unfortunately, it was too late to do anything about it now.

Her thoughts were interrupted by Attiyeh. He was not through.

"Miss Sarah, please forgive me. I never said that word in the presence of a woman before. But I have no choice. Sadly, I was not the only one who saw Dr. Abdullah leave your apartment last night. Your aunts watch and listen to every move anybody makes in this compound – especially you. They called me to their apartment early this morning and told me to tell you. I beg your pardon, but they insisted I use their words." Attiyeh could not continue. He put his hand on his forehead, closed his eyes, while his body tilted slightly sideways.

Jim reached and grabbed him. Attiyeh removed his hand from his forehead. His face was covered with a death-like pallor.

"Attiyeh. You need not worry," Sarah said. "We're not here to punish you for bringing us a message. Let's hear what my aunts had to say."

Attiyeh searched Jim's face for reassurance. Jim's frozen stare remained immaculately still. Attiyeh continued, eyes downcast. "They ... They told me to tell you this is not America. In Jordan, forgive me Miss Sarah. They said in Jordan prostitution is against the law. You have also brought shame to the family honor. They are willing to overlook that and they will not report you to the authorities if you leave the country immediately. They're adamant about it."

Sarah's anger mounted with each word Attiyeh spoke but she managed to keep it under control. She chose not to dignify her aunts' demand with an answer. It would serve no purpose. It pained her to realize how low her relatives were willing to stoop and how opportunistic they were. The murderous expression on Jim's face was another reason. And she figured if her aunts had something to say to her, they should have done so themselves, instead of through an intermediary.

"Are you finished?" It was Jim.

His abrupt manner surprised Sarah, but not overly so. Always kind and generous towards those treated less than humanely by most people because of their social and economic standing, Jim drew the line when someone he cared about was subjected to torment.

"Jim, it's all right," Sarah said resigned. "He's under enough stress as it is. Let's not put the blame on him when all he's doing is bringing a message."

"I prefer for the earth to open up and suck me in." Attiyeh swallowed the sobs building in his throat. "But Miss Sarah's aunts said if she does not leave Jordan in three days they will report her to the police."

Attiyeh's eyes remained glued on his slippers.

Sarah felt the man's pain. His livelihood depended on her. He did not know her well enough to know when, or if, or how she would react to such accusations. But he knew he had to do it – regardless. Sarah thanked him for the bread and the mulberries and asked him if he had anything more to say.

He shook his head no.

Jim dragged his big body to the armchair without once looking at Sarah while Attiyeh slipped out the door. Jim filled the huge armchair, his face taut, his brows curled up, his hands tight on the armrests as though intent on holding the armchair in place lest it disintegrate underneath him.

"I'm open to any suggestion you might have." Sarah did not like the way her voice sounded and stopped.

He spoke without passion, without elaboration. "The solution is simple. I can get rid of them – the doctor and your aunts. But of course you won't go for it."

She often failed to predict the extent of his response from the bland way he expressed himself. But the words were clear. What he casually referred to as a simple solution was what very few would contemplate after all else failed. "What about a less drastic measure," she asked with forced calm. It was a day that had pushed her to the limits of her tolerance, a day that would find permanent residence in her psyche with the picture of Dr. Abdullah with his pants down around his ankles parading ceaselessly in front of her mind's eye. Regardless, she had to restrain herself, conceal her pain, and hope he'll be less apt to resort to extreme measures.

"This is just a preview of what's to come," Jim said wearily. "Women don't live alone in this culture. It is considered an open invitation. Women are not allowed go to the movies even with their fiancées unless accompanied by a male relative. How do you propose to deal with these conflicting issues? As a one woman Salvation Army?"

Sarah felt exhausted and ready to snap. "If that's my only option, then so be it."

Jim rose. "I had to try." He opened the front door. "I won't be back tonight. Do not leave your apartment and make sure you keep the front door bolted when you're in."

She did not know where she got the energy from but she sprang off the sofa where she had plopped herself after Attiyeh had left, drained, her mind clamoring for her to shut the outside world out until further notice. Regrettably, it was not to be. "Jim, wait," she said louder than she had meant to. "Please promise you won't do anything foolish."

Jim stepped out. "See you tomorrow."

The next day, at four in the afternoon, a messenger delivered a package addressed to Sarah Sultan. It contained two permits; one allowing the use of the vacant units as classrooms, the second, a permit to teach. She tore open a separate envelope from inside the package with her name scribbled on it. It read: – In the future, if you need further assistance for your project, kindly contact my secretary. Signed, Ahmed Abdullah.

Sarah's stomach did a somersault. She reached for the phone. "Dr. Abdullah is indisposed." His secretary informed Sarah she was not at liberty to discuss what was wrong with the doctor and did not know when the doctor would be back. Her worst fears confirmed, Sarah grabbed her keys and went looking for Attiyeh. Attiyeh was in the courtyard, sweeping the grounds. He saw her but continued sweeping. Strange. No matter what he was doing, he always stopped when he saw Sarah approach. It would be disrespectful not to do so. But not this time. Fear, she sensed made him cling to his broom. "Was Master Jim here last night?" Sarah asked.

Attiyeh stopped sweeping, hesitated, "Yes, Miss Sarah."

"Are my aunts O.K." Sarah started to walk towards her aunt's apartment.

Attiyeh leaned on the broom for support. "Please Miss Sarah, don't go there. They hate you. They told me I'm a trouble maker. They will teach me a lesson I will never forget. Please Miss Sarah, tell me, what did I do wrong. They insisted. They forced me to give you the message."

Her fears were justified. Her aunts considered Attiyeh to be a helpless victim who would be made to suffer the brunt of their fury. But there was more. "They did not want Jim to know, right?" Sarah asked.

"I guess. They said they will have me deported." Attiyeh began to cry. "Jobs are very scarce in Egypt, Miss Sarah. For an unskilled laborer like me practically nonexistent. I have a family to support."

"You have a work permit, don't you?"

"I do. Your father got it for me. But if your aunts decide to make trouble for me, it's real easy. All they have to do is complain to the Ministry of Labor that I stole from them. My permit will be canceled and I will be deported immediately."

"I'll talk to Jim about it." Sarah knew Attiyeh's apprehension was justified. A more loyal, hardworking, honest employee would be difficult, if not impossible to find. Her aunts were well aware of Attiyeh's qualities and expectedly would stop at nothing to get rid of him, to make her life miserable. Her aunts underestimated her.

"Master Jim can fix anything, Miss Sarah."

The way he said it made Sarah pause. Fear of divulging unpleasant information to a person of higher social standing, especially if that person was involved, was often preceded by generalized comments. It was customary to dispense the news in small doses to better anticipate further disclosure. Sarah pulled back and studied the man. She was loath to guess. "What's that supposed to mean?"

"Master Jim knows what he's doing." Attiyeh tightened his grip on the broomstick.

It was clear he was trying in his own convoluted way to inform her about something he felt she should know. "Have you talked to Jim about my aunts threats already?"

"Oh, no. I have not talked to Master Jim today. He stopped

by your aunts' place last night and again this morning ..."

Sarah felt exasperated. "I hate it when you do that Attiyeh. Say what you have to say and get it over with, or don't get started in the first place."

Attiyeh cast a quick look around. "Last night, a couple of men beat Dr. Abdullah up – beat him real bad. They stuck a broomstick up his ..." Attiyeh covered his mouth with his shirt sleeve to stifle an embarrassed giggle.

Sarah gasped. "Who told you?"

"Dr. Abdullah's driver. He was there. He saw it happen."

"Oh, my God." Sarah walked to the stone steps and lowered her body on the first step she reached. It could mean trouble. Big trouble. "What else did he say?"

"Not much. He expected worst. Not to worry. It will die a quiet death."

What was she thinking of. Of course it would. Ahmed Abdullah was too much of a coward to contemplate action.

Attiyeh moved his broom, back and forth, on the same one foot space. Sarah sensed there was more on his mind he wanted to unload. She did not have to wait long.

"I was thinking," Attiyeh said, "Perhaps this year I should cancel my vacation."

"Why?"

"Miss Sarah, my vacation is next week, for a week. It is a very bad time. I hear and see things which are not nice. Your cousin Ramzi is back. I heard he was in London. Your father's relatives pretend to be God fearing people. Maybe they are. But not when money is the issue. Unlike your father, they love to take, not give. And they don't care who gets trampled in the process."

Although she relied heavily on Attiyeh's help and advice, it was inconceivable for Sarah to deny time off to a man who worked hard and was on call for the tenants twenty four hours a day, every day, fifty one weeks a year. Attiyeh saw his wife and children, once a year, for a week. That was it. "I think you should take your vacation as planned. Postponing it won't work. I have the permits and the plans all ready to go. School opens in a month. I will need your help."

Attiyeh did not reply. He remained bent on the broom, eyes glued to the ground.

"What's on your mind, Attiyeh?"

"I don't want to go. Believe me, Miss Sarah. If I go, it is all over for me. I will not be allowed to reenter the country. I know these people. They have already told me as much. If they try to deport me, they know you will interfere. But there is not much you can do if the authorities don't let me back in. They will put me on the next flight to Egypt right from the airport."

Sarah did not think that would be a problem. "Jim knows a couple of high ranking customs officials. I bet he can help."

Attiyeh shook his head, distraught. "I will not be able to reach you or Master Jim. Customs is specifically designed to prevent contact between passengers and outsiders."

"You won't have to. We will be there."

Attiyeh refused to be pacified. "It is too big a risk. At least twenty people back home live off the income I make here. I can't afford to loose my job."

"What do you propose we do? You can't go on working forever without a break – at least to visit your family. You work too hard as it is."

"I am not complaining, Miss Sarah. Many men would be overjoyed to change places with me. I work hard but my compensation is far more than I deserve, and I work for the daughter of a man who next to God was the best thing that ever happened to me. No Miss Sarah. I thank God – five times a day, every day when I pray. My happiness would be complete if only ..." Attiyeh burst into tears. He could not continue.

It was clear Attiyeh was holding back something. Sarah was not quite sure what. However, she sensed fear of losing his job did not seem to be the only reason for his distress. She realized, in desperation, he had divulged more than he normally would, and to a woman. Gradually, as she mulled over different possibilities, she had to admit she could not find a plausible explanation. "If only what?" she asked.

"I like to work, Miss Sarah. I forget my troubles when I work. But no man can work twenty four hours a day, every day. At night, when I go to my room I find my problems waiting for me. Being thousands of kilometers away from my wife does not help."

He is home sick Sarah thought. And yet he refuses to go home. It did not compute. "You are contradicting yourself, Attiyeh. You just finished telling me you don't won't to go home." Then it dawned on her. He did not say family, children or home. He said wife. The man must be sex starved. And that meant, he probably planned to marry again and in his own way was preparing her for it. "What is it you really want, Attiyeh. I need to know the truth. Otherwise, I can't help you."

Attiyeh fell on his knees, opened his palms, raised his head and poured out his grief. "A son, Miss Sarah. I want a son. A son that lives. All my sons die before the age of one. I am cursed, Miss Sarah. I need God to remove this curse from me."

If he goes home, he will have a chance, Sarah thought. Is he adamant about not going to Egypt because he has found someone here he wants to marry? She decided to ask him.

"No Miss Sarah." He seemed shocked that she would entertain such a thought. "I gave your father my word. It was your father's only request as a condition of my employment. I promised to take care of my wife, my daughters, my parents, my brothers and sisters. But I want a son so bad it is like an open wound in my heart. It is killing me."

"Then you definitely should go home. Maybe this time it will work. Let's hope you will have a son and let's hope he will live. Jim and I will make sure you can return to Jordan."

Attiyeh lowered his head and sobbed. Between sobs he said, "Miss Sarah, please don't force me. Too many people depend on me. God will have mercy on me some day soon.

He will give a son who lives. Maybe. I have to have faith, or I'll lose my mind."

They had come full circle. "All right then," Sarah said without hesitation. "We will bring your family here – to Jordan. If that is what you would like."

Attiyeh countenance changed suddenly. He looked stunned. For a moment he could not speak. Then slowly he looked up. It was the first time he had raised his head in Sarah's presence and almost made eye contact. "You ... You ... you would do that for me? The ... The ... The possibility never crossed my mind. You ... You mean it? You do, don't you? The ... The Prophet. He is listening today. God and the Prophet. Oh, my God. Oh, my God. What have I done to deserve such good fortune." He almost toppled over himself as he rushed over, grabbed Sarah's hand, and covered it with kisses.

Embarrassed, Sarah slowly drew her hand away. "I don't know why I did not think of it before. It will be good for you, your family and me. Especially since you have children. I have heard my aunts cannot tolerate other people's children. Maybe we will get lucky. Maybe they will move out."

Chapter 10

YOUNIS, THE WAITER FROM THE restaurant Salute, stood at the gate of Mukhayam al Baka'a, the Palestinian refugee camp where he lived with his teenage wife and son. His son was asleep on his shoulder. The suture marks on the child's head stuck out like little watermelon seeds, plum red in the summer sun. Tiny hair shoots curled over the rest of his shaved head. Yet Younis was a happy man. Dr. Tuqan had assured him the tumor was benign, the prognosis good, and return to normal health to be expected. Younis's gratitude had no bounds. Sarah was the angel sent by Allah to save his son. He'd do anything for her.

Sarah pulled her noisy VW bug slowly to the curbside by the gate, and was immediately mobbed by refugees who had been prepared by Younis to receive an illustrious guest, a rare opportunity not to be missed. Sarah felt more like a woman who had taken on a mission so complex, the only way she could restrain herself from landing on a psychiatrist's couch was to plunge head on into the project and deal with each problem as it occurred. "Here we are," she told Jim with forced cheerfulness. Jim reached for the paper bag full of candy, American candy, tactfully extracted from a friend at the U.S. embassy with commissary privileges. Sarah walked over to talk to Younis while Jim summoned the children to his side. Jim distributed the contents of the bag equally among the children after they promised solemnly to have only one candy a day – American candy. Wow! Delighted, the children ran to their homes treasures clutched tight, pressed against their chests.

During the day Younis drove a taxicab. Every hour away

from work meant income lost which Younis could ill afford. Sarah thanked him and insisted he go about his business. Younis's wife and son stayed with the rest of the crowd, while Younis introduced Sarah and Jim to the leader of the camp waiting to meet them in front of a shack like all the rest of the dwellings in the camp. After the introductions Younis excused himself and left – albeit reluctantly, to go to work.

The leader, a man in his middle twenties, spoke without looking at Sarah. He said his name was Muhammad. He was in charge of running the camp. His father, a mullah, took care of religious matters. He invited Sarah and Jim to his one room shack. The room was bare except for a ragged two by three feet carpet placed directly across from an ancient black and white television set entertaining Muhammad's father with Bonanza. As custom dictated, Muhammad's father, Abu Muhammad had proudly changed his name from Hassan to Abu Muhammad, meaning the father of Muhammad, after the birth of his first son. Abu Muhammad acknowledged the presence of the guests passively, returned to counting his worry beads with one hand and smoking a water pipe with the other. Meanwhile, an old woman hurried in with a straw mat, spread it out and invited Sarah and Jim to sit down. Sarah had no trouble sitting cross-legged on the mat. She was used to it from her childhood in Saudi Arabia. But Jim had to struggle to keep his appendages from flying in unintended directions. A few minutes after he finally managed to bring his huge body down on the mat and crossed his legs, a young girl hurried in with a wooden stool and offered it to him. Jim, took it, thanked the girl, then whispered his lips barely parted, "Thank God for little mercies." Doubtless relieved from a position which must have been sheer torture for him.

Coffee, Arabic, pure extract, in small cups with no handles was served almost immediately. It was so strong, and so bitter that although Jim sipped it drop by drop, his facial muscles contorted, live picture of a man struggling to subdue the somersaults in his stomach with no success. Refusal to drink or eat what the hostess offered was regarded as the ultimate insult. Sarah watched and chuckled inwardly. Poor Jim. He put up with so much – on her behalf. No one could ever accuse him of being a patient man. He was about as impatient as a man could be, especially when faced with, in his opinion, injustice, and still be acceptable in polite society. She was grateful he had accepted to stay and work with her, especially since he was knowledgeable, experienced and above all loyal – loyal without conditions or demands. Well, maybe a few demands. The demands he made were for her protection. None other. With each new experience she appreciated him more. Operating in a man's world without a man could easily turn into mission impossible.

Sarah and Jim spent many long nights discussing her project: the approach to take, the obstacles they were bound to face and how best to resolve conflicts with centuries old roots. They tried to anticipate objections that undoubtedly would be raised by the parents of the children, and by self-appointed leaders who controlled the lives of the parents and the children in the camp. After lengthy discussions, often with input from Dr. Tuqan when he could take time off from his busy schedule, it became clear that schooling girls alone would fall short of the desired goal. If the male population remained mired in its myopic view of females, women would have little chance of improving their lot in a society where men were almost in full control. Had been forever.

Out of respect for his guests Muhammad waited, an occasional twitch of his facial muscles betrayed his impatience. Sarah's reverie ended when he cleared his throat a second time.

"We have in mind," said Sarah, "to start a school for boys and girls at no cost to the parents. Transportation, books and meals will be provided – also at no cost. We need your help."

"Why?" Muhammad had been briefed by Younis prior to Sarah's and Jim's arrival. Nevertheless, he was convinced no one would embark on such a project for others without expecting something in return. And that something might be a price they were not willing to pay. He had told Younis as much. Younis's attempts to reassure Muhammad about his misgivings had failed. As far as Muhammad was concerned, for Younis Sarah was an angel sent by God. It was impossible for Younis to see beyond that point. Muhammad was convinced life did not spring up surprises of that magnitude without exacting a price. It did not – not in his world – not unless they had negative impact: if not immediately then in the future.

Any show of weakness on her part could have disastrous results. She decided to present her request with a few carefully chosen words. "A benefactor who wishes to remain anonymous has left a large sum of money expressly for this purpose. He has trusted me with the job. Mr. Jim Bateson here is my assistant."

Muhammad lit a cigarette and studied the ascending smoke as though the solution to the world's problems lay concealed in the rings he exhaled. Eventually, he addressed Sarah, his eyes shifting from Jim to his rubber thongs. "Why don't you, like all the others who are left with a large inheritance, take the money and enjoy life? Why do you want to bother with a bunch of refugees no one has use for and the world has long forgotten?"

Muhammad had done his homework. Her gamble at secrecy had failed from the start. Nevertheless, he had not tried to intimidate her, or argue out of blind prejudice because the offer was made by a woman. But would he cooperate? A fundamental rethink of the whole social system was necessary. And that's why she had to pursue the matter with finesse and diligence. "Because this is my parent's wish and my wish as well," she said in a manner reminiscent of a consummate politician at a fund raising event. "This might be hard for you to believe but it is a selfish thing, really. I get more pleasure watching children learn than wearing a ten carat diamond ring."

Muhammad threw the cigarette on the dirt floor and crushed it underneath his thong. "And I love walking through alleys deep in mud and living in a tin-roofed shack. Just like this one. Madame, please try and give us the real reason for your generosity."

Sarah had not expected her proposal to be greeted with applause. Even so, she found Muhammad's contemptuous response extreme and quite shocking. "What do you think is the reason, Muhammad?" Seeing the squalor around her it was not hard to fathom Muhammad's hostility and distrust. There were many multimillionaires among the Arabs in all the neighboring countries fully aware of the deplorable conditions the refugees had to endure: kings, sultans, sheikhs, princes, awash in money not earned by their efforts but bestowed upon them by chance, by geography, by world demand for oil. Few bothered to help those less fortunate than themselves. And when under pressure they relented and gave, it was mostly for political reasons – and at a price.

Abu Muhammad stopped smoking his water pipe. "My son is young and rash but he makes a valid point. Maher Sultan was not a devout Muslim when he was alive. He was married to an infidel. Some say a Jew. Why did he suddenly have a change of heart? And why have your parents chosen us?"

Offended, but not willing to dignify the old man's outburst with an answer, Sarah's attention shifted to Jim – immediately. Jim Bateson was not kind to those who spoke ill of Maher Sultan or any member of the Sultan family, or questioned their motives. He did not care who that person was or what the consequences of his response would be. His reaction was instantaneous.

He sprang off his stool, lost his balance and his huge body came crashing down. He pulled himself together at once and managed to settle precariously back on the stool meant to carry the weight of a child. As he spoke, he emphasized each word to leave no doubt in his listeners mind about his intense irritation and the pains he was taking to keep his anger in check. "Maher Sultan believed in the brotherhood of men – all men. So did Mrs. Sultan. If there were more individuals like them, this would be a much better world to live in – especially for people like you."

"Why us, and why now," the old man persisted oblivious of the limits of Jim's tolerance.

"You have not been chosen for a specific reason," Jim replied in the same manner as he had done before. "We'll be making the same offer to the other refugee camps. There is nothing new about it either. Mr. and Mrs. Sultan have helped support the refugee camps in Jordan and Lebanon for the past twenty years. At their request their contributions were kept anonymous. If you are interested, I can provide you with the records. I know. I kept them. They did not ask for anything in return then, and they are not about to after their deaths."

"What about the daughter," the old man's suspicious mind seemed to need more reassurance. "She's young. The youth of today is after having fun not troubling themselves with refugees."

"Fun," Sarah said as kindly as she could, "means different things to different people."

Sarah's words were greeted with an eerie silence.

After a brief pause, Muhammad spoke. "We don't want charity. We have schools and mosques where boys are taught the Koran. What's the use of learning more when you can't get a job?"

Although Sarah had made it a point to mention the school would be for boys and girls, she realized, in their conversations, neither Muhammad nor his father mentioned the word girl. Not hard to guess why.

Unemployment, up to eighty percent in most camps, was fertile ground for bitterness and hatred, especially among the young, and provided an endless supply of recruits for terrorist training camps. But lack of jobs could not be the sole reason for Muhammad's refusal to cooperate. Assuming there were other reasons or objections not yet aired, and Sarah had no doubt there would be several, it was essential to find a way to manipulate the situation to her advantage. She could not accept defeat. This was the worst camp she had ever seen. Even the barest, most basic necessities were out of reach of its residents, considered luxuries. Malnutrition, poor health, filth were the way of life, the most precious commodity being water, an endemic problem in the Middle East – far more so in the camps. Yet, somehow, the refugees drew on seemingly inexhaustible reserves which defied comprehension, and survived. The real killer though was politics – refugees, the pawns. "We don't intend to disrupt the existing system," Sarah said, hoping to get the message across with soothing words. "We want to supplement it with accelerated courses in English and science. If we work together, we will have schooled youth educated for today's markets and the jobs will follow. We can do it – if we work together."

After a long pause Muhammad spoke. "You're new here, aren't you?" he said, his lips curled downwards. "There are no jobs. It's that simple. Not even for Jordanians. We are unwanted guests in Jordan, a poor country, a country which does not have enough resources to take care of its own people. A good number of our young men used to work in Kuwait. The Gulf War closed that last door to us as well. The Kuwaitis don't want us. They think we helped Saddam Hussein when he invaded Kuwait. We have been branded as traitors. The other Gulf states are already super saturated with imported workers mostly from the Far East. Where do you propose we look for jobs?" Muhammad had yet to make eye contact with Sarah. He addressed himself to Jim or the space around Sarah. Sarah was not insulted. Arab men were not in the habit of dealing with women directly, especially about business matters. Perhaps abroad. If they had to. But not in the Arab world.

Sarah could not think of a quick answer. Jim came to her rescue. "I don't agree. There's a lot that can be done in Jordan. The potential exists. We should investigate."

"Like what?" Muhammad lit another cigarette.

"I certainly know of one." Sarah had no trouble recalling a recent experience she had had. "I took my laptop computer all around this city to have a small problem fixed. No luck. I had to ship it back to the States. I have questions about the software I need to use. No one has answers. A good technician could easily make a fortune here. I see a lot of computer stores but no support system available anywhere."

"Computers, huh?" Muhammad took a deep drag from his cigarette.

With those two words Muhammad had betrayed his fallibility. An opportunity not to be missed. "We'll make a deal with you," Sarah said, barely able to control her excitement. "We will arrange for you to train at a good school, as a computer technician, repairman, problem solver, whatever you choose, if you help us recruit students and talk to their parents."

Muhammad stood motionless, his face mask-like, his mouth slightly open, speechless.

A moment to savor. An idea hit her almost as an afterthought. "And if you agree to come back to Jordan and teach a few hours a week," Sarah added casually. "With pay, of course."

Muhammad's demeanor changed suddenly. As though he had woken up from a dream, from a trance. He snubbed his cigarette in a saucer on the window sill with too much force, turned around and almost made eye contact with Sarah. "I don't like jokes at my expense," he said as he lowered his body slowly onto the dirt floor, pushed his head back against the wall, closed his eyes as though waiting for the inevitable disappointing blow to follow.

"It's no joke." Not the reaction Sarah had expected, but, no doubt she had hit the right nerve.

Muhammad shot up like a puppet pulled by a string, rushed over, reached for and shook Jim's hand. "It's a deal," he blurted, the words spilling out of his mouth. "I ... I have ... never wanted anything more in my life."

Jim smiled. Muhammad was delighted to accept Sarah's offer but could not bring himself to shake her hand. "Young man," he said, "You're right on. It's a deal. But not before the basic rules are clarified. There's no charity involved in this deal. No one is giving you anything. In America we say there's no free lunch. We do something for you, you do something for us. We have room for approximately twenty students to start with. We want ten boys and ten girls, ages five to fifteen."

The words were barely out of Jim's mouth when Muhammad's father threw his worry beads down, swiveled around on his mat, raised his head towards Jim, and yelled, "No girls. No girls of any age, at any time. A girl's place is at home, a woman's place is in the kitchen. No girl is leaving this camp. I will not permit it."

"That's not a problem." Sarah pretended not to be bothered by the old man's outburst. "We will set up school here, in the camp, if that makes you feel better."

"No girls." The old man was emphatic.

"No girls, no deal," Sarah replied calmly.

Muhammad rose and paced the tiny room, fist pounding palm. "Why girls?"

"Why not girls?" Sarah asked softly, struggling to camouflage the turmoil within her.

Abu Muhammad motioned for Muhammad to approach. He whispered in his son's ear.

"You think everyone is," Muhammad countered without bothering to conceal his annoyance with his father's deduction.

Sarah did not have to be told what the old man whispered in his son's ear. She knew she was being accused of being a spy. It was a common enough occurrence. She rose, wrote her phone number and gave it to Muhammad. "Let me know what you decide. I can wait till tomorrow – noon."

Muhammad fidgeted. "Where abroad?" A touch of excitement and angst betrayed by those two words.

"Probably the United States. Or, wherever Jim can find a good technical school strong in computer technology. You'll

be on probation the first year. You'll have to maintain at least
a B average. If you don't, the funding will stop."

"The U.S. embassy does not give visas to Palestinians."

"That's not true," Jim said. "If you are accepted by a
school in the U.S., you can get a student visa. Not to worry,
though When the time comes, I'll take care of it for you."

Muhammad's mood bounced from sheer joy to panic a
few seconds after mulling over Jim's assurance. "This is all a
joke, right? I speak two words of English. Hello and goodbye
and you're telling me I can go to America and study to be a
computer technician?"

"Sure you can." Jim replied firmly. "Thousands of foreigners who don't speak English study in America every year.
We have special, accelerated programs to teach English to
non-English speaking students."

Muhammad smacked his forehead with his palm. "Damn.
Damn. Damn it all."

"That's not what's really bothering you, is it?" Jim was
annoyed and showed it. "It's the fact that we want girls."

"Muhammad," Sarah asked with an edge to her voice,
unwilling, past the point of caring. "Do you agree with your
father? Do you think girls should not be educated? Have you
ever stopped to consider how expensive ignorance can be?"

Muhammad looked at nowhere in particular while he
drew hard on his cigarette between breaths as though his life
depended on it. "I don't know what to think," he admitted
slowly, reluctantly. "When I listen to women like you, I wish
my mother and sisters were as knowledgeable, as at ease with
themselves and others as you are. Then I realize that if they
were, I would not know how to deal with them."

"A woman's role is to work for a man's pleasure, right?
And if they are knowledgeable and sure of themselves, they
might not be as compliant as you are used to having them. Is
that what you're saying?"

"I guess so."

"We like our women the way they are." Abu Muhammad

interrupted impatiently. "What do women need education for? When women get educated, the family as we know it is destroyed, finished. Nothing is ever the same again."

"Amen!" It sounded like Jim had had enough. He was ready to walk out.

Jim was right. It was useless to argue. The prejudices, the social and religious baggage the previous generations grew up with were too deeply ingrained – impossible to shake, much less change. But the more a situation seemed impossible, the more exciting a challenge it became for Sarah. Hence her determination to pursue her goal – regardless – definitely. If she could somehow teach women to stand up and fight for their rights, arrogance, which males considered their birthright would suffer a serious blow, total control would be a thing of the past. In most instances neither the very old, nor the very young presented the real problem. It was rather the age group in between. The age group which could not figure out what mind set was best for them to accept. The confused, the partially educated, the misinformed. For the time being there was nothing left to be said or done. Sarah turned to Jim. "I think Muhammad needs time to think. Let's go."

The blistering afternoon sun had sent the occupants of the camp to their shacks in search of shade except for a little girl, eight, perhaps nine, with a younger child, a boy about two years old precariously balanced on her hip, crying. The girl approached Sarah and Jim, timid, wobbling under the load she carried. "One of the neighbor's boys took my brother's candy." She too started to cry.

Jim had given away all the candy. Sarah decided to stay with the girl while Jim went back to the apartment to bring more. Iffat said she was the ninth of ten children. Her parents, older brothers and sisters were out looking for work. Her father and brothers took whatever was available. Sweeping streets, collecting garbage, carrying parcels from store to store in the souk. Her mother and sisters waited at a designated spot downtown where the wealthy came to look for servants, daily workers to do odd jobs around the house. Sometimes her family found work, other days were totally wasted waiting.

"Would you like to go to school?" Sarah asked the girl.

Powerful sun rays joined the waltz in space with dust particles and dirt kicked in the air by the occasional wind tunneling through the camp. Iffat squinted as she raised her head. "I don't know, Ma'am. I've never been to school."

Life offered few choices to these people. On the rare occasion when it did, aside from the traditional social and religious restrictions, the economic hardships weighed heavily upon their decisions. If Iffat went to school, who would take care of her little brother?

Sarah had a lot to think about. The problems were daunting, the solutions few. She often felt the only way out was to take the next plane leaving Jordan – destination irrelevant. But then she looked into the little girl's eyes and knew it was not time to buckle under. There was far too much to do.

It was an exhilarating thought, like a high on drugs. Only more so. From what she'd heard, with drug induced highs, the low never failed to follow when the effects of the drug wore off. But a challenge of the magnitude she had to deal with was bound to absorb all her energy, imagination and diplomacy. She suddenly felt great.

While Sarah chatted with Iffat, other children drifted towards them to ogle the stranger among them. She was not a stranger for long. Sarah talked to them, asked them about themselves, their families, their aspirations, their hopes, their dreams. The hunger to improve their lot, to help the family shake off the yoke of poverty, was on every child's mind at a surprisingly young age. They were eager to learn and their minds were not yet polluted. Taught analytical thinking they'd be armed to meet any challenge and decide for themselves what course of action to pursue. It was a golden opportunity not to be missed. Also not to be missed was the ratio between age and open mindedness. Children ten and older seemed to be already inhibited mentally by codes of conduct displayed by their elders. Doubtless, the solution had to come through education, gradually, over many years, perhaps decades and would require large sums of money to achieve the hoped for results. Although having the resources to meet the monetary challenges made her feel good, she knew that was only part of the solution.

Iffat's little brother woke up after a short nap, looked around, saw a boy licking a lollipop and began to cry again. Sarah checked her watch. Jim had been gone over two hours. The camp was half an hour's drive from her apartment on the road to Damascus, the traffic often heavy. Even so, Jim should have returned. Perhaps the car broke down. She thought of phoning the apartment but there were no phones in the camp. She decided to wait for a while before attempting to find a phone.

Meanwhile, a girl, about eight, dirty, in rags, who had stood a few feet away from the crowd, approached Sarah cautiously. "Is it true that you will help us go to school?" she asked, her voice cracking.

"Would you like to?"

The girl wiped her nose on her sleeve. "Oh, yes, yes lady. I'd love to. I worked for a couple of months for a rich family with a woman from our camp. They had a daughter about my age. The daughter taught me the letters of the alphabet. I know them by heart," she declared proudly.

Sarah felt a stab in her stomach. If Muhammad and his father refuse her offer, what could she do? Who could she turn to. That she'd eventually succeed was never in doubt in her mind even during moments when frustration added to more frustration pushed her to the verge of despair. "What's your name?" Sarah asked.

"Fatme."

"I promise, there will be a chair and a desk waiting for you when school opens the first of September. All you have to do is be there."

Fatme eyed the stranger silently for a moment, pulled her

skirt above her ankles and ran down the dirt road to a hut, like a child possessed. Within minutes faint cries filled the air, the cries of a child. Sarah stopped and listened. The screams grew louder. Suddenly, a small body came flying out the hut where Fatme had entered, followed by a man in his early twenties. He marched down the dirt alley where Fatme had fallen in a heap, bleeding from her nose and mouth and stomped on her. "This will teach you never to talk about school again." The young man yelled, kicked, spat, turned around and walked back to where he had emerged from, chin up, shoulders back, his duty as the guardian of the family honor duly fulfilled.

Sarah rushed to the child's side, lifted her gently into her arms, wiped her nose and mouth, as she ran up the dirt road to the exit in search of a taxi. While she ran, she heard a man call her name. It was Younis. He had returned home early. It was an unusually hot day, the city deserted. Rather than waste gas roaming the streets in search of passengers, he had returned to the camp and had been watching Sarah entertain the children from a short distance.

The taxi was parked around the corner. Younis asked Sarah to wait in the shade at the entrance of the camp while he brought the car around. The bleeding from Fatme's mouth dribbled down to her chest. Sarah was momentarily distracted as she reached into her purse in search of tissue paper. At that moment, unbeknown to Sarah, the girl's brother who had followed them, grabbed his sister's legs and tried to yank her out of Sarah's arms. They struggled, Sarah was knocked down and Fatme dragged back home by her brother.

When Younis returned with the taxi, Sarah begged him to return to the camp. Fatme needed medical attention. "Do whatever you can, please. Make sure she's checked by a doctor. Take her to the emergency room at the University Hospital. Ask for Dr. Tuqan. Tell the clerk to bill me. Please hurry."

Drained, blinded by tears welling in her eyes, she walked up to the street corner to wait for a cab. Mercifully, a taxi dropped off a passenger within yards from where she stood.

She took it.

Traffic was light. She was home in thirty minutes. She hurried to her apartment, key in hand. She didn't need it. The door was wide open, the place ransacked, and two police officers were busy assessing the damage.

Chapter 11

JIM WAS IN CUSTODY. AN anonymous caller had reported a burglary in progress in Unit 52 B. The police responded immediately. When they arrived, they found Jim in Sarah's living
room, paper bag in hand. Caught off guard, Jim attempted to
explain, realized the futility of it and gave up. He was handcuffed and driven to the police station for questioning.

Sarah's condo looked like a hurricane had blown through
it. Everything was scattered everywhere. All the contents of
all the drawers were spilled on the floors. Even the kitchen
cabinets had been emptied. Broken glass was piled high in the
kitchen sink. It looked like someone had deliberately broken
whatever could be broken and let the pieces fall wherever
they might. Glass and china bits glittered all the way from the
kitchen to the dining room. The two policemen who were still
in the apartment said they were at a loss as to why or how
such a thing could have happened. They claimed it was the
weirdest burglary they had ever seen. Why break glasses? The
noise would be enough to alert the neighbors. Not to worry,
though they assured Sarah. They had caught the thief red
handed. Still, they could not understand what prompted the
man to break just about anything that could be broken then
stand in the middle of the room waiting to be caught. As a
matter of routine they asked Sarah to check her belongings
and give them a list of missing items.

There was nothing of great value in the condo. Like her
parents, Sarah hated clutter, lived on the barest minimum. A
burglar would be hard pressed to find anything of value to
make it worth his while, he would not waste time emptying
the contents of drawers, nor would he break glass to alert the

neighbors as the police suspected. "I don't think anything is missing." Sarah fought to control the anger rising in her at the speed of her racing heartbeats. "You've got the wrong man in custody. Which police station was he taken to?"

The officers simply stared at her looking more confused.

Sarah turned to go.

"Miss." One of the policemen called her back. "You can't go. We've been waiting for you for over an hour. You must check your belongings first. We need a list of what's missing."

"To hell with my belongings. Where did they take my friend?"

"Your friend?" asked one of the policemen.

"That's what I said. Do you know to which police station he was taken?"

The policemen looked at each other, said nothing.

"You don't know, or you won't tell." Sarah was close to losing it.

The policemen exchanged glances – again. Neither man spoke.

Sarah stepped out, hurried down the stairs, ran through the courtyard to the parking lot in hopes of finding her car. She kept a spare key in her purse for emergencies, for when she'd lock her keys in the car. The VW was there, parked in its usual spot. She jumped in, then jumped right out. Invariably, when-ever she came and went, Attiyeh let her know he was around, and if there was one person who could shed light on what had happened, perhaps even who had done it, it would be Attiyeh. She peeped into his apartment. His door was locked and he was nowhere to be seen. Strange. Attiyeh did not leave the compound for any length of time without informing her. But she'd been gone all afternoon. Sarah got back in her car and drove up the street. She stopped at the small grocery store where she did most of her shopping to ask about the nearest police station. The grocer had gone to the mosque for evening prayers. His teenage son, Mahmoud, was in charge. Mahmoud often helped carry Sarah's groceries to her car.

Sarah liked the boy. Whenever she found an opportunity she spoke to him about the joys of learning, the advantages it brought to the mind and the pocket book – to all of life. Mahmoud listened fascinated, resigned, confused. "Why are you doing this to me," he once snapped back angrily. "You know I can't go to school. I have to help my father." Although in his early thirties, Mahmoud's father, Abu Mahmoud, had already fathered sixteen children from three wives and consequently had a hard time making ends meet. But it was the will of Allah and who was Abu Mahmoud to contest God's will.

"Have you seen Attiyeh today?" The store was less than a hundred yards from the compound. Attiyeh shopped there frequently for tenants of the compound, mostly for items tenants forgot to buy, or realized unexpectedly they had an urgent need for – usually cigarettes. Attiyeh was happy to oblige. It meant tips.

"He was here this morning," Mahmoud replied. "He grabbed a few items and ran. He said he had to go to the airport. His family was due to arrive from Egypt early this afternoon."

Of course, Sarah knew that. She had made all the arrangements herself. It had simply slipped her mind. She wrote down the directions to the nearest police station, thanked Mahmoud and left.

The officer in charge was about to release Jim when Sarah walked in. He was cordial, apologized. "I knew we had made a mistake the moment I saw Mr. Bateson," he said calmly. But, he explained they could not end the investigation because the culprit was still at large. "This is a strange case." The officer scratched the back of his head as he spoke. "You say nothing of value is missing. To ransack a place, break china and glass. Why? It doesn't make sense. Unless you have enemies we don't know about, someone who doesn't like you. Or, is trying to scare you for some reason."

"Perhaps both."

"Do you know who that person might be?"

Sarah thought for a moment, decided not to divulge her suspicion. She had to be hundred percent sure before she accused anyone. She shook her head. "Not really."

The officer assured her and Jim he would investigate the matter thoroughly. Sarah thanked him and they left. Back in the bug, Jim slumped in the passenger seat, morose, silent. Sarah herself was too upset to make small talk. She drove home.

There was still no sign of Attiyeh.

The front door of the apartment was closed but unlocked. The policemen were gone. Sarah and Jim stepped in. Sarah stopped at the entrance disbelief, anger, disgust stewing inside her as the magnitude of the havoc slowly sank in. It would take all night to dispose of the broken glass, sort out the stuff strewn all over the place, and perhaps a day or two to put everything back where it belonged. Where to begin?

Jim walked to the bedroom. The window was still open. He looked down for a long moment, turned back and said, "I think he broke his leg."

Her suspicions, only slightly in doubt, confirmed, she was swept with a feeling of revulsion, vindictiveness, anger. Feelings she despised, feelings she hardly ever permitted herself. "Was he alone?"

"I am not sure. I must have surprised him. I rushed to the window, saw his back as he jumped out, saw him hobble on one foot to the back of the apartment. I ran downstairs, checked the back and the front of the building. He was gone. Either he had an accomplice, or someone not knowing what happened, must have opened a door and let him in." Jim sighed. "What an idiot. Even though the condos are only two stories high, the courtyard is stone. He could have broken his neck."

"Ramzi does not burden his brain with thought. At best, he equates action with accomplishment – regardless of consequences." Sarah reflected for a moment. "Even if his leg is not broken, he will want it x-rayed. He's a hypochondriac. A sniffle, and his parents insisted the doctor make a house call."

"He probably went to the University Hospital. When you were sick, he said it was the only hospital he trusted."

"Let's find out. It's worth a try." Sarah reached for the receiver. The line was dead. "The phone is not working," she said as she replaced the receiver. She checked. The line had been cut. "Why am I not surprised?" she said, and she wasn't. She decided to go to Nabila's place to use her phone – if Nabila or her husband were home. Otherwise, she told Jim she would go to the grocery store and use their phone.

Nabila was home alone. She received Sarah politely but without the usual display of joy and gratitude. It looked like she was packing. Partially filled cardboard boxes were in the kitchen and living room. Although puzzled, Sarah put aside her concern momentarily and called the X-ray department of the University hospital. A recording informed her regular hours were from seven a.m. to six p.m., to call in the morning if it was a routine matter and gave another number to call for emergencies. It was a few minutes to eight. Sarah tried Dr. Tuqan next. His secretary said the doctor had been called to the emergency room, a child – battered. The secretary had no idea how serious it was, nor when Dr. Tuqan would be done. She did not expect him back in the office, as it was almost closing time. If Sarah wished, she could leave a message with the emergency room nurse for Dr. Tuqan to call her back.

Could it be Fatme Dr. Tuqan was taking care of? Sarah sure hoped it was. The secretary knew nothing more, not even the gender of the patient. If it were Fatme, it would mean that Younis had succeeded in convincing Fatme's brother to allow the girl to be treated. A great relief. Perhaps not. Sarah was too upset to think straight, was most probably seeing more than she should into an unrelated matter. Yet battered child meant a female – almost always. Males were revered and pampered. If it was Fatme, she was lucky. Battered females hardly ever made it to the emergency room for treatment. And if the battery resulted in the death of a female – so be it. It was the will of Allah.

Mixed emotions. Hope triumphed – momentarily. Sarah put in a request for repair with the telephone company while Nabila walked about aimlessly. She looked distraught. Sarah reached for her friend's hand. "What's the matter, Nabila? You look troubled. Anything I can do to help?"

Nabila burst into tears. "We can't take it anymore. We have to move out. Your aunts are here every day, threatening us, telling us you have come to destroy the youth, to force decadent Western ideas on unsuspecting poor people, to destroy Islam, and that we are helping you do it. They say you have the money to do it, you are a spy, you are a Jew. There is no end to it."

"Do you believe them?"

"I don't know who to believe or what to believe anymore. They say if you were a decent woman, you'd be married, home, taking care of your children. We are God fearing people, Miss Sarah. If you plan to teach anti-Islamic stuff to youngsters, we cannot be part of it."

"You are an educated woman." Sarah was amazed at how quickly she had become numbed to the repeated, idiotic, baseless accusations. "Do you think that teaching children to read and write, teaching them to think is anti-Islamic?"

Nabila threw her hands up in the air. "The truth is – I don't know what to think. Since the day Khomeini came to power, Muslim women have had the most difficult time of their lives. Who should we listen to? Who should we believe? The clergy eager to control every aspect of our lives, including our government, our parents who are often more confused than we are, or the Western media with its disdain for traditional values. Should we disregard what we have been taught to cherish and respect from childhood? And embrace what? The bombardment is relentless, Miss Sarah. What is right? What is wrong? Who is to say? And yet there is a whole other world out there. All you have to do is watch television. This is a very complex issue. Do you really believe you have the answer?"

Sarah chuckled. "Me? Of course not. No one does. There

are no absolute truths. But that does not mean we have to accept the status quo. We can work for change. Let us take one example. Don't you feel outrage at the sight of extreme forms of Islamic dress now being paraded all over the world by females of all ages? Little girls, three, four years old, their heads, foreheads and shoulders covered with scarves. How do you explain to a child what it is all about? And why? Defiance? Contempt? Superiority? Where does it say in the Koran that covering yourself from head to ankle makes you a better Muslim?"

Nabila shrugged. "Like I said, I don't know, but I feel the pressure – intense pressure. When we left Kuwait, although we lost our jobs, I was happy. I thought I would no longer have to live my life by the dictates of others, at least not to the extent I had to in Kuwait. I was wrong. In Saudi Arabia and Kuwait you know where the lines are drawn. You know you have been put on this earth as a receptacle for male sperms, to produce sons, to make life for the men in your life as comfortable as you can, be as invisible as you can. Otherwise, you'll pay a steep price, often with your life. Your limits are etched in cement when you are born without male genitalia and there isn't a damn thing you can do about it. However, I find it much more confusing and demeaning in countries like Jordan, Egypt and Syria. You have the modern mixed with the ancient and many versions in between. When you are young, inexperienced, and challenged daily by conflicting ideas, you are bound to take the path of least resistance. As a woman your survival depends on it. And that is what I'm doing – getting the hell out of here before one more neurotic, old woman accuses me of complicity in the destruction of my religion."

Sarah listened, a fixed expression on her face. "Have you found a place?"

"No. I called my cousin, Mona. They are here for the summer from Kuwait. They are getting ready to leave. They received permission to return, but her father does not know if he has a job or not. Hopefully, we can rent their apartment till we find a place of our own."

It was the same family Sarah had met on the flight from Damascus to Amman. She was pleased Mona's family was allowed to return to Kuwait as most Palestinians were denied reentry visas by the Kuwaiti government after the Gulf war ended.

Sarah walked to the front door. "I promised to call Mona, but I've been so busy I haven't had time. Say hi to her for me, please. And let me know if I can help you move."

Nabila thanked Sarah. She opened the front door for Sarah to leave. They were immediately greeted by angry shouts from a small crowd gathered in the courtyard about fifty feet away. They listened. Seconds later, Nabila turned to Sarah. "I think I heard my husband's name called. I can't see him though. There it is again. Excuse me, please." Nabila hurried towards the crowd.

Sarah followed.

It was a pathetic sight. A crowd of about twenty was gathered around a young man and an old woman. The old woman was screaming at the young man loud enough to pierce his eardrums. The old woman was Sarah's aunt Hamideh. She was wearing one slipper and holding the other in her right hand, held high, threatening to hit Nabila's husband, Samir, demanding to know why they had not moved out yet.

"We're not moving out," Samir said unperturbed.

Hamideh hit him on the head with her slipper. "Think twice young man," she yelled. "Otherwise your cooperation with my infidel niece will be amply rewarded. Just like she was."

Neither Samir nor Hamideh noticed Sarah and Nabila join the crowd. "And what is that?" Samir asked baffled. He had no idea Sarah's apartment had been ransacked. Involuntarily, a nervous smile crept across his face.

"Don't smirk, you son of a dog. You don't fear me. You think I am too old to harm you. Think again. I am not alone in opposing the infidel's grandiose plans. Those who refuse to cooperate with us will receive their just rewards."

Samir shook his head in disgust and started to walk away.

Hamideh hobbled after him, grabbed him by his shirt sleeve, and let out a profusion of curses. "We don't want that bitch here. She is a curse. As long as you and your wife keep helping her she will not leave."

"I don't see that it is any of your business."

Infuriated by Samir's blasé attitude, Hamideh tried to hit him, again, on the head. Samir caught her hand in mid air but that did not stop her fury. "I think you need to be taught a good lesson," she yelled, as froth spilled from her mouth.

Samir tried to walk away again but did not get far. The crowd had thickened.

"You will live to regret this." Hamideh's voice grew louder as her frustration mounted.

"I'll take my chances." Respect for elders is taught to children in the Middle East at a very young age. Sarah watched as Samir fought to keep his anger in check.

"You and your wife have been warned repeatedly." The veins in Hamideh's neck bulged more as the pitch of her voice rose. Sarah was concerned. If her aunt did not stop her hysteria soon, she might have a stroke or a heart attack or something. But Hamideh was not through yet. "Those who deal with the devil," she added while she wagged her index finger in Samir's face, "are no better than the devil himself. You leave us no choice. We will have to do to you what we did to that infidel. Perhaps more."

Samir turned around once more, never raising his voice, curious, cautious, confused. "And what would that be? Pray, tell me."

"Go to her place and see for yourself. The black man is there. He will let you in. Sarah is not home."

Sarah and Nabila stared at each other at a loss for words. Sarah stepped forward. A hush fell over the crowd. She walked over and faced her aunt. "Thank you for the confession my dear aunt. With these many witnesses, I will have no trouble putting you and your accomplice, Ramzi, behind bars."

Hamideh's mouth opened, and remained open, with her square chin resting on the fold bulging beneath her neck. The color drained from her face as she looked around quickly as though to assess the disposition of the onlookers and the degree of damage her indiscretion might have caused. What she saw could not have pleased her. With a look of disgust on her face, she threw her slipper on the ground, stuck her foot in it, pulled her abaaya down on her forehead, and marched towards her condo.

The crowd, mostly tenants, studied Sarah briefly then dispersed without comment, slowly, in small groups, murmuring among themselves. Samir joined his wife and Sarah. "I'd like to talk to you, if I may," he said to Sarah. "It is important. Let us go to our place."

School was due to open within a week. Samir was in charge of furniture and supplies. A tough job. Quality supplies were difficult to find and when available carried monstrous price tags. Samir worked long hours, without complaining, kept scrupulous record of all the purchases he made, and reported daily to Jim. Sarah considered herself fortunate to have found a man of Samir's caliber and integrity. The thought of losing him disturbed her immensely. She was concerned about the effect her aunt's attack might have had on him, and apologized for subjecting him to such an unpleasant confrontation. Samir shrugged it off. "I'm worried about you. What you propose to do is not an everyday phenomenon. Naturally, word about it has spread fast just about everywhere – from the grocer to the Ministry of Education. I heard from several sources – two today. They expressed serious doubts about your motives. Your father's family is doing the best it can to fuel the fire. Money is the issue with your relatives but not the public. They are genuinely concerned that what you bring as a gift might end up by being a curse in disguise."

"I don't get it. How?"

"What I sense out there is confusion. Too much of it. Initially, I thought educating women was the crux of the problem. I have learned that's only part of it. Some men are faring quite badly too; educated men – men who have lived and studied in the West. They find it difficult to deal with the rising tide of religious pressure, difficult to carve common ground between contradictory values, and impossible to escape either. We have a tough road ahead of us, and don't for a second entertain the thought that reason and logic will prevail. It never does in matters heavily laden with emotion, especially when laced with religion – not in the Arab world. Here we rely on how we feel not what we think."

Sarah wasn't sure she understood him well. "What do you have in mind, Samir? Of course men are affected, and they will be more affected when more women get educated. That's the reason we want to offer schooling for boys and girls. Are you suggesting that we give in at the first sign of trouble?"

His wife answered for him. "It is not the first sign of trouble, Miss Sarah, and it will not be the last. We can't wait for it to get worst. That is why we have to move out."

Sarah noticed Samir's demeanor change suddenly.

"That is precisely why we will not move out." He emphasized each word his gaze focused on his wife. "My conversation with Miss Sarah was meant to make her aware of what is waiting for her out there – a lot of apprehension, a lot of uncertainty, a lot of negative feelings. It should make no difference to us. Regardless of what I hear from different sources, I believe Miss Sarah's intentions are genuine, and her offer to help educate any child who wishes to be educated, a terrific opportunity not to be missed. Our concern stems from ignorance. We have simply not been exposed to people who are truly interested in the welfare of others without expecting anything in return. Like freedom, it is a difficult concept to get used to when you have spent all your life trying to survive against all odds."

"Thanks, Samir. I appreciate your trust in me, and I assure you, as long as there are people like you whose support I can count on, we will succeed – despite the misconceptions the public is being led to believe."

Nabila remained skeptical. "Maybe we should choose a different course, one that's not so controversial. At least to begin with," she suggested.

Samir walked over and put his arm on his wife's shoulder. "Educating a person to enable him or her to make choices based on knowledge rather than blind obedience, based on thought rather than emotion is the greatest gift of all. It seems to me our actions and reactions are mostly based on how we feel, not what we think. I fully agree with Miss Sarah. The only solution is education."

Nabila laughed a nervous laugh. "My dear husband, there is no sense in dancing around the issue. No one objects to educating males. It is we females, our men like to keep under cover, in our kitchens, preferably pregnant, preferably with male babies."

Samir rubbed his wife's shoulder. "Precisely. And that is the core of our problem. It is great for men in the short term, yet we fail to realize the price we pay. Forget the social consequences, the economic costs are enormous. It seems to me, the surest way out of poverty for any nation, is not to ignore the potential of half its population. If our women were educated, they could become agents of change, and in no time contribute to the economic welfare of the family and the country." He turned to Sarah. "Take my wife and I. We make almost double the amount of money we would have had it been only me working."

Sarah wished there were more men like Samir, men who did not walk around with a suffocating load of emotional baggage tied around their necks dragging them down every step of the way, men who could look beyond the immediate into the future and see reality for what it was. "You are both terrific. I am pleased Samir that you want to stay. But, if Nabila prefers not to, you really shouldn't."

Nabila hastened to defend herself. "Sarah, I love this

place. In my most blissful dreams I would not have dared dream that someday we would live in a beautiful condo like this, have friends like you and Jim, have a job. I have to learn to think positive – like Samir. He is a great role model for me and in due time, I will. We should have these discussions more often. It clears the air."

"We will. We agree on the basics, the details can be worked out, patiently, in time, by consent. I am convinced we will succeed if we work as a team, ignoring the naysayers. I can't believe there is a single woman, sound of mind, who agrees willingly to be a second class citizen, or, who believes the Prophet who brought so much improvement to women's lives in his time, would advocate the abuse and exploitation of women."

Nabila and Samir agreed. They were convinced, over centuries, the Prophet's message had been distorted by those trusted with its interpretation and propagation. Muslims who adhered to the basic teachings were trustworthy, kind people who helped those less fortunate than themselves and lived as pure a life as their circumstances permitted. Many claimed to be devout Muslims, but real Muslims were easy to spot. "They don't behave like your aunt Hamideh," Samir joked.

"That woman is dangerous," Nabila said. "I really think she will stop at nothing to get her way."

"Oh, no." Samir it seemed could not bring himself to say something bad about anybody, even a woman who had humiliated him in public. "It is not her. She is told what to say. She is an old woman. You take her and her sister Khadijeh too seriously. Let them talk. They have nothing better to do."

"You are minimizing their atrocious behavior in order to pacify me," Nabila replied, not in the least mollified. "They are not the harmless, old women you portray them to be. I know you are concerned with all the rumors you have been hearing. Those rumors start right here – in this compound, by two women determined to destroy the person who stands between them and a fortune."

"I understand, my dear. We will simply have to work that much harder to prove to them the futility of their efforts. Eventually, people will come to realize what an extraordinary opportunity we are being offered – no strings attached."

"I have heard it called by other names," Nabila replied, out of concern – not hostility.

"I know. My motives have received an incredible number of adjectives." Sarah needed this couple and was willing to do all it took to win their trust. "Among us there are those who are masters at twisting minds to suit their purposes. No logical person can condone such misinterpretation of facts. We have to do whatever it takes. Learn all we can, teach all we can. Teach anyone willing to learn. Teach logical thinking. If that is un-Islamic, if that is blasphemy, then so be it."

They were interrupted by the ringing of the doorbell. Samir opened it, spoke to a man briefly, and returned to the living room. "It is for you Miss Sarah, a young man. He said his name is Younis. He said it's urgent."

Younis shook his right leg impatiently while he smoked a cigarette. His face brightened when he saw Sarah approach, but only for a second. "We have trouble, Miss Sarah, bad trouble. When I returned to the camp, Fatme was alone in the room, semi conscious, bleeding from her nose and mouth. I looked everywhere but could not find her brother. I asked Muhammad for help. Fatme has no family except for that brother. Muhammad decided we should take advantage of your offer and take the girl to the hospital. We did. Dr. Tuqan, may God give him long life, left his practice and came to the hospital to check her."

Sarah's heart skipped a beat. "Is she all right?"

"Dr. Tuqan said she is doing OK – considering."

"What's the problem? Her brother?"

"No. We can handle her brother. While Muhammad and I were waiting for Dr. Tuqan to treat Fatme, a man, about my age, on crutches, and an old woman were waiting for X-ray results in the waiting room."

Quite a coincidence – if her suspicion proved true. "Can you describe him?" Sarah had to be sure.

The description fit Ramzi perfectly.

"Go on," Sarah urged.

"The man thought he'd broken his leg. He said he had fallen while stepping out of a taxi. Apparently, the driver pulled away with his left leg still in the car. I told him I drove a cab too. We got to talking. He asked why we were at the hospital. That's when I made the mistake of mentioning your visit. They said they knew you and wished they didn't. They claimed the sole reason for your generosity is to destroy Islam. The old woman said some other horrible things about you, and the young man called you ugly names that I will not repeat. We argued. Muhammad got angry, asked them to stop. Instead, the man taunted him with more ugly names directed not only at you, but your father and mother as well. Muhammad tolerated it as long as he could, but the man was so wound up he could not stop. To taunt Muhammad more, he stuck his face in Muhammad's face and asked, 'What is it to you? Has she slept with you too?' Excuse me Miss Sarah for repeating such impolite words. I have no choice – I have to; so you understand what happened next."

Sarah was not sure she wanted to hear any more unpalatable filth dispensed by Ramzi or her aunt. Unfortunately, she did not have that option. Younis had more to say.

Younis continued leaning wearily against the door. "That's when Muhammad lost control. He punched the man in the face. Like a child, this loud mouth threw himself on the ground, yelling and cursing. The old woman insisted the nurses call the police. The police came, handcuffed Muhammad and took him away."

"Where?" She should have been upset. And she was. But she could not ignore the implications of Muhammad's action. Muhammad had stood up for her. He had fought for her – a woman. There was hope.

"I don't know. The man saw blood dripping from his nose

and started screaming like a lunatic. Dr. Tuqan had stepped out of the treatment room to talk to us about Fatme, just as the police drove away with Muhammad. He told me to leave immediately – to let you know what happened. Miss Sarah, please believe me. Muhammad was not at fault. There was something weird about this man." Younis stopped and thought about it for a few seconds. "He displayed a remarkable lack of decency. He has a sick mind, if you ask me."

"Forget the young man," Sarah interrupted Younis impatiently. "Do you know where the police took Muhammad?"

"I have no idea. But Muhammad should not have to pay the price for that man's arrogance or his foul mouth. He needs bail. That's why Dr. Tuqan sent me to you. He said he didn't have time to post bail for Muhammad himself. He had left an office full of patients to come treat Fatme."

"How can I bail him out if I don't know where he is?" Sarah's anger was fast turning into revulsion. She did not like herself when she was not fully in control of her emotions. Her parents had taught her to have respect for what they referred to as 'differences of opinion' and to ignore ugly rumors. Her aunts' and Ramzi's opinions were definitely different – and destructive. Rather than ignore them, she had to put a stop to them – before the rumor mongering destroyed her and her plans. First though, Muhammad had be bailed out, a job difficult for a woman to do, especially without knowing which police station Muhammad had been taken to. "Mr. Jim is in my apartment," she told Younis. "Please, go tell him Muhammad is in jail, he needs to be bailed out. Mr. Jim will take care of it."

Sarah headed towards Hamideh's apartment. The place was dark. After several rings and a brief wait, she walked next door to Khadijeh's apartment where she thought she saw light in the hallway. But before she could ring the bell, the door opened, a pair of crutches appeared, one crutch missed the step above, Ramzi lost his balance and crashed at her feet.

Chapter 12

SARAH STEPPED BACK, SURPRISED. SHE had assumed he'd be in the hospital having his leg put in a cast or something. She could see it was badly swollen when he fell. Perhaps it was only a sprain. She bent down to help him. He pushed her away. "Leave me alone. I don't need your help."

"You wouldn't need anybody's help if you'd keep your nose out of other people's business."

Ramzi raised his head and shot her a penetrating glare. "What's that supposed to mean?"

Her childhood friend, cousin, self appointed boyfriend, and now resolute enemy, was up to his old tricks – always hiding behind someone's skirt while he did his dirty work. "You're lucky you didn't break your neck. My bedroom window is at least five meters up from the yard. You should tell me what you want instead of risking your life to get it. Perhaps, I would oblige."

Ramzi grabbed his crutches, pulled himself up, threw his head back and studied her for a couple of seconds. "Come to think of it, you can help," he said, his voice cracking. "Just go. Go away. I don't care where. I made the biggest mistake of my life when I asked you to come to Jordan. I did not think you'd come to stay. We don't need the likes of you here. You pollute everything; our lives, our culture, our way of thinking, even the air we breathe. The Queen with her so called 'modern ideas' is more than this place can handle."

Always a chauvinist, Ramzi considered it his God given right to be blessed with privileges the rest of his countrymen did not know enough to dream about, never gave his special status as a male a second thought, or concerned himself with those born with less than himself. It was the will of Allah. His problem was dealing with those who had more, especially those who had much more. That too, he conceded, sometimes, reluctantly, was also the will of Allah. But at other times, the wealth of the rich, especially his uncle Maher's, sent sharp, shooting pains through his being and drove him mad with envy. Later, however, before his uncle's death, he had come to believe that he really did not have a problem. All that wealth would automatically be his by marrying Sarah. It was not as if money was the only reason. They had grown up together and he loved her – in his own way. But not anymore. She'd betrayed him by associating with other men – Dr. Tuqan and the black man. She was always with the black man. Maybe there were other men, men he did know about. He hated it and let her know in no uncertain terms, before she was discharged from the hospital, what he thought of her association with other men. She in turn informed him, in no uncertain terms, it was none of his business who she associated with.

It took days for Ramzi to get over the shock. It had never occurred to him that she might have a say in the matter as important, as delicate as who she would or could associate with. He had taken it for granted that tradition would prevail. They were cousins. They would marry. Cousins always did. That was all there was to it. In his mind he had declared war on change, change of any kind affecting women. He had too much to lose with this so called 'women's liberation' thing. Western men had been forced to capitulate. He for one would make sure it never happened in the Middle East.

His parents and relatives poured as much fuel on the fire as they could. If the opportunity was not there, they created it. Sarah had many defects most glaring of which was her insistence that she was equal to men and had to have all the privileges and responsibilities men enjoyed. She could not be trusted to be pure – morally, sexually, and definitely not religiously. Her mixed heredity was the greatest negative for her relatives to accept – or so they claimed. They had never reconciled with the fact that their brother Maher Sultan, the business genius, the most sought after architect in the Arab world, the most eligible bachelor had stooped so low as to marry a non Arab – half Jew, half Christian and with no visible assets. It was absolutely imperative for Ramzi to find some other way of laying claim to the Sultan fortune.

Ramzi's relatives were not stupid. After many hours of consultation they had agreed to turn Ramzi's attention away from Sarah because they knew it was a lost cause. Sarah had never made a secret of the fact that she had no intention of marrying Ramzi – ever. They knew she meant it. Ramzi however chose to delude himself, convinced, eventually, she would be unable to resist his good looks, his charm, his love for her.

"What are you afraid of Ramzi? Have you been so brainwashed by your parents and your aunts that you can't think straight?"

"I don't have to listen to this. Do yourself and us a favor and get the hell out of here. Otherwise..."

"Otherwise what, Ramzi. What can you do to me that I can't do to you. I'm not one of your meek, oppressed women afraid to fight back. As a matter of fact, if you, your parents, and your aunts don't stop pestering me, don't stop meddling in my affairs and snooping around in my apartment, I will press charges against all of you."

"Really? And how will you prove it."

"Not to worry. This afternoon, Hamideh announced your adventures to a crowd gathered around her while she had a fight with Samir. She said you would do to Samir and his wife what you had done to me."

"Who?"

"Come now Ramzi, don't play the innocent with me. You know very well who. I bet it was your idea to confront a couple you feel should not be helping me – with encouragement from your parents and aunts of course. But you wouldn't do it. You sent an old woman instead. You always had others do your dirty work for you. Why should it be different now?"

Ramzi raised his eyebrows a defiant look on his face, pulled the door shut, and started to walk towards the yard. "You, my dear, are in my territory now. I am a man, and you are not. We know how to dispose of inconvenient women. Actually, it is real easy. We create a scandal, make life hell for her. Sooner or later the woman realizes the futility of fighting back and retreats – that is if she still can. Good bye, my dear. Your turn will come."

"Dream on." It was Dr. Tuqan.

Ramzi swung around, slipped, lost a crutch and fell. Dr. Tuqan lifted him off the ground, gave him his crutches. He said, "Every time I see you you're having an argument with someone. You seem to enjoy harassing men and domineering women. I think your time would be better spent taking care of your ankle." Dr. Tuqan explained to Sarah how, in the emergency room, learning the treating physician on duty was Dr. Tuqan, Ramzi had let out a torrent of curses, grabbed his crutches and walked out.

"I wouldn't let you touch me if I were dying." Ramzi hobbled across the yard, towards the street.

Dr. Tuqan's voice followed him. "Do yourself a favor. See an orthopedic doctor. Your ankle is pretty badly shattered."

Ramzi did not look back.

Sarah's admiration for Dr. Tuqan grew with each encounter. She knew doctors in the Middle East were revered not only as healers but also as wise men. Many had trouble accepting the adulation graciously. A few felt they were failures because they found it impossible to live up to the public's expectations. Suheil Tuqan however, seemed to have no ego problems. He did not consider himself wiser, or more intelligent, or better informed than others. He was a physician, trained to do a job and he insisted on doing it well. "I'd invite you to my place for a drink," Sarah said. "Unfortunately, I don't think I have a single glass left which has not been broken." She told him what had happened.

"I'll be content with just a spot to take the weight off my feet. I need to talk to you."

On the way to Sarah's apartment, Dr. Tuqan apologized for his impromptu visit. The reason was Fatme. She had cuts and bruises, her nose was broken and her right cheekbone crushed. After treating her, Dr. Tuqan wanted to discharge her and follow her progress as an outpatient. Hospital beds were scarce, demand excessive. But Fatme cried and begged to stay. She was afraid to go home. Dr. Tuqan then discussed the matter with Muhammad. Muhammad felt Fatme's situation was quite hopeless. Thirteen and not spoken for. She had polio as a child – limped pretty badly. No one would marry her. Her brother used her as his own private servant.

"Thirteen?" Sarah repeated shocked. "She looked more like an eight year old."

"She is malnourished, at the mercy of her brother who is unemployed and dependent on the relief provided by United Nations."

Attiyeh greeted them at the door, head down, voice barely audible. He and Jim had cleared the kitchen and the dining room of broken glass and cleared the floors, piled clothing in one corner, paper in another. Dr. Tuqan stood in the doorway a look of disbelief, shock apparent on his face.

Attiyeh approached Sarah. "Please forgive me, Miss Sarah. Had I been around none of this would have happened. But I couldn't leave. They detained my wife and daughters for six hours – for no reason." He shook his head. "I don't understand. All their papers were in order. The official at passport control said they were. But another official stopped them, took them to a room and told them to wait. Six hours. I waited for them in the lobby, called your number several times but there was no answer. Then suddenly, without explanation the door opened, my wife and daughters were let go. We took a taxi and came home immediately."

Could it be the work of Ramzi and or her aunts? Was it a

ploy to keep Attiyeh away from the compound long enough for Ramzi to ransack her apartment? Or was it vengeance misplaced: to make Attiyeh pay for his loyalty to Sarah, for getting his apartment back? It did not matter. "Is your family home now?"

"They are, Miss Sarah. The girls are tired and hungry. Their mother is fixing dinner. Tomorrow my wife and I will tidy up this place, make it spotless, like nothing happened."

Sarah thanked him, gave him a fistful of Dinars, told him to take his wife and daughters shopping instead. "Thanks Attiyeh, you've done a great job already. The rest of this stuff needs sorting and reorganizing. That's my job. You take care of your family. Buy the girls school clothes and warm coats. I hear it gets pretty chilly in Jordan, in winter."

"School ... School clothes? For ... For the girls?" Attiyeh's eyes widened, his gaze, as always, directed at any point away from Sarah. "Miss Sarah, girls don't need school. They will marry soon. They're already spoken for." His voice was barely audible, his facial muscles contorted, the picture of a man in pain.

"How old are they?" Big mistake, Sarah admonished herself. She should have told him that she would want the girls in school when she offered to bring them to Jordan. She had assumed that he would expect as much. She was wrong.

"Thirteen and eleven."

Sarah shook her head and walked to the kitchen. For the moment, she was too tired, her nerves much too frazzled to continue the discussion.

Attiyeh looked around for an encouraging sign from Dr. Tuqan. There was none. He murmured, "Thank you. Good night." And left.

"He won't get much sleep tonight," Jim chuckled.

Suheil Tuqan had collapsed on the sofa. "What a crazy day I had today, more so than most days. I am exhausted and utterly disgusted with the violence I have to deal with on a daily basis. The physical damage I can handle – most of it anyway – that is aside from those who land in the morgue: repeat patients, patients with severe internal bleeding, and head injuries. What I can't deal with is the arrogance, the folie de grandeur our male population thrives on. It drives me crazy. Do you realize that over ninety percent of the patients I treat are females and almost all their injuries are inflicted on them by male members of their own families?"

"Hey," Jim yelled from the kitchen, "do not despair. Sarah will fix it all – if she does not get herself killed in the mean-time."

Jim's concern for Sarah's welfare often clouded his judg-ment. He had promised Maher Sultan to look after his daugh-ter like Maher Sultan himself had done. Jim was a man who took his promises very seriously. Sarah was grateful yet knew it had to be checked occasionally because it could easily spin out of control. "Jim, If you don't approve of what I am doing, please, feel free to leave. Don't expect me to reverse my deci-sion because men in the Middle East abuse women, or, because some jerk chose to rearrange my apartment. I am under no illusion that change will occur overnight or even in a decade or two. But if those who can help give up because they don't like trouble, the escalating fanaticism we face today will reach a point of no return in no time, and we will have no one to blame but ourselves."

Jim threw up his arms in despair. "All right then, let's try another place, somewhere far from your father's relatives. It is tough enough to deal with a project like what we have in mind in untested waters, single handedly, against what many would consider to be insurmountable odds. We will certainly be better off without interference from a bunch of malicious, selfish bigots."

"You're wrong, Jim," Dr. Tuqan interjected. "Sarah's chances of success are better here than anywhere else in the Arab world despite the antagonism of her relatives. She prob-ably hasn't given it much thought, but she has allies here. Despite overwhelming political, economic and foreign policy problems the King and the Queen have to deal with, and the minimum resources available to them, they are committed to education, to the logical interpretation of the Koran, and to helping the citizens of this country reach their full potential. That's more than you'll find any place else."

"Granted," Jim argued, "but there should be a limit to what a person is willing to bear. When that point is reached, it's time to bid farewell."

Jim's remarks sparked an immediate response from Sarah. "Jim, I think you underestimate the human potential to bear hardship, especially mine. If there are no challenges, no obstacles, no problems to wrestle with when you're struggling to achieve a goal, than in all likelihood your goal is not worth working for. I prefer to regard hardship as experience, an opportunity to learn and profit from."

"Right," Jim snapped back. "It's easy to forget what's important in life. In your case I'd say your safety is far more important than what you call experience. It's like landing blindfolded in an unmarked minefield. Removing the blindfolds does not diminish the danger. You're dealing with ruthless people here, people who will stop at nothing to lay their hands on your parents' fortune. At least in another country we won't have to concern ourselves with a bunch of crazed relatives."

Sarah smiled sweetly. "Look at me, Jim. I'm a big girl. I can take care of myself, and I will deal with each situation as it presents itself. Even if my relatives got rid of me, they would not be able to touch the money. You know that and they know that but refuse to accept it. Perhaps, in due time they will come to their senses and give up their hopeless schemes."

Jim was not convinced. "They won't. There's too much at stake."

"Maybe so," Dr. Tuqan said, a soft-spoken man, not given to hyperbole. "But problems with her relatives pale in comparison to what Sarah would have to face elsewhere. In any other Muslim country she will have to deal with leaders who are desperately clinging to power and who are unwilling to alienate the clergy – regardless of the price their citizens are forced to pay. Saudi Arabia, Kuwait, Qatar, and the rest of the gulf sheikdoms come to mind. Many others are dictatorships, disguised as democracy Middle Eastern style: like Syria, Iraq, Yemen, Oman, Iran and the smaller sheikdoms. The citizens of those countries are always under the watchful eyes of the secret service and a few countries like Saudi Arabia and Iran have in addition the religious police to contend with. Often, the religious police are more feared than the regular police. That leaves Egypt – another disaster in the making. Since the start of Islamic Fundamentalism, Hosni Mubarak is finding it more and more difficult to control the Islamists. They attack tourists, kill and maim them: tourists who bring desperately needed dollars to a desperately poor country. A huge army and a secret service network spread throughout Egypt has been unable to stop the terrorists. Do you know that famous women singers, entertainers, even belly-dancers have had to give up lucrative jobs after they and their families were repeatedly threatened with death, and this, in a poor, over-populated country where tourism is the only source of income for many? The way I see it, Sarah's choices are limited, limited indeed."

"You're right, they are. It's like telling her 'pick your poison'. In my opinion she should forget the whole thing. I don't think her parents realized the enormity of their request, nor did they realize how difficult it would be to implement it. Maher was firmly convinced that if Arabs who could help did so, it would raise the standard of their people, and the world, especially the Arab world would be a better place to live in. I personally believe it is way past that point and definitely not the job of one woman – even if money is not an issue."

A sagacious man, Jim was a difficult person to convince. But Sarah had to try. Her commitment was total. Jim had to understand and accept it. "Like I told you many times before Jim, I won't know until I try. I believe in education. Those who are educated will have a better chance finding jobs, they will be able to raise well-informed children and face the world with understanding rather than hatred. We don't need any more terrorists. We need dialogue – intelligent, informed dialogue. This small world is getting too crowded. Unless and until we learn to talk to each other instead of killing each other, we can not claim to have progressed from the Stone Age."

"Have it your way, Sarah." Jim reached for the front door. "You are my primary concern. The Middle East is much too complex for my simple mind to comprehend. But if educating children is what you want, then so be it. I have a favor to ask of you before I leave. Bolt your door tonight and every night. Attiyeh said he heard rumors that Ramzi is determined to run you out of town. Bye."

Sarah did not respond. Her thoughts soon drifted miles away, to Fatme – handicapped, penniless, female, and with no place to go. Sarah knew no solution could be worked out without the approval of Fatme's brother, Ali. Yet the mere thought of dealing with that brute, churned her stomach. Still, something had to be done. It was unconscionable to keep Fatme in the hospital while acutely ill patients waited to be hospitalized for lack of beds. She thought of taking Fatme in temporarily. Would Ali permit it? Perhaps Muhammad could help. Dr. Tuqan disagreed. It would set a precedent which could lead to trouble in the future. There were too many children living under similar or worst circumstances. A more comprehensive approach was needed.

Sarah jumped up excited. "A boarding school!"

Suheil Tuqan shook his head – no.

"Right. I'll be lucky if they allow the girls to attend day school. Did you see Attiyeh's face when I mentioned school clothes for the girls? It is not like it is the first time he heard about it. He knows my plans. I bet he thought his daughters would not even be considered because he is only a caretaker. The challenge grows bigger by the day. Jim says like Sisyphus, I'll be pushing the rock uphill, but it will always come tumbling down, probably on my head and he is probably right."

"He's not. He told me privately how much he admires your resolve, but he had not counted on the hostility of your relatives. He is worried about your safety."

Sarah worried about Fatme's safety, felt she was to blame for her hurt – at least partially, and wondered what to do. Dr. Tuqan urged her to discuss the matter with Muhammad.

"He's supposed to call by noon tomorrow. He might and he might not."

"He will. His gratitude was infinite when he learned it was you who had bailed him out. Actually, I felt he was awed by your generosity. Awed and perplexed. It's not often that a beautiful, young woman finds helping those less fortunate than herself a rewarding adventure."

Sarah returned from the kitchen with two glasses of wine and sat next to him. "I had not thought of it as an adventure. An experience, maybe. I like the beautiful, young woman part though. It feels good to be pampered."

He reached for both glasses, placed it on the coffee table, hesitated for a moment, then placed his hand on hers and watched for her reaction. She let it be. After a moment's hesitation, he moved closer, wrapped his arms around her and murmured softly, "You. You had to come into my life when I had given up all hope. I walk in a daze from the hospital to my office, unable to concentrate, incapable of thinking about anything or anyone except you, and yet I know I can't have you." He held her tight and kissed her hungrily, a look of despair in his eyes.

She studied his face for a clue. "What makes you say that?"

"It's obvious, isn't it?"

"Enlighten me."

"You can have any man you want. Why should you want me? I have so little to offer."

She snuggled closer to him. It was the first time she felt totally relaxed since that fateful phone call from Ramzi informing her of her father's illness. It felt good – real good, especially so because Suheil was one of the few men she had met in the Middle East who did not feel the world revolved around him. She responded to his caresses with a smile, clung to him to let him know it was all right. She was not the untouchable person he was convinced she was.

His face lit up as if a veil had been lifted from it. "I ache for you," he said softly while he showered her with kisses. "I was fully prepared to be thrown out – couldn't help myself – love you too much – lost control." Then quickly pulled himself back as though fearful of pushing his luck too far. "Please forgive me."

"I love you too," she replied simply.

He remained motionless, expressionless, assessing her words, not convinced he heard right. It did not take him long though to notice the shine in her eyes, and the inviting smile on her face. "It's for real. I can't believe it." He grabbed her, carried her in his arms, and whirled her around.

"On one condition." She pulled her hair away from her face. It fell softly, naturally, in big curls over her shoulders.

"What? What? Anything. Name it."

"No more gloom and doom."

"Are you kidding? You and I will conquer the world."

"We will if you put me down before you get a hernia."

He let her down reluctantly while his lips roamed over her neck, her hair, her face, overjoyed, acting more like a teenager than a thirty year old man, six foot two, with the looks and physique of an Arabian prince. Yet he seemed to be totally unaware of it – a rare phenomenum in the Arab world.

The phone rang. It was Muhammad. The conversation lasted a couple of minutes. Sarah put the receiver down and yelled, "Yes. Yes. We're in business. Muhammad has decided to accept my offer. He was too excited to wait till morning. You were right. He says he is willing to do anything for me. I need only ask."

"I knew that. We had a long talk in the hospital.

Muhammad is a smart man. He said his father opposed his decision vehemently. The old man believes education is detrimental to females, to their families and to society. He relented when Muhammad promised to pay for a trip to Mecca his father has been dreaming about all his life. After Muhammad completes his studies abroad and returns to Jordan, he is confident he can find a good paying job which will enable him to pay for his father's trip. I told him he could have a job in my office – guaranteed. When something goes wrong with our computers in the office or in the hospital, no one knows what to do." He stopped and studied her for a moment. "You're not with me. What's on your mind?"

Her thoughts interrupted, Sarah quickly confessed her mind had wondered to the task ahead of her. Her imagination's portrayal of the classroom, the children behind desks, their eager minds, like sponges waiting to be soaked, had taken priority. However, one desk was unoccupied. The desk assigned to Fatme. Fatme's excitement at the thought of attending school was an experience Sarah could never forget. "I promised her," Sarah said as she fought back tears.

"Promised who? What?"

"I promised Fatme schooling and look what happened. She can't even go back home."

Suheil Tuqan watched her pain quietly. A man of few words, he had spoken more in one night than he usually did in a week. He reached for her hand, kissed it repeatedly as though apologizing for her suffering which he somehow seemed to feel responsible for. She dropped her head on his shoulder, forced herself to relax and instantly an idea popped in her head. She shot up. "Let me run this by you and you tell me what you think. What about Ali taking over Muhammad's job as leader of the camp. Do you think Muhammad will agree?"

"You're going for the jugular, right?"

"You bet. In return, he will have to permit Fatme to go to school and promise not to touch her."

"Ramzi was right. You are a terror."

Chapter 13

SARAH'S AUNTS DEMANDED AN URGENT meeting with her a month after the children started school. They claimed the noise the children made during recess, their comings and goings, and the Islamic principles trampled underfoot by having boys and girls in the same classroom, was too much for them to bear. They were willing to move to Kerak, to Sarah's father's house, if she'd give it to them for free.

After refusing numerous generous offers to buy their condos, her aunts' sudden decision to move out puzzled Sarah. From the moment she had arrived in Jordan they had made her business their business. What caused them to change their minds? How could they know what was going on at the compound if they were not there? Would they have someone spying for them? Kerak was her father's home, where she could feel his presence, be with him occasionally. And, eventually, if her school plans in Amman worked, she intended to start schools in small towns and villages all over Jordan. Kerak was first on her list.

It hit her – suddenly – like a snowball – out of nowhere.

"All right," she said, "you can move to Dad's house – free, if you will sell me your condos."

"No," both aunts yelled in unison.

"Why not? The children and I are here to stay. You can't stand the children or me. You prefer to live in Kerak. Why not sell the condos? I'll pay you whatever the market value is."

"No."

Sarah thought they were holding out for more money. "All right, then, I'll pay you more."

"Don't waste your time." Khadijeh spoke with the

warmth she usually reserved for people she disliked.

Sarah was not surprised, but to learn the true cause for their demand she had to probe deeper. "You want me to give you a huge piece of property, property which means a lot to me, property worth a lot of money, because you have decided to pretend to move out?"

"Pretend?" Hamideh's shrill voice rose by several pitches when she got excited.

"That property belongs to us," countered Khadijeh.

"No it does not, and yes pretend. This has to be one of Ramzi's brilliant ideas: plotting to get something for nothing – never satisfied. He should get a job, go back to school, do something. Just leave me alone."

"So you will have a free hand to do as you please. I promise you, it will never happen." The disdain in Khadijeh's voice intrigued Sarah. There seemed to be no limit to the amount of hatred Khadijeh could harbor towards Sarah, hatred which had been brewing ever since Khadijeh was forced to leave her brother's house in Saudi Arabia for trying to circumcise her.

Their reptilian efforts to demonize her were in vain. Sarah refused to be intimidated. "I figured as much. Unfortunately, scheming for Dad's money is a waste of time. It has all been spoken for. Ramzi should know that. Surely he learned that much from Dad's lawyers when he went snooping around in London."

The women exchanged angry glances. "You're just like your mother," Khadijeh shot back angrily, "stubborn. She had to have her way – always. And of course your father never found anything wrong with that. But Maher is no longer with us, and you're not going to get your way like your mother did." She rose, pulled her abaaya down on her forehead, while her sister gathered her voluminous self together and they marched out of Sarah's apartment muttering curses under their breaths.

After her meeting with her aunts, for two exhilarating

weeks Sarah's plans continued to work without a hitch. Two classrooms full of eager, excited children learned and played with unparalleled joy. Nabila took charge of one classroom, Sarah the other. There were twenty students in each class. Double what Sarah had hoped for when her imagination unfettered by reality ran loose. Even Attiyeh, who was initially horrified at the prospect of sending his daughters to school, and later objected to his daughters being in the same room with boys, relented. Out of fear that he might loose his job he agreed to allow the girls to attend school – provided they were given desks at the farthest corner of the room, away from the boys.

Jim and Samir took care of the school's day to day business.

Muhammad was doing great too. Sarah received two letters from him and had a long phone conversation with him the night before. Jim had arranged for Muhammad to live with a family in Bellevue, Washington and attend school at Bellevue Community College – computer classes during the day, and special English at night. But Muhammad had a major problem he did not know how to deal with. It had nothing to do with the usual difficulties foreign students faced in a strange country, especially when they did not speak the language. He was much too euphoric to bother with such minor detail. His problem had to do with who he was. Muhammad had been taught ever since he was a child, who the real enemy of the Palestinian people was – America. Without America there would be no Israel, there would be no Palestinian refugees, there would be no war, no Intifada, no problems. Americans were a Godless, Jew-loving, Arab-hating nation, responsible for the sufferings of his people, the Palestinians. He had agreed to come to America not because he wanted to but because it was the only choice Jim gave him. Now, however, everything he ever believed in was totally shattered. Americans, total strangers went out of their way to help him without expecting anything in return. They spent hours teach-

ing him English, getting him acquainted with his school, his
surroundings. They listened to him without interrupting even
when his comments were tainted with emotion and were fac-
tually incorrect. They did not hate Arabs, were not rich like
everyone abroad assumed they were, and had to work hard to
cope with every day problems like people everywhere.
Mostly though, he found them to be fair. And that he could
neither explain nor understand.

"You've ruined me," he joked. "How can I return to
Jordan, deal with people who think the way I used to. I'll be
crucified."

"Now that's a fine word for a Muslim to use," Sarah
teased back. "Don't you know crucifixion is strictly for
Christians?"

"Maybe. Except now I don't know who or what I am. I
can't thank you enough though, for drawing the poison out of
me – you and Jim. Jim is a great guy. I don't know what it is
about him that fascinates me so, but I aim to find out."

"No need for thanks," Sarah reassured him. "I look at it as
an investment and I intend to recoup my investment fully –
with interest."

"You will. I promise."

For Sarah, that phone conversation alone was worth all
the agony she'd been through. And Muhammad's letters,
painstakingly written in English to keep her abreast with his
progress, reaffirmed her belief that her decision to help others
less fortunate than herself, was the right decision.

For a while, she almost forgot where she was. She had not
left the compound except when absolutely necessary, and it
had paid off. Even when she was in an euphoric mood,
brought upon by an unexpected achievement in her attempts
to start the school, she had not imagined it would be as
smooth an operation as it had been to date, nor as gratifying.
Yet there was a gnawing pain at the pit of her stomach cautioning her not to let her guard down. Problems of the magnitude she faced could not have disappeared in a few months.

They had not.

Fatme, Sarah's favorite and best student, and six other female students did not come to school on Saturday, following the Muslim weekend on Thursday and Friday. The children present in the class had no idea why the others were missing.

Concerned, Sarah found it hard to concentrate on teaching that morning. Short of driving to the camp, or sending a messenger over, there was no way of contacting Fatme's brother, Ali, or someone who might know the children's whereabouts. Should she wait? For how long? For what purpose? The children lived more than thirty to forty minutes away by car – depending on the traffic, had no transportation other than the school bus, and were not permitted to leave the camp except to go to school supervised by one of the mothers who rode the bus with the children. No mother had ridden the bus with the children that morning. As the morning wore on, Sarah's anxiety wore her down. She could not think of a plausible explanation, but the warning sign was there. The missing children were all girls. Sarah reviewed her options over and over again. The distraction was taking its toll. She could not relax until she made the decision to drive to the camp immediately after classes were over for the day.

A few minutes past eleven, the door opened, Ali stuck his head in and inquired if he could have a word with her.

"Of course." Sarah's voice betrayed her relief. "Come in."

"I'd like to talk to you in private."

Sarah stepped out. Ali looked distraught. Her stomach did a quick somersault. "What's wrong?"

Ali studied his sneakers, his entwined hands, back to the sneakers while he fidgeted non-stop before he could bring himself to blurt out, "Too much. To begin with, I did not expect to be ostracized to the degree I have been when I accepted Muhammad's job. People are calling me 'pimp.'"

She had expected worst. "People? Who are these people?"

"They say I am a pimp. I have prostituted my sister for

position and money. I have never been in a situation like this before. My honor is all I have. I can't deal with it."

"Are you going to allow a couple of old women to run your life for you?"

Caught off guard, Ali's voice was barely audible. "How ... How did you know?"

"What's there to know. They've been at it since they learned I was here to stay. Where is Fatme? Fatme and six girls are missing this morning. The bus driver said he waited, asked around, but no one seemed to know where the girls were. Do you?"

Ali shrugged his shoulders.

Sarah could feel her anger rising. "We have an under-standing, Ali. If Fatme does not attend school, you don't have a job."

Ali shifted his position but did not answer.

"Need I remind you that it is also your duty to make sure every child gets on the school bus every morning, unless they are sick. And I need to know that. You said you couldn't be happier when Muhammad appointed you camp leader, that you were a changed man. You have not hurt Fatme, have you?"

"No Miss Sarah. I gave you my word. I have not touched her and I won't. There ... There ... is too much to discuss ... Serious matters ..." He turned his face away, reached for a cig-arette, lit it and smoked.

"If you have other problems we will have to discuss it some other time. I have a class to teach."

Ali stared at the ground.

"The children are my immediate concern. I want them here tomorrow morning and I expect you to make sure they get on the bus – every one of them."

"I'll try. I can't force them."

"That's not good enough. If you talk to the parents, remind them of the agreement we have, the consent forms they signed, there should be no objection."

Ali did not answer. His eyes remained glued to the ground.

Sarah found his hesitance, his seemingly reluctant attitude, unnerving. "Ali, go home and think about it. Would you rather have a decent, well paying job, or wait for charitable handouts? You know how difficult it is to find a job. Don't let remarks by ignorant people dictate your decisions."

Ali threw his cigarette on the ground, crushed it, moved as close as he dared to Sarah and whispered, "It's not me alone, Miss Sarah, they talked to the parents of all the girls in the camp. Everyone is upset. They said the girls are taught to hate Islam, its codes of conduct, its traditions, their parents, all men. It was terrible. There was a young man with them. He claimed to know you. He said you want the girls to become like you, independent, to do as they please, to disobey men. Your ideas are destructive to family, to religion, to social conventions we know and respect. He went on and on. It was awful."

None of it surprised Sarah. She wondered what had taken them so long. She asked, "Ali, can you read?"

"Yes, of course." Ali replied proudly. "I finished elementary school."

Sarah stepped back into the classroom, picked up a book from the desk of one of the children, stepped back out. "Here," she said, "Read, then tell me what you think."

Ali scanned a few pages, returned the book to Sarah. "It's the same book I had in school."

"That's right. We have to comply with all the requirements requested by the Ministry of Education. Otherwise, we lose our license. Also, by law, we have to teach the children an hour of religion every day. A teacher we have contracted through the Ministry of Education teaches our students religion. The government decides what he teaches, not we. Go back to the camp and explain to the others what you learned here. The people who spoke to you are not interested in your welfare or the children's welfare. What you witnessed was self-interest masquerading as concern for others. Bluntly put, they want the money I spend on the children for themselves. Money is all they care about."

Ali kept shifting his position but did not answer. He looked tortured, overwhelmed with problems he was ill prepared to cope with. Sarah had thirteen pairs of eager eyes watching her through the window, waiting patiently for her return. Ali, a skeleton of a man, shifted his weight from foot to foot, again and again. He seemed reluctant to leave, yet unable to bring himself to speak what was on his mind. He had interrupted the English class, the class the children loved most and looked forward to. Although the children waited patiently, quietly, Sarah wanted to get back to them. Actually, the antics of her relatives, annoying at first, had become totally boring, tiresome. Nonetheless, it would be rude to ask Ali to leave, so Sarah invited him to join the class, see and hear for himself, if he wished.

Ali declined. He said he had seen enough and trusted Sarah fully. The camp was in turmoil. He took his job as camp leader seriously. He had to get back. But, before he left he wanted to ask Sarah a question to clear his own mind, to better understand why – why did females need education? After all, they would soon marry, take care of their husbands, children, home. It seemed to him, the time, money and effort would be much better spent on men who had to go out to a harsh world to earn a living.

"We discussed that issue at our last meeting, when you took over Muhammad's job. It's possible I did not clarify it enough. Is that what's bothering you? Is that why you came?"

"No. That's not why I came. You did discuss it. But I need to hear it again to resolve the conflict in my own mind, to have answers ready when your relatives come around again, and for the mothers of the girls who are totally confused. They don't know whom to believe. To date, our women have not been educated and we have done all right."

It was the same argument Sarah had to listen to whenever

the subject of women's education came up. The last to be accepted, the first to be discarded, especially among the poor, girls' schooling was the first place parents economized, even when not hampered by religious dictates, even in a country like Jordan where the government encouraged education, regardless of gender. A house is built brick by brick Sarah reminded herself. If I succeed in changing the thinking of one man, especially the camp leader, who knows how far his influence will go. "Ali, how often did you see your father when you were growing up?"

"Hardly ever."

"That's quite common here, right?"

"Yes. Most men have several wives and a lot of mouths to feed. They are hardly ever around."

"Think about it Ali. Wouldn't you have been better prepared to cope with life had you had a mother who was educated?"

Ali fidgeted, rubbed his chin, seemed to mull it over, but did not answer.

"You're not worried about waste, Ali. You're worried about losing control. That need not happen if we approach it sensibly. If we remain stuck in the past, we are doomed. If we copy the West blindly, we are doomed. If we find a balance that works for us – as a nation, we can pull ourselves up and reach heights we cannot now imagine exist."

"We don't need to educate women to do that."

"Sure we do. If we deny knowledge to half our people, that's what we will be. Half a people." Sarah peeped into the classroom. Eyes full of great expectations remained focused on her every move. "I'd like to get back to the children," she said. "Come tonight. We will talk."

Ali stepped back, stopped, examined the cigarette between his fingers for a long moment, opened his mouth as though he had more to say, but did not. Sarah waited. He smoked, drag after drag, but did not speak. She shook her head baffled. He left her with an uneasy feeling, with the impression that he did not have control over whatever it was that was bothering him. She assumed it was due to his inability to process contradictory choices, choices not to his liking. Yet choose he must. It was hardest on the young, caught in the crossroads. Although some cultures had already taken great leaps forward into the twenty first century, others remained mired in the past, distorting ancient cultural values, religious teachings, social doctrines – to promote their personal agendas – to retain control. With the advance of technology and the speed of communication bringing diverse cultures and values to practically everyone's living room, Sarah wondered for how long centuries old traditions, codes of conduct, misconceptions, prejudices and superstitions could face the onslaught without losing out? Distortion of the truth, misinformation, lies, helped confuse unsophisticated minds like Ali's. 'Pimp.' They called him 'pimp,' because he let his sister attend school – school with boys in the classroom. An unforgivable sin. I have a long, hard road to travel, Sarah thought. But the harder they make it for me, the more the challenge, the stronger my resolve.

She watched from the classroom window as Ali walked away, slowly, reluctantly, head bent. Her previous meeting with Ali was when Muhammad had brought him over to her place to introduce him as the new camp leader, the man who was to replace Muhammad. Young, proud, ready to take responsibility, Ali was a happy man. Not at all the brute she had to deal with when he had dragged his sister, hurt and bleeding from Sarah's arms back to the camp. In Ali's mind he was doing his duty, what society expected of him as the adult male in the family: protect his sister from corruptive outside influences and guard the family honor. There was no family except for him and his sister. But that mattered little. He could not nor would he shirk his responsibility. Sarah hoped Ali would come that night so they could have a good discussion, to prepare him for further assaults, assaults she fully expected to intensify. For the moment, she had a job to

do, children who waited patiently, children for whom being in
a classroom was such a great privilege that they did not dare
make a wrong move, much less noise. She made a conscious
effort to put aside her discussion with Ali and concentrate on
her work – with moderate success. She was not too concerned
with Ali's opinion about women. He didn't know what to
believe or whom to believe, but seemed eager to learn. It was
the incessant interference, the ever more resourceful ways her
relatives devised to obstruct her efforts that irritated her more,
mostly because she had to take time out to deal with them.
She admonished herself. What a fool she was to let the calm
of the past two weeks lull her into thinking that she had hopefully endured the last of their assaults. The worst was the
banality of it all, the same accusations, the same demand –
money.

Late that night Sarah received a phone call from Ali giving her a detailed account of what happened after he left her.
At Ali's request, Sarah taped it. "I will describe it to you as it
happened," Ali said, "in minute detail, because my life might
depend on it."

Exiting the main gate, lost in thought, head still bent
down, Ali said he stepped out and accidentally bumped into a
young man. A package the young man was carrying got
knocked out of his hand and into the street. Ali rushed to the
street oblivious of the oncoming traffic, forcing cars to come
to a screeching halt, retrieved the package and gave it to the
man. He apologized for his carelessness and was about to
walk away, when he stopped and looked around. Then, almost
as an afterthought, he asked, "Excuse me. Do you work
here?"

"Who wants to know?"

Ali said he explained who he was.

"I work for Miss Sarah. What can I do for you?" Samir
introduced himself.

"It's important. Can we talk in private?"

Samir pointed in the direction of his apartment and the

two men walked there. Ali said he kept looking over his shoulder repeatedly until they reached Samir's apartment. He told Samir he knew they were not home. They were at the camp, and that is why he had come this morning. But he was worried about the young man – the young man who always came with them had not come.

"Who are you talking about?" Samir asked puzzled.

"Miss Sarah's aunts."

"You know them?"

"Met them last weekend."

"What were they doing at the camp? It's so far. How did they get there?"

"I have no idea," replied Ali. "But they've been there everyday since."

Samir opened the door and invited Ali in. He told Ali to take a seat on the sofa in the living room. As custom dictated, Samir quickly fixed Arabic coffee, poured it into two small cups and offered one to Ali. He sat across from Ali in an armchair.

"I came to talk to Miss Sarah about an important matter, but couldn't," Ali explained.

"Why not?"

"I don't feel comfortable talking to women – especially about delicate matters."

"What did you want to talk about?"

"I ... I really don't like what she's doing. I mean this business of teaching girls can easily spin out of control. Any man in his right mind wants to keep women where they belong – at home, where they are safe, where they can be protected." Ali stopped and sighed. "There I go again. I did the same thing to Miss Sarah."

"If you have already talked to Miss Sarah, why are you repeating it to me?"

"No, no, that's not it at all. I did not come here to discuss girls or schools. I can't bring myself to talk about what I came for."

"And what's that?" Samir was getting impatient.

Ali's voice quivered. "She has been extremely kind and generous to me. I'll never forgive myself if I don't warn her."

"Warn her about what?"

After an awkward pause, Ali took a deep breath, rubbed his hands together, studied Samir briefly, and said, "I think her life is in danger."

Samir gazed unblinkingly at the young man. It was preposterous. Who would resort to such an extreme measure? And Why? He did not believe Ali but felt he had to listen to him just in case. "Interesting. Very interesting. Miss Sarah told me this morning, for the first time, a number of students were absent. Is something going on we should know about?"

"A lot more than you think."

"How did you find out?"

"By chance." Ali explained his father had four wives. Um Hassan, the third wife, worked as a maid for the Itani family, Ramzi's parents. She had been working there for years. She disliked her employers because they treated her like she was less than human, and stupid, because she was poor. But Jordan was full of refugees and jobs difficult to find. She had six children to feed, and after ten years of service was allowed every other weekend one Friday off. All her efforts to find another job had failed. So she continued to work for the Itanis year after year. Last week, Ali explained, she came home on Wednesday unexpectedly. She came to see me half bent over, unable to stand straight. She said I should tell my father he has to provide for his children until she finds another job. She was through working for the Itanis. Apparently, Ramzi Itani kicked her in the back with his foot. His foot is in a cast. When she fell down, he threw a huge ashtray at her head because the kick hurt his foot. She was only twenty-three years old, but feared Ramzi had broken her back thus rendering her helpless and useless.

"Why did he kick her? What did she do?"

"He wanted her not to take that Friday off. They were

expecting guests, important people. He wanted her to work."

"I gather she refused."

"No. She said she would if they paid her extra. He got furious, called her an ungrateful bitch, kicked her, ordered her to leave and never come back."

"You've lost me."

"Sorry. I saw the incredulous look on your face when I told you I was worried about Miss Sarah and knew that if I didn't give you the details of how I came to know about Miss Sarah's life being in danger, you would not believe me."

"Go on."

Um Hassan, like most other women in the same predicament had few weapons to fight back with, Ali explained. When she realized it was all over for her, she started spilling the entire dirt about the Itani family. Our camp is like a beehive. Everyone buzzes every tidbit of news, gossip, whatever, to everyone else. Most are idle with nothing better to do. Um Hassan, like the rest of us at the camp, has heard all about Miss Sarah and her work with the children.

"Excuse me," Samir interrupted, exasperated. "I don't understand what Um Hassan has to do with Miss Sarah or the children?"

"You will, in a moment." Ali continued, as if driven by an enormous compulsion. "Ramzi wanted Um Hassan to work on that particular Friday because the Itanis were expecting visitors, clerics who had been to their house four times within the past three weeks. Visits by clerics had never happened before, not since Um Hassan started to work there over a decade ago. Ordinarily, Ramzi had nothing but contempt for them. Apparently, it was Ramzi's idea to involve the clerics. They came to discuss a serious matter – closing Miss Sarah's school."

"Clerics? What have they got to do with it? She's running a school, for God's sake. Not a seminary."

"That's the latest – after the Minister of Education refused to help them. It seems the Itanis donated money to the mosque in their neighborhood, told a lot of lies to the top cleric about Miss Sarah, and managed to recruit him to help them remove this detrimental woman from their midst. The top cleric wrote a letter to the Minister of Education urging him to close the school. A month later, after a thorough investigation, the Minister advised the top cleric to forget the whole thing. But they persisted – sat in the Minister's office every day waiting for him to step out. Finally, the Minister told them his brother, the Minister of Health, Dr. Abdullah, had definite information about contacts Miss Sarah had in high places, and that the King and the Queen had heard about her work and were delighted with it. They should do themselves a favor and leave Miss Sarah alone."

Samir was getting restless. "So, what's the problem? Look. The package you knocked out of my hand came special delivery for Miss Sarah. I promised I'd make sure she gets it. You said you thought her life was in danger. Did I miss something?"

Ali reached for yet another cigarette, studied Samir briefly, smoked, finally he placed the cigarette in the ashtray on the coffee table and threw his arms up. "All right, I'll spell it out for you. When the Minister of Education refused to discuss the matter further, the clerics met the Itanis at their home and discussed possibilities."

Instantly, the color drained from Samir's face. 'Possibilities' was a word used by Palestinian terrorists when the person in question was undesirable – in other words marked for elimination. "Possibilities?" Samir repeated incredulously over and over. "No. I don't believe it. It can't be. No one can stoop that low – not even Miss Sarah's relatives. Um Hassan must have heard wrong."

"I had the same reaction you did. I questioned her, asked her to repeat the words she heard exactly as she heard them. I made her swear on the Koran. She did."

"I still find it hard to believe."

Ali shook his head knowingly.

"Are you sure?"

"Absolutely."

"You trust this woman?"

"In this matter, yes. What motive does she have to lie? Her children are not in Miss Sarah's school. The Itanis would not permit it. And she knows fabricating a lie involving clerics could be costly – especially a lie with such serious implications. And why should she? Her quarrel is with the Itanis. She mentioned the clerics not to implicate them, but to show how low the Itanis were willing to stoop to rid themselves of Miss Sarah. However, the matter is far from resolved. According to Um Hassan, the clerics want to have complete authority to do the job. They want the aunts to leave Amman immediately, not to discuss their niece or what she is doing with anybody and they want Ramzi Itani out of the picture. She said Ramzi readily agreed when the clerics were present. After the clerics left, he told his parents he would do as he pleased. No stupid cleric was going to tell him what to do."

Samir shook his head. He said he knew Ramzi well from high school. The Ramzi he knew was a pampered, spoiled teenager, although even then he made no secret of his love of money. He wanted lots of it, but did not impress Samir as a person who would resort to extremes to get it. He was too much of a coward and had neither the imagination nor the guts to think of 'possibilities'? However, no doubt he'd love it if it happened to fall in his lap.

"Like you, Um Hassan is baffled too," Ali said. "She said Ramzi did the usual teenage stuff: the loud music, the loud friends, parties when his parents were away. But she insists he was never rude. Actually he had very little to do with her until this summer."

This summer, the men agreed a fortune was introduced into the equation, a fortune which in Ramzi's mind belonged to him because he was a male – first in line. Money did strange things to people. Ramzi would never agree to the cleric's demand that he stay out of the picture. He had too much to loose.

"Miss Sarah thinks Ramzi and her aunts are the only ones opposed to what she is doing," Ali continued. "She does not know a fraction of what is going on. The religious community is vehemently opposed to education for girls, especially nowadays with their influence on the rise they are not about to allow it to be threatened by a woman – a Westernized woman. Some say a Jew. The chief cleric of the district Miss Sarah lives in has appealed to the King to have Miss Sarah expelled from the country. I have heard that they did not have much luck there either. They are desperate."

They must be, Samir agreed. Whatever information Ali had might be crucial. "Did Um Hassan," Samir had trouble finishing his sentence. "Did Um Hassan ... Did she give you any details ... I mean details about – 'possibilities'?"

"No, none. She didn't have to. Their method is simple. Elimination – in the name of Allah."

Of course it was. Samir knew it well – having lived in Kuwait and Saudi Arabia. In their minds, Miss Sarah had sinned. Her teachings were anti-Islamic. The clerics in Jordan did not have the influence the clerics in other Islamic countries like Saudi Arabia enjoyed, and they were not prepared to loose what they had, least of all to a woman. If they could not remove the threat legally, plenty of other means were readily available to them – free – by martyrs. Samir thanked Ali and promised to relate the information to Miss Sarah. He told Ali he realized it took a lot of courage for him to come to the compound to report what he knew. Unfortunately, he was quite sure Miss Sarah would dismiss it as yet another nuisance. Jim, her assistant, had heard similar rumors from different sources: rumors to run her out of the country, hurt her, but not possibilities. He tried to warn her. Apparently, it was beyond her comprehension that anyone might want to harm her. "God, I hope not," Samir said. "I have yet to meet a person I respect and admire as much."

"Respect, yes. Admire, yes. But also confused," Ali confessed. "No matter how I try to rationalize it, I come up short. Why should a beautiful, rich, young woman want to waste her life among refugee children? What's in it ..." Ali stopped in mid sentence, cocked his head to the right and listened. "What's that noise?" he asked.

"What noise?"

Ali listened again, shook his head, then turned his attention back to Samir. "Just my nerves, I guess. I thought I heard a ticking sound."

"We don't own a clock."

Ali rose. "It is late. I have to get back to the camp, talk to the mothers. Miss Sarah wants my sister Fatme and the girls in class tomorrow, or I loose my job. I think I can convince the girls' parents. It shouldn't be too difficult. The girls don't go to school – the parents don't get their allowances. It's that simple. But my problem is not simple at all. I don't know where my sister is. I have searched everywhere. She is always the first to get on the school bus. She did again this morning. But when the driver rounded up the other kids and was ready to leave, there was no Fatme to be found anywhere. I've got to get back to look for her. Miss Sarah would never forgive me if something were to happen to her."

Concerned, Samir scribbled his phone number on a piece of paper and gave it to Ali. He told Ali to call him if he needed help to search for his sister, to call him immediately, any time, day or night if he heard anything new about 'possibilities.'

Ali assured Samir he would. He opened the front door and stepped out. "Even if she won't listen," Ali pleaded, "please tell Miss Sarah to be careful."

Samir had left the package in the kitchen. "I will. I promise," he said. "I'm on my way to see her right now. Let me grab the package."

Ali claimed within seconds, a powerful bomb exploded. The kitchen, the package and Samir were blown to pieces.

Chapter 14

AFTER THREE DAYS OF INVESTIGATION, the police concluded the explosion was due to a faulty valve on the gas tank which supplied gas for the cooking range – a gas leak, perhaps a smoldering cigarette. There was no piped in gas in the country and because the explosion was powerful enough to kill a man, demolish a kitchen built of cement, and blow its contents over a hundred feet in all directions, and because this was a country where explosions hardly ever occurred and there were no trained investigators, the assumption was easy to make and the findings were not questioned. It did not surprise Sarah or Jim. It managed to compound their fears. Encouraged by the lack of preparedness by those in charge, Sarah and Jim expected the perpetrators of the crime to strike again and soon. Ali's description of what had transpired between him and Samir left no doubt in Sarah's mind that the bomb was meant not only for her but for the children as well.

"The perpetrators message is clear," Jim said when Sarah told him and Suheil Tuqan about the phone call from Ali. "Stay away from Sarah. Otherwise it might cost you your children's lives."

The police report changed all that. Hence their fear that the criminals might strike again. The parents had no reason to doubt the police report that it was an accident, thus negating the intended effect of the explosion. It seemed like a job meticulously planned and executed except for the chance encounter between Ali and Samir. In Sarah's opinion, the thoroughness of it automatically excluded Ramzi. He did not have the imagination or the know how, and Sarah doubted, in this particular instance, he would trust someone else to do the job for him. Her aunts had disappeared. She had no idea where they were and couldn't care less as long as hey were not around to torment her. Would clerics resort to such extremes to get their message across, to protect their self-interest? Jim had no doubt. Sarah refused to believe any human being could stoop that low.

Slumped in an armchair, Jim had dozed off momentarily, exhausted from three days and nights of vigil. When Sarah decided to stay in Jordan, Jim had moved from the hotel to an apartment within a few minutes of walking distance from the compound. But his distrust of those opposed to Sarah's work was so intense, and his concern for her safety so overwhelming – especially since the bomb incident that he refused to let her out of his sight. Grateful for his concern, Suheil Tuqan brought Jim a change of clothing every morning and waited in Sarah's apartment until Jim showered, after that he left for the hospital.

Sarah paced the small living room oblivious of the world around her, sleepless, head pounding, stomach growling from three days of deprivation self-inflicted on mind, body and soul.

Once again, before leaving for the hospital Suheil begged Sarah to take a tranquilizer, perhaps a glass of milk, something, anything. Otherwise, he would be forced to admit her to the hospital. He could no longer watch her waste away.

She heard him but not much registered lately, especially when it had to do with her. It was the fourth day after the incident and Dr. Tuqan's passionate pleas were ignored – again. This time though, he refused to take no for an answer. He would not leave unless she relented and took some nourishment.

"Please go," Sarah pleaded. "I need to know how Nabila is doing."

Nabila was in the hospital under heavy sedation. The sight of her husband's body pieces scattered all over the courtyard was too great an emotional trauma for her to handle. Seconds after witnessing the disaster which had struck her husband and home, she had lost consciousness. With the help of Dr. Tuqan, Sarah managed to have her admitted to the University Hospital under the care of an internist recommended by Dr. Tuqan.

"I spoke to her late last night after the police report was published," Dr. Tuqan said. "She believed it and it helped her calm down. A natural disaster is the will of God. She wants to go home – today. I could not convince her to stay. Amazed me."

Jim pulled his body up slowly. "What home? I have guards around the clock watching her apartment. There is a big hole where their kitchen was. How will she live there, a woman, alone, with those two witches and their nephew still on the loose."

"Something has to be done," Sarah said. "I can't go on cooped up in this apartment much longer either."

"Maybe we should convince Ali to go to the police," Dr. Tuqan said without much conviction.

"What good will that do," Jim countered. "No one will believe him, and if they do, they will pile the blame on him. Ali is not stupid. I bet he figured as much and is long gone."

"Any news from Fatme?" Dr. Tuqan did not wait for an answer. "God what a crazy world we live in. Where on earth could that girl be?"

"She's not at the camp," Jim said. "I had an investigator check it out. No one has seen her since Saturday morning. She got on the bus, first – as always. When a few of the girls did not show up, the driver went to look for them. When he returned, Fatme had disappeared. Her books were on the bus seat, the seat she always sat in. But she was nowhere to be found. The driver searched everywhere, questioned everyone he could get hold of. No one had seen or heard a thing. Something tells me she was kidnapped."

"Don't say that," Sarah snapped. She dropped her weary body on the carpet. "I'm sorry. I did not mean to yell at you."

"I am expecting a call from an agency which provides discreet protection for the royal family," Jim explained. "We have to work an arrangement whereby you, Nabila and the children are protected. Nabila is the problem. How to convince her of the need for protection if she is not told the truth."

"I think we should tell her," Sarah said. "We should tell her about Ali's phone call. She might accept it as truth and she might not. She has a right to know."

Dr. Tuqan objected. "I don't recommend it. Now is not the time. It will devastate her emotionally and mentally. I will see her some time today, talk to her, and assess her condition. I will also talk to her treating physician. Let's take it from there."

"What about a psychiatrist or a mental health worker? Maybe therapy is in order here. I don't know. I do know though we must help her somehow."

"We have no mental health workers and Nabila refused categorically to talk to the psychiatrist. She said she was not crazy. Can't say I blame her. The stigma here borders on irrationality." Dr. Tuqan's answer did not surprise Sarah. She knew the answer but hoped she was wrong.

"Still no visitors?" Sarah's thoughts were constantly with Nabila. She felt helpless, frustrated. She was not permitted to reach out and comfort her friend, not even phone her, while her friend had to deal with the most painful situation of her life.

"No Sarah. I won't know until her doctor checks her this morning, and you won't know because I'm not leaving until you eat something." Suheil went to the kitchen poured a glass of milk and handed it to her.

She drank it slowly, without protest, and almost immediately felt better.

Suheil Tuqan glanced at his watch. "Before I leave, I want you to promise me you'll eat. Otherwise, you'll hear very little about Nabila from me."

Sarah promised, much too tired to argue.

Suheil dashed out the door. He was late to work.

If only the pounding in her head would stop.

She sat on the carpet, legs folded, bent over, her head held in her hands. The agony of defeat, the terrible pain caused by her good intentions, the absurdity of greed, the intolerance of small minds, her stubborn refusal to acknowledge the impossibility of the task she had charted for herself, the enormity of negative forces determined to thwart her efforts, her unrealistic expectation that logic would prevail, had resulted in the death of an honest, loyal, innocent young man. Was this only the beginning of things to come? She could no longer delude herself. There was no guarantee that in the end she would prevail because her intentions were good. At this point, she was not sure she really wanted to prevail. Perhaps the naysayers were right. Perhaps some things in life were meant to be the way they were. Perhaps change was not in the best interest of those she insisted needed change. Although Jim spared no effort in assisting her to realize her dream, and had stopped urging her to leave, he let it be known he did it because he cared for her, not for her goal. Yet to pack up and leave was out of the question. It was the first time in a long while she felt needed, she felt she made a difference in the lives of children whose only experience prior to her arrival, in the place they called home consisted of filth, stench, mosquitoes, flies and hunger. She could not and would not break her promise to the children. Besides, she had no intention of giving Ramzi and her aunts the pleasure of her absence.

Most of all, she felt, if she quit, she could not live with herself.

The phone rang. It was for Jim.

After a brief conversation Jim turned to Sarah. "It's Attiyeh. The guards I hired are outside the main gate. I told Attiyeh to let them in. Two men are assigned specifically to guard you, two others will guard the children and four men will cover the compound around the clock. I have also asked the agency to keep me informed about the camp."

"How?"

"If we don't hear from Ali, and I doubt we will, he will be replaced by an insider."

"What about Younis? He can take over until we hear from Ali."

Jim disagreed. Younis made good money in tips, from the restaurant. No doubt he'd quit his job and take over the running of the camp to please Sarah, but it wouldn't be fair to him even if Sarah compensated him for the loss. If Ali returned, he would want his job back and Younis would be hard pressed to find work.

"Ali will call. I'm sure." He has to, Sarah thought. Where could he have disappeared?

"I don't think so. He knows police often tap phones and he knows the police report is a cover up. I am sure he also knows they'll be waiting to arrest him. He was the last person seen with Samir. Several people saw them together. The police have questioned three persons already."

"Whom?"

"Attiyeh, his wife, and a tenant whom Ali collided with as he dashed into the street to retrieve the package he had knocked out of Samir's hand."

Sarah thought for a moment. "I can vouch for him. He came to see me before he talked to Samir. He did not have a package with him. He had nothing with him. Half a pack of cigarettes. That's all."

It took Jim a while to convince Sarah truth might not be necessarily what the police were looking for. They needed a scapegoat, someone to put behind bars to prove they had done their job, someone without clout, someone who did not have the resources to fight back – someone who could not prove his innocence.

The pounding in her head intensified. "That will make it a lot harder for us to locate Fatme. Where could she be? Why would anyone want to harm a handicapped, innocent child?"

"To get even with you, to ..." The door bell rang before

Jim could finish his sentence. Jim stepped out, closed the door, conversed with two men, opened the door and stepped back in accompanied by the two men. Jim introduced the men to Sarah. They thanked Jim and left. "They are your guards," Jim said. "They are British trained, come highly recommended. You probably won't see them much, but they'll be around, day and night and don't you dare dismiss them."

"Aren't you overreacting a little? I mean there is no real proof it had anything to do with me. Do I really need protection twenty four hours a day?"

"Humor me."

"All right. Have it your way."

"I said I will work for you," Jim teased. "I did not say I will always do what you want me to do. And now if you will excuse me, I want to go to my apartment, soak in a hot tub, maybe have a drink or two. Call me if you need me. Bolt the door after I leave."

Soon after Jim left Sarah collapsed on the sofa and in moments fell asleep, a fitful sleep, full of short, interrupted dreams; dreams – intense, fervent, demanding with an undeniable immediacy to them. Her father appeared twice, handsome, young, erect, smiled, disappeared. A large kitchen table, a woman Sarah never saw before, in a coarse, black outfit, grabs her, forces her onto the kitchen table, flat on her back, wraps a big roll of white bandage around her body. Immobilizes her. The woman reaches for a partly rusted razor blade she had previously set on a small table nearby. Suddenly, a commotion. Screams. Khadijeh launches at Gwynne, Sarah's governess. She pushes Gwynne, Gwynne pushes her back, knocks her against another woman standing behind her. Gwynne shoves the woman in black aside, throws herself on the kitchen table, tears the bandages to shreds with the razor blade, pulls Sarah off the table, presses her against her ample bosom and marches out of the kitchen. Her father reappears, embraces her, she stops sobbing. He disappears.

Comforted by her father, Sarah dozes off once again.

Moments later, a young girl, nine, maybe ten years old, with a black hood on her head, trembling, wailing, dragged to the public square by a man in a sleeveless black shirt with bulging muscles. A mullah reads a prepared statement. The girl is condemned to death accused of adultery. Rocks begin to rain on her from all directions, immediately, incessantly, for over an hour. The girl's body twitches one last time. The wailing stops. Their driver's ecstasy at being fortunate enough to participate in such an entertaining event is etched in Sarah's memory forever. Could a similar fate be awaiting Fatme?

Sarah sprang off the sofa, perspiration pouring down her face. I've got to find her, she said to the empty room. I've got to find her. She grabbed her purse and dashed out the door.

Outside her apartment, at the foot of the stairs, a young man sat reading a newspaper. Following her footsteps, two men cautiously waited for her next move. Sarah got in her car, the men got in their car parked next to hers. They smiled. She smiled back, an uncomfortable smile, like a caged animal in a zoo unable to escape the gaze of onlookers.

She drove to the camp.

They followed her.

The autumn breeze helped dispel part of the stench that filled the air at the camp. This was the fourth day her students were on an unexpected vacation. Sarah noticed two of her students, both seven years old, heads bent over a book, a few feet away. They did not see Sarah walk towards them. They were ecstatic when they saw her.

"Have you come to take us back to school, Miss Sarah," asked one of the girls, her voice full of expectation.

Before Sarah could answer, the second girl jumped up, "Please, please, Miss Sarah. Could you please take us back to school?"

"We'll try to have you back in school tomorrow – if I can find the bus driver. If not, definitely Saturday morning even if I have to come get you myself."

Then it dawned on her. She had not heard from the bus

driver since the previous Saturday when he drove the children to school minus Fatme and the six girls. After the incident, Jim had to drive the children back to the camp because the bus driver was nowhere to be found. Sarah had not given it much thought. It was a chaotic afternoon. The compound was immediately surrounded by police. No one was allowed in or out. But four days had passed since. Why hadn't the driver called? She'd been much too preoccupied earlier to think about it. She walked over to Muhammad's shack to talk with Muhammad's father. Even though Abu Muhammad did not approve of the girls attending school, he had a lot to lose if they didn't. Muhammad had made it very clear to his father that if the girls did not attend class, he would not go to Mecca. Hopefully, Abu Muhammad could shed some light as to why the six girls were absent.

The old man was at his usual spot, smoking his water pipe, counting his worry beads, and watching television. His wife followed Sarah with a straw mat for Sarah to sit on. Sarah gave them the news about Muhammad, his studies, how his English had improved and how happy he was.

Muhammad's mother pulled a corner of her abaaya and wiped the tears that had welled in her eyes. "How can we ever thank you?"

"When will he be back?" the old man asked impatiently without waiting for Sarah to answer his wife. "This place is a mess. No one knows where Ali is, and I am too old to deal with all the fighting and bickering that goes on around here."

"I don't know where Ali is but we will get someone to help you real soon. I was wondering if you knew why some of my students were absent last Saturday?"

"Ali takes care of that. Not me. And don't go telling my son it was my fault."

"It isn't. It's Ali's and the bus driver's responsibility. Do you know where the bus driver might be."

"No, I don't."

"He moved out four days ago," said Muhammad's mother.

Moved out? Sarah found it hard to believe. He had been given the job because he lived at the camp, was desperately poor, had two wives and eight children to support. How could he have moved out? She had not paid him for that month yet. Where did he get the money to rent a place? There was too much to sort out. She decided to tackle that problem later. Her immediate concern was for Fatme. Muhammad's father and mother assured Sarah no one had seen her or heard from her since she got on the bus Saturday morning.

Her last hope was Younis, or his wife. Younis was out driving his taxi, the boy was asleep and his wife did not have any more information than the others did. "Do you know where Um Hassan lives?" Sarah asked. Um Hassan was probably her best bet if what Ali told her was true.

Younis's wife walked with Sarah to Um Hassan's home.

"She's out looking for work." The oldest child, a girl, barely ten years old was given the duty of taking care of two brothers and three sisters. The girl carried the youngest, a baby in her arms. The baby looked like it was a few months old. "The Itanis fired her."

"Did your mother mention why?"

"Their son. He doesn't like her."

"Her back must be better if she's out looking for work." It was the only way for Sarah to find out if Ali was telling the truth.

"Not by much," the little girl replied. "But my father let her know he too was out of work and could not support us. She has to find a job."

"I see." Sounded like Ali was telling the truth. Perhaps Younis could arrange for her to talk to the woman. "Could you please have Younis call me as soon as he returns. Tell him it is important."

The sight of those children dirty, hungry, no mother or father around was more than Sarah could bear. She stepped outside, dug into her purse, pulled all the money she had, something she normally resisted to do, and gave it to Younis's wife to be passed on to the children's mother when the mother returned home. Younis's wife was advised not to tell Um Hassan where the money came from. No doubt it would not be hard for the woman to guess. But at least, it would make Younis's wife and the woman think twice before spreading the word around.

Younis's wife promised not to tell anyone about the money. She said she did not know when her husband would be home, but she would definitely give him Sarah's message.

Disappointed, her concern mounting as time passed, the whereabouts of Fatme still a mystery, Sarah had no idea what to do next. She got in her car and drove back to the city, lost in thought. When she neared the apartment, on impulse, she changed her direction and drove to the mosque, her shadows not too far behind.

There seemed to be a cohesion, a concerted effort behind the recent happenings and someone, somewhere, was responsible. She was determined to find out.

A mullah opened the door of the mosque, greeted her politely, but did not invite her in.

Sarah introduced herself and asked to speak to the cleric in charge.

The mullah told her to wait. He crossed the yard, entered a house and returned a few minutes later. He said the chief cleric wanted to know what her business was.

"Please tell him I have come to make a donation to the mosque," Sarah thought of it on the spur of the moment. If not, her chances of meeting the chief cleric were slim, without an appointment, practically nil.

She was received politely by the chief cleric, a man in his late forties, heavy set, a little over five feet tall, sharp eyes, protruding abdomen. The cleric offered her a chair across from his desk. Polite. Stiff.

Sarah introduced herself. The cleric's blank expression did not change.

"I have a few questions before I make a donation to the

mosque," Sarah began.

"What questions?"

"I have reason to believe that a number of people including my own relatives are opposed to my running a school in the compound where I live. What's your opinion?"

Caught off guard, it took the cleric a few seconds to gather his thoughts. "It depends," he answered.

"On what?"

"On what you teach."

"That's fair – assuming you don't believe we follow the Ministry of Education directives. I have a proposition for you. Come to my classes sometime, anytime you choose and learn for yourself what goes on. What could be more simple."

The cleric rearranged his body in his chair, said in a terse voice. "I am a busy man. I don't have time to run around checking schools."

"That's fine. Send a trusted assistant. It can mean a donation of ten thousand dollars to your mosque."

His face taut, his hand tightly wrapped around his chin, the cleric studied her for a long moment. "What is it you really want?"

"Let me do my job, without interference, without resorting to extremes upon the instigation of old women, without giving credence to lies fabricated by vicious people. That's all I ask."

The cleric chuckled. "I bet you'd like that. Yes I bet you would. But that's not how it works. We will not sit back and watch while you poison the minds of our young. No amount of money is worth it."

The message was clear. The price was not right. She had learned the art of negotiating early in life – from her father. Without it survival in the Middle East was difficult if not impossible.

Sarah took a deep breath, pulled herself together and let the insult pass. At least he did not deny her assertions. "While I waited for your assistant to notify you, I noticed the mosque was in pretty bad need of repair. Have you had it looked at?"

"Indeed, I have. I am in charge of four other mosques. This one is the newest, in better shape than the others. Although we receive generous donations from our members, the day to day expenses and the basic upkeep of the mosques drain the treasury. There's no money left over even for minor repairs."

"Did you get an estimate?" The cat and mouse game went on.

"One hundred thousand dollars." The cleric did not elaborate. Was that sum necessary for that mosque alone, the other mosques included, or was it a figure he expected Sarah to donate simply because it's a number that occurred to him on the spur of the moment. It did not matter. They both knew the reason was irrelevant.

Sarah rose, thanked the cleric and walked to the door. "It will be a pleasure for me to take care of the repairs. On one condition."

"What condition?" The cleric knitted his brows with an intent look on his face.

"Anonymity."

The cleric stood up and followed her to the door. "Of course. And I assure you your contribution will be greatly appreciated. But I remain puzzled. Why?"

"Why not?"

"Rumor has it that the real purpose for your altruism is your absolute hatred of religion, namely Islam. Is it true?"

She refused to dignify his question with an answer. She simply stared at him.

"You're wrong." The cleric remained unfazed. "If you think that a hundred thousand dollars will buy you our good graces, think again."

Sarah felt angry, exhausted, drained and in no mood to argue a point which invariably came up in one form or another whenever her motives were in question. "I have studied the Koran ever since I was a child. My aunt Khadijeh, who portrays me to the world as a monster, was my first teacher. After she left, my father had a special tutor come to our home twice a week to teach my mother and me the Koran and I had it daily in school. I find Islam to be a magnificent religion, a religion that can improve our lives morally, physically and spiritually. And I believe that is the reason why it is the fastest growing religion in the world. I find those who practice the true teachings of the Prophet to be extraordinarily good people. However, I don't appreciate those who distort the same teachings to mean what they want them mean – to further their own agendas while they give Islam a bad name."

"That's not very wise," the cleric snorted contemptuously. "The Koran is interpreted by learned men, men who devote their lives to it."

"No doubt about it. But it is also misinterpreted by many so-called 'guardians of the faith.' Maybe misinterpret is the wrong word. Interpret to mean what they want it to mean is what I really had in mind. More needs to be done to show the world the true image of Islam. I am not a scholar. Neither am I an authority on the subject. Yet it is impossible not to see the good it does to people who practice the pure form of Islam, and the pain it causes those who are misled or forced to believe interpretations not intended by the Prophet. I am sure you know this is not unique to Islam. Every religion has been abused in one form or another by those in authority to perpetrate their power, to maintain control." She kept her eyes deliberately focused on him.

"My dear, all life is about control. Religion is only a part of it."

"Coming from a chief cleric, that's most surprising."

Fascinating, Sarah thought. At least he's honest about it.

"It shouldn't be. It has always been and always will be about power and control – not only in humans but the animal world as well. Do not delude yourself, my dear. You're no exception."

This was no ordinary cleric. He was intelligent, well

informed and shrewd. "I assume you're referring to the fact that my father left me an inheritance."

"Money, my dear, money. It's power: translation – control." The cleric chuckled. "Do you really believe I'd be standing here talking to you if you did not have money?"

It was Sarah's turn to chuckle. "I don't delude myself for a minute. I know money opens doors for me and I know the power money has. But, I also know that power corrupts. That same power can be put to good use helping those less fortunate than us. It seems to me using more than a certain amount for personal gratification borders on vulgarity."

The cleric looked amused. He continued to study her for a long moment, a crooked smile briefly curling his lips. "I think I am beginning to understand the real reason for your altruism. You think you have the answer to our problems. You think you can change the world. You are here to show us misguided souls the true path – a path much superior to the one we follow – a path carved by more illustrious minds in the West. I commend you for your foresight and I admire your courage."

His sarcasm was not lost on her. She smiled softly, "I have no illusions about changing the world. Like all other religions, Islam has its fanatics who do more harm than good in the name of religion. What I want to do is teach – teach children to think. Islam has been through centuries of thought as it grows and spreads. You should have nothing to worry about."

Chapter 15

SARAH HAD LEFT FOR THE camp in the afternoon while the sun shone brightly. As she approached her apartment, she noticed the lights were on. She was not overly concerned. Jim – probably. He dropped in often. If she was not home, he waited for her entertaining himself with the vast collection of jazz and classical music Maher Sultan had left behind.

At the bottom of the steps, leading to her apartment, the ashtray Sarah had given the guard was on the steps, full of cigarette butts. But the guard was not there. Her steps slowed instinctively as she pondered over the possibilities of what might have happened. She heard voices coming from her apartment. Not loud and not in whispers. None sounded like Jim's and there was no music. Quietly, she turned back and hurried towards Attiyeh's apartment. It was dark. She checked the door. It was locked. She walked away apprehensive, not quite sure what to do next. She lingered for a few moments, aimlessly, too scared to cross the courtyard. Three rows of stone steps around the courtyard and a broad sidewalk separated the apartments from the entrance to the compound and the street. She chose the top step next to the gate, sat down and tried to figure out what to do next.

She cast a quick glance at her watch. It was ten minutes past nine. Although the courtyard had light posts all around it, several of the bulbs were burned out and the place was in semi darkness. Sarah made a mental note to have an electrician install better lighting and soon. Suddenly, she heard a noise – like something moving. She shot up, all her senses on maximum alert. It came from near by. This is ridiculous, she admonished herself and walked over to check, ignoring her protesting legs.

She saw two men. They were her guards.

"Do you know what's going on in my apartment? The lights are on. I heard voices."

The older man shook his head. "Mr. Jim said we should keep our distance from you – not to interfere unless it was a matter of your safety. We saw you approach the apartment and quickly turn back. We were discussing what to do next when you came over.

Sarah thought for a second. "Let's go check."

The guard who was assigned to guard her unit was still no where to be seen and the voices had died down. The older guard rang the bell.

The guard responsible for her apartment opened the door. He stuck his head out, looked around. "Glad you're back." His remark was directed at Sarah. "The guards caught a girl trying to sneak into the compound."

Sarah stepped in. "It's Fatme, Miss Sarah," Attiyeh said. "She has locked herself in your bathroom. She won't come out."

"Fatme? You mean Ali's sister, Fatme? Oh, my God." Sarah rushed towards the bathroom, knocked on the door. "Fatme, it's me, Miss Sarah. Open the door, please."

Nothing happened.

"Fatme, please," Sarah pleaded. "I'm here. No one is going to hurt you. Open the door."

Slowly, cautiously, the door opened a crack and two anxious eyes assessed the situation.

"It's me, Fatme. You have nothing to worry about. Come on out."

The girl hesitated.

"She is terrified of the guards," Attiyeh said. "I am sure she will come out if they leave."

The three guards conversed briefly. "We will be downstairs if you need us," said the oldest of the three.

Sarah had a difficult time camouflaging her emotions

when Fatme stepped out of the bathroom. She was a pathetic sight, her hair disheveled, her skin pale, her limp exaggerated, and her clothes looked like she had been living and sleeping in them for days. The girl wrapped her arms around Sarah's waist and sobbed. Sarah motioned for Attiyeh to leave.

Fatme stunk.

"Would you like to have a bite to eat?" Sarah asked. Fatme stopped sobbing, raised her head and nodded yes. Sarah fixed two egg sandwiches and poured two glasses of milk. She offered a sandwich and a glass of milk to Fatme, sat next to her at the kitchen table and waited for Fatme to eat. Within minutes, Fatme devoured the sandwich and drank the milk.

"Here," Sarah pushed her plate towards Fatme. "I'm not hungry. You can have my sandwich too."

Fatme hesitated, but only briefly. The second sandwich took slightly longer to finish.

Fatme had yet to speak.

Sarah moved closer, put her arm around Fatme's shoulder and gave her a gentle hug. She was instantly overwhelmed by the odor from Fatme's body. It hit her nostrils hard, especially when Fatme moved – not sweat, not dirt, but an odor like rotten eggs or some kind of fermented beans or something. It took a few seconds for Sarah to control her nausea before she could speak. "If you're done eating, I think it will be a good idea for you to take a bath. The problem is I don't have clothes that fit you and it's too late to go shopping. Any ideas?" A bath would relax her, help distract her from whatever distressed her so, and hopefully get rid of the stink.

Fatme covered her mouth with her hand and stared into space. Strange, Sarah had not seen her act that way before.

"I know," Sarah said pleased with the idea she had thought of. "We'll borrow some clothes from Attiyeh's daughters. His older daughter is about your size. That should work."

Fatme raised her head slightly, their eyes met for an

instant, then Fatme shifted her gaze. Slowly, almost inaudibly, she asked, "May I go home now, please?"

"I'd rather you spend the night here. I don't like to drive that far this late at night."

Fatme put her hand back on her mouth, slumped in her chair and said nothing.

"Even if I did drive you home, I couldn't leave you there alone."

Fatme stared into space for a long while. Afterwards, slowly, her voice betraying her fear, she asked, "Ali ran away, didn't he?"

"Whatever gave you that idea?"

"Is my brother all right?" She covered her mouth as soon as she finished what she had to say. Not only covered it but squeezed it – real hard. Sarah wondered if that was her way of making sure she uttered only the words she had to – fearful perhaps that the wrong word might come back to haunt her. Sarah had not seen Fatme cover her mouth in class. She decided to question her about it later, after her fears about her brother were allayed.

"Your brother was quite all right when I spoke to him last Saturday night."

For a few seconds Fatme stared at the table, her hand still tightly wrapped around her mouth. She removed her hand only when she had to speak. "They will hurt you if they find out I am here. I ... I did not know where else to go." Fatme began to sob uncontrollably.

Sarah tried to make sense of what Fatme meant, but failed. She had to make a conscious effort to regard Fatme not as a child, even though Fatme looked no more than eight, but as a teenager a few days short of her fourteenth birthday. Normally, a girl's birthday was not an event a family bothered to register or keep track of. Most men preferred not to think about the birth of daughters or pretended it never happened. It was different in Fatme's case. Her mother had died during childbirth. To qualify for special United Nations assistance, namely milk for newborns, the birth had to be reported. Sarah had known Fatme for a couple of months, yet she felt she did not know her well enough. Fatme was in class eight hours a day, every day. She had not missed school except the previous Saturday when she was kidnapped. She was timid, quiet, hardworking, kept very much to herself. Academically, she was Sarah's best student. Even the cleric, who taught the Koran at the school, found Fatme's grasp of the teachings of the Prophet remarkable, especially since she barely knew the letters of the alphabet when school started.

"Who are *they*, Fatme?"

"I ... I don't know."

"You don't know or you won't tell."

"I'm afraid." Fatme shivered, her teeth knocked. She rubbed her arms with her hands, pulled her headscarf down on her forehead, wrapped her sweater around her chest, and then sat still. But only for a few seconds. She continued to shiver while the tears rolled down her cheeks.

Sarah moved closer, rubbed Fatme's shoulder gently, until Fatme relaxed and almost stopped shaking. "Sometimes I heard full sentences, sometimes only a few words," Fatme said. "I think they kidnapped me because they knew Ali would come looking for me. They talked about a bomb. They wanted Ali at the school when the bomb went off. Ali is the only family I have. I think because I am a girl, if Ali was told that I was not on the school bus and he couldn't find me in the camp, he'd eventually come to question you about my where-abouts. I think they don't like Ali because they believe his work at the camp is a cover up. They are convinced he works for you. Was there a bomb Miss Sarah?"

The shaking resumed. Sarah hurried to the bedroom clos-et, grabbed a blanket, returned and wrapped it around Fatme's shoulders.

Fatme raised her head, smiled and thanked her. "I feel cold – sometimes. And sometimes I feel real hot. Was there a bomb Miss Sarah?"

Sarah would have preferred to answer that question some other time – seeing the troubled state Fatme was in. But it seemed to weigh heavily on Fatme's mind. Perhaps knowing the truth would help alleviate her fears and make her feel better. Sarah tightened her grip around Fatme's shoulder despite the nasty turmoil the odor produced in her stomach. "There was a bomb, Fatme. It caused death and destruction. School has been closed since last Saturday. I hope we can resume classes this coming Saturday."

"Did you say death, Miss Sarah? Is my brother dead?"

"No. Ali was not hurt. Samir, Miss Nabila's husband was killed."

Fatme covered her face with her hands and sobbed, quietly. "Mr. Samir was the nicest man I ever knew. Why would anyone want to kill him?"

"He was a nice man. But we have to be brave – to help Nabila – to help the other children, to prove Samir did not die in vain."

"Why, Miss Sarah? Why? What had Mr. Samir done to deserve death?"

"Nothing. The bomb was not meant for him. It was meant for me – for all of us. That's what your brother came to warn me about."

"But they told the police Ali did it. I heard them."

"You have yet to tell me who *they* are."

"Miss Sarah, I don't know. I heard voices. That's all. I was locked up in a room in the back of the mosque. A young Mullah brought me food in the evening, pushed it in the door and left. There is a room next to the one I was in where the voices came from. I heard more when they left the door open. This afternoon I heard them say tomorrow they will send me to Gaza to work for the brother of the chief cleric. They referred to the chief cleric as Sheikh. That's when I resolved to escape. Actually, it was easier than I thought. I waited till the mullah brought me my dinner. I told him I had to go to the bathroom. The bathroom is down the hall. He did not suspect anything because I had gone to the bathroom many times before, and I think he would find it hard to believe that a young girl would dare venture out alone at night. He told me to put my plate outside the door before I went to bed and he left."

Sarah heard little after Fatme mentioned the word mosque. "A mosque? Did you say a mosque?"

"It was a mosque – definitely. They had my head covered with a cloth until we reached a room at the back. But I was not blindfolded. I could see down. I saw shoes, many shoes, neatly arranged in front of a big door at the entrance to a huge hall carpeted with many Persian rugs. At night, and at dawn, when the mullah called the faithful to prayer, I could hear him loud and clear. The loudspeaker was directly above the room I was in."

Could it possibly be the same mosque, the mosque Sarah had visited that very same evening? It was the nearest mosque to the compound, the only one within walking distance. Had she spoken to the same Sheikh who had probably engineered the plot to kidnap Fatme, the same cleric she had promised to give a hundred thousand dollars to? Was that why the Sheikh had answered her questions with a smug, condescending look on his face? A shiver coursed down her spine. She asked Fatme how long it took her to reach the compound.

"I don't know. I don't have a watch. Twenty minutes. Maybe half an hour. Something like that. I ran most of the way – whenever I could."

It did not compute. How did Fatme know where to run? To her knowledge Fatme hardly ever left the camp before she started school, and even then was never allowed to roam the streets alone, especially miles away from the camp. An adult was always in the bus with the students on their way back and forth to school; except the previous Saturday when six students and the adult chaperone had not made it to school. The school bus did not pass by the mosque, not even close. How did she figure out where she was?

"I am surprised you didn't get lost," Sarah said.

"I know this area well, Miss Sarah. Rich people live here. The mosque is on the other side of the main road. Occasionally, when they had too much to do, women from the camp took me with them to help clean homes in this neighborhood. Sometimes the lady of the house sent me to the store to buy cigarettes or a forgotten item she needed urgently. I couldn't wait to go to work, not because I was crazy about cleaning floors, but because there was a chance I could go somewhere all by myself." Fatme's demeanor changed suddenly. "You won't tell my brother I went to the store alone, will you?"

Sarah assured Fatme she wouldn't. From the description Fatme gave her Sarah was quite sure it was the same mosque. It took Sarah a few minutes to drive home from the mosque but it would be much harder for Fatme to cover the same distance in less than twenty minutes or more. She could run with her limp – but not for long. Sarah felt numb. The information Ali had given her was proving to be remarkably accurate. Accurate and disturbing. The cleric she went to for help, the Sheikh, had to be the same person who had taken over from her aunts to put an end to Sarah's 'stupid experiment' – as Ramzi called it. What irked her most was the fact that she had promised the Sheikh a lot of money, money which would very likely end up in his Swiss bank account. She was furious with herself.

The phone rang. She expected the call. Dr. Tuqan either came or called every night before retiring to check on her. And lately to report about Nabila. He was relieved and pleased to learn that Fatme was with Sarah – safe. There was a pause. She sensed something was on his mind. "How's Nabila?"

It took a few seconds for him to answer. "Not so good. The newspapers are full of stories about a suspect who was seen running away from the compound immediately after the bombing. She's upset. She wants to leave the hospital immediately."

"I bet she's upset. Who wouldn't be? She's welcome to stay with me until her unit is fixed, or she finds a place of her own."

"Sarah, my love, my darling. This is Jordan – she is an Arab, a woman, and young. Living alone is not an option for a women unless she is very old and has one foot in the grave. Look at what you have had to put up with in the few short months you have lived here on your own. Most women in this part of the world cannot afford to feed themselves much less hire body guards."

Women could and would Sarah fought back in her mind – if only men would stop imposing their will on them, using self serving codes of conduct supposedly dictated by religion as their weapon. Sensing the futility of her thoughts, she made a conscious effort to put those thoughts on hold for the time being, and force herself to deal with the matter on hand – with reality. I must think like an Arab, especially in matters pertaining to women as long as I am here, she reminded herself. She asked Suheil if he had any suggestions.

"I don't know. Her cousin Mona is with her now. Maybe she can stay with them."

"I doubt it. Nabila told me earlier Mona's father got clearance to return to his job in Kuwait. He's gone. The family will probably follow him soon." Sarah felt totally drained. She was not pleased with herself. She should have talked to Nabila, told her the truth. Nabila was an intelligent, sensible woman. She would have understood. "I'd like to talk to her, Suheil, if I may."

"Now is not a good time." Suheil's voice was soft but firm. "She's quite distraught – on the verge of hysteria. I will go back to her room, calm her down, give her a sedative and hope to God she takes it. There's not much else we can do in the middle of the night."

"Suppose she refuses, then what?"

"She'll pass out, Sarah, trust me. She's ready to fall apart."

She knew Suheil was protecting her, and she knew he was right. Nabila needed medical attention – not Sarah's explanations. "Call me after you're done talking to her, please. Let me know how she does."

"If it's not too late when I finish my work, could I stop by for a drink?"

"Absolutely. I'll be up. Fatme and I have a lot to discuss."

"I love you."

"Love you too."

Sarah went to the kitchen to fix herself a cup of tea. Though she tried to be understanding and open minded, the restrictions, the religious and cultural taboos, the illogical demands and expectations placed on women, were often impossible for her to tolerate without fighting back. But how did one fight a mirage? With whom? No one took responsibility. Responsibility for what? It was the way things were done, always, ever since any one could remember. What was wrong with the way things were done anyway, she was often asked? Why shouldn't women stay home, have babies, take care of their families? What was wrong with that? Did she think in the West, where women were allowed all the freedom they wanted, fare any better? Look at the broken homes, the divorce rate, the dysfunctional families, the violence, the drug problem, they pointed out. How could she possibly expect them to copy the West when what they saw horrified them?

The irony seemed obvious only to her and few like-minded friends. The same situation existed in the Arab world too – in Jordan – right under their very own noses. Abuse and exploitation of women in the name of religion did not result in less dysfunctional families, or in less immorality, or in less violence, or in less drug abuse. Yet it was perceived to be so – mainly because the media did not acknowledge or report it. Such events were not considered newsworthy. The public did not hear about it – did not talk about it. How could there be a problem? Since Western leaders were not as privileged and therefore lacked the authority to control the press and its citizens, it was easy to claim that only the West was infested with it.

Sarah considered herself fortunate. She was taught early in her childhood to differentiate between fact and the media's version of fact. Whenever her parents came across a discrepancy or misinformation in something they read or watched on television, they pointed it out to her and made sure she understood the difference. However, Sarah knew this was not the norm. In the Middle East, like most other countries, people got their information about the West from newsmagazines, television shows, and movies. This portrayal by the media was assumed to be an accurate picture of the West. No question about it. Initially, not yet callused by the constant bombardment of the same misconstrued ideas, half truths and outright lies, Sarah argued fervently – not in defense of the West, nor in condemnation of the East, since that was not her objective. But in defense of objectivity. She longed to take a subject, any subject and discuss it logically, devoid of shackles placed on it from the past – relevant to the present, not only felt but thought through. Somehow we all need to learn to deal with the problems we face with more thought and less emotion, she said out loud to no one in particular, then laughed. I, more than anyone else, am often guilty of doing the opposite of what my gray cells tell me I should be doing, she admitted to herself – albeit reluctantly.

Fatme watched and listened with total concentration while Sarah conversed with Dr. Tuqan. "Is Miss Nabila sick?" she asked when Sarah finished talking to herself. Maybe it was her handicap, or her insatiable appetite for learning that had attracted her teacher's attention. But Nabila had shown special interest in Fatme from day one. Fatme in turn adored Nabila. Nabila was her role model, the perfection Fatme strove to be someday.

"Sick? No. Upset? Yes," Sarah told Fatme. "At first she believed her husband's death was an accident, the will of God. Now she has heard newspaper reports about a man escaping from the scene and is understandably terribly upset."

Fatme's hand quickly returned to cover her mouth. Sarah knew what she was thinking. Her brother was involved – somehow. Why else had he come to school that day, and why had he disappeared after the incident?

"Fatme, I know what you're thinking, and I understand how painful it is for you to think that your brother could have hurt the husband of someone you care about so much. It's simply not true. Ali did come to see me on Saturday. He had half a pack of cigarettes in his shirt pocket. That was it. If he was carrying a bomb, I don't know where he could have hidden it."

"Why did he come Miss Sarah, why?" Fatme's voice sounded like it came from an old record player, the needle groping its way through the dusty grooves.

"To warn me about rumors he had heard, but he explained later that he couldn't. Perhaps I didn't give him a chance. I was upset. A third of the class was missing that day. So were you. Ali acted nervous, confused, smoked incessantly, and asked questions I was in no mood to answer. You know, the usual stuff – stuff we often talk about in class. Why do women need education and so on. The children were waiting. I told Ali if he wanted to talk to me he could come back later, in the evening and I returned to the classroom. I think I was a little to harsh on him."

Fatme dropped her head, on her folded arms, on the kitchen table. Just dropped it, as though the weight of the problems crowding her head made it too heavy for her to keep it upright. Eventually, slowly, she raised it back up, just enough to make herself understood. "They talked to the police the same night. They said they knew who did it. They said it was Ali." Fatme shuddered, severe, like her body received a jolt of electricity.

The word 'they' grated on Sarah's nerves. Fatme seemed to get more agitated as the discussion progressed. Still slumped in her chair, she brought her hands together, entwined and examined them as though she'd never seen them before, then shook again – for a few seconds, just as severe. The shaking stopped as unexpectedly as it started. After that she seemed to be all right.

It can't be fear alone, Sarah thought. Something is wrong. "Do you have pain somewhere?" she asked.

Fatme assured her she was feeling fine. She was worried about her brother, Miss Nabila and felt very sad for Nabila's husband. That was all.

Sarah had a lot more on her mind that needed to be sorted. "Do you know who talked to the police? Was it a man or a woman? Could you tell?"

"It was a man. The same man."

The same man? Could it be Ramzi? "Was he young or old? What did he look like? Would you recognize him if you saw him again?"

"I am not sure. I did not look at his face except briefly when he entered the bus, before he spotted me."

"Entered the bus?" Sarah was aghast and her voice betrayed it.

Fatme hesitated, but a quick look at her mentor must have convinced her to continue. "Yes, Miss Sarah. The man entered the bus with a black piece of cloth over his left arm. He told me to follow him. I said I couldn't, I might miss the bus to school. He said Ali wanted to talk to me. I said I just left home. Ali left too to round the children to board the bus. Ali did not say anything about wanting to talk to me. The man said something happened right after I left. He said it was urgent, that it would only take a minute. When I stepped out, he threw the black cloth over my head, pushed me into a car parked next to the bus, and drove off. That same man called the police. I did not see him after he dropped me off, but I recognized his voice."

"You mean the man talked to you, you followed him, got off the bus – without taking a good look at his face." Sarah regretted it immediately. She knew better. Occasionally, however, caught between cultures, her mind found it difficult to make the transition from one culture to the other – instantaneously. Arab girls were taught not to look men in the face, not to make eye contact. I was ayb. A general term meaning shame.

"I could have, I guess. But I saw no reason to. He was a mullah. I trusted him."

A mullah? Sarah reviewed the day's events in her mind. She had gone to the mosque partly because of the information Ali had given her over the phone, and partly because she had hoped to see or hear something which would prove that information false. She was right on the first count, wrong on the second. The facts pointed to a well-planned campaign to intimidate her, to force her to put an end to her so called 'stupid experiment' before it spun out of control. Yet she could not bring herself to believe that they wanted her dead. Her death would mean an end to the charitable donations she had been doling out generously since her arrival in the country. Anonymously, of course – supposedly. Anonymity was more wishful than fact. Everyone involved knew who the donor was. However, there was a twist in the plan that did not make sense. Sarah was convinced that the clerics had taken over the job of getting rid of her, and in all likelihood, her aunts had either moved to another town, or were still in Amman but were keeping a low profile as requested by the clergy. Why?

Ramzi was a different matter. When money was the issue, his creativity would blossom. He could muster resources from within himself – inconceivable to most. She expected him to strike anytime. Where? How? She couldn't fathom. She had no doubt though that he would. He never gave up. Sarah knew him well. She had not questioned the accuracy of the information Ali gave her precisely for that reason. The events Um Hassan said occurred in the Itani household resulting in her dismissal did not surprise Sarah. That's exactly how Ramzi would behave. Because his greed often made him resort to irrational acts, Sarah figured it would be best to take a wait and see attitude. For the moment the proper approach to the clergy consumed her thoughts.

She had to win them over – somehow. A tough proposition. The clergyman she had encountered earlier that evening, the Sheikh, had not impressed her as a man with an open mind willing to listen to other points of view – especially if the other point of view was the opinion of a woman. He would consider it a waste of his time – guaranteed. He had agreed to talk to Sarah earlier either because she had mentioned a donation, or because he had recognized her family name, or both. Was money the answer? Would it win him over? She had her doubts. The more she gave, the more he would demand. It was a dilemma her father often struggled with before his death. How much to give? To whom? Would it reach the people it was intended? Who should handle the money and how? Having failed to find an acceptable solution, her parents must have concluded that they could only trust their own, and thus chose her to execute their will instead of some high-powered agency or firm. It was customary for wealthy people to will the funds intended for charity to a particular mosque to be handled by the clergy as the clergy saw fit. Sometimes the money was put to good use, other times it lined the pockets of individuals trusted with managing the funds.

Sarah's father, though generous to a fault, was extremely careful whom he trusted with his money. Sarah was learning slowly, the hard way. Predictably, a few requests for alms were interspersed with veiled insults by small minds envious and resentful of a woman who they believed had it all. But, she reminded herself, that did not license her to walk away. The need was grave, the right approach imperative.

Perhaps money was not the answer. If not money, then what? What made her think that bribing, which admittedly her offer to pay for the repairs of the mosque was, was the answer. What guarantee did she have that the Sheikh was the only cleric she would have to make a donation to? Where did it all end?

Jim is right. I should buy a yacht – sail the seas, fly to

Paris – hop nightclubs, or shop till I drop. What a joke. She lowered her exhausted body onto the sofa, lost in thought.

Meanwhile, Fatme had dozed off, her head on her arms, on the kitchen table.

A gentle knock on the door put an end to Sarah's reverie. It was Suheil. He walked in, gave her a hug and a kiss, and they settled on the sofa in each other's embrace. Unresolved issues that engulfed her like dark shadows, relentlessly, when she was alone, faded into nothingness when the man she loved and respected held her in his arms. She needed him and he needed her. In a society where emotions reigned supreme, finding a man like Suheil was almost like a miracle. He assured her Nabila had calmed down, and yes Sarah could visit her the next day. "I am off this weekend," Suheil said. "What about a trip to the Dead Sea. It will do us both good."

"I'd love it." She planted a kiss on his lips. "It will be wonderful to get away from it all. I need a drink. What about you?"

"A Scotch, please."

"One Scotch and a glass of wine coming up."

"Shouldn't she be in bed?" Suheil asked when Sarah returned with the drinks. Fatme had not moved since falling asleep on the kitchen table.

"I guess so. She was tired. I should put her to bed. But ..."

"But what?"

"She smells something awful. At first I thought it was because she probably had not had a bath or a chance to wash herself locked up in a room with no facilities. But it's not body odor. I can't figure it out."

"I smelled it too when I came in. It's a familiar smell – like a festering wound. We come across it sometimes – mostly in patients coming from the villages. Does she have a wound anywhere?"

"I don't think so. She was reluctant to bathe. I don't know why. It couldn't be her period, could it?"

Suheil thought for a moment, rose, walked over to Fatme

and smelled her. "That's not the smell of blood," he said. "That's definitely a festering wound."

Baffled, Sarah stopped to think. Where could a festering wound be? She could not think of a plausible explanation. She asked if she should wake Fatme.

Suheil pushed Fatme's hair to the side and put his hand on her neck. He turned to Sarah. "Do you have a thermometer?"

Fatme opened her eyes, looked around, dropped her head back on her arms, and went back to sleep.

Sarah searched the bathroom cabinet and emerged with a thermometer that had been used and another that was still in its factory wrap. They decided to use the new thermometer, one that her father had bought in the U.S. It was in Fahrenheit. Fatme had a temperature of a hundred and four.

Although Suheil had taken care of Fatme after her brother beat her up, he felt the girl might refuse to allow him, a man, to touch her in a non-hospital environment. Sarah tried to wake Fatme but she seemed groggy, too sleepy to cooperate. Sarah carried her to the sofa, laid her down, rushed to the bathroom, grabbed a towel, hurried back and placed it under Fatme's buttocks. Sarah's right hand, the hand she had placed under Fatme's buttocks to carry her to the couch, was smeared with a foul secretion unlike any she had ever smelled.

A disturbing thought crossed Sarah's mind. She dismissed it. Impossible. She stopped, searched Suheil's face, let out a scream and dropped herself in the armchair next to the sofa.

Fatme opened her eyes for an instant, struggled to keep them open, but her upper eyelids descended slowly like a curtain shielding a room from the sun.

"She is in no shape to object," Suheil said. "Help me remove her clothes."

They had butchered her. The clitoris and all the external genitalia had been cut off, the area was covered with a rag, pus and blood oozed from the wound. Some of the discharge had dried and caked around the pelvic area, some had sipped through the rag, dried and cracked on her thighs.

Sarah threw herself in the arms of the man who she knew felt her pain. "Why, Suheil? Why would anyone carry on such a barbaric act on a helpless girl?" She sobbed uncontrollably.

"They probably thought they were doing her a favor." Suheil Tuqan said without conviction. He reached for a tissue paper and gently dried her tears. "I would like to think that that was their motive. But to entertain a thought like that is to delude ones self. They did it because they figured it was a neat way to get even with you. It really doesn't matter what their motive was though. She is doomed for life."

Chapter 16

SARAH SPENT THE NIGHT WITH Fatme in the emergency room where Fatme underwent treatment with massive doses of antibiotics, infused in her to save her life. By morning, her temperature had dropped – some, but not enough to stop her drift in and out of consciousness. Jim came early in the morning. He wanted to come as soon as he heard from the guards that Sarah had left for the hospital, but Sarah convinced him to wait so he could relieve her if need be. She needed time out to see Nabila, to talk to her. Suheil had warned her Fatme's treatment was not a matter of hours, but days and there was no guarantee that Fatme would recover.

"I thought I saw you." Sarah spun around to check the familiar voice behind her. It was Nabila. The women rushed towards each other and embraced. "Actually, I thought I also saw Jim headed towards the emergency room. So I followed him. What's wrong?"

"It's Fatme. She's not well. Jim came to relieve me." Sarah was overjoyed with how well Nabila looked. However, Nabila seemed momentarily distracted by the familiar figure in the emergency room, oblivious to the commotion around her. Fatme was Nabila's star student and her favorite. Nabila shook her head in disbelief. "Did Ali beat her up again? I heard he has escaped – gone no one knows where."

"Ali had nothing to do with it. Let's go someplace where we can talk."

"They're cleaning my room," Nabila said, "How about the cafeteria?"

"Lead the way. I've been in the emergency room all night. I can use a change of scenery."

Only after Nabila assured Sarah she was feeling all right did Sarah bring her up to date about new developments – Ali's phone call, her trip to the camp, and other events thereafter. Nabila listened, without interrupting, fully absorbed as Sarah related everything she knew, and those who she thought were responsible for the deplorable state Fatme was in.

"Forget Ramzi," Nabila said without hesitation. "He couldn't have had anything to do with the bomb or Fatme's circumcision. – at least not physically. Mona was at the airport seeing her family off, when they spotted Ramzi with his parents at the British Airways terminal, in a wheel chair, waiting to board a plane for London. The same plane goes to Kuwait first, then London. They recognized him from when he came to pick you up at the airport – when you first arrived. It seems he neglected to take care of his ankle shattered in the jump from your bedroom window, developed some kind of complication and had to be flown to London for emergency treatment. He blamed it all on you. He claimed you brought your relatives nothing but grief since you arrived in Jordan, and are working hard to inflict worse grief on unsuspecting, poor people who have reluctantly joined your schemes for the monetary benefits they receive from you for allowing their children to attend your school. Mona said he went on and on."

The idea of sharing ones wealth with others was so alien to Ramzi, that he probably would have had a stroke just thinking about it. Nevertheless, Sarah should have felt relieved that Ramzi was not involved. And she did – to a point. It was believable. Ramzi was a hypochondriac, and a man who could focus on one issue at a time. Period. If his ankle bothered him, he'd concentrate on that and not much else. Her aunts were old. It was inconceivable that they could pull a stunt of that magnitude without help. If Ali's father's wife, Um Hassan were to be believed, the clergy must have taken full control. Would the clergy resort to such extremes without more to go on than the word of two old women? Nabila had no doubt the clergy would snuff any threat to their authority, imagined or real, swiftly and ruthlessly. "It's a question of power," she told Sarah. "If they feel threatened, especially now that Islamic Fundamentalism is on the rise, an opportunity they would not have dared dream about before Khomeini came to power, an opportunity they relish, they are not about to take any chances."

"We're running a school based on the directives of the country's laws." Sarah was and sounded exasperated. "The government appoints the person of their choice to teach religion. How did we manage to offend the clergy?"

Nabila chuckled. "You're teaching girls, aren't you? That's unacceptable to closed minds. Actually, I think men are scared of us. I really do. They're smart enough to realize, without much prompting, that when women learn to read, they will learn to think more analytically – which means, eventually, they will demand equality. That is a concept the interpreters of the Hadith, (what the Prophet said and did) have managed to suppress most efficiently ever since the Prophet's death. But it shouldn't surprise us. The way things are suits most men just fine. They're not about to let anyone, especially a woman, upset the balance they've so diligently maintained for centuries – totally in their favor, I might add."

"Granted. But the world is getting smaller by the day. Islam is a religion that advocates decency, human rights, and equality for all – man, woman, black and white. There's no discrimination advocated anywhere in the Koran, regardless of how hard the interpreters manipulate it. Instead of spreading the basic values of Islam, its true message, we seem to be distorting it, twisting it to suit our personal interpretations – for self-interest. I was horrified the other day when I read about a group in Afghanistan, religious students known as Taliban who have decided to become the Taliban militia. In the areas they have conquered, almost immediately after the creation of the militia, the Taliban have shut all schools for girls, forbidden women to hold jobs outside their homes, and ordered women to cover themselves completely in public. Women are urged to stay in their homes – not to appear in public unless absolutely necessary. And women includes girls three years and older. Television and radio have been banned as un-Islamic. The mind balks at such degradation. It's absurd, barbaric. Even in Iran with all its hard-liners professing strict adherence to the teachings of the Koran, schools for girls were not shut down. If the fanaticism in Afghanistan spreads to Arab countries, I hate to think what price we will have to pay."

"We are already paying the price Sarah. We always have, and most likely always will. Look across the barbed wire at Israel. Their women contribute as much to their family and country as their men do, if not more. They have the benefit of all their adult population. We have half – and that half is warped."

"There's got to be a way." Sarah's frustration was evident in her voice.

"There is. We should not be intimidated. I had a lot of time the past few days to think, to think back. I find subjugation of women has been a fact of life ever since cave men discovered they were stronger physically and could have their way by brute force. Until recently, women in the West had to fight for their rights – even the right to vote. In the West it was under the guise of social and political disapproval. Here it is religious. Different names for the same thing – control, power. Call it what you will. Why are you staring at me like that?"

Sarah smiled. "You baffle me. I thought you would want nothing more to do with my 'stupid experiment' or me – not after what you've been through. But here you are ready to take on the world. My good fortune, more than I had a right to expect, scares me."

Nabila studied her friend for a long moment with a look of intense concentration on her face. Then she said in a deceptively calm voice, "It's precisely because of what I have been through that I will do everything in my power to make sure my husband did not die in vain. He was unique in his way of thinking, in his attitude and in his ceaseless efforts to promote human rights. He hated injustice, particularly in the Arab world where it's been going on for so long that no one notices it any more. He was elated when you offered us jobs. For him it was a dream come true, an opportunity to do what he always wanted to do. My stay in the hospital was God-sent. Until late last night I was full of anger, self-pity, hatred, especially when I learned that it was not an accident. Although Jim, Mona and I spent hours discussing the issue and possible options, it seems to me our choice boils down to just one. We must fight for our rights at all cost. If we don't, who will? If we don't, what have we got to live for?"

"Has Jim been to see you?"

"Every day. Twice a day. Morning and afternoon. You should see my room. There's not a spot that's not covered with flowers. He thinks your father was the greatest man who walked this earth. I think, perhaps without realizing it, in his own way, Jim tries to be like your father. He seems to want to take over where your father left off."

Sarah shook her head in disbelief. The gentle giant, as she always thought of him, meticulously sensitive to the sufferings of others, unforgiving of injustice regardless of who the perpetrator was, made it his business to help where and when he could – without prodding, without fanfare, never expecting anything in return. How very gratifying it was for her to have the support of such a great man. Her father was wise indeed to have recommended that she work with him. Without Jim, she'd have a terrible time coping. She didn't even want to think about it. He was her guardian angel, advisor, critic, morale booster, brother, father, friend, all rolled in one.

"What they did to Fatme," Nabila continued, "is another reason I cannot and will not give up. We must press on. Denying oppression of women happens, as is often done by most Arab leaders, means we have to work that much harder to convince the world the practice is alive and well. Actually thriving. Governments can pass all the laws they want. It's meaningless. Take Egypt for example. This morning, Jim brought me the September 26th 1994 issue of the *Time* magazine. He wanted me to read an article about the United Nations meeting in Cairo, the International Conference on Population and Development. The article discussed the changing attitudes of rural women towards family planning. The reporter was surprised to learn that poor, illiterate, Egyptian women were eager to take action to limit the size of their families. Why should it surprise anyone? It's not as though women had choices before. They have not had access to birth control pills, and even if they had access they could not afford to buy it. Their husbands refuse to take the most basic precautions. And if a wife refuse to have sex, she either gets beat up – or if she's lucky, the husband moves on to one of his other wives. If he, for some reason does not have another wife, that's not a problem either. He can get one whenever he wants. The man must have his sex, when he wants, with whomever he wants, consequences be damned."

"Sometimes," Sarah admitted reluctantly, "sometimes I wake up in the middle of the night in a cold sweat and I realize the enormity of the problem has me gasping for air. I am terrified, especially when I witness the daily deterioration of all that we are fighting to improve. I see and read about more and more girls, younger, covered, at least with a big, white scarf on their heads, even while attending school in countries where by law all children must attend school. A picture of three girls, seven, eight years old, covered completely in black garb, in a street in Paris was front page news, a few days ago, in a French newspaper. It described the plight of African Muslims living in France. The cultural, social, religious clash was portrayed in meticulous detail, encouraging the extremists in France to ask their government to do something about immigrants who cannot or will not assimilate. Most of these children were born in France, elsewhere in Europe, the United States or wherever. I often wonder what type of scar such forced customs leave on developing minds. How do you explain to a child that her body has to be covered? How do you tell her she should not have contact with males of any age except her brothers and father until she is married to a man she has in all probability never met before? How do explain the sexism in our society? What are our reasons? And could someone please tell me why?"

"That was not all Jim wanted me to read," Nabila said. "Wait till you hear the rest. Jim insisted I read the article on the opposite page as well, entitled 'A Rite of Passage – or Mutilation.' It was about a film footage shown at that same conference, by Christian Amanpour, a correspondent for CNN. She starts by warning the audience the following footage would be 'very hard to watch'. The camera zooms in on a ten-year-old girl who peers into the lens with anxious eyes. It's a novel occasion. The girl is baffled by the appearance of TV cameras and crew. The combination of factors tells her something out of ordinary is about to happen. But she has no idea what, and she does not have a clue as to why she has been chosen to be the center of attention. The small room is crowded with relatives laughing and ululating as they prepare to celebrate the occasion. The ululating dispels the anxious look from the girl's face momentarily. But almost immediately it is replaced by a terrified expression as her hands are wrapped around her ankles and her legs spread up and out. A florist and a plumber are in charge. While the florist holds the girl, the plumber sticks his head between the girl's legs and snips off her clitoris. It is over within seconds. The girl gasps with pain. With the next breath, she jerks her head forward and screams at her father with a voice that booms over the ululating. 'Father! Father! A sin upon you. A sin upon you all!' The blood gushes over the girl's pubic area then down legs. The florist reaches for a rag, places it on the wound, is paid by the father and together with the plumber they take their leave. Mission accomplished."

As she spoke, Nabila choked on her words more than once. She had to stop, dry here tears and then press on. When she reached the part where the girl screams "Father! Father!

A sin upon you. A sin upon you all." Nabila's voice rose several pitches. When she was through, everyone in the cafeteria was staring at her.

It did not faze her. She leaned back in her chair, a defiant look on her face.

Sarah felt the girl's pain as acutely as Nabila did – despite the brave façade Nabila presented to the onlookers. Sarah's eyes rimmed with tears and her thoughts glowed with pride. Here was a woman who had only days ago been subjected to a traumatic experience few could cope with, and had emerged stronger, more open minded, with a can do attitude. Conventional wisdom shaped by centuries of tradition based on social, cultural and religious dictates she had grown up with, and expected to abide by all her life, had an undeniable influence on her until her husband's death. Yet somehow, the death of the man she loved had triggered her to reverse gear. Nabila seemed to take pride in lashing at the so-called 'wisdom of centuries' she blamed for most of women's woes and let it be known she for one had no intention of walking that same walk.

"You know," Nabila continued. "Jim said nothing to me about Fatme, and I couldn't figure out why he wanted me to read that article when he did. It all makes sense now. Knowing the Arab world as well as he does, he knows these rituals go on. Eighty percent of all Egyptian women are circumcised for the sole purpose of depriving them of sexual pleasure, and supposedly to ensure their fidelity. I challenge anyone from the highest-ranking clergyman, to the peasant in the field, to show me where this stupid custom has ever been mentioned in the Koran. The Prophet would have never sanctioned such a barbaric practice. Yet, hundreds of years later, the article states, several thousand girls are circumcised daily in Egypt alone. The same thing happens here, and in many other Arab countries, not to the same degree as in Africa though. There it's routine. But it happens. No one talks about it. That's why the Egyptians got angry when CNN singled them out."

"That's great," Sarah said. "I mean the fact that the world got to see what really goes on, especially in areas rarely visited by the news media. It's much needed publicity – publicity we could use a lot more of."

"Listen to this," Nabila could hardly contain her excitement. "They asked Hosni Mubarak about the CNN report, and he said he thought the practice had disappeared from his country. Can you believe it? He is the president of the country and he does not know what goes on in his country? And he expects people to believe him? There's no Egyptian law that bans the practice. There is a ministerial decree issued in 1959 which bans the procedure in facilities affiliated with the Ministry of Health and permits only physicians to perform the surgery. However, it's not enforced. It can't be enforced. The decree is for show. Everyone knows it goes on all the time – except it seems the president of the country. What a joker!"

"Was anything done about it? I mean now that it was there for the whole world to see."

"Of course. Never underestimate politicians," Nabila said. "The authorities arrested the father of the girl, the plumber, the florist, and the free-lance producer. The free-lance producer was later released, but there's no report on the others. When questioned, the girl's father insisted he believed as a Muslim he acted properly. He had not heard of CNN before and was under the impression that CNN was producing a documentary on Islam. The Egyptian government claimed CNN had abused Egyptian hospitality and tried to discredit the footage by claiming it was staged. However, much to their dismay, the footage was widely discussed by the participants of the conference and with all the readers *Time* magazine has, I bet the whole world has heard about it by now."

The information sent Sarah's mind reeling back to her own experience in Saudi Arabia, to those who were less fortunate than herself, to those who had to live with the scars, physical and emotional the rest of their lives. What puzzled her most though was the older generation, like her aunt

Khadijeh who because of her own similar experience and its after effects had suffered all her life. Here was a woman who was left barren from an infection following her circumcision. After her first husband discovered she could not have children, the word spread and no one would marry her. She had to live with relatives. Yet she made it her business to see to it that all the females in her family as well her neighbors were circumcised by age eleven – the latest.

The answer had to be, as her parents had foreseen, in education.

The task ahead was immense, incredibly complex, a task which had defied solution for centuries. Sarah had no illusions about it. She needed help, and needed it desperately – hence her gratitude for Nabila's positive, can-do attitude. She considered herself fortunate to have the support of such a strong woman, especially an Arab. What a terrific role model Nabila could be for her students, for her friends, for other women. The realization that she had at least one woman who was courageous enough and eager to help, quickly invigorated her. She could not wait to get back to her students.

As though Nabila had read her thoughts. She said, "Let's get on with it. There are capable nurses here. Fatme will be fine. Let's go, round up the children, and do what we're supposed to do."

"Right. But we have another problem. The bus driver has disappeared."

"They probably threatened him," Nabila replied. A matter she did not seem to need to think about at all. "He is a simple man. They must have threatened him – convinced him not to work for you, because, unknowingly he was contributing to your anti-Islamic activities. Just use your imagination Sarah and it won't be long before you can actually anticipate how the minds of our antagonists work. If it's logical, they want nothing to do with it."

I bet he is unemployed and his children are going hungry, Sarah thought. She knew though, that Nabila's guess was probably correct, and that it would be futile to try and convince the man to change his mind. It would also be futile to hire another driver. Whoever convinced the first driver would probably not waste much time before he worked on the new hire.

Suddenly, a thought occurred to her. "Nabila, do you know if a special permit is needed to drive a school bus in Jordan?"

"I don't know. I never asked. But I am sure the drivers will know. Why do you ask?"

"Let's go. We'll drive the bus to the camp. Younis will know. If we are stopped, it will not be for the lack of a permit. It will be because of our gender. At least in Jordan women are allowed to drive. In Saudi Arabia it's absolutely out of the question along with a zillion other rights most women in the world take for granted."

"Women are allowed to drive in Jordan – for now," Nabila said. "Privately owned cars only. We're taking monumental steps backwards – to the Middle Ages. I hope we still have a chance to turn things around. Who is Younis?"

"A waiter I met at a restaurant. He works as a driver during the day."

"Don't even think about it," Nabila misinterpreted Sarah's statement. "Whoever we hire will be forced off the job. I think we will end up by having to do the driving ourselves despite the displeasure we are sure to cause by our unorthodox behavior."

Sarah knew better. Younis would work for her. She need only ask. Younis broadcast repeatedly his undying gratitude to the woman whose generosity had saved his son's life. The reason for his extreme adulation was the fact that the life saved was that of a male. People listened and understood. They respected him for it. After all, who would not be grateful to such a person? Had it been a daughter afflicted with the same illness, in all likelihood, Sarah would not have even heard about it. Sarah was convinced it would take a lot more than threats to force Younis to quit. The unwavering loyalty of people like Younis, people who never took for granted or forgot kindness, was the adrenaline which pumped enough courage in her to keep doing what she was doing against all odds.

Yet she could not and would not ask Younis – precisely because he would insist on doing it, and in the process was likely to jeopardize his as well as his family's safety. Cross that one out, Sarah told herself.

She and Nabila could drive. Perhaps take turns. But her gut feeling was that it would not work. The clergy could easily hire thugs to drive them off the road. To subject a school bus full of children to possible danger was out of the question. She discussed it with Nabila. Nabila thought about it and had to agree – albeit reluctantly, that they were vulnerable, their concern centered on the children

"Hi there," Dr. Tuqan said, as he walked into the cafeteria. "May I join you?"

Suheil Tuqan pulled a chair and sat between Sarah and Nabila.

"To what do we owe this honor?" Sarah's eyes betrayed her feelings for the man she loved. It did not go unnoticed by Nabila.

"I was looking for my patient." Dr. Tuqan turned to Nabila. "I have good news for you."

"Me?"

"Your treating physician claims you have made a miraculous recovery. You're free to leave. Anytime you're ready."

For a few seconds Nabila was quiet, staring vacantly into space. Sarah sensed her trouble. Mona's family had left for Kuwait. Mona was staying with relatives until Nabila recovered. Where could Nabila go? As an Arab, a woman, a young widow, living alone even in her own house was an option she could not entertain. The risk to her reputation, to her family's honor, to her safety was a definite possibility. She had no family in Jordan and hence her dilemma.

"When is Mona leaving for Kuwait?" Sarah asked.

"Soon. I'm sure," Nabila replied. "She doesn't want to go. But she can't live with her relatives much longer. Her relatives have a tiny apartment and their fifth baby is due any time."

Suheil watched, as both women seemed to quietly weigh their options.

"Forget it." Nabila was quick to read Sarah's thoughts. "It won't work. Her moving in with me doesn't change matters in the eyes of those determined to see nothing but whores if women so much as dare live alone." Nabila's expression changed quickly. "Sorry, Sarah, I did not mean to imply that you're a whore because you live alone. But you know it will be difficult and right now I want one less problem to worry about."

"Actually, I was wondering if Mona's mother might come live with you and Mona if she had a place to stay here, in Jordan. While we were flying in to Amman, I remember her saying how much she preferred Jordan to Kuwait, mostly for her health. She said she couldn't tolerate the heat in Kuwait. I'm not sure though if she'd be willing to leave her husband."

"I doubt it," Nabila said. "She should, but she probably won't. The old man has another wife in Kuwait, a young woman, a Kuwaiti. That's why Mona's father was so eager to return to Kuwait. He visits Mona's mother occasionally, when he misses her cooking. Whether Mona's mother will leave him in Kuwait, alone, with his new wife, is a question I can't answer."

"Why not ask Mona to ask her mother," Dr. Tuqan suggested. "In the meantime, you're welcome to stay with us. We have a big house. My mother, two sisters and occasionally I, live there. There's plenty of room. My father shows up once in a while, when there is time left over from his business and other wives. He doesn't stay long – a couple of hours – at the most. Like I said, you're more than welcome to stay as long as you like."

Arab generosity and hospitality never ceased to amaze

Sarah even though she herself was half Arab, and, no doubt would have made the same offer given the circumstances. Yet in Suheil's case she knew he made the offer because he was a person who cared, who cared about what happened to others, especially a woman whose options were practically nil, thanks to a society which made sure she did not have any.

Sarah's eyes welled with tears. Dr. Tuqan was a man rare in any country, not just Jordan. If only there were a few more ... like him – in responsible positions, her job would be as easy as a pleasant dream. Only now it was more like a blood-curdling nightmare.

Nabila's voice cracked. "Your offer is most generous. I owe you so much already. You said my recovery was miraculous. It was – thanks to you and Jim. You helped me get back my life – my sanity. Pulled me back from the brink, from my determination to destroy myself. It would have been the coward's way out and you let me see that. However, as desperate as I am, I cannot live with your folks. They will expect me to mourn, to cry, to live in seclusion, in despair, totally lost without my husband. I am an individual in my own right. I want to live – for my husband and myself. I want to work for the dream we had. It is easy to portray it as an impossible dream, but Samir is with me, always, and I won't rest until I make a difference." Nabila had to stop to wipe the tears coursing down her cheeks. But she was not through. "Soon after Sarah offered Samir and me jobs, we talked late into the night about our good fortune. Our prayers were answered. We could do what we always wanted to do. Work for justice: a lofty ideal – its arrival long overdue. We keep losing ground because we expect someone else to do the job for us. That someone else has to be me, Sarah, Jim, you, and whoever has a conscience and hates injustice, regardless of how well camouflaged it is in religious, social or cultural guises."

Dr. Tuqan observed his patient for a long moment an expression of delight mixed with surprise spread across his face. He rose, stretched his hand out, and shook Nabila's hand with enough force to convey his feelings. "Like I said, you're always welcome in my house. My sisters and mother can learn a lot from you." He turned to Sarah. "I have to go. I have a full schedule. Fatme is in good hands. If I finish early, I'll stop by tonight. Maybe we can work on a plan for the weekend."

"The weekend?"

"Dead Sea. Remember. You promised."

Sarah smiled. "Of course. I'd love to."

Suheil said good bye and hurried out of the cafeteria.

Sarah turned to Nabila. "Have you been to the Dead Sea? Usually I gather as much information as I can about a place before I go. But lately I haven't had time. Suheil feels it will do us both good to get away even if it is just for a weekend. Strange as it may sound, I know very little about the Dead Sea."

"You should go," Nabila replied. "It's a must see place. I advise you though not to wear a skimpy bikini. European women do. But they don't always get away with it. Lately, there have been a lot of rumblings by the clergy about indecent public exposure by foreign women. They fear it will set a bad example for Arab women, who of course it is assumed cannot think for themselves and will copy anything Western. Actually, it would be funny if it wasn't so tragic. A few weeks ago, Samir and I went to the Dead Sea for the day. A group of Germans, mostly women, wearing bikinis, strolled down the walkway, into the sea. Nothing out of the ordinary. Regular bikinis – bikinis worn by women all over Europe. The men in the café, who until then had not cast more than a passing glance in the direction of the water, turned in their chairs and focused their attention on the water, on the spot where the women congregated. The sea is not good for swimming. You can't drown if you want to. But it's supposed to work miracles for all kinds of ailments. I don't think the Germans had any ailments. They were just there for the experience – to have fun. After a while they stepped out of the water and settled right next to a bunch of Arab women covered from head to toe, in their abaayas, in black, in the heat of the summer. A few feet away, the Arab men whose number seemed to have unsurprisingly multiplied during that brief interim, ogled the German women completely absorbed in every move the women made. After a while, the Germans got up and started walking towards the walkway to board the bus that had brought them there. Suddenly one of the women screamed. She collapsed right there on the walkway. She was hit by a rock in the back of her head. Samir saw her fall down first. We ran and offered to help her. She had fallen next to the rock. The rock was quite large, the size of an apple. It must have broken the skin. We could see blood slowly wetting her hair and the back of her neck. Samir introduced himself to the woman, and offered to drive her to a hospital or a clinic to be checked. While Samir spoke, the woman touched the back of her head where she was hit, looked at the blood on her hand, pulled herself up, and let out a torrent of words in German. She seemed terribly upset and with good reason. But we had no way of knowing what her words meant. Her companions however, did not mince their words. Those who spoke English let us have it. Basically, it boiled down to the fact that they thought we were barbarians. One of them said, 'I think there are two Jordans. One as advertised in the tourist brochures, and the other, the real Jordan, which no one wants to admit exists.'"

Unfortunately, Sarah thought, the situation was not unique to Jordan. Many countries hungry for tourist dollars, worked hard to present a polished image to the world, an image which ill prepared the unsuspecting tourist about ugly undercurrents that often popped out when least expected or wanted. Like in Egypt, Algeria, Turkey and other less publicized countries where bombs were used routinely to intimidate, maim and kill tourists – when the livelihood of many of their countrymen depended on tourist dollars. And it was all done in the name of Islam. It was so terribly ironic. To her knowledge Islam advocated peace and justice – not terrorism.

Nabila's words came to mind. 'It's a matter of power, control. Religion is merely a tool.'

Nabila had it right. Religion was often blamed for many man made ills of this world. Religion is not the problem, we are, Sarah thought. All our absurd notions, misconceptions, stem from our refusal to admit man as he really is, selfish, self centered, power hungry, insecure, desperate to control.

But did anybody care?

Sarah felt claustrophobic. She had to step out. When overwhelmed by sensory overload it became difficult for her to breathe. It was time for some fresh air.

"Do you need to go to your room before we leave?" she asked Nabila.

"It won't take but a minute. It might take a while though for me to take care of the hospital bill."

"Don't worry about the bill. Jim will take care of it."

"Jim will take care of what?" Jim's familiar voice was always welcome.

"Nabila's hospital bill," Sarah said. "She and I want to drive to the camp, round up the children, drive back to the compound and resume classes. What do you think?"

Jim shook his head in disbelief. "Am I missing something here? How do you propose to transport forty kids in your VW?"

The women exchanged glances. "We wanted to drive the bus," Nabila said.

"Nabila, dear, Sarah often forgets where she is. I attribute it to her many years in Europe. But you have lived in this part of the world all your life. Have you ever seen a woman drive anything but her own private car, that 'privilege' being limited to a handful of countries in the Middle East."

"Maybe we can start a new trend." There was lot of pent up anger brewing inside Nabila, anger that sometimes escaped the tight clamp she kept it under.

"Sure you can. Chances are you will be forced off the road by some maniac who would love to teach unconventional women like you a lesson you will not forget – quite possibly injuring your and innocent children as well. Or, you might be lucky and land in jail for driving without a special permit. Don't look at me with pleading eyes, Sarah. Even if I could, I would not get you a permit to drive a school bus in Amman." Jim's eyes darted from Sarah to Nabila. "All right. You win." Jim pretended to be reluctant. "I'll drive the bus until the storm blows over, but only if you two promise not to do anything foolish."

"Wow! This is my lucky day." Sarah was overjoyed. "It's still early. We can put in a full day. I'll check on Fatme while Nabila packs her stuff and you take care of her bill."

Nabila looked at Sarah perplexed as though wondering why Sarah should take it upon herself to pay her bill. Jim smiled. Her thoughts were transparent. "Your friendship means a lot more than money to Sarah," Jim said. "She needs more friends like you, not money. Let's meet at the front entrance in ten minutes."

Within a few minutes, Nabila was at the crowded entrance anxiously looking for Jim. She spotted him at the front desk going over her hospital bill. Relieved, Nabila rushed towards him. "Come quick," she said. "We need your help. I went with Sarah to check on Fatme before going to my room. Fatme's cubicle is surrounded by police and a couple of clergymen who claim Sarah kidnapped Fatme from the mosque. They want the police to arrest her."

Chapter 17

THE YOUNG MAN IN THE emergency room cubicle staring at Fatme was the mullah who had opened the door of the mosque for Sarah the previous afternoon when she had stopped by the mosque after her desperate search for Fatme had failed to reveal any clues about her whereabouts. The older cleric next to the mullah was also familiar to Sarah. He was the chief cleric, the Sheikh. When Sarah first saw the two clerics in the emergency room and heard the Sheikh inquiring about her, she could not fathom what could prompt the clerics, especially the Sheikh to follow her to a hospital emergency room. Had the Sheikh had a change of heart? Had he come to pull a stunt to extract more money from her? She had been quite forthcoming in her eagerness to donate money to the mosque and had without hesitation raised her offer from ten thousand to a hundred thousand dollars. But why couldn't he wait for her to return home? Was there an emergency? Did the Sheikh need money urgently? Perhaps he knew Fatme was not well and had come to see her. None of it was very convincing.

There was more at stake. There had to be. The matter had to be real serious for the chief cleric to take time out to come to an emergency room – for a girl. Sarah suspected the Sheikh planned to use Fatme's disappearance from the mosque as an opportunity to blame the escape on her, and thus have her deported – hopefully, permanently. She had to admit, albeit reluctantly, accusing her of kidnapping the girl – true or false was a brilliant ploy. Immoral, but brilliant. If the Sheikh chose to press charges, like it or not, those charges had to be resolved in a court of law.

She could also be wrong. She could be over reacting. Perhaps the chief cleric had decided on accusing her of kidnapping, to scare her, to force her to abandon her activities. But what proof did he have that she had kidnapped the girl? Did he need proof?

"Are you in charge?" The Sheikh asked a police officer who had just entered the room.

The officer nodded while he looked around seemingly assessing the situation.

"Your name?" The Sheikh did not bother to introduce himself.

"I am the assistant to the chief. An officer." He gave his name but asked that he be addressed as 'officer.'

"I want this woman arrested." Sarah heard the Sheikh stress the word arrested. He pointed at the two policemen standing at the entrance of the cubicle where Fatme lay in bed. "I spoke with your men who are here on my request – told them to arrest this woman. We have laws in this country – laws that apply to the rich and the poor alike."

"Why?" The officer looked baffled. "Why should we arrest her?"

Yes, Sarah wondered, why? Did the Sheikh expect Fatme to back whatever lie he was about to present to the police? Did he expect her to do it out of fear? Fatme had been terrified, hidden in Sarah's bathroom and refused to come out until the bodyguards left and Sarah was alone in the room. Besides circumcising her, what had happened to Fatme while she was locked up in the mosque? Strangely, the night before, in Sarah's apartment, Fatme's concern had been more for Sarah than herself, although her fear of someone or something had surfaced with each sentence she uttered despite her rather skillful efforts to suppress it.

"I explained all that to the police chief when I called the station." The Sheikh's anger was audible in his voice. "Don't ask me questions. Your duty is to arrest this woman." His index finger was pointed at Sarah but he avoided eye contact.

My suspicions are well founded, Sarah thought. My running a school must be a bigger problem than I imagined if he is willing to forego a hundred thousand dollars to get rid of me.

The officer paused, his gaze swept the room, yet he seemed in no hurry to do what he was asked to do despite the fact that the request came from a religious leader. There were two possibilities; either he had instructions not to, or, Sarah suspected he was not convinced there was a problem. After all, the patient in the emergency room was only a girl, she did not look like she was going anywhere, and neither did Sarah. Why the pressure to arrest her? When questioned by the two policemen earlier, the emergency room nurse told the men it was Dr. Tuqan who brought Fatme in, not Sarah. The officer, arriving later, had conversed with the men before entering the emergency room. Probably that was the reason he looked bored – as though wondering what all the fuss was about.

"You have not given me a reason," the officer replied calmly. "I cannot arrest someone because I am told to do so."

"I don't have to give you a reason." The Sheikh's eyes bulged like they were ready to pop out of their sockets. "Do as you are told. Your keeping your job might depend on it."

Faced with a situation the officer seemed to find difficult to deal with, he explained he needed to call the police chief for further instructions. He told Sarah to stay put until his return, cast an uneasy glance in the direction of both clergymen, and walked out.

The commotion around Fatme must have awakened her. She opened her eyes, located Sarah, smiled, and then drifted back to sleep. Meanwhile the emergency room nurse approached Sarah. "Dr. Tuqan is in surgery. He will probably be there for another two hours. Is there someone else you would like me to contact?"

Jim and Nabila walked in.

"No, thanks," Sarah told the nurse.

The chief cleric's eyes darted from Sarah, to Jim, to

Nabila, to Fatme. Yet the blank expression on his face made it difficult to interpret his thoughts.

"What's the problem?" Jim moved slowly, like a big, bored bear cramping the cleric's space.

"It's none of your business," the Sheikh snapped back in perfect English with a strong British accent.

Jim smiled – a smile not to please but to warn. "You remember me, don't you? I worked for Maher Sultan – took care of business. And now I take care of Miss Sultan's business. Whatever it is you're after, has to go through me."

"Then you better get her a good lawyer. We are charging her with kidnapping, kidnapping a girl from our custody. And we have proof."

"Interesting." Jim cocked his head to one side. "Very interesting indeed. You truly amuse me, man. Tell me, how and when did this kidnapping occur."

The Sheikh pulled a handkerchief from his pocket, wiped the perspiration from his forehead, then shoved it back in his pocket. His eyes quickly penetrated and locked on the woman he was intent on victimizing – but only for a second. He did not vocalize his thoughts.

Once again, Fatme opened her eyes, searched the room, her gaze rested on Sarah for a long moment. "Miss Sarah," she said softly, turned her head and went back to sleep.

It was almost as if the Sheikh had been waiting all that time to hear the girl speak. His demeanor reversed immediately, "See," he exclaimed barely able to control his excitement. "The girl knows who did it. She is calling her by name."

"Did what?" Jim moved his massive body closer to the diminutive cleric.

"Kidnap. Kidnap the girl. How many times do I have to say it!" The cleric huffed, wiped his forehead, shrugged his shoulders, turned to his assistant, the young mullah, and said in a voice barely above a whisper, "Black people are dim. They don't understand."

Instantly, an eerie quiet swept across the room. The Sheikh had assumed that Jim did not understand or speak Arabic. Unfortunately for him, Jim was fluent in Arabic plus several of its dialects.

Sarah's heart skipped a beat. She held her breath. There was no telling what Jim might do when unduly provoked. She and Nabila exchanged horrified glances, but neither woman moved or spoke.

Jim did not move either. He was already standing much too close to the man whose appalling statements hung like a radioactive cloud above the heads of the occupants of the room. "You have thirty seconds to clear out of here." Jim's voice was deceptively calm.

If he was aware of his stupidity, the Sheikh did not let on. "Really?" he asked a crooked smile on his lips. "What gives you the right to ask me to clear out?"

"We're paying for this space and you're not."

"So what."

"Get out." Jim's soft voice had a frightful edge to it.

The Sheikh did not move. He couldn't.

Jim's belt-buckle was in the cleric's face. "Get out, now!"

The Sheikh cast a quick glance in the direction of the two policemen at the entrance to the emergency room as though expecting them to intervene on his behalf. They did not. With a disgusted look on his face, the Sheikh stuck his chin out, pushed his shoulders back, motioned for his assistant to follow him, and marched out. Before stepping out, he somehow pulled himself together, turned and yelled, "You'll pay for this." And then almost as an after thought added, "Dearly, very dearly, I assure you."

"So will you." Calm as an autumn breeze, Jim made it clear he would not permit the Sheikh to provoke him no matter what he said or how loud he yelled.

That's what Sarah feared most. Jim rarely expressed his anger in public. Usually, later, when Jim felt it was the appropriate time, as in the case of the Minister of Health who raped her, Jim taught the perpetrator a lesson he would never forgot. But there was an unknown factor in this equation. How would the Sheikh react to the humiliation he'd been subjected to – and in public? Sarah feared the worst.

Alarm bells began to ring in her head. "Now we will really have a problem on our hands," she whispered to Jim. The man was not a simple cleric. He was a high priest, a Sheikh who custom demanded be revered and respected. Sarah had restrained herself from making any comments so as not to aggravate the matter further. Nevertheless the situation had spun out of control – regardless. She could not blame Jim. The Sheikh's indiscretion was gross – and that was an understatement. She gagged at the thought of anyone, much less a religious leader, thinking or vocalizing an idea as hideous as that, but especially so in the case of a Muslim religious leader. Islam was not the monopoly of Arabs. It was a universal ideology that had spread all over the world, particularly Africa where most believers were black – and so were many Arabs.

"It's the only language his kind understands." Jim replied. "You can't wait around for him to dole out more shit. He's got to be stopped."

The Sheikh and his assistant had not moved far. They were right outside the emergency room – waiting. Within minutes, the officer returned and was explaining something to the clerics. From the Sheikh's gestures it was apparent he disagreed – disagreed vehemently. In a moment, the officer left the clerics and entered the emergency room. "My superior wants both parties to come to the station," he explained. "He would like to have the complaints submitted in writing."

"Let's go." Jim took a step forward.

Sarah stopped him. "Did the Sheikh agree to come?"

"No. He refused. He said they won't come." The officer shrugged his shoulders. "He said by the time they return the girl will be gone. What's so special about this girl anyway?"

Jim ignored the question. "Why don't you insist? He has a complaint, he has been asked to put it in writing, why should he have the privilege to refuse?"

"I can't force a chief cleric to go to the police station if he doesn't want to." The officer sounded frustrated.

"Why not?" Jim asked. "I thought Jordan was one Arab country where the law applied equally to all. Is my information wrong? Do you have one set of rules for the public and another for clergymen?"

"I don't make the rules," the officer shot back, his patience tested first by the Sheikh and now by Jim. "If you have a complaint, I suggest you take it up with the police chief. He is waiting for all of you at the station."

Jim's reaction was swift. "I will submit my complaint at the appropriate time. You can bet on it. But if the Sheikh and his assistant refuse to go, it doesn't make sense for us to do so. The Sheikh's excuse is rather flimsy. We don't trust them here with the girl either."

The officer threw his hands up in despair. "I have never come across anything more mind-boggling than this. For a girl, nonetheless. Will someone please tell me what's so special about this girl?"

"She is a human being," Sarah blurted out, knowing full well her words meant nothing – nothing at all to the officer.

The officer stared at her as though she had just landed from outer space, an alien with crazy notions in her head. He shook his head and walked out.

Meanwhile, Jim was busy searching his pockets. Eventually he gave up. With a disappointed look on his face he explained he wanted to get in touch with the lawyer Sarah's father retained in Jordan but did not have his phone book with him. That morning he had left for the hospital in a hurry and forgotten all about it. He didn't want to leave Sarah and Nabila alone in the hospital, although the guards were inconspicuously a few yards away. They were there to protect Sarah not to intervene in disputes. His past experiences with telephone operators in Jordan and elsewhere in the Arab world had been an exercise in frustration. With no phone directories available to the public, Jim wondered if he should try the operator anyway – later perhaps, when it would be safe to leave the women alone briefly.

"Don't waste your time," Nabila said. "Where do you keep your phone book? I'll get it for you."

Sarah looked surprised.

Jim looked relieved. He gave her his car keys and the keys to his apartment. He told Nabila the special phone book was in his desk drawer – locked. He reached in the front pocket of his pants and gave her a small key. Nabila took the keys and left.

The look in Jim's eyes when he spoke to Nabila and the sparkle in Nabila's eyes sent a warm feeling through Sarah. The fact that he gave her his keys, which he always kept on himself even when he went to bed, was in itself an indication of how far the relationship must have progressed in just a few days. There's a balance in nature, Maher Sultan loved to remind his daughter. A little agony, a little ecstasy, and life goes on.

The officer reentered the room. "I talked to my supervisor again. Since the clerics refuse to leave the premises, my boss said he would come to see for himself what all the fuss is about. He didn't believe me when I told him it was about a girl, a refugee from the camp, an orphan."

"I bet he didn't," Sarah and Jim murmured in unison. Actually, Sarah thought, his supervisor is right to suspect there is more involved – right in a convoluted way. It's not about a girl. She's just a pawn. It's about stopping forty children from getting an education, about removing an undesirable, evil individual, me, from their midst. Nabila was right, damn it. We've got to fight. And fight we will.

Other possibilities crowded her thoughts. Are they suspecting that we will resume classes? She asked herself. Could this be a delaying tactic? I bet Ramzi made a big deal of my being obstinate and convinced them not to accept setbacks causing temporary stoppage as an indication of lessening of my resolve. Even as a child it was always a sore point with him – when he did all he could to force me to change my mind to his way of thinking and I refused. He said I was like a hyena determined to get my prey – regardless, laughing all the while at the obstacles I found in my path.

Fatme moved restlessly in her bed. Sarah reached for her hand and caressed it. Fatme opened her eyes, searched the room, and then with obvious relief pulled herself up to a semi sitting position.

Delighted, Jim approached the bed. "How do you feel?" he asked.

"Did they leave?"

"Who?" Jim asked and immediately stopped.

"The mullahs." Fatme voice was barely audible. "Please, Miss Sarah, please, don't let them take me. If you do, I will kill myself."

"Don't worry. I won't. I promise." Sarah squeezed Fatme's hand gently.

"No one is going to take you anywhere," Jim said emphatically. "No one. You have my word."

Fatme seemed to be tiring. "They wanted to send me to Gaza ... to work ... for ..." Her voice trailed off.

Fatme struggled to stay awake, worried – worried the clerics will once again be in a position to decide her fate – worried her luck would run out the second time around. That's what Sarah figured was happening to her protégé. That's why Fatme fought to remain conscious.

If only they could settle their disputes amicably. Sarah hated confrontation and this had been one unpleasant morning. Jim's idea of a lawyer was good. Why not allow the lawyer to settle the matter with the Sheikh? Find out if there was anyway to ameliorate the Sheikh's concern over Sarah's educational activities, dispel his notion that Sarah was after poisoning young minds, help him see the distorted picture her aunts had created and worked diligently to maintain.

Strange. She had not heard from her aunts – for quite a

while now. However, that did not mean they had given up their anti-Sarah activities. No one could convince Sarah of that. She knew better. It meant they were brewing a concoction, a concoction only her aunts were capable of fabricating, since they were the only people who knew her and her family well enough to do so with credibility and without impunity.

It hit her suddenly. "Jim," she asked, "how did the Sheikh know Fatme was in the hospital? How did he know who brought her here?"

Jim knitted his brow more deeply than usual, reflected for a long moment, then said, "I hadn't thought about it, but now that you mention it, it does need looking into. You, Suheil and the guards were the only people who knew you were headed for the hospital. Correct?"

"And Attiyeh."

"You think?"

"No way. I meant Attiyeh knew. He saw us leave. He came running from his apartment, offered to help. Suheil told him to go back to bed. We'd manage."

"You're right. It's not him. If he had any such inclination, he would have pretended to be asleep."

The pressure in her head was about to blow her skull apart. Lately, prone to migraine headaches, she had taken to carrying Tylenol in her purse. She did not know when the knocks would be too hard to overcome with will power alone. She swallowed a couple of capsules and waited for her nerves to settle. Meanwhile, her frustration erupted in waves of nausea in a stomach that had been punished with massive doses of caffeine and not much else.

But she could not dismiss the thought. No doubt the clerics were informed by someone. But who? Did they have a contact in the compound – contact in the pay of the clerics, her aunts, or both. Who? Not knowing was driving her crazy.

"Think Jim, think," she said. "Who could it be?"

"I am thinking. A lot of people live in the compound. It's hard to tell."

Sarah jumped up. "My phone. I bet it's my phone. Suheil called the hospital before we left so the nurses would be ready for us. I bet my phone is tapped."

"It was. I took care of it. And I check it regularly. It's not your phone."

"Damn." Sarah had trouble containing her anger.

Sarah pulled a chair, dumped her body in it, threw her head back and waited for the pounding to lesson. Jim paced the small cubicle a couple of times. He was too big – the cubicle too small. He grabbed a chair and joined Sarah in the waiting game.

It was a long wait. Exhausted, eventually they dozed off.

A soft tap on his shoulder awakened Jim. The police chief accompanied by his assistant greeted him and introduced himself – in Arabic. No doubt warned by the Sheikh.

Sarah woke up, rose and approached the men. The chief continued talking to Jim, ignored Sarah.

Sarah moved closer. In a small cubicle there was little room to maneuver. Nonetheless, she tried. Still there was no acknowledgment of her presence. She stretched her right hand out. "My name is Sarah Sultan," she said to the police chief. "It's a pleasure to meet you."

The police chief nodded politely. He did not give her his hand or his name.

Sarah withdrew her hand. The insult was duly noted and stored, with all the others, in a special compartment in her brain, reserved specifically for such data. A long, hard road lay ahead, perhaps an impossible task as the attitude of the male elite was not about to change soon, if ever. These acts were intentional, meant to emphasize a woman's place in society, to dissuade any attempt at change. It had worked for centuries. Men had women exactly where they wanted them; at home, in the kitchen, or raising children when they were not busy working for their husband's pleasure. The few who dared struggle even for the most basic rights, found them-selves shunned by a society controlled by codes of conduct which condoned abuse and exploitation of women – all in the name of Islam.

Preposterous. It had absolutely nothing to do with Islam. The reason Islam had survived through fourteen centuries and grew daily was directly related to the Prophet's teachings. Equality and justice for all: men, women and children. For all races, all colors. Somehow, she and other like-minded women had to get this message across to men. They had to.

"He probably doesn't want to appear friendly while the Sheikh is scrutinizing his every move." Jim whispered in Sarah's ear – always alert to any change in her moods.

Sarah took a small step back, took a deep breath and struggled to regain her composure.

"What do you want with this woman?" The police chief's words were addressed to Jim.

Sarah noticed Jim's facial muscles tighten. "You should ask Miss Sultan, not me. Obviously the Sheikh has filled you in on his demands. I suggest you sort it out with the parties involved. I am sure you know Miss Sultan speaks excellent Arabic."

"I was told you were in charge of her business affairs."

"I am. But that does not exclude her. After all, the Sheikh is accusing her of kidnapping. She has a right to know why."

"This is the most ridiculous dispute I have ever had the misfortune of dealing with. The Sheikh insists the mosque is responsible for the care of orphans, widows, and the homeless. He says Miss Sultan had the audacity to hire thugs who took the girl from the mosque and brought her to Miss Sultan's apartment. Don't you call that kidnapping Mr. Jim?"

"Of course that's kidnapping," Jim quipped. "Except nothing like that happened. The girl escaped because she had been circumcised without being consulted, and overheard the Sheikh tell his assistant to send her to Gaza the next day to work as a maid for the Sheikh's brother."

"He's lying." It was the Sheikh. He had entered the room encouraged by the presence of the police chief. "The girl expressed a strong desire to follow Muslim tradition. She wanted to be circumcised. Since she has no family, I went trough great trouble to arrange it for her."

"Yeah, right." Sarah could not control her anger any longer. The subject of circumcision never failed to snap the wrong cord in her. "It's she who is going through great trouble fighting for her life. The infection is so severe from the great favor you did for her that it will be a miracle if she pulls through. She was not kidnapped, sir. She escaped."

"Sure she did. And my mule climbed a tree." The Sheikh was frothing from the mouth. "How do you expect anyone to believe a story like that. The girl limps so bad, she can hardly walk."

The officer listened to both parties without comment and without changing the expression on his face. He pulled two forms from his pocket and asked each party to write down in detail what they were charging each other with.

"Why?" objected the Sheikh. "Why do you need anything in writing and why from her. I'm telling you it is impossible for that girl to have escaped from the mosque and reached the apartment of this woman, on foot, on her own. Impossible. That's all there is to it, and that's all you need to know. Now arrest her. You should have done so hours ago instead of keeping me waiting – wasting my time."

The Sheikh made sure his back remained turned to Sarah throughout his diatribe.

Sarah chose not to be intimidated by his rudeness. She addressed her words to the police chief. "And I am telling you I have three independent witnesses who will swear on the Koran that that is exactly what she did. I was no where near my apartment when Fatme was caught trying to sneak into our compound. I have witnesses who I have no doubt will vouch for that as well."

"You also have a lot of money. You think you can buy your way out of any situation unfavorable to your schemes."

"I don't need to," Sarah replied calmly. "There are many

honest people in this country – people capable of sorting truth
from lies. And others who defy the country's laws, commit
illegal acts like circumcising a young girl, and claim it was
her request."

The bickering, the cumulative affects of the contradictory
statements seemed to increasingly confuse and frustrate the
chief officer. He finally had had enough. "I told them exactly
what you asked me to tell them," he said to the Sheikh. "I
know as a religious leader you will not want to accuse anyone
falsely. I am not a judge, nor is this a courtroom. If you still
want her arrested, I respectfully urge you to please put your
request in writing."

The Sheikh looked furious. "Are you trying to tell me that
you are accepting a woman's word against mine?"

"Absolutely not. We have to follow procedure. Unless I
have your complaint in writing, I cannot arrest her."

The Sheikh tightened the wide black belt around his
waist, huffed and said with droplets of sputum flying across
the room, "It requires no leap of faith to believe in what your
religious leader tells you, but it is a sin to put credence in the
words of women."

"Really? And where in the Koran is that written?"

Sarah could have as well been speaking in the wilderness.

The officer shook his head. "It depends on the woman,"
he said. "Your version is totally different from hers. I fear perhaps you have been misinformed."

"Misinformed? Misinformed? What kind of nonsense talk
is that? The girl was kidnapped. Obviously this woman did it,
or, hired people to do it for her. Otherwise she wouldn't be by
the girl's bedside all night. How much more proof do you
need to make an arrest?"

"With all due respect, sir, I still think you've been misinformed," the officer replied. "My understanding is that this
woman has done more charitable work in this country, in the
short time she's been here, than many of us combined will do
in a lifetime. I also received a phone call from our top securi-

ty chief before coming here to be sure and obtain all the facts before doing anything rash. And that's exactly what I am doing."

Jim and Sarah exchanged perplexed looks. Who could have called the security chief? Who knew about Fatme's medical problem and how?

The Sheikh looked even more perplexed.

Meanwhile, slowly, fearfully, Fatme pulled herself up ever so slightly, opened her eyes wide carefully examining every person in the room. When her eyes caught sight of the mullahs, she stared hard for a second, quickly pulled the bed sheet over her head and crawled back in bed.

The Sheikh paid no attention to Fatme. The perplexed look disappeared giving way to an appearance of authority. "We are not here to discuss the virtues of this woman." He still had his back turned to Sarah. "Her charitable work, as you so rightly mentioned, is not done out of her convictions as a true Muslim. It has no religious basis. She does it because she is on a mission. And her mission is simple – to poison the minds of our youth. Why you may ask? Why does she want to bother with us? Is it because she has more money than she knows what to do with? No, my friends, that's not the reason at all. She'd like you to believe that that is the reason. But it's not. She is here because it will delight her to see our society destroyed."

The police chief shook his head in disbelief. Everyone else just stared at the man whose contorted imagination seemed to stretch beyond the scope of human comprehension. The cleric had a unique gift. He could twist any situation to suit his purpose – facts and logic being the least of his requirements – his attitude one of 'I dare you to question the authenticity of my statements.'

Almost on cue, Jim shoved his hands in his pants pockets. Sarah knew exactly why and prayed he'd keep them there. Jim turned to the cleric. "Pray enlighten a dim wit like me." He spoke softly with just the hint of a smile. "Why should the destruction of your society bring such joy to Miss Sultan?"

The Sheikh's pitch black eyes scanned the room faster than a rabbit in a forest full of wild animals. "Because," he hesitated, then blurted as if the thought had suddenly occurred to him. "Because she has Jewish blood in her. That's why." He pushed his shoulders back looking rather pleased with himself.

Jim chuckled. "Come now, Sheikh. You can do better than that. Mrs. Sultan's being half Jewish has never been a secret. Yet it did not stop you from accepting large donations from the Sultans before. As a matter of fact, the mosque you are in now was built entirely with money that I personally handed to you donated by Mr. and Mrs. Sultan. Anonymously, of course. But you knew who gave it and accepted it with great pleasure. Why the sudden change of heart?"

The Sheikh fidgeted, pulled his pants up, tightened the belt around his waist and wiped his forehead. "Things are different now," he grumped. "Times have changed."

Jim laughed out loud. "Yet only yesterday evening you accepted a donation of one hundred thousand dollars from Miss Sarah claiming you had four other mosques which needed repair. How come times changed so dramatically between yesterday evening and today noon?"

The Sheikh tilted his head back, gave Jim a drop-dead look, tucked again on his belt and stepped back. "Like I said, we are not here to discuss the virtues of Miss Sarah." He turned to the police chief. "There is no end to the delaying tactics of these people. I ask you for the last time to do your duty and arrest this woman."

Sarah tried to speak but was cut off – again. Her frustration mounted which each passing moment. This was a man's world all right. It seemed her opinion did not count despite the fact that it was her fate that was at stake. Jim sensed her frustration and had taken over. Nevertheless, keeping her rage under control sapped most of her energy.

"Excuse me Sheikh," the police chief interjected. "Since

the girl is in no condition to escape, and as you mentioned earlier, unable to do so on her own, let's all go to the police station and sort this out. We will resolve it if we can. If not, you're welcome to press charges. To put your mind at ease, I will ask one of my men to guard the emergency room. That's the best I can do."

The chief then tried to work his way out of the cubicle. As he did so, he collided with Dr. Tuqan who was rushing into the emergency room. Dr. Tuqan apologized profusely and asked the chief to please take a moment and brief him on what was going on while he checked his patient.

Fatme's temperature had dropped to a hundred and one, her skin was no longer cold and clammy like the night before, but she still trembled whenever a man touched her. Pleased with his patient's progress, Dr. Tuqan approached the men who had congregated at the foot of the bed and asked the cleric casually what he wanted to do with the girl.

"Take care of her, of course."

"No!" Fatme shot out of bed, yelled, then slipped back in again.

"Why her?" Dr. Tuqan's voice and manner intrigued Sarah. He was a man of few words, yet suddenly he dominated the conversation. "The refugee camps are full of children in need of care. Is there a reason why you want this particular girl?"

"I have had enough, doctor." The Sheikh's voice was intense to let everyone in the room know his displeasure with the lack of respect he was being shown. "This girl's brother is a wanted criminal. He has escaped. She has no other relatives. As the religious leader of this community, it is my duty to make sure she is placed in a respectable home, with a good family."

"No!" It was Fatme again. "No. Please. Don't let him take me."

"Will someone shut that girl up," demanded the Sheikh.

Something was on Dr. Tuqan's mind, something that had

him really going. It scared Sarah. It was almost one o'clock in the afternoon. His surgery, according to the ER nurse would be over by eleven that morning – the latest. Where had he been the past two hours? Was he the one who called the Security chief? What else had he been up to?

"Fatme is welcome to stay with my mother and sisters," Dr. Tuqan offered without hesitation. "We have a big house. It will be no trouble at all."

He's going to end up by turning his home into a place for women who have nowhere else to go. I bet much to the dismay of his mother and sisters. I've got to talk to him about it. Sarah made yet another mental note to be dealt with later.

"That's out of the question," the Sheikh countered. "She's coming with us."

The police chief threw his head back and roared with laughter. "Never, ever, have I witnessed so much fuss over of all things, a girl. May Allah help us."

"You don't understand," Dr. Tuqan said smiling broadly at the police chief. "They want the girl to cover their tracks. The girl is not important. Dead would be better."

The Sheikh narrowed his eyes, studied the doctor for a few seconds, cocked his head to one side and asked, "What are you talking about?"

"You know very well what I am talking about. But I'll humor you, anyway. Fatme's medical condition is not due to her circumcision only. She was raped repeatedly, the past few days while she was in your care. Would you happen to know who could have done such a horrible thing to a helpless, innocent child?"

Sarah gasped, searched the face of Dr. Tuqan hoping to detect a sign which might indicate it to be a mistake, perhaps a fabrication – to intimidate the clerics. She checked herself. It had to be the truth. Suheil Tuqan was incapable of such deviancy.

Other than Sarah's gasp, the doctor's words had induced a deathly silence in the room. The Sheikh's eyes rolled back, he swayed ever so slightly, grabbed his assistant's arm, followed by a deep breath. Sarah wished she could stop the pounding of her heart and hoped no one else could hear it. But her concern was for the Sheikh. She was fearful he might have a heart attack or a stroke. At least we're in a hospital, she told herself. Instantly, her thoughts shifted back to Fatme. No wonder the girl yelled 'no' every opportunity she got.

It was not long though before the Sheikh regained his composure. He pulled his belt up – again, an act he seemed to repeat whenever he was nervous and asked, "I assume you have proof for such an accusation?"

"I do indeed." The doctor's cool, calculated manner seemed to agitate the Sheikh more – accomplishing its intended purpose. "We have samples of sperms – not from one source but two, and enough tears on the girl's genitalia to make it resemble the tracks of a train terminal."

The word two grabbed the Sheikh's attention momentarily. He swung around, his face red with anger, locked his gaze on his assistant for a split second, and as quickly shifted gear. "Liar." He lashed out at the doctor. "You're a liar." Perspiration coursed down his face, and the veins in his neck bulged ready to burst.

Sarah was terrified. She was sure the Sheikh was about to have a stroke.

A sudden scrambling in the bed riveted all eyes on Fatme. She sat up, pulled the bed sheet up to her neck, to cover her body to hide her trembling. Sarah could see her shake uncontrollably. She looked terrified but determined. "Please sir," she pleaded in a tremulous voice, her words directed to the police chief. "Please arrest those men. I would hate to see the same thing that happened to me happen to other women."

Her finger was pointed at the clerics.

Chapter 18

THERE WERE SEVERAL MESSAGES FROM Younis on her answering machine, the last message recorded late that morning. Sarah had left word with his wife for him to call her not expecting to spend the night in an emergency room. Since he did not have a phone, assumed it was important, and worried about her not answering the phone, he said he planned to stop by her house sometime that evening.

There was also a message, from Muhammad, from Bellevue, Washington. He wanted Sarah to call him as soon as possible. He said it was important.

Sarah wanted to take a hot bath and disappear in her bed – for a day – at least. She was exhausted, not so much physically – but emotionally and mentally.

She dialed Muhammad's number.

A young woman answered. She called Muhammad to the phone.

"What's going on at home?" Muhammad asked.

"You mean here, in Jordan? Lots. How did you hear about it?"

"Ali called me yesterday – collect."

"Ali? Where is he? Did he say?"

"He did. But it's better not to discuss it over the phone. He's worried about his sister and has no money. I sent him all I had – hundred fifty dollars."

"I'll have Jim refund you."

"No need to. I got a part time job at school. Janitor's assistant. Is this the greatest country in the world, or what?"

"I'm glad you're enjoying yourself. Jim will give your allowance to your parents. I'm sure they can use it."

"Thanks, Miss Sarah. But I think I'm being selfish. I think I should return to Jordan. My father is too old to take care of the camp by himself."

"I'd rather you didn't. We'll find someone. Someone your father approves – can get along with. Younis, the waiter is coming to see me this evening. He will help. I'm sure."

"I know he will. Younis is a good man. But it's a thankless job. He will find few takers."

"We'll manage. You can help – by staying where you are. Keep up the good work. Leave the worrying to us. We've hired a lawyer and investigators. We'll do everything we can to clear Ali. It will take time. Meanwhile, please stay in touch with him. We'll help him with his needs until he can return safely to Jordan."

"You don't think he did it."

"I know he didn't. And I know who did. Proving it is another matter. Lately though, some events have taken place which have shed unwanted light on the connivers, their sources, and their intentions. It's important for you to finish your education. I need you back here educated and empowered to help our people understand what truth really is."

"Actually, Ali did not call me to ask for money. I know he doesn't have any money and when he told me what had happened, I offered to help him out."

"Thanks, Muhammad. I sure appreciate your thoughtfulness. I offered to help him too when he called. He said he would call later, give me an address. He hasn't – so far. Ali has rough edges but he's a fine young man. I owe him a lot. He had come to warn me. That's how he got in trouble. I was nervous and really concerned. Seven girls were missing that morning, including Fatme. I'm afraid I was rather curt and short-tempered with him. I thought he knew where the girls were, or had something to do with their not coming to school. I know better now. But that won't do him much good – wherever he is. A fugitive. I feel terrible."

Muhammad assured her he'd keep her posted and wanted

to know if they found the girls.

"We did. All but Fatme, initially."

"Why do I feel left out? There's more – right?"

Sarah gave Muhammad a detailed description of the events of the past two weeks. It was detailed to impress him with the enormity of the problem not considered an issue for centuries, to broaden his recently acquired budding sense of justice, and help rid his mind of previous misconceptions, misconceptions he grew up with, misconceptions he firmly believed in until he landed in the States.

Her words were received in total silence. When several seconds passed without any reaction from Muhammad, Sarah thought they had lost the connection. She called his name twice. Finally she heard heavy breathing. Sarah urged him to please calm down, be patient and for the time being refrain from telling Ali.

"That's the reason he called," Muhammad replied. "He was worried about his sister. Family honor and all that. He wanted me to ask my parents to take her in until he could send for her. You realize of course what this means. The family has been shamed. Ali will rush back to Jordan to kill those who were responsible – and Fatme, even if she was an innocent victim. It's his duty. The family honor cannot be compromised."

Sarah's concern mounted to the point of panic. "He doesn't have to know right away, does he?"

"He'll hear about it. Guaranteed. The way you described it, there were a number of people in the room. I assure you, by now, it's topic of the day at the camp, everyone has heard, and someone will make it his business to inform Ali."

The same exact fears had been nagging her since the incident occurred. A chill shot through her body. It was a serious matter that should not have been discussed in an emergency room, in the presence of many. After that, damage control was impossible. Visions of Fatme stabbed to death, paraded in front of her mind's eye. The sensory overload was too much to deal with after a long, sleepless night and a hectic day. Search for options drew a blank. She could almost see the glee on her aunts' faces when the news reached them. It wouldn't be long. Although lately her aunts had not openly interfered in her day to day running of the school, the reports she got indicated they were still very much on their crusade in the camp to persuade the participants in the school program to quit before the wrath of Allah was unleashed upon them.

Her thoughts were interrupted when she heard her name called repeatedly. It was Muhammad. She told him she was listening, thinking, had no answers.

"Where I come from," Muhammad said with a troubled voice, "no man worth his name will tolerate the shame to the family honor such an incident inflicts. He might as well be dead."

"Muhammad, Fatme does not have a family. Ali is it. If he steps in this country, he'll land in jail before he gets near the mullahs or his sister."

Muhammad chuckled. "Miss Sarah, the borders we have are very porous. Ali can sneak back in any time he wants to. Trust me. If he hears about it, God almighty will not stop him."

Sarah took a deep breath. Anger, frustration, helplessness crowded her psyche forcing her to revise her earlier assumptions and decisions. It goes back to my taking on a project I'm ill prepared to handle, an idea impossible to execute, and an atmosphere getting murkier by the hour, she admonished herself. And stopped immediately. I'm falling in the trap they have set for me. To hell with self-pity. With each incident, with each stumbling block they place in my path, I should see the disease not the symptoms. The need for change is pressing and the need to strengthen my resolve even more so. There's got to be a way to acquiesce our opponents and I'm going to find it.

"Miss Sarah, are you there?"

"I'm here. Just thinking."

're not thinking about quitting, are you Miss Sarah? selfish as it may sound, and it is, my life will be total- tered if you do, and so will the lives of all the children have come to depend on you. It's only in the past few months, since I came to the States that I feel like a human being. Never did before – wouldn't have known what it was like if I had been hit in the face with it. I was so full of hate."

Her introspection over, her reaffirmation to proceed as planned infused her with an energy she always had but thought she'd lost under pressure from the bombardment of recent events. Muhammad's words were sufficient reward in themselves. To hear a young man, a very bitter young man, admit his life had changed to the point where he finally felt human, could not have come at a more appropriate time. "No, Muhammad," she said, cool and composed. "I won't. There are many who would like to see me do just that. But we can't please everybody, now, can we?" Even her sense of humor had crept back.

"Does that mean you will continue to help us?"

"We're in this together Muhammad. When you're done with your schooling, I expect you to return and shoulder your share of the responsibility. And don't think for a moment that it is going to be an easy job. You have been warned."

"I will. I promise. My life has changed – drastically. You remember when I first met you what a cynical, angry man I was. I hated life. Every night when I went to bed I used to pray not to wake up – ever. I could see absolutely no way out of the rot we were all in. Then, from nowhere, comes this guardian angel. Do you believe in miracles, Miss Sarah?"

"We still have a long, long way to go," Sarah reminded him. "But I've got a few terrific helpers. I was having night- mares about what to say and how to cope with Nabila. I need not have. She is determined to carry on despite what they did to her husband. In fact, her husband's death is the reason behind her decision to fight – to fight for equal rights and jus- tice. It's strange. She was the person I expected to bail out the first opportunity she got. She tried to – earlier. My aunts were pestering her, warning her about participating in what they have branded as my 'anti-Islamic schemes.' Her husband argued with her, changed her mind."

Muhammad laughed. "Your aunts are quite diligent. They've been to see my parents every week to persuade them not to send my sisters to school. What's their problem?"

"Money."

"That explains it. I think we should call it greed. Ali told me your father provided very generously for all his relatives, especially his sisters. His father's wife, Um Hassan told him."

"But my father made a big mistake," Sarah joked. "I am a woman. I don't count. The way they see it, the 'real money' should have gone to my cousin, Ramzi. They're trying and I don't expect them to give up. Not to worry, though. The money is safely tucked away – overseas, where they can't touch it."

The irony of their conversation did not escape her. She could not have had such a discussion with Muhammad had he not been exposed to a different culture, a culture which was not faultless, but was a democracy, a culture committed to resolve differences by consensus – not by force. Muhammad was a man for whom equality and justice were mere abstract terms, a man who initially had found the shock from his new social and cultural environment insurmountable. Yet within a few months, he confessed, acquainting himself with the values of the new culture was a challenge he looked forward to with enthusiasm, a novel feeling he did not know he had.

He loved it.

"When I return to Jordan," he said, "and get a job, I want to give ten percent of my earnings to help someone else get an education. It probably won't be much, but will help a little. I don't know how else to repay you for all you've done for me."

"Tell anyone who will listen the truth. That's the best way to repay me."

After a long pause, Muhammad said, his voice full of sadness. "Only lately, have I come to realize the havoc lies and half truths have caused in our lives. Misinterpretations, which we automatically assumed were the teachings of the Prophet because our religious leaders told us they were, have very little resemblance to the actual philosophy or the teachings of the Prophet. The more I learn, the more I admire the Prophet's message. It's a whole way of life, with the highest morals, equality and justice. Not at all what some men have distorted it to be."

"That's great!" Sarah could hardly contain her excitement. "Where? How did you learn all this? And why this sudden interest in religion." It became clear this was not a show Muhammad put on to please her benefactor that is what Sarah had suspected from his earlier calls. This was a man who was going through a genuine transformation and thank God he was not doing it at the expense of his religion.

Muhammad was on a roll. He asked, "Remember when I questioned you at your place about your religious beliefs, and reminded you repeatedly that you were being accused of having anti-Islamic intentions?"

"I remember."

"You said Muhammad, Islam is a beautiful religion. If it weren't, it would have gone the way many other religions have. But it's here and growing faster than any other religion. There's nothing wrong with Islam or Christianity or Judaism. There's lots wrong with us – humans. We take from religion what suits us and distort it to satisfy what we mistakenly think we need – namely power and control. A true believer has no use for either. He is a person who has achieved the highest form of spiritual purity. When you find such a person, you will find the true meaning of religion. Miss Sarah, I did find such a person, in a mosque, in Seattle. I had to. I could not deal with the contradictions I was faced with, the misconceptions I had so firmly believed in all my life. I was going crazy. My English teacher suggested I talk to a councilor at school. The councilor said she would investigate and get back to me.

She did. She advised me to contact a man called Omar Askari. He helps students like me who come from overseas adjust to their new environment. The best thing about him is his sense of humor. He says students from overseas resemble Siberians dressed in many layers of clothing who are accidentally dropped on the beaches of a tropical island. The layers of clothing represent the preconceived ideas we come with. He helps us shed them, layer by layer. We have learned that it is not a duel between which culture or which religion or which society is better. It's about learning to respect each other through values common to all of us. That he said is the true message of the Prophet. Dr. Askari is a professor of religious studies at the University of Washington. He works with our group every Sunday morning for a couple of hours. I am beginning to understand the true interpretation of the Koran. It's fascinating."

The best thing that could happen to you, Sarah thought.

She had sensed the potential in him during their first meeting. Behind the 'I hate-the-world facad" she saw a young man desperately pleading for help. The high she got from listening to the change of attitude he had undergone in a few months away from the suffocating, oppressive atmosphere of the camp, made the agony she had to endure from her opponents seem almost insignificant.

"I think you'll end up as one of my great success stories." She found it hard to express more eloquently the pleasure she got from the progress he was making, how little it took for him to gain an insight into what real truth was, as opposed to what he was taught to believe. "Call me collect when you hear from Ali. If you sense trouble, call me any time day or night."

Muhammad said he would and after they said goodbye, Sarah stretched on the sofa. She eyed the bathroom longingly, but could not get her body to move. She passed out. The hot bath would have to wait.

It was dark when she woke up.

No sign of Nabila or Jim. They had stayed behind to

arrange for Fatme to be transferred from the emergency room to the surgical unit, while Sarah went to the police station with the police chief.

She thought they might have gone to a café, but had to check herself. Nabila was in mourning. Custom demanded that she do just that – mourn. Wear black, weep, feel sorry for her loss – herself. But Nabila was not the Nabila Sarah knew only a week ago. She probably would go ahead and do whatever she fancied, custom be damned.

Sarah figured she'd know soon enough. It was time for that hot bath she'd been hoping for all day.

It was not to be.

She had barely stepped in the bathroom, when someone pounded on the door.

Sarah stepped back out.

Jim and Nabila stood facing her, looking totally frustrated. "They've disappeared," Jim said, his voice shaking with anger. "They've simply disappeared. No one seems to know where or how. Only that they're gone."

Jim dropped his protesting body into an armchair in the living room, threw his arms on the sides, pushed his head back and said, "I've got to find those bastards. I must."

"I assume you're referring to the mullahs." Sarah simply wanted Jim to know she shared his concern. No doubt few others would arouse such fury in a man as disciplined as Jim.

Jim did not answer. He was grinding his teeth.

Nabila went to the kitchen with Sarah for a drink. She said after the police chief took Sarah to the police station to have the incident in the emergency room recorded, the two policemen the chief had left behind to guard the mullahs until a special police van arrived to pick them up, had a long wait. They waited over an hour. No van arrived. One of the policemen left to call the station. He was back within minutes. Said a special car had arrived, not a van. They got in and drove off.

"Damn." Jim punched his left hand with his right fist.

"We quickly transferred Fatme to the surgical unit, Jim

posted guards at her door, we got in Jim's car and were on our way to your place, when suddenly Jim turned the car around and drove to the police station. He said he wanted to make sure those. . . Never mind what he called them. . . were safely locked behind bars."

"Yeah, right." Sarah had rarely seen Jim so upset.

"He almost punched the police chief," Nabila said. "I had to beg him to get out of there."

"Get this." Jim jumped out of the armchair. "After all that happened in the ER, the police chief had the audacity to tell me that the clerics were allowed to go after their business because it was the word of a child against the word of a clergyman."

"You know better, Jim," Nabila said. "That was just a cover up. I bet he received a call from some big shot to keep hands off the clergy. It's political dynamite. No one wants it. The police chief had no choice."

"And we are led to believe that Jordan is the least corrupt, most orderly, law abiding country in the Arab world without being a dictatorship?"

"Oh, Jim." Sarah felt she had to help Jim snap out of his negative feelings. "These things happen all over the world. And yes, Jordan is better than many other countries which easily come to mind."

"I'm going to find them," Jim shot back. "I don't care where they hide. I will find them."

Sarah was horrified. Her thoughts started to spin faster than the wheels of a race car in competition. She managed to drag herself to the sofa to sort out her options. She had none. When Jim decided on a course of action, not much could be done to deter him.

The doorbell rang.

It was Dr. Tuqan. "Terrific guards you have out there, Jim. They searched me again, although by now you'd think they'd know who I am."

"Can't be too careful."

"What's the matter with everybody?" Dr. Tuqan asked searching their faces for a clue.

"Scotch and water?" Sarah asked Dr. Tuqan.

"Just what the doctor ordered."

"Anybody else want a drink?"

"Make that two," Jim said.

Sarah and Nabila prepared the men their drinks, poured themselves wine, then joined the men in the living room.

"So what's up?" Dr. Tuqan persisted. "Fatme is doing all right. What's all the gloom about."

"Don't fall out of your chair," Jim said with a rueful smile on his face. "But the mullahs are gone. I'm urged to accept it as a fait accompli."

Suheil did not look surprised at all. After a long pause, he spoke with resignation. "Of course they're gone. No police chief dares put a Sheikh behind bars. His life won't be worth a damn if he does. But there's much more to it than that. The whole thing was planned, staged."

It came as a thunderbolt. "What did you say?" Sarah could not believe that Suheil could sit there and tell them calmly that the whole thing was staged.

"I had a long talk with the police chief and earlier with Fatme. I surmised from the bits and pieces I gathered that it was not a simple matter of exposing the culprits. We were naíve to think that Fatme could escape from the mosque. They let her go because they were afraid she would die in the mosque. Calling a doctor to check on her was out of the question. Any doctor would immediately know what had happened. The Sheikh expected her to end up here. Too far to walk to the camp. She has no family, no friends – at least no one she can count on. They followed her, were relieved she made it here and hoped that we would take care of her, treat her without letting anyone know what had happened."

"It still doesn't make sense." Sarah figured her aunts must be keeping the clerics informed about her visitors. Otherwise how would they know Dr. Tuqan would be around to treat her.

"I cannot believe that they would expect me to cover up for them," she added.

"Fatme is a very brave girl," Suheil replied. "That's because she has suffered much. The Sheikh made her swear on the Koran not to tell anyone that he had so much as touched her. What he didn't know was what happened after he left her bed. His assistant saw him go to her room every night, spend about an hour, sometimes more, then quietly sneak down the hall and return to his quarters. The assistant knew he had it made. He waited impatiently, frequently peeping through the key hole until the Sheikh left. After that, it was his turn."

"Oh, my God." Sarah was in tears. Fatme being raped by both men had already been disclosed, but the cumulative effect of all that had happened had begun to take its toll.

Dr. Tuqan moved to the sofa, sat next to her and took her in his arms. All pretense at friendship was put aside. "Please don't cry," he begged. "I truly cannot take it."

He pulled her closer to his body and caressed her hair.

Sarah wiped her tears. "I'm sorry. I didn't mean to upset you."

Jim sipped his Scotch and waited. Finally, he said, "Doctor, the revelation that they allowed her to escape is most interesting. Please go on."

"Think about it, Jim. The room had no windows. All they had to do was lock the door. Which they did, every night, until the night before last."

"What's so special about the night before last." Jim shook his head confused.

"The night before last, the Sheikh went to the room where Fatme was locked up like he had done the nights before. He thought she was asleep and tried to wake her up, but couldn't. He decided she was acting up and went ahead anyway. When his body touched hers, it felt very hot and the wound had festered and begun to smell foul. Fear that she might die in the mosque prompted him to put his clothes back on and leave.

"He wasn't gone long," the doctor continued. "He returned – to his assistant's room a minute too late to catch his assistant step out of Fatme's room. He told the assistant to prepare himself to take Fatme to Gaza the next day to work for his brother."

"The assistant had had the same experience with Fatme. Since he was in charge of taking care of her, he felt he should let the Sheikh know that Fatme was ill and in no shape to travel. Apparently the Sheikh went back to his quarters but returned within the hour and instructed his underling to leave her door unlocked and not to mess with her if she tried to escape."

The women listened to the doctor quietly, totally absorbed in what he had to say. But the unfolding of the events seemed to make Jim edgy. He fidgeted, pulled his legs, pushed his arms and looked like he was ready to explode. "Where did you dig up all this?" he asked. "And how?"

"A lot from Fatme. She was not out of it as she pretended to be. She knew she had a fever and she knew her wound was infected, but she was not unconscious as she pretended to be. She heard most of the conversations between the Sheikh and his assistant but wasn't aware that they wanted her to escape. I doubt it would have changed her mind though. And the rest of the information came from the Sheikh's assistant. The police chief is a capable officer trained in England. He advised the Sheikh to leave the country immediately and not return until tempers cooled down, namely yours, Jim. He then advised the assistant to tell him everything he knew, otherwise, the police chief warned, he would make sure the mullah spent the rest of his life in jail. The assistant knew he was in trouble because Fatme had pointed her finger at him and the Sheikh in the ER, despite having sworn on the Koran not to."

"It doesn't compute," Sarah said. "If Fatme swore on the Koran not to tell, she wouldn't."

"She didn't want to," the doctor replied. "She did it after we had a long talk. I explained to her that God would forgive her because she had sworn under duress, when she probably had a fever and could not think clearly. That did not impress her too much. So I revised my approach. I told her they will blame Miss Sarah for what happened to her. That got her attention. How she wanted to know. I said the Sheikh will deny having ever touched you, and apparently that's precisely what he did, and his assistant will claim you asked for it. You asked for it because Miss Sarah is filling your young minds with crazy ideas like freedom for women, sexual equality, human rights and so on.

"She was quiet. I asked the nurse to change her dressing, came to the coffee shop, talked to you, and when I left, I made it a point to stop by and check her temperature. I wasn't sure I was getting through to her. She seemed quite drowsy at times, but she was responding to the antibiotics, and her temperature had dropped somewhat. She did have periods when she was quite alert. I checked her chart but did not speak to her. As I was leaving, she said, doctor, please wait. I approached her bed, she tried to bring her face close to mine. I moved closer. Her voice dropped to a whisper. She said she prayed and Allah told her he will forgive her. Allah said Miss Sarah should not be blamed for the sins of others. She should tell the truth."

Sarah was speechless. For a fourteen year old ,who, until a few months ago had only been exposed to traditional values, values which taught breaking a vow as one of the greatest sins – for her to rationalize and emerge with a solution, was beyond Sarah's comprehension. The fact that so much change had taken place in Muhammad and in Fatme, change she had neither suspected nor expected – as yet, infused her with an enthusiasm she found hard to contain. Her efforts were not in vain. All the young needed was a chance, a helping hand. The harvest followed.

Immediately, thought of Muhammad reminded her of Ali. She told them about her conversation with Muhammad and his fears about Ali's reaction when he learns of his sister's rape. "We did the right thing, for the right reasons, at the wrong time, in the wrong place. We've got to put our heads together and come up with a plausible alternative. I have no doubt in my mind, if Ali returns to Jordan, there will be bloodshed."

Sarah waited for a response but none was forthcoming. Jim stared despondently into space, his brow furrowed, his body still. Whenever he sulked, Sarah worried. Nabila had said little since the doctor's arrival and the doctor seemed to be in another zone. "Drinks, anyone?" Sarah could not think of how else to get their attention.

"I've got to go." Jim rose.

Nabila mumbled something.

"I'll drop you off at Mona's place if you'd like," Jim said.

"You're welcome to spend the night here," Sarah offered. "It will give us time to discuss Ali's problem and perhaps come up with a few ideas for a place for you and Fatme."

"Fatme will probably not live long enough to need a place." Nabila broke into tears and sobbed uncontrollably.

Jim rushed over, put his arm around her shoulder and tried to comfort her. "I won't let that happen Nabila. I will do everything in my power to see to it that it doesn't."

Sarah's eyes welled with tears, but she managed to remain in control. Nabila pressed her face on Jim's chest and wept quietly.

"It will do her good." Dr. Tuqan poured himself another Scotch as he spoke. "It's time she let go, give herself a break. We should all take time out. Decisions made under pressure have a way of coming back to haunt us."

"We don't have time to take time out," Nabila protested between sobs. "Ali will be here soon enough and then it will be too late to stop him."

With a look of intense anxiety on his face, Dr. Tuqan walked back from the kitchen, drink in hand. "Your concern is definitely justified," he told Nabila. "Like you all, I too worried about the repercussions if the rape were to become public knowledge. But upon further consideration it became clear to me that there was no way for such a matter to remain secret – even briefly. Half a dozen employees, nurses, interns, residents were in the ER when it became evident that we were not dealing with an infection following a clitoridectomy. She has stitches all the way to her rectum. Had the clerics not been exposed when they were, the way they were, there's no doubt in my mind an innocent person would end up paying for their lust – namely Fatme. With her life."

Jim permitted himself a laugh, ever so sardonically. "Who says clerics don't have a sense of humor."

Nabila struggled to bring her sobbing under control. "What has happened to Fatme," she said, "speaks volumes about the devastating effects the combination of injustice, sexual discrimination, violence and domination have upon the innocent. Even if by some miracle Fatme manages to escape her brother's wrath, she will be condemned to a life of misery. She will not be able to show her face in public, she won't have any friends, she has no family, which in this case is probably a blessing, no money, nothing. She will be branded as an immoral woman. How is she going to survive?"

Negative ideas never failed to arouse an intense reaction in Sarah. She moved close to Nabila, reached for her hand, and pressed it between hers. "That's what we're here for, Nabila. With Fatme's guts and our determination, there's no battle we can't win."

Chapter 19

IT WAS AS THOUGH THE Holy Spirit had descended from heaven to arrange a truce between the warring factions. Or, perhaps, it was the Sheikh's absence. It did not matter. Life was good. Now in her early fifties, and living in England, Sarah's nanny, Gwynne, with whom Sarah had remained in close contact, was invited by Jim to come live with Nabila and Fatme. Jim had meant to surprise Sarah and make it possible for Nabila to live in the compound without being hassled. Sarah managed to live alone but she had paid the price. Rape was not an experience to be overcome easily, she was also only half Arab and could pack up and leave anytime. Nabila had no options, only a self appointed protector – Jim.

Maher Sultan had not forgotten Gwynne. She received enough money to live comfortably the rest of her life. Hence, Sarah's complete surprise when Gwynne showed up, the day after the incident in the emergency room delighted to be close to Sarah again. Meanwhile, construction workers worked from dawn to dusk to rebuild Nabila's blown out kitchen, since that's where she preferred to live together with her husband's memories. In the meantime, Nabila, Fatme and Gwynne lived in one of the vacant apartments in the compound. Sarah's father had been unable to sell seven units after his sisters moved in.

Jim drove the school bus, Younis categorically refused to back down from his insistence that he take care of the camp until Ali returned. Nabila took Fatme home from the hospital to live with her. Sarah's aunts had returned to their homes two days after the incident in the emergency room and the Sheikh's unexpected departure. Both women moved about completely covered, in black, from head to toe, even in the compound. Ordinarily, they wore a headscarf when they visited their neighbors in the compound or wanted to talk to Attiyeh. Lately though, they were always together, spoke to no one, walked directly to their separate units on the rare occasion that they left their homes.

"Something is cooking," Jim remarked. "I've never seen them so tame."

"They have their orders, I am sure," Nabila said. "It's time out, like you Americans say. My guess is they're waiting for the Sheikh to sneak back into the country to tell them what to do."

"It's not time out for their weekly trips to the camp," Jim said. "The guards tell me the same taxi comes every Friday afternoon about two o'clock, drives them to the camp and brings them back late in the evening."

"It gives them something to do, I guess," Sarah said. "We have not had a single absentee since we resumed classes. Hopefully, someday soon, they'll tire and give up."

They learned through Attiyeh that Ramzi was back in town. Attiyeh saw him in the bazaar downtown, walking with a cane. "He'd lost so much weight, he looked like a stick himself," Attiyeh said.

Meanwhile, Nabila had gained weight and kept on gaining. Occasionally she took a couple of hours off, took a taxi, went somewhere and returned. Sarah and Jim did not know what to think of it. They assumed she went to the cemetery to visit her husband. Lately though, she was withdrawn, hardly ever initiated conversation and answered in few words when spoken to.

In due time, Nabila's deepening depression became intolerable for Jim – especially her refusal to see a doctor about it. Jim contemplated having one of the secret service agents follow her on the rare occasions when she went out, but Sarah insisted it would be counter productive if Nabila ever found out. Jim agreed – reluctantly and confessed he could think of no other options.

The situation worsened with each passing day inducing a heavy dose of depression in Jim as well. Although he did all that was required of him and more, he remained morose, uncommunicative.

Like Jim, Sarah's concern mounted steadily. However, she did not want to pry. Delayed depression following her husband's death seemed like the only plausible explanation. Even time, the one element Sarah had hoped would work in her friend's favor seemed determined to cheat her of it.

Sarah finally relented and discussed her concern with Jim.

Jim was in love with Nabila. Yet he dared not reveal his feelings to anyone but Sarah and Gwynne since tradition demanded that Nabila mourn her husband's death at least for a year, and not remarry later unless her family chose someone for her, usually a close relative.

Nabila had no family. They were killed during one of the many Israeli bombing raids. She happened to be in a friend's house when a bomb wiped out her home and family. Mona, her cousin, was the closest relative she had. Mona had brothers, but they were in their teens. However, Nabila's husband had two brothers. Nabila had mentioned earlier that presently Samir's brothers were in Kuwait but were planning to immigrate to Brazil together with their parents. Three hundred thousand Palestinians had been kicked out of Kuwait and Saudi Arabia for backing Saddam Hussein in the Gulf War of 1991. Samir's brothers suspected their turn would come soon enough and therefore planned in advance for a place to immigrate.

"I've lost sleep over it many a night, wrecking my brains," Jim admitted. "I can't come up with anything. I've talked to her several times – pleaded for her to confide in me, assuring her I'd take care of whatever it is that's bothering her. She says she feels fine. Not to worry about her. End of conversation."

"Such behavior is troubling," Sarah said. "Before she left the hospital, she was full of vim and vigor. She couldn't wait for classes to resume and was real eager to get the children back on track. I have to admit though, she does a terrific job with the children, but it's almost as if something or someone has snatched her love of life out of her practically overnight. There's no drive, no laughter, no anger, nothing. She's more like a robot."

Gwynne lived with Nabila in the same unit and she was a shrewd judge of character. Jim and Sarah decided to consult her hoping she could shed some light on the matter.

Gwynne was as baffled as they were. "She's scared of something. I don't know what. Whatever it is, she keeps it to herself. She hardly eats – drinks milk. That's just about it. But she keeps adding weight. I can't figure it out, really."

It was two days before Christmas, more than two months without incidence. With Gwynne's help, Nabila and Sarah taught the children how to make decorations for the Christmas tree. After much soul searching and consulting principles of other schools, and the Ministry of Education, it was decided that the children should learn about the signifi-cant holidays of major religions – namely Islam, Christianity and Judaism. Christmas was first on the calendar.

The children simply devoured whatever they were taught, the hunger great, their privileged status branded on their as yet unpolluted minds. This was more so with Fatme than any other student. She had made a remarkable recovery from her infection under the superb care of Dr. Tuqan, worked dili-gently at whatever task she was given, took care of the younger children, prayed daily to thank Allah for sparing her life and hoped Allah would be kind enough to protect her brother – wherever he was. She was badly scarred physically but not incontinent of stools as had been feared. If she was scarred emotionally and mentally – she did not let on. She did a superb job of going about her business as if nothing ever happened.

No one had heard from Ali since his last conversation with Muhammad. All efforts at locating him, thus far, had failed. Although his absence meant relief from the constant worry of what he might do to his sister when he returned, Sarah could not help imagining the worst. To help placate her fears, Jim hired a private detective to search for him. The detective had little to go on. Muhammad had written Sarah a letter and sent it by registered mail to inform her about Ali's whereabouts – what he knew from the one phone call Ali had made, the phone call Muhammad had discussed with Sarah earlier without mentioning Ali's whereabouts.

Panicked, apparently Ali hitchhiked to downtown Amman immediately after the bomb blast. He went to the garage where he had worked at odd jobs the previous summer. It was a garage where truck drivers gathered to load produce destined for Baghdad. He asked a driver he had worked for before to give him a ride, claiming he had received word that an uncle was quite ill, in a small town, in Iraq. The truck driver was eager to oblige. It meant company for the long, boring trip through mostly desert area. Within a couple of hours, the driver and Ali crossed the border into Iraq. At his request Ali was dropped off at Ar Rutbah. With only a few Dinars in his pocket, and his concern mounting for his sister, Ali had called Muhammad from the local post office – collect. Muhammad promised Ali he would contact Sarah to inquire about Fatmé. He also offered to give Ali what money he had to help him out. Muhammad's offer could not have come at a more appropriate time. Ali promised to call as soon as he received the money. Muhammad had yet to hear from him. That was the extent of Muhammad's knowledge.

After months of investigation, the detective Jim had hired was ready to give up. The detective had located the truck driver and verified the fact that he had indeed given Ali a ride to Ar Rutbah. But the trail ended there. "It's like landing behind the iron curtain," the detective said. "Can't go to Iraq. Too dangerous."

"Perhaps the truck driver might be willing to help," Jim said, urged on by the anxious expression on Sarah's face. "For the right price."

"Believe me, I tried," the detective said. "They are issued special permits to go into Baghdad, empty their truckloads and leave. No one is allowed to stay without special permission. While they're there, their every move is watched by Saddam Hussein's secret service."

"I wonder if Ali knew the risk he was taking when he decided to go to Iraq." Sarah was scared. Her voice betrayed it.

"Where else could he go?" Jim argued. "Syria? Iran? They're all the same – despotic regimes, secret servicemen everywhere. It's also possible that he did not have a choice. He had to go where the truck driver had to deliver the load he had."

"That's precisely what happened, I'm sure," the detective said. "The truck driver said he did not believe Ali's story about a sick uncle. He figured Ali was running away from something – but didn't know what. He had not heard about the bomb blast as yet. He thought perhaps a robbery, or a fight – common occurrences in the camps, especially nowadays with most young men out of work."

"In Iraq, all long distance phone calls are tapped," the detective continued. "My guess is simple. They must have listened to Ali's conversation with Muhammad, heard he was promised dollars from America and pounced on him as a spy."

Sarah took a deep breath and struggled to control her anger at the impersonal manner in which the detective had analyzed the situation. "So where do we go from here? Do we just let an innocent man rot in an Iraqi jail? An innocent man whose only crime was his concern for my safety. You have given us your interpretation of the events – and that's fine. I think you're probably right. But the problem remains unresolved. What we need now is action. Do you have any suggestions?"

"I don't." The detective shrugged his shoulders. "I am as frustrated as you are and that's why I have decided to drop this case. Don't misunderstand me. The money is good and I would love to continue. But I'm a religious man. It would be wrong to take your money when I know in all probability there is very little I can do to help locate this man."

"Don't you have any contacts in Iraq?" Jim asked. "There must be some way to find out if he is in fact in jail. Maybe he really has relatives in Iraq, maybe he found odd jobs in the border villages to support himself until he can return home. There's no sense in assuming the worse. Please don't give up."

"I'll work on it, if you want me to. But I make no promises. My conscience has to be clear that we understand each other. So far, I've been groping in the dark. It will take time and money and even then it might end up completely dry."

Sarah caught Jim's eye.

"Go for it," Jim said. "Whatever happens. Keep us posted. I bet even in Iraq, for the right price, you will be able to get the information we seek."

"I feel responsible for what happened to Ali." Sarah's voice cracked. "Please spare no effort."

"Anywhere else it would be easy." The detective paused. "A substantial reward almost always brings results. Unfortunately, in Arab countries, especially in Iraq, chances of being caught are horrific and no reward is large enough for that."

Jim raised an eyebrow and took on a serious look.

"But," the detective added quickly, "since you insist, I will persist. God be with you."

And with that, the detective took his leave.

The next day, day before Christmas, Attiyeh and his wife brought in three turkeys that had been bought alive, killed, plucked, cleaned and ready for the oven. Sarah wanted the children to experience a traditional Christmas dinner. It had taken over a week of planning, as most of the ingredients, including the turkey were not readily available. But Jim and Attiyeh had somehow managed, and the turkeys were distributed among Nabila, Sarah and Gwynne to be baked.

It was a meal the children would never forget. Not because it was the best meal they had ever had, but also because while they were in the process of eating, with Gwynne and Sarah explaining the tradition to the children, suddenly the classroom door was flung open and two clerics walked in, unannounced, uninvited and demanded an explanation. "What's this," demanded to know the younger mullah his finger pointed at the Christmas tree.

It had taken a week for Jim to find a lopsided Christmas tree at a price he had difficulty articulating.

"And this," the same mullah said, this time his finger pointed at the food on the table. "How dare you try to convert Muslim children to Christianity."

The older mullah did not say a word. He seemed totally captivated by the beautifully decorated tree, the Christmas decoration all over the classroom, the children's festive outfits, and the tables laden with food.

It never fails, Sarah thought. My aunts have been at it again. Somehow, she mustered enough courage to keep her cool, walked over to the entrance where the clerics stood, introduced herself and invited the clerics in. "Come join us, gentlemen please come in. There's no religion involved here. We are simply enjoying a meal together in celebration of the holidays."

"What holidays? Why are you confusing these children? Who gave you permission to teach Christianity to Muslim children, in a Muslim country" The same mullah seemed determined to do all the talking.

Sarah was about to answer when she noticed the expression on Gwynne's face. When Gwynne put her mind to take matters over, Gwynne took matters over.

She rose, pushed her chair back and marched towards the clerics. "Gentlemen, sit down, please." Gwynne was a strong woman, spoke with an authoritative voice. Objecting was not an option, and she did not wait for any. She pulled two chairs and plopped them in front of the mullahs and waited, hands hugging her hips.

The mullahs sat down.

For some reason which Sarah found difficult to fathom, Arab men, in general, showed more respect to Western women than they did to their own.

"It's like this," Gwynne explained as she piled food in two plates. "Those who sent you here are malicious, old women. You don't need them to tell you what children should be taught. The Prophet himself admired and respected Christ. You will not find a more true believer than Miss Sarah. She was raised to believe all religions have basically the same goal: to achieve spiritual purity. And all religion should be respected – none more than the others. Now pull your chairs closer to the table and help us celebrate."

The mullahs exchanged looks. The older man seemed eager, the younger man hesitated.

"You need not worry," Sarah said, "I checked with other schools and with the Ministry of Education. I was assured it was perfectly all right to teach the children about any religion we liked."

"That's a lie." It was a woman's voice. Khadijeh and Hamideh barged in. They had been listening, huddled behind the door.

Both mullahs jumped up.

Covered in black, with only their eyes showing, the two women stopped at the entrance of the classroom and immediately Khadijeh started a diatribe about immoral women filling the minds of innocent children with everything forbidden by Islam. Hamideh took over when her sister, short of breath, took time out to breathe. Their niece, Sarah, she claimed, did whatever she pleased and no one dared stop her because of the immense wealth left in the hands of a young, inexperienced, Godless woman, by her father who should have known better.

For the children, arguments, fights, were common occurrences at the camp. To survive, they had learned to block it out whenever possible, or wait patiently for it to end. They waited for it to end.

But Sarah was furious. She walked to the entrance where her aunts stood and faced them.

"I don't remember inviting you in," she said the pitch of her voice partially under control. "This is private property. Please leave."

"Make us." Khadijeh's voice was full of contempt.

Caught off guard, Sarah stepped back and reached for the phone.

Gwynne quickly grabbed her hand and pressed the receiver back in its cradle. "Can't you see? They want you to call the police. It will give them the best opportunity to blow this thing out of proportion." Then she whirled herself towards Sarah's aunts, the look in her eyes deadly serious, her face a few inches from theirs. "Get out. Now," she growled through clenched teeth.

They did – muttering curses under their breaths.

Gwynne closed the door and turned back to face the classroom. For a moment no one spoke. There was an uneasy quiet. Once again, Gwynne came to the rescue. "Eat. Eat," she told the children. "Your food is getting cold."

After a moment's hesitation, the mullahs rose. "We must be going," said the older mullah reluctantly.

"Indeed not." Gwynne seemed determined to have her way. "There's food in your plates, good food. Let's not waste it. Come gentlemen, let's eat. We can't permit a couple of sick minds to ruin a scrumptious dinner it took us days to prepare."

The mullahs looked at each other as if to ask 'is this woman for real?' They sat down. The aroma of the food must have been too much to resist. They proceeded to eat with vengeance.

Jim had stayed behind to put the last touches on the Yule logs he had spent two days baking and decorating. He entered the classroom, followed by Attiyeh carrying two trash bags with gifts for the children, their families and every other child in the camp. Upon seeing the two clerics at the dinner table, Jim came to a quick stop, searched the faces of the women, then headed towards a table in the corner where he placed the Yule logs. He walked over near where Sarah sat. "I have not had the honor of the acquaintance of these gentlemen." He said it the way an Arab would say. Without waiting for a reply, he stepped forward, stretched his right hand. "Jim Bateson. Nice to have you here with us."

Both mullahs rose and shook hands. They said they came from a mosque near by but did not give their names. The older man said they were having a great time – contrary to what they were led to believe.

Jim turned to Sarah. "Did you know your aunts are outside – in the cold. They saw us coming, they hurried and hid behind the building."

"They've already paid us a visit, thank you." Sarah cast a quick glance in the direction of the clerics. "Their representatives are here to check on us."

"Wonder what it's costing your aunts to buy the services of these clerics." Jim planted a huge smile on his face as he pulled a chair next to the older cleric and proceeded to serve himself dinner. He ate a few bites and declared it was the best turkey he had had in a long time.

It was the turkey Nabila had cooked. She smiled, said nothing. Jim thanked her, then quickly turned his attention to the uninvited guests much to Sarah's consternation. It took little to ignite a fuse in Jim, and the clerics, especially the younger man, had not impressed her as being very tactful. Uneasy, Sarah went about making sure the children were served desert and received gifts for themselves and their families.

After dinner the children sang a benign Christmas song applauded enthusiastically by everyone except the young mullah.

Sarah chose to ignore him.

Meanwhile, Nabila collected the used plates and piled them in a garbage can. It was the first time the children had seen paper plates, cups and cutlery, courtesy of Jim through his connections with the American Embassy. The children kept the cutlery they had used to take home, a treasured item.

Soon Sarah relaxed. Jim and the older mullah were engrossed deep in conversation. Whatever the topic, both men seemed to be enjoying themselves. The younger man ate and ate. Finally he seemed to have had enough. He wiped his mouth with his napkin and placed it next to his empty plate. Nabila walked over, asked if he was through eating and was told he was. She reached for his plate. The younger mullah, in his middle thirties, regarded her curiously as though he had become aware of her presence only then, pushed his head back and said smugly, "You are Muslim, aren't you?"

It was a question asked often of women, more so lately, by self appointed guardians of the faith when they thought the woman in question did not abide by the dress code meted out to them by men. In Saudi Arabia, it would land a woman in jail, instantly, with worst to come. Fortunately for Nabila, she was in Jordan. She cast him an icy glare, picked his plate and moved on.

The mullah jumped out of his seat, his face red with anger. "You are a disgrace," he shouted as forty little faces stared at him uncomprehending, terrified. "A woman should be covered in the presence of men, she should lower her gaze and be modest. What sort of example do you think you are setting for these children?"

Nabila was dressed in a simple long sleeved, black shift, reaching her ankles. "The best," she answered and walked away.

Nabila was in a testy mood.

The mullah grabbed the edge of the table in an attempt to control his shaking.

Sarah's knees turned to jelly. She pulled a chair, lowered herself in it slowly, and prayed for divine intervention. She hated confrontation and never ceased to be strongly effected by it.

Gwynne, who had been busy cutting the Yule logs, stepped up front from behind the table and placed a slice of Yule log in front of the mullah. "Eat," she said with a voice meant to intimidate.

The mullah stared at her in disbelief. "Eat. She says eat. Did you hear that? Can't you see we're in the midst of an important discussion?"

"You are," Gwynne shot back. "No one else is. Don't be so judgmental. You should consider yourself privileged that someone with the moral fortitude of Nabila is here to teach these children."

"What moral fortitude?" the mullah retorted angrily. "It is the duty of a true Muslim woman to obey the dictates of Islam. Women should not draw attention to themselves. It is clear to the believers of the faith that seclusion of women, when possible, or at least full cover is essential to safeguard herself, her family and the society."

"Oh, lay it to rest," Gwynne said without missing a beat. "Why don't you save your sermon for the mosque. Let's worry about religion some other time. Now we want to have fun."

The mullah had worked himself into frenzy. He had barely returned to his seat when he jumped out again, cast a quick glance at his colleague as though hoping for reinforcement. His colleague ignored him. Undaunted, the mullah rambled on. "Fun. She says fun. You ... you want us to have fun when we're faced with women who ... who ... trample on our religion. Trample on it like old newspaper?"

Gwynne pushed him back in his chair – not so gently. "I suggest you calm down and join the fun. If you don't, you might end up having a stroke."

Sarah was delighted with Gwynne's presence. Gwynne had lived most of her life in Arab countries. She knew how to deal with Arabs, especially the men.

Annoyed by incessant bickering of the mullah, Jim and the older mullah had to stop their conversation. They could not hear each other talk. However, much to their dismay the younger mullah continued his verbal abuse seemingly gripped by an irresistible urge to prove to one and all his devotion to his sanctimonious duty. "He takes himself quite seriously, doesn't he?" Jim loved verbal duels, especially when it revolved around injustice of any kind, when he could watch devious minds at work. It fascinated him.

"He does," answered the older mullah. He turned to his colleague. "This is not the time or the place for you to preach. The English woman is right. At this rate you're headed to an early grave."

Caught off guard by the reaction of the older man, the younger mullah went on the defensive. "You were busy talking. You don't know what happened. That woman is a widow." His finger was pointed at Nabila. "You would think she would have enough sense to cover herself in the presence of strange men – at least her head."

"They had no idea you were coming. You invited yourself."

The reaction of the older mullah sent a faint smile to Sarah's face. Ordinarily, she avoided arguments, especially arguments advanced by individuals less interested in talking about objective facts than about subjective feelings on a matter. But not when the argument was about women's issues. Overcome suddenly with an urge to vent months of pent up frustration, she said, "The gentleman has a right to his opinions and the right to voice them. Thanks to an enlightened King and Queen who made free elections possible in 1993, we live in a democratic country. The only democratic country in the Arab world, I might add. But free speech and free press are not privileges to be abused. The gentleman needs to face facts. In a democracy we have freedom, but freedom comes with responsibility. We cannot trample on the rights of others."

The mullah's face got redder as Sarah spoke. It was apparent he had not anticipated or expected resistance or talk back, from, of all people, a woman. He stuck his right hand out, shook it at Sarah and yelled, "Rights? Who said anything about rights? We're talking duty. A woman's duty as a Muslim is to respect the teachings of the Prophet. It has nothing to do with democracy or rights. It has everything to do with obeying the moral code clearly outlined in the Hadith. These traditions about the life and sayings of the Prophet are all we need to guide us through life. Democracy is a degenerate, Western concept we can live without. We need the teachings of the Prophet. Nothing else."

"And what are those teachings, sir." Sarah decided to speak her mind, damn the consequences. "Should a woman sit at home and have kids? Should a woman make sure she caters to every whim her male relations have. Should she submit, let her husband's word be law, have no life of her own, no demands, no desires, preferably invisible, except when needed to satisfy a male requirement. Sir, do you really believe that that is what the Prophet, in all his wisdom advocated for women? Or is it a convoluted reading of the Koran, the distorted interpretations of the Hadith conveniently concocted by men like you to suit their own egos that you now insist on advocating as the truth."

The mullah's eyeballs bulged as an expression of disbelief swept across his face. He tried to, but could not speak. His lower lip and beard shook. He reached in the pocket of his black garb, pulled out a large handkerchief and blew his nose.

The older mullah cast a quick glance around, then quickly turned his attention back to the man who seemed paralyzed by his own anger. "Sit down," he urged, in a voice meant for the younger man's ears only. "It's enough."

His colleague's complacency fired the young man's anger even more. "What's enough? How can you call yourself a mullah, a man of God, yet still accept an intolerable situation like this? How can you listen to a woman tell a man what he should and should not do and like a helpless spectator turn around and tell the man it's enough?"

Jim chuckled, the nasty, cynical chuckle he reserved for individuals whose genetic impulse for irrational thought left him mildly amused, mostly annoyed. "You're right. No woman should tell a man what to do. Women should not be seen or heard – except when they're victimized."

Jim's comment failed to register on the young mullah's over heated gray cells. "You're right," he said without diffidence and obviously pleased at least one person agreed with him. "They should know their place. It's better for everybody."

Exasperated, the older mullah grabbed the side of the younger man's garb and pulled him down. "Bear in mind that you invited yourself. It's extremists like you who give religion a bad name."

Tall and thin with a triangular face the young mullah had an odd look about him as his anger guided his actions. He had not yet fully recovered from the verbal lashing he got from a woman. He wiped his forehead with the same handkerchief he had used to blow his nose, shot his colleague a contemptuous look, remained standing. A crowd of blank faces must have convinced him he was wasting his time. He looked down at the man who had failed to support him. "You seem to have forgotten that we came here to put a stop to the actions of these women out to destroy our religion. It seems to me they bought you with a turkey dinner."

The man's countenance changed immediately. He stood up, placed his napkin next to his plate and said for all to hear. "It is my misfortune to have to deal with someone with limited intelligence and less common sense. Our religion spreads because of its humanism, its universal character, its compassion and its advocacy of human rights and dignity. That's the accurate image of Islam, not the distorted version you want to force on people – especially children. What kind of role model do you think you are for them?"

The younger man sighed a deep sigh, threw his hands up as though to impress the onlookers with the futility of trying to impress the older man's weak mind with his brilliant assembly of facts. "Your words make it harder for me to get any respect. I simply asked her if she was Muslim. That's all."

"And then you proceeded to accuse her of improper conduct."

"It is improper. If women were allowed to do as they pleased, who knows what kind of forces that might unleash. And what guarantee do we have that those forces will not spin out of control."

Jim threw his head back and laughed uproariously.

The older man simply shook his head.

"I've had enough. Let's leave." Jim's laughter seemed to have grated on the young man's nerves.

"I'm not done yet with my dinner and neither are the rest of the people here," replied the older mullah. "I need the car. If you want to leave, you'll have to walk."

The young cleric sat down slowly, aware of the eyes focused on him, aware his absence would be greatly appreciated, aware he could not retract what he had said even if he wanted to. Seething with anger, he continued his diatribe aimed at no one in particular. "The best!" His voice cracked. "Just like that. She said the best and walked away her head in the clouds. Who the hell does she thinks she is? Has anyone had the misfortune of witnessing such impertinence? From a widow nonetheless."

"You are headed to an early grave. That's for sure." The older mullah savored every bite of the Yule log, cleaned his plate in moments. Gwynne plopped another slice for him to attack. She winked at Sarah as she did so indicating she liked the man.

"Khadijeh was right," the younger man continued unperturbed. "These women are at work for the express purpose of polluting the minds of our youth, of our women, of all of us – with their Western ideas, their notions of democracy, and Allah forbid, women's liberation. But Allah is great and Allah willing we shall soon put an end to this travesty."

"The travesty comes from you," Nabila replied calmly. Until then she had ignored the man, intentionally, not looking in his direction when the attacks were directed at her. But by then, she seemed to have had enough. "Why should women be expected to sacrifice their comfort and freedom to satisfy codes of conduct concocted by men like you whose only purpose is to force women into submission – to humiliate, exploit and degrade us. You show me where in the Koran the Prophet gave men authority to force women into seclusion and I will show you an immense body of Hadith, where the Prophet insisted on the rights of all humans, male and female, and praised women's sexuality and their right to sexual pleasure. You feel women's bodies pose a threat to social stability. I beg to differ. Repression leads to ignorance. And that's where we are now."

With a horrified look on his face, the mullah covered his ears with his hands. "I never thought ..."

Sarah kept a straight face but laughed inwardly. The word sex, referring to women, uttered by a woman, a Muslim woman, must have sounded much too harsh for the young man's delicate ears – an intolerable situation compounded by the fact that it was directed at a cleric. Hopefully, Nabila would not have to pay too steep a price for her outburst.

"Excuse me." Nabila dropped the plates she was carrying in the bin and left the room.

The only sound to be heard in the room was the younger mullah's heavy breathing. He bounced to his feet, gathered his garb around him and declared for all to hear that he was leaving. He paused momentarily and added, "I did not join the clergy to be insulted by women." Chin forward, shoulders back, with sure steps the young cleric cast one last glance to impress his colleague with his disappointment and marched out of the classroom.

Gwynne followed him and shut the door. "We better get this party wrapped up," she said. "Your poor aunts must be freezing out in the cold."

Sarah glanced at her watch. "It's almost seven. I didn't realize it's so late. Come children. Everyone, grab a bag, gather your stuff, and off you go. Remember to share your gifts, and remember there's no school tomorrow."

The words 'no school' were the two least liked words by the children. Their faces drooped, their heads bent low.

"Come now," Sarah said as she helped them with their coats. "It's only for one day. Mr. Jim will be at the camp to bring you to school day after tomorrow."

Each child planted a kiss on Sarah's cheek, followed by a kiss on Miss Gwynne's cheek and hurried to the bus. For the first time Nabila was not there to see the children off. Timid, a little worried looking, Fatme approached Sarah. "Miss Sarah is Miss Nabila sick? She didn't look well when she left."

"I'm not sure. We'll check on her as soon as the children leave and we tidy up the classroom a bit."

Fatme helped the children get on the bus, then rushed back to clear the tables together with Sarah and Gwynne. Attiyeh and his wife, silent throughout the evening, put together what was left of the meal to take home with them – told to do so by Sarah. Attiyeh took the garbage out – returned to clean the classroom. Sarah insisted they leave the cleaning of the classroom for the next day. She asked them to take their daughters home after a long day.

The older mullah had yet to leave. He sat back and watched, without comment, until everyone, except Gwynne and Sarah were gone. He rose and approached the women, sad, gentle eyes pleading for understanding, perhaps forgiveness. "Thank you for a fabulous dinner, and thank you for the work you are doing with the children. Please forgive my colleague. He is a rash, young man, his words the product not of reason but emotion. It is tempting to believe that in due time he will change. Fanatics hardly ever do. I leave you in peace. Allah be with you."

"We enjoyed your company immensely." Sarah shook the clerics extended hand. "Thanks for coming."

"Careful out there," Gwynne said as she opened the door for him. "The courtyard is rather poorly lit. God be with you too."

Sarah checked the time. Suheil was supposed to come to the party, if he finished his work early. Anticipating delay, Sarah had saved a serving of turkey and desert for him. She was contemplating whether she should take his meal to her apartment or wait for him in the classroom, when there was a loud knock on the door.

The women exchanged glances. "I'll go." Sarah rushed to open the door.

It was Dr. Tuqan. "Call an ambulance," he said. "Quick."

Gwynne hurried to the phone.

"What happened? Who?" Sarah rushed past Suheil to the courtyard.

The huge courtyard remained in semi darkness despite torchlights all around. It didn't matter how often Attiyeh changed the bulbs. Most failed after a week or two. Sarah looked with intense concentration. She saw nothing, heard nothing.

Suheil caught up with her, reached for her arm, and directed her towards the unit where Gwynne, Fatme and Nabila lived. "Don't panic," he said, as they hurried. "I was late to the party. I took a short cut, came in from the south side of the compound, was rushing over, when I heard a moan."

It had to be Nabila. The units on the south side built after her aunts moved in were the units which had remained unsold.

"Is it Nabila? I was afraid of that. Oh, my God. Where is she? Is she all right?"

"Afraid of what?"

"Nabila and one of the two clerics who dropped in, courtesy of my aunts, uninvited, to check on us, were at each others throats." Sarah explained briefly the exchange between Nabila and the mullah.

Suheil looked puzzled. He could not understand how the

cleric could have attacked Nabila in the courtyard since Nabila had left the party before the cleric.

"She must have seen the children board the bus and decided to come help clear the mess in the classroom. Actually, I was kind of expecting her. She's not a person who shirks responsibility. She knew there was a lot to do. I bet she was on her way back to the classroom."

"But you said the mullah left after she did. Do you think he came back?"

"No. I think he left the classroom but not the compound. My guess is my aunts were waiting for him. When he came out of the classroom they took him to their apartment, kept watch to see who was coming and going. They must have seen Jim leave in the bus with the children and Nabila on her way back to the classroom. They must have followed her."

In the semidarkness, an ear piercing scream. A woman's voice. Nabila.

"My god! Sounds like she's dying." Sarah saw a dark pile barely ten feet away. She disengaged her arm from Suheil's grip and ran towards the voice.

Nabila immediately reached for Sarah's hand, grabbed it and let out yet another scream.

Terrified, Sarah turned to Suheil. "Do something, please. She must be hurt."

"Some ... one hit me ... on ... on the back of ... my head ... knocked me down." Sounded like her pain was so intense, she had trouble breathing. As soon as she could breathe, she let out yet another scream as she tightened her grip even more on Sarah's hand.

Sarah was losing it. Paralyzed by the suffering of her friend, and guilt, she could not move. She just trembled and ground her teeth.

Dr. Tuqan was on his knees holding onto Nabila's other hand. "Is it your head, Nabila?" he asked, his voice full of pain. "The ambulance should be here soon. Please, try to stay calm."

The loudest yell yet echoed throughout the compound before Dr. Tuqan completed his sentence. It lasted a few seconds only. Heavy breathing coupled with a deep sigh as though finally relieved of a heavy burden followed the final scream. An eerie quiet soon replaced all noise as her friends watched her every move anxiously.

"It's ... too ... late," Nabila murmured. "My ... my ... water broke. I ... I ..."

She had to stop talking.

One more scream, the mother of all screams and it was all over.

Within seconds, the quiet was barely disturbed by the faint cry of an infant.

Chapter 20

A BABY BOY.

Born forty days before due time, nevertheless, a boy – a little over five pounds, head covered with a bushel of black hair, strong cry from miniature healthy lungs.

A boy – first born – an occasion for celebration in the Middle East, a God-send to mothers and fathers alike. Time to rejoice, time to celebrate, time to change the father's name to the child's name by adding the word abu, meaning father, in front of the child's name. This centuries old practice is meant to let the world know the father is a man, a real man, and the mother has done her job by giving her husband the best gift a man can receive – a son. Paradoxically, in the future, when the father and the mother grow old, it is the duty of the son to look after his parents. The pampered, the indulged, the overly protected and spoiled in effect becomes their social security – almost always. To this day it is up to the first born son to make sure his parents' needs are met when the parents are no longer capable of doing so for themselves. Often, one or both parents live with their son and his family until they die. The wife of the son has no say in the matter – only the obligation to care for her in-laws as long as they live. And almost always it is the first born son who is blessed with his parents adoration and later burdened with their care – a dubious blessing at best, but one that's rarely challenged.

It's the custom. Has been forever.

This is not to say that only the first born son is treasured. All males are. But looking after the welfare of the extended family is the responsibility of the first born son unless he is incapacitated or deceased. That being the case, the son next in line is expected to take over the responsibilities of the first born son.

There was no rejoicing in Jim's apartment where Nabila had insisted on being taken immediately after the baby's birth. Actually, she wanted to be someplace other than the compound – didn't really matter where as long as she and the baby were away from the prying eyes of Khadijeh and Hamideh and the rest of the tenants. Hopefully, no one had heard the baby cry immediately after he was born and before mother and son were whisked away. The units were built around a vast courtyard, each unit clearly visible to all the others. Nabila had managed to keep her pregnancy to herself until the very last moment. Now that it had come to an unexpected early end, she was adamant about not letting anyone except her closest friends learn about the birth of her son.

Physically Nabila had come through birthing with no problems despite delivering the child in the courtyard and despite the nasty blow to the back of her head. While pregnant, she had deliberately chosen not to take the gender test to determine the baby's sex, fearing her ability to cope with her pregnancy would be seriously compromised. She had not even gone to a doctor for prenatal care to assure her pregnancy remained secret. No mean achievement considering the circumstances she had to live under, and the fact that she had to cope alone. However, upon learning she had given birth to a boy, unpredictably, she had immediately gone into hysterics – overjoyed, panicked, laughing, sobbing uncontrollably all at once, while her friends watched helplessly not quite sure what ailed her or how to help her.

What could possibly instigate an intelligent, perfectly sensible woman to behave in such an unusually neurotic manner? Perhaps it's her husband's absence at such a joyous moment. Sarah whispered to Jim. Jim disagreed. "There is more here. We just don't know what."

It took Nabila a couple of hours after her baby's birth, and after she made each of her friends, including Fatme swear to secrecy that she was willing to discuss what she had agonized over the past eight months. And why her pain had intensified to unbearable levels with the birth of her son. Nabila told them she learned she was four months pregnant three days before her husband's death. Ordinarily, it should have been a great consolation for a widow to have a part of her husband come to life. And it was, especially for Nabila, since theirs was a love union. But there were factors beyond her control that would and could snatch her child from her – at will. "And therein lies my problem," Nabila added gloomily.

Her words were greeted with eerie silence.

Jim fidgeted in his seat, put his fist on his chin his eyes focused on Nabila, immersed in thought.

Nabila understood. Jim would not rest until he heard the very last detail. She wept as she told them about her husband's family. Her husband, Samir, had two brothers. Either brother could choose to take her child away from her. Although the practice was illegal in Jordan, its occurrence was quite common. The mother had little say, often could not afford a lawyer, and had to hope for the goodwill of her husband's relatives to be able to keep her son. A daughter was much less of a problem. Hardly anyone would fight to claim a female child. In Nabila's case the issue was compounded by the fact that her in-laws had been against their son choosing and marrying a woman on his own. It was not a marriage arranged by her husband's parents with her parents, as custom dictated. And worse still, the woman their son had chosen to marry without their consent had no family to speak of. She was an orphan.

Grounds for disowning a son.

Consequently, to impress their son and his wife-to-be with their displeasure, no member of Nabila's husband's family had attended their wedding or tried to contact them. From the moment they learned that their son was determined to marry the woman he loved and refused to buckle under family pressure – regardless of the consequences – they had nothing more to do with him.

After marrying Nabila, Samir had made numerous attempts to establish normal relations with his family. He had failed. He received only one message from his family through a third party advising him to divorce his wife if he wanted to be a member of their family again. Nothing less than a divorce and complete disassociation with the woman he had married was acceptable.

"They did not come to his funeral either," Nabila said, after a brief pause, as the tears coursed down her cheeks. "Everyone who knew Samir came – except his family."

The implications were enormous – and ruthlessly clear. Sarah held her breath and hoped it was the end of the story. She was not sure she could handle any more.

Cool and composed, Jim focused his attention on the woman whose existence lately had become synonymous with agony. "No one is going to take your son away from you," he said with finality. "No one. I'll do whatever it takes. You have to stop torturing yourself and learn to trust your friends."

Sarah was in a catatonic state, too shocked to speak. She held onto Nabila's hand while Nabila rested on the sofa, her head over an ice pack. Sarah had been too involved with her own problems to notice the suffering, the despair her friend must have endured – for months – alone. She should have known. It had to be a major issue. Nabila was much too strong a woman to succumb to minor problems. She had demonstrated that strength by the totally unexpected way she had coped with her husband's death. Contrary to custom, Nabila had not spent her time wailing, begging for sympathy, celebrating numerous dates of her husband's death – mandatory for all who abide by the cultural dictates of the society they live in – meaningless or not. She went to the cemetery by herself when it was least crowded, told her husband about the baby's progress, told him she loved him and returned home. Even her closest friends had no idea where she went when she took a couple of hours off occasionally. That was the extent of her overt mourning – unheard of in the Arab world.

And now Nabila feared the baby she had nurtured for eight months, the only precious possession she had or cared about in her otherwise constrained life, could be snatched from her anytime by her husband's brothers. The only interest Samir's brothers had in the child revolved around satisfying the rules of tradition and repaying in kind the woman who had the audacity to marry their brother without their approval – and for love. Her husband's family had no use for her. She had trampled on tradition and married a man she had no business marrying.

Not surprisingly, Nabila's husband's family held her responsible for their brother's death. They were convinced Samir had agreed to work for Sarah under pressure from his wife. They believed Nabila was so eager to have fancy living quarters that she was willing to sacrifice her religious beliefs and had forced her husband to do so as well. It was a closed issue for them. Their brother could not possibly afford a luxury apartment like the one he and his wife lived in, in an exclusive part of the city on a teacher's salary. Sadly, his wife's greed had cost him his life.

Nabila was therefore considered to be an unfit mother. Yet being fit or not had nothing to do with her in-laws claim to her son.

The centuries old tradition had come about because it was generally assumed, and with good reason, that a woman on her own would find it difficult to provide and care for a child – especially a male child. The fact that Nabila had a good job and could provide quite well for her son was immaterial. Her in-laws were not inclined to use logic, analyze the circumstances, or make exceptions. Ancient customs had to be respected and Nabila punished for imagined wrongs.

I should be blamed for the loss of their brother, Sarah protested in her mind. Not Nabila. She had nothing to do with it. I should be blamed for Samir's death not only by his family but also by Nabila. Had I not pressed on zealously to proceed with my project and urged everyone who worked with me to do the same, undoubtedly Samir would be alive today. Yet Nabila has never in words or actions indicated that she holds me responsible for her husband's death. On the contrary, her husband's death has brought about a new inspiration in her coupled with determination and courage to meet the challenges of our undertaking head on – a project she had planned to walk away from before her husband's death.

Nabila confessed in a toneless voice that she was worried about when this scenario would occur – not if. She felt numb – helpless – chances of keeping her son were zero – her will to fight dead. Jim's comforting words did not assuage her concern. She knew the culture better than Jim. She was of it. There was no doubt in her mind that her in-laws would not hesitate for a moment to come for her son as soon as they heard about the boy's birth. The birth of a female child, considered a curse by many, was highly likely to be ignored. A boy? Not a chance.

Sarah managed to get a grip on herself. "What makes you so sure, Nabila? I recall someone, I believe it was Samir, mention something about his family's plans to immigrate to Brazil? He talked about it because he wanted to see his family before they left Kuwait and was upset when they refused to see him. He said they had relatives in Sao Paulo – two uncles. I gathered it was a done deal. Wouldn't adding a baby to the list complicate matters for them?"

"Not at all. I doubt they'll give it a second thought. They consider it their duty. Stop and think, Sarah. What will people say? That's what we live for. What will people think about us? What will they say?"

"Nobody is going to take the baby from you," Jim interjected emphatically – again. "Not as long as I am alive." Rage invariably defined Jim's facial muscles. They were bulging. It was scary.

I bet if we put our minds together we can come up with a solution. We have to, Sarah thought. Otherwise, Jim's patience tested mercilessly lately, especially when it affects the woman he loves, is about to vanish. Jim smoldering like a volcano ready to erupt was cause for serious concern. He had not said a word about the blow to Nabila's head, the blow that had led to the infant's premature birth. Invariably, when pushed to the limit, Jim reacted swiftly, quietly, mercilessly. She had to find a way to get through to him. She had to somehow convince him not to correct what for Jim was an 'inexcusable injustice' – by brute force – Jim's venue of choice whenever provoked beyond human endurance.

Precedents gave her ample cause for concern.

The Sheikh, who had raped Fatme and had skipped town, had yet to return to his mosque. Rumor had it that he was last seen in a hospital in Damascus suffering from multiple broken ribs, a collapsed lung and a broken leg – identify of the assailants unknown. Sarah did not need to hear more.

Actually, the rumor was soon confirmed as fact. Sarah learned through Dr. Tuqan that the hospital in Damascus, Syria had contacted the University Hospital where Dr. Tuqan worked to arrange for the transfer of the Sheikh to a hospital in Jordan, namely, the University Hospital where the Sheikh's private physician practiced. It seems the Sheikh did not approve of the care he was receiving in the hospital in Damascus and wanted out ASAP – back to Jordan. He didn't have to worry about going to jail for any of the crimes he had committed. No one would dare touch him.

Since the Sheikh had yet to arrive in Jordan, Suheil Tuqan and Sarah agreed to keep the news to themselves until the actual transfer took place.

Sarah's reverie was cut short by Gwynne.

"Having spent many years of my life in different cultures," Gwynne said, as she brought tea and biscuits for everyone. She handed Nabila a cup, "I have found the hardest thing to fight is ingrained customs and traditions. They have energy all their own. They turn humans into robots. We do what is expected of us – the way it's always been done. It's easier. Less effort – no thinking required. Logic be damned."

"We humans," said Dr. Tuqan as he rose with weary help-lessness, "we pride ourselves on our intelligence. But when you think about it, we can also be quite dumb. I have to go." Suheil Tuqan planted a kiss on the forehead of the woman he loved and prepared to leave. A surgeon turned instant obste-trician, the front of his suit covered with blood and gook.

"Thank you for everything." Nabila raised her voice a pitch. "I don't know what we would do without your help – if we could not count on you we would all be at a loss with our medical problems."

Suheil Tuqan advised Nabila to keep the ice pack over the swelling on her head, on and off, for at least another hour. "We are fortunate the baby is in such good shape, and if the bathroom scale is accurate, I don't think he will need special care. I'll stop by tomorrow. In the meantime, if you need me call the switchboard of the hospital. They know where I am at any given time. Good night."

It was a few minutes past midnight.

Fatme had curled in the corner of the living room waging her own little battle, forcing her eyes to stay open, fighting to stay awake.

"If you think you can manage," Gwynne said to Sarah, "I'll take this child home. She looks exhausted."

"I'm fine," Fatme protested meekly.

"You might be. I'm not." Gwynne lifted her up. "School bus or the VW?"

"Take the bus," Jim said. "Sarah might need her car."

Like a mother cat looking after her kittens, Sarah ran to Jim's bedroom and checked the baby wrapped in Jim's flan-nel shirt, asleep in the bottom of the chest of drawers. Every ten minutes or so she repeated her anxious trip to the bedroom and back until Nabila burst out laughing. "Don't worry about the baby. He'll be fine. I took care of my sisters and brothers, all six of them before they were ..." Her laughter turned instantly into tears.

Sarah rushed over and rubbed her friend's shoulder ever so gently. "I'm so sorry. I did not mean to upset you. You've had more than your share of tragedy and at such a young age. But look at it this way, Nabila. However brief your time with your family and your husband was, at least you had them, you enjoyed them, and the memories of your times together will be with you to enrich your life – forever. In the end, that's all anybody has got left. Don't you agree?"

Nabila pulled herself up and embraced the woman who had replaced the family she had lost. "I'm so worried about losing my baby that I fear I have lost my self control and am about to loose my mind. I know Samir would never tolerate weakness. Yet I feel helpless, defeated by fear of the unknown, not the unknown who, but the unknown when. Sarah, if ... if ... I lose my baby, I cannot be held responsible for my actions. I swear I can't." And that brought a fresh flood of tears. Nabila sobbed out of control.

"You're not listening to me. No one is going to take your baby from you," was Jim's icy reply – yet again. "You have my word." Jim moved from the armchair to the sofa, sat on the edge, and took Nabila's hands in his. "Trust me. No one."

Between sobs, Nabila managed to say. "You don't know my in-laws. The only way to avoid trouble is not to let them know the baby is mine."

Her words uttered in pain sparked an immediate response from Jim. "Not yours? How is that possible? You have to breast feed the baby and take care of his needs, don't you? Whose baby will you tell the world you're caring for?"

"I don't know. It's so terribly difficult to figure out what to do. When I was pregnant, I thought perhaps we could pretend either Sarah or Gwynne adopted the baby from an orphanage. It was a stupid idea, I know. But it was the only possibility I could think of, the irrational solution I concocted for myself to cling to what was left of my sanity."

"I would agree in a snap," Sarah said. "But it won't work."

"You are right. It won't. I realized it the minute I set eyes on my baby. He is Samir come to life – come to life to renew mine – a gift from heaven. A cruel gift." Nabila buried her face in her hands and sobbed.

Sarah's thoughts were in turmoil. To deflect the pressures closing in on her in her solitary agony, Nabila must had led herself to believe that she had no other option. There was no lack of detail or ambiguity in Nabila's expectations. Only stupefying fear. And, it was contagious. "You did not answer Jim," Sarah had a hard time keeping her troubled voice in check. "Do you want to breast feed?"

"Of course."

Sarah chuckled nervously. "There you are."

"We are not without resources." Jim said with barely con-cealed exasperation. "We'll do everything humanly possible to protect you and the baby. You have to stop torturing your-self – thinking about your in-laws taking him from you as a fait accompli. But we'll need your help to put an end to your worries."

Jim's words sent a chill down Sarah's spine. So far Jim had managed to get away with dispensing justice a la Jim on unsuspecting culprits. However, Sarah feared despite all the caution he used, if he were caught .... She could not continue. It was much too gruesome a thought to dwell upon. And even more so was the violence he resorted to, when convinced no other tool would provide the desired end result. Sarah abhorred violence and had yet to convince Jim to change his ways – if for no other reason than the fact that it disturbed her immensely. It did not matter who or what was at stake, Sarah sought ways other than violence to deal with the problem and did not give up reminding Jim to do the same.

His answer was the same – always. It is the only language those who perpetrate injustice understand – here, in the States, everywhere. And I resort to it only after all else fails. So stop worrying about it.

"Jim, please." Nabila's pain was evident in her voice.

"You don't understand. Samir's older brother is an experienced player in this game. He lived in the States for seven years, married an American, had a son, divorced his wife, kidnapped their son and returned to Jordan, then moved to Kuwait. I met his wife in Kuwait. She came to ask Samir for help. She has lost her home, her job, spent all her money on lawyers and crossing continents to get her son back. She can't even get to see the child. When she gets hot on her husband's trail, he disappears with the boy. That's when we heard about his plans to immigrate to Brazil. Earlier it was Australia. No one knows if it's true. Brazil does not have extradition treaty with the United States. Or so I'm told. Maybe they will immigrate. Maybe they won't. Oh, Sarah there are days I hate being a woman."

"We all do, dear. It does not matter what society or culture we live in. There are always more restrictions for women to deal with than for men. Unfortunately, in the Arab world it is totally out of control – beyond all human endurance."

"Jim, I know you want to reassure me, and I have no doubt in my mind that you will do everything in your power to protect me and my baby. But I fear we don't stand a chance. Only recently I read in the paper about another woman, a German. The father kidnapped both their sons. After several failed trips to Jordan, the mother managed to convince the German ambassador to get her an audience with the Queen. The Queen herself has to keep a very delicate balance. She's American, was Christian but converted to Islam to marry the King. She is too Westernized and not from a Jordanian family. Many prominent Jordanian families had their hopes dashed when the King married yet another foreigner instead of one of their daughters. Everything the Queen does is minutely scrutinized. She tried but could not help the mother. Every so often, the media reports about similar cases. I wonder, don't women read or hear about these reports? I mean, most Arab women don't have a choice. They have to marry whomever their parents arrange for them. But non-Arabs?

Americans? Why would an American woman marry a man who might take the child she gives birth to from her? Why take such a horrific chance?"

"They think it won't happen to them," Sarah replied. "Yet it happens quite often. And there is astonishingly little outrage from the public when they hear about it."

"I cannot imagine a more terrifying situation to deal with," Nabila concluded gloomily. "I prefer death to the loss of a child."

"Snap out of it, ladies," Jim said as he headed for the bathroom. "That's why we're here, remember? Complacency, defeatism, are the coward's way out – not ours."

"Jim ..."

"Listen my dear. If they fight dirty, we'll fight dirty. If they listen to reason, there won't be a problem. Let me handle it."

It was precisely what Sarah had feared. From what she had heard thus far, it did not sound like Nabila's in-laws were disposed to listen to a reasonable proposition even if that proposition was sweetened with money since their hatred of their daughter-in-law would probably outweigh any monetary compensation. Sarah refrained from mentioning her concern to Nabila. It would only heighten her anxiety.

Nabila looked drained physically, emotionally and mentally. Sarah coaxed her to go to bed. "I think I'll spend the night here so you won't have to worry about being alone with Jim in his apartment."

"Worry? Why should I worry? Have you ever known a more terrific guy than Jim? I mean the man is a hundred percent devoted to your welfare, to my welfare, to anybody that matters to him."

"That's not what I meant, Nabila. It's better not to provide fodder for the gossip mills – a woman alone with a man in his apartment. We can't flaunt all the rules this society has so generously portioned to us. We can only hope to bring about change gradually, in small doses, wherever and whenever we spot an opportunity. Now off you go to bed, Mama. You must get some rest. I'll keep an eye on the baby, and tomorrow we will work out a plan. Your in-laws might be clever, but I bet we can outsmart them if we use our brains instead of our emotions." The last sentence was more to convince herself than her friend who had a lot more to lose.

Nabila seemed to welcome the suggestion. She grabbed the side of the sofa and tried to stand up, wobbled and collapsed back on the sofa as Jim stepped out of the bathroom.

It took Jim a few quick, long steps to reach her. He cradled her in his arms, marched to his bedroom, placed her gingerly in his bed, pulled the covers up, and planted a small kiss on her forehead. "Sleep well my love," he whispered in her ear. "Have no fear. You are not alone."

A similar scene, in Saudi Arabia, would have qualified the woman for death by stoning. Actually, even the occurrence of such an event is immaterial. If four witnesses testify claiming the event actually took place, the woman's life would not be worth a damn. Sarah recalled vividly an incidence while living in Saudi Arabia. Her mother had shut herself in her room for days with no food or water. She was a child then and could not understand what had happened to debilitate her mother to such an extent – to cause her such anguish. Out of sheer spite, for refusing the advances of a business associate of her husband's, the business associate and his friends had ganged up against the woman and accused her of adultery. After that – it was all over for her mother's friend.

And yet stoning is never specified as punishment for adultery in the Koran. The Koran says that adulterous wives should be confined 'to their houses until death overtakes them.' It was later, under the rule of the second Caliph, Omar, that repression of women was incorporated into the religion and stoning legislated as a means of an adulterer's execution.

Sarah smiled inwardly and thanked her good fortune for being in Jordan, and for Jim. Jordan was the most progressive Muslim country, thanks to the rule of a wise monarch and an enlightened queen. The only trouble she had with Jim was the method he used to deal with his adversaries – albeit only when he absolutely had to. Other than that it would have been quite difficult for her to achieve a fraction of what she had achieved thus far without his help. And since he had fallen in love, it was as though the world could finally get to see the real Jim. A huge man, yet gentle to a fault, a man who walked like he would topple over with one misstep, yet light as a boy of five when need be. She had come to rely on him as a friend, an advisor, a solid block to lean on – a man who had all but replaced her father. He had done it quietly, with no conditions and no demands. The chance of having a loyal friend, when needed, under exceptionally demanding circumstances, was as rare as an encounter with a UFO. Sarah never took her blessings for granted.

"O.K. Let's hear it," Jim said as he stepped out of the bedroom. "What's on your mind?"

Sarah checked the bedroom door. It was closed. "Jim, what are we going to do?"

"I love the woman. I'd marry her tomorrow, if only she would agree."

"She's crazy about you too, Jim. But you know she can't. The only way for her to marry you is to move away from Muslim countries. That's not what she wants to do. She wants to be here – work for change – help improve the abominable conditions under which women are forced to survive. That's her life's ambition. That's what keeps her going. She made that very plain to me in the coffee shop, at the hospital, and several times since. That's why I couldn't figure out what was bothering her when she was so despondent and for so long."

They had few options. None satisfactory. It was becoming more difficult, almost daily, to justify her conviction that change was inevitable. Change was taking place, but not what Sarah and her friends had in mind and had hoped for. The change in progress was not a quantum leap backwards as in Iran, but a subtle change permeating every level of society:

less women given opportunities at jobs, fewer promotions, harassment, sexual and otherwise and no recourse. Sarah and Nabila had coined a new word for it. They called it the cement ceiling. Push hard enough and you might succeed in breaking glass. Cement however had no give. It kept women where they were or with the help of its weight forced them out. There was considerably more sexual harassment in the work place. Women who worked outside the home were considered to be less moral than women who stayed home. Complaining to management or the person in charge was a waste of time. No one would listen. And if they bothered to listen, they would not waste their time correcting the situation – or the complaint would be used against the woman who did the complaining. She would be fired. Suing was not an option either. It would mean money wasted on lawyers. Women knew the outcome was a foregone conclusion with practically all-male lawyers and judges in charge, and very few laws to protect them.

More disturbing signs manifested themselves most every-where: more covered women in the streets and at younger ages, a democratic government after centuries of autocratic rule, slowly permeated by Islamic hard-liners demanding reversal of the few hard fought gains women had eked over decades of struggle under an enlightened monarchy. The hard-liners tried to introduce perceived religious restrictions and demanded for those restrictions to become law. Yet even when Islamic extremism failed to win support in the Jordanian Parliament, it continued to press its views on the public gradually forcing the society to succumb to its demands. Public entertainment was targeted first – that's where the young of both sexes congregated. Hotels were pressured to post regulations against mixed sex swimming in their swimming pools, soon bikinis were frowned upon, no public display of affection was tolerated and gradually mixed swimming, discouraged at first, was changed to segregated swimming. Different days were assigned for males and females. Before Khomeini came to power and Islamic Fundamentalists took control in Iran and gradually penetrated the neighboring countries, mostly the old and the less educated were persuaded to comply with the so called 'dictates of Islam' since few dictates were the direct result of the teachings of the Prophet. However, lately, it was becoming extremely painful to watch the number of educated, so called Westernized men and women come under the spell of fanatics.

Yet compared to other Muslim countries the influence of the hard-liners in Jordan was skillfully controlled by their enlightened monarch. In Algeria, fundamentalists have been killing civilians, men, women and children for over a decade in the name of religion. In Afghanistan a group of religious students called Taliban, backed by arms from Pakistan, in control of eighty percent of the country, have sworn to replace the existing government with a pure Islamic state – the Taliban version of pure, in its most extreme, where all women are forced to stay in their homes, all girls' schools are closed, and any woman caught showing an inch of skin in pubic, if she dares appear in public, bound to receive punishment according to Islamic laws of Taliban choosing. All TV and radio are banned. In Egypt, radicals have tried to topple the secular government with indiscriminate bombings to scare the tourists away – a major source of income for an impoverished, overpopulated country. Many women entertainers have been forced to quit unable to cope with the harassment and death threats to themselves and their families. In the Sudan, ruled by extreme fanatics, women probably fared better during the Middle Ages than they do at present.

Not surprisingly though, extremist hard-liners have made least headway in countries ruled by absolute secular dictators like Syria and Iraq. That's not to say that hard-liners have given up on those countries. For them, it is only a matter of time for the present dictators to be replaced by one of their own. Even in secular Turkey, under the watchful eyes of the military, the rumblings intensify with each passing day.

Turkey is feared to be the next in line to fall to the demands of fanatics.

Basically it was the culmination of decades of frustration that led to rebellion against Western influence. It was felt that the West, instrumental in the establishment and survival of Israel was responsible for the misfortunes of Arabs – for many Arabs, the West is held responsible for all their misfortunes. Their secular leaders had failed them, nationalism had led them to defeat in war, the West had conquered and colonized them, perhaps it was time to revert back to their roots, give religion a chance; a religion which had given them centuries of glory.

Yet another negative Western influence often cited was decadent Western morals. A couple of weeks earlier, Sarah was invited to a dinner party in Abdoun, an affluent suburb of Amman, where palatial homes grace the landscape, by a Jordanian family who knew her father and had heard about her work. The discussion at the dinner table focused mainly on Hollywood and the way the Western media glamorized loose morals and its affects on young minds eager to embrace indiscriminately. They claimed it led to the break up of families, to single parent homes, to drug abuse, teenage pregnancies and more. In the opinion of many in the Middle East, these ills of society were preventable by observing strict moral codes – namely Islamic moral codes. The degree to which people recast the teachings of the Prophet to conform to their views, never ceased to amaze Sarah.

"What's the difference," Sarah asked. "There's plenty of divorce in Muslim countries in addition to polygamy. At least in the West a woman has some rights. In the Arab world, a woman loses her children, gets no support from her husband, and since she is last on her parent's priority list to get an education, if ever, and the first to lose it during hard economic times, she is least prepared to face the world on her own. Most women are forced to stay home to care for their families. When a husband decides to divorce his wife, with little or no education and few skills to support herself, her only chance is to return to her parents home. Is that really conducive to promoting family unity?"

Her host was quick to admonish her. "You have a myopic view of the cohesiveness of families in Arab countries. I suspect it comes from many years of exposure to Western culture. Families here are much more closely knit than the West. I do business with Europe and the United States and I travel back and forth often. In the West, everyone lives for himself."

"Right. And here the world rotates around men, while women are delegated to subservient status – to toil for the pleasure of men. I assure you, you wouldn't like it one bit if the roles were reversed." Studying the faces of the group staring at her, the so called elite of the country. Sarah had to admit her dream, what she had hoped would be her life's work, was probably nothing more than a delusion, a mirage.

After listening to Sarah and her host argue, a woman physician in her early forties had tapped her wine goblet with a spoon and demanded to be heard. Earlier that evening, she had told Sarah she had recently resigned from her post at the University Hospital in Amman because of constant harassment by her male colleagues. In addition she claimed she was not promoted from her position in four years despite a contract which stipulated yearly promotion. By the end of dinner, quite drunk, she wanted everybody to join her in a toast. She wanted to drink a toast to all women who due to the devastating combination of circumstances and the lack of a piece of flesh dangling between their legs, were condemned to a life of misery.

That said, she had drained her glass.

Her words came as a thunderbolt. The crowd of forty was speechless.

She was drunk. But for Sarah it was a moment to savor. Perhaps there was hope after all.

A gentle tap on her shoulder startled her. "What? What's the matter? Where's the baby?"

Jim stood towering over her. "Why don't you lie down on the sofa."

"I'm O.K."

"You fell asleep in the armchair. You'll be sore tomorrow." He slipped his hands under her armpits, lifted her, and eased her onto the sofa. "I'll get a blanket."

Sarah was about to lie down when she heard a faint cry, jumped, and rushed to the bedroom to check on the baby before he woke his mother up. He needed a change of diaper, actually, a hand towel. That's all they could find in Jim's apartment. Nabila had bought nothing for the baby figuring there was still time and not wanting to arouse suspicion.

Sarah took the infant to the living room.

"It's very becoming to you," Jim said with a huge smile.

"Ouch! I just stuck the safety pin in my finger."

"Allow me."

Neither Jim nor Sarah had ever changed a diaper before.

Jim pulled and folded the towel different ways but could not shape it to fit the tiny form patiently lying on the sofa, oblivious to the effort it took for two grown ups to relieve his discomfort.

"It's my turn." Sarah reached for the safety pin then gently nudged Jim away with her hip. After a few tries she gave up the struggle with the safety pin, placed one towel under the baby's buttocks, another over his genitals and she was done. "Can't do much more with hand towels. Watching women in the camp take care of their babies never ceases to amaze me. They have rags to work with and yet they manage. And here I am. Can't substitute a hand towel for a diaper."

"You did great," Jim teased. "You can easily become a pro. Makes me think you should stop turning down Suheil's proposals, otherwise, Arab beauties waiting in the wings will pounce on him. He won't wait forever for you to make up your mind."

"Marriage is at the very bottom of my priority list, Jim. Suheil understands that."

"Sure he does. But he's also a human being."

"And so am I."

"Precisely. This is not a country where he can move in with you, or spend any length of time alone with you. He has no friends he can have a decent intellectual conversation with. And his thinking is totally opposite the doctors he works with. That leaves him with few choices."

"Jim, explain please. How do I marry an Arab, admittedly an enlightened Arab, after the horror stories I hear about and witness almost daily? How do I know that after we're married Suheil won't change and become like the rest of them? Foreign wives I have talked to – without exception – agree on one point. Their husbands were terrific guys before they were married and changed dramatically soon after. So I'm half-Arab and quite familiar with the customs and traditions that shape this very complex society. Does that give me whatever it takes to fight injustice, humiliation and feeling less than human? Suppose we marry then decide to split. If my child is taken from me, do you really believe I can cope with a blow of that magnitude?"

"That won't happen with Suheil."

"Perhaps not. Still, no one knows what the future brings. Witness our friend in your bed. Do you think when Nabila found out she was pregnant, do you think she ever imagined some lunatic would blow her husband to bits and she would lose her mind trying to figure out a way to hide her baby? A perfectly sensible, intelligent woman at the end of her wits and the only solution she can come up with is to disown her baby so she can keep him. Does that make sense to you, Jim? It's not so much the man a woman marries as it is the family, the culture, the society and the country. There's no quick fix. We all know that."

The few pounds of flesh on the sofa moved its arms and let out a loud cry as if to say "I'm here. Don't forget me."

"Do you think something is wrong with him?"

"He's probably cold," Jim said. "I'll raise the heat."

Sarah got her jacket hanging at the entrance and wrapped it around the baby.

The infant stopped crying. A surge of emotions, warm giddying swept through her being. Face it, she told herself. Nabila is right. Losing a child has got to be one of the hardest things to deal with.

She knew she couldn't do it.

"Suheil loves you."

"I know he does, Jim. And I love him. But the price is too high. Especially if we plan to live here."

"He hates it here."

"Then he should leave."

"Yeah, right. Only he can't and won't because the woman he adores happens to be here with crazy notions in her head about changing the world, notions that are not too different from his, I might add."

She regarded his curiously. "What are you talking about?"

"Haven't you noticed how he wears the same few outfits over and over again? Didn't you see the look on his face when his best suit got messed up delivering the baby?"

"Yeah ..."

"I'm told he's a real good surgeon and is paid exceptionally well. They don't want to lose him."

"You've managed to confuse me – again."

"Well, how's this for clarification. His pay, minus a few Dinars, goes directly to family planning – has been since he returned from the States and started to work in Saudi Arabia first, and now in Jordan. He spends money only on the barest necessities. In his opinion overpopulation is the greatest threat the world faces. He has decided to do his share to help, to make a difference no mater how minute."

With eyes that probe and evaluate, Sarah studied Jim while he poured himself a drink. She and Suheil had often discussed overpopulation. She agreed with him. It was a serious problem – especially in developing countries – a problem Sarah felt could be best corrected by educating women so they could have control over their bodies. And the doctor had agreed with her. But he had never said anything to her about sending his pay to family planning. Why would he tell Jim?

"He didn't tell me," Jim said as though reading her thoughts. "I found out by accident. When Nabila was leaving the hospital and I went to pay her bill. The clerk asked me to wait. He said he had orders to contact Dr. Tuqan before any of his patients were discharged. I asked why. He said Dr. Tuqan does not charge those who can't afford to pay. I told him it was not necessary for him to do so for Nabila – that we would pay the bill. He said he had to. Those were Dr. Tuqan's orders. Otherwise he would get upset. Does it happen often I asked the clerk and he assured me it did. That doesn't leave him much to take home, I commented. He said it didn't matter. Dr. Tuqan did not take more than a few Dinars a month anyway. He said they mail the balance directly to the central family planning clinic."

Sarah leaned wearily against the back of the sofa. "It's ironic, perhaps tragic. I'm not quite sure which."

"You're playing my game. What's ironic?"

"The few invitations I have accepted since I came to Jordan almost always ended unpleasantly. My business seems to be everybody's business here. We're not engaged or anything. Yet it never fails. Someone, either the host, or a guest makes it his or her business to pull me aside and warn me about marrying Dr. Tuqan. 'Beware, he is after your money,' is what it boils down to. I know every form, shape or convolution that sentence can be camouflaged in – especially subtle are the ones coming from men and women who are looking for wives for their sons."

"It is ironic," Jim replied. "They would die if they knew what you have done with the money with Suheil's and my blessing."

Chapter 21

LATE AT NIGHT, THE NEXT day, Nabila returned to her condo with her baby – discreetly. Jim had guards posted around the clock to watch over mother and child. Upon Sarah's insistence Jim had let go of the guards he had hired earlier for Sarah's safety. But he refused to listen to Sarah or Nabila when the peace of mind of the woman he loved and the well being of an innocent infant were at stake.

Then, he took off.

He was gone for three days. Didn't say where. Returned with an impish grin on his face, like a conquering hero, dismissed the guards and proceeded with business as usual. Baffled, the women questioned him to no avail. "I assure you," he said to Nabila, "no one will touch you or your baby."

Slowly, albeit cautiously, Nabila came to trust Jim totally. In reality, she had learned to trust him soon after their friendship blossomed. But when customs and traditions practiced for centuries were involved, it was her contention that no one could help.

She was wrong.

When a month passed and still there was no sign of anyone coming for Nabila's baby, Samir Junior, Sarah suspected Jim was somehow involved. A letter from Mona, Nabila's cousin who had returned to Kuwait, informed them that no one from Samir's family would be coming for the baby. Apparently, all kinds of rumors circulated in the community. The rumor most repeated was that Samir's family chose to believe the baby was not their brother's. Their brother was dead. They knew the woman their brother had married could not be trusted – at least that's the version they fed friends and relatives.

The implication was clear. Nabila being an orphan, and without close male relatives to 'protect' her, must have conceived from a man other than their brother.

Nabila showed Jim Mona's letter in hopes of triggering a reaction from him. She did get a reaction. But it was quite different from what she had hoped for.

Jim shrugged his shoulders. "Let them think what they want. It's easy to prove whose child the baby is. I understand Samir's older brother was educated in the States. Unless he is a total idiot he would know it's a matter of a simple blood test to prove or disprove paternity."

"I wonder ..." Nabila did not finish her sentence. She wanted to ask Jim if he had anything to do with the turn of events but she did not have a chance.

Jim interrupted. "Give me the list of the school supplies you said you needed." Jim's manner was clear. The subject was closed.

Nabila's fears were not totally allayed. Maybe her in-laws had not come for Samir Junior due to a reason she was not aware of, or thought of. Maybe they kept her waiting to catch her off guard. She wanted to believe Jim. But, except for Jim's assurances, what guarantee did she have? If they don't show up, Nabila thought, something drastic must have happened to change their minds. Nabila's in-laws were not inclined to break tradition, nor were they known for their generosity towards the wives of their sons, especially when the fate of a male child was at stake. After many attempts at brain storming, neither Nabila, nor Sarah, nor Gwynne could come up with a plausible explanation as to how the change had come about.

"They have to go through me to get to that child. They do indeed." Gwynne had taken over the care of the infant from the moment he was born. Nabila had her time with the baby, nursing and playing with him. After that Gwynne took over like it was a natural progression of events.

For Nabila, Gwynne was God-sent – a free, trustworthy nanny. It freed her to attend to her students and to her own needs without guilt or worry.

Yet fear – fear of losing her baby, fear of when it would happen, had her in knots. She seemed condemned to live and work under a dark cloud of perpetual anxiety.

It was too much for Sarah to bear.

After giving it a lot of thought, as a last resort, Sarah decided to call the ruler of Kuwait, a close friend of her father's. She had his private number given to her by her father, upon the insistence of the ruler who had asked that she call him personally, if she ever needed assistance anywhere, anytime if she thought he could be of help. There was little that went on in Kuwait the ruler did not know about. In the intricate business of navigating through mind-numbing rules and regulations, the ruler's input had been invaluable to Sarah's parents while her mother opened bridal boutiques in a country where business was strictly the domain of men. In return for the ruler's help, Maher Sultan had built for him the most magnificent palace in all the Gulf States.

The ruler's gratitude had no bounds.

Sarah wanted to know if Samir's brothers had asked or received an exit visa – or perhaps another member of the family was trusted with the job of bringing the infant to Kuwait. After the Gulf war, most Palestinians who left the country, even for brief visits, were denied reentry visas. The Kuwaiti government believed they had been less than loyal during the war. Could it be the concern of Samir's brothers as well? Could that be the reason why no one had come to claim the infant?

Sarah dialed the ruler's number.

The ruler himself answered delighted to hear from Sarah. After expressing his condolences for Sarah's father's death, he said in a matter of fact way, "That family is forbidden to leave the country." He proceeded to explain that about a month ago he received a request from a man who worked for

Sarah's father, a man called Jim Bateson, a man he knew well, to forbid the exit of the whole family. "They are under investigation," the ruler added, and when Sarah asked why, he said it did not matter why. Their passports were being held by the Ministry of Interior and would not be returned until Mr. Bateson informed the Ministry of Interior, or the ruler, it would be all right to do so.

Sarah had the ruler on the speakerphone.

"What if they have paid a third party to do the job for them?" Nabila whispered in Sarah's ear. "Please ask him."

"Mr. Bateson brought that problem to our attention," the ruler said. "You have my word. That infant will not be permitted to enter Kuwait. The family has strict orders to refrain from any contact with the infant and that includes contact through none family members. If they disobey my orders, both brothers will take a long vacation in jail – to give them time to think about their action."

"What happens when the family eventually leaves Kuwait?" Sarah repeated Nabila's question.

"In return for their cooperation," the ruler said without hesitation, "we have given the brothers good, long term jobs. They'll be here for years to come. Fear not. Even if they were to leave Kuwait, we have ways of dealing with those who do not cooperate with us."

"I am the mother of the boy." Nabila spoke into the speakerphone, tears of joy welling in her eyes. "Please accept my thanks and sincere gratitude. Words fail me. Suffice it to say that you have given me the biggest gift of all – my son, and you have given my life back to me. I will forever be indebted to you."

"Think nothing of it. It is the least I can do for Maher Sultan."

Sarah thanked the ruler profusely, put the receiver down, punched the air with her fist and yelled, "All right. Jim did it – again."

And that did it for Nabila. She turned into a volcano in

action. She said, "Let's get this show on the road." A statement she had learned from Sarah. She urged Sarah to put an ad in the daily Arabic and English paper to recruit teachers, to expand to every village, every town, and every possible location, not only in Jordan but also in villages in Egypt where the need was far greater than Jordan.

Sarah obliged – reluctantly – believing few individuals, if any, would be willing to subject themselves to the relentless harassment the applicants for the jobs were sure to experience.

To Sarah's surprise, the response was phenomenal. Dozens, mostly women, applied for each position. Women in their early forties, educated before Khomeini and his revolution gained a foothold in Arab thought, women with grandiose dreams of freedom from 'protection' by their male relatives, women who wanted to have the right to make decisions for themselves – the chance to be human beings in their own rights – excited, eager and impatient to be part of a project they had often dreamt about, talked about, but could not act upon due to lack of funds. During their interviews, Sarah was astonished by the degree of rebellion, outrage, anger, and extreme hostility suppressed for over a decade surface with pent-up energy unparalleled when a subject other than women's rights was discussed. The applicants were intensely resentful of the fact that since Islamic Fundamentalists came to power in Iran, women were expected to take a giant leap back to the Middle Ages – at times forced, at times insidiously. It seemed ironic for the enforcement of such a shift to succeed, especially at a time when easier, faster and better communications had kindled distinctly different hopes in most women: hopes of liberation from the yoke they and many generations before them had had to endure, fear of the future for their daughters – fear of further deterioration of women's rights making it more impossible for future generations to reverse the trend.

"You shouldn't be surprised," Nabila remarked. "Women

don't walk around like big, black tents with slits to see through because they want to. They don't automatically turn into housekeepers, cooks and bottle washers when their families arrange marriages for them. Neither do they willingly submit to be one of several of their husband's sex objects. Being at the mercy of men is not a prospect any woman in her right mind cherishes. They do it because they have no choice."

It was heartwarming to get to know the real feelings of women – especially young women. There was hope – definitely. Sarah was not alone. With the help of like-minded women, over two dozen willing to be assigned anywhere, they could make progress faster than previously imagined. And they did. The women who accepted positions in Egypt, had the support of their husbands, idealists willing to relocate to stem the tide of fanaticism which they felt was destroying their religion. There were only a few idealists, but enough to make a difference. By the summer of 1995, they had six schools in Egypt, four in Jordan, and several more possibilities under study. The only stipulation was that the classes in each school be at least fifty percent female, and each student had to promise to help educate others for one year after graduation. With pay – of course.

They were not fancy schools – a room or two conveniently located within walking distance, mostly in villages where the only education available was for males. Boys were taught to read and write and learn the Koran usually in the village mosque. Almost all villages, except the very small ones had at least one mosque.

The parents were compensated for the loss of income from their children's labor thus eliminating the most commonly used excuse not to permit children, especially girls, to attend school. Encouraged by Sarah's progress, Dr. Tuqan sold a piece of property he had inherited and used the money to build small family planning clinics in the same villages where Sarah opened schools.

To the surprise of everyone except the women them-selves, Egyptian women flocked to the clinics eager to take advantage of advice and birth control pills. Since no other options were available to them, they were relieved to finally be given a chance at taking control of their own bodies, at least to a degree. Sarah took many quick trips to Egypt, accompanied by Dr. Tuqan whenever his schedule permitted, and was amazed at the hunger among women to better their lives. All the research Sarah and Jim had done indicated they would meet fierce resistance by the public for any type of change they planned to introduce. There was resistance. But not from women – definitely not from women of child bearing age. It came from the older generation and from extremist Islamic groups bent on destabilizing the secular government, the same group that assassinated Anwar Sadat, the previous Egyptian President.

Fortunately for Sarah and many Jordanians, King Hussein of Jordan was a survivor, the Queen, a liberated, intelligent woman who worked quietly and effectively to better the lot of all Jordanians. Faced with unrelenting, fierce opposition by religious fanatics as well as traditionalists, without the royal family's enlightened leadership, Sarah was convinced, progress would have been far more difficult to achieve, if not impossible.

Egypt was different. Hosni Mubarak's government had to deal with religious fanatics determined to transform the gov-ernment into an Islamic state by acts of terrorism. Radicals attacked family planning clinics claiming it was a conspiracy by the West to limit the number of Muslims in the world. Those in charge, like Dr. Tuqan were branded as traitors and stooges of imperialist Western powers, or better yet in the employ of the CIA. Schooling, as advocated by the West was proclaimed unnecessary. For males, the fanatics insisted, knowledge of the Koran was sufficient. For females, early marriage, giving birth to boys, taking care of their husbands and children, was what the Koran called for. Never mind the fact that the Prophet himself did more for the improvement of the lives of women in the seventh century than anyone had done before, and had fought throughout his life against abuse and exploitation of women. The Prophet called for justice for all – even slaves. Not only men.

Those aspects of the Prophet's teachings somehow never found their way into the thinking of men whose purpose it did not suit. They twisted what the Prophet had said and done to retain control over the lives of women, as they had done for centuries and planned to keep on doing. Since the death of the Prophet, the Prophet's words have been interpreted by men, for men, except for Fatima Mernissi, a woman sociologist in Morocco who is barely known in the Arab world. She interprets the Koran clearly, accurately, based on extensive research and an inexhaustible supply of examples of the pronouncements of the Prophet.

The loud, persistent ranting often aimed at family planning clinics and at girls attending school, could sometimes be contained with a donation to a cause often never heard of before. Other times it got ugly. On May 19, 1995, Sarah received a phone call from the woman in charge of one of the schools in a village south of Asyut, south of Cairo. Unknown assailants had attacked two girls walking to school that morning. They had thrown sulfuric acid, known as 'fire water' on the girls' faces. One girl had managed to turn her face away just in time. She had a few burn spots on her neck, otherwise she was not hurt. The other, a thirteen year old, was badly burned in the face and neck.

The incident happened in Attiyeh's village, the first village in Egypt chosen by Sarah in appreciation of Attiyeh's unwavering loyalty and hard work. Attiyeh realized it was an honor, but was not sure he wanted the honor. It was all very confusing. Miss Sarah was a woman he had great respect for. She could do no wrong – except ... Well, Attiyeh could not understand why such a fantastically intelligent person did not see the futility of educating girls and the horrible effect such an undertaking would have on a society not used to dealing with women on an equal basis. Why the obsession with girls? After only six months of schooling, his daughters had already begun asking questions – questions the answers to which he could not begin to fathom. It certainly was a different world from the village he came from and now that village would no longer be the same. These were great times for Attiyeh. He had never had it so good. He worked, his wife worked, and he got compensation for both girls. His wife was pregnant, thank Allah with a boy. Miss Sarah had promised the very best care for the baby so this infant boy, unlike the others, would survive – would live – would make Attiyeh a happy man. Yes, life was good. Very good indeed. But girls in school? Tough pill to swallow.

Dr. Tuqan insisted on flying to Egypt with Sarah.

They rented a car and drove to the village.

It was a quiet place, about thirty mud huts, dirt streets, an open produce market, swarms of flies and a mosque.

The woman who ran the school met them. Afaf seemed nervous, agitated. There had been more trouble since her phone call to Sarah. She explained that while she rushed with the girl who had been attacked to the nearest town on a neighbor's motorcycle to get medical help, the father had come home and beaten the wife to a point where she now sounded incoherent. "He hit her on the head with a chair." The rise in the pitch of Afaf's voice betrayed her outrage.

"How's the girl doing?" Sarah was afraid to ask but did so nonetheless.

"Can't tell. They washed the acid off. She said she can't see out of her right eye and the right side of her face is badly burned. Third degree, I was told. Needs special care. Definitely not available around here."

"Why her?"

"She's thirteen. She had her head covered but was not wearing an abaaya. They wanted to make an example of her."

"I'm surprised she's not already married," Dr. Tuqan said.

"She was – to a man seventy years old – when she was ten. He divorced her last year because he decided she could not conceive. I met Hind on my first trip here, bright, intelligent eyes. She was working in the fields. While all the other children gathered around me, she remained aloof, fearful, a resigned, defeated expression on her face. Later that evening I fetched her out and spoke with her – tried to convince her to come to school. She didn't answer. Of course I knew what the problem was. As you had instructed me, I offered her father more than enough compensation. He agreed."

"Have you contacted the police? Any clues who did it?"

"There's no police to speak of here. The closest police booth is in the next village. He said he would look into it. He won't. He won't want to be involved."

"Perhaps we should bring it to the attention of the authorities in Cairo," Sarah suggested.

"We could," Dr. Tuqan said somewhat apprehensive. "But they have their hands full. The tourist trade has declined sharply because of terrorism by the extremists. The livelihood of millions of Egyptians depends on it. That's their priority. I doubt they will be bothered with the burned face of a thirteen year old girl."

"Still, we have a great deal to be grateful for," Nabila said. "My colleague in the next village informs me it is much worse in places like Algeria and the Sudan. They kill and maim innocent people all in the name of Allah. Algerian radicals have spread their activities to France attacking Muslims who they feel are being corrupted by non-Islamic influences. Throwing acid in women's uncovered faces apparently is an immensely popular form of punishment the Algerian Islamists use. So their counterparts in Egypt copy whatever the more radical rebels in Algeria do. It's like a disease out of control."

"What about the mother?" These situations drained so much out of Sarah that it took all the courage she could muster to stop herself from saying or doing something she might regret later.

They had reached the house – a one room shack hardly eight by ten.

The father, in his late sixties or early seventies, sat on a wooden chair at the entrance of the shack smoking his water pipe. At least a dozen boys played nearby. No girls. The women were in the fields, working.

Afaf introduced Sarah and Suheil to the father of the girl. The old man raised his head briefly, looked at them as though in a haze, then returned his attention to his water pipe. Afaf asked if they could go in. Abu Yahya, the father, said the women could go in, but not the man.

"He's a doctor." Afaf knew it was useless but had to try.

Abu Yahya sucked on his water pipe as though his life depended on it, then shook his head no.

Afaf whispered to Dr. Tuqan her back turned to Abu Yahya, "He'll pass out in a few minutes. It's the same every afternoon. All the money we give him goes to buy pot."

They waited for a while but Abu Yahya kept sucking on his water pipe.

Sarah was restless. She wanted to go inside – to check on the girl and her mother.

Afaf agreed. The women stepped inside. Dr. Tuqan had to wait outside.

One look at the girl and Sarah's knees turned into a bone-less pile of flesh and the iron control she prided herself with melted instantly forcing her to reach for Afaf's arm to steady herself. The mother, both eyes swollen, left eye swollen shut, crumpled in a corner in the fetal position, raised her head slightly, stared at the visitors, contours of her facial muscles defined by the intensity of her pain. She repeated a few words in a drawl. Sarah and Afaf listened closely but could not understand what she was saying.

Sarah dragged herself out of the room. She had to. She felt lightheaded, claustrophobic. She could not stand the stifling air in the room and the million flies in clusters feasting on whatever lay underneath their bodies.

"You look like a ghost." Dr. Tuqan's said anxiously. "Is the girl that bad?"

Sarah put her hand on her forehead to shade her eyes from the bright, desert sun and hoped the fresh air outdoors will give her stomach temporary respite from the nausea burning like a torch in her stomach. It was not to be. The sight of children with myriad flies poking at the pus in the corner of their eyes, and the green mucous dribbling from their noses, aggravated her already rebellious stomach even more. The children were gathered around the visitors. It wasn't often that they had such an opportunity.

"Is she that bad?" Dr. Tuqan repeated his question again.

Sarah turned her back to the children, dropped her face in her hands and burst into tears.

Dr. Tuqan whispered soft words in English to comfort her, but could not do much more in public.

Sarah wiped her tears, pulled herself together and slowly turned around. Hopefully the children had not seen her break down.

Curious, the children moved closer Sarah. Abu Yahya seemed annoyed. He shooed the children away – told them to go play somewhere else. He wanted to rest.

Meanwhile Sarah and Dr. Tuqan waited for the old man to fall asleep.

It was a short wait. Abu Yahya's head soon fell forward.

"Let's go in. Afaf was right. It didn't take long for the old man to pass out."

Dr. Tuqan gave Sarah's hand a gentle squeeze. That small gesture told her his pain was no less than hers. Quietly, they sneaked into the room.

When the girl saw a man enter the room, she immediately reached for a corner of the blanket to cover her face. Afaf reached for the girl's hand. "Hind, it's all right. He's a doctor. He has come to help you."

Hind did not seem appeased. The blanket remained on her face, sending shivers down Sarah's spine. In addition to the flies, fear of infection from the blanket covering the exposed flesh on her face, sent Sarah's apprehension to new heights.

Meanwhile the mother kept muttering words, incomprehensible, accentuated by an occasional call for Allah's mercy. There was no response from Allah. "Perhaps the cruelty, the stupidity of it all is too much even for Allah to tolerate." Afaf said feebly.

"We should fly the girl to Jordan," Dr. Tuqan suggested. "The burn unit at the University Hospital is better than anything they have in Egypt."

"I'm all for it," Sarah said without conviction. Somehow she did not recognize her own voice. It sounded like it came from a distance, from a stranger.

"Are you serious?" Afaf looked baffled.

"They won't let her go, will they?" Sarah knew the answer. But she was an optimist. She did not give up hope easily.

"That's not the only problem," Afaf said. "Dealing with bureaucracy here is a nightmare – even if you were willing to bribe from the gate man to the top bureaucrat, it would still not guarantee results. Hind is a female, has no birth certificates, no ID, nothing. She might as well not exist, and for all practical purposes, she does not. And yet she does."

"Occasionally we forget what kind of an insane world we live in," Dr. Tuqan admitted. "It will probably take, who knows how long, to obtain the necessary travel documents – if and when we succeed to convince the girl's father – with a generous sum of course."

Sarah crouched next to Hind on the dirt floor. Hind lay on an old blanket. Her mother was on the dirt floor. It was unbearably hot in the room, with only a small opening on the side for ventilation and light. Hind sobbed softly, her hands in Sarah's hands. Despite her best efforts, Sarah could not control the tears slowly dripping down her cheeks.

"Did you see the man who threw the acid in your face?" Sarah uncovered the girl's face gently. She wiped the girl's eyes with tissue paper from her purse.

"There were two of them. They drove by on a motorcycle. Am I going to be blind?" Hind struggled to control her sobs.

"How much can you see?" Sarah asked.

"I can see a little with the left eye only."

Dr. Tuqan approached the girl.

"No. Please, no." Hind sounded terrified. "You're a man. My father will kill us both."

Dr. Tuqan turned to Afaf. "Do you think you can keep an eye on her father for a couple of minutes. Cough or say something in English if he wakes up."

"Sure can. If he wakes up I'll cough to let you know. Then I will distract him till you step out."

The pot the old man smoked had done its job. Abu Yahya was asleep, his head resting against the wall of his shack, his mouth wide open, flies promenading fearlessly in the toothless cavity.

There was damage to both eyes. However, Dr. Tuqan was not an ophthalmologist and could not tell for sure if the damage was permanent. He talked it over with Sarah, in English. They decided to tell Hind the truth. She would have to be checked by a specialist. Aside from her eyes, the damage to her face, especially the right side was extensive. She would need care – a lot of it. They would make sure she got it.

Hind turned her head towards the wall and sobbed quietly.

Dr. Tuqan approached the mother. "Let me help you sit up."

The woman cringed – pulled her abaaya over her nose. Only the bruised eyes were left uncovered.

Sarah moved next to the woman, slid her arms under the woman's armpits and tried to raise her. "He won't hurt you. He is a doctor. He is here to help you." Saying what she didn't mean irked her. The woman was concerned because Suheil Tuqan was a man – not because she was worried he would hurt her.

"Abu Yahya is asleep," Dr. Tuqan said in a low voice.

The mother seemed to drift in and out of consciousness,

or was it simply unbearable pain. It was hard to tell.

With Suheil's help Sarah pulled the mother up. The abaaya slipped off the mother's head while strong sunlight from the opening in the wall cast a heavy shine on her face.

Sarah straightened herself, and as she did so, she took a good look at the woman's bruised face. Her youth was apparent despite her swollen eyes, cut lips and bleeding nose.

Um Yahya, as the mother was known, like the father, named after the first born son, seemed to come to life under the gentle attention of her guests. Although her movements were labored, and she winced with pain as she tried to open her eyes, she immediately reached for her abaaya and pulled it back over her head. Keeping the female body covered was so deeply embedded in the Muslim psyche that only death would keep her from not doing so almost automatically when there was a male present.

Sarah reached in her purse, grabbed a package of tissue paper and proceeded to wipe the blood from Um Yahya's face and more blood pooled in the corner of her mouth. "Is Hind your oldest?"

Um Yahya looked at Sarah through dazed, uncomprehending eyes.

Sarah repeated the question.

The mother nodded yes.

"She can't be more than twenty five." The words blurted out of Sarah's mouth. Although well aware of early, arranged marriages, especially in rural areas, Sarah could not get used to it. Naturally, the victims were young girls, condemned to a life of misery by their own parents. Why? Because that's the way it had always been done. Just thinking about it made Sarah's blood boil.

"If you don't stop torturing yourself, you won't be around much longer to help anybody."

"Sorry."

"She seems to listen to you. Talk to her. I'd like to check her."

They tried. Um Yahya refused to let the doctor touch her. Afaf stepped back in. "The old man is snoring."

"Can you talk to her. She won't let me examine her."

Afaf tried. "She's terrified. Maybe later." She turned to the mother. "Um Yahya, your neighbor brought a bucket of water from the fountain. She thought you might want to clean up a bit. Can you walk?"

Um Yahya pulled herself together, tried to rise, stumbled, was grabbed by Sarah and Afaf and helped to stand up. "It's ... neither ... the first nor ... the last time." She sighed, seemingly resigned to whatever life had in store for her. "I have ... to walk ... whether ... I like it or not. I ... have ... ten kids ... to take care of."

Sarah felt the knot in her guts tighten yet another notch. How? How did one cope with a situation like this? What could she do to help? Was there anything that could be done? Was she adding to their misery? In her zeal to improve the lot of women, had she overlooked the unintended consequences that might eventually cause irreparable damage rather than accelerate reform. Was it worth it? "What we have achieved can be lost in the wink of an eye," Suheil often reminded her. She felt paralyzed by fear, fear that warnings in word and action, well meaning and otherwise, were a premonition of things to come.

Sensing her pain, Suheil took her by the arm and tried to walk out with her.

Sarah pulled back. "Wait a minute. We can't leave that child in a corner by herself. This is outrageous. It can't be allowed to continue." Sensing she was about to lose it, she admonished herself. No need to vent your anger at the only Middle Eastern man who understands and respects your values. "I'm sorry, Suheil. Please forgive me."

He could read her mind from day one. He pulled her close to him. "Don't be so hard on yourself. Ignorance we have in abundance. Sadly, common sense has become rather uncommon. It is impossible for it to coexist with fanaticism. I'll dress Hind's wounds. You watch the father. Let me know if he wakes up."

He didn't.

Suheil had come prepared and this time Hind did not object. Her mother had left the room. She did not bother to cover her head or face, but held tight onto the edge of the blanket – just in case. Dr. Tuqan dressed the wound, gave Hind eye drops to wash her eyes with, and pills for pain. He reassured her they would do everything humanly possible to help her. Then he had to step outside. The pained, hopeless look in the teenager's eyes probing his, was more than he could handle. Dr. Tuqan had a serious problem. Despite years of treating pain and suffering, he had yet to get callused or even used to it.

"Darling," he said, in a shaky voice. "Let's find a spot to sit down, discuss the predicament Hind is in, and see what solution we can come up with."

Except for a dirt field, there was no where to sit down. Presently, Afaf, with Um Yahya leaning heavily on her right arm, and a straw mat on her left, walked towards the house. She entered the room, spread the mat next to Hind, helped the mother lie down, then joined Sarah and Suheil. "Let's go to our place. We have chairs. Nothing fancy. Wooden chairs. A place to sit down."

Afaf and her husband were educated in England, practiced Islam in its purest form as a way of life, and were strong supporters of women's rights. There was no contradiction in their minds. On the contrary, they believed justice for all was an integral part of the teachings of the Prophet – and that did not exclude women. End of discussion. Both came from prominent, wealthy Egyptian families. Idealists, they chose to live simply, to devote their lives to help better the lot of women in the Middle East. It was only after talking to them extensively that Sarah was convinced they were genuine. So rare was the phenomenon in the Middle East that it took a leap of faith for Sarah to believe such men and women existed in the Middle East – especially men.

On their way over, Dr. Tuqan asked, "Is there a phone in the village? I'd like to place a call to Jordan, to the hospital, to have a bed ready for Hind. Maybe, just maybe we'll get lucky."

"There's only one phone. It's in the mosque. It works – sometimes. But please, let's have a cold drink first. I'm parched. I'm sure you are too."

Sarah agreed. However, a few unanswered questions kept rattling in her head. Perhaps Afaf could help. She'd probably never learn who the culprits were. Even if the villagers knew, fear of retaliation would clamp their mouths shut. The assailants had to be outsiders. The villagers were all related. They would have probably given the girls a good beating for what they considered improper attire, but they would not resort to throwing acid in the girls' faces.

Afaf had no answers. But to Sarah's questions as to why Abu Yahya beat the mother, why so badly and how could an old man inflict so much injury on a young woman, Afaf had plenty to say.

She said Abu Yahya had agreed to allow his daughter to go to school, reluctantly, for the compensation money. He had worked as little as possible when he was young, and now that he was old, he spent his days in the company of his water pipe and let his wife and daughters do the working. They did – in the home and outside the home. Nevertheless, the mother still got blamed for not making sure the daughter was always fully covered when she stepped out of the house. The fact that the mother left at sunrise to start work in the fields and could not be back to check on her daughter, since her workday did not end until sunset was irrelevant. "There's not much she can do to protect herself when he attacks her, crazed by drugs. And don't forget. Islam means submission – submission to God of course. But men have mastered the art of bestowing that 'privilege' solely upon women – submission to God and men. In effect, men have appointed themselves as our gods."

Sometimes, it was harder to deal with outbursts of bitterness, exasperation, helplessness and hopelessness most women found difficult to keep under control – harder than the abuse and exploitation in the name of Islam. And bitter they were – especially those in the know. Bitter not only because they could see no way out, but also because at every turn, invariably, bigger and more restrictive boulders were thrown in their path.

Afaf's hospitality worked like a miracle. An hour and a half later, refreshed and feeling much better, they left the two room, sparsely furnished, spotlessly clean house, and headed for the mosque. Sarah was relieved to learn that Afaf had all matters pertaining to the school under control – except the acid-throwing incident.

The mosque stood in the center of the village.

Mullah Rashid, a man in his forties, with a thick, unruly beard, intense black eyes greeted them politely. He offered to help place the call.

As expected, the operator informed them there would be a wait. The operator did not know how long the wait would be. All external lines were busy. While they contemplated what to do next, Yahya the first son born to Hind's parents came running to the mosque. "Miss Afaf, Miss Afaf, come quickly. My mother is vomiting blood."

Afaf did not stop to think. She rushed to the door, then dashed back. "Sorry. Here I am doctor, nurse, teacher. Name it, I am it." She turned to Dr. Tuqan. "Please, can you help?"

"Certainly. If Abu Yahya will let me." He turned to Sarah. "Can you wait for the call?"

"Of course I can. Admissions OK, or you want me to talk to someone in particular."

"Tell admissions to reserve a bed. Tell them I guarantee payment. Tell them it's an emergency."

It was a tiny office, with a small wooden table on which the phone rested, and a wooden chair that wobbled on the uneven floor when touched. The cleric offered her the chair.

Sarah thanked him, explained she was not tired and did not need to sit down. After that brief exchange, Mullah Rashid settled on the chair and proceeded to study Sarah with a concentration that made her nervous. She avoided eye contact, opting to look out the window instead.

Slowly, the cleric's breathing grew heavy. It filled the room. "When you go against the word of God, there is always a price to pay." He followed it by reciting a verse from the Koran.

"Excuse me."

"If God wanted women to be educated, he would not have given them an organ with which to receive and nurture life. You are fighting a losing battle."

"Really? How so?"

"An educated women is a curse, a danger to her family, to her society, to her religion and most of all to herself."

She shook her head totally at a loss for an answer. "These ... These ideas ... These beliefs you have. Are they your personal opinions?"

"Of course. What sort of question is that."

"What do you base them on?"

The mullah's chin quivered. "Women who ask questions are trouble. If you have money to throw around give it to the mosque – like the Koran tells all believers to do. The clergy will decide where the money goes. Not the donor. It will definitely not go to incite the villagers with heretic ideas."

"That's a matter of opinion."

"Indeed it is. And this is my village and here it is my opinion that counts. You have caused enough damage. I suggest you take your staff and leave."

"I shall do nothing of the kind. I have permission from the government to operate a school in this village and that is precisely what I am going to do even if I have to post a guard to protect each child who goes to school."

Her stubborn stand seemed to have a weird effect on the cleric. "Interesting." He rose and walked across the tiny room towards her. "Very interesting."

A part of her warned her to stop before she went too far. Instead she faced him. "You are a young man. Can't you see how detrimental these archaic traditions are? Can't you see how much they're hurting our people? Why can't you work with us to help improve their lot? Isn't that God's work as well?"

Was that a smirk, a smile, or muscles twitching from anger? Hard to tell. Slowly, the cleric cocked his head to the left and said with measured words, "Perhaps, perhaps. We could work out a deal."

"No deal. That's not what I meant at all. I will work with you to help the villagers any way I can. But if you expect cash for your cooperation, you can forget it. That's not how I operate."

He put his hand on his chin and studied her for a long moment. "I think you're a phony."

"Think what you wish. Frankly, I couldn't care less." I should have quit when I first thought of it, Sarah admonished herself. This is getting ugly.

"Why should it matter to you? You can't use the money you have in ten lifetimes."

It was the number one advice her father had consistently pressed on her. Bribery, in a part of the world where most deals, even simple transactions depended upon, was to be her last resort, a means when all else failed. Bribery, Maher Sultan was convinced, did not solve problems. It often led to complications. The more one gave, the more the recipients demanded, and the favors received shrank respectively. "It's like blackmail," Maher Sultan told his daughter. "Once you agree to it, the only thing you can count on is the escalation of demand. There's no end to it."

"I told you, that's not how I operate. But if the harassment does not stop, I'll have no choice but to move the school to another village."

"It's a natural reaction." The cleric chuckled. For what

reason, Sarah could not fathom. "Change disturbs people," he added casually. "Especially change imposed upon people with traditional values, inhibited mentally by codes of conduct they are born and expect to die with, values deeply embedded in their psyche – I'd venture to say almost impossible to reverse."

It was Sarah's turn to study the cleric. "I don't follow you."

"Of course not. You're on a mission. You want to change the world. Like you, I had similar ambitions, and like you I was stubborn and refused to budge from the path I had chosen. But the society we live in crushes anyone who dares introduce even minimum diversion from the path they have carved out for people to follow. Naturally, I had heard about you, a lot. Afaf talks about you every chance she gets. And I have done my own investigating. My words were meant to test you, to assure myself of the degree of your commitment."

"You amaze me." In her mind she said, 'will the real man please stand up.'

"I have learned that you have suffered much in the hands of clerics, but you were not hostile towards me. I have also learned that a fierce storm is brewing. Those opposed to your activities are in consultation with radicals, to pressure you to leave Jordan. Don't. I had to leave. I did not have the money to fight them. I left Cairo in search of a less oppressive society to live in, to teach the faith, to spread the word by living an exemplary life. Not by terrorism. That was to be my Jihad, my holy war. The villages seemed like the reasonable answer." Mullah Rashid stopped, paced the room. In a moment, he picked up where he had left off. "There's no difference – none. Today you witnessed a day in the life of all the villages in this country, or, for that matter, any Arab country. The prejudices and social baggage we are born with is a curse I fear we will not be able to overcome – at least not in my lifetime."

Incredible, mind boggling, came to mind. Warning lights

flashed cautioning her. It's a game. Perhaps a game two can play. "I'm often accused of being too hard on myself. I think that right now you surpassed me. Maybe I am naíve. Maybe I am so hopelessly mired in the hole I have dug for myself that I fail to see the warning signs. The storm you mentioned. How did you learn about it? Have Egyptian extremists joined hands with their Jordanian and Palestinian counterparts to put an end to my 'evil schemes'?"

Mullah Rashid had a pained smile on his face. "You might think this is a religious witch hunt. It's not. Religion has little to do with it. It's political. It's about power, about control. You're disturbing the balance, a balance meticulously maintained for centuries. Every member knows exactly where he stands. Don't you think they can foresee what will happen to that balance if women get educated? Once educated, what's to stop women from demanding equality? And," Mullah Rashid added his voice full of cynicism. "And after that, what's to stop them from demanding sexual equality – God forbid."

There was hope. If at least one cleric could be this well informed, Sarah figured, then there was hope – definitely – if he was sincere – if he truly believed in what he said.

"You asked how I learned about the storm. In the type of atmosphere we live in, ignorance can be very costly. Therefore, I make it my business to be informed. The Sheikh in charge of the mosque on Mecca street in Amman and I were classmates at the Islamic University of Al-Azhar, in Cairo. His interpretation of the Koran is quite different from mine. He believes oppression, acts of violence, even terrorism are essential in teaching the faith and spreading the word. He is convinced bloodshed, sacrifice, repressive interpretation of the Holy Law, help us preserve our society, our culture and our religion. Fanaticism is his weapon of choice to fight our enemies real and imaginary."

Enough said. She knew precisely whom Mullah Rashid was referring to. "He's been back for a while," Sarah replied. "Several months, I believe. Not much has happened so far.

Routine harassment we've come to expect. Not much more."

"Be on your guard at all times and make sure you have your assistant by your side as long as you are in Jordan. He's the only man they fear."

The phone rang. It was the hospital in Amman. The connection was clear. Sarah relayed the message, thanked her host profusely for his hospitality, the stimulating conversation and his warning. She glanced at her watch. It had been twenty minutes since Suheil and Afaf left. Engrossed in conversation she had lost track of time.

"I'll go with you," said the cleric. "The old man has to be reminded of his manners – often. Otherwise, we'll have a real tragedy on our hands soon."

The tragedy was already in progress.

Hind was in the street covered with the blanket she lay on in the room, trembling.

Having learned that a man had visited his wife and daughter while he slept, Abu Yahya had grabbed his favorite weapon, stormed into the shack, and broke the chair on his wife's head. Meanwhile Hind had escaped. His fury not quite spent, he then apparently shoved his son who was trying to protect his mother to the ground, turned to pull his khanjar, a dagger he kept in his belt and lunged, yet again, at his wife.

Only it wasn't his wife he had stabbed. It was his son.

Chapter 22

THE NEXT MORNING, YAHYA'S BODY wrapped in a bed sheet with different shades of yellow stains over a grayish white background, was placed on a stretcher improvised from a large wheat sack – four corners tied to the ends of two sticks – U.S. wheat printed across the sack in bold, red letters. A group of women gathered inside the shack, around the body, wailed and pounded their chests. Outside, men crouched around Abu Yahya, talked when the cigarettes they were smoking were not in control of their lips. Sad-eyed children, scared, hesitant, stared at each other slouched against the mud wall of the house, resigned to the beating from the merciless rays of the desert sun and the uninvited company of swarms of flies.

The previous afternoon, concerned about his mother, Yahya had run back to his home from the mosque after alerting Afaf about his mother vomiting blood. Dr. Tuqan and Afaf had arrived at the house a minute too late – after the stabbing. While Dr. Tuqan tried to stop the boy from bleeding to death and eventually failed, Afaf whisked mother and daughter to a relative's house before Abu Yahya, still in a daze after his violent outburst, got another chance to impress his wife and daughter with his displeasure.

In accordance with Muslim custom, the boy had to be buried as soon as possible – the next day at the latest. "The burial will take place tomorrow after noon prayers," Mullah Rashid made the announcement standing in the doorway of the hut – the women gathered inside the boy's home, the men outside. Mullah Rashid's voice shook and his body shook. He left without another word and walked away on a dirt road leading everywhere. Dr. Tuqan and Sarah spent the night with

Afaf and her husband Bassam. Sarah wanted to make sure the boy got a proper burial, some kind of restraint would be put on the father, and mother and daughter would be protected from the father – in the future, somehow. She did not have a clue as to how. Nevertheless, she had to think of something. Violence was an everyday affair for these people. No one seemed particularly upset or concerned enough to do something about it. Customary rituals of wailing, beating their chests and pulling their hair – an unwritten law delegated the responsibility of this ritual to women. The women did their duty. The rituals were respectfully performed. Everyone agreed. Too bad the 'accident' had happened to the first born son. There was no disputing the will of Allah, and Allah willing more sons would follow soon. The dead got buried and the living continued with the business of surviving. That's the way it had always been and that's the way it was now. Nothing to get excited about.

While the woman prepared the boy's body for burial. Abu Yahya occupied his usual spot outside the door. He smoked his water pipe and occasionally waved his hand lethargically in a futile attempt to get rid of the flies busy feasting on a festering sore on his foot.

Eventually, every one in the village drifted towards the shack filled with the wails of women. A couple of men approached Abu Yahya to express their condolences.

Abu Yahya kept his lips glued to the mouthpiece of the water pipe. He had nothing to say to anyone.

Soon, the wailing grew louder indicating time for wailing inside the home was coming to an end and time to prepare for departure to the cemetery had arrived.

The old man sucked on his pipe.

Two 'poll bearers,' cousins, in their teens, entered the dwelling. Moments later they exited, one cousin up front the other in the back,carrying the U.S. wheat sack on sticks – with the boy's undernourished body wrapped in the bed sheet barely making a depression in it.

Abu Yahya did not move or speak. He clung to the mouthpiece of his water pipe.

The mourners waited for a few minutes for everyone to gather.

Abu Yahya did not move.

Eventually, a man walked over, put his hands under Abu Yahya's armpits, lifted him, walked with him and propped him up behind the make shift casket but did not let go. Abu Yahya looked like he did not know what planet he was on.

Mullah Rashid arrived immediately after the noon prayers and prepared to lead the procession to the cemetery. He looked at no one, spoke to no one. The cemetery was outside the village – a fifteen-minute easy walk. Sarah approached Mullah Rashid cautiously. He looked pale, gaunt, almost as if he had aged a decade overnight. She greeted him and asked if there was anything she could do to help. He stopped, stared at her for a long moment, then said totally without emotion, "I doubt there's anything anyone can do."

Prophetic words – perhaps. Feelings of helplessness was an emotion Sarah always had trouble accepting. As she tried to suppress the raw fury building inside her, she could feel her own heartbeat echoing through her.

It was almost as if Suheil had an in-built barometer tuned to sense Sarah's emotions. He reacted instantly whenever he felt the barometer had risen beyond her tolerance level and immediately offered his support. As she took a deep breath to calm herself, he reached for her arm and walked with her slowly, a few steps away. "Rashid is right darling," Suheil said with a soothing voice. "You can't go on torturing yourself. You were up all night pacing. Now it's time to let go."

They stopped where there was a small patch of shade cast by the west wall of the dwelling. Sarah dropped her head on the doctor's shoulders and sobbed. "I feel like an angel of death. Pain and death seem to follow me wherever I go. Is there no sanity left in this world, Suheil?"

He wiped her tears, caressed her hair, then lifted her chin

up and planted a kiss on her forehead in full view of men lingering outside the shack waiting for the procession to begin.
These were men who would consider honor killing justified
in a similar situation of public display of affection between
the sexes if one of their own was involved without hesitation.
In this case, they stared at the couple with disapproving eyes.
Suheil ignored them.

When Sarah raised her head she saw tears well in Suheil's
eyes. She felt grateful for the deep love he had for humanity,
for justice, for her. If all her projects failed, the fact that she
had come to know a man of such sensitivity, kindness and
generosity was reward enough for her time in the Middle
East. She had often wondered what it felt like to be in love, to
love someone other than ones parents. Were there special
indications a person could rely upon? Unique signs? Feelings
not yet experienced. How did one know those feelings were
genuine? What did being in love mean anyway?

She got the answers by looking in the eyes of the man
holding her chin up.

Meanwhile the procession to the cemetery got under way
– eight men, no women, about two dozen children – boys.
Inside, the women sipped tea – their mission accomplished.
No more wailing.

Sarah did not own an abaaya. Neither did Afaf or any of
the women who worked for Sarah. They refused to cover
themselves no matter what the reason – on their own, not
urged or recommended by Sarah. These women were the
rebels who simply would not comply with man-made restrictions – regardless of the consequences. It was a matter of principle – of setting an example for the children and the women
who considered them their role models. That meant of course
that they could not go to the cemetery. There were no restrictions for women with proper attire to attend funerals or visit
the cemetery.

Although reluctant to leave the women behind, Dr. Tuqan
explained he thought he should accompany the mourners.

"Mullah Rashid looks like he can use moral support," the doctor said with a rueful smile. "I better join the procession."

As the small group of mourners, with Mullah Rashid up front, headed towards the open field which served as a cemetery, and where a small grave was dug for the boy the night before, the cleric bent down and whispered something to the younger brother of the dead boy. The boy stopped, eyed the cleric, seemingly not quite sure he had heard right. The cleric bent down and whispered again.

The boy, about nine years old, shrugged his shoulders, left the group and approached Sarah and Afaf. Afaf had joined Sarah to take refuge in the only shady spot there was against the wall of the shack. "Mullah Rashid would like you to accompany him," the boy said to Sarah apprehensively.

Caught off guard, Sarah consulted Afaf. "You know these people better than I do. I don't have an abaaya and am not about to borrow one. Do you think we should go dressed the way we are?"

"No, it's best not to." Afaf asked the boy to tell Mullah Rashid it was much too hot to walk in the sun and that she and Sarah prefer to wait for the return of the mourners at her house. "Rashid is upset," Afaf told Sarah. "It is his way of lashing back at a world he understands but fears he cannot change."

"Ditto." The oppressive heat was taking its toll on Sarah. She felt like she was on fire, she was parched and feared a heat stroke imminent if she did not move to a cooler spot.

"There's no shortage of ignorance here," Afaf said, as the boy, obviously relieved hurried back to report to Mullah Rashid and rejoin the procession. "Mullah Rashid is the most brilliant cleric I have met in all my life and I come from a family of clerics. Like you and Dr. Tuqan he wants to help his people. He is highly educated – studied with the best in top schools in Cairo and London. He comes from a family of wealthy landowners. He has distributed all his wealth to widows, orphans and the poor – with a special fund reserved for the sick poor. He keeps only enough for his simple needs. Yet he is hounded like a common criminal. He receives death threats almost daily. Ultimately, they will get him. I'm really worried."

"What is it that they don't like about him?" The more Sarah learned, the more she was baffled until the cleric's words came back to mind. It is not religion, he had said. It is politics. Indeed it was. And the people were the pawns in a game of chess played on an enormous battlefield. The prize crystallized in one word – power.

"They don't like his ideas. They think he is out to establish a new religious order. Lies. All lies. Fabricated by his enemies and believe me, he has quite a few of them. The man knows the Koran so thoroughly, and so well, that no one can argue with him and win. He wants to emphasize the positive message of Islam – to teach the highest morals, wipe out prejudice and superstition and eliminate abuse and exploitation in the name of Islam. Does that sound bad to you? He wants to get rid of the social baggage we have been burdened with for centuries. He wants to do away with codes of conduct which inhibit us mentally by denying us freedom of thought – issues already mostly resolved in more advanced countries."

"That's a tall order," Sarah replied dismayed. "How does he propose to do it by himself?"

Afaf chuckled. "Listen to you. He is not by himself. What about you and Dr. Tuqan? How many people do you know who would willingly sacrifice a life of luxury to endure all this agony instead? Mother Theresa? Perhaps. But Mother Theresa does not have the financial resources you have. I have to admit though, with Mullah Rashid it is an obsession. He has lost his mother and two sisters because of some of our retarded customs that actually have nothing to do with Islam but have somehow become an integral part of it. His mother was constantly abused by his father and eventually killed over a cup of tea his father felt was not prepared to his liking, and a sister he was very close to was killed by a brother – stabbed seventeen times. Honor killing the brother claimed. No punishment – none – zero. Not even a hearing in a courtroom. The reason for the killing? Rashid's brother saw his sister talking to a stranger – a man – in the street. Later, much too late for his sister, they learned the man was a foreigner asking for directions."

"It sounds like Mullah Rashid has had more than his share of pain." An oppressive feeling of déhà vu paid a brief visit to Sarah's psyche reminding her of the countless men and women who had for centuries been through the same experiences with no recourse whatsoever. "And yet it does not seem to have discouraged him to the point that he would want to quit or slowed him down. May be there is still hope for us."

"What I told you is a fraction of what he has been through. Yet another sister bled to death at age ten, soon after being circumcised by a man Rashid refers to as the 'butcher.' Not surprisingly, his greatest concern is for women in our society. He feels the only time women are not invisible are when they are victimized. Rashid the boy therefore decided to become Rashid the mullah, to work for change – to fight fire with fire, so to speak. Change he insists can come only with the right weapon, and that weapon is knowledge."

"Perhaps there are others like Rashid." It was the one hope that Sarah clung to whenever all else looked bleak, whenever the world seemed determined to close in on her. That hope gave her the energy to go on. "Men and women not looking for revolutionary changes, not demanding excessive privileges, not even fairness – only a reasonable balance. I bet they are out there. We just don't know about them."

"Close, maybe. Like him? Don't count on it. He is one of a kind and how long he will last is anybody's guess. The acid that destroyed Hind's face was meant more for Mullah Rashid than for Hind. It was a warning – to let him know they are watching him. He teaches Islam as a universal ideology, a way of life, equality for all, justice for all. The extremists working to tighten the noose around women's necks are not exactly pleased to see their hard work systematically disman- tled – by a cleric, nonetheless."

"How long has he been doing it?" Sarah was surprised that a strong liberal thinker like Mullah Rashid, a man, especially a cleric, had managed to function and stay alive in such turbu- lent times – in a country swarming with terrorists – terrorists brutally hunted down and executed by a government deter- mined to eradicate them. Instead they kept on multiplying.

"In this village, a little over two years. It took a while for the extremists to catch on, but now they are on to him. There have not been any female 'circumcisions' – Rashid calls them genital mutilations – in the village he is in charge of. He won't permit it. He spends hours arguing with anyone who makes the mistake of telling him it has to do with the Prophet's teachings. He has a small publication he puts out monthly at his own expense, spreading the truth of Islam without the pollution added by interpreters. He tours all the surrounding villages, reads to the public and explains every sentence the Prophet spoke within context – especially within its historical context. He insists it is the only way. If the historical perspec- tive is not kept in mind, the Prophet's teachings can easily be altered to mean what the interpreters want them to mean – as is often the case. During the Prophet's time, when humanity was steeped in ignorance and superstition, the problems were different and had to be dealt with in a manner appropriate to the times. The prophet tried his best to introduce a balanced synthesis between worldly life and spiritual purity. Unfortunately for Mullah Rashid, there is a lot of ignorance and superstition now as well. But he presses on. If there are any literate men, he leaves copies of his publications with them – if they want. Usually, they don't. For them, he is an enigma. A few call him 'mullah majnoon.' Crazy mullah. Still, he has earned the extremists' wrath. They're not in the business of taking chances."

Sarah shook her head baffled – although the scenario was

familiar by then. "Of course not. Losing control is their worst nightmare. But think about it Afaf, if, if a few more men, especially clerics, or men of position could be found with similarly liberated thinking, we'd be able to operate with far more efficiency and face far less road blocks. Perhaps we have not been sufficiently diligent in our search for like-minded men and women, or clerics for that matter."

"We don't have to. There are many intellectuals among Arabs – free thinkers, especially here in Egypt. Art, music, theater, movies have originated here and have spread to other Arab countries for decades. If only it was so simple. Nowadays, any idea not propagated by Islamist extremists is categorized as anti Islam, and those propagating it are considered heretics. Anti extremist sentiment is simmering. Individuals find it difficult to fight terrorism when governments seem paralyzed by it. They either leave the country or keep a low profile hoping this nightmare will blow over – hopefully soon."

"No harm in dreaming, right."

"A dream it is." Afaf moved the fan closer to Sarah. Perspiration coursed down Sarah's face as though she was in a Turkish bath. The oppressive heat, coupled with emotional blows of the past two days, had sapped her energy. Gently, Sarah repositioned the fan between herself and her host. "Don't worry about me," Afaf said. "I'm used to the heat. But you look dehydrated. Would you like something to drink?"

"Water, please."

Afaf went to the kitchen, filled a pitcher with water, took a step towards the living room then stopped suddenly. She stepped back into the kitchen, looked out the open window, pulled back, looked again, shook her head and walked slowly back to the living room with a pitcher of water and two glasses. "I could have sworn I saw someone looking inside," she said still shaking her head in disbelief. "But there's no one there now. Where could he have disappeared in a few seconds?"

"Did you recognize him?"

"No, not really. Perhaps it is just my imagination, or lack of sleep, or the events of the past twenty four hours playing havoc with my senses."

"Amazing how much damage a senile, old man can do." Sarah pulled her T-shirt, soaked with perspiration, away from her chest.

"Drugged old man is more accurate. He was not senile, and he was not old when he decided to take on a new wife and have more children. Young or old, in our culture a husband's word is law. That is what is so pathetic."

Sarah dropped her head back, immersed in thought. Discussion with friends and enemies, at times, infused her with renewed energy., At other times, fear of failure took over – but only briefly. Old anxieties consciously shelved in the dark corners of her mind resurfaced warning lights flashing. Be that as it may, she refused to consider abandoning her mission. Failure, when so much was at stake, was worse than death.

"Stupidity is always amazing, no matter how used to it you become. That's a statement of Jean Cocteau." Afaf poured more water in Sarah's glass. "It is to Abu Yahya's type – the old, the poor and the uneducated that the extremists have their greatest appeal. That is why I feel, I hope and I pray that we are on the right tract, and that is why I believe we will eventually win. We have to, actually. Failure is not an option we can afford."

"We will not fail." It warmed Sarah's heart to witness others who felt as strongly as she did, and who were willing, despite serious risks to themselves and their families, to fight for a better future for women – especially in the Middle East where Sarah felt certain it was needed most. "No, Afaf, we will not fail. You can count on it."

"In the long run, I sure hope so. Short term, you can win if you have a weapon you can use to stem the tide. And that is where the difficulty lies – in short term. Terrorism, in my opinion is almost impossible to control unless the perpetrators and the government reach some kind of agreement or compromise. We have no answers. Our only hope is time. Because, here in Egypt, we have to deal not only with terrorism but with a new phenomenon as well."

"A new phenomenon? You mean the young – the brainwashed – those you feel are beyond help?"

"For the time being I have given up on those." Afaf impressed Sarah as a woman with an analytical mind perfectly capable of sorting out complex issues and making the appropriate choices. The young, diehard radicals were the greatest challenge they faced. Afaf must have concluded to reserve her efforts where it would do most good. Sarah listened and learned.

"I am more concerned about our legal system," Afaf continued. "Lately, militant fundamentalists have changed their tactics. Their campaign of shootings and bombings aimed at Egyptian Christians, the police, tourist sites and tourists has backfired. At least thirty tourists have died recently. Egyptians are religious people, yet they were filled with revulsion as fanatics escalated their attacks, innocent people were killed, are still being killed, and businesses associated with tourism lost income. For a poor, overpopulated country, the devastating affects can hardly be overstated. The negative public reaction has helped the government of Hosni Mubarak to crack down on the dissidents. Thousands are in jail under atrocious conditions. But that does not mean that the extremists have given up. They have not. They have increased their efforts and diversified. Have you heard about Sheikh Yusuf el-Badry?"

"Is he the imam who was in New Jersey a couple of years ago?"

"That's the one. He is shrewd, loves attention, and wants publicity at any price. He has shifted his tactics from bombs to lawsuits. He uses the Sharia, his version of Islamic law, to enforce his claims involving mostly family matters: marriage, divorce, custody, inheritance. Whatever has to do with the family. It serves his purpose magnificently."

"I thought Egypt's government was secular." Sarah had concentrated mostly on learning all she could about Jordan. Only recently, after deciding to open schools in Egypt, had she delved more deeply into research about Egypt. She had a lot of unanswered questions floating through her mind but had yet to find time to seek answers. She knew that Egypt's highest Islamic authority from Al-Azhar – a religious university, routinely censured books, magazines, movies and plays – and the so-called democratic government tolerated it. But lawsuits by clerics were news to her.

"Egypt is secular – more or less," Afaf said. "The courts recognize some elements of the Sharia. Hosni Mubarak's government has a delicate balancing act to maintain. Our president does not want his predecessor's fate. Anwar Sadat underestimated the zeal of the fanatics and paid for it with his life. The Shah of Iran vacillated, and paid for it by the loss of his kingdom. President Mubarak knows he has to keep the fanatics in check. The question is how and by how much. Unfortunately, the fanatics are not the only problem he has to deal with. It's hard to believe, but often, the Egyptian Organization for Human Rights has more to say about Mubarak's government's handling of political prisoners and prohibition of religious parties, than it does about innocent people being maimed and killed in the name of religion. For Mubarak, for Egyptians, for all of us there are no ready answers. Mubarak has a tough job. So far he has managed quite well. He gives a little and takes as much as he can get away with."

"I guess lawsuits are better than killing innocent people." Sarah sighed, her mind in turmoil. Lawsuits were fine, but she had a gut feeling it was mostly to polish a much-tainted image of Islam – courtesy of fanatics convinced they are doing believers a big favor. No doubt, if thwarted, they would revert to their old tactics without a moment's hesitation. Perhaps that was why Mubarak, the shrewd politician that he is, permitted the lawsuits to be heard.

As though reading her mind, Afaf said, "Don't let me give you the impression that terrorism has been scrapped as the weapon of choice here, in Egypt. It has not. Different extremist groups strike when or where they choose. El Badry's followers represent a small group of Islamic Fundamentalists, who have discovered to their great delight that they can use the courts to their advantage, and consequently not have to worry about the government cracking down on them or face public outrage. It is all nice and legal. Unfortunately, el-Badry has succeeded over and over again in obtaining court orders banning books, films, magazines and any publication he considers anti Islamic. He does not limit his lawsuits to family matters. More often, he uses Hisba – legal action to protect God's rights. It has nothing to do with God but everything to do with his glorification. At present, under Hisba, he has sued a prominent Egyptian intellectual, a highly respected professor of Islamic studies at Cairo University. The intellectuals of this country and the rest of the Arab world are waiting anxiously for the court's ruling. El-Badry contends that the professor, Nasr Abu Zeid, is an apostate because he has published works which claim the Koran is open to modern interpretation. He also advocates separation of religion from government. Because el-Badry has branded him an apostate and because as an apostate he cannot be married to a Muslim woman, he must divorce his wife."

"That is outrageous. It can't be true." Sarah blurted shocked. She did not want to believe it. To be declared an apostate by an imam, a chief cleric, had serious implications – implications far more devastating than divorcing a wife. It could literally cost the accused his life.

"It is true. The ruling comes next month. If the case is not dismissed, there will be a flight of intellectuals from this country like it has never happened before."

Sarah was speechless. She recalled having read about the case in Jordanian newspapers on and off for months. Modern interpretation of the Koran advocated by professor Abu Zeid was widely welcomed by the Jordanian media. Separation of religion from government was considered imperative, if, as the countries involved claimed, they were to be recognized as democracies. Either the media had not reported that the professor had been declared an apostate or she had missed reading or hearing about it.

"Do you think el-Badry has a chance? I mean, how can he expect to win a case on such ridiculous grounds – against a well known scholar, nonetheless."

"Never underestimate the power of a fanatic, Sarah. El-Badry is opportunistic, dishonest, self-centered, arrogant and a master manipulator. He has some of the shrewdest lawyers working for him and has won cases considered to be jokes by many. So far he has outsmarted them all. He had the best reserved for last. He claims judges who rule against him have been known to go blind. Can you believe it? So rather than fight him the judges rule in his favor. We're talking about educated, professional men – judges – not ignorant peasants."

Had the religious fog become so dense that seeing beyond it had become impossible?

Prevarication had reached punitive levels.

Shaken, as anyone would be, the word apostate triggered a nasty reaction in Sarah – fear. Fear that actions like those of el-Badry would make her worst nightmare come true – the exodus of the intelligentsia – the group most needed to foster progress in countries in desperate need for the contributions the intelligentsia had to offer. She said, after she subdued a spasm of rage, "This is a serious matter, Afaf, exceedingly serious. If my understanding of what being branded an apostate by an imam is correct, now that el-Badry has declared the professor an apostate, according to the Sharia any Muslim can kill him. Right?"

"Absolutely. Actually, I don't think el-Badry gives a damn about Professor Abu Zeid divorcing his wife. He wants attention and he doesn't care how he gets it. I hate to admit it, but

so far he has succeeded exceptionally well. The fundamentalists use every opportunity to take legal action against anyone
who does not comply with their ideas, their wishes and their
commands. According to the Center for Human Rights Legal
Aid based in Cairo, last year alone fifty four cases of Hisba
were filed against leading cultural figures."

"Have they won any cases?"

"Most. They have lost a few minor ones – to make it seem
legitimate. It is generally assumed that el-Badry will win his
case against the professor. To presume otherwise is sheer
folly. The judge appointed to the case is one of el-Badry's
stooges. The professor and his wife are long gone. They were
not about to wait around for the outcome of a predetermined
verdict."

Precisely what Sarah had feared.

"People like Professor Abu Zeid are leaving in droves,"
Afaf added. "They go wherever they can, to whatever country will give them a visa. Talk about brain drain! If el-Badry
wins this case, we won't have the brain drain problem anymore. There will be no one with brains left to drain."

Afaf fascinated Sarah. She had a master's degree in history and political science, a graduate of the American
University of Beirut. After graduation Afaf had spent two
additional years traveling and doing research about the
Middle East in the Middle East, Europe and the U.S. She was
married to a man with similar qualifications. Afaf and her
husband were euphoric when they learned about Sarah and
her search for qualified teachers. They applied and enthusiastically joined Sarah's school ventures. Sarah paid the going
rate plus benefits. Although Afaf and her husband came from
wealthy families, they lived simply. Very simply. Living simply when you have wealth is not a common occurrence in the
Middle East. Ordinarily, people do their best to impress
others with much more wealth than they actually have.

As Sarah studied the woman without whose help running
the school in Egyptian villages would have been quite diffi-

cult, she noticed Afaf's gaze focused either on her shoulder or behind it. There was nothing behind her except a window that was stuck and could not be opened. Perhaps she feels the heat as much as I do, Sarah thought while she wiped the perspiration dripping from her face. Within twenty minutes Sarah and Afaf had finished a full pitcher of water.

"Would you like more water?" A weird look on Afaf's face made Sarah pause.

"Don't move." Afaf stood perfectly still. "I can see the reflection of someone in the glass behind you."

"Man or woman?" Sarah asked.

"Looks like a boy. In his teens. I'd say fifteen, perhaps seventeen. He sticks his head out, peeps, then pulls it back immediately." Afaf spoke in whispers.

"You think?"

"I don't know. Nothing surprises me anymore."

"He could be armed."

"I doubt it. Guns are expensive, the supply limited and difficult to get hold of even if money is not an issue. He probably has a knife."

"Why don't we corner him? Two against one. We should be able to do it."

Afaf said she preferred to wait. It was a small house built on an open field. By the time they stepped out the boy could run in any direction and eventually disappear before they could catch him. Afaf was worried that if they chase him, they might miss the opportunity to find out who he is.

"I'm surprised they are not back from the cemetery yet," Sarah remarked. "It's been over an hour. Do burials always take this long?"

"No, not really. Actually, I was wondering about that my ..." Afaf stopped in mid sentence.

They could hear a scuffle outside.

Both women dashed out.

Afaf's husband, Bassam, had a boy in chokehold at the spot where Afaf had seen the person peeping in.

Bassam was in charge of all the schools in Egypt funded by Sarah. He also studied the Koran with Mullah Rashid daily. This day was different though. He had stayed in the village to attend Yahya's funeral.

"What's your name?" Bassam asked the boy.

The boy trembled. He looked exhausted, his face, clothes, shoes and hair covered with dust – like he'd traveled on foot – a long way.

Bassam loosened the chokehold. He faced the boy. "Speak."

"I have business with Mullah Rashid." The boy shook uncontrollably.

He looked like he was about to pass out. "Are you sick?" Sarah put the palm of her hand on the boy's forehead. "He looks like he's been cooking in the sun."

"Water, please."

Sarah ran inside, grabbed a glass of water and ran back out. "Drink it slowly," she advised.

The boy's eyes rolled back and his extremities went limp.

"Looks like heat stroke," Sarah said. "Let's take him inside."

"It could be a trick." Bassam sounded uneasy.

"It is not a trick, Bassam." Afaf said echoing Sarah's concern. "His face is red like a tomato and he can't stand up. What's he going to do? Attack three of us? Let's go in."

Bassam dragged the boy inside the house.

"There's no sign of the others. How come you're back before the rest?" Afaf asked her husband.

"I couldn't take it anymore. When we reached the gravesite, Um Yahya was already there. I bet she was grateful to be covered with the abaaya so no one could see her abused body. But I could see her eyes. That was enough for me. I had to leave, or kill that bastard husband of hers. I decided he wasn't worth my spending the rest of my life in jail."

"Are they almost done?" Sarah asked.

"Just about. Dr. Tuqan is with Um Yahya trying to convince her to leave the gravesite. Abu Yahya has prostrated himself on his son's grave. He looks worse than dead, but no one is paying much attention to him, especially Rashid. He kept his back turned to the old man the whole time."

Afaf helped the boy sit on the sofa, gave him some more water, while Sarah brought a wet towel and put it on the boy's forehead.

The crowd of mourners could be seen emerging from across the field returning home.

"I'll wait outside for Suheil," Sarah offered. "I think the boy needs help."

"No need to," Afaf replied. "The sun is a killer this time of day. I'm sure Dr. Tuqan will figure out you're here with us. He will come here."

Slowly, after small, repeated sips of water, the boy said he felt better. Occasionally, he looked at Bassam but made a conscious effort to avoid eye contact with the women. He was from a town north of the village, a day's walk. He had anticipated arriving at the village late that evening at the earliest, but he had managed to hitch hike rides on a donkey back and a short distance on a motorcycle.

"Why are you here?" Bassam gazed at the boy intensely.

"I have business with Mullah Rashid."

"Is he expecting you?"

"No."

"Go on."

"When I got here, I went straight to the mosque. There was no one there. I walked around the village. There was no one anywhere. I kept looking. From a distance I saw this house – I saw someone move. I came closer. I looked. I saw two women."

"You still haven't told me why you were peeping inside my house."

The boy addressed his words to Bassam, his face turned away from the women. "I was looking for a man to ask him where I could find Mullah Rashid."

Sarah and Afaf exchanged knowing glances. The boy did not want to be seen talking to strange women. No problem as far as he was concerned by it could mean serious trouble for the women.

"Mullah Rashid had to direct services at a funeral. He's on his way back now. If you're feeling better we can go out to meet him."

"Oh, no." The boy looked terrified.

Bassam pulled his chair close to the boy's chair. "What's your name?"

"Iyad."

"Would you want to tell me what business you have with Mullah Rashid?"

"No."

Bassam turned and spoke to the women in English. "He is scared of something. I don't know what. Keep an eye on him. I want to go talk to Rashid. He's in bad shape – took it very hard. Yahya was a student Rashid had great hopes for – a sensitive, intelligent young man." He turned to Iyad, asked him to stand up and searched him from head to toe. He found nothing. "Stay where you are. I'll be back shortly."

"You ... You ... mean ..."

"It's O.K." Bassam said with barely concealed exasperation. "The women will not bite you."

The boy, of course, was worried about the consequences of being in the company of women – alone – women who were not covered.

It must be all so very confusing. Sarah thought, for the young, and the old for that matter, to be caught in such conflicting, contradictory attitudes. In the Middle East, most teenagers struggle to survive and they barely manage to do so. Discovering one's self, different attitudes, beliefs, East versus West – what a heavy dose of reality for a young mind to sort out. Overwhelmed, no wonder they often chose the painless, easy way out – ignorance.

"Don't be so hard on him." Afaf spoke in English while

Bassam walked towards the front door. "I know you are concerned about Rashid's safety, but I think you are wrong to suspect a teenager. He can hardly stand on his feet. Give him the benefit of doubt."

Bassam was not pacified. "Radicals have been known to use nine and ten year olds to do their dirty work for them. This one probably got caught before he had a chance to do whatever it is he was sent to do. Be careful until I return."

Bassam did not return for over half an hour. Afaf looked out the window every few minutes, her eyes darting nervously back and forth. "What happened to the mourners coming across the field?" she asked unable to mask her anxiety. "They are no where to be seen." A look of panic remained frozen on her face.

"Would you like me to go check?" Sarah asked. "I don't care if they don't like the way I look. I don't live here."

"I don't care either, and I live here. I'm fortunate to have a husband who has somehow escaped the tyranny of our oppressive customs. Sitting here waiting, neither you nor I can do much but drum our fingers and worry. If watching the boy is not a problem for you, I'd rather go myself."

"No problem. You mind if I fix something for him to eat," Sarah asked. "He looks like he could use it."

"Please, by all means. I should have thought of it myself, but I am not all-together today."

Afaf stepped out.

"Do you go to school, Iyad?" Sarah did not approach the boy, nor did she face him or try to make eye contact.

"No. I finished elementary school. There are no other schools in the village." Iyad's eyes remained glued to his hands placed on his knees.

"Do you work?"

"Sometimes."

"Would you like to go to school?"

Iyad did not answer.

"How about something to eat?"

Iyad hung his head low in an embarrassed manner meaning yes.

Sarah rose, went to the kitchen, warmed a plate of chicken and rice pilaf she found in a pot on a burner. She called Iyad to come to the kitchen and eat.

She could tell he was starved. Although he never looked at her, he devoured the food in a few minutes, wiped his mouth on his sleeve, all the while avoiding eye contact.

There was still no sign of anyone returning from the cemetery. Sarah wanted to look out the window. She also wanted to make sure she could see the boy at all times. She was about to ask him to move to the living room when she heard the tires of a car, her rental car, the only car in the village, take off with a screech from the rock filled dirt courtyard. She rushed to the window and watched, shocked, as Afaf drove the car, like a mad woman, across the field. Sarah was puzzled, a little concerned and quite intrigued. What could prompt Afaf, a perfectly sensible woman, to get behind the wheel of a car which did not belong to her, and drive like she was on a suicide mission? Should she investigate? Should she take the boy with her or trust him to stay put where he is and go alone?

She decided to wait a few minutes.

About five minutes later, the car returned driven by Dr. Tuqan, speeding across the courtyard the same way Afaf had done. He must have taken leave of his senses, Sarah decided. There were others in the back seat, but the doctor drove past so fast that Sarah did not get a chance to see who they were.

She collapsed on the sofa feeling a bone-deep weariness brought about by repeated stress. But it did not last long. She grabbed the boy by his hand and rushed out of the house, the boy protesting all the while.

"What's your problem?" Sarah asked exasperated by the boy's refusal to cooperate.

"I can't tell you."

"Then you are coming with me whether you like it or not.

I have to find out what's going on. If you won't come of your own free will, I will have to drag you."

Iyad started crying. "My father said I should be seen by Mullah Rashid only. The villagers are not supposed to know I'm here. My father said they can't be trusted."

"Iyad, do I look like one of the villagers to you?"

"Please, lady." Iyad's eyes were brimming with tears. "My father gave me strict instructions. He will punish me severely if I don't follow his orders. My business is with Mullah Rashid. Please let me stay inside the house, or anywhere you want me to. Lock me in the bathroom if you wish. The plan was for me to arrive at night and go straight to the mosque." Iyad wiped his eyes with his hands. "It's bad enough that three people have seen me already. If my father hears about it, he will kill me."

Sarah threw her head back and tried to get a grip on herself. The pressure of uncertainty as to what was happening outside the house tested her patience sorely. Yet there was nothing she could do but wait.

It was not a long wait. Within minutes she saw Mullah Rashid walk with determined steps, past the house, towards the mosque.

"There goes Mullah Rashid," Sarah said, happy the wait was over. "We can follow him to the mosque if you like, but the villagers are not too far behind."

"Do you have an abaaya?" the boy asked with a little more bounce in him than Sarah had noticed previously.

"I don't. If you want to see Mullah Rashid, you'll probably have to run across the field to the mosque."

"The lady who was here. When is she coming back?"

"I don't know. Why?"

"I thought perhaps she might have an abaaya, and if not maybe she could ask Mullah Rashid to come here – since you don't trust me here by myself."

"You think I should?"

Still Iyad had not made eye contact. "That's up to you. I

am not a thief and I am not a bad person. My father is a Hajji, a religious man. He is also a very cautious man. I have urgent business with Mullah Rashid. After that I shall immediately head for home."

Sarah weighed her options quickly. Although she had promised Afaf she would watch the boy, she did not think the boy was a threat to anyone. "Stay put," she said and headed for the door.

She hurried to the mosque but realized on the way over that she could not enter the mosque without covering herself. Mullah Rashid did not care but if there were others in the mosque, they could create problems for the cleric for allowing a woman to enter the mosque without cover. She went ahead nonetheless. Perhaps, if the door was open, she could call him or find someone who would.

Fortunately, Mullah Rashid was in the small room where the phone was located, at the entrance to the mosque furiously dialing a phone number. Sarah need not have worried about covering herself. She let out a deep sigh of relief and knocked on the door.

Mullah Rashid opened the door quickly then rushed back to the phone without waiting for her to come in or speaking to her.

A moment later, he put the receiver down. "Can't get a connection," he said.

"Problems?"

"Lots."

She did not like the look of desperation in his eyes, or the pallor of his skin.

"Can you handle more?"

"Do I have a choice?" He regarded her curiously as he sank into the chair behind the desk.

"There's a teenager, fifteen, maybe sixteen, at Afaf's place. He says his name is Iyad and that he has urgent business with you, but he has strict instructions from his father not to be seen in public. Do you want to check him out?"

Mullah Rashid studied his hands folded on his chest for a long moment.

"A teenager you say. Afraid to be seen in public. I have to admit I'm intrigued. I'll go." He gave her a phone number scribbled on a piece of paper. "Try calling this number. It's the hospital in Asyut. If you get through tell them to prepare for an emergency."

A chill shot through Sarah's body. Although aware something drastic must have happened at the cemetery, she hesitated about asking the cleric but could not help herself. She had to know.

"What kind of emergency?" Sarah could barely speak.

"I think he's dead. But Dr. Tuqan insists he can hear heart beats."

It was Sarah's turn to ease herself into the chair. "Who?"

"Abu Yahya. After the boy was buried and I had finished praying, he asked everyone to leave. He said he wanted to be alone with his son one last time. Soon after everyone left, he pulled out his dagger and plunged it in his heart. I should have known. He'd been acting strange since the boy's death, but I attributed it to guilt, to grief, to the pot he smokes all day. But the old man did it." Mullah Rashid shook his head baffled. "I would have never believed it had I not seen it with my own eyes."

Shocked into almost total silence, Sarah could only gasp.

"I never trusted the man. I kept looking over my shoulder. People here refer to him as the village idiot. Once again he lived up to his reputation. The crowd rushed back. Dr. Tuqan rushed back – pulled the dagger out of his chest. He tried everything. I can say without hesitation, I have known very few men like Suheil Tuqan and certainly no doctors. You are a woman blessed."

She was also a woman filled with terror and revulsion.

Blinking back tears, incapable and unwilling to voice her pain, she saw with ruthless clarity the trap ignorance had set up for these people. The wasted lives, the irreversible damage to body, mind and soul and the ignorance that fueled it multiply right before her eyes – incessantly. The so-called experts who advocated and perpetuated outmoded social, cultural and religious codes designed to hold and tighten their grip on an unsuspecting, submissive, trusting public forced her into a sense of desperation which had never been more profound.

Mullah Rashid permitted himself a touch of sardonic comment. "I'm often reminded that life is for the living. Man, what a life!" His voice trailed off. He opened the door and stepped out.

Sarah dropped her head in her hands and wept.

A few moments later, she rose. Her parents had always encouraged her to speak out, cry if necessary – to vent her pain, her anger, her frustrations. Never keep inside you what ails you, her mother advised her every chance she got. Her parents believed firmly in the therapeutic value of sharing one's pain and sorrow with family and close friends. In the past, that advice had served Sarah well. She reached for the receiver and dialed the number Rashid had given her.

She couldn't get through. However, she did not stop trying.

She was dialing the number yet again when the cleric opened the door and walked in with the boy.

"Can't get through." Sarah felt compelled to make a remark about the obvious – just to make conversation. "I tried repeatedly. Sometimes it rang busy, sometimes nothing happened, and sometimes it rang and rang but no one answered."

"Don't bother. Often it takes days. I figure at some point even Dr. Tuqan will give up, turn around, and return to the village. I spoke to Bassam before they left. I told him to convince Dr. Tuqan not to waste his time on a dead man. Dr. Tuqan is a man in bad need of a vacation. He told me when you return to Jordan, come what may, he plans to take you to the Dead Sea for a week. I understand it is a unique experience not to be missed."

Why is he discussing the Dead Sea when he knows I'm

waiting not too patiently to hear what the boy had to say? Luckily, I can keep a blank expression on my face while I'm boiling inside.

He kept staring at her unabashedly, as though calculating what he planned to say or do, but said nothing.

Perhaps he wants me to leave so he can be alone with the boy. In his polite way he probably wants me to understand that what the boy has to say is none of my business. Sarah headed for the door. "I will wait for Suheil at Afaf's place."

"Please don't go," he murmured his voice barely audible.

"The boy. He wants to speak to you – privately. He said so several times before you returned from the cemetery."

After an awkward pause, the cleric reached in his pocket, pulled out a piece of paper and handed it to Sarah. "I know you can read Arabic and I know I can trust you."

Sarah hesitated. Whatever the message, she wasn't quite sure she wanted to get involved.

His voice calm, measured, Mullah Rashid said, "I have often come dangerously close to sharing my intimate thoughts with the walls of my room. If it is not too much to ask, please read the note and let me know what you think."

Chapter 23

"I CAN'T LEAVE NOW," Mullah Rashid protested. "And please call me Rashid."

It was past midnight. Sarah, Suheil, Afaf and Bassam had spent the past four hours urging Mullah Rashid to take steps to protect himself. Iyad's father, Abu Iyad, a pious man, among the few who admired and appreciated the work done by Mullah Rashid, had come to know the cleric on one of the many pilgrimages he took to Mecca. It took a lot of guts to risk his and his son's safety to warn the cleric, but it was not a surprise to his friend. He was the one man Mullah Rashid invariably pointed to when he wanted to impress others with what the Prophet's teachings could do for the spiritual well being of an individual.

Abu Iyad was a very wealthy man who lived an extremely simple life; helped the poor and the widowed, had married only once, treated his wife as an equal partner and his sons and daughters were loved equally by both parents. He kept an open house for abused women and children. They could stay as long as they wished – often permanently. Abu Iyad abhorred violence and fighting injustice was his crusade in life – hence his close relationship with Mullah Rashid.

The note advised Mullah Rashid to leave Egypt – immediately. Abu Iyad had information through his contacts in Saudi Arabia that Muslim activists belonging to a secret organization known as the Saudi Hizballah were in Egypt looking for Mullah Rashid. It was their contention that his teachings were anti Islamic, therefore he was an enemy of the people, and therefore had to be eliminated.

They also regarded with disdain the fact that Mullah

Rashid encouraged the same kind of teaching in recently opened schools under his supervision. Their main objection however, was the unyielding refusal of the cleric to permit clitoridectomies. Clitoridectomies were an integral part of a girl's initiation to womanhood, although it had nothing to do with Islam – a fact no fundamentalist Muslim was willing to admit. No cleric had the right to take that privilege away from families who had practiced it for centuries and felt deprived if prevented from doing so.

"That's supposed to be a top secret organization backed by Iran, revolutionaries fighting to overthrow the present regime in Saudi Arabia," Sarah said. "These fundamentalist dissidents are no better than the repressive governments they are working to overthrow. I know. They wanted money from my father, aware of his aversion to injustice. They met with him twice, in London, claiming to be true representatives of the faith. My father pointed out to them the irony of their statement when their weapon of choice was violence. You must think as the Hizballah do and do as they say – or else they snuff the life out of you. It's that simple."

"She's right," Suheil added. "When I was working in Saudi Arabia, what we referred to as the executioner's square, and foreigners called 'chop-chop square' was often cited as an example of the extreme harshness of the Saudi government's handling of dissent. I ask you, what difference does it make if an executioner slices your head off in a public square, or a fanatic puts a few bullets in you in some dark street corner. In both instances the destination of the victim is the same – a grave."

They had all gathered in Afaf's house after delivering the body of Abu Yahya to his wife and sending Iyad back home in the rented car with a trusted employee of the mosque.

Mullah Rashid dropped his head in his hands seemingly lost in thought. Eventually he looked up as though at an invisible audience. "The unthinkable," he said, "has become the unstoppable in no time at all. Who would have believed only

fifteen years ago, that Islam, once again, would be used to ter-
rorize the world when all the Prophet strove for all his life was
for peace. The only consolation for those of us who care is
that the other religions have had their share of abuse as well."

"Those who care are in the minority," Sarah said, "especially among the clergy. That's why you must leave. We can't
afford to lose you."

"Perhaps Abu Iyad is over reacting," Mullah Rashid said
without much conviction in his voice.

"Do you really think he would risk his and his son's life,"
Sarah asked with forced calm. "And you know that's exactly
what would happen if the Hizballah were to suspect him.
He'd be dead man and Iyad would be dead as well. Do you
really think Abu Iyad would go through the trouble of warning you without being positively sure about the accuracy of
his information when he knew how much was at stake?"

Mullah Rashid looked at her with eyes that seemed to
probe and evaluate. Eventually he said, "You are far wiser
than your age. But you set a bad example. If anybody should
leave, it should be you. You are a woman. Your job is far
tougher than mine."

Sarah let out a nervous laugh. "You call a death threat by
Islamist holy warriors less worrisome than the occasional
harassment I'm subjected to trying to educate children? Come
now Rashid, I am sure we can work out some kind of arrangement. A short vacation perhaps – until the storm blows over. I
am sure Bassam and Afaf can cover for you for a while.
Maybe not your clerical duties. But all the rest of the stuff you
do around here."

"Occasional harassment," the cleric murmured to no one
in particular. He seemed to be on a totally different wavelength. "She calls it occasional harassment. Allah have mercy
on us all."

Sarah heard him. Said nothing.

Bassam and Afaf assured Mullah Rashid they would be
more than happy to help. As for religious matters, Bassam had

been studying with Mullah Rashid the past two years and felt confident he could fill in during the cleric's absence, or if the cleric preferred they could ask for a temporary replacement from Asyutí.

"No." Sarah's voice was full of apprehension. "No one must know Rashid is leaving – not before he leaves. Bassam, while he's gone, if you have a religious problem you cannot solve, you might consider requesting help. Meanwhile, all you know about Mullah Rashid's absence is that he has disappeared."

Mullah Rashid, still distant continued talking to himself. "A vacation?" He laughed – like it was a word he had not heard before. "I have never had a vacation in my life. I wouldn't know what to do with myself."

"Then it's time you found out," Suheil spoke for the first time. "You'll come with us to Jordan. We have a small cabin at the Dead Sea. Remember? I talked to you about it. It's an ideal place to relax. We'll even allow you to bring your books. What do you say?"

Mullah Rashid rose and paced the room. But not for long. He stopped, faced Sarah and Suheil, a hazy expression on his face. "So much has happened in the past two days that we have forgotten why you are here in the first place. We have a young girl totally disfigured, who cannot expect help from anyone but us. We know you can't take her to Jordan. The formalities will take months – if at all possible. And, we also know that regardless of the impediments, we have got to get her treated. The most appropriate location in my opinion is Cairo. We can inquire, find a good plastic surgeon and hope he can help her. Someone has to take responsibility to get the job done, though. I think that someone has to be me. Hind's eye ... her face ... she ..."

"You're talking months, many months, perhaps a year," Dr. Tuqan said. "You can't take that much time off even if you wanted to. We have to arrange for her to stay with a family."

Mullah Rashid did not answer immediately. He resumed

his pacing of the room. A minute later, he turned slowly to face Suheil and Sarah. "And why did I suddenly decide to take a vacation?"

Why indeed? Sarah thought except that you look like a man who minutes ago walked away from a plane crash, a man at the end of his wits, a man so tortured you're zoning out while you speak. Yes indeed. You are a man in desperate need of a change of scenery.

Dr. Tuqan leaned forward in his armchair palms clasped beneath his chin. His eyes narrowed and his jaw tightened for a full minute before he said, "As a physician I recommend that you take a vacation immediately to give your nerves much needed rest. My being here is no secret. Therefore, it should not be a problem."

"Who do you have to answer to?" Sarah asked.

Rashid did not reply. He paced the room.

Sarah waited a few seconds then repeated the question.

Rashid's gloom seemed to deepen. "No one, really," he said tonelessly. "I minister on my own. But I feel I should notify the central mosque in Cairo – just in case. They have not appointed a cleric for this region because they know I'm here."

"You really think you should?" It was Suheil.

Rashid said he didn't know what to think.

"In his note Abu Iyad urged you to leave Egypt immediately," Sarah reminded Rashid. "Who knows how long it will take to notify Cairo then wait around for an answer."

"Also," Suheil added, "you might be putting the lives of Abu Iyad and his son in danger. I reckon Abu Iyad sent his son on a long journey, on foot, to warn you, because he did not want to phone you at the mosque. You have been marked for elimination. Therefore, your phone is tapped. Abu Iyad knows as much. If you call Cairo and the terrorists learn about it, don't you think they'll figure out you were tipped off? Don't you think they will want to know by whom?"

Mullah Rashid dropped his body in an armchair, a far-away look in his eyes. He did not respond.

"Your only option is to leave Egypt as soon as possible." Sarah felt and sounded weary.

Afaf and Bassam joined in the conversation after serving everyone a glass of cold lemonade. They urged Mullah Rashid to leave immediately for his own sake and for the peace of mind of those who cared about him. They reassured him they would do the best they could until his return.

Mullah Rashid was not convinced. He felt they were wasting too much time figuring out what to do to help him, instead of concentrating their efforts on finding a solution for the problem that had brought them to the village in the first place.

"Sarah and I will leave for Cairo in the morning," Suheil said. "I met a couple of surgeons from Cairo last year at the surgical conference in Amman. If I can locate them, and I think I can. I'm sure half our problem will be solved."

"I'll go with Hind to Cairo," Afaf offered. "They won't let her travel alone."

"That's great." Sarah was impressed with the way Afaf took charge of matters – quickly and efficiently. "We'll call you from Cairo as soon as we have all the details worked out."

"It's settled then," Suheil added. "We'll notify Jim. Rashid will go to Cairo – from there to Amman, and we'll catch up with him in Amman after we make all the necessary arrangements for Hind in Cairo."

Mullah Rashid was again on his feet pacing the room.

"What's on your mind?" Sarah asked. "You don't seem to think much of our suggestions."

Rashid paused, shifted his gaze from the walls of the living room to Sarah and Suheil. "Consider this," he said. "By coming to Jordan, I will not only risk your lives but the lives of those left behind. Hizballah is small and secret in Saudi Arabia, fearful of the swift and terrible response they will undoubtedly receive if discovered. They are extremely limited in what they can do. Yet they managed to send two members to track down and eliminate an individual who refuses to tow their line. Let me remind you also that they have no such restraints outside Saudi Arabia. The organization has branches in all Arab countries and Europe, bankrolled by Iran. Now how long do you think it will take them to locate me, especially after they learn that you two have been here."

Frustrated, angry, Sarah rose, went to the kitchen for a drink of water and to think. The problems in the Middle East were like the many-headed hydra of mythology. Cut one off and think you're done – think again. But you won't have time. Many more pop up in its place – immediately. There was truth in what Mullah Rashid had pointed out. Hizballah, by any perspective was a ruthless organization, Jordan a stronghold. They'd be on to them in no time. Mullah Rashid's concern for others was also justified. Hizballah members were well known for their lack of compassion towards those who did not cooperate with them, be it giving information, or turning in individuals wanted by the organization. But what about him? There had to be a place he could go to, at least for a little while.

Then it hit her.

Although Hizballah most probably had small cells in the States, she had not read or heard anything to make her think that they were as active in the U.S. as they were in the Middle East and Europe.

"What about a trip to the States?" Her words came tumbling out.

The cleric acquired a grave look. He stared at her for a full minute before responding. "I truly appreciate your concern. All of you. I want you to know that. But I don't expect you to know how long it takes to get a visa to the States. I mean people spend days outside the embassy to eventually submit their applications and then wait and hope that they will be granted entry. I'd love to go to the States. I have good friends there. I'm afraid though, by the time I get a visa, if I get a visa, it might be too late."

Mullah Rashid pulled a chair, dropped his body in it and let his head fall back resigned.

"Getting a visa is not a problem," Sarah said without elaboration. "We can get it for you."

The cleric shot up like a missile, disbelief apparent on his face. "You're kidding, right?"

"No."

She could almost see the debate raging inside his head. "Rashid, don't torture yourself. You're no good to anyone dead and that's what you will be if you don't leave this place and leave immediately. We don't need martyrs – just honest, well informed, open-minded individuals devoted to spreading the truth. To see how the rest of the world lives will give you a better perspective of life in all its aspects. When this madness is over, you will return and do your work in a less hostile environment. Hopefully. Maybe."

"I have to admit. You are very convincing. And the thought of going to the States is an improbable dream I have dreamt about many a time. But I can't simply pack a bag and leave. What about all the people who depend on me? I can't dump all my responsibilities on Afaf and Bassam and take off. I ... I ... need time to think, time to ..."

He was interrupted in mid sentence by a loud noise, like an explosion, from a near distance. The vibrations reverberated across the house shattering glass, displacing objects not anchored in place.

Instantly every one in the room took refuge on the floor.

Within seconds, it was absolutely quiet again.

"The lights." It was Mullah Rashid.

Bassam reached for the light switch.

The intense heat which had previously forced Sarah to down gallons of water, had little effect on her as a chill coursed through her being and made her shiver. After that, she was covered with a cold perspiration that seemed to want to remain stuck to her flesh.

Minutes passed. No one dared moved or speak. Sarah shivered and listened.

Slowly, Suheil crept close to her, put his arm around her shoulder and his body next to hers.

Although still terrified, her body relented and gradually shook less.

Minutes more passed. Except for the Mullah's labored breathing, nothing more could be heard.

"I think it's over." Rashid's voice was subdued, barely audible.

"Sounded like a gas tank," Afaf whispered.

"That was no gas tank. It was a bomb." Mullah Rashid's teeth chattered.

Sarah gasped. The violent trembling resumed.

"They must have gotten here sooner than we imagined." Bassam crawled next to his wife.

"You think?" Suheil asked.

Sarah opened her mouth to speak but no words came out.

Suheil pulled her close to him.

"No doubt," Mullah Rashid replied his voice a whisper. "In the villages people go to bed soon after dark, especially in these parts where there's no electricity. The mosque has a generator. Afaf and Bassam have one too. But the villagers don't. I suspect they scouted the area, figured where my quarters were, expected me to be there and took action."

"If you're right," Suheil whispered his voice cracking, "that's bad news. The lights here were on and we might be their next target."

"Not until they learn I was not in my quarters. They follow orders. That takes time."

"Meanwhile," Suheil said, "the best thing we can do is to figure out a way to get out of here undetected. You, Sarah and I."

"Keep your voices low," Afaf reminded everyone. "The windows are open."

For a while, no one spoke. Everyone was thinking.

Bassam was the first to break the silence. He suggested they shut the windows, turn on a couple of fans he'd recently bought in Asyut, but not turn the lights back on. There were no streets or streetlights in the village. Only one dirt road. The villagers used kerosene lamps. If they had heard the blast, and there was no way they could have missed it, they would not light their lamps so as not to attract attention. "If what Rashid suspects happens to be true," he said, "then no doubt they noticed our lights were on. I will go out and head for the mosque. If I am stopped and questioned, I will say my wife is sick. I am on my way to the mosque to call a doctor. Afaf should be in bed and the rest of you hide in the bathroom until I return."

"Can't let you do that," Rashid objected.

"Sorry, but this once I will not take your advice," Bassam replied. "If no one has a better idea, I should be off before our friends from Hizballah pay us a visit."

"My guess is they won't," Rashid said. "They probably took off immediately after the explosion. They don't want to be caught and questioned."

"Maybe, maybe not," Bassam replied. "It's better to check."

In the darkness, Sarah, Suheil and Rashid made their way to the bathroom. Afaf took her clothes off, slipped into a nightgown and crawled in bed. Bassam stepped out, flashlight in hand.

He was back within the hour.

His report forced the mullah to shelve any objections he might still have entertained. The clerics quarters; two small rooms, a kitchenette and a bathroom attached to the mosque, had been reduced to a pile of bricks, broken glass and dust. Complete demolition. Nothing was left of it. Nothing except a frying pan which somehow had landed yards away from the cleric's quarters. Bassam had accidentally kicked it on his way to the mosque. Except for the wall to which the cleric's quarters were attached, there was no damage to the rest of the mosque. Not the work of amateurs Bassam concluded. He had searched the area as well as he could with his flashlight. He had seen no one but he had noticed impressions of car tires on the dirt road leading from the mosque north.

"In a way," Sarah said, "this is good news. They'll think Rashid is dead. Until they learn otherwise, we can sneak him into safety."

"How?" Suheil looked quite upset. "We don't have a car until morning. We sent the boy back with it, remember?"

Think, Sarah told herself, think. There's got to be a way.

"Buses start passing through the village at five every morning," Bassam said. "I suggest Rashid get rid of his religious garb and his beard, cover himself with an abaaya, get on a bus and go as far as it will take him. There are buses all the way to Cairo. I admit it's not the most comfortable form of transportation, but at least chances are he'll get there without being recognized."

Rashid shook his head in disbelief. "You want me to pretend to be a woman? Surely you jest."

"Not at all. The longer it takes for the terrorists to know your whereabouts, the better your chances. With that beard and clerical garb you can't be missed. As a woman, covered, you'll have no trouble."

"Hey," Sarah joked. "Maybe being a woman is not so bad after all, and maybe we can use the abaaya to our advantage – for a change."

"It's crazy," Rashid replied. "It's crazy." A moment later he added, "But it might, just might work."

Sarah was surprised that the cleric accepted the word of Bassam and based upon that, without checking the place out for himself seemed to agree.

He sensed her misgiving. "It's not the first time they've tried to get me," he said, with a voice devoid of emotion. "I've lost count – except that the level of violence escalates with each renewed attack. I had hoped that they would leave me alone in the villages. Obviously I was wrong. They get a lot of feedback from the Sheikh in Jordan. I am a thorn in his side. Doesn't matter where I am, what I do. He'll find something I've said or done and use it to single me out as an enemy of Islam."

"Why?" The word tumbled out of Sarah's mouth before she could stop herself.

"Because he's an immoral man. He abuses his position to rape, lie and steal. And he knows I know."

Sarah and Suheil exchanged knowing glances.

"He's one of the principal reasons I don't want to vacation in Jordan."

"But he's in Jordan and you're here in a remote village. Why should it matter to him? Who keeps him informed?" All kinds of questions crowded Sarah's thoughts.

"He's in Jordan now but he was in Cairo before where my family lives. He is the cleric, who, without our knowledge forced clitoridectomy on my sister, my sister who eventually bled to death. He does them himself. I think he derives some kind of sadistic pleasure from it. No I don't think. I know he does. He told me so himself." Rashid eased his body into a chair, put his face in his hands, shook as he struggled to control his anger.

"We heard he was in an accident in Damascus," Bassam said after awhile. "But he's like a cat with nine lives. He always recovers."

"He's known as 'the butcher' by the villagers," Afaf said. "He'd go to the village of his choice and perform mass clitoridectomies masquerading the procedure as a religious dictate. It's an obsession with him." Afaf stopped, then whispered, "Did you hear that?"

The knocking on the front door was repeated.

Bassam approached the front door, slowly, cautiously, turned the outside light on long enough to see who the person at the door was. It was Yahya's younger brother. "My mother said to come warn you. Two men are snooping around asking questions."

Bassam grabbed the boy by the arm and pulled him inside. "What kind of questions?" He quickly switched the light off.

"About Miss Sarah and the doctor."

"What did your mother tell them?"

"She said they should go to the mosque and ask Mullah Rashid."

"What else?"

"Nothing. They wanted to know if the doctor and Miss Sarah were still in the village. My mother said she had buried her first born son today, was sick, in a relatives house. Had no idea who was where."

"How come they came over to your place?"

"Hind woke us up. She was in a lot of pain. We had to light the lamp."

Bassam thanked the boy and told him to return home quietly and thank his mother. He'd talk to her first thing in the morning.

"Wait." It was Dr. Tuqan. "I had left some pills with Hind for pain. Do you know if she took them?"

"She said they didn't help."

"Give me the flashlight." Dr. Tuqan reached in his medical bag, found the pain killer pills he was looking for and handed them to the boy. "Tell Hind to take one tablet now and one more in four hours if she still has pain."

The boy stuck the pills in his pant's pocket and slipped out the door quietly.

"It doesn't compute," Bassam said, as he groped his way back to the living room. "Like Rashid mentioned before, why would they take a chance at being caught. Enough time has passed for security to learn about it. Anyone living in Egypt knows the government has an extensive network of agents all over Egypt, especially in the villages. That's where the fanatics focus their efforts most – to indoctrinate and recruit."

Of course it doesn't compute, Sarah thought. I bet there's more than one group at work here. The mere thought of it brought back the gnawing feeling at the pit of her stomach – with vengeance. She winced from the pain.

"They'll probably check us out next," Afaf said.

"No doubt about it." It was Bassam. "They'll see the house even though there's no light outside. There's enough moonlight."

"We must be prepared." Afaf went to the bedroom and came out with two blankets. "And it's late. We could all use a little sleep, I'm sure. There's a spare bed in the other room. Maybe you gentlemen can sleep on the floor and let Sarah have the bed. If they come, they'll have to deal with Bassam and me."

Aided only with illumination from the flashlight, it took them a few minutes to find a spot for their blankets and for Sarah to get to bed.

Someone hammered on the door.

Bassam switched the lights on and opened the door.

Two men pushed their way in guns bulging from their belts.

"We saw the light above the front door of your house come on for a few seconds then go off. Did you have visitors at one thirty in the morning?"

"Excuse me. Who are you? What do you want?" It sounded like fear forced Bassam to control the level of indignation in his voice, yet let his visitors know they were not welcome.

"An answer." One of the two men did the talking. The other made sure Bassam noticed his gun.

"Are you from security?"

The two men exchanged glances. "We ask the questions." It was the turn of the man who spoke to rearrange the position of his gun. "Why did you switch the lights on?"

"Is there a law against having the lights on in one's own house at one thirty in the morning?"

"Bassam," came a voice from the bedroom. "Could you please hurry up. Bring me a bowl or something. I can't hold my vomit much longer."

Bassam faced the men. "Excuse me gentlemen. My wife is ill. She's been throwing up all night. I have to help her."

As he turned to go, one of the men said in a loud voice, "Why don't you have the doctor check her?"

Bassam turned back slowly, a blank expression on his face. "What doctor? Do you know something I don't?"

"Where have you been, Mr. ..."

"I believe you heard my name called. I was touring the surrounding villages the past two days as I always do every Sunday and Monday."

"Bassam," Afaf yelled from the bedroom followed by serious noises like vomiting, followed by a brief period of quiet. "What's keeping you so long. Could you please hurry up."

Bassam opened the front door. "Gentlemen. I don't know what you want from me and I don't believe it's any of your business. But if you must know, I turned the front lights on to go to the mosque to call a doctor. My wife would not let me. Sometimes it takes hours to get through. She didn't want to be left alone in the house."

The men exchanged glances, shrugged their shoulders, hesitated, then walked out.

Bassam was about to shut the door when he heard the man who had done the talking say to his partner, "Let's check the mosque."

It was only after he shut the door that the full impact of the gravity of the situation hit him and he collapsed on the couch, the lights still on. Afaf rushed out of the bedroom, while Sarah cracked the door of the room they were in and peeped. "Come on out," Afaf urged. "They're gone. I think Bassam needs help. He looks like he just saw a ghost."

"Two ghosts," Bassam corrected. "Bloodthirsty ghosts. Actually there was nothing ghostly about them. They were very real, they were here, and they made sure I knew they were armed. One wrong word, one wrong move is a guarantee for a quick trip to the mortuary." Bassam sounded weary, overwhelmed. He shook his head vigorously, again and again. Sarah could not fathom why. Finally he stopped and said, "Funny thing though, one of the men did not say a word."

"That's because he was Palestinian," Rashid said. "He was here with an Egyptian to help him locate his victims. That's how they operate. If the Palestinian spoke, you would know right away he's not Egyptian and could not possibly be from security. We were listening. When you asked them if they were from security, the man who spoke in Egyptian dialect changed the subject."

The same gnawing pain at the pit of Sarah's stomach was back again. Bassam was having a hard time accepting there was more than one group at work, in one night, in a village with thirty mud huts. So did Sarah. Rashid's explanation made sense. Had the Palestinian spoken, it would have betrayed his nationality thus making him suspect, it would have also made it easy for Bassam to figure out that he was not with the Saudi Hizballah. The Saudi dialect is distinctly different from the dialects of other Arab countries. Did the two groups know about each other, or was it just coincidence that they happened to plan their operation for the same night in the same remote village. The Sheikh immediately crossed her mind. Could he, Sarah wondered, could he have possibly been involved, perhaps even planned both operations. Her gut feeling was that her suspicions were well founded. He would not be suspected. He was in another country and how was he supposed to know that Sarah and Dr. Tuqan were in Egypt. And even if he knew, how could he have time to put into action any plans he might have devised on short notice.

"You think too much," said Rashid interrupting her thoughts.

She told him her suspicions.

"Come now, Sarah." She saw the hint of a smile curl Rashid's lips for the first time. "You can't be so naíve. You underestimate the man. He is magnificently endowed with a gift which analyzes the reaction of people to certain situations. He creates the situation, waits for the reaction from the intended victim, proceeds with his plan. He knows he can't hurt you in Jordan. He's not too crazy about having more broken bones. What better opportunity could he have created to get back at you?"

It hit Sarah like a bolt of lightning. She was speechless. How did such devious thoughts take control of a person, of his life? Incredible.

"And we fell right into his trap." Suheil looked as shocked as Sarah.

"Not much we can do about that now," Bassam said. "It's important for us to find a way to get you three out of here as soon as possible without help from our night visitors."

"How?" Sarah asked. "On donkey back? I see no other option."

The constant bombardment of unanticipated conse-quences from the events of the past two days had frazzled Sarah's nerves to a degree which began to scare her. "I'm sorry, everybody," she added quickly, "But perhaps a dose of reality is in order."

Rashid agreed. He suggested scouting the village and surrounding areas before dawn. There was always the possi-bility that the men who bombed the mosque and the men who were looking for Sarah might be lurking in some unexpected spot waiting for their prey to step out.

It was futile for anyone to go to bed. It would be dawn soon. Sarah parted the drapes ever so slightly, every few min-utes to check. When situations forced her to feel helpless, she balked. That pushed her gray cells into overdrive. She groped her way close to Afaf. "Any chance we can borrow a couple of abaayas from one of the women in the village?"

"Sure. But how to get there is the problem."

"I could go," Bassam offered. "But what explanation can I give? Afaf makes a big issue of persuading women here and everywhere she gets a chance, to get rid of their abaayas. What do I say she wants it for?"

"Go to the mosque," Rashid said. "There's a closet at the entrance where there's stacks of them. They are delivered to the mosque courtesy of the Saudi government so no woman can use lack of funds as an excuse for not covering herself. I usually burn them. But there's more arriving all the time. Sometimes the workers stick them in the closet before I have a chance to see them."

"I don't think it's a good idea for Bassam to go to the mosque, unarmed, when there's definitely the possibility that any one of those men could be out there." Sarah had reached the saturation point with violence and was not prepared to face more. At least not right away.

"They're gone," Rashid said without hesitation. "They will not wait for sunrise when the whole village wakes up, everybody knows everyone else and they're sure to be questioned as to the purpose of their visit. They're not worried about the villagers. They're concerned about security officers masquerading as villagers. Hosni Mubarak's government leaves nothing to chance."

"Even so," Sarah said, "it would be wise for Afaf and me to take a good look around before we proceed with any plan."

"No." It was Dr. Tuqan. "You shouldn't go Sarah. It's too dangerous."

Daylight seeped into the house, through the curtains with blinding rays as the sun climbed to its almighty position in the bright, blue sky. Sarah walked over, planted a kiss on Suheil's forehead. "I'm not in the habit of asking others to do my dirty work for me, darling. I'm a big girl, quite capable of taking care of myself."

Suheil rose, shifted his weight from one foot to the other. He wanted to know how far Abu Iyad's home was and when Rashid's assistant was likely to return with the rental car.

"It's only about fifteen kilometers from here," Rashid said. "However, the roads are real bad. I told him to spend the night and drive back in the morning. Morning means dawn here. If he spent the night there, which he probably did – he should be back any time now."

Sarah watched Suheil ease himself slowly onto the sofa engulfed in deep thought. There's a malignancy spreading around these countries, a malignancy fueled by ignorance, perpetuated by violence and repression. It has disaster written all over it. Tyranny marches on unabated affecting the lives of every man, woman and child. If, the select few who, maybe, just maybe, have a chance to help stem the tide of fanaticism quit when the going gets rough, then they have no right to think of themselves as any different than the perpetrators of the same chaotic social order they so vehemently condemn. She approached Suheil. "There's no need for doom and gloom, darling. Remember, that was the one prerequisite of our relationship. If we get discouraged, frightened, or worst yet, quit, we would have satisfied every wish the extremists have. It would also make it that much harder for others to follow in our footsteps now or in the future. I really feel you should snap out of it. You're no good to anyone, much less yourself in a state of perpetual anxiety."

Suheil rubbed his eyes with his hands and rose. "O.K. What do you want to do? You want abaayas so you can scout the area. Fine. Go ahead. I'm sure Rashid knows what he's talking about. Maybe they're gone. Maybe they left a contact behind. Who knows? I don't feel comfortable sending you out there."

"It's got to be done, Suheil. That's all there is to it."

Bassam stepped out the door in his stocking feet, put his sneakers on, stuck his head inside the door before he left to remind everyone, if questioned, to say he went to the mosque to call a doctor for his sick wife. Rashid gave Bassam the keys to the front door of the mosque and the key to the adjacent room where the telephone was located.

He was back in fifteen minutes carrying two abaayas. He gave the abaayas to his wife and the keys to Rashid. "I did not need the keys. You left the doors open."

The cleric just about fell off the sofa. "Say that again."

"The doors were open."

"God have mercy on us. Did anything seem out of order, broken, whatever?"

"No. I didn't see anything out of place. I checked your quarters, I mean what's left of it. The rubble from last night looked bigger, but then I could only look at it with a flashlight before."

Rashid stroked his beard as he rose and paced the room.

"You saw no one in the mosque."

"No."

"You checked."

"Of course. There isn't that much to check. It's just a room."

Rashid continued to pace the room. "The closet. Was the closet open?"

"No. It was shut but not locked."

"It never is."

"Are you sure you locked it?" Suheil asked the cleric, his concern mounting as he watched the cleric pace his lips tightly shut.

"Absolutely. My most precious possessions, my books, I keep in the mosque. Locked in bookcases. There's not enough room for them in my quarters."

Afaf motioned for Sarah to follow her. "We'll go check."

They put on their shoes always left outside the door of the entrance to the house – a custom Sarah appreciated and followed. Then they unfolded the abaayas.

Only the eyes remained uncovered under the black tent which now covered the women. The village was just beginning to wake up but few had ventured out of their homes yet. The women decided to check the mosque first.

Bassam had not exaggerated when he said Rashid's quarters were totaled. Even the frying pan, their first encounter, was bent out of shape. Sarah's attention was caught by a set of tires leading to the entrance of the mosque. She walked to the back. Two set of tire imprints had left their mark on the dirt road. Once again, it did not compute. One car came to the mosque and two cars left. Impossible. There had to be another explanation. Afaf was as baffled.

They decided to check inside the mosque. Rashid's books which worried him so, remained locked in their bookcases. Or so they hoped since they did not have keys to open them.

Suddenly Afaf whirled around. "Did you hear that?" she asked.

"Sure did. Let's get out of here."

The women pulled the abaayas over their faces, opened the door of the mosque, and were about to step out when two policemen blocked their way.

Chapter 24

Y OUNG, SLEEPY-EYED, IN UNIFORMS WHICH looked like they had been bought from a used clothing store a decade ago, the two policemen, mustaches stretching from ear to ear, stared at Afaf and Sarah looking shocked, flabbergasted. Eventually, the policeman with the bushier mustache pulled himself together and demanded an explanation.

"Keep yourself well covered," Afaf whispered to Sarah in English. She turned to the policeman who had spoken to them."We heard a loud noise. It sounded like it came from the mosque. We thought maybe something had exploded – a gas tank perhaps."

"When did you hear the noise?"

"Soon after midnight. We were scared. We wanted to wait for sunrise to come check."

The policemen looked at each other.

"I don't recognize them." Afaf restricted her conversations with Sarah to English, in whispers. "I know everyone in the surrounding areas. These men are outsiders. It shouldn't be too difficult to get rid of them though. Their pay is so pitiful. Any amount will do. Do you have any money on you?"

"I left my purse at your place."

"Where are your husbands?" The other policeman asked with forced authority in his voice. The way he said it left Sarah with the impression that he wanted to be recognized too.

"Look who's here," Afaf murmured as a man appeared from behind the building.

"Where are your husbands?" The policeman who had asked the question before repeated it with obvious annoyance.

Neither Sarah, nor Afaf, was surprised by the question. In the society they lived in, women their age had husbands. If not, they were widowed. And women did not do investigating – anywhere – and much less at dawn.

"Oh, yes, excuse me," Afaf said, like someone caught day dreaming. "Our husbands ... Our husbands are home – asleep."

"Your husbands are asleep and you are out here for who knows how long. How come you did not wake them up. How come you chose to come out here in the middle of the night when it is more than likely that something drastic has happened."

"Damn," Afaf murmured under her breath as she searched her pockets. "I often find money in my pockets."

"You'll have to come with us," said the policeman with the bushier mustache. The frantic searched in her pockets sent an unfortunate message to the two policemen. It was not hard for them to guess the women had no money to give them.

"Fawzi." Afaf raised her voice as the newcomer approached hesitantly to check the situation. "Go ask my husband to come here right away."

Rashid's assistant, a young man in his early twenties, stopped, stared, rubbed his eyes, stared again. "Is that you Mrs. Afaf?"

His voice cracked badly. Sounded like he was about to cry.

"It's me, all right. Hurry up. Go call Bassam."

Fawzi did not move.

Angered, Afaf marched towards him. "Can't you see the police are here. What are you waiting for?"

Fawzi trembled, stuck his hands in his pant's pocket, pulled one hand quickly back out, and rubbed the back of his head. "I called the police Mrs. Afaf. Mullah Rashid is dead. They killed him. Have you seen his place? It's a pile of rubble." The man broke down, dropped himself on the dirt ground, held his face in his hands and sobbed hysterically.

Afaf bent down cautiously, her back turned to the police-men. "Mullah Rashid was not in his quarters," she whispered in the man's ear. The assistant uncovered his face, searched Afaf's, and immediately his face lit up. "He's at our place." Afaf pretended to help Fawzi pull himself together as two confused policemen watched her every move. "Get up slowly, excuse yourself, then go call Bassam."

All eyes at once turned towards the dirt road. A jeep turned the curve spewing dust and rocks in all directions. It came to a stop in front of the mosque. Two men in civilian cloth stepped out, pulled the policemen aside, conversed with them. The policemen walked to the back of the mosque, got in the police car and drove off.

"Now what?" Sarah whispered.

"I have no idea."

One of the men wore a suit – the other, younger, a white shirt and pants. The man in the shirt walked to the back of the mosque where the cleric's quarters had been. The man in the suit approached the women. "Where do you live?"

Afaf pointed to her house.

The man in the suit told them to go home and stay there until they heard from him.

The women waited for the officer to walk away before taking a deep sigh of relief. Acting as normal as they could, they walked, with cautious, measured steps until they were out of hearing range.

"Wow!" Sarah took a deep breath. "That was close."

"My heart dropped into my pelvis," Afaf said laughing softly.

"Yours and mine."

"Wonder what they have in store for us."

"Questions. Lots of questions." Sarah's abaaya slipped down her head unto her shoulders. She had been struggling to keep it on her head all the while the police were interrogating them. "Afaf how come your abaaya stays in plays but mine keeps running away from me?"

"Practice, my dear, practice. When I was a teenager, I use to take my mother's abaaya, wear her high heels and walk in front of the mirror. At the time, I felt it was neat. I would look mysterious. I could go where I wanted and do what I wanted and no one would know who I am. Little did I know what a curse it could be."

They were almost home.

"Well," Afaf ventured, "the men would love to tell us I told you so. But they won't. At least I hope not. Can you imagine how horrible it would be if the men in our lives were a bunch of self-serving hypocrites like most men in the Arab world?"

"Fortunately, there are a few. I think if they say anything it will be out of concern for our safety. They don't trust the government and they don't trust the justice system. That practically forces every person to look out for himself or herself. Don't you think so?"

"No. The security system in this country is the best thing we have going for us. Otherwise, the extremists would do exactly as they please, drunk with newfound power and obliged to answer to no one. Like in Iran. Revolutionary Guards there are as powerful as the mutawas – the so-called 'religious men' in Saudi Arabia. Self appointed guardians of the faith. Everyone is terrified of them."

"The mutawas are volunteers in Saudi Arabia," Sarah said. "It's a power trip. That's all."

"It's the same with the Revolutionary Guards in Iran," Afaf replied. "But Power is not always bad. It gives great results when used toward a positive end. Look at the military. Without it no army can function. But here we are faced with power without discipline, without respect for those who the person or persons with power have the authority to act upon."

"It starts with the leaders, Afaf. If they have self-respect, they will have self-discipline. That in my opinion is real power. Like in Jordan and King Hussein. He has gradually introduced democracy in a country despite dire warnings from all his advisors. His advisors were wrong. They are doing great."

Bassam was rushing out the door when the women arrived. They removed their shoes and went in.

Within minutes, the man in the suit could be seen walking towards the house.

Peeping from behind the drawn curtains, Rashid saw the security officer approach. "This is my lucky day," he said rubbing his hands together.

Everyone stared at him baffled.

"Well," said Rashid, "I first managed not to be at the right place at the wrong time. Look at me. I'm still alive and in one piece. And now I see my friend Anwar walking towards this house. What more can a man ask?"

"Anwar who?" Sarah heard Suheil ask Bassam.

Bassam shrugged his shoulders. Told Suheil he did not know.

Rashid did not wait for his friend to ring the doorbell. He rushed to the front door and opened it. They embraced, kissed each other on both cheeks Arab style, and headed towards the living room. They had hardly settled in their respective seats when Bassam arrived with a tray carrying Arabic coffee – coffee he had prepared earlier to be drunk when his wife and Sarah returned.

Afaf motioned for Sarah to join her in the kitchen. Customarily, women withdrew to their quarters when male visitors came to visit a family. Although Afaf loved to defy custom and tradition whenever she felt she could get away with it, the gravity of the situation and her curiosity forced her to reconsider. "Let's leave them alone for a while until we find out what he wants," she told Sarah. "Dictates of custom don't bother me, but the men of our culture speak more freely when there are no women present. Anyway, we can hear them quite well from the kitchen. If he is Rashid's friend, we have nothing to fear. He might even help us. Maybe. If we're lucky."

"Do not travel together," Sarah heard the man say to

Rashid. "The woman should not travel alone and you should not travel with them. Separately is much better."

"We have only one car," Suheil reminded the men.

Anwar was quiet for a long moment. "Bassam's suggestion is the best so far – for Rashid. The doctor and his friend – I'm not so sure. Definitely not the rental. Let me think about it."

"Can we rent or buy a car from somewhere near by," Sarah asked Afaf.

Afaf thought the nearest place would be Asyut, the best Cairo. "I really don't know. I have not looked into it. The prices are astronomical – even for cars with hardly any life left in them. Bassam uses a bike and I use my feet. Can't ride the bike. The villagers will have a fit."

The question was how to get to Cairo. The buses were ancient relics, broke down frequently. People had to wait for hours by the roadside for another bus that might or might not have room for them – not even standing room. There was no telling how long it would take to make the trip.

"Do you have any idea who the perpetrators of this crime were?" Suheil asked Anwar.

"We do and we don't. There are so many groups, splinter groups, extremists of one kind or another – all power crazy. They hate the West and they hate the East. They like only themselves. It all boils down to one thing – control. Everybody thinks they are better qualified to run the government no matter who is doing the governing. What they really want is power. Power to control as much of the lives of others as possible."

"I'm going in," Sarah told Afaf. "I have a few questions to ask. If it insults their manhood, they can always throw me out."

"I'll follow you. As soon as I have the cold drinks ready."

Sarah entered the living room, walked over to the security officer, shook his hand and introduced herself. In a conservative traditional Muslim home, the mere act of a woman introducing herself to a man would not be tolerated – men and women visiting in the same room, unacceptable – not a subject for discussion. The toughest problem for most people caught between different social conducts was to assess the level of tolerance in a given situation where diametrically opposed attitudes came face to face with established customs.

Instinctively, almost exclusively, Sarah followed her gut feeling. Fortunately, the officer took it as naturally as if it was an everyday occurrence. It was not – definitely not in rural areas. That was enough to indicate to Sarah that she could talk to him.

"I know who you are," the officer said. "I worked in Saudi Arabia for four years training guards for the palace your father built. Brilliant mind, a most compassionate man. Where's your father now?"

Sarah told him.

He was quiet for a full minute and when he spoke he literally stuttered. "I hope God forgives me. But it was wrong of Him to take away a man of his caliber that early in life. We need men like him here – in this crazy world to help us find and keep an acceptable balance."

"God works in mysterious ways," Rashid opined. "Perhaps otherwise we would not have had a chance to meet his daughter. I hear she's working to make her parent's dream come true."

Sarah blushed – tried to change the subject. "I heard you mention to Suheil that we should not use the rental car to drive to Cairo. Since our options are rather limited – like that particular rental car or nothing. What do you suggest we do."

"You won't make it to Cairo in that car. It's marked. I have been thinking of a solution. I can think of only one. We wait. When darkness falls we drive the jeep to Asyut. There I rent a car in my name and you can drive it to Cairo."

"I have a full schedule at the hospital tomorrow," Dr. Tuqan protested. "We were supposed to be back home today."

"What happens to the rental car?" Sarah asked.

"It should be destroyed. We will have to compensate the rental agency. But cars are very expensive here. We will probably overhaul it completely, sell it, and send you the money."

Sarah explained to the officer money was not the issue. They had agreed to return the car to the agency in Cairo. She felt uncomfortable not keeping her end of the agreement. "It's a good little car," she added.

"I'm sure the rental agency will have no problem accepting cash for it."

"All right then," Sarah said, "I'll leave the details for you to work out. When the car is overhauled and safe to use, I'd like for Afaf and Bassam to have it. Bassam travels a lot from village to village. I'm sure it's not much fun to be on a bus, or a bike, in hundred twenty degree temperature."

It took a few seconds for Afaf to digest this latest development. Although Afaf and Bassam came from wealthy families, they refused to ask for financial help from their parents. They lived on their teachers' salaries by living simply. The only luxury they had was the air conditioner and because of the high cost of energy they used it sparingly. Afaf rushed over and hugged Sarah. "How can we ever thank you? We'll put it to good use for all the villagers' needs, not just ours."

That kind of emotion always left Sarah embarrassed. Blood rushed to her face making her look like she had first degree sunburn. Consequently, she found it hard to express herself. She forced herself to do so to reassure her friend. "You have thanked me enough already. The fact that I don't have to worry about the running of the schools here in Egypt is more than enough gratitude."

"I have an idea." Rashid's big, black eyes had a mischievous look to them. "If I am to wear an abaaya to get to Cairo, why don't the good doctor and his friend do the same. Then they won't have to wait for nightfall to leave this place." His smile broadened as he spoke.

Sarah and Suheil exchanged glances. "I cannot imagine

any thing I dislike more." Sarah knew Suheil was allergic to the sight of that black piece of cloth. To him it symbolized abuse – abuse of his religion, abuse of women, abuse of power. "I'll wait until nightfall." Suheil was not a man who compromised on his principles. "I will not wear an abaaya."

"That's not fair," Sarah teased. "I dislike it as much as you do. I wore one. Why can't you?"

"You might have to wear one," Anwar said, "even if we travel at night."

While Anwar spoke, Sarah's thoughts gyrated in wild circles. How did the officers learn about the explosion? Had the policemen contacted security before leaving the station? But the policemen seemed as surprised as she and Afaf were to see the security men arrive. Perhaps Rashid's assistant, Fawzi had called the police and security. Should she ask? Did it matter? The same thoughts demanded her attention unceasingly. She decided to ask him.

"How did you learn about the explosion? The villagers are just now beginning to wake up and we didn't call. Did Fawzi contact you?"

"Who is Fawzi?"

"My assistant," Rashid said, caught off guard.

"He must have called the police. We did not know about the explosion until we got here."

The gnawing pain at the pit of her stomach forced her to take a deep breath to relax.

She couldn't. To survive in the Middle East, it was imperative not to accept anything at face value. She had learned that lesson very early in life. It seemed to her there was more to the visit by security than Anwar let on. But she felt uncomfortable pressing him for more information.

Meanwhile, Rashid's eyes narrowed as he studied his visitor. "I thought you'd come to investigate the explosion," he said.

"We will of course investigate the explosion," Anwar assured Rashid. "But the purpose of our visit, I mean my assistant and I, was to check on Bassam and Afaf."

"Us?" Husband and wife spoke in unison.

"This early in the morning?"

"Rashid." Anwar turned to the cleric. "Can you guarantee the loyalty of these people?"

"Absolutely."

Anwar explained that security had intercepted a coded message from Jordan the previous evening ordering members of an extremist group to kidnap a woman by the name of Sarah Sultan. The extremists were instructed to kidnap her and keep her in Egypt until they were contacted and given further instructions. Anwar said he was not quite sure who Sarah Sultan was as Sultan is quite a common name – although Sarah is not. He made a few phone calls and his suspicions were confirmed. Sarah Sultan was indeed the daughter of Maher Sultan, a man he had worked with for four years, and a good friend. Concerned, Anwar and his assistant had driven all night to arrive at the village before the kidnappers did – while two of his colleagues tried to locate the kidnappers hideout.

Rashid knitted his eyebrows looking puzzled. "Where do Bassam and Afaf fit in? I thought your asking me about their loyalty had something to do with the explosion."

"I know it's hard for you to deal with yet another problem soon after a serious incident like an explosion," Anwar said. "But I figure the explosion was the work of yet another group. A coincidence – perhaps. But most probably not. The leaders of the extremists assign different jobs to different groups at the same time. Usually neither one knows about the other. The leaders feel the impact of their acts will be greater and they can control their followers better."

Sarah opened her mouth to speak but no words came out. She felt as if someone had lifted her up and thrown her in a bottomless pit. She kept falling like a rock expecting to hit bottom any moment, but there was no bottom to hit. As the information whirled through her head with urgency, she sensed panic setting in. If true, it meant that the agent had competently obtained information about a potentially dangerous situation and taken upon himself to make it his business to come warn her. But was it true? A cold sweat sprung all over her body. Weird thoughts crowded her mind. How could she be sure Anwar was telling the truth? He looked decent, sincere. Why would he lie? Money? How could she be sure anyone was telling the truth? She stopped herself. She was becoming paranoid. If Anwar were not trustworthy, he would not be Rashid's friend. She made a conscious effort to push those ugly thoughts to an obscure corner of her brain. Still, she was unable to comprehend how a simple undertaking like teaching children could ignite such drastic measures from people who did not know she existed a few months ago.

Suheil was by her side immediately. "It won't happen," he said, his voice breaking. "We won't let it happen. The extremists might be ruthless, and they are definitely armed. But I think we are smarter. We can outwit them."

"That's why I'm here," Anwar said. "I couldn't tell you initially because in this business we have to be very careful. We know two thugs are on their way over here – and you are right doctor, they are armed. We launched an extensive manhunt immediately. But since I have not heard from my contacts up to now, it is safe to assume that the men will be here within the hour."

"Oh, my God." Afaf quickly covered her mouth with her hand. Her husband rushed over put his arm around her.

"We need your cooperation – all of you," the security agent continued. "We need for you to wait here till they come. They are not going to rush over immediately. First they will want to make sure Sarah has not left the village. Or the doctor for that matter. They know Sarah and the doctor came together and will most likely leave together."

"You want to use Sarah as bait to apprehend the terrorists?" Suheil asked, a horrified look on his face.

"You and Sarah. Yes. That's what we would like to do.

You can refuse, of course, and I will send an escort with you all the way to Cairo to assure your safety. But, like I said. We have an opportunity to put a couple of terrorists away. We should take advantage of it. When you're losing a war, no strategy should be left untried. And believe me my friends we are losing this one fast."

"I'm staying," Sarah said without hesitation.

Suheil asked her quietly to follow him to the kitchen. He closed the door, took her hands in his and asked, "Suppose there is shooting, killing. I know how much you dislike violence. Can you deal with it? It's not like American movies. It does not end well – hardly ever. It can be deadly and it will haunt you forever even if it is the bad guys who get killed."

"What do you propose we do?"

"I think we can use the car we rented. It seems to me Anwar is exaggerating the risks to keep us here so he can score."

"I hope he does. I'm staying, Suheil. You should leave if you're not comfortable with the arrangement."

Suheil tried to explain his concern was for her, not for himself.

"Then there's no problem," she replied, planted a light kiss on his forehead and walked out – a brave façade outside, terrified inside.

"We don't have much time," Anwar reminded his hosts.

A few minutes later, Rashid emerged from the bathroom minus his beard, practicing keeping the abaaya over his head and body. He couldn't. It kept slipping off his head from one side or the other and off his body.

Afaf watched and chuckled. Still smiling she came to his rescue, showed him how to keep it in place – wrapped tightly around his head and body. Rashid was nervous. He did not think he could do it, cursed the person who had thought of it in the first place, and those who perpetuated the demeaning practice whose demise in his opinion was long overdue.

Bassam had been waiting at the entrance of the village for

the early bus. He came running to the house to notify Rashid it had arrived. Rashid said quick good byes and hurried to the bus. As he did so, the abaaya flew off his body completely and fell on the ground. Bassam, who was still outside the house rushed over, helped Rashid cover himself. There were only two passengers on the bus and the bus driver. But Rashid had to turn back. If they had seen him, and he did not know if they had or not, he could not get on the bus. He returned to the house, threw himself on the sofa, frustrated, angry, resigned. "I need time to – to practice. It's the stupidest thing. I don't know how women do it."

"You don't have time." Bassam leaned against the wall of the tiny hallway.

"They'll clobber me to death if they learn I'm a man masquerading as a woman. Did it occur to any of you that there is a distinct possibility that I might be caught?"

There was ample truth in the cleric's statement. Everyone was silent hoping the next person would offer a more plausible option. There was none. Eventually Rashid turned to Bassam. "Would you mind if I travel as Afaf's husband. I thought perhaps we could take Hind with us. I'll disguise myself as much as I can. I doubt anyone will recognize me once we pass the neighboring villages."

With his beard gone, he looks like a different man, Sarah thought. It might be worth a try.

"You've got to be really well disguised," Anwar advised. "You're dealing with pros. I saw from the window what happened to you. An abaaya is not the answer."

The arrival of the buses was highly irregular. Sometimes a bus arrived early in the morning and no more buses came until evening. Sometimes they arrived after each other – depending on how many buses were operational on that particular day. Everyone agreed Rashid should leave as soon as possible, as disguised as possible.

Afaf hurried to the dwelling of the deceased Abu Yahya to convince Um Yahya to let Hind go to Cairo. She was not sure what the mother's reaction would be. It was not a problem. Um Yahya expressed her everlasting gratitude for the concern and help she had received from the doctor and from that charming lady from Jordan. She was sure her daughter would be in good hands and seemed thrilled at being given a chance to make decisions on her own – for a change – without interference from her husband. Something she had never been allowed to do before.

Um Yahya was fortunate. Her husband had no male relatives in the village to order her behavior.

Um Yahya was not told Mullah Rashid would be traveling with her daughter – for her own protection – in case she was questioned by the terrorists, then or later.

Mercifully, the wait for the arrival of the next bus was over in a half an hour. Rashid wore a pair of dark sunglasses, removed his clerical hat and garb, put on a long, white shirt like outfit and hat like ordinary Egyptian men do. Afaf, Hind and Rashid said their good byes and left to board the bus. Afaf and Hind covered themselves with abaayas. Afaf's concern was for Rashid. If they recognized her, they were bound to check Rashid more closely since they were from the same village. For the second time in the same day, Afaf had had to shelve her principles for safety's sake, and she was not at all pleased about it.

Suheil got even more restless as he watched them driven away. "Why can't we disguise ourselves too, get on a bus and leave?" He addressed his words to Anwar. "I know you're concerned about our safety, but I don't see how delaying our departure makes a difference."

"I don't advise you to travel by bus. I know you want to get to Cairo before the girl gets there. You will. You have my word. The arrival time by bus is anybody's guess. Daylight worries me because neither you nor Miss Sarah look like Egyptians. Besides an abaaya we have nothing more to disguise you with. You said you don't want to wear an abaaya. I don't blame you. You saw what happened to Rashid when he tried using it. Wearing an abaaya looks easy when women do it. That's because they start when they are barely six or seven years old. Without disguise it will be easy to spot you. In case of trouble we don't have enough agents to prevent a catastrophe."

Sarah listened intently. The security agent's explanation made sense although she too was quite restless and getting progressively more nervous. However, she did not want to endanger Suheil's life or the agent's life by a rash act. She could of course wear an abaaya and leave, but Suheil would not let her go without accompanying her and she wasn't quite sure that the an abaaya alone would the trick. If questioned, an Egyptian would have no trouble spotting her as a non-Egyptian from her dialect and her I.D. card would confirm the rest.

"If you leave now," Anwar added, "the villagers will be at risk as well. They will know you have left and when questioned they will tell what they know unaware of the consequences."

A disturbing thought suddenly rattled in Sarah's head. What was to stop the kidnappers from coming to the village and carrying out their mission? Sure it was more risky, but she had read numerous accounts of terrorists carrying on acts of sabotage, kidnappings and bombings in broad daylight in Algeria, in Egypt, even in France. Only two days prior extremists had managed to throw acid in the face of two innocent girls – also in broad daylight. And of course suicide missions, dying for the cause guaranteed the terrorists a first class ticket to paradise. It happened all the time in Israel. Car bombs, killing of innocent people – routine. The agent's statement that they were short of manpower to help prevent a major mishap had triggered the concern now demanding her attention. She explained her apprehension to the agent and to Suheil.

"Of course there's always that possibility – even as we speak. The information the kidnappers received was detailed and quite accurate. I figure they must be getting it from a reliable source." Unexpectedly, suddenly, Anwar turned and faced Bassam who had been listening to the conversation but had said nothing. "Perhaps you can help us." His voice was calm, not threatening. "Can you think of who could possibly be feeding information to the terrorists? Working as closely as you do with the villagers perhaps you have heard or seen something which at the time might not have seemed relevant to you, but in the light of these new developments I thought perhaps you might be able to help us."

Bassam must have sensed the precarious position he'd been placed in. He suddenly had a terrified expression on his face. At first he could not talk, but soon found his voice as Sarah and Suheil watched him completely shocked. "This might be hard for you to believe," Bassam said when he found his voice, "but I did not realize at the time what I said might cause problems. Two men got on the bus I took to the village coming from Asyut. They started a conversation, asked me to stop at their village for a cold drink. I told them I would love to but couldn't. I had to get back home as soon as possible. We were expecting important visitors. They asked a lot of questions. I answered. It never occurred to me that they were after Miss Sarah." He could not bring himself to look at her. "I'm sorry. I really am, Miss Sarah. I would never do anything to hurt you." He was on the verge of tears.

"I am glad you came clean," Anwar said. "We knew it was you but found it hard to believe. From now on if any one asks you questions about Miss Sarah, about the schools, about anything whether the person is asking the question looks innocent or friendly, or whatever. Give no information. None. Is that clear?"

Aware of the harsh treatment which awaits traitors, Bassam looked like a man who had been hit by lightning but had been lucky enough to escape death. "I'm ....I'm really sorry," he stuttered. "It was only after you mentioned the detailed information the kidnappers had, that I realized my mistake. It will never happen again."

"It better not," Anwar shot back. "You could languish in a not so comfortable jail the rest of your life had I not watched you myself this morning and had you not come forward with the truth."

Bassam thanked the agent profusely then apologized to Sarah.

"It was an innocent mistake," Sarah said. "Forget it."

Anwar was not through with Bassam yet. "Did you see the same two men or perhaps someone else, after Abu Yahya's funeral or anytime yesterday?"

Bassam put his chin on his fist lost in thought. "Last night, when I went to buy bread from the bakery, a man walked in. He asked about the funeral, when our visitors were leaving, lots of questions." Bassam smacked his forehead with his fist. "How could I be so stupid?"

The agent turned to Suheil. "I hope now you understand why we can't leave this morning. They know you plan to. I have my assistant snooping around, pretending to be an Islamist militant hoping they will get desperate and show their faces."

"You think?" Suheil did not seem convinced.

"No. They're well trained and much too clever. But some-times desperate men do desperate things. If we are patient, who knows, we might be rewarded."

Still Suheil was not convinced. "They'll probably wait us out. Who knows how long we'll be here?"

"It's better than being out there – dead," the agent replied.

"Dead?" Suheil's voice rose a lot higher than Sarah had heard before.

"Suheil," Sarah interjected. "The terrorists are after me. There's no reason for you to stay."

Suheil rose, paced the room, scratched the back of his head. "I'm sorry. I'm frustrated, angry, and quite devoid of patience for the moment. It irks me to learn that our people will stoop so low as to kidnap a woman whose sole purpose in life is to improve the lot of innocent children. Let's say I'm having trouble dealing with it."

"It's not that simple," Anwar explained. "Their order is to kidnap – if met with resistance, to kill. Human life in this part of the world has so little meaning, it's pathetic."

She broke out in a clammy sweat, her knees knocked and her mouth went dry. The extremes fanatics stooped to was indeed difficult to fathom. Suheil was much more inclined to anticipate the worst and thus was more prepared mentally to face it. Her biggest dilemma was her unshakable belief in the goodness of human beings – man woman and child, and how to reconcile her belief with facts to the contrary – facts she was bombarded with incessantly.

Bassam sat in a corner looking like a condemned man waiting for the executioner to arrive.

It bothered Sarah to watch him agonize. "Don't be so hard on yourself, Bassam," she implored. "They could have had most of the information you gave them from any villager here."

Anwar reached into his coat pocket for a cigarette, lit it, took a deep drag, turned to Bassam. "How close is the bakery to the mosque?"

"About a hundred yards south."

"The market?"

"Next to the bakery."

"Let's see," Anwar murmured. "That means you pass the mosque on your way to the bakery and the market. Am I right?"

"Right."

"Go buy bread or fruit or whatever. On your way over, as you pass the mosque, check on my assistant. I should have heard from him long ago. Do not go near him or talk to him. If you see strangers, keep going. Do not stop. Do I make myself clear?"

Bassam shook his head vigorously, yes. He rose, and walked out.

He was back in twenty minutes with a loaf of bread in one

hand and a bag of fruits in the other. "He's there," Bassam said, his voice shaking.

"What was he doing?" Anwar asked.

"He was talking to two men – not villagers."

Anwar stiffened noticeably. He lit another cigarette, drew deeply on it several times before he asked, "Did they see you?"

"I'm not sure. There were several other people on their way to the market and the bakery."

"Did you see them?" Anwar took on a serious look.

The security agent's questions did not escape Sarah's notice – nor Suheil's. "Only divine intervention can save us now," Suheil said to no one in particular.

"I saw them briefly," Bassam replied to Anwar's questions fearfully, reluctantly.

"Are they the same two men who questioned you on the bus?"

It became chillingly clear to Sarah that she was in a predicament unlike any other she'd been in before. Unfortunately, those associating with her, unsuspecting, and through no fault of their own, found themselves in the same predicament as she was – often. This time, Bassam and Suheil were the victims, and perhaps Anwar and his assistant.

Bassam fidgeted, his eyes darted back and forth. "Yes."

Anwar did not seem surprised by Bassam's answer. "The jeep?"

"It's there."

The situation seemed absurd, surreal. Sarah wondered about the courage of those two men. If their objective was to kidnap her, or kill her, why would they appear in broad daylight in a village where everyone was related, a stranger immediately recognized.

Anwar acquired a grave look. After a brief pause he stuck the pack of cigarettes in his pocket, walked out the front door after telling everyone to stay in the house.

He returned within minutes. "I know who they are.

Palestinians. Bloodthirsty members of Hizballah. It looked
like they were about to leave." He handed Bassam a key.
"Wait a few minutes then go to the mosque. If the strangers
are still there, ask to speak to my assistant in private. Tell him
your brother sent me. Your brother needs the jeep. He will
understand. If the strangers give you trouble or question you,
tell them the vehicle belongs to security. That, I think will
make them stop and think."

After about five minutes Bassam took the key reluctantly
and headed towards the mosque. When he got to the mosque,
neither the assistant nor the men were there. He immediately
jumped in the jeep and drove around looking for them. They
couldn't have gone far. Didn't have enough time. He searched
every where he could think of. The men had disappeared into
thin air.

Meanwhile, Anwar chain smoked and paced.

Bassam returned with the disturbing news. Anwar's
expression changed from frustration to fury. He reached into
his coat pocket, pulled out a cellular phone, said two words,
jumped in the jeep and drove away like a man possessed.

"Great!" Suheil threw his hands up in the air. "What do
we do now?"

"We think and we find a solution," Sarah shot back.
"Remember the terms of our relationship. No gloom and
doom." Suheil was not a man who functioned well under
pressure when the woman he loved was involved and it took
far less to discourage him than it did her. It upset her when it
happened. However she did not dwell on it for long. She drew
his attention to it and carried on with whatever she was doing.

Sarah had a lot of quick thinking to do. An idea, a possibility came to her mind. "What about a boat?" Sarah asked
Bassam. She could hardly control her excitement. Whoever
the kidnappers were, no matter how good they were at what
they were doing, she doubted they would look for her on a
boat, especially since she had used a rental car to come to the
village. Most cities, towns and villages in Egypt were located

on the shores of the Nile. Sarah figured it should be possible to hit a major town by boat, rent a car and drive to Cairo.

"It's forty five minutes walk from here." Bassam's face lit up.

"North or south?"

"It's difficult to explain. If you don't know the way, it's easy to get lost. I'll go with you."

Bassam's offer to accompany them said a lot to Sarah about the man. If he was a traitor, he would want to stay behind to give information to those who would probably reward him handsomely for it.

For the first time in two days Sarah saw a smile turn into a grin as Suheil said, "What are we waiting for?" He opened the front door. "Let's go."

The long walk to the port was god-sent. They felt relaxed and invigorated. There was a solitary boat at the port. No one around seemed to know where the owner / operator was. After a brief search Bassam located him in a nearby café drinking tea. But the man refused to budge. It was noon. It was hot. He wanted to wait for evening, cooler weather.

Sarah approached the man to ask how much he normally charged passengers traveling to Asyut. The man's eyes roamed from the top of her head to her shoes, then back again. Sarah ignored him. She knew exactly what he was thinking. Her Arabic is really good, the accent – not Egyptian – perhaps Lebanese Christian Arab. A tourist. Otherwise she'd wear an abaaya. After a moment's hesitation while he appraised her ability to pay and by how much he could raise his price, he quoted a figure. She turned to Suheil. "I bet he will leave immediately if we double the fare. What do you think?"

"You really want to?"

"No. But I think I have to. You are restless. Your patients are waiting. We might as well."

Suheil chuckled. "This is quite a shift from the Sarah I know – the Sarah who always claims money is best spent where it does most good – the children. Allow me to pay, please."

"We'll split it. Agreed?"

"Do I have a choice?"

"No."

"Let's go."

They said their good byes to Bassam, told him to keep them posted, and the boat sailed away after Sarah and Suheil paid him double full fare for the twenty passengers the boat would normally carry. The owner claimed they would have to wait until evening for the boat to fill up as few Egyptians traveled in the blazing noon heat.

It was Sarah's idea not to stop at Asyut as previously planned just in case her pursuers were waiting for her, expecting them to return the rental car. They continued on to the next city, El Minya. They arrived late that evening, located the downtown area, but could not find an agency to rent a car. At a used car dealership they met a young man who offered to drive them to Cairo – at an exorbitant price. They figured it was cheaper than spending the night and less hazardous to their health. From the looks of the city it did not seem like they would be able to get clean, comfortable accommodation, regardless of cost. And they wanted to reach Cairo as soon as possible. They agreed to the man's terms.

Their boat trip and car trip were uneventful. They reached Cairo close to midnight, found a small hotel, prayed it would be clean, registered under an assumed name, and went to bed. They agreed to stay away from the big hotels where it would be easy for the kidnappers to locate them.

Early the next morning they took a taxi to the airport. Suheil did not want to spend any more time in Egypt for fear of jeopardizing Sarah's safety. "I'll make the arrangements for Hind from Jordan," he said. "Maybe Rashid will get there before we do. Then we'll know where to reach Afaf and Hind."

"I gave Rashid Jim's phone number. Told him to call Jim from the airport."

"Good. Hopefully, we'll be out of here and soon."

Then they hit trouble. The flight to Amman on Royal Jordanian Airlines was fully booked, including first class. Their flight had been scheduled for the day before which they had missed. All flights were booked solid to the end of September and they had a long waiting list.

Sarah and Suheil tried the other airlines. Same story.

"It's mind boggling," Sarah said. "We got tickets on the spur of the moment three days ago. How could they sell out all the seats, on all flights, in three days?"

"Jim, right?"

"Yeah... He did not indicate he had a problem getting the tickets, though."

"Let's give him a call," Suheil said. "That man has more connections with more people than any one I know."

"My father had business all over the Middle East, Egypt, the Sudan and England. Jim went where my father went. That's why."

Sarah asked the operator to connect her with Jim's number. She prayed he was still home as she waited for him to answer.

Jim was home getting ready to drive the children from the camp to school. Despite massive advertising, unlike the overwhelming results they had had advertising for teachers, they had yet to find a driver willing to drive the school bus. Those who accepted the job, three in all, quit after a few days, courtesy of Sarah's aunts and the Sheikh.

Jim loved driving the school bus. He brushed aside Sarah's objections, claimed it gave him a chance to be with children. It was an excuse. The real reason was his concern for the safety of the children. When he was in charge, no one would dare kidnap a child from the bus like they had done Fatme.

She explained the problem.

"Departure time?" Jim asked.

"Forty five minutes."

"Call me back in ten minutes."

Talking to Jim always gave a boost to her spirits. There was no such word as impossible in Jim's vocabulary. The 'can do' attitude was his trademark.

A stream of passengers lined up at the Royal Jordanian Airlines counter to check in. From the length of the queue there was no doubt in Sarah's mind that it would be quite unlikely for them to find seats on that aircraft.

"Let's grab a cup of coffee," Samir suggested. "We have time. Looks like they have overbooked heavily. I'd say our chances of getting on this flight is next to nil."

"Maybe first class." Sarah said without conviction.

Suheil did not think so. There were many Saudi Arabians waiting to check in at the first class counter. The Saudis invariably traveled first class. No airline bumped them off.

"Coffee sounds good," Sarah said

Their choice was limited to instant coffee or Arabic coffee which was served in tiny coffee cups, in tiny amounts, a teaspoon or two of pure caffeine – the extract. Sarah asked for a cup of instant coffee and so did Suheil. The cafeteria was packed with travelers. No place to sit. They walked to the hallway in search of a telephone. The telephone Sarah had used before was being used by someone else.

Sarah took a sip of her coffee, realized she had to wait a while before she drank more. It was much too hot. As she raised her head, her eyes locked with the eyes of two young men coming from the opposite direction.

"See those two men coming towards us," she said in a low voice. "They were looking at me in a weird, calculating manner."

"What's new about that," Suheil teased. "Any man who sees a beautiful woman will look at her."

"Suheil, I'm not joking. I don't like the looks of those men."

Suheil suggested they continue their walk and see what happens.

The men walked with quick steps past Sarah and Suheil and were lost in the crowd.

Sarah sighed relieved. They resumed their search for a telephone she could use to make a long distance call. There were phones at the airport but only a few with access to long distance dialing.

Suddenly Sarah felt a hand grab her arm. She heard a man's voice say through clenched teeth, "Walk nice and easy now. Just as you were doing. I have a gun. Don't force me to use it. Yes, that's it. Nice and easy."

Pretty strong grip the man had on her arm. Her hand was getting numb.

A quick look to her right confirmed her fear. Suheil was in the same predicament. Both men seemed terribly young, eighteen, nineteen, at the most. New recruits, most probably. A quick analysis of their predicament convinced her she needed a fail-proof response. Without further ado, invigorated with a sudden rush of energy, Sarah whirled around and threw the hot coffee in the face of the man holding her arm. Instantly, the young man let go of her arm. Sarah took a step back and screamed for help.

Chapter 25

"MISS SARAH SULTAN, MISS SARAH SULTAN, please contact Royal Jordanian Airlines. Urgent."

Sarah heard the message for the second time, but could not move. She was surrounded by a crowd of at least two dozen people who had rushed to her rescue when they heard her scream for help. Many came to help, a few approached cautiously out of curiosity. Unfortunately, the culprits had escaped the minute they heard Sarah scream, and Sarah's would be kidnapper could open his eyes – eyes momentarily blinded by the sting of the hot coffee Sarah had thrown on his face.

The message was repeated again by Royal Jordanian Airlines.

"Excuse me," Sarah said as she forced her way through the crowd. "I'm being paged. I have to go. Thank you all very much." Sarah ran to the counter, followed by Suheil, leaving a baffled crowd behind.

Sarah and Suheil were told by the manager of Royal Jordanian Airlines to follow him. The manager took them through a narrow passage reserved for employees. Once they were out of hearing range of the rest of the passengers, he told them to proceed to the first class cabin of the aircraft immediately. "Please proceed as discreetly as you can," the manager pleaded, "while walking to the aircraft and while boarding. The aircraft can be easily seen from the waiting lobby. We don't want to anger the passengers waiting in line, especially our first class passengers."

After a few minutes, the doors of the aircraft were closed by flight attendants and the plane started to taxi before take off. Soon they were cruising in a clear blue sky, the wings of the aircraft glistening in the bright sunshine. Sarah and Suheil held hands, happy to have foiled the kidnapping, grateful to have someone like Jim on their side, and relieved the ordeal was finally over.

"I need to take a few lessons from Jim," Suheil said. "When it comes to medical problems I hardly ever give up. But dealing with people, especially with people in the Middle East where emotions rather than thought govern most people's actions, I find myself totally at a loss."

"You are good at what you do and he is good at what he does. What really matters is that we managed to foil the attempt of my pursuers and we found a way to get out of Egypt. That was a close call, though. I shudder when I think about it."

Sarah rubbed her arms with her hands to actually stop herself from shaking.

"Are you all right?" Suheil asked. "Would you like me to order something hot for you to drink?"

"Tea please."

Sarah was quiet after that for quite a while, thinking, sipping her tea. The events of the past couple of days had given her ample cause to reflect.

"What's on your mind?"

"Fear," Sarah replied. "Fear of the kidnappers. Whether my luck will hold out in the long run or not. Fear of what Jim might do if he learns about the kidnappers and all that happened in Egypt the past two days. I have to admit it was the longest two days of my life. It seems more like a week when I think back."

"How will Jim know if he is not told?"

"What about Rashid? Maybe he's already in Jordan – with Jim. But Rashid and Afaf were gone when the security agent warned us about the kidnapping. Nevertheless, I can't keep a secret from Jim. Not for long, anyway. He always finds out."

"On second thought," Suheil began to worry aloud. "I

think it's important for Jim to know – for your safety and my peace of mind. I'm at the hospital all day, every day, and often late into the night. You don't like it and neither do I. But it is still a man's world and a damned dangerous one at that."

Despite the pressure from those that cared about her and were worried about her welfare, the idea of relying on some-one else other than herself regardless of the reason remained heretical for Sarah. Sure she was scared – petrified was more like it. She also knew that it was inconceivable for anyone to really protect her if her enemies wanted to get her. Primarily she had to rely on herself.

Predictably, Suheil knew what Sarah was thinking. "We don't want to make it easy for them. We have witnessed the extremists operate without fear, in broad daylight, right under the noses of security guards, in an international airport. The last person to arrive after you screamed was an airport security guard dragging his feet. It seems to me he took his time get-ting there. And when he finally arrived, he started to question me while I was trying to tell him which way the assailants ran. Why me? You did all the screaming. The answer is not hard to guess. He probably thought I was your husband and did not want to get involved – not in violence cases. So what if a man beat his wife. It happens all the time. That's why he took his time getting there. Egyptian society all but condones attacks on women. The usual incompetent, uneducated peasant made law enforcement officer courtesy of his uniform and we're wondering how come terrorists operate anywhere they want, anytime they want," Suheil added. "What have they got to fear? We were lucky you got paged. Otherwise it would have taken us hours to disentangle ourselves from questioning by Egyptian security had they found out what really happened."

Of course Suheil was right. Sarah had to admit to herself; she counted on Jim consciously or unconsciously – for minor and major issues. Now more than ever she needed his help. Since the efforts of her assailants were frustrated, and they had lost the opportunity to kidnap her outside Jordan, she had no doubt they would try again – in desperation, in Jordan, or wherever she might happen to be. She also recognized the fact that if they were determined to get her, neither Jim, nor Jordan, nor darkness, nor half a dozen bodyguards could possibly guarantee her safety. The only answer she could think of was to somehow convince the Sheikh it was not to his advantage to pursue harassing and threatening her.

But how?

She did not have a clue. She had tried money. It had not worked. Jim was quite sure the Sheikh's behavior was only partially influenced by Sarah's aunts. Granted, Sarah's aunts had brought Sarah's activities to the Sheikh's attention and very likely supplied him with detailed information about Sarah and her parents. Sarah had also heard rumors that her aunts helped the Sheikh with circumcisions of young girls in the camps whose parents they would either bribe or threaten. Other than that their contribution was limited. It was Jim's contention that the Sheikh was in the pay of the Saudis who aided and encouraged extremism in all Muslim countries. Their wealth made it easy for them to promote the interpretation of Islam best suited to their ultra conservative way of thinking. At times Sarah found it hard to believe this was the twentieth century: a time when men had already been to the moon, the space shuttle traveled into new horizons routinely, and technology put the remotest corner of the world on anybody's fingertips who had a computer and a modem. At times like that Sarah had to shake her head vigorously to get rid of the cobwebs. Otherwise, the irrationality of the world, particularly her present world, frustrated her and sapped her courage.

She had asked Jim why. Why would the Saudis want to perpetuate such extremism?

It's the only way the Saudi family can stay in power, Jim had explained. In power and with absolute control over a people who have no say in how they are governed, where women fare no better than a commodity to be used for a man's pleasure and discarded when her usefulness for him becomes irrelevant. In the past, few people outside Saudi Arabia were aware of the extent of oppression the authoritarian regime of the Saudi family used to govern its people. Of course Western governments knew all along. But cheap oil invariably gained priority over human rights. It still did. Recently, however, the Iranian revolution with its successes and excesses sent shock waves through the rulers of Saudi Arabia giving them a God-sent excuse to tighten the noose yet another notch rendering life, especially for women, inhuman by any standard.

What about human rights organizations? Sarah knew about conditions in Saudi Arabia first hand. Not a day passed by without her visualizing the death of the thirteen year old girl by stoning in the public square, her fear of the mutawas – the religious police, every time she and her mother, or she and Gwynne stepped out of their house in Saudi Arabia – just in case the mutawas would find something improper in their attire.

Because it is a closed society, Jim told her. Human rights organizations cannot speak out unless they have proof. And even if they have proof and speak out, it gets buried in the back pages of some newspaper. Western powers want to keep the status quo and oil money takes care of the rest – like making sure people like you whom they consider to be an enemy of Islam, do not succeed in educating women for fear they will distance themselves from Islam. That's what they feed the international media. The truth is they prefer their women isolated, subservient, subhuman and at their mercy from the cradle to the grave.

And to date they have succeeded fabulously.

I believe, Jim had added, that the Saudi rulers would dearly love to see their brand of governance by the strictest laws of Islam, tailored to fit their version become reality in all Muslim countries. They consider money spent for that purpose, money well spent. It keeps the Saudis in power, and the world no longer able to single out Saudi Arabia as an oppressive authoritarian regime – if not the most oppressive. Actually, so far their money has worked quite well for them. Abuse of women has become endemic, a way of life and gradually getting worst.

As was often the case, Jim's assessment was brutally honest. Even broken bones had not dissuaded the Sheikh from resuming his vendetta against Sarah almost immediately after his return from Damascus. She recalled the disdainful look he had given her when she had offered him funds to help repair the mosque. She now understood money was not an issue for the Sheikh. He could get all he wanted from the Saudis. But a dangerous woman like her was definitely an issue to be prevented from doing more damage – at all cost.

Engulfed in her own narrow escape, Sarah had not thought of much else the past hour or so. Soon enough though, another problem jarred her thoughts. It had taken Jim's help for her and Suheil to get two seats on a flight out of Egypt – first class seats. Previously, she had not given Mullah Rashid's departure from Egypt much thought. She had assumed that tickets were available. Rashid was supposed to contact Jim when he landed in Jordan. Other than that they had no way of reaching him, or Afaf – until Afaf called to let them know where she and Hind were staying. The number of convoluted steps they had to resort to to escape the wrath of extremists was stupendous and it pained her deeply. She felt helpless, vulnerable – feelings she detested, yet due to circumstances unable to suppress those feelings fully.

Afaf did call about an hour after Sarah arrived at her apartment. They had made it safely to Cairo. She and Hind were with her parents. Afaf's parents had offered to keep Hind and make sure she got treated. They would wait to hear from Dr. Tuqan. Afaf gave Sarah her parents' home phone number. "The bus ride was awful," she said. "We had to change three buses to make it to Asyut. All three broke down. We rented a car in Asyut and drove to Cairo."

"What about Rashid?" Sarah asked. "Did anyone recognize him?" The good news about Hind was most comforting. Sarah had envisioned serious problems finding the proper home for a disfigured teenager, a female, someone who needed a lot of medical attention, someone who had never stepped out of her village and was incapable of doing much for herself. Hind had no resources. She had never been to see a doctor before much less been treated by one. Finding a plastic surgeon and an eye doctor would have been beyond her reach.

"No. We had no problems," Afaf replied. "Rashid left for the airport after he dropped us off at my parents. He was like a little boy babbling about his forthcoming trip to the States. He couldn't stop talking about it – and about his beard. Or I should say lack of it. He wondered what his friends would think about a cleric without a beard. Would they believe him if he told them what the real reason was? He said he understood from his friends that people in the States believe terrorism is something foreigners do to one another in third world countries. Why shave your beard when your destination is the States. He thinks his friends and colleagues will find it difficult to believe the degree the situation in Egypt has deteriorated."

"His beard will grow back," Sarah remarked candidly. "I'd be surprised though if he makes it to Jordan in the foreseeable future. The airlines are booked solid. We had trouble getting first class tickets."

Afaf was quiet for a couple of seconds. Sarah thought they were disconnected when Afaf came back on the line. "That's bad news," Afaf said. "He didn't give that matter any thought at all perhaps because he has not done much traveling lately. He does have family and friends here in Cairo, though. Let's hope he can go on standby or something. He has Jim's number and I gave him yours. I hope you don't mind."

"Of course not." Sarah was relieved to know that Rashid had some place to stay and would not have to wait at the airport not knowing how long it would be before he could find a seat on any airline. She thanked Afaf, said good by, then turned her attention to the messages on her answering machine.

One message in particular drew her attention. It was from Muhammad, from Bellevue, Washington. He had done great in school throughout the academic year, was planning to go to school full time during summer, and he expected to complete the requirements for his computer classes by the end of spring 1996. To date, he had not heard from Ali. The reason for his call was to ask Sarah for her approval regarding a delicate matter. He was in love with the daughter of the host family and she was in love with him. He would like to marry her and return to Jordan with her. He wanted Sarah's opinion.

Jim had already listened to her messages as Sarah had asked him to do and was waiting for her reaction.

"He can't be serious," Sarah said, her mind racing with zillion reasons as to why not.

"He is." Jim poured himself a Scotch and offered to fix a drink for Sarah.

"I'll have a glass of wine. You said Amy is seventeen. Can you imagine what it would be like for a seventeen year old who has never been out of Bellevue, Washington, to be suddenly faced with a culture that is one hundred eighty degrees different from what she is used to, or can ever imagine? Can't you just see her wearing an abaaya, staying home, cooking, cleaning and having babies? Can you see her living under conditions where the husband's word is law and where the mother-in-law runs the household and the wife has no say in it or in anything else for that matter?"

Jim returned with the drinks, lowered himself into the armchair facing Sarah, leaned back, rubbed his eyes and sighed. "I talked to Amy." His voice sounded weird, as though he was subduing a scream. "I told her everything you're telling me. It's no use. She is determined to go through with it. She will be eighteen in the spring of 1996, free to make her own decisions."

"Did you talk to her parents?"

"I did. They are very upset. They want me to find some other home for Muhammad as soon as I can. Being under the same roof makes it difficult for Amy's parents to have much control over their daughter."

"Any ideas? Muhammad has another year to graduate."

"The Wilsons are my friends. That's the main reason Muhammad is in Washington state and the fact that the University of Washington has a terrific program which he might be able to enroll in after he completes the basics at Bellevue Community College. There are families that accept foreign students. I have to look into it. I'm sure it can be arranged. My concern for the moment is not Muhammad. I sense there is more to it than they are willing to tell us."

"Who's they?"

"Muhammad and Amy."

"Like what?"

Jim sipped his drink slowly. "I guess it was mostly Muhammad. Not what he said so much, but the way he said it – like he was reading from notes or something. Didn't sound like him at all. Amy, however, was quite forceful with her message. No hesitation whatsoever."

"You think she's pregnant, right?"

"I think she is and I think they are already married."

Stunned disbelief was Sarah's immediate response. Jim was not in the habit of making meaningless remarks – remarks made for the sole purpose of shocking someone. "What makes you say that?"

"Just a feeling. I asked a lot of questions when I talked to Muhammad last night and afterwards to Amy. Like I said, he was very careful with his answers – almost as if he'd been tutored. And she in effect told me to mind my own business. I don't think Amy's parents know. They like Muhammad. They like him a lot. He has been a model guest so far. I suspect they would be opposed to the marriage because of the cultural, social and religious differences – from the little they know about it. And believe me it's little – practically nil. Amy's parents are devout Catholics and I doubt they knew where Jordan was located before they met Muhammad. They know he is Muslim, though. I made sure they knew before they agreed to have him stay with them."

"Did you mention to Amy that Muhammad can have at least three more wives, can divorce her whenever he wants to, and there's no law to protect her if her husband decides to take their children away from her?"

"I think you can guess the answer to that. Like every other American woman who marries out of her culture, she is sure it will not happen to her. She assured me Muhammad would never do a thing like that."

Initially the differences charm and attract, Sarah thought, but soon after marriage they raise their ugly heads demanding special attention. How can a seventeen-year-old fathom what the differences are, what impact they will have on her life. At twenty-seven, and with all the exposure she had had to both cultures, she found most age-old traditions difficult to comprehend and almost impossible to tolerate.

She decided to sleep on it. The next day she would write a letter to Muhammad, a letter to Amy and a third letter to Amy's parents. But if Jim's suspicions proved to be correct, probably nothing she wrote, said, or did, would make an iota of difference, if they were already married and or she was pregnant.

Jim advised her to wait at least a couple of days. "I forgot to mention," Jim said. "Muhammad told me he sent you a letter, a couple of days ago giving detailed explanation about the same subject. Let's wait for his letter before we take action."

"Letters sometimes take weeks to get here. We should probably check into the possibility of another host family and perhaps into the possibility of admitting Muhammad to the University of Washington. You're right. They have a strong computer department there. If my information is correct, they give priority to minorities and they have fraternities and dormitories. They fill up quickly though. That's why I think we should not loose time. Maybe a new environment will give Muhammad something new to think about. Of course that all depends on the assumption that they are not already married and she is not pregnant."

"I'll look into it. Despite the intensive schedule he has and despite all the private tutoring, I doubt Muhammad will qualify for admission to the university. The requirements are pretty tough. His English has improved but his general knowledge is awfully lacking. Even if the University or a vocational training school accepts him, we will still have to figure out a way to solve the problem in regards to his relationship with Amy. And it will be a lot harder to solve if Amy is pregnant."

"That's just a guess right, Jim?" Her question was meant more to placate her frazzled nerves than expect a denial from Jim. "Neither Muhammad, nor Amy, told you out right that she is pregnant, right?"

Jim smiled, rose, went to the kitchen to pour himself another drink.

"More wine?"

"No, thanks. I've got enough cobwebs in my head. Another drink will knock me out."

Jim returned to the living room drink in hand.

As Sarah mulled over the complexities involved in marriages undertaken without examining the inherent difficulties which were a large part of the picture, she realized it happened more often than she liked, and would probably continue to do so regardless of what she said or did. Witness foreign wives chasing ex-husbands across oceans to catch a glimpse of their children. All those women, like Amy, refused to believe that the person they planned to marry would ever 'do something like that.' For the time being, at least until Muhammad's letter arrived, the best course of action was to be prepared for the worst.

"You and I are about to embark on a similar venture," Jim

said, as though it was a foregone conclusion. "I'd marry Nabila right now if she would agree, and you are practically married to Suheil. How can we, in all fairness tell Amy and Muhammad the road ahead is full of pot holes?"

"Jim, I'm not against mixed marriages. Obviously, as the world becomes smaller, and contact among different cultures becomes an every day affair, we are bound to see more people of different backgrounds attracted to each other. If they are aware, or knowledgeable about the differences in each others backgrounds and feel they can cope with them, then it's the best thing that could happen to this world of ours which at present is full of false pride and prejudice. Unfortunately, I sincerely doubt that those who really make the plunge have the foggiest notion what they're getting themselves into. And even then, it would not worry me so much if no children were involved. That spells double trouble should the marriage not work out."

"That's why we're here, right? To make a difference, to narrow the gap – hopefully, maybe. More likely, we are deluding ourselves." Jim leaned back in the armchair seriously examining his drink.

"Come now, Jim. All you have to do is observe the children's faces in our classrooms. It gives me more satisfaction than, than ..." Sarah stopped unable to articulate her thought in words. Eventually she said, "I can't think of a thing that would give me more satisfaction."

Jim cocked his head to one side and studied his protégé for a full minute before he spoke. "You're crazy. You know that. Worst than your father. And even worst than your mother. Neither your father, nor your mother ever connected with the stupendous amount of wealth they had. While Adnan Kashougi was being hailed as one of the richest men in the world and reveled in the media attention piled upon him ad nauseum, your father, who had far more wealth than Kashoughi had or will ever have, never once made an issue of it. Hardly anyone knew about it. I think your parents simply did not connect. It was as though they had compartmentalized it. The money in one compartment, your parents in another, making contact only for their needs."

Mention of her parents, never far from her thoughts, brought tears to Sarah's eyes.

Jim walked over and gave her a big hug – a bear of a man, a bear of a hug. "You and I are blessed to have known individuals like your parents. It is very rare, especially in the Arab world to come across a man of your father's noble stature, or your mother's generous spirit. They always said after a certain point what you're wearing or eating does not matter any more. And you know what? The more I think about it, the more I am fascinated by the minds of those who can think like that. Me, I am a simpleton and such noble thoughts are way beyond the comprehension of my ordinary mind."

Sarah dried her eyes and let a faint smile cross her lips. "If you had an ordinary mind, Jim, you couldn't have worked with Dad for decades, and you wouldn't be here making sure his daughter lives up to her father's expectations."

Jim laughed, a hearty laugh, shook his head, sipped his Scotch.

"Any news about Ali?" Sarah asked. "It's been months."

"Lack of news is not the problem," Jim replied. "It's figuring out what to believe and what to shelve. The investigator has located a shepherd near Trebil, on Iraq's western border with Jordan. The shepherd says he has seen a man of Ali's description with a group of bandits who are terrorizing the new, modern highway – highway 10. Apparently, more than five years of sanctions have crippled Iraq's economy to such an extent that any goods the bandits steal from passing motorists can be sold on the black market, at exorbitant prices in no time at all. I am told the most sought after goods are cigarettes."

The information was comforting in some ways and disturbing in others. Trebil was the closest point in Iraq to the Jordanian border, three hundred miles to Amman. It also meant that their fear of Ali having landed in an Iraqi jail was perhaps no longer valid. Sarah figured Ali had probably joined the bandits out of desperation, as he had no money. "Isn't the highway patrolled?" Sarah asked.

"It is – to some extent."

"Which means?"

"Depends if the bandits are lucky, if the guards on patrol duty feel they have been adequately compensated to look the other way, and if the same guards are on duty when the bandits stop motorists to rob them the next time around."

"Do you think it is Ali, Jim?"

"More than likely. The shepherd said the young man spoke Arabic but not the way Iraqis do. The Iraqi dialect is harsher. He said the man spoke the same way the truck drivers from Jordan speak. He was sure the man he saw was not from Iraq."

It stands to reason, Sarah figured. The dialect the shepherd heard the young man use was most probably Palestinian, same as Jordanian – the speaker Ali. Aside from tanker trucks to Jordan carrying Iraqi oil and trucks transporting produce to Iraq, few Jordanians or Palestinians carrying Jordanian passports ventured into Iraq or cared to. It was important though to make sure the individual in question was definitely Ali. If so, what were his chances of being caught? Had he moved closer to the Jordanian border to sneak back into Jordan at the appropriate time? They could do nothing but wait – a situation synonymous with life in the Middle East. 'Wait. Have patience. God willing, tomorrow everything will be all right.' Most everyone repeated those phrases regardless of how serious the situation was. "Never heard worst rubbish in my life," Sarah grumbled sullenly.

"Do not despair my fair lady," Jim teased. "Tomorrow is another day."

Sarah rose, went to the kitchen to fix herself a cup of tea. She was about to pour the boiling water on the tea bag in her tea cup, when her hand let go of the kettle without warning, spilling boiling water on the kitchen counter and the floor. Fortunately, she jumped back just in time. Only a few drops landed on her bare feet.

Jim rushed to the kitchen. "You haven't been yourself since you came back, Sarah. Something is bothering you. Something you are trying to hide from me. What is it?" Jim took her by the arm and returned with her to the living room. "Sit still. I'll clean up the kitchen and I'll bring you a cup of tea. Put your feet up, your head back and relax. Whatever is bugging you is best shared – when you're ready."

She did try to relax. The events of the past three days had taken their toll. Her hands shook, her voice shook, her stomach ached. She had to tell Jim. Suheil had made her promise and threatened to tell Jim himself if she did not do so – that very same night. Suheil made no secret of his dislike for the Sheikh. He believed firmly that the man was evil and capable of the vilest deeds. In his opinion, a man who hired thugs to kidnap a woman whose ideas he opposed, was a most despicable character – the lowest of the low. The fact that the man was a cleric made the doctor loathe him that much more.

"You have been going around in circles all evening long," Jim said as he handed her a cup of tea. "It's time you unloaded whatever is on your mind."

She had to. She had no choice. And she felt she needed to. After all, for the time being, he was the only invariable in her life. "Hopefully, you'll soon be receiving a call from a mullah," Sarah said, not quite sure where to begin.

"A mullah? What would a mullah want from me?"

"I gave him your number thinking he would be in Jordan before Suheil and I got here."

Jim listened with intense concentration as Sarah told him briefly most of what had happened in Egypt – pointing to the contrast between Mullah Rashid's approach to Islam and life in general, with that of the Sheikh in Jordan.

Throughout her description of the events in the village as well as the airport, Jim's expression did not change. And much to Sarah's surprise he did not interrupt her or ask any questions as he invariably did when a matter that serious and concerning her was being discussed.

That is not until she had said all she had to say. When she stopped, he said, "Start from the beginning and give me all the details. And I mean every detail whether you think it's insignificant, irrelevant, or whatever. Leave nothing out."

She pondered his request quietly for a few seconds. Distorted Islamic teachings were responsible for ruining many lives, mostly lives of women – most recently Um Yahya's. In less than forty-eight hours, Um Yahya's daughter's face had been burned with acid, her first born son had been stabbed to death by his own father, and the father had ended up taking his own life. Never in a million years would he have done it for killing a daughter. And Um Yahya was struggling to recover from the second beating she had received from her husband in less than twenty four hours for allowing a man, a doctor, to enter their dwelling. Where as knowledgeable religious leaders wanted to spread Islam through persuasion and were succeeding marvelously with converts from all over the world, there were other clerics, fanatics, in equally prominent positions eager to use whatever it took, including force, to spread their version of Islam. And they were in a hurry, in a hurry to ride the crest of the wave of religious revival sweeping the region.

Egypt is the birthplace of Arab feminist movement, gaining the right to vote in 1956. Yet a woman could not leave her home without her husband's permission until 1979. If she managed to run away, the husband had the right to force her to return home and have sex with him if he chose to, whether she wanted to or not. It was a wife's legal obligation. It is – to this day, in many Arab countries and in Iran. Sarah recalled an article in the *Wall Street Journal*. The headline read, Divorce Iranian Style: In Court, Islamic Law Honors the Husband. The subtitle stated, 'The Wife Has Few Rights The Mullahs Will Concede; Battering Is No Grounds.' Another headline

read, Islamic Law, as It Is Practiced, Forgives Husbands
Everything, Even Wife Beating. The writer, Peter Waldman
goes on to state, "The problem, of course, isn't Islam, which,
in the Koran, reveres women and instructs men to 'live with
them on a footing of kindness and equity.'"

Yet in Iran, to date, divorce is nearly impossible for a
woman without her husband's permission. Under Khomeini,
the mullahs gained back the power they had lost under the
Shah and then some, and proceeded immediately to transform
the society into a society like it was in the seventh century
during the Prophet's life. And they did the same with government through a legal system based on the Koran and Islamic
law, the Shariah. Mr. Waldman goes on to say, "Women have
paid the price. The Tehran family court today is like a horror
chamber." Despite the severity of their complaints, few
women are granted divorce. The judges are male, clergymen,
the privileged, enforcing Islamic rule.

Women's misery does not end even if by some miracle
they obtain a divorce. Where children are involved, custody is
automatically given to the father for boys older than two and
girls older than seven. This is according to the Sharia.
Frequently, though, the father ends up by taking custody of
the children at whatever age the children might be if he so
desires. A woman's voice is hardly ever heard in a court of
law.

Soon after returning to Iran after the fall of the Shah,
Ayatollah Khomeini in his zeal to rid the country of Western
decadence declared, "There is no fun in Islam." Works of
hundreds of Iranian artists, musicians and writers were
destroyed by the Ministry of Culture and Guidance. Works
glorifying Islam was the only art form encouraged and
accepted.

A sense of desperation engulfed Sarah. Conditions being
as they were the hostility she faced no longer surprised her.
Perhaps her efforts were misplaced. Perhaps the rising tide
was much too strong for her, Jim and all those who worked

with her to cope with. Yet whenever she felt overwhelmed by seemingly insurmountable problems, she reminded herself of the countless invisible women who worked tirelessly in a male-dominated world to bring a semblance of dignity and basic human rights to women. This was true more so for women in the Muslim world where the few gains women had fought for for centuries, evaporated overnight with the over-throw of the Shah of Iran and the coming to power of Ayatollah Ruhullah Khomeini.

The constant insidious increase in the gravity of the prob-lem left an indelible impact on Sarah's psyche, a psyche which had already been exposed to much more trauma as a child than most adults in the western world are exposed to in a lifetime.

Soul searching invariably left her depressed until, once again, she reviewed mentally the sacrifices other women throughout history had made for the benefit of their gender as well as all humans deprived of basic rights. First to come to mind was Rigoberta Menchu who played a crucial role in opposing and defeating the government of President Serrano who wanted to impose an authoritarian regime in Guatemala. This was a woman whose father, mother and brother were tor-tured and killed by authorities who insisted on perpetuating the plight of the indigenous people forced to live under slave conditions. Rigoberta Menchu's book, *I Rigoberta Menchu*, and her tireless efforts won her the Nobel Peace Prize in 1992.

Sarah first read Rigoberta Menchu's book soon after it was published in 1983 and often parts of it whenever her mind could use a morale boost. Rigoberta Menchu was a woman Sarah admired. Recently her book has come under attack. Many of the events she describes as happening to her apparently were false or exaggerated.

Vera Chirwa was another woman, who, along with her husband worked to gain independence from Britain for Malawi. She was abducted, charged with treason, and sentenced to death. After her husband's death in prison, she was released in 1993 at age sixty due to intense international pressure. Despite it all, she has not succumbed to adversity. She has concentrated her efforts on human rights education in Malawi. In her opinion, the slow but sure way of preparing future generations to respect human rights, equality, and justice for all, could only be achieved through education.

Precisely what Sarah's parents were firmly convinced of.

Megawati Sukarno-Putri is similarly involved in Indonesia.

Yet Sarah's role model, the woman she admired above all, was Hanan Ashrawi – the spokeswoman for Palestinians – the founder of Palestinian Independent Commission for Citizen's Rights. A Christian, married to a Muslim, she speaks out fearlessly against intolerance, against abuse of human rights, and by her courage sets an example to other Arab women to fight for their rights. However, she does not limit her struggle to women's issues alone. If Israel acts irresponsibly towards Palestinians, Mrs. Ashrawi is quick to speak out against them and equally quick when Palestinians are at fault.

No doubt countless other women not in the limelight, women we don't hear about, fight for human rights, dignity and tolerance in any way they can. The brutal truth, Sarah realized, was that giving up was not an option – not anymore.

Jim agreed. "The stakes are high, the prize is power. Therefore, our struggle must go on." Nevertheless, Jim felt violent Islamic militancy in the Middle East had crested. "It could also be the lull before the storm," he admitted reluctantly. "Public revulsion over the violent methods used by the extremists and disillusionment with established Islamic regimes like in Iran, and the Sudan, has helped some to decelerate the rising tide of fanaticism. The excesses the extremists have resorted to, the brutal crackdown by the Egyptian government – in response, and the civil war waged by extremists in Algeria and the Sudan are in the news daily. In Algeria alone over 50,000 human lives have been snuffed out in the name of religion, followed by more almost daily. Militants feel free to cut throats, explode bombs, shoot and maim indiscriminately to impress the world with their zeal for their religion. The toll in Algeria keeps rising. The Taliban in Afghanistan are even more rabid followers of strict Islamist rules of their own making. They have closed all schools for girls, have ordered all women including foreigners to be accompanied by a male relative when they leave their homes, and no woman – professional or not, can work outside her home. Even health care for females is restricted. All these factors have left a negative impact on people of all religious beliefs. Unless there is a radical change in their tactics, I believe the negative impact will eventually determine the outcome."

"Meanwhile, all we can do is educate – and hope it works," Jim added.

"Time," Sarah said. "That's what's important. It might work for us or against us. I have always felt that the world is getting smaller by the day, making insularity almost impossible. Clerics are no longer worried about an enemy attack by the Big Satan they call Amrika. Their worst nightmare is reserved for VCRs, TVs and satellite dishes. The onslaught of their culture by western technology is feared more than guns. The impact of television all over the world is impossible to overstate. Pictures, unlike words, speak volumes. Their impact is greater and lasts much longer. No wonder the main topic of discussion recently in the Iranian parliament was how to stop the proliferation of satellite dishes mushrooming all over the country."

Jim nodded. "They worry about western influence on their culture not because they value their culture, but because it will put a permanent stop to the abuse of power which men in this part of the world have enjoyed for centuries. They are deluded by power. Don't expect them to give up their privileged status without fighting to the bitter end. Clerics across the board, maybe with the exception of a few, consider Michael Jackson and MTV to be their worst enemies."

After a moment of reflection, Sarah recalled the arrogance of the men in the villages, not only in Egypt but in Jordan and all other Arab countries as well. It seemed to her the less educated the man, the more eager he was to prove his power, to make sure everyone knew he was in control – he was a man. These men dressed their insecurities in religion in hopes of giving it a respectable look. How long did it take to change a mentality like that? Decades? The image of Um Yahya eyes swollen shut, curled in fetal position lingered in her mind. Hind with her disfigured face and very likely blinded in one eye. Hind's brother, a young boy of eleven – stabbed to death. The father dead. The reason? Ignorance. It did not matter how she tried to twist and turn the events in her mind to give them some kind of rationality. She couldn't. Ignorance was the only explanation she could come up with. She feared those images would remain imprinted in her mind permanently to remind her of the challenges ahead, the adversities involved, the searing agony – and yes maybe, just maybe success – some day – perhaps.

"I'm waiting," Jim grumped.

Her thoughts interrupted, Sarah looked askance at Jim. "Waiting? For what?"

"Whenever you're in the mood to reminisce, it indicates to me that your gray cells are working overtime, sorting out your options. It goes something like this. Should I tell Jim or not? I suggest you tell Jim whatever it is you're not telling Jim. You think I have a short fuse, I overreact. I do. If I didn't, you probably wouldn't be here now. Unfortunately, I can't advise you or urge you to leave like I used to in the past. I'm just as involved as you are. And now that that's off my chest, let's hear what more the Egyptians entertained you with."

She knew that eventually she would have to tell him. The encounter with the kidnappers at the airport had given her a terrible scare. Intimidation, rape, imprisonment, torture and death were all a part of the deal, endured by many women throughout history. Hazards of the job. She had come to expect the same for herself. Her adversaries were diligent, dangerous men, tools in the hands of power crazy clerics with 'respectable faces.' Yet despite it all she was reluctant to make a big deal of it. She had managed to take care of the incident quite well actually. Hadn't she?

You were damn lucky, an inner voice reminded her.

Jim waited patiently, his manner making it clear he expected her to confide in him regardless of the reservations she might have, and regardless of the gravity of the matter. It was an understanding they had with each other, an unwritten law if you will. Actually, it was the only condition Jim had stipulated in agreeing to work for her – total honesty. Since then, although he was not a patient man, he had learned to bid his time until she was ready to take him into her confidence. It was a unique relationship, unlike father and daughter, or brother and sister, or even friends. He was her self-appointed guardian, her protector, and her keeper – the only way he knew to help make her dream a reality, the only way he knew how to get the job done.

"I was downtown shopping yesterday," he said to keep her focused. "Actually I was in a watch repair shop to get my watch fixed when I ran into your favorite cousin."

"Really?"

"He asked about you – cool, composed, like we were long lost friends. He cocked his head to one side, a crooked smile on his lips. 'How is my over privileged air head cousin?'" he asked.

That was enough to warn Sarah Ramzi either knew about the kidnapping or was somehow involved. And the way Jim relayed the message, it indicated to her that Jim suspected Ramzi of some vile deed – in keeping with Ramzi's character.

"I gave him a disdainful look," Jim continued without waiting for Sarah's answer, "turned my back and proceeded to explain to the watchmaker about the problem with my watch. Ramzi has the patience of a starved hyena at a banquet. He grabbed his cane and stomped out of the store."

"Poor Ramzi," Sarah said smiling, "Life has been so unfair to him. Think how much better off he would have been had he inherited my father's wealth. After all, he is the next male heir in line. If only my father had been aware of the error of his ways, he would have respected tradition, and given Ramzi what he wanted. Ramzi could then live the life he always assumed he would – like Adnan Kashoughi, or better. It would have at the same time brought joy to the hearts of all my father's relatives. Instead, my unconventional father made secure arrangements, in London, away from Arab countries, in his daughter's name. Just thinking about it must drive Ramzi crazy – absolutely mad."

Jim sipped his Scotch slowly, seemingly lost in thought. "Do not underestimate Ramzi," he said softly. "He is not a man who gives up easily. Not when billions are involved."

Millions, billions, whatever, Sarah thought. After a certain point it does not matter any more. Why should it all go to one man or one woman for that matter, just because he or she happens to be related to a person who had wealth? Especially since it is that person's explicit wish for poor and underprivileged children to be his beneficiaries. And why can't Jim stop reminding me of Ramzi? Could it be that there was more to it than a chance meeting?

Jim rose, stretched, walked to the living room window overlooking the courtyard. After a while, he turned around slowly and faced Sarah. "That man had a smirk on his face when he asked me about you. Like he knew something I didn't. I thought of grabbing him by the collar, forcing him to talk to wipe that stupid smile off his face for good. I didn't. The man is a wimp. He'd probably make a scene, scream for help, or collapse. Whatever. I was sure he would do something stupid. I could tell he was itching to anger me. Unfortunately, I was not in the mood for theatrics. I let him go – for now."

Sarah got the message. In his own gentle, persuasive way,

when her safety was at stake, Jim invariably extracted the information he needed, irrespective of the effort or time it took. It intrigued Sarah. Jim was a man with little tolerance for small talk, no patience with stupidity, and less with injustice. But when an issue involved Sarah, it did not matter how long it took, or what price his reaction would cost him mentally, physically or emotionally. He got the job done. "All right, Jim. You have made your point and I agree. You have a right to know. I came close to being abducted at the airport in Cairo soon after I called you." She told him in detail the warning by the Egyptian security agent, their travel by boat and the incident at the airport.

"You know what worries me most about you," Jim shot back angered by her reluctance to talk to him about it. "You think you are immune to the crazies of this world, you think just because you knowingly will not hurt anyone that the rest of the world will react the same way towards you. So then when you find yourself faced with an unpleasant, or should I say life-threatening situation, you do your best to hide it from me. We cannot work together unless we are honest with each other. I want that understood clearly."

"What do you want me to do, Jim. Come running to you each time I have a problem?"

Jim came and sat next to her on the sofa. "Please listen carefully. There are only a few of us against a whole fanatical crowd – individuals who removed the word 'think' from their vocabulary sixteen years ago when Khomeini came to power. They have substituted it with feel. Using logic will get you nowhere. Education beginning with the young – will. But it will take time – a precious commodity we have very little of. When and where necessary we have to fight fire with fire. Otherwise, you can forget about making a difference. You will not be around long enough to do it. So you might just as well leave."

"Aren't you being a little over dramatic, Jim? Of course I expected to have to overcome obstacles. I think we have to take each day as it comes and ...”

“And what? Wait for them to kidnap you and force me to pay ransom? You know very well, regardless of how important you think your contribution is to the needy in this place, there are those who think otherwise and they would dearly love to see you departed or dead.”

Sarah felt exhausted, drained. Of course Jim was right, and of course he had reason to be angry, and it did complicate matters further. “What do you want me to do, Jim?”

“Greed brings the worst out in most people, Sarah. You must understand that. Ordinarily, those who have money are impressed by it and by the awesome responsibility that goes with it. Unfortunately, like your parents, you don’t connect with your money. Consequently, you find it difficult to foresee the unintended consequences that result from it. I implore you to please, please, for your safety, for the safety of all those who are committed to work with you, and for my sanity, do keep me abreast of any new developments.”

Sarah was quiet for a long while mulling over options she might have to prevent further mishaps. “Why not make announcements in the local newspapers that whatever money her parents had, has been put in a trust fund to be used for educational purposes – only, for children mostly.”

Jim shook his head in disbelief. “That’s what your father’s lawyers in London told Ramzi. He did not believe them. And the clerics did not believe Ramzi. In a way, that’s to our advantage. It would have been worse if they had believed him. They will feel infinitely threatened if it becomes evident that besides your determination, they will also have to cope with all the wealth left by your parents channeled for educational purposes.”

Sarah was running thin on patience. “Why me, Jim? There are literally hundreds, perhaps thousands of very wealthy Arabs – men who could part with millions and not feel it at all. Why are they not threatened?”

“The Arabs you speak of are males, mostly oil wealth,

ultra conservative. Whenever necessary, they make a donation to the clergy and all is well. You, on the other hand are a
female who insists on educating females, spending your
money teaching children to think. They can't understand why
a beautiful, wealthy, young woman like you should waste her
time and money on a bunch of underprivileged children –
unless of course she has an ulterior motive."

"What ulterior motive? Do they think I am a one woman
bulldozer here to sweep their children into the land of
Godlessness?"

"Sarah, listen to me. Money is the issue with Ramzi, but
not the only issue for the clerics. You did offer money to the
chief cleric, and the other clerics know you'll give if they ask
for it. They are not stupid. They know what you're up to. You
are a threat to their newly found power through religious
revival – a power they are so desperately struggling to cling
to. You call it education – they call it subversion. I don't see
much common ground to work with."

"Religious revival? There's a serious misconception here.
It seems to me Khomeini style fanaticism is being peddled as
religious revival."

"Call it what you like. The clerics love it. They call it
Islam."

"Except that it's not the true teachings of the Prophet. It's
their version of it – the version that guarantees power, almost
absolute power to the clergy, and to men, any man over his
wife and daughters. I have to admit Jim, the more they harass
me, the more they plot to intimidate me, the more I'm challenged, and the more determined it makes me to fight even
harder. We're talking basic human rights here. Women beaten
half to death by husbands who have the right to divorce them
any time they please by simply uttering three times 'I divorce
you' – women whose children can be taken from them anytime their husband's so desire – women who have to slave day
and night for their husbands' pleasure – women who cannot
leave their homes without their husbands' permission –

women who are treated no better than slaves. Their crime – born without a penis. Does that make sense to you, Jim? Does it make sense to any fair-minded person – especially when those powers are deceptively attributed to religion?"

"Few things in life make sense, Sarah," Jim replied cryptically. "I'm with you – to a point, and not for the same reasons. I'm a cynic. I don't believe people change. I prefer to do my thing, and let others do theirs."

Sarah pondered Jim's statements quietly for a few seconds. Gradually, it became clear to her that the poverty of that type of a mindset did not represent Jim at all. Behind the tough guy exterior, Sarah had witnessed, on many occasions, Jim practically falling apart when someone he cared about was mistreated or an innocent person victimized. It was Sarah's turn to suspect Jim. She wanted to know if she was correct in assuming that Jim was hiding something from her?

"Your actions speak volumes about you," Sarah said, "but they have never presented you as man who is cynical, self centered or selfish. I think you are throwing that line at me for a reason."

"I hate to admit it, but you are right. At times, though, I do wish I were less of a ... of a ..." Jim shrugged his shoulders. He didn't know what to call himself.

"Less caring?"

"That's it. I do. I really wish I could care less."

"I'll tell you what, Jim. It is my turn to accuse you of not coming forth with info you're concerned might upset me. You are playing the same game I played earlier."

Jim smiled. "What makes you say that?"

"You are waiting for someone or for more information. I'm not sure which. I'm a big girl. I can take it. Now let's have it."

"Am I that transparent?"

"Jim!"

Jim rose and walked back to the window, looked out at the darkness outside and returned. "Are you expecting Suheil tonight?"

"No. He had a lot of catching up to do at the hospital. He figured it would be past midnight before he was done. Why do you ask?"

Jim lowered his huge frame into the armchair facing Sarah. "You are not the only one threatened with kidnapping," he said, anguish shadowing his eyes. "I have reason to believe Suheil is a marked man."

"Why Suheil?" Sarah's voice betrayed her indignation, as though her indignation would somehow change the message. But she couldn't help herself.

"He's been branded as anti-Islam."

"Oh, my God." Sarah broke out in a clammy sweat. That meant any one who considered himself a true Muslim had the right to kill him. "Because of the family planning clinics?"

"Of course. What did you expect? And, because he's in love with you. Allow me to enlighten you. You, my dear are a spy – for Israel and for America. What you plan for Arab children is nothing short of the destruction of everything Islam stands for."

"Reliable source?"

"Very." Jim explained he had hired the same firm investigating Ali's disappearance to assign two well-qualified agents to keep tabs on the activities of the Sheikh.

Sarah rested her head against the back of the sofa fighting to control a strange rage building inside her. She could tolerate attacks on herself, verbal, religious, political or whatever they felt like throwing at her. But not Suheil. What evil lurked in the minds of those who accused a man of Suheil's integrity of being anti Islam when he spent practically all the money he made, as well as his medical skills on those less fortunate than himself without fanfare, without ever asking anything in return.

Another thought raised its curious head. Jim left nothing to chance if he could help it. No doubt he had the Sheikh's phone tapped and knew about the kidnapping in Egypt. He had acted strange when Sarah called him from Egypt. First quiet, then a great sigh as though he was relieved of some heavy burden. Sarah had not given it much thought at that time, preoccupied mostly with the unavailability of space to fly back to Jordan. But why had he not warned her?

"I had no way of reaching you," Jim said, reading her thoughts. "After many debates with myself, I had decided to seek help from our embassy in Egypt when you called. I was so surprised and relieved that I practically fell on my face. I knew then that the plot had somehow been foiled."

"And?"

"That's it. Soon after the Sheikh was informed of the failure of the mission. He was not too happy about it. And that's an understatement."

"Is Suheil covered?"

"As much as anyone can be."

Unaccustomed to the constant bombardment by events she had no control over, Sarah felt disillusioned, numb – especially when others were made to account for their actions solely because of their association with her. "Will you let Suheil know?"

"I have not made up my mind yet. He is just as difficult to convince he needs protection as you are, and when Mullah Rashid gets here, we will really have a job on our hands with all three of you, and myself, on the top of their hit list."

For a few brief seconds Sarah felt paralyzed physically and mentally and overwhelmed emotionally. Too many instances of ruthless solutions for individuals branded as anti Islamic – by arrogant men who had appointed themselves as guardians of the faith – their version of the faith – and who stopped at nothing to make sure their version prevailed. And the few fighting to bring the truth back to their religion faced with the most daunting challenge of their lives from the time Khomeini had arrived on the scene. These thoughts crowded her mind. She had no satisfactory resolutions other than education – a long-term proposition. Short term consisted mainly of frustration, pain and agony. The intensity of it all and the fast pace of progression alarmed her immensely. If there was more death and destruction, she was not sure she could deal with it – especially if she was a contributing factor, actually, the main contributing factor – at least to the present crises.

"Do not torture yourself," Jim said as he walked to the front door. "The Sheikh might be ruthless and cunning, but despite what he thinks of blacks, he is not nearly as smart as I am."

"You don't have to put up a brave facade for me, Jim. Our quarrel is not with a lone clergyman, but a whole culture. I could be more optimistic if I did not witness the daily erosion of our efforts, and the results of unintended consequences we cannot foresee or control."

"Does that mean you're ready to quit?" The astonished expression on Jim's face did not surprise Sarah.

"No, Jim. It means we have to try that much harder. What about you?"

"Me? I'm thoroughly enjoying the challenge. Why would I?"

"As they say in the Middle East," Sarah said smiling, "there's always tomorrow. Goodnight, Jim."

Chapter 26

Suheil Tuqan was not amused.

Two weeks of intense, around the clock 'protection' had exacerbated his already strained mental state as it reminded him constantly of the circumstances that necessitated such an extreme measure. Although the men assigned to guard him were highly trained professionals and tried to be as inconspicuous as possible, he felt frustrated, claustrophobic. They followed him everywhere he went – except for the operating room and the bathroom. On those occasions the guards waited outside.

Jim teased the doctor mercilessly. "You have joined the ranks of royalty," he said, a crooked smile on his lips. "The King, the Queen, and their children have to live under identical circumstances. You should feel privileged, not claustrophobic."

Sarah was not amused either. Living under constant threat left her with an uncomfortable feeling, like having unwanted constant companions. She waited a week until Suheil caught up with his work at the hospital then invited Jim and the doctor for a meeting, over dinner at her place. "We should talk to the Sheikh. We have to try," Sarah urged. "We won't know until we do."

"It's a waste of time." Jim had no desire to deal with the cleric. "There's a lot more involved here. The Sheikh does not want to be just another cleric in charge of a mosque. He wants to be the Khomeini of Jordan and eventually the religious representative of all Arabs. That's why nothing we say or do short of putting an end to our activities and our presence here will satisfy him."

"His chances are nil," the doctor replied. "There are far more qualified clerics, especially in Egypt eager to take advantage of what they believe is an awakening, a deep desire among Muslims of the world for a leader who can lead, a leader who can show the world the true meaning of Islam. Khomeini did not represent the Prophet. He represented himself, his vengeance against the Shah for forcing him into exile, and for murdering his son. The Sheikh does not have Khomeini's patience nor does he have Khomeini's following. But he does have an infinite hunger for power, the ruthlessness to wipe out his enemies, and the financial backing from the Saudis to accomplish his goal."

"But he doesn't have the smarts," Jim added.

The discussion between the men continued. Sarah understood and agreed with their comments. Nevertheless, she felt she had to talk to the Sheikh – regardless, even if Jim and Suheil felt it was useless and refused to do so. She had nothing to lose. Or so she thought.

The next day, after classes were dismissed for the day and while Jim drove the children back to camp, Sarah got in her VW bug and drove to the mosque.

The Sheikh's attitude was totally reversed on this her second visit. He was all smiles as he opened the door for her – cynical, chin up, head back, chest out, like a conqueror. Of course he had time for her. He invited her into his office, sat behind his desk, and waited for Sarah to speak.

It was mostly his smile. It sent shivers down Sarah's spine. She made a conscious effort to ignore it, pretend it had no effect on her, but found it difficult to control the pitch of her voice whenever her nerves were on edge.

"I've come to ask you to forget whatever misunderstanding we had in the past. Let's start fresh. You want the welfare of our people and so do we. Instead of fighting each other we should work together."

The Sheikh raised one eyebrow and took on a serious look. Palms clasped resting on the desk he leaned forward as he spoke, his voice calm, measured, with a light touch of sarcasm. "Go on."

Perhaps it was not only the smile but also the manner in which he looked at her, undressing her with his eyes. "That's all," she said and hoped she sounded just as calm.

The Sheikh pushed his shoulders back, raised his head and studied her for a long moment. "What brought about this change of heart?" His question was followed by a smirk. "Did something happen in Egypt to make you see the light?"

Mention of Egypt caught Sarah off guard. It took her a few seconds to realize he was setting up a trap. She smiled and replied looking cool on the outside, turmoil brewing inside, "It did indeed. Mullah Rashid has worked miracles with the villagers in Egypt."

It was not what the Sheikh had wanted to hear.

Mention of Rashid's name wiped the smirk off the Sheikh's face instantly. Sarah figured he probably was waiting to hear about the acid-throwing incident and how it had effected her. She watched the rage build inside the cleric, a rage he desperately fought to control, a rage manifested by the twitching of his facial muscles down to his beard. But it did not stop the Sheikh's eyes from roaming up and down her body. He stopped, pushed a writing pad to the side of the desk, and then said, "Interesting. I find your observation about Mullah Rashid most interesting. Perhaps seeing the results of the work done by a cleric will convince you to leave the job of educating our children to us. It is extremely important for children to be taught by clerics. Don't you agree?"

"No, not quite," she replied without hesitation. "Mullah Rashid handles the religious aspect of the children's education. Regular teachers teach the rest of the curriculum. I think religion should be taught by clerics but the other subjects should be taught by teachers qualified in the subjects they teach." She paused, then threw at him the line he had thrown at her earlier. "Don't you agree?"

The cleric listened with I'll-humor-you-for-a-few-more-seconds look. It did not last long. Soon, his eyes went up and down her body – again – as though he was measuring her for size. "Let's stop this charade," he said taking on a serious look. "What are your intentions? What do you really hope to accomplish?"

"My intentions are simple. I want to educate children, teach them how to think." She stopped, put on a charming smile, asked, "What are yours?"

Her question startled him. "What do you mean, what are yours?"

"Exactly what I asked. What are your intentions?"

The Sheikh narrowed his eyes until they looked almost like slits. "What makes you think I would divulge my intentions or plans or whatever it is you're after to you, to a woman – to a woman who has spent the past year doing everything she can to destroy me and my religion?"

Her smile turned innocent. "You're giving me far more credit than I deserve. I'm only good at teaching children. At least, I hope I am. Destroying those who disagree with me and or their religion is not an option I care to entertain."

He kept his gaze focused on her but said nothing. It was not difficult to sense the contempt he had for women in general and for Sarah in particular – especially when forced to deal with a woman on a one-on-one basis.

Sarah rose. "Thank you for your time. I knew my visit would be a waste of time. But I had to give it one last try."

The cleric's eyes persisted on their journey up and down her body, reminding her of cattle auctions where the buyer examines the animal closely for defects prior to purchase. Suddenly, the Sheikh's face lit up like a man who had accidentally come across a solution to a vexing problem and was eager to share it. "No, no, your visit is not a waste," he said, an impish grin blossoming on his face. "You can help our people immensely. There's no magic to it. Simply transfer the funds you inherited to our mosque. Since you claim educating underprivileged children is your goal, we'll make it easy for you. We'll do it for you."

Was it conceivable that he could think she was that naïve? No matter. It was time to go. "Thanks for the offer. But I like my work. As a matter of fact I like it a lot. And I have absolutely no intention of giving it up." Sarah reached for the doorknob.

"Wait." The cleric rose quickly, walked around the desk and stopped a few inches from Sarah's face. "A beautiful woman like you should not waste her time with children from refugee camps. Go to Europe. Go to America. There's a big world out there. Go. Enjoy yourself."

His face was much too close to hers and his breath stunk. "I have lived in Europe and I have lived in America. This is where my life is and this is where I plan to stay." Sarah turned, tried to reach the doorknob.

The Sheikh took a step back, planted himself against the door, effectively blocking it.

"Don't, don't you." He sounded so excited, he could hardly talk. "Don't you wonder at times how others who have money live? You can't possibly be sane and want to stay in a small, desert country, surrounded by filthy, ignorant children."

He kept blabbering.

She did not hear much of what he said. Had no use for it. And the fact that he was blocking the door was weighing heavily on her mind. "I'll tell you what," she said, acting as though nothing was amiss and she was in full control, "When you tell me what you plan to do with your life, I'll tell you what I plan to do with mine. Now if you will excuse me, I'd like to leave."

He studied her, his head cocked to one side, the corner of his lips twisted downwards. "I have a proposition to make," he said, his voice smooth – minus the usual edge, to the point where he sounded almost civilized and made her almost gag. "If you agree, all our problems will be solved."

He did not have to spell it out for her. Nevertheless, to give

herself time to find a way out of her predicament she decided
to continue with the charade. "What's your proposition?"

"Can't you guess?" The grin on his face broadened and
the expectant look in his eyes manifested a true picture of his
over-sized ego. No doubt a woman who took upon herself to
break all taboos to come see him, in private, for the second
time, was asking for it, and he in his graciousness was ready
to oblige.

Sarah's determination not to lose her cool was being sorely
tested. She had to be blind not to see the lust exuding out of
every pore in his body. With barely concealed exasperation
she replied, "I'm not good at guessing. Why don't you tell
me."

"I can do better than that." And without a moment's hesitation he threw himself at her, grabbed her head in both his
hands and forced his lips on hers. Quickly his right hand
moved down over to her shoulder, while his left hand held her
head tight against his lips.

Sarah was about to puke. She struggled to free herself
pushing him back with all her force – to no avail. The harder
she pushed, the more he clung to her, and the more labored his
breathing got. His grip felt like the embrace of a boa constrictor and his breathing sounded like a dog panting after a
long chase. In desperation, Sarah lifted her right leg and
smacked her knee in his groin – hard.

The cleric let out a sharp scream, doubled over his hands
instinctively releasing her to provide cover for his genitals.
Meanwhile, his cleric's turban flew off his head half way
across the room.

Sarah opened the door and dashed out.

She shook violently for a few seconds, her legs limp like
cooked sausage, her heart pounding, protesting violently
against the abuse it was subjected to. She ran her fingers
through her disheveled hair, forced her body to cooperate, and
headed for her car parked in the street across the mosque.
Once there, she dropped herself in the driver's seat, took a

deep breath to tame her electrified body, put her head on the steering wheel and made a conscious effort to pull herself together before attempting to merge into the unruly traffic. A few minutes later, she was home parking her car in the underground garage when she realized she did not remember how she got there. Her mind had been floating on a completely different wavelength.

The guards parked behind her seconds later.

She had forgotten all about them.

Nabila was also in the parking lot. She rushed towards Sarah relief apparent on her face. "Am I glad to see you."

Please God. I don't need another shocker. Not today, Sarah muttered to herself. "What are you doing here? What's wrong Nabila?"

"Attiyeh's wife delivered – at home. We didn't have time to find a cab to take her to the hospital."

"Oh, my God. Is she all right? How did you manage?"

Nabila smiled. "The best thing that could have happened to us is Gwynne being here with us. Attiyeh's older daughter, Asieh, came running to our apartment panic stricken. She said her mother was about to deliver the baby. They needed help. Gwynne rushed to Attiyeh's apartment while I went looking for you. I couldn't find you. I knew Jim was not around. He drove the children home. So I ran to the street to grab a cab. By the time I got back, five, six minutes at the most, Gwynne was holding the baby in one hand and trying to cut the umbilical cord with the other. Cool as winter sunshine. I was shaking like I had just seen a beheading in the public square. Gwynne was not impressed. She plopped the baby in my arms and proceeded to cut the umbilical cord, like she'd done it all her life."

The two women headed towards Attiyeh's apartment but after taking a few steps, Nabila stopped. "May I borrow your car?" she asked. "That's why I returned to the parking lot, to see if you had returned. We need feminine napkins for Mrs. Attiyeh."

"Of course you may." Sarah handed her the car keys. "Where's Attiyeh?"

"In the kitchen – crying, praying, whining. Take your pick."

"He's worried about losing the baby, right?"

"You guessed it. He says God has given him four boys so far. This is the fifth. And each time God has taken them back before they were a year old."

Sarah made a mental note to talk to Attiyeh, to reassure him. It was Attiyeh's firm belief that God found something he did unacceptable and consequently punished him by taking his most prized possessions from him. In Sarah's opinion a more honest, devoutly religious, loyal man was hard to find. Although Attiyeh was illiterate, he had more common sense than many men who had spent years in school. Unfortunately, the loss of his sons, in a culture that practically worshipped sons, seemed to weigh ever more heavily on his psyche, especially since the newborn was also a son. Hence his fear that the fifth son would follow the fate of the previous four.

Asieh met Sarah at the entrance to the room where her mother had delivered. Her younger sister, Najwa was with her. "Miss Gwynne told us to wait outside," Asieh said. "She's helping Mother wash herself."

"Let me know when she's done. I'll go talk to your father."

Sarah waited till Attiyeh rose from his face down position, folded legs, palms up begging Allah for his mercy, promising to do anything Allah wanted him to do, if Allah in His wisdom and generosity saw fit to bestow long life on his newborn son.

"What will you name the baby?" Sarah asked.

Eyes brimming with tears Attiyeh tried but could not easily articulate a response.

Sarah felt his pain. Attiyeh was the product of the culture he lived in. It meant so much for a man in the Arab world to have a son. At least one. For Attiyeh it was doubly painful as he buried a son a year, for four years, sons who, to his way of thinking, were supposed to immortalize him. The birth of yet another son, he admitted while his wife was still pregnant, condemned him to live under a dark cloud of perpetual anxiety.

"I have not thought about names," Attiyeh said after an awkward silence. "Some people suggested I wait until the baby is born. They said to decide on a name before a boy is born brings bad luck. I have had enough bad luck already. I don't need more."

"What about Marwan?"

For a few brief seconds, Attiyeh's face seemed to glow with pride. After that it went blank. "It's a great name, Miss Sarah. But ... But a thought crossed my mind occasionally after I learned the baby would be a boy. If you have no objection, I would like to name him after your father. I would like to name him Maher. With your permission, of course."

Caught off guard, Sarah did not know what to think. Was it out of respect for her? Or for her father perhaps? Was it because Attiyeh felt sorry for a man of Maher's wealth not to have had a son who could carry his name, who would immortalize him? What am I? She asked herself. A hologram? A substitute to be tolerated in the absence of a male successor? Precisely what they think. No doubt about it.

To Attiyeh she said, "That's fine. If that's what your wife also wants to name the baby, it's fine with me."

"My wife? What for?"

"Yes, Attiyeh. Your wife. Shouldn't you consult her?"

"Why?"

What an alien concept for this poor man to deal with, Sarah thought. To him she said, "She happens to be the mother of your son. She carried him for nine months. Doesn't that mean anything?" She wanted to add and all you contributed was a sperm. Why should you have all the rights? But refrained.

His gaze glued to the kitchen floor, Attiyeh shifted his

weight from foot to foot. He did not answer. How Sarah felt about women's rights was no secret to Attiyeh.

Not only was she the mother of his children, she worked outside her home to help her husband in all the chores of the compound, and in addition had to take care of the chores at home – until the moment she delivered. And not once had anyone heard her complain. Women, especially from rural background were born to not much more status than slavery. Few fought back, the futility of it imprinted on their psyche soon after birth, when the meaning of being female slowly sank its tentacles in their flesh to take root and multiply for as long as they lived.

The long silence prodded Attiyeh to respond. "My wife will agree to whatever I decide."

"Of course she will, Attiyeh," Sarah shot back. "What choice does she have?" At times, Sarah's youth betrayed by her lack of patience indulged her in venting her frustrations. Moments when her self-control, bombarded by too many irksome attacks left her with lowered guard were rare. But they did happen. Sarah regretted her outburst. She knew better. Holding an uneducated man, a man born and raised in a culture imposed on him, a man who had not been exposed to any other culture, a man who did not know different, was wrong. But it was done. There was nothing she could do about it.

A simple man, Attiyeh had missed the point.

Asieh came to the kitchen to inform Sarah her mother was done washing. Sarah followed the girls to the room. The mother was sitting up in bed tears coursing down her cheeks, the baby wrapped in a blanket in her arms. Only his face showed, kind of wrinkled, eyes closed. Sarah gave the mother a hug, congratulated her, and assured her the baby would get the best medical care available. She thanked Gwynne with a big embrace and wanted to make a hasty retreat before Gwynne asked her to hold the baby. She suspected Gwynne might. That look in Gwynne's eyes had not escaped Sarah's notice. She had never held a baby before. It terrified her to do so. Just as she turned to leave, Gwynne plucked the baby from his mother's arms and placed it in Sarah's not so ready arms. "It becomes you," Gwynne teased. "Time you thought of having a couple of your own, my dear."

Attiyeh had quietly followed Sarah to the room. Gwynne took the baby and placed him back in his mother's arms. "You're shaking so bad I thought you might drop the child," Gwynne joked. "I promised Attiyeh I'd make sure you held the baby. He thinks it will bring the baby luck."

Attiyeh stared at his son and beamed. "Miss Sarah is the angel Allah sent to us. I hope she brings good health to my son."

Immediately after, he dropped on his knees sobbing uncontrollably.

"He is obsessed with fear," Gwynne said. "Each time he sees his son or thinks about him, he breaks down and cries. His wife blames herself while he blames himself. I think they both need therapy."

Perhaps we all do, Sarah thought. She moved closer to Attiyeh. "Dr. Tuqan has arranged with a colleague, a pediatrician, to take your son under his care. But your son is not going to do well unless you and your wife change your attitudes."

"I'll do anything, anything at all, Miss Sarah."

"He's becoming hysterical." Gwynne approached Attiyeh. "I suggest you wait and see before you decide every son you have will not make it. Your wife should do the same. Otherwise, the quality and the quantity of her breast milk will be effected and then your son might really not make it."

Attiyeh stiffened noticeably, wiped his face with his sleeve, stood up.

Gwynne motioned for Sarah to follow her out. "Someone needs to knock some sense into that man's head. His wife was O.K. until her husband began acting up. Can you imagine what will happen if the child falls sick? Can you think of a child that doesn't? They'll lose their minds. That's what they'll do."

"They'll probably be more receptive to advice after a few days," Sarah said without much conviction. "Right now I think he's in shock. So is his wife."

"It's horrible." Gwynne sounded outraged. "Not once did either parent stop to think what effect their stupid hysteria was having on their daughters. The girls remained cringed in the corner feeling guilty. Guilty to have lived while their brothers died. Does anything happen in this society for which females are not blamed or victimized?"

Sarah had had a rough evening, needed to unwind. Gwynne, always attune to her moods, suggested they take time out for a cup of tea. They headed for Sarah's place.

Gwynne had spent decades in Arab countries, always working with the zeal of a missionary to enlighten the minds of those she came in contact with, to help improve the lot of women. Despite very little evidence of change, Gwynne was not discouraged – not much anyway. It takes time, a long time to change people's attitudes she often warned Sarah when they both felt like idiots for even thinking that such a phenomenon was possible. It has been this way for fourteen hundred years. If it takes a hundred years to reverse it, it's well worth the effort. She sounded sincere – sometimes. Other times, she was the first to admit she wasn't so sure.

Lately though, even Gwynne with a will strong as Genghis Khan's and nerves to match, occasionally showed signs of despair. It was impossible not to notice the changes taking place – minor, gradual, nothing tangible, yet palpable everywhere. All negative.

Sarah served Gwynne tea and cookies.

"If it disturbs you and me so deeply even though we are not obliged to live by the dictates forced on women in this society, can pack up and leave any time we want to, can you imagine how oppressive, how very demoralizing it must be for women who have absolutely no say about their own lives and absolutely no way out?"

Gwynne always drank her tea hot. She had yet to touch it.

Perhaps, Sarah thought, after more than three decades, even Gwynne could find little to pin her hopes on. "You've always been an inspiration to me but you sound quite discouraged today."

"Discouraged. No. Angry. Very. Look at you. Look at Nabila. At Fatme. You've got guards around you day and night. It's not much better than being in jail and we're probably in the most enlightened Muslim country." She sighed, reached for her tea, and to Sarah's surprise took a sip without noticing her tea was no longer hot. She continued to sip slowly, eyes wrinkled, lost in thought. "Ah, what the hell. Tomorrow, when we watch the faces of the children light up like majestic firecrackers as they open their books, the world outside becomes irrelevant. That's why we must press on."

Sarah reached over and gave the woman she adored a great big hug. "I'm so glad you're here. It makes the loss of Mom and Dad a lot easier to bear."

"I can say without reservation that I miss them as much as you do. It's thinking of them that makes the burden here bearable."

The door bell rang.

"Are you expecting anyone?" Gwynne asked.

"Probably Jim." Sarah went to the door, opened it. Suddenly, a surprised look, coupled with joy, followed by an exclamation of delight, prompted Gwynne to head to the door as well.

Jim, accompanied by Rashid, both men with naughty grins on their faces waited to be let in.

"One of these days I'm going to get even with you." Sarah stuck her face close to Jim's, almost touching it. Then turned to Gwynne. "This is the man I've been so worried about and all the while, this man, who calls himself my friend," Sarah's finger was pointed at Jim. "All the while this man was conniving behind my back." Sarah teased as she invited them in.

It had taken two weeks, but somehow Jim had managed to get a seat for Rashid on a flight out of Egypt, meanwhile keeping Sarah in the dark so as not to worry her.

"I'm sorry you had to wait so long to get here," Sarah said. "I had no idea we'd have trouble finding seats until Suheil and I got to the airport and tried to buy tickets."

"Actually," Rashid replied, "it worked out quite well for me. I spent some time with my parents. I had not seen them in over two years. Also, I had an extremely informative and illuminating time with my sister who was visiting my parents. She is married to a Turk, lives in Turkey, studied law, and is the leader of Modern Lawyers' Association. Although we don't hear about it as much as we should, Turkey is fast sliding back into darkness. There is great fear among Turkish women that if the Muslim-oriented Welfare Party comes to power, and all indications are that they will, secular Turkey will be history."

It was not news to Sarah. Lately, the *Economist*, her favorite magazine, a magazine her parents encouraged her to read, had several articles predicting the inevitable takeover of the Turkish government by Islamic fundamentalists. Secular reforms decreed during the nineteen twenties by Mustafa Kemal Ataturk, the founder of the Turkish Republic was heavily supported at that time by women who opposed the restrictions which Sharia, the law of the Koran (as interpreted by clerics who claim to have monopoly on the meaning of its messages) imposed on them. To date, Turkey has been the most secular country in the Middle East, its secularity guaranteed by the army which considers itself the guarantor of Turkey's secular system. However, the army has had to interfere three times already in the last forty years and ran the government until a civilian party emerged which could be trusted with the fate of the country.

"My sister is horrified at the undercurrents gradually eroding the rights of women in that country," Rashid said. "She fears that if Islamic fundamentalism gains a foothold in Turkey, it won't be long before other Muslim countries with secular governments are toppled. She is organizing meetings,

speeches, rallies, protest marches, whatever she can, to prove
to the world that anti-fundamentalist sentiment is strong and
widespread. Thousands of women show up at meetings she
holds, agree to carry signs and march through the streets of
Ankara. She showed me the contents of a few signs she was
working on. One of them read 'Down with the Sharia.'
Another, 'Women will not be pushed back into the Middle
Ages.' Yet another 'Do not turn back the clock. Darkness will
follow.' Women played a crucial role when Ataturk struggled
to remove the shackles weighing down his country and pulled
them into the twentieth century. My sister is not a Turk, but
she's a woman and a human rights advocate, an extremely
dedicated advocate I might add. So is her husband who is also
a lawyer. She teaches law at the University of Ankara. She
said she noticed lately a number of female students had begun
wearing head scarves. When questioned they said they were
pressured by their families who had only lately become more
religion conscious themselves. All of them blamed the
Welfare Party which has spared no effort, especially in rural
areas, promising dramatic improvement in the lives of the
inhabitants if they help support Islamic fundamentalism.
Invariably, the first victims of Islamic fundamentalism are
women. Although there is a ban on women wearing veils or
head scarves on public university campuses and in government offices enforced from the time Turkey was declared a
republic by Ataturk, the Welfare party is seeking to end these
restrictions claiming it infringes on freedom of choice. Since
almost all students depend on their parents for financial support, they have no choice but to comply."

No one in the room looked surprised. Every Muslim
country in the world seemed to be faced with its share of
problems as a result of the so called religious revival, twisted,
then molded to attract unsuspecting societies into conformity
– loss of basic human rights, men excluded. Colonialism,
imperialism, western moral decadence were often cited as
contributing factors. The sentiment expressed by new con-

verts was to give religion a chance since almost all else, in their opinion, had failed them. "That's a tough assignment," Gwynne said. "I hope she won't be the lone voice in the wilderness."

"She knows it's tough and dangerous. She has no illusions about it." Without his beard, Sarah found it difficult to think of Rashid as a cleric. "That's why she has asked me to help her."

"How?" The question tripped off Sarah's tongue.

"If it's not too late and you're not too tired I'd like to discuss that with you."

"Of course not. What is it you'd like to discuss?"

Rashid turned to Jim. "Your friend here has gone through a lot of trouble to bring me here and I cannot begin to tell you how much I appreciate all he's done for me. He has also assured me that you can get a visa for me to visit the U.S. like you said you could. I'd like to know if – Jim said you call it rain check. I'd like to know if I can have a rain check."

Sarah studied the man who did not cease to fascinate her. "Sure. If that's what you want."

"It's not a matter of want. Going to the States would have been a dream come true. But my sister needs my help. The plan is to start an organization with branches in as many Muslim countries as possible, to show the world who the real Muslims are – not those who want to turn back the clock. An organization capable of fighting for human rights, an organization ready to protest against the policies of any state which introduces religion into government. She knows the tide is rising fast. She wants to be prepared to meet it. It would be disastrous for women in Turkey, or any other Muslim country, to be caught unprepared the way Iranian women were. We're at the end of the twentieth century for God's sake. Women don't want to spend their lives under a black tent, nor do they look forward to living a life of servitude with no way out."

Rashid had not mastered the art of keeping his outrage to

himself, especially when the issue was human rights. But he was among friends – his confidence evidenced in his words and manner.

Still, Sarah could not fathom how Rashid, an Egyptian, a cleric, could play a role in an undertaking organized by women, for women – for human rights. This was not an organization which intended to limit its activities to Turkey. In several countries like Iran, Saudi Arabia, the Sudan, Tunisia, Morocco, Yemen and other gulf states, religion already played a major role in government despite fierce resistance exerted by many. If Rashid joined the group, he'd be an outcast in the eyes of the religious establishment – if lucky. Branded an apostate – more likely. Already in disfavor with hard line clerics, was he ready to face more of their wrath?

She asked him about it.

"A week ago," Rashid said, sadness creeping back in his voice, "while I was in Cairo, an Islamic group called Gama'a al-Islamiya, the largest of the militant organizations, killed my parents next door neighbor and his family. Friends for forty years. Their crime – the father was a Coptic priest. They have killed seventy six Copts since 1992 when they began their violent campaign against this religious minority. Copts are descendants of ancient Egyptians. They have lived in Egypt forever. They're being persecuted by a bunch of fanatics because Copts are Christians. This is not what Islam is about. It's supposed to be a model for tolerance, harmony, spiritual purification. The word Islam means peace, submission. Not killing of innocent people. If I don't help stop these misguided, misinformed extremists from inflicting more damage on innocent people and giving a horrible reputation to Islam, then I'm no better than they are."

The room was quiet, all eyes on the cleric whose shoulders sagged more as the night wore on as though the weight of injustice he had chosen to fight grew heavier as he spoke.

"It's hard to understand what motivates these people, what turns them into psychopathic killer machines – but easy to underestimate," Jim said, his face tense, his brow furrowed. "No doubt your contributions will be of immense value for women risking all odds to fight for what rightfully belongs to them. As a cleric you'd be God-sent – a tremendous boost to their image. However, I see a big drawback in your involvement. You don't impress me as a man capable of violence. The thought of it seems to devastate you. You want to use logic. You question, you analyze, you gather information and you reach a conclusion. Commendable traits – useless when dealing with radicals, extremists, fanatics. Call them what you will. By definition, a fanatic is inordinately and unreasonably enthusiastic. The key word here is unreasonably. Reason, logic, or dialogue, play no role in their thinking. If they did, we would not have opportunists imposing a brand of primitive Islam on Muslims, often by force, when the way of life Islam teaches, its humanism and universal character, if presented accurately, are more than adequate to promote the true image of Islam."

Rashid asked if he could please have a glass of water. Sarah rose, apologized for her lack of hospitality. Too involved in the discussion. Fetching drinks was a welcome momentary diversion. She asked everyone what they wanted to drink and headed for the kitchen to fix it. Jim followed her.

"We've got to stop him," Jim said, keeping his voice low. "He'll be a marked man the moment he takes on any undertaking considered anti-Islamic by his colleagues and enemies. He won't last long."

"I doubt we can change his mind. He sounds determined."

"Try. It might have more impact coming from a woman."

They returned to the living room, served the drinks and settled back in their seats.

"Rashid," Sarah said, "What exactly does your sister expect you to do?"

Rashid drained his water, placed the empty glass on the table, rubbed his hands together, looked upwards like a man waiting for divine advice. "My sister does not expect anything from me. I offered to help. The southeastern portion of Iraq is heavily populated by Shiites. It borders on Iran. Not surprisingly, Saddam Hussein's government has welcomed my sister's organization's initial inquiries with open arms. Saddam Hussein is a Sunni, a dictator. He wants the organization in Iraq, in the south. The towns and villages bordering Iran, practically worship Khomeini. Saddam Hussein has strict guidelines about that. No rivals. His ego will never tolerate such lack of reverence."

When Rashid mentioned Iraq, for a moment Sarah thought she had either misunderstood or he had lost his mind. But neither was the case. "Are you telling us that you plan to work in Iraq?"

"My dear, don't look so horrified. Look at Turkey. It is a crime in Turkey to advocate an Islamic state. The army is quick to remind anyone who forgets, with tanks and heavy artillery even if a fairly mild attempt is made to introduce religion into public life. Yet politicians, turned religious crusaders, find countless ways to advance their agendas. In the south of Iraq, in the absence of politicians, Shiite clerics, encouraged by Khomeini's success next door, are more than ready to wield their clout. Religion has no place in government. We as clerics have enough work teaching our people traditional values and Muslim brotherhood. Governing should be left to politicians. And if I do not get involved when I have had the good fortune of literacy to enable me to learn about my religion as it truly is, I would have no respect for myself and no right to complain about the lack of involvement by others, would I?"

Sarah pushed a strand of hair away from her face. "When do you plan to go?"

"As soon as I make contact with a couple of Iraqi officials. I plan to go to Baghdad first. A couple of my classmates work in Baghdad. I want to consult them. They are both truly great clerics – believe strongly in separation of religion from government. To my knowledge they've had no problems with

Saddam Hussein's regime. They get all the help they need from his government. The Minister of Interior has promised the same to us. Financial support and in our case, around the clock protection, which no doubt means keeping our activities in line with the dictates of the regime. And that's perfectly all right with us. So you see my dear, it will probably not be as bad as you think. At least I hope not. But with a man like Saddam Hussein one can never tell."

"If that's the case," Jim said, "I don't think you need to worry. Not about Saddam Hussein, anyway. Your problem will be the Islamists who are no less brutal when crossed than Saddam Hussein himself. And they'll probably be more so since they'll feel betrayed by one of their own."

"Not exactly. I am a Sunni. The south of Iraq is Shiite. I'll be working as a regular person, not a cleric."

That explained why he was still clean shaven. Sarah teased him about it just to lighten the conversation.

"It's no joyride," Jim reminded them, "with or without a beard."

Rashid shook his head in agreement. "At times I feel like our society is in an irreversible downward spiral and even intervention by an army, like in Turkey, will merely postpone the inevitable. Who would have thought, not too long ago, that the Shah of Iran could be toppled and a theocracy established in its stead, with the ease it did, an ally of America, in this day and age. Consequently, I have convinced myself not to give up, to push harder, until reason and logic come to prevail."

Sarah and Jim exchanged glances. Gwynne, as far back as Sarah remembered had never kept quiet while someone else dominated the conversation. But she seemed to be mesmerized by what the cleric had to say. Yet Sarah had a new idea sending her thoughts into high gear. To give herself time to think, she went to the kitchen to pour fresh drinks for everyone.

Jim followed her to the kitchen as she had hoped.

She turned to Jim. "Are you thinking what I'm thinking?"

"Yup."

"You think we should?"

"It's worth a try."

Sarah returned to the living room with the drinks, settled back on the sofa and said, "Rashid, we'd like to ask you for a favor."

"Of course. What is it?"

Sarah told him about Ali, about the time and effort they had spent so far trying to locate him and their concern for his well being. She also mentioned about what the shepherd had said. Did Rashid think, on his way over to Baghdad, there was a chance he could inquire from the villagers if anyone had seen a person of Ali's description. "I hate to ask you," Sarah said. "But we're desperate."

Rashid thought for a few seconds before he said, "I will be driving on highway ten. That's the only highway from Amman to Baghdad. No problem there. I will stop and inquire. It seems to me though I have heard something about this man. Quite a while back. Anwar, my friend, the security agent was contacted by an agent in Baghdad because the Sheikh had lived and studied for many years in Egypt. Iraqi security had intercepted a message sent by the Sheikh to a colleague in Iraq asking him to investigate the whereabouts of a young Palestinian man wanted for murder. Supposedly he had escaped to Iraq after throwing a bomb in a large complex and killing a man. The Sheikh claimed the dead man was his relative. Iraqi security has no use for the Sheikh and would have probably eliminated him long ago. But they have him where they want him, unaware that he's feeding Iraqi security a lot of information about the efforts used by Muslim revivalists and his own grandiose ambitions. Anwar asked me about the Sheikh because he knew we had been classmates at al-Azhar."

Sarah was so shocked, she couldn't speak. That meant Iraqi security knew about Ali. She looked at Jim and Jim understood.

"Did they get him?" Jim asked.

"They did."

Sarah could not hold back. "Is he ... Is he ... alive. Do you know?"

"I don't. But I have contacts. I can find out."

Chapter 27

MUHAMMAD'S LETTER ARRIVED TWO WEEKS later with little new information other than the message he had left on Sarah's answering machine. Concerned, Sarah called him.

She got the Wilson's answering machine – for a whole week, several times a day.

"Perhaps they went on vacation somewhere," Jim said.

"Where's Muhammad then. I doubt he went with them. I don't think they would have wanted him to. And furthermore, he's got summer school." Sarah was at a loss. She did not know what to do next. She could wait. That was all.

A week later another letter arrived – from Muhammad – written in Arabic.

June 20, 1995
Dear Miss Sarah,

I write this letter to you in Arabic so I can use the right words to express myself. The day after I mailed you a letter earlier this month, I moved out of the Wilson's home to a friend's apartment. It took me a week to gather my courage to write to you, to let you and Mr. Jim know what really happened here in Bellevue, at the Wilson's home. When I spoke with Mr. Jim on the phone, I could not be completely truthful with my answers. Amy was standing next to me and I wasn't quite sure how to handle the situation. Ever since the Wilsons accepted me as an exchange foreign student, I have seen nothing but kindness, generosity, helpfulness and love. They've done much more than I had a right to expect, and I will be forever be grateful to them for everything they've done for me, especially helping me overcome my bitterness – by simply being themselves.

However, a couple of months after I began living with them, Amy stopped dating her boy friend and gradually wanted more and more of my attention. For some reason, which I do not understand to this day, neither her father, nor her mother objected to it. I was getting quite uncomfortable with the progression of events. I did not want to give her any indication that I, in any way, was interested in her. But Amy persisted. She has decided that she's in love with me and if I don't marry her, she'll commit suicide.

Don't get me wrong. I love her perhaps more than she loves me. Who wouldn't? She's beautiful, kind, generous to a fault, and stubborn. Like most teenagers her age. And that is where our problems begin. I have spent many hours describing to her the almost insurmountable differences that exist between our cultures, the age difference between us. Twelve years is hardly an issue in our culture. As you know men in their eighties marry teenage girls. But I understand it is a concern here. I pointed out to her the distance from everything she's familiar with, the deprivations she'll have to endure – all to no avail. She has no doubt love conquers all. Don't get me wrong. I'd love to marry her. In my wildest dreams I would not have dared expect to have a wife who would come even remotely close to Amy, her beauty, her youth, her innocent loyalty. But even if I were to become completely westernized, and I'm not sure I can or want to, living in Jordan, surrounded by a totally alien culture, at age eighteen when we return to Jordan, will present her with challenges she is ill prepared to cope with. I know how hard it was for me to adjust to this culture, and I did not have to put up with an iota of what she will have to deal with if she were to live in Jordan. Here, being an only child, she has it all. Her parents indulge her, her life is easy. Homework and tests are her only concerns – occasionally. Just like our women back home, right? Just kidding.

Amy almost always gets what she wants. I sense that her

frustration is mainly due to her desire to have me and my reluctance to oblige. There's no convincing her that it's for her own good.

I have become an enigma to the other students at school as well, especially the few Muslim students, mostly from Iran. Muslim students, actually a number of foreign students included, do all they can to get the attention of American girls. A few to gain residency, others because they want to show the world they have become westernized. Some have even changed their names – Westernized them. No one I know is in it for love. My schoolmates often ask me why I don't take advantage of a girl who is literally throwing herself at me. My answer is simple. I do not believe I have the maturity, the education, the financial resources, or the right to subject the woman I love to what I have come to realize are primitive, demeaning, in my view, barbaric conditions which she will invariably be faced with since that's the culture I come from, and that's where I want to return. I am not a genius, and I have not suddenly had a revelation. What I have had are two most fortunate events that have permanently changed my life.

Miss Sarah, I want you to know that no woman, or the lure of permanent residency, or any lucrative job offer of which I have already had two, will have any effect on my decision to return to Jordan immediately after graduation. It's a privilege I look forward to, dream about, talk about. My life revolves around it. And I will be grateful to you all my life for giving me this opportunity. But gratitude is not enough. You have kept your part of the agreement and then some. Soon it will be my turn. I intend to fulfill my part of the agreement and more. Short of death, nothing can stop me.

You're probably shaking your head and wondering what happened to the bitter, angry young man who had a totally negative view of the world barely a year ago. I'll tell you what happened to him. He's dead. It was a lingering death, kept kicking back, but finally, he's gone. Thanks to you, Mr. Jim, Professor Askari, my friends at school and the mosque, and the opportunity to live in the most wonderful country in the world, I can now see clearly that adjustments have to be made in our attitude. We must work diligently towards a better understanding of our religion, learn to appreciate the human rights approach it advocates and to extend those rights to all –especially our women. Our women have to be free from exploitation and we have to do what we can to right the wrongs of the past, the present, and make sure it does not raise its ugly head ever again.

You might wonder why then I do not marry Amy, bring her to Jordan, and have a partner in our fight to change a lifestyle so deeply ingrained in us. She is a living example of a liberated woman. Why not let her be a role model for future generations of women in the Arab world?

Because love is not enough. Amy is too young, too inexperienced, and definitely not prepared to deal with a culture she does not even begin to fathom. Youth's greatest drawback is its lack of experience. I know. I was there myself and still am at times when I let my guard down. Although by age seventeen she has been exposed to far more of the world through better education and the media than I ever was, she has no way of relating to life in other cultures. How can she? All I have to do is think back. What I thought of the U.S. and Americans before I came here had absolutely no resemblance to this country or its people.

But I have a problem, Miss Sarah, a problem I don't know how to deal with.

My problem is how to make Amy believe me. I entertained thoughts of taking on a second job, saving the money, and sending her on a trip to Jordan – to see, to experience the country and the culture for herself. Professor Askari convinced me otherwise. He does not think she'll commit suicide if our relationship does not lead to marriage and he thinks she's much too young to benefit from a solo trip abroad. And since by necessity the trip will have to be cut short, it won't be worth the time, the money, and the effort required.

He was also concerned that a second job will jeopardize my academic performance. Professor Askari keeps close tab on me. He advised me to cool my relationship.

I've tried – every way I could think of. That's the reason I moved out. I don't know what the outcome will be. Her parents have taken her to Los Angeles to visit relatives. I'll know when they return if not being under the same roof with me will help cool her passion. I will keep you posted.

In closing, I would like to thank you and Mr. Jim for all you've done and are doing for me. I aim to make you proud of me. I am grateful for the faith you had in me while I had none in myself or anyone else. I love computers. My grade point average this term was four point zero.

Please let me know if you hear from Ali. I wrote a letter to Fatme as well. She's alone in this world and I figured she could use a little morale booster.
Respectfully,
Muhammad.

A warm, gratifying feeling coursed through Sarah's body as she read the letter. It gave her energy, a boost to her often battered mental state, renewed fate in her fellow human beings. The mean and the ugly would always be around, but they were few and hopefully could be kept under control by means other than brute force. She felt good, real good. Even if she never accomplished another goal, to have given hope, optimism, help clarify complex issues Muhammad would not have had a chance to do otherwise, get him to think, was more compensation than she had dared hope for. How fortunate I am to be in a position to help, she mused to herself, how fortunate to have had the parents I had.

Jim beamed with pride as well. "It's a tough fight, but there are many young men and women out there just like Muhammad. All they need is a break. And no Sheikh or anyone else is going to stop us. Right?"

Jim always had a weird look in his eyes and a smirk on his

face whenever he wiggled his words to extract information from Sarah, information he already had, but nonetheless wanted to hear it from Sarah herself.

"Sometimes I think you use threats to our safety as an excuse to employ guards to spy on us," Sarah teased. She did not bother to ask him how he knew. Guards or no guards. Somehow, Jim always did.

"Leave the rearranging of the Sheikh's anatomy to me. That's a ruthless man. You should never expose yourself to such danger." Jim's expression changed suddenly to one of rage. "Perhaps I should let you in on a little secret. Perhaps in my zeal to protect you I have deprived you of crucial information. Do you realize that now the Sheikh is no longer satisfied with forcing you to leave the country. He has hired a professional killer to eliminate you. Those are his words. You know what that means, don't you?"

Sarah threw her hands up in disgust. "I know exactly what it means. More body guards, more restricted movement, more precautionary measures. Thank you very much."

"The arrangement the Sheikh has in mind can work both ways."

"Jim, for heaven's sake, I did not stay in this country to turn it into a killing field. I stayed to change all that – to solve disagreements by dialogue, by use of logic. Not bullets. Violence begets violence. Please, don't ever bring that up again, or entertain such thoughts."

Jim laughed out loud. "Dialogue? Logic? I thought that's what you practiced on the Sheikh. Look how far it got you. You're on his death list. I promised your father I would not let any harm come to you as long as I lived. That's precisely what I plan to do and no one is going to stop me. Period."

"Which means?"

"I'll do what it takes. Those involved will be duly warned."

"You're crazy," Sarah blurted out.

"I sure am. It's far less dangerous than using logic with

those who only understand force. I have an aversion to wasting my breath on fools. So far it has served us real well."

Sarah's stomach growled reminding her of the abuse it had been subjected to lately. Frequently, involved in situations which demanded her immediate attention, she forgot to eat. "Attiyeh brought over an Egyptian dish earlier. I think it's Mouloukhieh. Want some?"

"I'll join you. My stomach is not growling like yours, but I am kind of hungry."

Sarah stuck her head in the refrigerator, pulled the container with the food Attiyeh had brought, dished some for herself and some for Jim, zapped them in the microwave and they settled in the kitchen to eat. "We took Attiyeh's son to the pediatrician during lunch break today," Sarah said. "He checked out fine."

"I doubt it makes any difference to Attiyeh what the pediatrician says."

"You're right. Hopefully, albeit slowly, we'll make progress. Today I made a great discovery. When I was in Seattle, I read an article about SIDS, sudden infant death syndrome. The advice to parents was rather simple. Do not put your baby to sleep on his stomach and make sure the mattress the baby sleeps on is firm. I talked it over with the pediatrician. He was familiar with the publication and advised me to check the baby's crib when we got home. In his opinion, next to diarrhea, soft mattresses, believed to be gentler on the baby's spine, was the biggest killer of infants in cultures where the practice prevailed – like in the Middle East. Although laying a baby on his stomach was uncommon, soft bedding, especially for boys, was considered a must."

"That's Attiyeh's curse, most probably," Jim said between mouthfuls.

"I discussed the doctor's suggestion with Gwynne. It made sense to her. She and I went over, checked the baby's bed, and sure enough, the bed was so soft, the sides folded over the baby's face. The pillow was softer than the mattress.

The mother thought she was doing the right thing, giving her baby a soft bed to sleep in. Something she admitted she had not done for the girls. The girls crib was a blanket on the dirt floor. No pillows. Cost too much. For once ignorance worked in the girls' favor. The pediatrician spent an hour with Mrs. Attiyeh, explained in detail, showed her diagrams. Mrs. Attiyeh could not wait to rush to the store to buy a firm mattress. No such luck. I did not realize how difficult it was to find mattresses in this country. We were told people made their own. One of the many stores we visited told us about a fancy baby boutique, newly opened. We ended up buying a pretty good imported mattress paying for it ten times its worth. At least I have peace of mind now, and I hope it will calm Attiyeh's nerves as well. Amazing how that man has changed. He's a total wreck, walks in a daze. Call his name, and it takes a few seconds to register. What else can we do to reassure him?"

Jim shook his head. "Don't know really. We'll just have to be patient with him, I guess – at least until the baby has past his first birthday."

The phone rang. Sarah answered. After a brief conversation, she hung up and returned to the kitchen. "Yes," she yelled, delighted. "They accepted my offer – both of them."

"How much time do we have?"

"We're quite late as it is. Kerak should have been attended to earlier. But Dad won't mind. I think he would approve of what we have accomplished so far, especially in regards to Muhammad, Fatme and Nabila. Fatme cracks me up when she tries to speak English with a British accent. Gwynne has taught her table manners, table manners to a teenager who had never held a fork in her hand before, or sat at a table for a meal, manners which would make Miss Manners proud. Of course we've had some setbacks, but considering the odds we've had to work against, I dare say, overall, we've done pretty good."

"I haven't checked on Kerak in months," Jim admitted

reluctantly. "I had too much going on here. Let's try to get there this weekend. Maybe Suheil and Nabila can join us. We haven't had a break – so far. None. Talk to Suheil and I'll talk to Nabila. My opinion being totally biased, I dare say I have rarely seen a baby as adorable as Samir Junior. That mobile you had shipped for him from Sears, he smiles, and gurgles at it, throws his arms up to reach it. Happiest baby I ever saw."

"Nabila glows each time she looks at the child. I don't know what I'd do without her help, without you, Suheil, Gwynne, even Fatme. She's fifteen now but it's more like she's thirty. Have you ever watched her take charge of the class when Nabila is busy elsewhere? Her transformation is little short of miraculous. To pick up reading and writing Arabic, speaking, reading and writing English as well as she does, in one year, makes me wonder how far she will go at this rate. Could you have our lawyers arrange a fund for her to continue her education for as long as she's willing to study?"

Jim thought it was a great idea. He promised to call London the very next day. "Now I have something for you," he said, with a look of I-know-you'll-like-what-I-have-to-show-you smeared across his face. "Fatme was typing away on the computer last night when I went to give the classrooms a final check." Jim reached in his coat pocket and produced two sheets of paper. "I left to check the rest of the place. When I returned a few minutes later, the printer had jammed and Fatme had her right thumb pressed against her upper teeth trying to figure out how to get it working again. I offered to help. She insisted it was she who had created the mess and it had to be her that fixed it. And she did. Opened the booklet, read the directions, checked the words she couldn't understand in the dictionary, and did it. She printed a copy of what she'd been working on and gave it to me." Jim handed Sarah the two sheets of paper he had pulled from his pocket.

It was a letter to her brother. It was heartbreaking. She began by telling him how much she loved him, how much she missed him and then proceeded to give a detailed account of her days, what a fortunate person she was to be blessed with the privileges which had magically come her way, and how little she deserved them. What was most gripping though was her confession that although her great love was for computers – she was totally fascinated by them, she had decided to study law. "You are innocent," she wrote in bold letters. I know, because you're not capable of such an inhuman act, and because Miss Sarah told me so. Actually, she told me how it all happened. She blames herself for not giving you a chance to talk to her. I suppose it will be a while before I graduate and will be capable of defending you, but it's better than spending the rest of your life in jail, or being executed for a crime you did not commit.

"I don't know where to send this letter. But I don't think it matters. I am convinced that in your heart you know how much I love you, and have no doubt we will see each other soon. When I was a child, I used to dream of miracles, of winning the lottery, moving to a fancy house, having servants, like the ladies I used to work for. Then I met Miss Sarah. Rumor has it that she is very wealthy. She has to be. How else can she spend all this money on us? But she doesn't have a fancy home, servants, or drive around in expensive cars. Observing her taught me there's more to life than money and I know now that winning the lottery does not really matter, and miracles do happen. It happened to me – the day I met Miss Sarah. Except for the pain of not knowing where you are and how you are, I have never known happiness like this before, did not think it was possible. I am happy because I have discovered a big world out there through education, a world I would have never believed existed. I hope you are happy too – wherever you are. I will write to you often. Miss Sarah and Mr. Jim are doing everything they can to find you. They tell me all about it. I will save my letters for when we meet my dear brother. I hope it will be soon."

Tears coursed down Sarah's cheeks as she put the letter

aside and reached for a tissue paper. "Why did you show it to me?"

"Don't look so glum. I gave her letter to you to read because I have news for you. Rashid has located Ali. He's not in the best of shapes, but he's alive. Not to worry, though. With the right amount of grease in the right palms, anything is possible. I'm working on it."

Sarah countenance changed instantly. She was besides herself with joy. She rose, rushed toward Jim and planted a kiss on his forehead. "When? When did you learn about it? How?"

"Before Rashid left, we worked out an elaborate system of communication so he could inform me about whatever he found out, over the phone, without delay. He called me late this afternoon. I will wire the money to his sister. She's leaving for Baghdad next week to help Rashid get started with the organization they want to set up. She'll give him the money."

"What's Ali being accused of?"

"They don't need a reason to put someone in jail. Not in Iraq. You know that."

"I'm surprised they haven't killed him yet." The thought of it sent shivers throughout Sarah's being.

"Remember the hundred fifty dollars Muhammad sent him?"

"Right."

"That literally has saved his life. It was intercepted and went into some official's pocket. The expectation that more will follow, kind of blood money to secure Ali's freedom is what has kept him alive to this day. But despite severe torture and demands to know if he had connections with someone who had money and was willing to bail him out, Ali has not mentioned your name."

Sarah listened, part of her proud of the fact that despite the torture he was subjected to, torture which most likely would have cost him his life, Ali had not divulged her name. Usually, when loyalty became inconvenient, most people conveniently forgot it. However, her logical other half was furious. Risking his life so as not to cause her trouble, was inexcusable. "Did Rashid get to talk to him?"

"Cost him five hundred bucks."

"Can you see to it that he gets refunded?"

"I tried. He won't accept it. He'll see Ali one more time before leaving for the south. He said he'll call and he'll give his sister a letter with all the pertinent details to be forwarded to us."

"Progress at last," Sarah sighed.

"We are lucky and so is Ali. Few people survive Saddam Hussein's detention centers – better known as graveyards by the Iraqis. Rashid has arranged for him to be treated less harshly – at a price – of course."

"Which he won't mention, right?"

"Right. But let's not fool ourselves. No amount of money would have worked if Rashid did not have Saddam Hussein's approval."

"How's Rashid doing?"

"Great. You can accomplish a lot in any country if you have the backing of an autocratic dictator. Rashid's difficulty is in dealing with the religious policies filtering through the border with Iran, and the Shiite clergy in Iraq determined to implement the dictates imposed from across the border. A man like Saddam Hussein does not take challenge to his authority kindly. Rashid finds convincing Hussein to use persuasion rather than brute force his biggest challenge, the misinformed clerics, his biggest headache. But if there ever was a person who could handle an explosive situation like that, I believe it is Rashid. I hope it doesn't cost him his sanity."

"Or life. Khomeini's henchmen are no less ruthless than Saddam Hussein's. The thought of Rashid in Iraq makes me have nightmares."

"He's been given around the clock protection. Trust me, he wouldn't last a day on his own."

That helped Sarah feel a little less apprehensive. "Still, no protection is full proof," she had to admit reluctantly.

Jim rose. "It's a choice he made willingly and knowingly. He's had to deal with extremists before. It's a challenge his brilliant mind is perfectly suited to undertake. I would not worry about him if I were you. He's under the protection of the elite Republican Guards. No one will dare touch him."

"That's a relief."

Jim opened the door. "I need to get to bed early tonight. Have to call London early tomorrow morning before the banks close to transfer money. We've pretty much depleted the last amount we had transferred."

"How much do you have to send to Baghdad?"

"Ten thousand dollars for beginners. No Dinars, if you please. People kill for dollars in third world countries, but it is worst in Iraq. The economic sanctions imposed by the UN have taken their toll. I have no idea what it will end up costing to gain Ali's release. I bet it will be a lot more."

"Can't put a price on human life."

"Of course not. Especially when we are mostly to blame for the misery he's going through." Jim reached for his coat. "I'll see you in the morning. If you get a chance to talk to Suheil make sure you ask him about going to Kerak and I'll ask Nabila. If we don't start preparations soon, we won't be able to open the school by September. I should probably go ahead and order the desks and chairs to be made anyway. Would you say twenty is enough to begin with?"

"I think so. But I wouldn't be surprised if we get a lot more. It is Dad's village, and this is a poor country. Chances are few children, perhaps I should say few girls are getting the education they need."

"It will be easier to make that judgment after we get there, after we've studied the situation more thoroughly. I hope Suheil is not on call this weekend."

"He's not. He'll either call or come tonight. I'll ask him. He won't say no. But it's really not fair to him. He's been wanting to go to the Dead Sea for months now. Each time we make plans to go, something happens and we postpone it. But we shall see."

After Jim left, Sarah reached for a magazine, stretched on the sofa, tried to read. She could not concentrate. She had too much on her mind. She reached for the phone and dialed Suheil's number. It was almost ten o'clock. Suheil said he had just finished his nightly rounds and if she did not think it was too late, he'd stop by to see her.

She told him she'll have a Scotch ready for him.

Suheil Tuqan was a man impossible not to love. As the night wore on and their passion rose to new heights, they made love repeatedly, until – exhausted, they fell asleep. Suheil spending the night at her place invariably left Sarah apprehensive. No telling what her aunts were capable of concocting if they knew. Sarah had no idea where her aunts were. She had not seen them in days. They came and went like shadows, appearing and disappearing noiselessly – a sign of trouble brewing. She had convinced herself the best policy was to ignore them and that's precisely what she had been doing.

Before they fell asleep Sarah and Suheil decided to make good on their promise to each other and spend the weekend at the Dead Sea. They would go to Kerak the weekend after.

Jim thought it was a good idea. It would give him time to prepare for Kerak. Nabila was delighted to join them – so was Gwynne. And Fatme went wherever Gwynne and Nabila went. For the adults, no special preparation was necessary, but Jim had to buy some kind of portable bed for the baby, not an easy task in a country where such items, considered luxuries, were rarely available. Fortunately, Jim had contacts in the U.S. Embassy and hoped to borrow a foldable playpen or 'some other contraption', as he put it, to make sure the baby had a safe and comfortable place to sleep in in Kerak.

Thursday morning, the beginning of the Muslim weekend, Sarah and Suheil left for the Dead Sea, elated they could finally get away. When they reached the Dead Sea, Sarah realized Nabila was right. There were two Jordans. The Jordan open to tourists in skimpy bathing suits oblivious of laser-like focused looks, and the Jordan where Arabs from different countries, men fully clothed, women covered from head to toe, in black, in the broiling sun, came to watch the exposed flesh of the infidels. For the men it was lust, for the women, it meant a glimpse of how the rest of the women of the world lived.

"Can you imagine what would happen to these tourists if they were at the Caspian in Iran?" Suheil said, "even if they were in less skimpy bathing suits, say a one piece."

"They'd be stoned to death. Period. Luckily they're here and not there."

"We should consider ourselves lucky, I guess," Suheil added. "Not much to worry about as long as tourists can come and can wear what they want."

Sarah and Suheil spent the day like two carefree souls, chasing each other, throwing sand at each other, floating on the water, dunking each other. Impossible in the Dead Sea – thus more fun. Swimming, an experience unlike any other, never to be forgotten. "The best day I have had since I came to Jordan," Sarah declared as they walked back to the cabin. "No reservations."

"Same here." He kissed her hand, their backs turned to the crowd.

Later that evening, they drove to a restaurant, had lamb kebab for dinner, then drove back to the cabin. Naturally, every where they went the body guards followed.

Tired, nice tired, they made love and fell asleep.

A few minutes after one in the morning, they were awakened by a soft but persistent knock on the door.

Suheil whispered to Sarah not to move. He pulled his robe on and staggered to the door.

Where are the guards, Sarah wondered. Maybe it's one of the guards. Maybe someone is sick, someone needs a doctor. Maybe a guard is sick.

They heard a brief, muted conversation. Neither could identify the voices.

"Has to be the guards," Suheil said. "They don't want to wake the neighbors."

Another knock.

"Who is it?"

Someone answered in whispers. Suheil and Sarah exchanged a quick, confused glance. They could not tell who the callers were. Hoping it was either the guards, or someone the guards did not object to, Suheil opened the door a crack.

It was Jim.

Sarah could hardly breathe. Nothing short of a disaster would prompt Jim to disturb them and at that time of night. As though on automatic pilot, her body sensing abuse, seemed to take leave of the rest of her. She made a conscious effort to regain control.

"We have serious trouble," Jim said, while he dismissed the guard and closed the door, confirming Sarah's fears. "Younis came in absolute panic a little while ago to inform me that the Sheikh and your aunts have managed to circumcise two girls, two of our girls from the camp. They were planning to do more when Younis found out what was going on, grabbed a knife and threatened them, forced them to leave. Furious, the Sheikh apparently went to the police station and returned with a couple of policemen to arrest Younis. Younis expected him to do just that, and immediately went into hiding until the police, after a thorough search, left the camp. He managed to grab a cab, went to your place first. The guards grabbed him at the gate. He told the guards what had happened. They got in touch with me. Younis and I went back to the camp, checked the girls. They were both hysterical. We left them with Gwynne and Nabila."

Jim had to stop. He was too angry to go on.

Sarah tightened her grip on Suheil's hand. She was too distraught, too besides herself to react rationally.

"I'll throw our stuff in the overnight bag," Suheil said.

"We'll go back immediately."

"The girls?" Sarah needed to know who they were, what shape they were in.

Jim took a deep breath. He looked like he was about to explode. It didn't seem like he had heard Suheil or Sarah. "Suddenly," he said, "suddenly, they were grabbed from behind and forced to submit to the mutilation, threatened with their lives if they made a sound. God, how I wish I had been there." Jim banged his right fist in his left palm. "Luckily Younis was – later, much later. He learned about it accidentally."

Jim stopped again. Sarah had rarely seen him upset enough not to finish what he had to say.

After a brief pause, Jim continued where he had left off. "Muhammad's father is sick. I knew about it when I dropped the children at the camp night before last. I told his wife to take him to a doctor and send us the bill. The old man wouldn't go. Today he couldn't stop coughing, but still refused to go to the doctor. So his wife asked Younis to go to the drugstore to get something for the old man's chest. Apparently, all that smoking and a bad cold gave him a hard time with his breathing. As Younis left the camp to go to the drugstore, he said he noticed a Mercedes parked at the entrance of the camp, with a man in the driver's seat. He questioned the driver. The driver told him the car belonged to the Sheikh. The Sheikh and two old women had arrived an hour or so earlier, told the driver to wait. They did not tell him when they would be back."

Younis suspected the old women were Sarah's aunts, Jim explained. They often visit the camp to stir up trouble, on weekends, always in the afternoons. It was not afternoon, it was past nine p.m. Also he could not understand what the Sheikh was doing there – late at night. The Sheikh was not in the habit of visiting camps day or night – ever. After purchasing a bottle of cough syrup from the drugstore, Younis got to thinking as to what could have prompted the Sheikh's impromptu visit. And then it hit him. The Sheikh is well known for his relentless pursuit of young girls reaching puberty. Circumcising girls gives him ultimate pleasure. Was it possible? Younis apparently ran back to the camp. Unfortunately, by then it was too late for two of the girls. But at least he managed to save the other two."

"The other two?" Sarah spoke but the words echoed in her head as though coming from another space, another time.

"Yup. He had them lined up. All ready to go. The more the merrier, I guess."

"Who? Where were the parents, at least the mothers of the girls?" The fathers were hardly ever around. Sarah had trouble articulating her words. "Where could they be late at night?"

"They were there all right. But, when the country's top cleric tells them it is their religious duty as true Muslims to abide by the laws of the Sharia, you can't expect people who don't know better to object. And they didn't. The girls did. Especially Farideh and Zeina. The two who got butchered. Hollered the place down – despite the threats."

"How do you know the Sheikh is not back there now?" Suheil asked. His voice broke.

"I posted guards at every entrance to that camp. That's why it took me a while to get here. It's not easy to find guards late at night. I had to ask the guards we have to contact their colleagues. At this point, we're spending more money on protection than on education, and my guess is it will only get worse."

"Oh, my god." Sarah had reached her breaking point.

Jim approached her, put his arm around her shoulder. "I need you. Those girls are in pretty bad shape. I need you, and I need Suheil. I also need for you not to question me as to how I am going to deal with the perpetrators of this heinous act."

Sarah stared at him, drained, uncomprehending.

Suheil threw their clothes in the overnight bag. He said he wanted to go to the coffee shop to phone the hospital to admit the girls. He also wanted to call Nabila and Gwynne so the girls could be taken to the hospital and Suheil could meet them there. He was gone briefly. Returned. Explained he couldn't call. The coffee shop was closed and there were no pay phones.

The trip back, with Suheil driving his car, followed by Jim in his, followed by the guards, remained etched in Sarah's memory. Suheil drove calm, outwardly composed, eyes glued to the road. No traffic to speak of. No conversation. Just a procession headed for more leaps into the dark.

Reality set in when they reached Amman. They went directly to the compound, to Nabila's condo.

Nabila was home with the baby. Meanwhile, Gwynne had rushed the girls to the emergency room as the bleeding from the crude carving could not be stopped on one of the girls.

Nabila looked like a bulldozer had ran over her.

She clammed up immediately after telling Suheil and Sarah where the girls were, the same way she had done after her husband's death. Quiet desperation, Sarah called it, and it scared her to death. She motioned for Jim to follow her outside.

Suheil followed them.

"I'll go with Suheil to the hospital," Sarah said to Jim. "Please stay here with Nabila. When she walks around like she is doing now, almost catatonic, I worry about leaving her alone."

"You're right. I debated about bringing the girls to her place, but then where else could I take them? I talked to the mothers. They couldn't understand what all the fuss was about. Nine year olds, blood running down their legs. What was there to be concerned about?"

Like herself, Jim occasionally had trouble coming to grips with reality. Not that Sarah was in better shape than Jim, but it was imperative that someone keep a clear head. Otherwise, matters were bound to spin out of control.

Jim shrugged his shoulders. "There's not much I can do at the hospital anyway."

Suheil shifted his weight from one foot to the other signaling his impatience. Sarah hurried back inside, gave Nabila a hug, said goodbye, thanked Jim and rushed out to join Suheil.

The new resident on duty in the emergency room, a woman doctor in her early thirties, had attended to both girls by the time Dr. Tuqan and Sarah arrived. The girls had been moved to the pediatric surgical ward. Dr. Badran felt they needed to remain under observation as the damage done was quite extensive. The clitoris as well as the external genitalia had been cut on one of the girls. The other girl however was in worse shape – the job interrupted, half done. After giving a brief report to Dr. Tuqan about the treatment Dr. Badran had given the girls, she said, her voice shaking, that she had notified the police. A recent graduate from Davis, California, Dr. Badran seemed terribly upset by what she had seen and treated.

"Welcome to the real world," Dr. Tuqan said. He did not bother to hide his anger. "Welcome indeed."

"I thought this sort of thing was forbidden in this country." Dr. Badran rubbed her arms with her hand to stop her shaking. "The girls told me they were circumcised by the Sheikh himself, without their consent. Actually, after much prodding, they both admitted they were subjected to the mutilation by force. I think the Sheikh should be held responsible for what he's done to these girls. What I don't understand is how and where clerics manage to get such power?"

"From the people they victimize," Suheil said. In a manner indicating the futility of debating the issue.

"Then they should be held responsible for their actions."

Suheil Tuqan smiled, a sad, painful smile. "How long were you away from this country? Or perhaps I should say this world of ours?"

"I was nine years old when my parents immigrated to California. I came back because I thought I could make a difference. I came back because I was taught talk is cheap. Instead of complaining about poor medical care in third world countries, my parents said I should do my best to make a difference. I am beginning to realize that neither their thinking nor mine were up to date."

Before Dr. Tuqan could give her an answer, the nurse on duty informed them two police officers waiting outside would like to speak to the doctor who placed the call to the police station.

Sarah, who'd been waiting at a respectable distance stepped out first, followed by the resident and Dr. Tuqan. Sarah wanted to see for herself what shape the girls were in.

"Gentlemen," Dr. Tuqan said to the police officers, "Dr. Badran and I will have to check the patients before we can give you an accurate report about their condition. My office is down the hall, the last one on your right. Please join us in about ten minutes."

As they walked down the hall, Sarah on his left, the resident on his right, Dr. Tuqan spoke, his voice barely audible, his words aimed at the resident, his gaze focused forward. "I wanted to talk to you before you spoke to the police. Do not raise your hopes too high. The Sheikh will not be punished. He considers what he does as his clerical duty. You can try to prove him wrong with all the teachings of the Koran, the Sharia, the Hadith, whatever you like. He brushes them off. It's a matter of interpretation as far as he is concerned, and his interpretation is the right one. He derives sadistic pleasure from what he does. I thought you should know."

"What about the government. There's a law against such a barbaric act, isn't there?"

"He doesn't care. He knows no law can touch him."

The resident seemed totally baffled. "What do you mean? No law can touch him. We're not in Iran. Or the Sudan, or Yemen. Or are we?"

"No, we're not. You're probably not aware of it. But lately, the clergy have become adept at exploiting the growing religious revival now widespread in most Muslim countries. The extremists are slowly getting their way, aided, or perhaps I should say propelled by a few clergy determined to win power for themselves. After all, if an imam like Khomeini could topple a Shah who called himself the Shah of Shahs, what could possibly prevent other clergy from aspiring to reach similar new heights?"

"I thought the clergy were supposed to attend to our spiritual needs," Dr. Badran said coldly. "Cutting a women's clitorises hardly qualifies as a spiritual matter. My mistake. I should say girls. Not quite ten years old, I might add. Either I am terribly naïve, or the lure of power has thoroughly corrupted the clergy. Why else would they need to resort to such barbaric acts? What are they out to prove? Who can victimize most those weaker than themselves? Is that really what religion is all about?"

"It has nothing to do with religion. Power comes in many disguises, my friend. It becomes all consuming. The abuse of it, the lure of it, the high it generates – no need for drugs. Few given the opportunity can resist it."

Dr. Badran stopped, faced her boss, her eyes bulging, her face blood red. "And in the process women get trampled underfoot because they are the least protected in Muslim society."

"You got that right." Sarah could not hold back any longer.

"What? What about the government? Perhaps in Iran, or the Sudan, the governments are part of the picture. But what about here? I returned to this country thinking it was working its way to becoming a democracy. Is this another one of those 'for popular consumption only' democracies?"

"Not at all. It is a democracy. I dare say the only democracy in the Arab world. Against all odds. Thanks to the King and the Queen. Otherwise, chances are we'd be more like Saudi Arabia than England. It takes a man of the King's political savvy to keep under control the suffocating religious policies, especially of the last few years, advocated by the religious party which has recently won seats in the Parliament. Wisely, the King prefers to have these extremists in Parliament rather than force them underground. Had it not been for his intervention, in 1993, when Ms. Toujan Faisal was elected to Parliament and was almost ran out of town, she could have never made a comeback. Harassing phone calls day and night, death threats to herself, her family, the works. Her crime; fighting for women's rights. Men in this country have interpreted democracy to mean freedom, freedom to do as they please. Freedom without responsibility. A special democracy – 'for men only'. I don't believe it crosses their minds that women are human beings too. Never mind the rights women are entitled to by their religion, by the constitution of their country. Those facts are meaningless in our society."

A painful matter for Suheil, a matter which never ceased to trouble him. Sarah felt good. At least there were a few men who cared enough to be troubled by it. And she also felt his pain.

"You stay and fight, or, pack up and leave," Suheil said in a monotonous voice. "The choice is yours."

"I need to sit down." The color had drained from Dr. Badran's face.

Sarah moved to the doctor's side quickly, put her arm around the doctor's waist to give her support. Meanwhile Dr. Tuqan found an empty private room and a chair for Dr. Badran to relax in. Dr. Badran felt better a couple of minutes later and insisted they check on the girls as planned.

They did. The hospital staff did not object to Sarah's presence anywhere, anytime. Word of her donations had spread to all – despite Jim's and her efforts to keep the donations anonymous. In a small country, with few donors, secrecy was a rare treat. Mercifully, both girls were heavily sedated and thus Sarah was spared the agony of giving them an explanation – for the time being.

Zeina, the girl whose clitoridectomy had been interrupted by the untimely appearance of Younis was hooked to a blood transfusion, Farideh to an infusion with antibiotics.

Although outwardly Dr. Badran looked O.K. and she said

she felt all right, Dr. Tuqan was concerned. She was the only resident on call that weekend. Suheil did not want to leave her alone. Not yet. And not to attend to emergencies. He urged Sarah to go home. For the time being there was nothing she could do for the girls.

As Sarah walked down the hall, the agony of defeat and the feeling of helplessness weighed heavily on her mind. Often, when the relentless bombardment of it all became to much to bear, she found refuge in fantasizing what she would do to Ramzi, to her aunts, to the Sheikh and to anyone who inflicted pain and suffering on others unable to protect themselves. Fantasizing helped guard her sanity. Her mind took flight, to the compound, where she would grab her aunts and shake them, shake them until they promised never to hurt another girl again.

Ramzi would self-destruct. No worries there.

The Sheikh ... She'd have to think about it.

As she approached the nurses' station, the night nurse came out of a patient's room, saw her. "I'll call you if there is any change in their condition? Please don't worry." The night nurse was doing her rounds. She headed for the next room.

Sarah thanked her, continued down the hall in a daze, wobbly, like someone who'd overindulged in cheap wine. She stopped at the nurses station to give the nurse's aide her phone number. They would call her if there was any change in the girls' condition. The nurses had been very cooperative in the past when Fatme was in their care. Sarah trusted them.

The nurse's aide was not at the desk. Sarah decided to wait for her.

After a few minutes, restless, bored, Sarah heard footsteps coming down the hall. She turned around. The two officers who had come to the hospital in answer to Dr. Badran's call were walking back from what seemed to be Dr. Tuqan's office. The two men were busy talking. She heard one of the officer's say. "What has this world come to. To request the police to come, at this late hour at night, to check on two girls who have had clitoridectomies borders on the ridiculous. Do they think we have nothing better to do?"

Chapter 28

AFTER A SLEEPLESS NIGHT, FIVE minutes before eight the next morning, Sarah dragged her protesting body to the classroom where the children were waiting anxiously to hear about the condition of their friends from the woman in whom they all had trust. Although both girls who were circumcised were from Nabila's class, Sarah knew the incident of the previous night had cruised through the camp with lightning speed and the students had already heard distorted versions of what really had taken place.

Across from the hall, Nabila's students, minus two, were waiting as well.

She needed to set the record straight.

Sarah greeted her students, asked them to have their English books ready, and to read for a few minutes until her return. Concerned about Nabila, Sarah walked across the hall to the classroom where Nabila taught. Nabila stood erect, shoulders back, head held high, a newspaper in one hand and a magazine in the other. She was about to speak when she saw Sarah enter the room.

"Good morning." Sarah tried to sound cheerful but knew she could not fool Nabila.

"It is a good morning," Nabila replied catching Sarah completely off guard. "It is a very good morning, indeed."

Sarah walked to the desk where Nabila stood and inquired if she was feeling all right.

"I am fine," Nabila replied with a forced smile. "With your permission, for the first hour of class I'd like to veer from our regular schedule – slightly."

Nabila did not wait for Sarah's answer. She faced the

classroom. "Today we are going to discuss a subject we should have discussed long ago. Female genital mutilation." Nabila was seething. Her voice shook and the pitch rose and sank as she spoke – out of control.

As though on cue, her students gasped collectively.

Sarah's eyes met Nabila's. Nabila looked away, her face red with anger. She continued – completely undaunted. Nabila's 'discussion' could have disastrous consequences. Any discussion of sex, even vague references to it was unacceptable. It was not even mentioned that mention of sex is forbidden in the classrooms. It was assumed that everyone knew not to discuss the subject openly, especially in the presence of children and especially with both sexes in the same room.

Sarah also knew not to interfere. It had to be done – consequences be damned.

The night before, while Gwynne had rushed the girls to the hospital, Sarah had been concerned by Nabila's demeanor and had asked Jim to stay with her while she and Suheil went to the hospital to check on the girls. However, she soon realized how similar Nabila's reaction was to the news of her husband's death. She came to expect and accept Nabila's excessive reactions to corrosive situations characterized by withdrawal first, followed by decision making, culminating in execution of that decision – sometimes in less than a day. "Moderation is not one of my afflictions," Nabila often remarked when coaxed to temper her often fiery opinions.

Sarah loved Nabila's energy, her determination to get things done, her fearlessness in face of guaranteed retaliation. Expecting the worse, she murmured to herself, "To hell with being religiously correct. We have to inject a dose of activism into our plans. Otherwise we're doomed." She'd been toying with the idea for months. "This could be our best opportunity yet," she told herself.

"With your permission," Nabila said to Sarah, her voice still wavering, "I'd like to have your class join us. I believe what I have to say is relevant to all of us."

Sarah nodded yes.

Fatme jumped out of her seat, rushed to the other room and transferred the children over. The classrooms were often combined for lectures. To facilitate joint sessions they kept extra folding chairs in each classroom. Soon after the children were settled, Sarah pulled a chair and sat in the back of the room, her thoughts a jumble, her apprehension mounting.

Nabila held the *Time* magazine, the September 26, 1994 issue, given to her by Jim when she was in the hospital, the issue about the circumcision of a ten year old girl in Egypt by a plumber and a florist filmed by CNN. She passed the magazine around, showed the picture of the girl with her hands tied around her ankles to each student, "Please observe this picture carefully," she said, as she moved from student to student working her way from the back to the front of the class. "I stayed up all night last night to translate this article to Arabic so each of you will have a copy to read and take home. Fatme stayed up with me. She put the article in the computer. Many of your parents can't read so you will have to read and explain it to them. What I have to say is crucial to every girl in this class – and indirectly to boys. To be sure that you understand what's involved accurately and since it is quite possible that it will be your turn next if you're a girl, I will read the article sentence by sentence and explain it to you."

An awkward quiet filled the room.

Fatme rose from her seat with a stack of papers in her hands and gave each student a copy of the article.

"Two of your classmates are missing this morning," Nabila said, as she fought to subdue a spasm of rage. She went on, soon after, as if driven by an enormous compulsion. "You probably know that Farideh and Zeina are in the hospital. Farideh and Zeina are not in the hospital because they are sick. They are in the hospital because someone cut them up."

Another collective gasp.

"However," Nabila continued without paying much attention to the gasp. "We are fortunate. We have a friend who is a doctor and he is a doctor who cares, we have a friend who is our benefactor and she cares. Hopefully, your classmates will get well – soon. It is estimated that a hundred million women, perhaps I should say girls, children mostly, have had circumcision done in dozens of African and a few Middle Eastern countries. But it doesn't end there. You don't have to be in Africa or the Middle East to be forced to undergo circumcision. Immigrants take their customs with them wherever they go and they insist on the procedure for their daughters in the countries they immigrate to – the States, England, France or wherever they may be. Legislation to prevent the practice has done little to stop it. Any decent human being, given time to think about it, should be horrified by it. This is not the simple procedure its proponents claim it to be. It comes in a wide range; from cutting the hood of the clitoris, to removing the whole clitoris and all the tissue at the entrance to the vagina, followed sometimes by infibulation where the remaining tissue is joined together"

The children had the most horrified look on their faces.

Who knows, Sarah said to herself, perhaps shock therapy is what they need.

"You saw the picture of the little girl, tied down," Nabila held the magazine up. "You can see for yourselves. She has no idea about what's going to happen to her. But she's not worried. She is surrounded by her family. How can anything bad happen to her with her mother and father looking on? Right? She wonders – why suddenly a man is tying her hands to her sides. She's still not worried. Mom and Dad are right there in the room with her. No harm can come to her. Right? Her concern mounts, has no idea, until, suddenly, the plumber leans between her legs and cuts off her clitoris with a pair of barber's scissors. The blood running down her legs and the intense pain make her scream, 'Father! Father! A sin upon you. A sin upon you all.' She is only ten years old."

The children, the oldest being Fatme at age fifteen, looked

like blocks of ice. Except for the tears flowing down their cheeks, nothing moved.

"In our culture there are a few subjects that are taboo. But none more so than sex." Nabila was on a roll. If the children's discomfort upset her, she showed no sign of it.

A few students gasped, ever so discreetly.

Nabila continued unperturbed. "You have been chosen to be educated and because you have you carry a big responsibility, the responsibility to share the knowledge you learn in this school. The most important issue for you to learn is responsibility. Responsibility for your actions. We cannot blame the country, the King, the Queen, our families, the Jews, America, the clergy, or anyone else that strikes our fancy for what is wrong with our society – if we are not willing to take a stand and do something about it. That something is learning the truth and passing it on. It sounds easy. It isn't. Our parents were taught differently. Sexual discrimination, neglect of women's human rights are a way of life here. We don't bother to stop and think about it. Our culture promotes it. It has for centuries. But if you really want to repay your debt to society, to the person who so selflessly has devoted her resources, and yes her life to give you an education, then you must help us spread the truth."

Nabila stopped to catch her breath. Her eyes scanned the faces of thirty eight pupils, transfixed, motionless, terrified. "Any questions?"

Silence.

Nabila shifted her weight from one foot to the other, pushed her black curly hair from her face as she prepared for her next move.

From the back corner, the voice of Fatme rang across the room. "How?"

Nabila turned her head, focused her gaze on Fatme. "When the rest of your classmates go home and show their families the article we gave them, their parents will be horrified. They will insist that the children not have anything to do with sex. It's shameful Not acceptable. Some will beat the children. They might even be forced to quit school. But if the children persist they'll be given lots of answers. They'll be told circumcision is the duty of all Muslims – the Prophet said so. The Prophet did not. It's a custom which existed long before the Prophet, in Africa and the Middle East. It has nothing to do with Islam. It is a degrading, humiliating, life threatening procedure and it is not like male circumcision where only the foreskin is cut. Don't believe anyone who tells you that. It is more like cutting off the penis."

A loud collective gasp. The word penis spoken by a woman in front of children, male and female. Catastrophe awaits us, Sarah concluded.

It was almost as if Nabila had forgotten the presence of the students. She spoke to them but she seemed to be on a different wavelength, letting off steam, saying what she had always wanted to say, felt the opportunity had presented itself, and was not about to stop.

She went on. "But your families are not going to be jumping up with joy that you have learned the real truth. Change is hard on people because of the ignorance they have been cursed with. Unfortunately ignorance cannot be shed easily even when people move to a more advanced culture. They take their ignorance with them no matter where they go. Sometimes it takes decades, sometimes longer to change ingrained customs and attitudes. Meserak Ramsey," Nabila held up the newspaper. "a woman who speaks from experience, is waging a one-woman campaign shuttling between states in Africa, the Middle East, Europe and America, pleading with anyone who will listen to her to stop this barbaric practice. After years of frustration she now boasts the support of Rep. Patricia Schroeder. Persistent pressure on law makers by Patricia Schroeder, coupled with the efforts of local human rights groups and activists worldwide to raise public awareness of this issue, and other human rights abuses, have prodded the American Congress to pass a law forbidding genital mutilation in women under the age of eighteen. You might say to yourselves how is that going to help a girl whose parents force her to have the procedure done anyway – and she is not yet eighteen. It might and it might not. There are no guarantees. In life there seldom is. But we know for sure it has drawn the attention of the world to the problem. It will not be as easy as it used to be to have the procedure done and get away with it."

"But Miss Nabila." Fatme acquired a grave look. "We have similar laws in this country. They don't seem to dissuade those who chose to perform it or force it on others. Not in the least."

"That's because they are not aware of the permanent psychological and physical effects the procedure has on its victims and because their victims are too young to fight back. That of course is all the more reason why we must fight – all of us – at all cost. Educating the public is the core of this matter. Fatme is right. Legislation by the government has little effect since most of these violations take place in the home, away from the public eye. We have excellent legislation here in our country. But the abuse goes on. Here. Everywhere. I came across an article recently which claimed that 160,000 females have been circumcised in the United States where the procedure is a federal crime punishable by up to five years in prison. Clitoridectomies are not our only problem. In many countries, nine, ten year olds are sold into slavery, forced to prostitute themselves, beaten, raped, circumcised. Actually, many girls are forced to be circumcised by their mothers who themselves had to endure the pain and humiliation of the procedure when they were children. Ask them why and they will be surprised by the question. They defend it as a rite of passage, as a social prerequisite of marriage and Muslims defend it as the duty of a true Muslim."

Fatme's hand shot up from the back of the class – again.

Nabila invited her to come to the front of the classroom.

The eyes of her classmates followed her every move.

Sarah glowed with pride each time she looked at her. She had a prize student in Fatme, a young girl raped, maligned and abused, yet saner than most who lived in the lap of luxury, and far too mature for her age. Fifteen going into thirty five, Sarah often joked. She was an excellent role model for her school-mates who came from similar backgrounds giving them reason to hope.

"What, in your opinion can we do to stop these abuses," Fatme asked.

"Silence is acceptance," Nabila replied calmly. "We must speak out – all of us, young, old, men, women, children, all of us."

"You can lose your life for suggesting less."

Sarah's heart skipped a beat. Fatme knew what she talked about. She'd been badly beaten by her brother for asking if she could go to school. Nothing unusual there. She'd been kidnapped, raped, mutilated. And although everyone knew what had happened to her, Fatme did not dwell on the past. She carried on totally focused on the present and the future.

Nabila studied her star pupil a puzzled look on her face. "Do you think we should keep quiet then, take all the abuse doled out to us by our male relations, by our clergy, or by anyone else who so desires?"

"I was thinking we should organize into groups," Fatme replied timidly. "women's groups perhaps. If men wanted to join us they would be welcome. We should devote our efforts to community education, to create an awareness in the public of the problems plaguing our society. We pretend they don't exist. Of course they don't. Only because we don't want to acknowledge that they do. But if we could organize into groups and make a relentless effort to bring into focus women's human rights, eventually we might be able to erad-icate many of the violations against us. Don't you agree, Miss Nabila?"

Sarah was speechless. For a fourteen year old to have come this far in one year was incomprehensible but most rewarding. She felt a warmth inside, a kind of good feeling she never got except when the fruits of her labor surpassed her expectations.

Nabila dropped her head to one side, continued to study the girl, all of fifteen years of age, the girl who she claimed never ceased to amaze her.

As though reading her mind, Fatme said shyly, "It's not my idea. I read about it in the newspaper. The one Miss Gwynne gets from England. Miss Gwynne helped me understand what it was all about. It was about the fourth UN World Conference in Beijing, about members of Equality Now, a group it said has been working with international human rights organizations, like Amnesty International to bring to the attention of the world the injustices suffered by women. It said we had to promote women's rights through international grass-roots activism. Equality Now apparently has been especially successful in its campaign against female genital mutilation. It was then that I realized how widespread this problem is, even in so-called advanced countries."

It was hard to tell if the children were even breathing. It was as if they had been encased in a steel cocoons. Sex, human rights, women's rights, were not subjects that were discussed – ever. Not in school, not at home, not anywhere, not at any time. It was taboo. Period. Fear of retaliation kept sex from being mentioned even among friends. And yet here they were – a bunch of kids from the most disadvantaged part of the country, perhaps the world, listening to a fifteen year old, one of their own, carry on an intelligent discussion with adults, seemingly not bothered by the consequences of her indiscretion, nor the price she'd have to pay – without a doubt.

Sarah had mixed feelings about the progression of the discussion. It was gratifying to know that her efforts were so amply rewarded. Of course she was elated. Yet fear of what might happen to Nabila and Fatme and definitely herself for allowing such matters to be discussed in her classrooms, tempered her exuberance – but only briefly.

To hell with caution. Sarah felt there had been too much of it already. We must act and act now.

She walked to the front of the class. "Children, we should all thank Miss Nabila for her ceaseless efforts to inform and educate us and we should congratulate Fatme for her interest in women's human rights issues, for the effort she puts into learning and keeping abreast with the subject. All of you know she has been the victim of abuse, rape and mutilation. However, you should also know that the same thing can happen to any one of you girls, anytime – like it did to your friends yesterday. Now, does that mean freedom for boys. Not if a boy cares for his sister, cousin, and/or friend. If, as we have been teaching you for the past year – if we oppress half of our people, than that is exactly what we will have. Half a people. A mother who is not educated cannot be expected to raise a child to his full potential. Are men doing themselves a favor by denying women basic human rights? I'd like you to think about it. Maybe you think we should ask the government to stop these practices. Of course we should. Government can help. But in many countries the government and the judges are men and they make the rules and the rules are for the 'benefit' of men. In Jordan we have good laws meant to protect women. Yet abuse goes on all the time with no end in sight simply because our culture accepts it. Therefore, we must organize, like Fatme said, and fight until our outrage becomes the public's outrage and men are forced to face the truth."

"And what is the truth, you may ask."

"It is simply this," Sarah answered her own question. "Women are human too. And if anyone really believes in her or his religion, no matter what that religion is, if he really believes, then there's no reason why he or she cannot accept a woman as an equal. No reason at all."

There was a sudden sparkle in Nabila's eyes. Until then, although she had not tempered her speech, she admitted she had been worried about how Sarah might react to the reversal of their previous attitude of not doing anything to upset the religious, social and cultural establishment. Education was great. But it took time, and time was what they had little of. If they were to make progress they had to couple it with grass-roots activism. The challenge was monumental, the stakes high, the perils terrifying, the outcome uncertain. "Best of all worlds," Sarah said. "Let's get on with it." Sarah thrived on challenge – the more complex the better.

"Congratulations are in order," Nabila reached for Sarah's hand and shook it eagerly. "We have a lot to lose and perhaps a lot to gain. Gentle persuasion has lost its luster. We must organize, educate, spread the word."

Sarah felt alive, felt good despite the internal struggle she was having convincing herself the girls recuperating in the hospital could have been saved the pain they were suffering had she had the courage to start an aggressive campaign against the practice and against all women's rights abuses sooner.

Sarah pointed at a student in the front row, an eleven year old. "Who do you think should be held responsible for what happened to Farideh and Zeina?"

Caught off guard, the girl blushed and started to cry.

"She's been there herself," Nabila said as she walked over to comfort the girl.

Nabila's words rendered Sarah nearly inarticulate. Her enthusiasm turned to irritation. Was there no end to this dilemma? A few feet away, the woman who had so forcibly and with such great courage captivated the class's attention minutes earlier, was quietly wiping the tears welling in her eyes. Was it possible?

"Could we go to my office for a minute, Nabila please?"

Nabila raised her head, gave her friend a resigned look, followed her to a small room next to Sarah's classroom. "Tell me it's not true." Sarah's voice broke. She could not keep her anxiety under control.

Nabila's tortured smile was all the answer she needed. It tore her apart.

"When?"

"Soon after my parents died. Arranged by an aunt."

Sarah reached over and embraced her friend. "I'm so sorry. I should have guessed. I should have known from the way you were affected whenever the subject was mentioned, or the procedure took place, from your taking in Fatme, from your devotion to the children. I had to have been totally blind to what so obviously called for my attention. Please forgive me."

Nabila reached for a tissue paper from a box on the desk, wiped her eyes. "It's too late for some of us. But we might be able to help others too young to help themselves."

"Why don't we give the children a break," Sarah said. "They've had a rough morning and so have we. Let's let them have a twenty minute recess."

"I'm not through yet Sarah. I know a lot of what I said was way above the children's understanding. But I had to get it out of my system. If they grasped a fraction of what we were talking about, it will help. We need to go back there and tell them in simple words to be on the lookout for that barbarian who calls himself Sheikh – the sadist whose great pleasure in life seems to be the genital mutilation of females, for older women who force helpless girls to undergo the procedure imposed on them when they were children. The children should be warned. They should be prepared. Like the little girl in the picture I did not know what hit me until it was all over. There's no telling who their next victims will be or when. But we know for sure Farideh and Zeina are not the last names on their list."

Sarah could not argue with that. But it would have to wait. Nabila was in no shape to work herself back into a frenzy – again. "You will go back, Nabila – shortly. Now I will go give the children their milk and snacks, then send them out to play."

When Sarah returned to her office, she found Jim perched over Nabila.

"Hi Jim."

Jim had a solid build body and a solid face – like a prize fighter. But when provoked the muscles on his face could easily be used to teach anatomy students the origin and point of insertion of each muscle. When Jim looked up, every muscle on his face bulged as though screaming to be let out.

Pangs of pain erupted in Sarah's stomach. Something had to be terribly wrong for Jim to look that upset. And then it hit her. The Sheikh must have disappeared – again. Rumor had it that the Sheikh feared Jim more than he feared the law or his religious superiors. Although the Sheikh did not have proof, he was firmly convinced Jim worked for the CIA, was against the Islamic revival now spreading from the Middle East to Africa and was determined to eliminate him. Working for Sarah was the cover he needed. Jim had powerful friends in the U.S. embassy in Amman. That, the Sheikh was sure of. And powerful contacts as well in Jordan, in the business community. Perhaps he disliked Sarah almost as much. On the few occasions the Sheikh had met Sarah and his investigations about her, had led the Sheikh to conclude that Sarah made donations to mosques not out of religious conviction but to advance her own agenda disguised as teaching underprivileged children. But he, shrewd as he was, knew precisely what Sarah's intentions were and told her so.

Jim pulled a chair and lowered his body slowly into it. From the bags under his eyes it was apparent he had not had much sleep. He stared at the ceiling hands entwined, in not so subtle an attempt to calm his nerves.

Sarah found herself restraining an impulse to question Jim. Not about the Sheikh, but the girls. Surprisingly, Dr. Tuqan had not called although he had promised to do so. As the day progressed, her level of anxiety rose.

Nabila wiped her eyes dry, turned to Jim. "Have you been to the hospital yet?"

Jim sighed. "Farideh is doing better – physically. Her mental state however, is terrible. No one can approach her bed. She cringes and slides down under the bedcovers."

Both women waited for Jim to continue. He seemed in no hurry to do so.

Sarah knew why. "Zeina is in bad shape, isn't she?"

It took a while for Jim to answer. Finally, with a resigned tone he said, "It seems when Younis interrupted the Sheikh's joy ride, the Sheikh did not get to finish the job he had started. He was only half done. He had made a deep cut to remove the clitoris completely but managed to remove only part of it. She was rushed back to the operating room to stop the bleeding which, unfortunately had been missed by Dr. Badran."

Nabila dropped her face in her hands and sobbed.

"Still in surgery?" Sarah asked.

"They started about forty five minutes ago. They had to wait for test results and the cardiologist before rushing her into surgery."

"Cardiologist?"

"They think she has congenital heart disease."

No wonder Suheil had not called. The deterioration of Zeina's condition made Sarah pause and take count. How many more girls would have to be sacrificed before she mustered the courage to do something about it? Something worthwhile, something that really made a difference. Could she? Could they? How? The obstacles placed in their path had seemed less formidable than they appeared at first. However, the suffocating religious atmosphere, especially of the last decade had made the task of introducing change a veritable contest. Opponents claimed it was an attempt to impose ones values on others – Western values on Easterners who have no place for it in their culture. It was the opinion of many that American women changed sex partners frequently because their sexual organs demanded more and more satisfaction. A hateful fate awaited young girls trapped in a culture, in a world they had no say in shaping. Sarah moved next to

Nabila. "Why don't you go home, rest a while. I'll take over
the classes."

"No." Nabila stiffened noticeably. "It's not time to think
of ourselves. It's got to stop. We've got to find a way. Only if
we demonstrate we have the guts to take on these problems
whether they are labeled cultural, social or religious, will
much needed change take place. We must attack on as many
fronts as we can. Good intentions alone are not enough.
Outrage, rather than patience, should be our weapon of
choice."

Sarah broke into a sweat. Nabila's militancy sent shock
waves through her. Unlike Sarah, she had her guts and her
brains to fight with but not much else. She also had a child to
think about. Sarah would never forgive herself if something
were to happen to Nabila thus depriving Samir Junior of both
parents. The guilt feeling regarding Samir's death was her
constant companion.

Jim must have sensed Sarah's discomfort. He pulled himself up from the slumping position he was in and said with the
sang-froid of a master intelligence officer, "Embracing
change in a culture which defies change is like embracing a
boa constrictor. Perhaps it would be better to accept matters
as they are and be done with it."

Nabila shot out of her chair her face red with anger. "You
don't believe that, do you?"

"What I believe is immaterial. People's attitude does not
change overnight. Unless you accept that, in your haste you'll
make the wrong choices."

"I made my choice while I was in the hospital. Even if you
and Sarah quit, leave the country, I believe so strongly in
women's rights that I will carry on the fight regardless of the
risks involved, the time and effort it will take and with less
hope for a positive outcome. But fight I must. It's the only
way I can respect myself, do justice to my husband and feel
there is a purpose for me occupying space in this world."

"You can be sure of one thing," Sarah commented calmly, without hesitation. "I'll be with you every step of the way. Jim always plays the devil's advocate because he worries about our safety. I respect that. We're not fighting just the Sheikh or my aunts, or Ramzi. Its a whole culture, attitude, state of mind we are hoping to reverse. Jim is right, though. We shouldn't raise our hopes too high, but we can move faster than we've done in the past. We should organize, have small cells, demonstrate, publicize and we must be relentless. Facts should speak for themselves. But that's no guarantee for success. We must persevere, understand less and condemn where called for. We must be fearless yet cautious. We've been too passive in the past. That's why I believe our progress has been so slow. Let's get on with it."

Jim rose. He found public displays of emotion difficult. Yet he managed to walk over, reach for Sarah's hand and shake it. He then reached for Nabila's hand. "I congratulate you both. The best time for you to start is now. Fearing reprisal the Sheikh took off for Cairo late last night. He thinks I don't know where he went. It suits me fine – gives us a window of opportunity to get our act together. But fear not. The minute he hears our activities have taken on a new twist, he will be here as fast as an aircraft can fly him here."

"I thought you did not approve." Nabila had a puzzled look on her face.

"Of course I don't. I can predict the outcome as of now with no trouble at all. But I know what I will have to put up with if I have two unhappy women to deal with instead of one. I call that double trouble," Jim teased.

"Where do we start?" It suddenly dawned on Sarah that she had absolutely no preparation for this sort of thing. It was easy to teach school, pat herself on the back and feel good about doing something worthwhile. True, forty students and Muhammad were benefiting from schooling. But at that rate it would take decades for any tangible results to manifest themselves. In the meantime, in a century galloping with technological progress millions were left behind mired in ignorance. Where to start? The question echoed in her head.

"I can get you help," Jim said. "But her identity has to remain strictly confidential. She will give you all the information you need on how to start, how to attract many who are out there and who believe as strongly as you do in women's rights, are afraid, or don't know how to go about doing something about it. She will show you how to attract the attention of the media, how to get your message across. Since you two are determined to press on, it's best for you to go about it well informed."

"How?" Jim never ceased to amaze her. He almost always foresaw her needs and made arrangements to meet them. In all likelihood, he expected a strong reaction from her and Nabila regarding previous night's incident. What he did not know was how strongly Nabila felt about it since she herself had also been a victim.

"I'll let you know. We'll probably meet in a coffee shop or restaurant. She works for our embassy. Our embassy does not approve of its employees getting involved in local issues. She has heard about your work and is eager to help but she must do it behind the scenes. She is a top ranking member of Equality Now. They operate through Women's Action Network, a volunteer organization. They handle appeals of specific violations – through public pressure – namely letters, faxes, the media. They document individual cases and mobilize grass-roots protests on their behalf. You have probably heard about Fauziya Kasinga, in jail for sixteen months, in the U.S., as an illegal immigrant. She apparently escaped from Togo, Western Africa so as not to undergo genital mutilation. Equality Now got her released through the public outcry they generated, got her political asylum. She is now in the U.S. legally. It seems they have been quite successful in their campaign against female genital mutilation. That's not all though. They campaign against domestic violence, sex trafficking, illegal abortions, rape and sexual harassment. They work with local groups to raise public awareness about human right abuses. You can write to them for more information if you wish. Here is their address." Jim reached in his wallet, pulled a piece of paper and handed it to Sarah.

Sarah was elated. A member of Equality Now with the know-how to run an organization. What a stroke of luck! "How soon can we do it?"

"Tonight. Quite possibly."

"Fantastic. As always." Sarah rushed over, gave Jim a big hug, then turned to Nabila. "I'm boiling with energy. Let's take a run around the compound before we resume classes. Do you feel up to it?"

Captivated by the information from Jim, Nabila had listened with an intense concentration Sarah had not witnessed before. "Could I come too, Jim? Could I meet this lady?" she asked.

"Absolutely. Now get on with the business of teaching those children."

"Fatme will take care of the classes. Sarah and I want to go running first."

Jim planted a kiss on Nabila's forehead, gave her a hug, said good-bye and left.

Sarah and Nabila put their running shoes on, kept in a closet in the office. They ran around the compound for about fifteen minutes. Exhausted, they sat on the steps close to Attiyeh's unit. Mrs. Attiyeh rushed over with two glasses of water, a ritual they were all used to by now – except they usually ran before classes started, not in the middle of the morning.

It was almost ten thirty. Ordinarily, time for recess for the children. Tenants and owners of the other units stayed indoors for twenty minutes, until the children returned to their classrooms. This morning, the children had recessed early and gone back to their classrooms. Sarah and Nabila were the only persons around, sitting on the steps in the hot summer sun.

In a moment, Sarah thought she heard noises coming from the south side of the compound where her aunts lived.

She cast a quick glance. Sure enough, Ramzi, with a slight limp cane in hand, and both her aunts, each carrying a suitcase stepped forward. They stopped suddenly when they saw Sarah and Nabila on the steps. Both women turned to Ramzi. He said something while he continued to walk. To exit they had to pass by Sarah and Nabila since Sarah and Nabila were on the steps in front of the exit, next to Attiyeh's house where they stopped every morning after running, for a drink of water. Sarah's mind raced. Where were they headed to suitcase in hand? Ramzi was not carrying a suitcase. Were her aunts planning an escape like the Sheikh? Where to? To her knowledge, they had not left Jordan in many years, Hamideh did not have a passport, Khadijeh's passport had to have expired years ago. Where could they go?

The compound was immense. Ramzi and his aunts were about a hundred feet away from Sarah and Nabila. Sarah's heart ached when she saw Ramzi limp. Her aunts, whom she had not seen for quite a while, especially Khadijeh, seemed to have gained a lot of weight. She had to wobble from side to side to walk. Since she was covered with the abaaya, it was hard to tell how much weight she had gained. Perhaps her suitcase is heavy, Sarah thought. She knew it would not cross Ramzi's mind to offer to carry the suitcases for his aunts.

Nabila chuckled when she saw the concerned look on Sarah's face. "My threat worked," she said as she wiped perspiration from her forehead. "Last night, after Gwynne took the girls to the hospital, I put Samir Junior to sleep. The more I thought about what they had done to those girls, the angrier I got. I looked out the window to see if by chance your aunts were home. There was light in Khadijeh's house. I asked Fatme to watch Samir while I went out for a few minutes. I rang Khadijeh's doorbell. It took forever, but eventually she opened it and was completely surprised to see me. After a moment's hesitation, she asked, 'What do you want?'

"I hear you and your sister have been quite generous with your gifts to Farideh's and Zeina's parents," I said for openers. She turned to Sarah. "Can you believe It? Your aunt actually gave money to people."

"The Sheikh must have asked them to."

"That's what I figured. Anyway, Khadijeh's disdainful smile quickly turned into a frown. 'What is it to you?' she shot back.

"I'll tell you what," I said, "If I were you I'd save my money. A few minutes ago, the English woman drove the girls you and your beloved Sheikh butchered, to the hospital. They were bleeding quite badly. Zeina more than Farideh. Therefore, we have decided to take you to court. You, your sister, and the Sheikh."

"Khadijeh looked me over carefully. Seething with anger, she yelled, 'Go to hell. You are a whore. You don't know what you're talking about.'"

"Oh, but I do," I said, by then pretty worked up myself. "We'll see in the morning who does and who does not know what she's talking about."

"She tried to close the door in my face. 'Go to hell,' she yelled. I tell you she was shaking so bad she could hardly breathe.

"I quickly put my foot in the door. 'I have no intentions of going to hell,' I said. 'I like it here. I like it a lot. Moreover, I have to stick around to make sure you receive your just punishment. I am not a nice person like your niece, Sarah. I don't forgive, and I never forget. You, your sister, that Sheikh and your nephew have gotten away with far too much. Someone has to make you understand that what you are doing is against the law in this country. Someone has to put a stop to it.'

"Shut the door on the bitch's face," Hamideh hollered from inside.

I answered, "No need to. I have said what I came to say."

It should have, but did not surprise Sarah. Very little did any more. But a lot of questions rattled through her head. "Lawyers cost money. How will you carry out your threat?"

"Easy. I have heard about a woman lawyer, a Jordanian. I

phoned her last night before I went to call on your aunts. She said she'd be more than happy to help. She said these cases were hardly ever brought to the attention of authorities – a cultural thing, happened all the time, nothing to be concerned about. That, according to her, is the opinion of her colleagues, almost all male, I might add, and the general public. So what if it is against the law."

"That's good to know. But that does not answer my question. You're always so adamant about not accepting financial help. How will you pay for it?"

"No problem." Nabila had an impish grin on her face. "It's free. She'll do it for nothing – any case involving women's rights. Free. That's what's so good about it. I tell you, there are people out there, men and women who think like us, eager to help. We should tap these resources. We have to find a way to reach them."

Halfway to the front gate Khadijeh stopped first, followed by Hamideh. Ramzi took a few more steps, turned back, waited. It looked like Khadijeh was having trouble walking. She lowered her body down to the ground, sat, and immediately pulled her abaaya to cover herself. Hamideh did the same. Ramzi looked angry, said something, but made no move to proceed. He leaned against the wall of the unit in front of which they had stopped and waited.

"It looks like Khadijeh is having trouble crossing the yard," Sarah remarked.

"That's because she has added weight. Last night when she got angry, I was afraid she'd have a stroke. She had to stop to catch her breath repeatedly."

As Nabila spoke, Sarah's apprehension grew. Her thoughts were on a completely different sphere. Where were her aunts planning to go? Were they leaving because they were worried that they might be sued? What was Ramzi's role? Was she imagining it all? Nabila had acted on impulse. Was Nabila's threat to her aunts reported by her aunts to the Sheikh? Was that why the Sheikh had left for Cairo? Since clitoridectomies were the Sheikh's passion, no doubt he knew it was forbidden by law. If the Sheikh was informed of the girls' hospitalization by Sarah's aunts, fear of Jim's wrath, in addition to carrying on a procedure forbidden by law, had to have been the reason for the Sheikh's unexpected departure. Did her aunts know the Sheikh had left the country?

It was probably a blessing in disguise, Sarah figured. Bringing the Sheikh to justice was no mean job. They had tried before and failed. Dealing with Jim's wrath was worst. When Jim entwined his fingers and stared at the ceiling, it sent warning signals to Sarah. Somehow, Jim managed to locate the perpetrators of the injustice he so despised, and dispensed his version of justice swiftly, without remorse. Explanation: the wheels of justice turned too slowly, especially in third world countries. Those who commit crimes should not go unpunished.

Jim will be livid, Sarah thought, when he finds out who tipped the Sheikh – albeit unintentionally. To Nabila she said, "Let's go. The children are waiting."

"A few minutes more, please," Nabila pleaded. "I've got to see Khadijeh's face when she passes by. Look. Your aunts are back on their feet already, headed this way."

"Nabila, please, let's go. Ramzi is not an individual you want to deal with. He can be quite nasty."

"Sit. Sit down, Sarah. This is too good to pass up. She called me a whore last night. I figure why not give her a dose of her own medicine."

"What good will that do? She's not going to change. Neither by words nor by threats. It's summer. They'll probably vacation somewhere, come back refreshed to do more damage. People don't change, Nabila. Not after age eighty anyway."

"I don't care if she does or not. I want to have my say. If it bothers you, go ahead, leave. I don't mind."

"You're a stubborn one." Sarah sat down reluctantly. "I don't trust you, alone. Not with my relatives. You don't know them like I do." Unlike Nabila, Sarah hated confrontation.

"You will be surprised," Nabila answered. A naughty smile briefly crossed her face.

Soon Ramzi and her aunts were a couple of feet away from them. They continued walking, their gazes focused ahead.

"Hey, Khadijeh," Nabila shouted, her voice moderately loud. "Running away, are you?"

Khadijeh ignored the remark, continued walking.

"What are you going to do for entertainment if you can't get girls to cut up?"

They continued walking.

"You had your say," Sarah interjected. "Now let's go." She knew Ramzi's patience was being sorely tested. No doubt, pushed more, he would react. No doubt, violently.

Nabila was not finished.

"Khadijeh, don't forget to take your friend with you. They say the Sheikh cannot live without you and your sister."

Khadijeh turned around slowly, cast a disdainful look at her tormentor, was about to say something, changed her mind.

"Don't answer her." It was Ramzi. "Don't cheapen yourself. She's a whore."

"Glad to hear you say that in public. Nothing will stop me now from suing you as well."

Ramzi spun around. "You want to sue me?" He shook his head in disbelief. "You want to sue me, my aunts, the Sheikh, everybody and anybody. You think you live in America? Wake up woman. You're in Jordan." He found his own words so funny he burst into laughter. He laughed so loud Attiyeh's wife came rushing out of her apartment to see what was going on.

Ramzi turned to Mrs. Attiyeh. "Take this woman," He pointed at Nabila with his cane. "Take this woman to a doctor. She has lost her mind. She needs help."

Mrs. Attiyeh did not move.

Sarah rose. "You need to learn some manners young man.

I doubt though you have it in you to realize how low you have sunk."

"Really?"

Sarah turned to Nabila. "Let's go."

Nabila could not be persuaded. "I have waited a long time to get a few things off my chest." She turned to Khadijeh. "The neighbors tell me you are a sick woman. You have heart failure. Your nephew is not here because he is a gentleman and wants to help you. He is here to make sure he gets everything you have when you die. His great love is money. None left to spare."

Khadijeh's eyes bounced from Nabila to Sarah, to Ramzi, back to Nabila. She opened her mouth but could not speak.

"I told you she is sick," Ramzi shot back barely able to control his anger.

"The person who sends bombs in packages and kills innocent people is sick. Not someone who tells the truth."

Suddenly the color drained from Ramzi's face, his knees knocked, yet somehow he managed to steady himself on his cane. "Where did you get that idea?"

"It's not an idea. It's a fact. We have proof – enough proof to make you pay with your life for the life you took."

Sarah's jaw dropped. She was speechless. Jim. It had to be Jim. Mostly, Sarah tried to consciously block the incident from her mind. But she did not always succeed. And when she thought about it, it seemed odd that Jim, always so sensitive about injustice, about violence, had let that one slip by without doing much about it. At times, she underestimated him, at times did not understand him at all.

Ramzi cocked his head to the left, studied the woman who would not stop tormenting him, as though assessing the validity of her words. A moment later, he asked, "Then why haven't you gone to the police?"

"Oh, but we have. We received the last piece of information last night. I believe Mr. Bateson is at the police station right now."

Chapter 29

ZEINA DID NOT MAKE IT.

Neither did Khadijeh. Her intended trip had to be substituted for a trip to the intensive care unit of the University Hospital. She clung to life for three weeks. On the twenty second day her heart called it quits, sent her on her last trip to face her Maker.

Sarah hoped God would have more mercy on Khadijeh than she found it in her own heart to do so.

It was a day Ramzi had prayed and waited for. He was the sole heir, destined to inherit the Khadijeh's house and the lump sum inheritance Khadijeh had received from her brother, Maher Sultan. The trouble was, Ramzi was nowhere to be found. He had vanished. Even newspaper ads placed by his parents urging him to contact them had failed to elicit a response.

Soon after Nabila's encounter with Ramzi and her aunts, baffled as to why Nabila had acted the way she did, Sarah mulled over the incident repeatedly, but could not come up with a plausible explanation. If Nabila had proof about Ramzi's guilt, if, as she claimed, she knew that Ramzi was the so-called messenger who gave the bomb to her husband, and Jim was at the police station reporting as to who the culprit was, then why did she tip Ramzi off. Why would she give Ramzi a chance to escape. It didn't make sense, not coming from an intelligent woman like Nabila. Why would she warn her husband's killer that the police would be soon closing in on him?

Unable to find an answer, Sarah decided to ask her.

Nabila listened without interrupting. When Sarah was finished, she said, "In this case hindsight is really twenty, twenty. The problem was we had very little to go on. Jim and I brainstormed. Rashid's presence in Iraq seemed to us like a good opportunity. We thought Ali might have seen something or someone – anything that might shed some light on this puzzle that has been torturing me day and night. We decided to ask Rashid to talk to Ali, to question him thoroughly, to find out if he remembered anything, anything at all about the incident. Jim has hired a lawyer, here in Jordan. The idea was for the lawyer to have something to work with until such time when Ali would be released from prison in Iraq and return home. Ali told Rashid he did get a glimpse of the man who handed the package to Samir, before he, Ali, collided with Samir while dashing out the main gate. The description fit Ramzi perfectly. However, Ali insisted it was only a glimpse. He doubted he could identify Ramzi if asked to do so. Jim consulted the lawyer. The lawyer did not think there was enough evidence even if Ali were to identify Ramzi positively. It would be Ali's word, a fugitive, a refugee from one of the poorest camps in Jordan, against the word of a man who comes from a prominent Jordanian family, a man who has never been in trouble with the law before. Who do you think they would believe, Sarah?"

"So you decided to trap him."

"I had to. I had to know. Not knowing who killed my husband was driving me crazy. Every time I look at his son, I see his father's eyes pleading, demanding I find the man who snuffed his life just when life had become worth living. I had to know – for my own peace of mind. And when my son grows up, he will want to know who made him an orphan."

"He couldn't have gone far," Sarah replied, aware of the fact that her relatives attitudes could no longer be wished away. "I bet Ramzi is right here in Jordan, hiding, and I bet his parents know where he is and are willing accomplices. You forget, Nabila. That bomb was meant for me, not your husband."

Nabila had a strange look on her face. "But ... But ... all those ads in the newspapers."

"It's a ruse, a trick. I know how their minds work. They are addicted only to whatever works to their advantage — which rarely happens to be the truth. In all likelihood, they have their own discreet investigation underway to determine if there was sufficient truth in what you said, or it was an educated guess based on suspicion. For them facts are nuisances, totally irrelevant. When they feel relatively confident that not enough evidence exists to prove their son's guilt, Ramzi will surface. He can't last long on his own. He's been pampered all his life and there's too much wealth at stake for him to disappear without a trace."

Nabila did not like what she heard. "There for a while I was happy. Not only because I finally knew who my husband's killer was, but also the fact that Ramzi had disappeared. With Khadijeh gone and Hamideh in seclusion, at least we would not have to worry about your relatives. I also fear that the Sheikh will return soon. I'm surprised he has stayed away, wherever he is, this long. He simply cannot afford to give us free reign."

"The last I heard from Jim, a couple of weeks ago, the Sheikh was on his way to Libya – probably to brush up on the latest advances in terrorist tactics. He's already been to the Sudan, teaching and learning from the radicals. Apparently, he's mostly interested in transforming secular governments in the Middle East into Islamic states. The King is fully aware of his activities. Be rest assured, when he returns he will be watched very carefully."

Nabila's fears were not assuaged. The Sheikh was powerful, his following growing fast even among the young who blamed all their problems on the unconditional support of the U.S. government for Israel. Also, the tendency in Middle Eastern countries with majority Muslim population was to reject the immoral ways of the West by embracing Islam – starting with the government. Nabila was sure, armed with new ammunition from his trips, the Sheikh would be much more difficult to deal with. But she had no doubt he would return when he felt he could do so safely. Jim had mentioned on several occasions that the clerics who worked for the Sheikh were in daily contact with him and assured him they would let him know when it was safe for him to return.

After due reflection, Sarah said, "That's fine. But until the Sheikh returns we will continue with our work like we've done the past three months. It's amazing how fantastic the response to our ads has been so far. No doubt there are many religious fanatics out there. But there are also those who can think and see clearly the results of fanaticism. All they have to do is observe Iran. We've got women from all walks of life: women doctors, lawyers, representatives of parliament, professionals and many homemakers eager to join and work with us – despite the repercussions that their actions are sure to exacerbate. Surprisingly, we also have a good number of men. It did not take long for us to attract these people simply because they are terrified that what happened in Iran might happen here and in other Arab states."

Nabila was quiet for a long moment. "Bear in mind," she said, her voice calm, measured, "that we do not face government opposition in Jordan. If the King and the Queen were not the enlightened rulers that they are, we could not accomplish a fraction of what we have done so far. It's harder in Egypt, the extremists are well funded and violent. But we've done quite well there too. The sad part is that all we have worked for, all we have fought for, and sacrificed for the past sixteen months, can be lost in the wink of an eye."

That's not very encouraging, Sarah thought but said nothing. When Nabila had something bothering her, Sarah had learned to let her be.

Sure enough, Nabila picked up where she had left off. "Sarah, think back. Remember the Shah of Iran. He tried to pull his people into the twentieth century. He had the money, the power and the backing of the United States. Maybe he tried too hard. Maybe he was too much of a dictator, a mega-lomaniac some say, or whatever. In the end, it cost him his throne and his people landed back into the Middle Ages in the blink of an eye. That was in nineteen seventy-nine, not too long ago. While the world bit its fingernails to the quick yet did nothing else, a bunch of radical clerics managed to topple the so-called fifth military power in the world. That's what gives clerics in other Muslim countries, like our Sheikh, the audacity to force their version of Islam on others. The victims – mostly us women, of course."

"I think it's a question of degree, Nabila. In Europe and the States although women have far more liberty than they do in Muslim countries, they still have to fight every inch of the way for many rights automatically enjoyed by men. It often borders on the ludicrous. Consider this, a woman and a man, doing the same job for the same firm, the woman will earn two-thirds the man's pay if she is lucky and she can do a better job than her male colleague can and still be the last to be promoted."

"That may be true but they are not forced to do so because of their religious beliefs. Distorted Islamic teachings are responsible for ruining the lives of the majority of Muslim women from Asia to Africa. Islamic revolution should come through persuasion not force. The religion itself poses no threat and it is important for us to treat different Islamists differently. Imposing a brand of primitive Islam does little to change the lives of men. Actually, in some cases it makes them a little more God-fearing, compassionate, more tolerant. It's the power crazy mullahs with their distorted messages blaring from mosques, heard all too clearly, who use religion to oppress women that gives our religion a bad name. And that's what we have to deal with."

"It's tempting to think," Sarah said, "that that's what makes the challenge worthwhile. We are not here to change the world. We are here to reinstate what's rightfully ours. Our destiny will be determined by our actions. Not by waiting for someone else to do it for us. That won't happen."

"At times," Nabila admitted, with bone-deep weariness brought on by frustration. "At times, alone, late at night, I find myself in a deep depression. I have searched but failed to find an answer as to why our minds work the way they do. The same gray cells that can send men to the moon can also kill and mutilate. Jeffrey Dahmer, Ted Bundy comes to mind. The same religion in the hands of different individuals can help meet the spiritual needs of its followers, help the poor, the sick, the widowed, the elderly, while denying the most basic human rights to women and forcing them to live a life of sub-servience under black tents. In our society, women are con-sidered subhuman. They are victimized – by their society, their culture and their religion. But mostly they are victimized by members of their families. Crimes of honor are perpetuat-ed by a society that not only tolerates it but also encourages it. The epidemic of violence against women is openly condoned by our religious figures. Women find Islamic rules most degrading and absurd. I have tried – I really have. Perhaps I need the Wisdom of Solomon to differentiate fact from fiction to understand the logic behind it all. Unfortunately, so far, it has eluded me."

Pondering these thoughts Sarah was impressed with the power of Nabila's intellect. Nabila was fortunate. She could speak to her about her pain. How many women were out there suffering a fate worse than Nabila's without being able to unburden their heavy hearts. An awful thought not to be dwelt upon. Men had been writing their own script for too long. "The religion in its pure form is a masterpiece," Sarah heard herself say. "It teaches the highest morals, satisfies the spiritual, cultural, mental needs and provides guidelines for a balance between worldly life and spiritual needs. I think the negative aspect we are experiencing is political, a backlash against the West. The so-called Islamic revival is what I fail to understand. Islam has always been live and spreading. What's new about that?"

Nabila nodded in agreement. It was a subject never far from her thoughts and often discussed. Simply because it affected every aspect of her life.

"Do not despair, my friend," Sarah tried to cheer her up. "I think the pendulum has swung too far out. It's bound to return to the center sooner or later. We want it to happen sooner rather than later. That's why we're doing what we're doing. Our best chance depends on educating women. An educated woman is an empowered woman. An educated woman has confidence, self-esteem. An educated woman can help herself, will not have to rely on a man for her very livelihood, as she must now. Armed with contraceptives, she will be less inclined to have as many kids and those she has will benefit immensely from her knowledge and enlightened attitude."

"I think one of the best ideas you had," Nabila said, "was the adult classes and the vocational schools we started in the villages. The change that has come over the women is phenomenal – even more so than the children. You are right. Knowledge is the best weapon for women. Or men, for that matter."

"We can't stop there though. There's much more to be done. We have to find ways to help the women find jobs or start their own businesses. Once they gain economic independence, they'll be less inclined to tolerate the abuse and violence of their male relatives. Suheil showed me an article about population control in China. It said 'by making women better off China is doing more for population control than all the states coercion ever managed.' The same will be true of religion. When women become better off, they will be much better prepared to fight for their rights themselves instead of relying on organizations which might or might not succeed in giving help when and where needed. It doesn't matter how many human rights organization strive to achieve some kind of basic rights for all. There are places and people they cannot reach – like Saudi Arabia, the Sudan, Iran. But we can't give up. If women are trained in basic skills and are literate, in due time, they will be capable of doing anything they want."

"They can and they will," Nabila replied. "And therein lies the problem. Consider this: Previously, that is until nineteen seventy-nine, women in Egypt could not leave their homes without their husband's permission or a court order, if you please. Then along came Gamal Abdel Nasser. He repudiated that law and gave women the right to vote in nineteen fifty-six. Delighted, women rushed out in droves to work outside the home. Unfortunately, when they returned home after working all day, they found the work at home waiting for them. Men in our culture don't share in housework. That boring stuff is strictly reserved for women. Consequently, women found themselves holding two jobs. Many quickly opted to take care of their homes and children and let men take care of providing for them. It's a whole mind-set, the mind-set of millions of people that needs to be changed I'd say by a hundred eighty degrees."

"You're implying then that educating women alone will not work."

"Precisely. We have a huge population that's illiterate. Like blindfolded mules, they follow ancient customs mostly because they have little exposure to much else. We should open the adult literacy classes to women and men. Like you always say, if we change the attitude of one person, it will snowball, it will all be worth it."

"You miss the point, Nabila. The reason we have classes for women only was based on the assumption that most men would not permit their wives or daughters to attend classes if men were present. We can however, for starters, have separate classes for men as well. Any ideas?"

"I was hoping you'd say that. I often ride the school bus with Jim. After dropping the children at the camp, Jim usually checks on Muhammad's family. Slips them money for the old man to buy medication. The old man is still not well. Actually, he's worse. Jim is worried about him. But he will

not go to a doctor. He says he never has and never will. And
then we linger a while, talk to whoever happens to be around.
A few days ago, we dropped the children in front of their
homes, made sure they went in, and we were walking toward
the bus when we heard a scream. Of course Jim rushed over
to check. Amal's father, the Amal in your class not mine, was
beating his wife something fierce. I had to restrain Jim, literally beg him to leave the man alone. I thought Jim was going
to kill him. Like a rag doll Jim grabbed the man, lifted him up
and threw him across the room. It took a few minutes for
everyone to calm down. I approached Amal's father. I said
that's not a good thing you did. He said beating our wives is
a God given right. No man should interfere. It is written in the
Koran. Trust me, even those who are illiterate know selective
teachings in the Koran. Whatever works for them, whatever is
to their perceived advantage – they know. Whether what they
think they know is correct or not is irrelevant."

"I can see Jim now," Sarah said, looking at the incident
through her mind's eye, witnessing the clash of opposites.
"Jim is going to get himself into real trouble one of these
days. I'm so glad you were with him."

"Me too. Otherwise, it could have been catastrophic. I
asked Amal's father where in the Koran does it say for you to
beat your wife and lo and behold he recites it for me. He can't
read, but he sure can recite. 'Good women are obedient,' he
said. He liked the sound of what he said and went on. 'As for
those from whom ye fear rebellion, admonish them and ban-
ish them to beds apart, and scourge them.' That really got my
blood boiling. Why don't you recite for me where the Prophet
urges kind, gentle treatment for women, I asked. I bet you
have not heard that verse, have you? So let me recite it for
you. That's what I said and did. The Prophet says, 'Some of
your wives came to me complaining that their husbands have
been beating them. I swear by Allah those are not the best
among you.'"

They were working late into the night, as usual, brainstorming, planning, evaluating plans that had been executed, plans to be executed, changes to be introduced. When Jim and Suheil were free, they joined the women. Ordinarily, Nabila spent as much time as possible with Samir Junior, now nine months old. An active baby, he usually crashed about seven in the evening and except for an occasional teething pain waking him up, he slept through the night. Samir Junior was everybody's baby, pampered, loved, and drowned in lavish gifts from Sarah, Jim, Gwynne and Suheil when he could take time off from his medical responsibilities to go shopping. At nights, when Nabila and Sarah worked, Gwynne and Fatme took care of the baby.

A few minutes before midnight Nabila dropped the ballpoint she was using on the kitchen table and rose. "Jim said he might stop by. Guess he got busy or forgot. I think I'll call it a day."

The door bell rang.

"Ah, better than never." Nabila opened the door.

Attiyeh's daughters stood shivering, clinging to each other.

Nabila brought them in, her arm around the shoulder of the younger girl.

They started to cry.

Why would two little girls, quiet, never in trouble, come to her door, obviously without the knowledge of their parents, at midnight. Perhaps the baby is sick. Sarah thought. She asked the girls if that was the problem.

"The baby has a cold," the older girl, Asieh said. She sniffled, tried to stop crying but couldn't.

"Do your parents know you're here?" Sarah asked. She was puzzled and disturbed by the unexpected appearance of the girls.

Sarah gave them tissue paper. "Do you want to talk about it?"

No answer.

"When your parents wake up and see you're not in bed,

they will be awfully worried."

"No they won't," Asieh replied between sobs. "My father doesn't care about us because we are girls. He doesn't care at all."

Sarah and Nabila exchanged painful looks.

"Unless you tell us what's bothering you," Sarah said softly, "we cannot help you. Remember how we discussed in class to be brave, to fight for your rights, to admit when you're wrong, to accept credit when you're right. When we have a problem, we talk about, try to solve it. We don't resort to violence, and we don't run away."

A panicked look landed on Asieh's face. She took her little sister's hand and headed for the door. Nabila and Sarah hurried toward the girls, brought them back, set them on the sofa and they sat on each side of the girls.

"I did not mean for you to leave," Sarah said, totally at a loss as to why the girls, especially Asieh was behaving in such a strange manner. "But for us to help you we must know what's bothering you."

"My brother is sick." Asieh burst into tears.

"It's nothing serious," Nabila said. "Samir Junior has a cold too. They'll be all right in a few days."

"My father said my brother will die. No one will call my father Abu Maher any more."

"From a cold?" Attiyeh's neurosis about his son's health was well known by all those who knew him. But a cold?

"My father says his other sons started the same way – a cold, then suddenly they stopped breathing and died. He says he is not going to wait for it to happen again."

It's really mind boggling, Sarah thought. How can this great divide between ignorance and reality be breached? What made me think I could play a role, even a minor role in an insurmountable, centuries, perhaps millennia old mind-set as I have been faced with. "What does he want to do? Your mother took the baby to the pediatrician this morning. She told me the doctor said it's a mild cold, his lungs are clear, and he could travel."

Once more Asieh burst into tears.

"She's normally a very sensible person," Nabila said. "Something has to be very much out of whack for her to behave like this."

Sarah caressed Asieh's hair and hoped she would relax and eventually explain what had forced her to leave her bed, at midnight, drag her little sister along and come to her place. Whatever it was, and it didn't seem like her younger sister, Najwa, had any idea what was going on, it had to be something terribly upsetting for them both. Yet her culture, full of intrigue, suspicion, distrust, made it difficult for her to confide in others, perhaps more so to someone she looked up to with reverence.

Nabila turned to Sarah, her head behind the little girl. She whispered in English, "Maybe that's what's bothering Asieh. Maybe she doesn't want to go."

The previous day, Attiyeh had stopped by Sarah's place and asked to talk to her. He said he wanted to take his family to Egypt for a week or ten days, with her permission, of course. At first Sarah thought it was strange that a man who literally pleaded with her not to go to Egypt the previous summer now was eager to do so – as soon as possible. But times had changed. Khadijeh had died, and without Khadijeh, Hamideh was not capable of much malice on her own. If anyone deserved a vacation it was Attiyeh. Sarah agreed, pleased with his request yet still not comfortable with his demeanor which had turned sour immediately after his son's birth and seemed to get worse each time the boy sneezed or had a loose bowel movement.

"Don't you want to go to Egypt to see your grandparents and the rest of the family," Sarah asked the girls.

"I do. I miss my cousins."

"She's terrified," Nabila said in English. "Perhaps she is worried about missing school for ten days."

"She is a very good student." Sarah was getting impatient.

"She won't have trouble catching up. I don't think that's enough to send her into a frenzy like this."

"Asieh," Nabila said, with a little edge to her voice. "Are you worried your parents will leave you in Egypt?"

"Maybe."

"That's crazy. Why would they do something like that." Sarah could not fathom what made Asieh so despondent, so negative. She was one of her brightest pupils, intelligent hard working, very reserved.

"My father said to my mother, maybe it is best we don't bring the girls back with us. Maybe they could stay with your parents. My parents are too old, he said."

Najwa had fallen asleep leaning her head against her sister's shoulder. Asieh pushed the hair from the child's face, put her head in her lap and sobbed – again.

The women waited for her to calm down.

"What did your mother say?" Sarah asked.

"She didn't."

"If that's what's bothering you, you need not worry. I will talk to your father. I don't know what his reason is. But I'll find out."

"Our flight is at six in the morning."

"I see." She'd have to wake up at four thirty in the morning the latest to get to talk to Attiyeh. The drive to the airport even early in the morning, in the congested traffic of Amman took over an hour.

"Could we stay here with you Miss Sarah?"

Sarah and Nabila studied the girl for a long moment. No doubt fear prevented her from sharing with them whatever problem she was facing.

"You may, of course," Sarah said, "But I have to let your parents know you are here so they don't lose their minds looking for you."

"They won't."

"They won't what? Lose their minds or look for you."

"My father doesn't care. My mother has to do what my

father tells her to do."

Nabila and Sarah exchanged looks.

"What makes you say that?" Nabila asked.

"It's not what I say Miss Nabila. It's the truth. My father doesn't care at all. It doesn't matter if my sister and I are hungry. He couldn't care less if we are cold, or have no clothes to wear. The only person that matters in our house is Maher. Everything is for Maher. My father sits in a chair next to his bed every night, half the night, because he wants to be sure Maher is breathing. Then my mother has to take over. My father says the hard mattress recommended by the doctor will break the baby's spine. My mother says the doctor said soft beds kill babies. He finds something wrong with everything my mother does or we do. It happens every time we get a brother."

"Asieh," Sarah said, "it might seem to you that your father doesn't care. But you know that's not true. Your parents are preoccupied with the baby. Your father is worried about losing him. Soon he'll find out his worrying is useless. Maher will be up and around in no time and your father will look back and laugh at himself for worrying uselessly."

Nabila frowned. "Having traveled down the same path myself when I was a little girl, I know quite well what Asieh and her sister have to live with. You learn real fast, soon after realizing the difference between you and the opposite sex. Worshipping male children can adversely influence the thinking of a female in her formative years, destroy her psyche. Girls feel unwanted, just like Asieh – a burden, a work horse. Not loved and cared for. When there's work to be done, a girl is the first to be remembered. When there is fun to be had, she becomes invisible. No one thinks about her except when her services are needed. When a man's lust demands satisfaction, he looks for a woman. But dare a woman want sex, and she is stoned to death. To make sure women never succumb to the temptation, they cut out her external genitals before she has the slightest idea what sex is all about. No, I can't say I blame

Asieh for the way she feels. It's a man's world. Yet despite it all, she must learn not to give up. We have to impress her with that. That's our challenge."

Sarah leaned wearily against the back of the sofa. Cultural, social considerations, religious restrictions and man's greed for power had bonded together to embalm the public in a straight jacket, a straight jacket obliterating free thought, free speech, logic. Next to her sat a tortured child, among adults from whom she had seen nothing but love and dispensing of knowledge, yet incapable of bringing herself to divulge the cause of her distress.

Asieh could hardly keep her eyes open. Sarah offered her a glass warm milk. Asieh sipped it quietly, staring despondently into the glass.

It was so easy to get discouraged. And yet the line between hope and disappointment was so thin, the balance so delicate. To treat Islam with the respect it deserved, the shackles pulling it down had to be removed – somehow, before it was too late. The increasingly confrontational manner of the clerical regime in Iran and their widening influence made it harder to resolve the dispute as to what constituted the correct interpretation of the Koran. Without it the interpreters would remain in full control – her great 'experiment' an exercise in futility as often predicted by her opponents.

She was no longer alone though. Many had joined her ranks and contributed greatly to the ever increasing projects they designed and executed. Despite their efforts, their society seemed to be in an irreversible downward spiral with radical elements increasingly gaining ground.

Sarah remembered the harsh treatment faced by the Egyptian professor of Islamic studies, Nasr Abu Zeid for suggesting the Koran is open to modern interpretation and advocating a secular state. She and Nabila were lucky though. The great repercussion Sarah had feared after Nabila's talk about female genital mutilation had not materialized thanks to the turn of events. Had the Sheikh not had to make a hasty exit, she hated to think what their fate would have been.

Asieh finished drinking her milk, took the glass back to the kitchen, slumped next to Sarah on the sofa. It was not clear if she was ready to talk. Sarah decided to try.

"Why do you think your father wants to leave you in Egypt?" she asked.

"He says he might lose his job if he brings us back."

She must be misinformed, Sarah concluded. There's no way Attiyeh is worried about losing his job. Either that or he made it up for reasons I fail to understand. "Did you hear him say that?"

"Yes. He said it to my mother."

"When?"

"About an hour ago. Before they went to bed."

"And where were you?"

"My sister and I had gone to bed earlier, much earlier. My sister slept, but I couldn't. My father was talking nonstop. He was nervous. He would throw stuff in the suitcase then take it out, scream at my mother, call her names."

Sarah couldn't believe what she was hearing. Of all the Arab men, especially from rural areas, Attiyeh was a rare specimen. He treated his wife rather well compared to other husbands – mostly because he had promised Sarah's father. He had not taken other wives although she had yet to give him a living son. He did not beat her, at least not to Sarah's knowledge. He did not consult her for any type of decision making, but that would be too much to expect from an illiterate peasant. Actually, until his son's birth he was a pleasant man, kind, considerate, obliging, grateful for the smallest kindness, worked real hard, never complained.

She had also never heard him lie.

"What else did he say?"

"He said there was no doubt in his mind if we did not go to Egypt that Maher would die."

"He must have lost his mind." Nabila said. She had refrained from interrupting but admitted she could not do so any longer. She switched to English. "Perhaps one of us should talk to Attiyeh. It almost sounds like a bad dream. If it had come from anyone else but Asieh I would have said it is definitely a bad joke or someone is hallucinating. What she has overheard doesn't make sense."

"Let's see if we can get to the bottom of this." Sarah turned to Asieh."I am assuming that your parents are asleep. That's how you managed to sneak out of the house. Am I right?"

"Yes."

"You want to sleep here till about four in the morning and then we'll take you home. Is that OK?"

The terrified expression returned to Asieh's face. "We don't want to go home. We want to stay here with you. Please don't send us back."

"All right then. I don't have an extra bed. You and your sister can sleep on the sofa. We will worry about the rest in the morning."

"No. Please. No." Asieh jumped off the sofa, grabbed her sister, and once again headed for the door, dragging her sister behind her.

Sarah stopped her. "Where do you think you're going?"

"I don't know."

Sarah closed the door. "Something is scaring you. You won't tell us what, and I am out of ideas. If you want us to help you, we have to know what's bothering you."

"I can't Miss Sarah. I can't. My father will kill me."

Sarah took the girls back to the living room, set them on the sofa then turned to Nabila. "Can you please keep an eye on them. I'm going to check. It's possible Attiyeh woke up, saw the girls gone and panicked. It's also possible he may have some answers for us."

"Please Miss Sarah, don't go. You can't change his mind. Nobody can."

"She's right," Nabila said. "When it's in regard to his son, Attiyeh takes leave of his senses. We don't have the guards anymore and that yard is quite dark at night. I don't think it's wise for you to go – or me for that matter. He will probably check with my place and yours before he calls the police."

"O.K." Sarah dropped her exhausted body in the armchair. "I'll set my clock for four am." She turned to Asieh. "Don't worry. We'll find out what's bothering your father and when we do, we will take care of it. Let's all get some sleep. Nabila, do you want my bed or the sleeping bag?"

"I'll be fine here in the armchair. No need for covers. It's too hot."

Sarah was not quite sure how long she had slept when she was awakened by the ringing of the door bell.

It was Gwynne.

"Attiyeh left our place a few minutes ago. He's looking for his daughters." Just then Gwynne saw the girls asleep on the sofa. "What in heaven's name has brought these children here in the middle of the night? Attiyeh says they were home until almost midnight when he went to bed."

"What time is it?"

"Four thirty. Daybreak."

"Where's Attiyeh?"

"I told him to go back to his apartment. Wait for me there. Our phone doesn't work. I told him I'll check your place, call the police if need be from your place."

"Let me throw a pair of jeans and a top on," Sarah said, half asleep. "I need to talk to Attiyeh. He has said and done things which make no sense, no sense at all. Asieh is much too scared to talk. We tried last night. Neither Nabila, nor I could get her to tell us what her problem was. Only that she and her sister did not want to go on vacation with their parents. They want to stay at my place."

"What sort of things?"

Sarah told her.

"It's the strangest thing," Gwynne said. "He is packed and ready to go but can't find his daughters. I bet I know exactly what Attiyeh is up too."

"You do? What?"

"I don't want to sound like an alarmist. But Attiyeh is so consumed with fear about losing his son that he is willing to do anything to prevent it. Let's go check it out."

From a distance they saw Attiyeh dashing back and forth, in and out of his apartment like a man possessed. He stopped briefly, went into his apartment again and this time closed the door behind him. When Sarah and Gwynne reached the apartment, the door was still closed but one of the windows in the living room was open. Attiyeh was speaking forcefully, through clenched teeth, evidently trying to keep his rage under control so his voice would not wake the neighbors up. His wife had to be the recipient of his diatribe as there was no one else in the apartment except the baby.

"I told you to take care of it," Attiyeh said to his wife, "before you left Egypt. But you had other ideas. You said they are too young. You said the butcher who does it is not there. You told me all kind of stories and you managed not to get it done. If something happens to my son, you can be sure this time, promise or no promise, it's the end for you."

Sarah and Gwynne were at the entrance to the apartment about to ring the bell. They stopped when they heard Attiyeh vent his anger at his wife. "Butcher?" Sarah asked in whispers.

"That's what the man said." Gwynne put her fingers on her mouth motioning for Sarah to keep quiet.

Attiyeh screamed a few obscenities.

No answer.

Sarah peeped through the open window. Mrs. Attiyeh sat in a corner, the baby in her arms, asleep, bags packed, time to catch the plane fleeting.

"It's not hard to guess what he is up to," Sarah said to Gwynne. "No wonder Asieh was terrified."

Gwynne smiled sadly. "No it isn't. Ancient customs are hard to get rid of."

Attiyeh continued with his monologue. "We're through. Finished. Wherever that daughter of yours is, she must have dragged her little sister along, and wherever she is, she probably heard us talk and is telling everyone about it. Otherwise why would she escape in the middle of the night. And where to."

Mrs. Attiyeh remained quiet.

"I've got to see this," Sarah said to Gwynne as she moved quietly toward the window. "I think we have an ally in Mrs. Attiyeh. She's always so quiet, it's hard to tell what she thinks. I have never seen Attiyeh so worked up. But the logic behind his words eludes me."

Sarah took a quick look inside the apartment and withdrew quickly. "He's running his fingers through his hair and pacing, getting ready for another bout. He seems very angry. He is looking at her in a real weird way. I'm afraid he'll hit her."

"I've been thinking," Attiyeh said, as Sarah made her way back to the window. "I checked to make sure Asieh was asleep before I discussed it with you. Ever since that incidence with Farideh and Zeina, she's been acting strange, awfully quiet. She looks at me with eyes full of questions, fear, hatred perhaps. What I am wondering about is who has been talking to these girls. Besides reading and writing, what else are they teaching them in that school. And I still don't understand why in the name of the Prophet, why a girl needs schooling. I don't understand."

Gwynne moved close to Sarah. "Smart woman Mrs. Attiyeh," Sarah whispered. "She let's him talk. Doesn't answer. He is moving close to her."

Gwynne sneaked close to the window, looked in. "He needs counseling. He's lost his mind. You'd think he's the only Muslim in the world who has trouble having or keeping a son. What a pity. Of all the men I have met in the Middle East he was one of my favorites."

The women saw Attiyeh whirl around suddenly. "I don't think," he said, his voice totally out of control. "I don't think Asieh heard us talk. I think you told her about it and I think you sent both girls somewhere." He raised his right hand and slapped his wife across the face.

"He's not my favorite, I tell you." Gwynne looked furious. "Not anymore. He's sick. We should take him to a doctor."

Attiyeh hit his wife again and again. "Where did you send them? Answer me you daughter of a dog."

Mrs. Attiyeh did not make a sound.

He hit her again. "I know where they are. And I'm going to go get them. You have ruined our trip, you have ruined our vacation, you have ruined our lives. But most of all you have ruined the chances for my son's survival. It's a pity. Without my son you have no place in my house."

Mrs. Attiyeh rose, the baby in her arms, found a rag on the floor, took it and wiped the blood dripping from her nose. She then returned back to the living room, sat on a chair and started to nurse the baby awakened by his father's screams. She never once looked at her husband.

"What has it got to do with his son's survival?" Sarah asked Gwynne.

"I don't know. We'll soon find out, I suppose."

Unfortunately, Attiyeh was not through with his wife – yet. He was so incensed he could not stop. "You know why?" he said, and approached his wife once more threateningly. "If he touches her again," Sarah whispered, "his chances of surviving my wrath are zero." Instead of hitting her, probably because she was nursing his son, Attiyeh cast a disdainful look at his wife and continued his monologue. "Do you know why you think you are better than most? You think so because some rich lady taught you how to read and write. They fill your heads with crazy notions, ideas which twist your feeble minds. If Allah wanted women to be educated, he would not have given them a uterus to bear children. A woman's job is to toil for her husband's pleasure, to give him sons, to take care of the family. I can say without reservation that that's not at all the case with you lately – not since you started those adult education classes."

Attiyeh kicked a the suitcases as he made his way to the front door.

"He's coming out," Sarah said to Gwynne. Gwynne had moved away from the window. With barely concealed anger, Sarah moved away from the window to the door.

Gwynne rang the doorbell.

Caught off guard, by the sight of Sarah and Gwynne at the door, for a moment Attiyeh seemed lost for words. He looked quickly from Gwynne to Sarah, then back again, as though assessing the damage, perhaps hoping they had not overheard him. In a moment he managed to pull himself together. He turned to Gwynne. "Did you call the police, Miss Gwynne, did you?"

"No need to. The girls are asleep in Miss Sarah's place."

Attiyeh acted as though he was surprised. He let his jaw drop. "In ... In Miss Sarah's place? Why? Why did they go there?"

"Cut out the charade, Attiyeh," Sarah said with more force in her voice than she had ever used with him before. "Cut it out."

Attiyeh turned ashen gray. He must have realized he was doomed.

Sarah pushed him aside and walked inside. Gwynne followed. Sarah made her way quickly to the living room. "Give me the baby, please. Go wash up."

Mrs. Attiyeh handed the baby to Sarah, a resigned expression on her face, conveying her pain with her eyes. Gwynne took her by the arm, walked her to the bathroom, helped her clean up.

Attiyeh stood at the entrance of his own apartment like an ice figure stuck on a stand unable to advance or retreat. When Gwynne walked out of the bathroom with his wife, Attiyeh kept his eyes glued to his slippers. Gwynne ignored him. She eased Mrs. Attiyeh down into a chair in the living room, returned to lash out at Attiyeh.

"I bet you feel like a hero, don't you?" A woman whom

few situations could intimidate, Gwynne did not give a damn that the culture she lived in did not tolerate female aggressive behavior toward males. "Your wife did not ruin anything for you, you did. You're a sick man. You need counseling. I dare say the sooner the better."

Attiyeh remained in his frozen state. He did not even blink.

Gwynne gave him a disgusted look. "I have to give you credit though. You are a great actor – but only when it's to your advantage. How could you possibly be so stupid?"

Sarah walked over with the baby in her arms and the mother next to her. She turned to Attiyeh, "You have upset me immensely. I hate to speak in anger. That's why we are going to leave. I am going to take Maher and his mother to my place until you come back to your senses and all of us have had a chance to cool down."

Before Sarah could take a step, suddenly, Attiyeh threw himself at her feet. "Miss Sarah, Miss Sarah, please, please, try to understand. Maher is sick."

"Maher has a cold. He's not sick. You are – in the head."

Attiyeh began to sob still prostrated on the floor at Sarah's feet blocking her way out.

"You don't know, you don't understand what it's like to dread the inevitable. It's driving me crazy. I have lost control. I don't know what I am doing or saying. Please, please forgive me."

"Rubbish," Gwynne retorted. "Absolute rubbish. What the hell does your son's survival have to do with your wife or daughter?"

Attiyeh wiped his tears with his sleeve. "I was desperate. I couldn't take it any more."

"What the hell are you talking about." Gwynne's outrage permeated the room. "What's there to take?"

"I am cursed. Me, my family. We are all cursed." Attiyeh directed his words to Miss Sarah conscious of the fact his future depended on her forgiveness. "Miss Sarah, please help us."

"Who told you you are cursed?" Sarah was livid, her ire directed at the man who so inhumanly had beaten his wife.

"I ... I went to the mosque. I went many times but the Sheikh had gone on vacation. Lately, the Sheikh had shown interest in me and my family. Unexpected, but appreciated, I might add. His assistant did not know when the Sheikh would be back. I went again, a week ago. He said the Sheikh had taken ill. I better look for someone else. I asked him to help me find someone. The assistant said he will arrange for me to meet another cleric downtown since I was so troubled. Three days ago the Sheikh's assistant stopped by. He gave me the name and address of someone he was sure could help me. I ... I went to see him. He said we have a curse on our family."

It became clear to Sarah she was not going anywhere for a while, not unless she could be callous, walk out and let Attiyeh stew in his own stupidity. But that was not her at all. The baby seemed to be getting heavier by the day, thriving on his mother's milk and good medical care. A healthy, beautiful infant, he gurgled and smiled, without a care in the world. Sarah pulled a chair and sat in it.

"How does he know?" Sarah shook her head in disbelief.

"Of course he does. He is the cleric in charge of the big mosque downtown."

"All right. Let's say he does and let's say he is right. What does that mean?"

"Miss Sarah, please."

Sarah's eyes met Gwynne's. This was not a show, a charade. The man was genuinely tortured. "Miss Sarah, we are cursed because we have sinned. Praying five times a day, giving alms to the poor, being a good Muslim is not enough. We have sinned. We are cursed." Tears flowed down Attiyeh's face. Gwynne dug in her pocket and handed a couple of tissue papers to him.

Attiyeh wiped his eyes, blew his nose and then he was quiet. The color had drained from his face. Always thin, his skin looked like an oversized coat carelessly thrown at his body to cover protruding bones.

Sarah waited till he calmed down. "Who is we, Attiyeh. Who is the sinner among you. And what sin is it that has brought this curse upon your family?"

Attiyeh's gaze, never too far off the ground, dropped a notch lower. He did not answer.

It didn't take a genius to figure out the answer. But Sarah was determined not to make it easy for him. If he wanted her sympathy, he had to say it, loud and clear. Amazing, Sarah thought, what a slow death old customs and traditions die, especially in the rural areas. Compared to his peers, Attiyeh has had much more exposure to alternate ways of looking at and solving many issues. Yet the village buried deep in his psyche never let's go.

She looked at him, a pathetic sight, not stupid by any measure, yet incapable of making choices. All his life he's been told what's white and what's black – no shades of gray, no possibility of change. What made her think she could coax people to do the impossible.

"Come child," Gwynne said, evidently concerned about the person she loved most in the world. "Sarah, let him be. We cannot change the world. Let's go."

Sarah rose reluctantly, rearranged the position of the baby in her arms, turned to Mrs. Attiyeh. "Come. We have to go. The girls must be awake by now."

At first Attiyeh did not move or speak. But just as the women reached the front door, he threw himself on the floor, grabbed Sarah by the ankle and implored, "Miss Sarah, please, please, I beg of you. Help me remove this curse from my house. Let me have the girls circumcised."

Sarah had not expected him to be that persistent or that bold. But desperate situations demanded desperate action. No doubt Attiyeh was desperate. She turned around one foot firmly nailed to the ground. "Let go of my foot."

"Miss Sarah, for Maher's sake, please, have pity on me. I hear thousands of women are circumcised every day. Their mother is. Why should my daughters be different."

"Because they are. If you don't stop your irrational behavior, you'll not only lose your wife, you'll lose your job, your home and your children. Maher is a healthy baby. Circumcising your daughters will not bring him better health. Here he has everything he needs to remain healthy. You won't be doing your son a favor by taking him to Egypt in intolerably hot weather. In the villages in Egypt, a serious infection or illness and no decent medical care has been the cause of infant mortality for as long as children have been born there. Do you want the same thing to happen to your son?"

Attiyeh heard her but the words did not register. Before Sarah could take another step, Attiyeh, still on the floor, grabbed her by the ankle again. "I will do anything you want, anything at all if you'll only do this little favor for me."

Gwynne was not known for her patience. Looking totally exasperated she reached down picked the man up without effort and forced him to stand straight. "Listen carefully," she said with a threatening glare. "It's against the law. Do you want to go to jail for it?"

Attiyeh shook his head vehemently no. "No one needs to know. We will have it done in Egypt, in our village. It's done on every girl by age nine – the latest. That's why I wanted to go."

"You're free to go." Sarah had a hard time keeping her rage under control. "I sponsored your family to come to Jordan. I am responsible for them. Unless they chose to go, they're not going anywhere."

Mrs. Attiyeh moved closer to Sarah.

Attiyeh raised his open hands and started hitting his own head calling on Allah the merciful to come to his rescue. "If I can't change your mind," he said as he cried and sniffled. "Maybe Allah can."

"Allah, in his wisdom, takes time out when fools like you decide to leech on to him." Gwynne never lacked for words. "I say God has more important things to do than listen to your babble. That's what I say." With that, she stepped out.

"Not to worry." Sarah grabbed Mrs. Attiyeh by the hand. "It will not happen."

They walked out, Attiyeh still prostrated on the floor, Gwynne leading the way.

Chapter 30

SARAH DID NOT FIRE ATTIYEH. Over two dozen people depended for their livelihood on his income – his extended family, his wife's extended family. She simply ignored him. However, finding accommodations for his wife and children, with all the vacant units in the compound turned into classrooms, presented a serious problem. Finding housing, even substandard housing was difficult, in the area where Sarah lived practically impossible.

Once again Jim came to Sarah's rescue. He arranged for a room for Attiyeh to move into in the basement of the apartment complex where Jim lived. Mrs. Attiyeh and the children remained in their home.

Attiyeh came to work at his usual time, soon after morning prayers at dawn, looking more like a dog deserted by its owner, than a man who beat his wife.

He lasted three days. The fourth day he was like a dog with his tail between his hind legs. He begged to return home. Name the price.

"Talk to your wife," Sarah said, "It's her decision."

It was the last thing Attiyeh wanted to hear. Couldn't Miss Sarah, please, just let him return home?

Miss Sarah could but wasn't about to.

Sadly, Mrs. Attiyeh was not given to making decisions. Any decision worth making was always made for her, early on by her parents, mostly by her father, after marriage by her husband. She asked Sarah for help. She did not want her children to grow up without a father, yet she was ready to raise her children without her husband if her husband's behavior did not improve. She was in a position to support herself and her children. She had learned to read and write attending adult literacy classes at night, and learned to sew quilts and caftans with tribal designs and patterns taught in the vocational school Sarah had started. The quilts and caftans were in great demand by tourists and wealthy Jordanians. The women who learned how to make them could not make them fast enough. They earned decent wages for their efforts and the project had the support and the encouragement of the Queen. There was no limit to the amount of income they could earn from their work. They were paid by the number of articles they made. The more they made, the more they earned.

Given her background, Mrs. Attiyeh's intelligence often made Sarah stop and think how far she could have gone in another country where people did not trample over women's rights, where women were not treated as subhuman beings, where circumstances nurtured growth instead of suppressing it. Unfortunately, this woman, like millions of others in the Middle East and Africa, was trapped doing menial jobs, deprived of knowledge, her world confined to her village and no larger than the distance her legs had strength to carry her – until she came to Jordan.

She was more fortunate than most of her peers. She did not live and die in the village she was born in. She had traveled to another country – in an airplane. The closest other women from similar villages or even towns and cities came to an airplane, was seeing it fly overhead.

Sarah had a long talk with Attiyeh. It was easy to lose tract of the real issue. The man was a victim of circumstances, not of his choosing, one of millions confused by an idea creeping slowly into their lives – lives not seriously touched by civilization ever since there was civilization. What was this crazy idea of equality for women? Who could come up with something so radical, so unheard of, so utterly impractical? If the Prophet advocated equality, then why hadn't he, Attiyeh, or anyone else he knew, ever heard about it?

Sarah could not help but feel sorry for him.

She let him return home after he swore on the Koran never to hit his wife again, never ever attempt to have his daughters circumcised and to put his trust in Allah, the God he professed to love and worshipped five times a day, to give his son long life.

Attiyeh was never the same again. He worked hard, like he always did, but he never smiled and he had little to say to anyone. His world had crumbled beneath his feet. He milled around like a zombie – seemingly devoid of emotions, distant, confused.

In his own eyes, he was no longer a man. His felt his life was dictated by women – by Sarah, by his wife, even his daughters. When he quoted the Koran, his older daughter, Asieh, promptly located the quote as well as different inter-pretations by learned men who explicated the real meaning of the Prophet's words. What had the world come to? How low could a man sink?

"He thinks we have taken his masculinity away," his wife explained. "He claims circumstances made it impossible for him to fight for his dignity and honor."

By that he meant he needed the job – desperately. Otherwise, no one would dare question his authority in his own house. "My biggest mistake was to let my wife and daughters come to Jordan." He had taken to talking to him-self. "How was I suppose to know that I would be forced to send my daughters to school? Allah the merciful in his wisdom has chosen to punish me. Even my wife goes to school. I think the Prophet said, 'This is what happens when misfortune subjects you to deal with women.' You lose con-trol. But Allah is great," he murmured to himself as he swept the yard. "Allah in his wisdom will show them the error of their ways. Please, make it happen soon," he pleaded. "I can't take this miserable state of affairs much longer."

Attiyeh seemed more depressed as time went on. Upon reflection, Sarah found herself wondering if individuals like Attiyeh could ever transcend the traditional codes of conduct so deeply ingrained in them. One morning, she observed him from her bedroom window sweeping the yard. He kept talking to himself – again. He stopped frequently, raised his palms up calling on Allah to please end his misery. "If you won't make things as they were before, put an end to my life, Allah the Great," he said his voice cracking. "A life lived in shame is not a life worth living."

The sight of a loyal, hard working, honest employee giving up on life bothered Sarah immensely. Was her fight for the rights of women an illusion – a dangerous illusion, perhaps? Was she in the wrong place, at the wrong time? There were millions of men like Attiyeh, in fact a lot more rigid in their beliefs than Attiyeh. Did she really think there was the remotest possibility for success? Who appointed me guardian and promoter of women's rights? She asked herself. Has it become an obsession? Am I subconsciously, greedily striving for power like the people I accuse of doing? Will the experience leave me disappointed, bitter? Should I quit before it's too late – before more people are hurt? Is it already too late?

Soul-searching was her constant companion – never far from her thoughts. Her youth and lack of experience in the issues she was tackling gave her cause for concern. Her consolation rested on the fact that she felt deep down that she was on the right tract – that she was doing the right thing. She comforted herself focused on the idea that although she might be a pessimist in the short term, she was an optimist in the long term. She had never really connected with the vast sum of money she was entrusted with. Somehow, spending billions for her personal pleasure, a point frequently brought up by friend and foe alike, sounded almost obscene.

Nabila laughed in her face. "No, my dear, you're not power crazy. This is not a one-woman crusade in search of power dressed up in altruistic garb. If it were you would relate to your money. You should check with Jim. He hands out over two hundred paychecks every month. You have a vague idea where it all goes and not much more. I know. Jim complains often that he has yet to convince you to make time to take a look at the accounts."

"Perhaps I feel disillusioned, skeptical at times because the negative forces we have to deal with are so radical, so extreme, and come in such punishing quantities. Perhaps my expectations are too high. I crave to see the world as it should be, not as it really is. I blame it on my youth, on my lack of experience. I wish it were that simple. In reality it never is."

"How can you blame yourself." Nabila studied her friend for a long moment. "You have a brilliant mind, a mind which despite its youth places value on the really important things in life. How many people do you know who can do that before the age of thirty?"

Sarah chuckled. "The world is full of brilliant failures, my dear. I would prefer not to be one of them."

"History is on the side of human rights." Nabila was always there for Sarah whenever the blows came too often and too hard. And Sarah was there for her. "I have faith. I am convinced, in due course, with the fall of the Soviet Union, political freedom will spread, and economic freedom will follow. Economic freedom will lead to better education opening new avenues for logical thought, informed choices. Hopefully it will help us get rid of our superstitions, prejudices, ancient traditional values – irrelevant, dangerous, unacceptable in today's modern world. I refuse to believe that the fight for human rights, especially the rights of women is futile. Women's rights will evolve, in time, like it has done in many countries already. While I was studying in England, I was shocked to learn that universal suffrage did not come to Britain until 1918. That was not so long ago. In my opinion women in this part of the world have waited long enough. No one is going to go out there and fight our war for us. We have to do it for ourselves. Unfortunately for us, the pendulum has swung too far out in the opposite direction. We are told it's best for Muslim women to return to the Middle Ages. I have to believe our masters will eventually fail. If we persevere, if

we continue along the path we have chosen, we will help ourselves and encourage others in the same predicament not to
press on, not to give up."

Sarah sighed. "We are, and I suppose we shall continue to
do so. Those who rail apoplectically against us, against our
commitment, hopefully, will tire eventually and let us be. But
I doubt it. Did Jim have any news about the Sheikh? I haven't
talked to Jim in days."

"Neither have I," Nabila answered. "I sense he is up to
something, something that's consuming all his attention. He
used to stop by every day to check on Samir Junior, morning
and evening. I haven't seen him the past five days. Younis is
driving the school bus. I don't know if you knew."

"He might be sick. Let's give him a call."

Nabila shook her head. "He's fine. Gwynne talked to him
this morning. He said to tell me he will stop by this evening
and that he's been busy."

"I haven't seen Suheil either." Sarah frowned. "He claims
he is busy too. I don't worry about Suheil though. He'll show
up eventually. But I get concerned when Jim immerses himself in whatever he is doing. It's usually something he doesn't
want us to know about until after it is all over. Whatever it is,
I hope it does not involve the Sheikh. The thought of it makes
me shudder."

It was a week before Christmas, nineteen ninety-six. They
had had a few months of relative peace from the constant
harassment they had come to expect – often rightly so. The
classrooms everywhere were supplied with the latest state of
the art teaching materials and tools. The children learned and
their creativity blossomed. The vocational schools and adult
literacy classes had waiting lists stretching to three years. It
became difficult to find qualified teachers to open more
schools. Moreover, Sarah did not want the project to get much
bigger for fear of losing control, and making it easier for her
opponents to claim she was in it either for the glory or a secret
agenda designed to destroy Islam. Why else would she waste

her time and money on the underprivileged. Most wealthy people simply made a donation, let the world know about it, and moved on. Why was she different? Why couldn't she pay others to do the work for her? That in turn would free her to do as she pleased.

She heard those comments so often that they no longer registered – effectively blocked by her mind.

"What's in it for you?" Many applicants wanted to know – their questions masked in different words. But the meaning remained the same.

Those applicants did not get jobs.

Although the schools in the villages consisted usually of a few rooms, the school in Kerak where her father was born and buried had twenty-three rooms. The school was built in memory of her father, to honor him – but only in Sarah's mind. There was no sign or plaque indicating the name of the donor. However, in a small country like Jordan, it was impossible to keep a significant project like that from attracting attention and the donor's motives questioned. Regardless, instead of building an elaborate burial place for her father as expected from the wealthy, Sarah respected her father's wishes and built a school with free education available for the townspeople, male, female, children and adults. Children attended classes during the day, adults at night. The construction started soon after she and Suheil returned from the Dead Sea to take care of the Sheikh's latest butchery.

A family clinic funded by Suheil was being built next to the school.

"I hope the Sheikh stays wherever he is," Sarah said, without much conviction in her voice.

"I doubt it," Nabila replied. "He'll show up back here soon enough. Let's forget him. We'll deal with him when we have to. He's done far too much damage and gone much too long without punishment. It's bound to explode in his face sometime."

Ordinarily, unless political, the actions of a chief cleric

were not brought to the attention of the government. However, a month earlier, the Minister of Health had resigned unexpectedly and left the country without his wife and children. It was rumored that he had married an American, a woman he had met on a trip abroad. Consequently, the job of Minister of Health was offered to Dr. Suheil Tuqan. To the surprise of everyone, except Sarah, Suheil Tuqan did not accept the offer. He was asked by the Prime Minister to explain his reasons, perhaps reconsider. Dr. Tuqan did not waste the Prime Minister's or his time. "As long as there are individuals in this country, who, with total disregard for the laws of this country force young girls to undergo circumcision to satisfy their sadistic desires, or perhaps I should say their lust, I prefer to be in surgery where I feel I can do more justice to my profession than behind a desk signing forms."

Pressed further, Dr. Tuqan refused to elaborate.

He didn't have to.

Normally, the death of a girl from a refugee camp hardly ever hit the newspapers. Yet although months had passed since the incident, invariably, the Arabic and English papers had something to say about it almost daily. Not only about the death of Zeina but about female genital mutilation no matter where it happened. It had become a hot subject with many readers writing letters to the editors, mostly women, calling on the government to enact stricter legislation and punish the perpetrators of the barbaric act. Many claimed they had been victims themselves. Many others claimed they had not realized the procedure was being carried on in their own country. Sarah made it a point to check the papers daily. She loved to read – a habit she had acquired from her parents, especially so since there was little of interest on television in Saudi Arabia where she had lived while she grew up. The fact that Zeina's death remained a subject of interest, at least for the publishers of the newspapers, intrigued Sarah. She discussed it with Nabila and Gwynne.

"It's probably Jim's doing," Nabila said. "You pay, they

publish – as long as it's not an attack on the Royal Family or a call to embrace communism."

"I think Dr. Tuqan and Jim have joined hands in making sure the issue doesn't die down," Gwynne opined. "They know that as long as it is in the papers, the Sheikh will think real hard before he returns to this country. I heard there is a warrant for his arrest. He is charged with murder. I doubt the murder charge will stick. My guess is they will use it as an excuse to put him behind bars if he ever comes back. I seriously doubt that he will. I am sure his anti-government activities are being closely watched. The King is a survivor. He's not about to lose his throne to a cleric the way the Shah of Iran did."

"If Jim and Suheil are behind these publications," Sarah said, "it's a brilliant plan. I must admit, in the past I have judged Jim rather harshly. When pushed to the limit, Jim does not worry about consequences. And that worries me."

The holidays were always rough on Sarah. Not for their religious significance so much, but for the fact that she felt alone, alone in a world she did not feel fully prepared to cope with. Yet her parents never wavered in their faith in her. She was always reminded that she could do anything she put her mind to. And so she did. She missed her parents – missed them so much it hurt. The hurt did not lesson with time. It intensified. She felt lonely, sad – despite Suheil's unconditional love for her. Gradually, her relationship with Suheil had deepened. It was a love based on mutual respect and total commitment to each other and to human rights. Human rights, especially women's rights, were indisputably the focus of their attention. She considered Suheil the only family she had, and he did likewise. Yet still she could not bring herself to say yes to the numerous times he had proposed, indeed pleaded on many occasions that they get married. When uncertain about how to respond to a situation, her thoughts brought her parents to mind. Given the same situation, how would her mother or father react? How would they expect her to react?

After months of deliberations in her own mind, Sarah came to realize that her own mother had married an Arab and a more compatible, loving, selfless love and marriage was hard to find anytime, anywhere.

"It's what's inside a person that counts," Sarah's mother explained. "The rest is immaterial. What's crucial today, may seem insignificant tomorrow."

She decided to surprise Suheil – agree to marry him. She planned on telling him the next time the opportunity presented itself. Only it was over a week that she had not seen him. He called, less frequently, but had not stopped by as he usually did. Although she had not minded it initially, as the days passed and he still did not come, she began to wonder if the real reason for his absence was the fact that he was busy.

Restless, in need of change, she asked Gwynne and Nabila how they felt about spending Christmas, or the New Year in Kerak. She wanted to visit her father's grave, talk to him and ask him if he approved of the progress so far. She wanted to ask him if he and her mother thought she was on the right track, that she was fulfilling their request. It didn't matter that her father could not answer her. Often, when deeply troubled, Sarah visited her father's grave, alone, explained the problem to her father and asked for his advice. Somehow, through vibes she wasn't aware of until later, the best way to deal with the problem became clear in her mind before she left the gravesite. He was always there for her. No one could convince her of the contrary.

While in Kerak, she could also check the progress on the work being done for the school and the family planning clinic – Suheil's pet project that he rarely had a chance to visit.

"That will be great," Nabila replied. "Should we wait for Jim and Suheil or go on our own?"

"I don't know about you," Sarah said, "But I haven't seen either man in days. Let's go. We will leave them notes. They can follow us there if they wish."

To Sarah and Nabila's surprise, Gwynne hesitated at first,

then tried to find excuses for postponing the trip. "I'd rather spend Christmas in Amman," she said, as though the thought had just occurred to her. "New Year in Kerak sounds a lot better to me. Christmas is not for everybody, my dear. You know."

Sarah was embarrassed. She had not thought about its religious connotation. She checked with Nabila. Nabila did not seem to care what holiday they celebrated, or where, as long as they went away for a few days. But Gwynne could not be persuaded. "Let's wait for Jim and Suheil," she said. "I'd rather we all went together."

Sarah relented. Gwynne was a woman who did not change her mind once it was made up. She was Christian and had every right to celebrate the holiday wherever she wished. Sarah would not leave her alone, especially on a day like Christmas. Yet it seemed strange that Gwynne, who had never made an issue of Christmas in the many years she lived with them in Saudi Arabia, had suddenly expressed a strong interest in it. And why couldn't she enjoy Christmas just as well in Kerak? She wouldn't miss anything. It wasn't as though the streets of Amman would be decorated for Christmas.

"Can't help you there," Nabila said. "I'm just as confused with her behavior recently. I get the feeling she's trying to avoid me. I can't figure out why."

That same night, Jim and Suheil came over and asked the women out to dinner. Both men acted as though nothing was amiss. No explanation about their absence, nothing. Just a normal get together. Nothing out of the ordinary.

The next day, still baffled at the strange behavior of both men, and unable to resolve it in her own mind, Sarah asked Nabila, "Do you feel kind of left out? Do you feel as if something is going on around us, something Jim and Suheil don't want us to know about?"

"You bet. They had that silly smirk on their faces all evening. The one that says I-know-something-you-don't. Whatever it is, I doubt they can keep it to themselves much longer."

"So it's not just my imagination."

"I think they have bought us gifts – with Gwynne's help. They want to surprise us."

"Gifts? What could be so special to warrant all this secrecy?"

"We'll know soon enough. I tend to agree with Gwynne's idea of staying in Amman for Christmas though. Although my experience was not so great last Christmas considering the confrontation I had with that mullah, still it was lots of fun. What do you say we do it again?"

And they did. Turkey with mashed potatoes, stuffing, even cranberry sauce courtesy of Jim's contacts at the U.S. embassy. The children were thrilled, not because they were served better food, since they got two good, nourishing meals and snacks at school everyday, but because the occasion was festive, and this Christmas they did not have mullahs sitting around questioning their teacher's motives and admonishing them for celebrating an occasion in honor of Christ – not a Muslim holiday.

To the surprise of both women, Jim and Suheil found the time and participated fully in celebrating the occasion. Jim baked the pumpkin pies as he had done the previous year and made sure the children received their gifts. Suheil brought a winter coat for each child especially purchased from England for the occasion. Yet the only Christian besides Gwynne, was Jim. Sarah was part Christian only – through her mother's father. But such distinctions did not seem to matter to any of the participants. Everyone celebrated it as a special day, a day to party, to have fun, to love.

Surprisingly, neither Sarah nor Nabila received gifts from the men who kept proposing and insisted on marrying them. And for some reason Gwynne, who always noticed the minutest detail, failed to comment about it. After everyone went home that night, Sarah and Nabila went to Sarah's apartment to review the curriculum vitae of a woman who had applied for the job of principal for the school in Kerak. They did not get very far. Nabila was upset, and to a lesser degree so was Sarah. "It isn't as if we are heartbroken or so insecure that we must receive gifts to feel worthy," Nabila said. The tone of her voice however suggested otherwise. "It's the thought that counts. It would have been nice if they had mentioned something like sorry or we were busy we didn't have time. Or any other dumb excuse. But to ignore us completely is inexcusable. For me that sort of behavior displays a remarkable lack of respect. I mean both men took the gifts we gave them and said thank you. And that was it. I never felt so stupid, so insulted in my life. Not that I recall, anyway."

"Something weird is going on," Sarah replied. "I hate to say it, but I think Gwynne is in cahoots with them. Do you think we should go tomorrow? When I suggested we spend Christmas in Kerak, Gwynne wasted no time telling me she'd like to spend Christmas in Amman. After Jim and Suheil came over and she got to talk to them, when Jim suggested we spend Christmas day in Kerak, she said she would love to. Why then did she say earlier that we should wait till New Year's eve to go to Kerak?"

Nabila shrugged her shoulders. "I don't know. I don't really care. Material things don't mean much to me. It's their attitude which bugs me more."

"Thou protestest too much," Sarah teased.

"Yeah, you're right. Let's go. It's easy to forget what's important in life and receiving gifts is not one of them. We can be – what's that word Jim uses often?"

"Cool."

"That's right. We can be just as cool as they are. Let's pretend it didn't affect us at all."

The next morning Jim and Suheil rang Sarah's doorbell. When Sarah and Nabila worked late into the night, Samir Junior, nicknamed Sam spent the night with his mother at Sarah's place, in a crib, in Sarah's living room. Sam was awake, waiting patiently for his mother to give him his breakfast. Upon hearing Jim's voice the child jumped up and down in his crib, obviously delighted to see the man who smothered him with love and brought him toys. So many in fact, that his mother often sent bags full of toys home with the children in her classroom to be given to their little brothers and sisters. Somehow, Jim never tired of bringing toys, nor did he mind that Nabila gave away what he had brought earlier, despite the fact that they were shipped over for Jim from the U.S., and the customs duty on imported toys, considered luxury, was horrendous.

Jim handed Sam a musical toy that made sounds of different animals depending on the button the child pressed. The picture of an animal popped up corresponding to the sound. Sam was fascinated with it. Jim took Sam's index finger and pressed a button. A cat popped out and mewed. Sam jumped up and down in his crib, delighted. He reached for the toy and tried to press another button.

Nabila walked over, thanked Jim for the toy, lifted her son and took him to the kitchen to feed him breakfast.

"Can we leave after Sam has had his breakfast?" Jim asked Nabila.

"It's all right with me. Check with Sarah."

Sarah walked out of the bedroom. She greeted the men politely, planted a small kiss on Suheil's forehead. She said, "I have no objection. Which vehicle do you want to use?"

"The school bus. It has room for all of us."

"Is Gwynne coming?" Sarah asked. I can play this game as well as you can, she told herself.

"Of course," Jim replied. "Why do you ask?"

"Because when I mentioned going to Kerak for Christmas, she said she'd rather spend Christmas in Amman. She suggested we go to Kerak for New Year. Has she changed her mind?"

Jim and Suheil exchanged glances.

Looking a little uneasy, Jim said, "We stopped by Nabila's place before coming here. She was ready. She wants to come. And of course Fatme will join us too."

Sarah took over feeding Sam his breakfast while his mother packed Sam's clothes and other necessities. Within the hour, everyone was ready. They piled in the van, ready to go.

Twenty minutes south of Amman, driving on the King's Highway, Jim quietly veered off the highway and headed toward a town called Madaba. The women were busy talking in the back when Nabila stopped suddenly with a puzzled look on her face. She said, "Jim, this is the way to Madaba. Why did you get off the highway?" She turned to Sarah and Gwynne, her eyes rimmed with tears. "This is where Samir was born."

"If you have no objection, I'd like Sarah to see the Greek Orthodox Church of St. George," Jim said. "This town is famous for its ancient mosaics. It's believed there are mosaics under every house. The Greek Orthodox Church has a magnificent piece of art, all mosaic. It's a map of Jordan, Palestine in the north and Egypt in the south, a well preserved piece of art worth seeing."

"Oh, no," Nabila replied. "It's fine with me. You're right. That's a must see."

They stopped at the church. Jim excused himself. So did Suheil. The women thought they probably had to go to the bathroom. The women roamed throughout the church, bought a few souvenirs, but the men were not back yet. "It's difficult to find bathrooms," Nabila explained. "I don't know where they went, but I can't think of a place here that has public bathrooms."

They stepped out of the church and started walking toward the van, when they saw both men hurrying in their direction.

Jim took Sam from his mother's arms. "Sorry we're late. Do you feel like walking a couple of blocks? I want to show you something but we have to walk there. There's no parking."

"What is it?" Nabila asked.

"Can't describe it. You'll have to see for yourself."

It was a sunny, crisp day. They walked down a narrow, centuries old, cobblestone street. Presently, Jim stopped in front of a large, two-story building.

A few steps before reaching the building, the color suddenly drained from Nabila's face. She looked so shocked, her eyes rolled back, and she was wobbly on her feet. Sarah thought Nabila was about to faint. She reached over and held her from beneath her armpits. "This ... This used to be Samir's home. Right here," Nabila said, between sobs. "What has happened to it?"

Jim hesitated, as though he wasn't sure whether to proceed or not. He opened his mouth but could not speak. They waited for a few seconds for Nabila to overcome her shock.

"Are you all, right?" Jim asked, concerned.

"Sorry, I didn't mean to upset everybody. I'm fine."

A middle-aged man waiting in front of the door ushered them in. Somehow, he seemed to know Jim, perhaps also Suheil. "Sorry, you had to look for me," the man said. "I went out to get something to eat." Jim assured him it was all right, not to worry about it. Jim walked ahead of the women. Sarah and Nabila followed, with hesitant steps – not quite sure they were ready to face whatever it was Jim wanted them to see.

The house Samir had grown up in was intact, hidden behind a newly built facade. Jim continued to walk ahead of the women. Suheil stayed behind, roamed around, did not say a word. They walked through a passage and headed for a two-story, new, brick building. Jim took a key out of his pocket, opened the door and asked the women to step in.

It was a large building, built around an Olympic size swimming pool filled with the latest state of the art equipment for sports and recreation.

Baffled, Sarah and Nabila waited expectantly for Jim to explain the purpose of their visit. Gwynne had walked away ostensibly examining the rest of the building.

Jim ignored their quizzical looks, continued to walk through the building, the women in tow, their perplexity mounting.

Nabila could not suppress her curiosity any longer. "Pray tell us," she said a touch ironically, "what are we doing here?"

"I thought you might have guessed by now." Jim replied, smiling broadly. "But maybe not. Let's go to the entrance of the building on the south side."

When Jim turned his back to walk ahead of them, Nabila shook her head and Sarah threw her hands up. "What's he up to?" Nabila whispered.

"I have no idea."

"We're not building inspectors," Nabila said. "Why is he giving us a tour of the whole place?"

"I don't know. We'll have to wait and see."

They reached the entrance, stepped outside. Jim pointed to a plaque on the door. It read, 'Youth Sports Activities Center'. Underneath it, in small letters, it read, 'In Memory of My Husband Samir Mahfouz'.

Sarah could not recall when she had seen someone look so shocked. Nabila simply froze on the spot she stood on, speechless, her hand quickly thrown across her mouth, tight, as she did when she wanted to scream but knew she shouldn't.

Jim handed Sam to Sarah, put his arms around Nabila. "Please accept it, darling," he said. "It's my Christmas gift to you."

Nabila dropped her head on his chest and sobbed.

Jim caressed her hair and waited for her to get over her second shock in less than a few minutes. In between sobs, she managed to say, "My ... My first Christmas. I'm not even Christian. How ... How ..." She reached in her pocket for tissue paper. "How did you manage to get a building built without letting anyone know?" She stopped. "Everyone knew – except me. Right?"

"Wrong. Only Suheil and Gwynne were let in on my little project. You're a difficult woman to keep secrets from. Without their help I don't think I could have held up much longer."

"What do you mean?"

"Come now, you know what I mean. Frequently, when I had to check on the workers here, I could not come see you and Sam. Later when I did come, I could feel the anger in you mounting. But you're too much of a lady to have made an issue of it."

"Wow! Am I that transparent?" Nabila smiled, and cried, and looked stunningly beautiful.

Jim clung to the woman he loved, once again her face pressed against his chest. He caressed her hair, kissed the top of her head and waited patiently for her to pull herself together.

"I love you." Sarah heard Nabila say a few seconds later, for the first time to Sarah's knowledge, and in public. Nabila was brave and unconventional when being conventional meant repeating the mistakes of the past. That was the easy way – not Nabila's way, especially since her husband's death. Somehow his death had ignited long dormant passions in her, essentially the passion for knowledge. That's what Sarah loved about the woman. Nabila was not encumbered with what people said or people did the way her countrymen were. She thought a situation through and took action the best way she knew how – consequences be damned, intended or not.

Obviously overcome with joy, Jim bent down and planted a kiss on her lips. "I love you too," he murmured. And the tough guy had to reach in his pocket for a handkerchief to wipe his tears.

Sarah cast a quick glance around. Thank God no one was around – except Gwynne who seemed to have appeared out of nowhere. Public demonstration of affection in many other Middle Eastern countries was a sure invitation for the severest form of punishment the system could come up with – the harshest punishment reserved for females. Sarah took a few steps away. Soon Sam got restless. He began to cry. "All right you two," Sarah said, "Let's get back in the van. I think Sam is thirsty. He needs a drink."

Jim let go of Nabila reluctantly. He walked over and took

Sam from Sarah. The infant stopped crying immediately. Gwynne joined them on the way back, strolling, looking everywhere but at the women, a naughty twinkle in her eyes. "I'm gonna get you," Nabila joked. "Here I thought all the while you were my friend."

Gwynne smiled and soon her smile broadened. "I would not exchange that look in your eyes when you saw what he had built for you for all the tea in China. No my dear, I would not."

Jim asked Suheil to take over the driving. Sarah moved up front, next to Suheil. Jim gave Sam a bottle of juice. In no time at all the child was asleep in Jim's arms. Surprisingly, Suheil congratulated Nabila, said he hoped she liked Jim's gift to her, but little else. He seemed preoccupied, not in the mood for small talk.

When they reached Kerak, Sarah asked to be let off at her father's grave. When she was done, she would follow them home on foot.

"How long do you think you'll be?" Suheil asked.

"Twenty, thirty minutes."

"I can come pick you up, if you like."

"Not unless you want to check on the clinic. I want to have a look at both buildings."

"I don't feel like it now," Suheil said. "Maybe later. I can come for you whenever you want me to."

"Thanks. I prefer to walk."

The van drove away.

Sarah said a prayer at her father's grave, told him about the latest events, asked and received her father's approval. She walked around the village for a while, then moved on toward her father's home, head bent, conflicting thoughts crowding her mind. She forgot all about checking the buildings. As her project snowballed, growing steadily, at an ever-increasing pace, so did her fear. It had been too quiet lately. Too good to be true. If past experience was any indication, trouble had to be lurking around the corner. Why? Why did women have to be treated in such shameful manner? Why did an innocent man have to land in jail, in Iraq no less, for a crime he had nothing to do with? Why did another young man have to die leaving a widow and an unborn child behind? Why were young girls mutilated, scarred for life? Did anyone care that those who were mutilated sometimes bled to death? Why was justice so difficult to obtain in this and many other parts of the world? Questions, questions. But there were no answers.

Sarah had reached her grandfather's house. She opened the door and walked in. She thought she heard a commotion, strange voices coming from the kitchen. She could have sworn she heard someone say, 'She's here. Hurry.' She shook her head. I need a couple of days off, she said to herself. I'm beginning to hear things. Nonetheless, she headed for the kitchen.

Upon seeing her, everyone shouted, "Surprise!"

Rashid stood at the head of the kitchen table, a can of Coke in his right hand, without his beard, lighter by at least ten pounds, exuding joy.

"Oh, my God," Sarah rushed over and reached for the cleric's hand. "What are you doing here?" She stepped back, faced Jim. "How could you keep something like this from me. It looks like this is the day for surprises. I will never trust Jim or Suheil – ever again."

"Me neither." Nabila was having a blast. "Never been happier either."

"You ain't seen nothing yet." Jim laughed.

"What's that supposed to mean?"

"Just kidding."

"Out," Gwynne ordered. "All of you. I'm starved. I want to fix us something to eat. Out of the kitchen, everybody."

No one argued with Gwynne. It was futile. They drifted to the living room.

A minute later, Gwynne walked into the living room dragging Fatme by the hand. She deposited her in a chair.

"Everybody means, everybody. Sit."

Fatme did.

"What was that all about?" Sarah asked.

"She won't let me help her," Fatme replied. "I don't know why."

Sarah shrugged her shoulders and resumed her conversation with Rashid, eager to learn more about Ali, what had happened to him, and how far Rashid had progressed with his project, when she heard footsteps coming from the stairs, the stairs that led to the upstairs bedroom. If she had seen her own reaction in a mirror, she would have realized she looked no less in shock than Nabila was earlier. Worse yet was Fatme. She promptly passed out.

Descending the stairs was Ali, dressed in a suit which looked like it was hanging on a skeleton held in place by Velcro, clean shaven, desperately struggling to smile.

Gwynne rushed over to take care of Fatme, while Sarah got a grip on herself.

"I don't want to hear it," Sarah said. "I don't want to know. He's here. That's all that matters."

Suheil moved close to Sarah. He put his arm around her. "I couldn't think of a thing to give you for Christmas, my love," he said softly. "I thought it would be nice to have Ali home for Christmas."

"It's the best gift you or anyone could have given me." Sarah rushed to the foot of the stairs to meet Ali and without giving it a second thought, threw her arms around him and gave the startled man a hug. Meanwhile, Fatme opened her eyes, looked at her brother, then her eyes quickly scanned the room. Gwynne helped her stand. Ali hurried over, and to everyone's surprise embraced his sister.

"I got your letters," he told his sister.

Fatme stared at him in disbelief.

After the excitement died down, Jim pulled Sarah aside. "Ali's presence must remain strictly secret," Jim said, "until I have all the documents he needs to travel ready."

"Where to?" Sarah asked.

"That's up to you. I had in mind the same proposition we made to Muhammad."

"Does he like computers?"

"I don't think he has ever touched one."

"Maybe we should let him decide," Sarah suggested.

"It was his idea, or perhaps I should say Muhammad's."

Sarah narrowed her eyes until they were almost closed. She studied Jim for a long moment, the man who had tried to be father, brother, friend, or whatever else the occasion demanded. She shook her head. "You mean to tell me Muhammad knew about Ali getting out of jail before I did?"

"Just barely."

The suspense was too much for Sarah to bear. "Jim, I've had enough excitement for one day. Tell me, how did Muhammad hear about Ali."

"You'll know in a moment." Jim dashed out of the room.

He was back a minute later accompanied by Muhammad.

"I don't believe this," Sarah said, the pitch of her voice higher than she meant it to be. She jumped out of her chair and practically threw herself at the man who eighteen months earlier had avoided eye contact with females at all cost. "This is a regular conspiracy," she said in jest, as her gaze shifted from Jim to Suheil. "I'll get even with you somehow. Both of you."

"This is the day for hugs." Sarah gave Muhammad another hug. His letters had sustained her through many difficult times. Muhammad was not startled. Not anymore. Not after eighteen months in the U.S.

"Dare I ask what brings you here?" Sarah asked.

"Jim. I have two weeks off for Christmas. He said I should do him a favor. Me – do Jim a favor. My father has been sick for months now. He won't go to a doctor. Jim called me up. He said to me, would you please come for a short visit. Maybe your father will listen to you. Maybe you can take him to a doctor. The next day, I got a call from Air France. They had my ticket ready. And here I am. Tell me, am I a lucky bastard, or what?" That said, he threw his arms around Sarah, thanking her profusely, startling her. "I can't wait to get back and start my own business so I can be in a position to help others."

"What will that be?" Sarah asked.

"They call it trouble shooter in America. Or computer nerds. Take your pick. You have problems with your computer, you call me, I come, I fix it."

"You'll have more business than you can handle," Suheil interjected. "No such business exists in this country. Not yet anyway."

Sarah was skeptical. It was hard to believe that two years of community college offered sufficient knowledge for such a venture. She did not want him to be disappointed though. "Do you feel prepared for the job?" she asked.

"Your concern is justified. Bellevue Community College teaches basics. I take courses at night at Lake Washington Vocational School. It's fabulous. I've learned a lot. I have also taught myself. I didn't want to tell you because I knew you'd insist on paying for it. I got a loan from Professor Askari, the professor from the University of Washington I met at the mosque. I'll pay him back. As soon as I make money."

"You're incorrigible," Sarah said, immensely proud and pleased with Muhammad's progress and his level of maturity, despite having gotten little help from his family or environment until he left Jordan.

"I want to take Ali back with me. He's a good man. He will work hard. He, Jim and I had a long talk. Even if he did not have to fear being thrown in jail here, if he stays in Jordan, slowly, insidiously, his mind will rot just like everybody else trapped in our situation who does not get a break in life. I hope you will agree."

"On one condition only. Ali has suffered a horrendous amount of pain not because he did something wrong but because he wanted to warn me. I owe him my life. I have to be assured by you, or Jim or whoever is taking responsibility for him that he will be given the best opportunity available and I will need full disclosure of all his expenses. It's the least I can do for him."

"Jim already told him that's precisely what you would say."

"Then we understand each other."

Muhammad's eyes welled with tears. "You have already done so much for just about everyone you have come in contact with. You not only help financially – you give a whole lot of yourself. At times it scares me real bad. I wake up to the laughter of men who laugh like hyenas. 'Wake up! Wake up! They scream and they point at me and they laugh. You've been dreaming far too long,' they say. Wake up!'"

Like Muhammad, Sarah was on the verge of tears. "For everything I have given you, you have given back tenfold. I hope you will be in a position some day soon to be able to give. Nothing feels as good as giving does – especially when it's done without expecting anything in return."

"I have to keep my promise to my father first. He is convinced the only way for him to get well is a trip to Mecca."

"Jim talked to me about that. I asked him to arrange for your father and mother to leave for Mecca as soon as your father is fit to travel. An idea just popped into my head. You could use the trip to Mecca to coax him to see a doctor."

Muhammad was caught off guard. "But, but Miss Sarah."

"I know, you promised to pay for it yourself. And that's fine. But your father is quite old and frail. If he doesn't go this year, he might not make it next year and you find it hard to forgive yourself. In return you can take responsibility for Ali."

Muhammad lowered himself slowly onto the sofa, too overwhelmed to say a word. A few seconds later he raised his head and said, his voice barely audible, "Thank you. Thank you for everything."

"Think nothing of it." Sarah looked around. "By the way, where is Jim?"

Suheil smiled, said nothing.

"Where's Nabila?"

Gwynne walked in from the kitchen. "They went out. They'll be back soon."

Jim and Nabila were gone for over three hours and when they returned, they did not return alone. They had Afaf and Hind in tow, yet one more surprise for Sarah on a Christmas day full of surprises, a Christmas day she would never forget.

The women embraced. Hind's facial scars from the acid burn were almost invisible thanks to extensive plastic surgery. She looked healthier but still as reserved as before. "Jim wanted everyone who had touched your life since you came to Jordan to gather in one place this Christmas," Afaf explained. "Unfortunately, our tickets were sent to the village while Hind and I were in Cairo for Hind to have her last surgery evaluated. I called Jim and told him I didn't think we could make it to Jordan by Christmas. By the time my husband sent the tickets from the village to Cairo, it would be too late."

Sarah shook her head at Gwynne. "That's why you couldn't decide where you wanted to spend Christmas in Kerak or not. You, conspirator you."

"It's most fun I've had in years, my dear," Gwynne said, and looked it.

"How did you manage to get here today?" Sarah asked.

"My husband drove the car you gave us all night. He was so eager for us to be here for Christmas, he couldn't contain his joy. We got the tickets this morning and here we are."

Sarah could only shake her head in disbelief. Jim had not missed a thing, not one thing. She walked over, thanked him and kissed him on both cheeks. "If you have no more surprises for me," she said, radiating happiness, "I suggest we all have a bite to eat."

"Well, I'm not so sure about that."

"No, Jim. Please, no more. I can't take it. I have no doubt you and Suheil spent countless hours planning and conniving.

It requires superhuman effort to make sure it all comes together. And it did. You have done your best. I can't thank you enough. I can't remember when I have felt so happy, so deliciously alive, so ravenously hungry."

"Give us a couple more minutes," Suheil said, a weird smile briefly fleeting across his face.

"A couple more minutes to do what?" There seemed to be a concerted effort to perplex her – almost as if it had been rehearsed. Obviously they were enjoying themselves immensely. Everyone in the room except Nabila and Sarah seemed to be in on the joke, and those in the know were evidently savoring the drama they were witnessing. Nabila's eyes kept darting back and forth from Jim to Suheil. She caught Sarah's eye, raised her eyebrow and shrugged her shoulders. Sarah answered her likewise.

Sarah had risen to go to the kitchen. She sat back down.

im said, "Remember what your Dad used to say quoting Winston Churchill. 'It's no use saying we are doing our best. You have to succeed in doing what is necessary.' And that we have yet to do."

Captivated by Jim's oratory, wondering what else she could have possibly missed, Sarah said, "Let's have it. The suspense is killing me."

"Me too." Nabila rose from her seat and joined Sarah on the sofa.

"That's perfect," Suheil said, practically jumping up with joy. "Stay where you are. Jim and I will be right back."

They were – in less than a minute, one hand behind their backs, a smile dancing in their eyes.

"You go first," Suheil said to Jim.

"I have a better idea," Jim replied. "Let's go together."

"This is crucial," Rashid chimed in. "Listen carefully."

And both men said, "Darling, will you marry me?"

And both women by then having anticipated what was in store for them replied, "I will."

At that moment, Mullah Rashid stepped forward, took the

small boxes the men had in their hands behind their backs, pulled out two simple gold bands from each, said a short prayer, put the ring on Sarah's finger first, followed by Suheil, Nabila, and Jim. He then said, "I pronounce you man and wife."